The Spectral Saga

With Star Tarots Spreads

Written By

Joanne Alain Cook

Cover Art by Janice Calvento
Tarot Card art by Joanne Alain Cook
Author art by Alaina Grace Batten
This is a collection of the Spectral Trilogy and includes *Spectral Analysis*
© *2022, Spectral Voices© 2022,* and *Spectral Redemption © 2022.*
This is a work of fiction. All the characters and events in this tale are
fictitious and totally made-up amusement.

Table of Contents

Spectral Analysis

Seeking Lost Souls

Star Tarot SA
Story Arc
the problem 1
XVIII
The Moon
past influence 4
0
The Fool
Future 6
I
The Magician
XVI
the outcome 7
The Tower
XIV
Temperance
IX
The Hermit
XVII
The Star
pos+ influence 2
neg-Influence 3
present 5

Chapter 1

Old Town Sacramento Janine

Emerging from the depths of Old Town Sacramento, Janine took a grateful breath upon reaching fresh oxygen. Below, on the original street level, a stagnant atmosphere saturated the tunnels. Stale, cold, and acrid in places, the underground section of the capitol city reeked with the stench of rat droppings and moist soil. Rumors of a haunted Old Town had lured the ghost-hunting team of *Spectral Analysis* to the Golden State, and most of the hauntings lurked in that dank darkness.

Old Town is considered the riverfront district of the California Capitol with Gold Rush era buildings, streets paved in cobblestones from the 1800s, horse drawn carriages, and fun novelty shops. Foot-worn wooden planks formed walkways along each block except in the back alleys where the ground dipped to the original level. Over a hundred years ago, the streets had been raised to combat against periodic flooding from the Sacramento River. *Spectral Analysis*, a team that filmed paranormal investigations, chose Pioneer Park as their entry point into the underground. The park sat on the lower level and provided easy access through the simple removal of a wood wall. They could pass directly into the tunnels and explore.

Scattered across the park, broken pieces of metal ironwork lay rusting and half buried. The technical crew, Carlos and Janine, waited patiently as the special talent for *Spectral Analysis* traipsed out of the opening and into bright sunlight.

"Can you believe the smell?" Carlos whispered. "We'll need gas masks."

Janine watched the tall scientist, Doctor Ian McNally, as he helped the petite Kiki Mellow out of the dark. Kiki ran her hands up and down her arms to warm up. The doctor scratched his head and gave the crew a little wave.

Janine's attention was drawn to his eyes as they squinted in the bright sunlight.

The doctor meandered toward their Sacramento guide to the underground, a short bald man from the Old Town Discovery Museum by the name of Jeff Lang. Lang sat on the edge of the wooden walkway wearing extremely dark sunglasses. His head tilted toward Kiki, giving the impression that he stared at her.

Kiki did not follow the doctor toward Lang. Instead, she gazed back into the tunnel. Kiki Mellow was a self-proclaimed witch and medium and stood just shy of five and a half feet tall. She was blessed with a curvaceous but slender build. Her naturally dark eyelashes framed bright green eyes, but the natural color of her smooth hair remained an enigma. Kiki's mane altered from dark brown to chestnut to strawberry blond on a rotating basis. She could appear anywhere from mixed West Asian to European depending on how she dressed and what she did with her hair. She had a flair for fashion and constantly changed her style. Steve rushed across the debris to cover her with a light coat.

"My hero," she gazed at him. His face broke into a smile.

By far, Kiki was the most famous asset on the show. Her colorful personality and very sexy persona kept the public wanting more. Sponsors always vied for Kiki Mellow to be their spokesperson. Following their first season, talk shows and speaking events begged Kiki to appear. She resisted over showing at outside engagements and often declined the invitations. Kiki obviously enjoyed keeping a more mysterious image. At the moment, Kiki studied the makeshift entrance to the underground with a puzzled expression on her face. Ian McNally strolled toward her, whispered something, and they nodded agreement with each other.

Ian towered over Kiki at about six-foot-three. As usual, his dark-brown hair was in a bit of a mess over his brow and his pretty blue eyes sparkled. He actually had a doctorate degree, so the crew felt justified in calling him *the Doctor* instead of just Ian. He earned his PhD at the University of Edinberg's Koestler Parapsychology Unit (KPU) and spoke in a fading Scottish accent that Kiki mimicked perfectly on occasion. Janine easily imagined what inspired the many fan letters from female viewers regarding the doctor. It was those pretty blue eyes, masculine jawline, and broad shoulders.

Ian could also be very funny and his dry humor worked well with Kiki's over-the-top personality. Their dynamic, more so than the ghost stories, provided the driving force behind a very popular first season. They easily bantered on almost any topic and they looked good together. On several episodes, Kiki got herself into a situation that called for the doctor to rescue, catch, or pull her to safety. A couple of times, they almost, just about, but didn't, kiss. The rescues began accidentally, but everyone knew the audience loved it. The doctor and Kiki came round to where the crew stood waiting.

"All right everybody," the doctor announced. "Our guide, Mr. Lang, tells me we're having lunch on the Delta King, our other destination. There are two ghosts on the boat, one of a little girl and one of an older man, so, it'll be a working lunch. We'll grab what we can on SBT voice, maybe a small portable EM box and also the camcorder. Then we'll come back to this underground entrance at nightfall."

"Ion detector?" Carlos suggested.

"Aye, good thinking. We'll just walk ahead."

The doctor and Kiki strolled ahead of the crew. They usually developed a rough game plan while Janine and Carlos gathered the needed equipment and followed.

Spectral Analysis just entered into a second season. Their breakthrough episode occurred in Providence Rhode Island at the very gaudy Biltmore Hotel. It was the first episode with a Kiki-Doctor romantic tease. Kiki had managed to lose her footing in the dark basement where animal sacrifices were once performed and the doctor caught her quite spontaneously, saving her from a nasty fall. Kiki then proceeded to faint languidly into his arms. Upon recovering, Kiki insisted the basement held the spirits of more than just animal sacrifices. She insisted that one angry entity caused her fainting spell, and then it invited her to a party in room 1404. After that episode aired, room 1404 at the Biltmore in Providence became booked out for months in advance. Viewers also began to speculate if the doctor and Kiki were an item.

Each episode started and ended with a lessor ghost story near their feature investigation, which they called bookends. They were short snips of a tale meant to capture audience attention. The bookends for the Biltmore episode revolved around a library near Brown University, the historic Providence Athenaeum. People claimed it was haunted by both H. P. Lovecraft and Edgar Allen Poe.

Kiki didn't agree. But she did insist that the Biltmore was haunted, extremely so, and Janine almost believed her. That hotel had spooked her more than any other film site. In the grand ballroom, her thermal-panger, a fancy thermometer, had plummeted to subzero temperatures, then, just as instantaneously, the temperature rose back to normal levels. Everyone felt the dramatic cold rush of air, and though it was snowing outside, not a single window or door to the ballroom had popped open.

"Unhappy spirits bring in the cold," Kiki had uttered through chattering teeth.

Spectral Analysis consisted of a very minimal and basic crew. Steve Hanks managed the computers, tape storage, and data-conversion software. He spliced the image and audio media, and took care of the computer equipment. He acted as their executive producer/director, as well as the editor/art director. He spooked easily and kept a safe distance from the action. Janine got the sense that his interest fell into creating a successful indie television show, not so much on their paranormal discoveries.

Ted operated the main camera. He trained his lens on the talent, the doctor and Kiki. He set up lights for the shoots and remote cameras for the angles they offered. Ted gave very little input to any of the events he filmed. He managed to stay quiet and almost completely off camera, much like Steve.

Carlos and Janine carried and operated the sensors, recorders, and other gadgets needed to document paranormal evidence. They trailed Kiki and the doctor and assisted as needed. They served as extra witnesses to unexplained spectral activity and offered nonexpert commentary. Carlos mostly provided wisecracks. They acted as onscreen receptors for the doctor or Kiki to analyze an interesting event. The doctor kept his discussions on the measurable data they collected, while Kiki rambled about her psychic feelings and the stories behind the ghosts. A few times, she spontaneously pulled Janine and Carlos into an impromptu séance. No one ever knew when Kiki Mellow would whip out a candle, or tarot cards, or a crystal ball.

During lunch on the Delta King, Kiki pulled out a small, translucent orb. She polished it with a blood red cloth.

The Delta King was a 285-foot riverboat permanently docked at the pier in Old Town. A giant, bright-red, immobile water wheel dominated the stern, and the main deck felt slightly tilted and warped. The manager opened up the Pilothouse Restaurant for the crew to gather and investigate the local ghosts. He offered them a free meal. Airtime on their show translated into free advertising for his boat.

The *Spectral Analysis* team gathered around a table in the center of the dining room. Out the back window, a spectacular view of the Sacramento River and the gold-painted Tower Bridge loomed. The operational drawbridge rose during their short lunch and a tall boat passed underneath. The metallic paint scattered beams of afternoon sunlight onto the water.

When their lunch had been cleared, Kiki centered her orb on the table. She used her red scarf to make a base and balanced the ball in the folds. She glanced at Janine.

"Perhaps us girls should stay in here to try to draw the spirits," she said.

Doctor McNally rose. "Carlos, let's hit the deck. Ted is going to tape Kiki and Janine inside while we try to get what we can on camcorder out there."

He gave Kiki a little nod, then smiled at Janine. His eyes lingered a moment. Did she imagine it, or did his eyes become a tad deeper blue? Every so often, Janine caught him gazing at her like that, like he wanted to say something but thought twice about it. His attention caused her nerves to buzz. Janine once told Carlos that she thought the doctor was making "eyes" at her, but Carlos just laughed. Carlos claimed the doctor often gave girls that same wrong impression. *He's a Scotsman*, Carlos said, *every girl thinks he's making eyes at them*. Carlos grabbed a portable LED electromagnetic field box and camera before moving out to the deck.

Kiki readjusted the crystal ball as Ted set up a tripod. The empty dining room fell quiet. Janine retrieved her thermal-panger and registered a micro-temperature rise. Kiki leaned into the table.

"Janine, I've got something to tell you." Kiki's eyes slowly swept the empty room. "This boat is not haunted."

"Really?" Janine let out a startled laugh.

"Really, there's nothing here. I don't feel a thing." Kiki reached across the table and took Janine's hands. "But we'll give it a major-league try. A little show to get those book ends." Kiki smiled sweetly at Ted. "Ready? We are going to call on the spirit of the little girl. Rumor has it, the girl is often heard singing *Ring Around the Roses*. We should call to her with her song." Kiki glanced at the door the server disappeared through. She looked back at Ted. "Do you think we could get some water?"

"Am I a waiter?" he snarled. Ted often snarled, so they were used to it. He turned toward the doorway and redirected his booming voice. "Hey! Can we get some water in here?"

"Better order a whisky sour too. Two if you want one," Kiki advised. She smiled at Janine. "I know you won't touch one, Janine, but we," she tilted her head toward Ted, "will be glad of them in that tunnel tonight."

"What do you mean?" Ted aimed the camera on Kiki.

Kiki put on her game face. "Main Street Sacramento is buried in a tunnel underground. On those streets six feet under, I felt panic, sorrow, anger, and greed. Desperation too. It is a gold strike on the original streets of Sacramento. A California gold strike of spectral energy."

"Nice," Ted said.

Kiki turned back to Janine and grabbed her hands.

"Now let's give this the old college try," Kiki said. "We'll need something for the bookends. It's a sure thing that Ian and Carlos will turn up empty handed out there, so we need to get something usable in here. Then, I want to catch a long nap. It's going to be an exciting night."

The doors to the *Spectral Analysis* van were splayed open exposing several blinking monitors. Steve Hanks lounged on the back bumper with a large drink in one hand and a double burger in the other. He often worked and munched at the same time and had a little pudge to show for it. His command console glowed and hummed behind him.

"Everything is ready to go. I set up a fan to air out some of the smell. Lang assured me that the stench is only near your opening. That's where the rodents and such will hang out. The further in, the less stench," Steve told them.

Floodlights created a bright circle that illuminated their gear. Two air cases sat side by side on the curb. On a makeshift miniature sawhorse, headsets were lined up with decals to identify them so no one would mix them up. Doctor Who for the doctor, Patriots for Ted, Captain America shield for Carlos, and a Wonder Woman "W" for Janine. Steve recently added two small lamps to the top band of each headset for emergency purposes: a red light to keep their night vision, and a white light for total illumination. Carlos called the white one "the scared little investigator" lamp and no one had used it yet.

Kiki refused to wear a headset. She clipped a small microphone onto her shirt instead. She required unencumbered senses to receive paranormal energy.

Ted, Carlos, and Janine geared up. For feature segments, they wore violet-colored coveralls topped with red vests and black work boots. Their color choice represented the two ends of the visible electromagnetic spectrum. The red fishing vest provided pockets for tools, random gadgets, and ponytail bands for Janine's long, auburn hair. Carlos loaded his pockets with gum, candy, and treats of different sorts. As the riverfront town drew a cool evening breeze, Janine was happy for the jumpsuits.

The doctor wore a button-down shirt under a lab coat to identify himself as a scientific doctor and the leader of their investigation. He topped it with a multicolored *Spectral Analysis* tie. Kiki wore whatever she wanted, which usually turned out to be an outrageous ensemble designed to tantalize the audience. Although Kiki was a very serious spiritual seeker, she realized their program involved show business. Plus, she loved attracting male attention and didn't appear shy in the least.

For the Old Town Sacramento segment, Kiki chose dangly gold jewelry and a Western-themed outfit. She strutted into their circle in red cowboy boots, black lace gloves, tight denim jeans, and a rhinestone-studded blood-red shirt unbuttoned to reveal her deep cleavage. She probably couldn't button it properly if she tried, Janine observed. Kiki had pulled her hair into a tight bun and wore an old cameo pendant which fell into the V of her shirt, drawing eyes to her shapely breasts. Her grab-bag of items resembled a leather saddle bag right off a Pony Express horse. Kiki paused to flirt with their guide, Mr. Lang, for several minutes.

Carlos didn't conceal his amusement. He laughed loudly and flashed his dimples at them.

"No one told me we were headed to a rodeo later."

Ted and Steve chuckled. Kiki blew them a kiss then promptly ignored them.

Janine popped open an air case and retrieved a small electromagnetic field reader with five LED lamps. She secured it to her vest with a carabiner. Set to automatic mode, the EMF recorded sixty minutes of wave activity in any section of the lower-than-visual-frequency range of her choice. Her recharged temperature reader, which they called a thermal-panger, was dropped into her front right pocket for quick access. Specifically designed by the doctor, the silver meter resembled a phallic device, as Carlos loved to point out. It stored thirty minutes of temperature fluctuations to the nearest one thousandth of a degree. Her headset hung snuggly around her neck while the transmitter-receiver was zipped securely into her arm pocket. Only the stubby antenna poked out between the zippered teeth.

Steve finished his burger, stood up, and climbed into the van with a big bag of french fries.

"I'm firing up!" he announced before shutting the doors.

The crew strolled down the street to Pioneer Park and Janine clumped down the steep steps in her heavy work boots. They formed a semicircle just outside the tunnel entrance. Pitched blackness loomed in front of them. It represented a doorway into a dark and forgotten era. The ultralow wattage bulbs on the remote camera's would give them little respite from that darkness. Adrenaline jumpstarted her heart as she recalled Kiki's "gold strike of ghostly energy" declaration.

Ted planted himself a few feet apart from the crew and panned his camera over their semicircle. Showtime.

As they invaded the blackness, Kiki rattled on about the charged feel of the atmosphere. Her voice level dropped as they rounded the first corner in their route. She mentioned heading toward the basement floor of the BF Hastings building under Second Street. The dim light from Ted's camera provided just enough luminosity for the crew to be aware of each other. Janine's heart beat loudly in her ears and she wished her night vision would show up to quiet that drum.

Kiki led the pack. Her cowboy boot heels clicked rhythmically, echoing against the tunnel walls and giving them something to follow. Kiki said the Hastings ghost story seemed to be the most credible of all the tales in Old Town Sacramento. Earlier that day, she sensed a very strong energy in the building directly under the front foyer floor. According to sources, three ghosts haunted that area: a cowboy, a former saloon girl, and a small child. They caused lights to flicker, footsteps to echo, and pockets of negative energy to manifest. Kiki had detected a lingering presence hovering in the building, perhaps even two. She felt certain one of those entities was a cowboy.

Steve's voice filtered into Janine's headset, clear as a bell.

"Ted, go down all the way on your luminosity input. I'm barely getting outlines." They paused for a moment. "And your sub IR settings, one step up on your lamp. Okay, that's beautiful. Now, I see you."

Kiki's boots began clicking again and the crew followed the sound. The stench in the tunnels altered from an organic acrid to earthy damp. It became more bearable with each step away from their escape door.

"*We seek yon souls of near to there, we call on you to us appear, reveal yourself for us to see, so I command, so mote it be*," Kiki whispered. "I am starting to feel something. Something is in this tunnel. Do you hear that?"

During an investigative shoot, Kiki often vocalized her stream of thought for the camera and crew. Her tone became sharper and her volume changed slightly when she addressed a spirit.

"*I hear you, cowboy.*"

Janine pulled out her audio recorder and turned it to super slow motion by feel, then slipped it back into her pocket. She glanced toward Carlos and could just detect his outline in the darkness. She didn't need to see his face to know Carlos wore a wide grin.

Eerily, the air did feel strange. A stagnant wall of cold seemed lodged inside the tunnel. If they were going to find a ghost, the underground of Old Town Sacramento seemed like a good place.

"Do you feel it?" Kiki whispered to the crew. "The tingle? All along your skin. There is definitely something lingering down here. It's stronger in this direction." The tone of her voice changed again, "*I'm here, cowboy. Talk to me.*"

The clicking of her boots slowed to a halt. She shuffled on the hard ground and it sounded like she turned around. In the darkness, it was near impossible to tell who Kiki addressed. She whispered.

"Do you hear him? *What's that, cowboy?* He doesn't seem to be a very happy fellow."

Kiki stood with her arms out as if she were an antenna trying to pick up a signal. Janine's eyes were quite adjusted and she could see Kiki's outline perfectly. The doctor circled Kiki, studying one of his smaller gadgets. He turned toward Carlos.

"I'm getting thermo-layers at that wall," the doctor said quietly. "High to low."

"I'll go ultralow band red, just below visible on video," Carlos said.

"He's saying something," Kiki whispered excitedly. "I think he's laughing. He feels like a crude fellow. Angry and accusatory."

Kiki's boots clicked right up to the wall and stopped. A sudden spike flashed on the main EMF box making them jump. Any night vision they developed was severely reduced in that flash. Kiki began breathing harder, hyperventilating. Janine's own heart beat faster as she listened to Kiki gasp in a frightening way. Janine did not like that sound and felt her tummy tighten.

Relax, relax, she told herself, but her tummy clenched into a severe cramp. The air molecules seemed to crowd around her and she began to feel claustrophobic. Did she feel a hand on her back? Janine spun around, but nothing was there.

"*No. No. What?*" Kiki gasped again. "I am really feeling something awful here. Does anyone else feel this dark energy? I feel like he's grabbing me. Oh my god, my stomach…"

Carlos panned his camera and suddenly stopped. "Geezus! What's that!" He squeaked. "Doc, Doc, take a look at this!"

Janine glanced at the infrared camera. A definite blotch pulsed against the far wall near the thermal image of Kiki. It showed clearly on Carlos's camera display. It roughly resembled the shape of a small human body. Yet the thermal blotch was not uniform like a human heat signature would be. Parts of it moved randomly and independently flared at times. Good grief! What in the world could it be? Cool cracks appeared throughout the shape. It moved and twisted in different directions.

Janine peered into the darkness but saw nothing, just the darker figure of Kiki bent over and clutching her tummy. Was her own cramping abs sympathy pain? Did any of the guys feel a tummy ache? She tried to breathe easy. Janine definitely felt a pressure bearing down on her, squeezing parts of her body. She began to break out in a sweat.

"He's very angry. I sense terrible rage. This is not a happy spirit. *I'm not lying. I am not lying to you!*" Kiki panted. "My stomach… *I am not lying to you, cowboy!*" Kiki's boots shuffled in the dark.

"There is an enormous level of ionized air popping off in here?" the doctor whispered. "Kiki, what do you say?"

"I'm feeling manhandled, literally. Like he's trying to rip out my guts," Kiki gasped.

Quite suddenly two red spots appeared, like tiny eyes.

Janine startled, and she instinctively stepped backward. She glanced to Carlos's infrared camera display. The heat signature near Kiki flare up once before bursting into fragments that shot out in every direction. Carlos yelped and dropped his camera.

At that moment, Kiki ran to the opposite corner of the tunnel and proceeded to dry heave. Alternatively, Janine felt her own abdominal muscles flex before loosening in relief. Her breathing eased as she swallowed down the bile. Could that have been a ghost she felt? The hair on the back of her neck stood on end and it took a lot of discipline to stand calmly.

"Christ!" The curse came under Ted's breath as he stumbled a bit.

Someone flipped on their red headset lamp, Carlos. He crouched over to look for his dropped camera. The doctor spoke calmly into his headset microphone and moved toward Kiki.

"Steve, confirm that you got all that," the doctor said. "Kiki, are you okay?"

Janine also moved toward Kiki, but the doctor got there first. His hand dropped to Kiki's back and he whispered something to her. Janine felt her own hands shaking. She took a deep breath and then let it out. She told herself it was nothing, only the power of suggestion.

"Just give me air." Kiki, breathing heavily, clutched the doctor's arm. "I need to get somewhere to breath. I need fresh air."

The doctor turned toward the crew and fixed on Carlos.

"I can get her," Carlos stepped forward and scooped Kiki up as if she were a child. She whimpered against his chest as he started shuffling down the dark tunnel toward the entrance. "What the heck!"

Janine watched him stumble, banging against the wall, almost dropping Kiki. Rats. Lots of rats ran past. They crisscrossed and scurried around. Where did they come from? The pitter-patter of rat feet echoed everywhere. Janine felt ready to pee her pants. At least the rats were running away from them.

"Are you two okay?" Excitement hovered just below the calm, cool of the doctor's voice. "Are we ready to move toward the Dingle's Coffee and Mill? We should get whatever we can down here. This is quite exciting. Did you see that flash of energy on the EMF box?"

After a moment, Janine nodded and squeaked out an affirmative.

"Christ!" Ted cursed. He hoisted the camera on his shoulders. "Give the recap as we walk. Walk and talk."

Their second destination lay under the Dingle Steam Coffee and Mill building. People cited a bad haunting with inexplicable moaning sounds and the random opening and closing of doors. An old legend blamed the spirit of Nathaniel Dingle, a rough pioneer of early Sacramento, known to be a harsh and dangerous man and who committed one of his daughters to a lunatic asylum out of spite. Dingle was found mysteriously dead in his basement workshop in 1897. The current owners still used his old workshop as a storeroom of sorts. A large picture window allowed them to spy into Dingle's old basement. Before Sacramento raised the streets in 1862, the basement door and window would have been the storefront. Janine tried the door and found it locked, or blocked rather. The knob turned just fine, but the door didn't budge. Kiki's sixth sense wasn't needed to hear the noise. A loud clacking and scraping increased in volume nearer the Dingle basement.

At the doctor's orders, Janine set up a low intensity electromagnetic wave boosting antenna in the forty to fifty Hertz range. The doctor pulled out a rather large coil of copper wire from the pack he carried.

"Instead of electric oscillations, we'll try to tap into the magnetic part of the wave. Boost the receiver to full throttle."

They instantly picked up super low frequency electromagnetic signals. Janine proceeded to clamp the extra leads onto the large copper coil.

"Next, I want to do a heat sig on those pipes," the doctor pointed to the plumbing running in and out of the Dingle basement. "They might be a clue to these phantom noises."

"Uh, Doc?" Ted spoke.

The doctor turned slowly to face Janine. His eyes grew wide and his brow furrowed with concern. Ted's camera, which usually points at Kiki or the doctor, was aimed directly at Janine. She straightened up slowly, wondering why they were staring at her.

"What?"

"You're glowing," Ted blurted.

"Aye, you are glowing," the doctor confirmed with his eyes glued to her. Her heart began to pound again. "And your lovely hair is standing on end. It's static electricity or something. Don't touch anything," the doctor warned. His eyes blinked rapidly as he glanced around.

"What are you talking about?" She felt nothing out of the ordinary but then noticed her hand. To her astonishment, a soft yellow/green halo radiated from her skin. She reached up and felt stray strands of hair from outside her pony tail floating.

"Somebody is going to get one hell of an electric shock when they ground you," Ted said. "You're getting brighter."

"Are you connected to something? The antenna? Are you stepping on something?" The doctor moved cautiously near, looking everywhere. His handheld lamp blinded her as the beam swept the floor. "Don't touch anything. Don't move," he repeated, fanning the light slowly, systematically. Janine raised her hands in surrender.

"Tell us how you feel." Ted kept filming her.

"I feel fine," she spoke calmly to the camera. "I feel like, nothing. Nothing."

"Do you hear the buzz?" he asked.

"The buzz?"

"You seem to be buzzing as well as glowing," the doctor made a second slow circle around her. "Crikes. What could be causing this?"

Janine turned ever so slightly and barely lifted one foot. A sudden flash of light, coupled with searing heat, rushed up her legs, through her body, and out her fingertips. From a faraway place, she spied the doctor lunging forward before she blacked out.

"Janine!" His voice sounded desperate in the blackness. "Steve, we need EMT. Steve, do you copy? Steve, come in… Ted, I think the com is out."

"Shit! Shit! Shit!" Ted spat out in the dark.

"Janine? Ja…" The doctor stopped suddenly.

Janine saw a bright light. Her fluttering eyes allowed the light in. She noticed the doctor staring right at her. He was bent down so close that he was practically nose to nose with her. As her vision cleared, his soft blue eyes locked right onto hers and they appeared worried. Her heart melted under his gaze. She watched the emotions in his eyes slowly dissolve into relief. Ian McNally had very expressive eyes. She felt her heart begin to flutter and wondered if she was still glowing. It dawned on her that she lay limp in his arms, staring at his eyes and lips, hands casually on his shoulders; not unlike a Doctor-Kiki encounter. She felt him shift as his hands moved along her back sending tingles down her spine.

"Hello there, lass," he said tenderly, in almost a whisper. "Can you speak?"

She wriggled out of his grasp and stood on her own. Her heart still raced and she could feel a flush rushing up her neck. She was embarrassment at having a Kiki-like moment with the doctor. It wasn't in her job description to play the damsel in distress. She took a step away from him.

Ted had illuminated the "scared investigator" lamp on the top of his headset so the tunnel glowed bright. Janine pretended to dusk off invisible particles to avoid the concerned eyes boring into her. *Just give me a minute*, she silently demanded. Other than feeling very warm physically, she felt just fine.

"Are we done here?" Ted sounded anxious.

The men exchanged glances.

Janine noticed that somehow the door to the Dingle Steam Coffee and Mills basement had cracked open. When did that happen? The doctor also noticed the door. The loud creaking noises had mysteriously stopped. The tunnel was stone cold silent and the air stagnant with a burnt smell.

"We should get you out of here and checked out." The doctor blinked at Janine.

"We should check out what's in there first." Janine defiantly indicated the open door. She stared down his concern and started to move toward the basement door.

The doctor took in a sharp breath.

"Shit," Ted mumbled. "Christ. Okay, I'm still rolling."

After the paramedics cleared her, Janine opted out of going straight to bed as they advised and instead joined the crew in Steve's hotel suite to debrief the night's events. The others always drank whisky and watched the film clips, discussing which parts would work best for the show. Sometimes they recorded a little narration, or voice-over, while the experience was still fresh in their minds. Janine rarely stayed longer than necessary, but this time she was eager to see the extra information on their static sensors and cameras. There must be a reasonable explanation for what happened to her in underground Sacramento.

As they congregated around the coffee table with shots of single malt whisky, the doctor came up behind Janine with a steaming cup of tea. He passed it over slowly, taking care not to spill. He used two Styrofoam cups to protect against the heat.

"Careful, it's a wee bit hot." Ian smiled at her. "Remember, the paramedic said to keep hydrated. I'm glad you're staying up a bit longer. We want to keep an eye on you. Just give that a bit of a blow before you try it."

Well, that made her feel about five years old.

They viewed the video of Janine's experience under the Dingle building several times. Everyone was curious to discover where and when the glow of electricity originated. It appeared spontaneously and spread along her perimeter from the feet up. Her ponytail levitated a bit, and red/gold highlights appeared in her hair. When she suddenly flared up, Janine cringed as her body stretch tensely before collapsing. It appeared much more painful on video.

Then, the doctor swooped in to catch her and cradled her tenderly in his arms. The way he gazed at her fluttering eyes caused her pulse to thump. She especially enjoyed that playback in slow motion. It was more tender than his Kiki moments and exactly how Janine fantasized such an event. She kept rooting for the doctor to lean all the way down and kiss her, but it never happened.

She glanced automatically toward the doctor and caught him staring at her. He immediately began blinking and turned his attention back to the monitor. Carlos was right, the doctor definitely sent mixed messages. She blew on her tea and took a careful sip. It was extremely sweet. Apparently, the doctor added lots of honey to it.

Steve made a comment that perhaps they might infuse a little rivalry for the doctor's attention into the current season. Who will win the doctor's affections, tomboy science geek or sexy ESP vixen? The audience would surely eat it up. The look Kiki kicked out made very clear her opinion on the subject, but Steve sounded pretty set on the idea.

"I think your new antenna malfunctioned?" Kiki purred, lounging like a cat on the sofa.

"The antenna is a receiver, not a transmitter," the doctor countered. "That energy did not originate from our devices. The battery in that EM box could not pump out that kind of power." He looked a bit embarrassed. "I guess, I should take another look at it."

"Janine. You got pretty pink when you first came to." Carlos chuckled. "You were either totally fried, or… you were hoping the doctor would lay one on you."

She could kick him. Carlos, the world-class teaser, knew how she blushed beet red in certain situations. He also knew she had developed a little crush on the doctor. Did he need to call her out like that? Luckily, no one ever paid attention to his off-color comments.

The rest of the Dingle film led to nothing of consequence. For all their adrenaline, the Dingle basement turned out to be just a dusty and quiet room. Not even a mouse scurried about. The noise recorded in the hall had ceased during her blackout and they attributed the racket to the pipes of fluxing temperature.

On the other hand, the first encounter came with hidden gems. The super slowed down audio from Janine's recorder revealed actual words. A distorted but understandable *swallow nails and spit corkscrews* emanated from the recorder. Steve set it to repeat over and over again. The group laughed at the creepy voice. Was it real? What did it mean? Sounds can often be warped into words when they are sped up, slowed down, or played backward, but this voice sounded very real and clear.

Kiki insisted they caught a clip the cowboy speaking. The cowboy said those words in her ear, with that voice, at the moment Kiki began to feel ill. She insisted that he attacked her and manhandled her. The spirit of a cowboy desired to harm her in a painful way.

"In life," Kiki sipped her single malt whisky, "The cowboy was likely an outlaw who died in the great flood, probably at the very spot his spirit lingers. I sensed that he killed someone. Maybe even enjoyed it. I sensed a particularly strong hatred of women. He doesn't trust women. He called me a liar more than once. I felt him pulling at my hair. Evidently, he was trying to rip out my guts. He felt animosity towards you too, Janine. Did you feel it?"

"Come on now, Kiki," Ted called from his corner of the room. His eyes were still closed. "It wasn't that whisky sour mixed with oysters at lunch you were feeling?"

Kiki threw a small square pillow at his balding head.

"Speaking of the lunch. We need something better to bookend the show. The Delta King was a total bust." Steve played with his computers, all three of them, moving as he spliced clips together. "My lord, those rats had me freaked. They still have me freaked. They are just freaking crazy. Do you think rats were pulling your hair?"

They reviewed the low infrared playback of the man shaped rat mass, a greenish glob that moved like an amoeba across the screen. Red blotches shot out rapidly in every direction as the rats suddenly dispersed. Odd behavior, even for rats.

"I'll bet they were outlining the cowboy on the very spot he died," Kiki mused.

General agreement trickled around the room. Kiki put a hand on Steve's shoulder, not an uncommon thing for her to do. Kiki had a flirty nature around all the men.

"Are you sure our little crystal calling can't be good filler? The look on our faces when the waiter joined in on Ring Around the Roses is priceless."

"It looks forced." Steve nixed it. "The underground stuff is sure to be audience pleasers. Inconclusive, but entertaining stuff. We need something with a little more appeal for the bookends."

"He's right," the doctor added. "We can have a bit of fun entertainment," he meant the little fainting dramas. "But not too much. We want to be the show that delivers the real goods. We don't want to muck up what we discover with forced intrigue or useless comedy. I know part of all this is show business, but our main goal is pinpointing real paranormal activity. Let's brainstorm. Where can we get a quick little side story?"

"F Street house," Ted said. "Dorothy Puente lived there. Remember that story? Little old lady luring her victims with cookies."

"Wasn't there a vampire of Sacramento?" Carlos added.

The doctor shook his head.

"No, no. We do not want serial killers. Not unless there's paranormal activity involved. And we want something relatively unknown, near here, near the capitol. I don't want to drive out to that deserted Bodie again. There has to be something good close by. That place is overdone."

"We could hit Rio Linda," Janine suggested softly.

"What's Rio Linda?" The doctor asked.

"A little town about ten minutes away," she told them. "It has hauntings. Out at Dreyer Road. A tractor trailer specter. The river too. Apparently, a little girl ghost lures kids into the water. Yearly drownings are blamed on the ghost by the locals."

"People believe this?" The doctor asked, "How do you know?"

"My gram lives in Rio Linda. I'm visiting over my break. The Dreyer Road ghost and the river ghost are well known tales in Rio Linda. When a kid plays all alone, people say they must be playing with the river ghost. People scare kids about the ghost. In fact, when I used to visit my gram, I had an imaginary friend, normal, like most kids, my gram became convinced it was the river ghost and sent us away that summer. She refused to let us visit until I grew older. She believed it that much."

Ted snorted. Steve Hanks appeared riveted.

"That is fantastic!" Steve said. "We have to check it out and reconnect you with that girl spirit. This is perfect. Seriously, with your glowing segment in the tunnel it will be the perfect side story for this episode. Kiki, think about it. You specialize in child spirits. Janine used to see a child spirit. You both had encounters, fantastic encounters, in this episode."

Enthusiasm grew in all corners of the room. Even Ted sat up to give the room a good positive glare with his thumbs up. Janine began to rethink opening her big mouth and offering up Gram's ghost story. Did she really want this extra attention?

"Do you think your grandmother would fancy a visit?" the doctor asked.

"She'd love it. This is her new favorite show and she actually begged me to bring you guys over."

Everyone agreed, they would head out to Rio Linda for a simple rural ghost story to bookend the Sacramento adventure. Janine needed to give Gram a heads up.

Carlos Fuente is the Fool

Chapter 2

Rio Linda Janine

Gram, aka Martha Williams Stinger, welcomed the *Spectral Analysis* team with open arms. She hugged every member of the crew as if they were each a grandchild of hers. Gram surprised Janine when she whipped out Doctor McNally's rare book on paranormal electromagnetic spectroscopy and requested his autograph. Gram further established her superfan status by showing off Kiki Mellow designer earrings. They dangled flamboyantly from her lobes as she poured the tea. She offered cookies and coffee cake in honor of their visit. Gram lamented the crew for failing to wear their *Spectral Analysis* uniforms. She really thought they looked cool. She raved on and on about the show, and at one point, she inferred that much of the show's excitement must be directly connected to Janine's efforts. If Janine could sink into the earth, that was the moment she hoped it would happen. Yet the crew appeared to genuinely adore Gram, and everyone agreed that Janine played a vital role in their success.

Until recently, Janine managed to keep a private, businesslike relationship with her coworkers, but Gram dashed it all in a matter of minutes. She blatantly exposed a more intimate side to Janine. She gossiped about their family and relayed tales of Janine's childhood antics. She bragged about Janine's perfect student record and sports accomplishments. Gram seemed determined to systematically help Janine dismantle her carefully constructed wall, brick by brick, a wall Janine built to obscure a painfully damaged past. Gram realized that she was ready for that wall to be demolished, and Gram knew that she needed help doing it.

After everyone felt completely at home, Gram embraced Janine for a very long time and whispered into her ear, "I love you, girl."

Even after their reconnection over the long weekend at Sammy's birthday, Gram treated her like she might disappear again. Janine felt ignominy about shutting her grandma out of her life for so long. It took until recently for her to feel recovered enough to face her family again. Her heart ached thinking of the ties she nearly severed during her depression. She vowed never to go into that dark place again.

Ted attempted to charm Gram by kissing her hand and noticing the decor. He asked where he could set up the camera.

"Really? I thought Jaja was joking with this old lady when she said you wanted to interview me."

"Jaja?" Carlos chuckled at Janine. "Jaja, did you not explain to the lovely Mrs. Gram that we are on an important mission? Jaja. I love that. I'm going to start calling you Jaja."

The doctor interrupted him, "Here's the plan. Ted and Steve will remain here and film Kiki interviewing Mrs. Stinger about the river ghost, and her memories of Janine. The rest of us will make ourselves scarce, so, maybe we'll ask around a local pub or someplace, about the local ghosts. Then, later tonight, we'll head out to Dreyer Road."

Ted gave his standard thumbs up and started setting up his camera.

"Is there a local hangout we could visit?" the doctor inquired.

Janine, Carlos, and the doctor found themselves at the Old Rio Linda Bar, a hole-in-the-wall worn-out building with frosted glass windows taped over with cardboard. Dubious of entering, they were pleasantly surprised to find the dark room was clean and well maintained with cushy bar stools and a nice pool table. For early afternoon in a small town, the bar already welcomed a sizable collection of older drinkers. Couples played board games at small tables and a few old men sat at the bar. Gram certainly sent them to the right place.

Janine imagined they were unassuming to that older crowd, so it was surprising when people recognized the doctor. Admittedly, his foreign accent and intellectual aura clashed with the local surroundings. The fans waited about three minutes before pouncing on the oak table to say hello. A waiter delivered beer on tap in frosted mugs.

"Are you investigating Rio Linda?" After the first sip, questions started flying at them.

People inquired about the Providence episode and asked if there actually was something in that old hotel. The New Orleans episode also sparked questions. Did the voodoo priest really make a zombie? Where did the zombie boy go? No one knew.

Janine studied the doctor as he smiled at each person who spoke. He took every question seriously and treated everyone with regard. No quick, witty responses from Ian McNally; he formulated his answers in a thoughtful way, indicating that there were no stupid questions. Janine decided that he must have been a very pleasant professor. She could listen to him babble all day. She quickly shifted her seat slightly away because she realized she was staring at him.

Other women also found the doctor attractive. Despite of the nerdy, kind-of-stiff quality he projected, his good looks and slight Scottish accent created an alluring image. His rough hands and muscular forearms gave the impression of a powerful physique hidden underneath his proper shirt. Janine flashed on that moment in the tunnel when she woke staring into his eyes. She recalled the pleasant warmth of those overlarge hands holding her up and wondered how a real embrace from Ian McNally would feel. Her pulse ticked up just thinking about it.

From the corner of her eye, she watched him interact with a woman who obviously flirted with him. The doctor somehow made her feel noticed without acknowledging the forward behavior. Was he giving her the wrong impression? The doctor caught her watching him and smiled pleasantly at her. She glanced away, annoyed with herself.

Her psychiatrist warned her that an increased libido might be an after effect of weaning off medication. Was that what was happening? How? The weaning ended months ago. Whatever it was, she really wished her little crush would go away. Her out-of-control daydreaming was getting her all worked up.

People asked after Kiki. Where was she? Would she join them at the pub? The Old Rio Linda Bar packed in a bit more since they arrived. Janine got the distinct impression that friends were calling friends to come see the paranormal investigators.

"Kiki's interviewing someone right now," the doctor told them. "We're looking into your River Girl Ghost and the Dreyer Road Specter."

Lots of folks put in their two cents.

"We once went out to Dreyer Road after the football game," a middle-aged woman confessed. "I saw a guy driving a tractor, just inching along, and I thought it was funny, him driving out there at night. I laughed so hard I dropped my beer. When I went to pick it up, I look up again and he's gone. There was nowhere for him to go."

"We saw him in the evening clear as day. In the rearview mirror, behind us. When I turned around to look for him, he wasn't there. Vanished!" A man in a plaid shirt added.

"I saw him in the rearview mirror too. I'm not kidding about this. We never passed a guy in a tracker, but he magically appeared in the rearview mirror anyway. I'm not kidding," a woman gave.

"That river bend is spooky. You can hear a little girl crying whenever there's a soft breeze," a man in a different plaid shirt told them.

"She only speaks to children. People say, if your little sister or brother sees her, they are required to drown in that river. The river ghost always takes children who play at the water edge, out near the bend, close to the rocks," a woman sitting very close to the doctor rasped, without a doubt, a serious smoker.

"Kids drown at that river bend all the time. Half the streets in this town are named for kids that drowned at the river bend. Everyone insists the river ghost lures them, or marks them, or some other nonsense. Some folks even call her Linda after the river," an old man in a red baseball cap sat at the bar. He turned full around and stared directly at Janine.

"Linda?" Janine asked him. "People say the river ghost is named Linda?"

"Sure." He took a slow sip of his draft beer and scowled. "You're Martha's granddaughter, ain't cha? I remember when she told me that you saw the ghost. You called her Linda too. Damn near gave Martha a heart attack, you seeing that ghost. Especially since she kept the river off limits to you and your sister. Insisted the ghost would never try anything with *her* granddaughters. 'Course, others have called the ghost Mary."

Janine silently considered the old man: salt-and pepper beard with thick, grey-patched brown hair on his head, light-brown eyes behind his scowl. He seemed familiar. Did she know him?

"Keep in mind, there's plenty of kids who never said anything about no ghost and went ahead and drowned in that river," he continued. "Certain times of year, after the snow melt begins, there's nasty currents, and the water runs pretty wild. Freezing cold too. There's a natural trap at the bend where a body can get stuck under the rocks."

"You say the streets are named for kids who drowned in the river?" The doctor's interest was piqued.

"Everybody knows that," a raspy voice next to the doctor said. She had luscious red hair, but wrinkled, cracked skin. "Some people say each little child ghost can be spotted on their namesake street from time to time. I've encountered the ghost of Eloise on Eloise Street more than once."

The man at the bar let out a gruff laugh. Clearly, he thought that bit of information was rubbish.

Janine eyed the old man. He turned his back to them and didn't offer any more information. Who was he?

They returned to Gram's house to retrieve Kiki for the drive out to Dreyer Road. Steve and the doctor took off in the *Spectral Analysis* van and the others followed in a rental car after Kiki finished getting ready. Kiki said that Martha Williams Stinger insisted on putting the entire crew up in her rather-large house that night. Gram pushed the offer numerous times. Janine's grandmother lived in one of the original farm houses in Rio Linda.

Although the house was huge, sections of the house were in dire need of repair: faded paint inside and out, chipped moldings, and areas of the wood floor were slightly warped. But Gram's beautiful antique furniture, refurbished and cozy, were all the rage of fashion again. The recently remodeled kitchen was filled with modern energy-saving appliances and finished with solid granite countertops. Best of all, the house offered plenty of room to spread out and relax.

In the interview, Gram told Kiki that most of the furniture came handmade from Europe over one hundred years ago. Antiques delivered during the main reconstruction phase in the early 1890s, after the great valley flood. As the first structure in town, the Williams house once hosted important visitors to Rio Linda. Janine was surprised to learn that Gram's house had such history and was filled with such old heirlooms. The Williams "mansion" boasted two wings, which were added to the original one-room structure during the Gold Rush era. Gram only used one bedroom in the main wing, while her roommate Misty used another bedroom in the smaller wing. Gram's roommate doubled as a cook and a maid.

Janine recalled Misty from childhood, always in the house but hardly ever seen. Gram always said that Misty feared crowds and detested being around people. Misty diligently kept the rooms dusted and aired for guests, even though guests rarely visited in Gram's old age.

Kiki agreed to spend the night. Not to worry, Kiki was actually very excited at the prospect. She looked forward to sleeping in the old farmhouse that once founded the town. Kiki said that she caught a tremor of a presence in Gram's backyard, and wondered if she would sense any other Rio Linda ghosts in Gram's old "mansion."

"Your gram is a treasure trove of history," Kiki gushed.

Sometime after the interview, Kiki changed clothes for the Dreyer Road excursion. She teased her hair into a bob, and she wore a shimmery pink jacket that shouted Pink Lady's. Kiki's kohl-lined green eyes bore into her.

"Your grandmother is totally tapped in, like me. Only, she doesn't know it, or admit it. Extrasensory perceptions like ours are genetic, Janine."

Carlos followed the GPS directions to Dreyer Road. They drove toward farmland and horse pastures. Very little traffic went past in the early evening.

"Your story chilled me," Kiki said. "Chilled me. Hey, Ted, was the story about Janine and her imaginary friend chilling or what?"

"Chilling," Ted agreed flatly. His eyes remained closed.

"What was so chilling about it?" Janine asked.

"You'll have to watch the interview to see how Gram tells it." Kiki reached out to cover her hand. "But the main gist of it is, you were targeted, by the River Girl Ghost. Targeted for death. Children who see that ghost are meant to drown. Oh, don't worry. You're safe now. Martha, Gram, insists that only small children are in danger of the ghost, because they don't understand and can be lured into the water. As a child, you were on her death list. Your Gram is sure of it. Everybody thought so, she says. You spoke to the ghost regularly. She was your best friend. You repeated things she said, things other drowning victims also repeated."

"Like what? What did I say?"

"Weird stuff, like *seek redemption, fill an empty spot*, but with no context or explanation. Crazy talk, your grandma said. She didn't know what it meant."

"Dreyer Road!" Carlos interrupted.

"We'll talk about it later." Her soft touch turned into a brief reassuring squeeze, then Kiki let go of Janine's hand. *When did Kiki find time to change the color of her fingernails*, Janine wondered. Tan last night, hot pink today. Kiki slipped into her quiet moment of meditation. She always did. Kiki claimed it centered her and opened her psyche to the other side.

The *Spectral Analysis* van idled on the shoulder of the pavement. Somewhere on that lonely rural road, they hoped to see the farmer and his tractor.

Experiencing actual paranormal activity is rare. Recording scientific evidence, practically impossible. On Dreyer Road, they ditched the EMF box because the power lines on both sides of the road provided too much close electrical interference. Water pipes poked up 15 yards off the shoulder of the asphalt, rare and unfortunate. Piped water often caused phantom noises. Carlos pulled out his handheld infrared camera. Luckily, the camera only took a scratch from the fall in the tunnel. Janine grabbed both an audio recorder and her thermal-panger, two meager gadgets used in the hopes of backing up their primary paranormal receptor; Kiki.

Kiki and the doctor set out on a casual stroll down the deserted road. They walked toward Ted, who held the main camera. Ted slowly moved backward while he filmed. A boom microphone stuck out on a short telescoping pole attached to the camera.

The doctor recounted several tales of the Dreyer Road ghost to Kiki and they discussed their authenticity. Kiki once said that viewers desired a rich ghost story more than anything else. They yearned for the lives behind the ghosts, more so than any blip on a box. Carlos and Janine followed about ten feet behind. Temperature readings on her thermal-panger jumped from the positive hundreds to the negative fifties.

Crap! Temperature fluctuated dramatically in natural settings, but this jumping around was impossible. Janine shook it; no change. She knocked it against her leg with a tap, tap, tap; nothing. She hit it hard with her open palm; still wild readings. An amused expression broke out on Carlos's face as he watched her abuse of the silver phallic-shaped device. She checked the battery level; good. She slipped it into her back jeans pocket with a frown and shrugged.

"I hope you're nicer to your boyfriends," Carlos snickered.

"In op," Janine ignored his comment. "I don't know what's wrong with it."

"Maybe it got fried. It was on you when you got fried in the tunnel."

An inoperative thermal device was bad news. Making a big deal out of changes in temperature was a huge part of her onscreen job. Janine definitely checked the silver panger the previous night and it seemed fine. Perhaps she should have run a reset on it. Hopefully, the doctor would not ask about temperature readings on their stroll down Dreyer Road. She focused on the visual display of her audio recorder instead. The needle jumped with Kiki and the doctor's conversation. She played around with the tuning to hit sounds beyond the sonic range.

"Take a look." The doctor waved Janine and Carlos forward. "We see something out there in the field, just off the road."

"I don't see anything," Carlos said.

"Look at the air above the ground," Kiki told him, "Close to that tree."

"It looks a little blurry," Janine offered.

"A bit like convection currents over hot asphalt? But at this time of evening, and in the grass?" the doctor offered back.

"Or maybe it's the start of a spectral mass—wait!" Kiki stopped and rotated around. She searched up and down the street. From out of a pink mushy bag, she pulled a tortoiseshell compact out and opened it. She peered into the oval mirror while slowly pivoting. She stopped. Her eyes squinted into the small mirror purposely. She frowned before snapping the compact closed. "I'm not getting anything."

Kiki often claimed that spirits were more easily seen reflected in mirrors than with direct observation. Carlos fondly pointed out that it was the exact opposite for vampires. Janine recalled that the man on the tractor often appeared in rearview mirrors, according to folks at that bar.

"Do you feel this?" Kiki bent down and put her hand on the ground. The doctor did the same. The two spoke about the ground vibrations while Ted slowly circled and filmed the conversation. Janine pulled out the thermal-panger. It still fluctuated wildly.

"Vibrations. Like a truck on the road," the doctor said. He looked up and down the street. "Yet, there's nothing out here."

Kiki's eyes widened. "It's stopped. No, it's still there. Stronger?"

A train whistle echoed in in the dark distance. They chuckled. Then the doctor shook his head and stood up. He offered a hand to Kiki and helped her rise.

At that moment, Janine noticed her thermal-panger blinking a constant 20.5 degrees Celsius. The gauge miraculously fixed itself. Janine glanced at Carlos and he winked.

The group moved forward, toward the tree. Upon closer inspection, the blurry spot turned out to be right over a drainage hole. The thermal-panger confirmed a temperature rise above the drain and Carlos's camera picked up warm thermal currents emanating from the opening. They hung out for another half hour before calling it a night. Any ghosts on Dreyer Road did not come out for *Spectral Analysis*.

The guys headed back to the hotel in the van while Kiki and Janine drove the rental car to Gram's house.

The next morning, Janine interrupted Gram and Kiki at the kitchen nook table. They were speaking intimately with their heads bent together. An enormous breakfast spread of bacon, biscuits, jams, butter, and fruit lay across the counter. Gram beckoned Janine over and directed her to sit in her normal place at the table, the same spot she always took as a little girl. She noticed that Kiki sat at Juliana's spot. Gram had placed Kiki in the superior big sister chair.

The early morning in that familiar kitchen had an odd effect on Janine, a feeling similar to being on too much cold medication. She felt slightly sluggish and laden down with images she couldn't quite remember. The aromas, colors, the very density of the air provoked a flicker of feeling from her distant childhood. Gram's wallpaper of small stenciled flowers unsettled her.

Kiki's hands were wrapped around an empty teacup. Her lips pursed as she stared into the delicate porcelain dish. Kiki poured a little more tea into the cup, swirled it around, and gave it back to Gram. Then she stood up.

"It needs a little more sediment in there," Kiki said. "Sip that slowly and I'll be right back." Kiki left the kitchen.

"Kiki is reading my tea leaves," Gram daintily sipped her tea.

Of course. Reading tea leaves turned out to be a very popular blip on the show during the first season. To date, Kiki only read leaves once on camera, but fans still wrote in about it. Even so, Kiki rarely agreed to do a tea leaf reading. She avoided it because she said she wasn't any good at prophecy.

Also, if she sensed anything frightful, she wouldn't want to look at the leaves and that left people upset at her. To demonstrate, Kiki read Ted and Carlos's leaves but stopped short when she got to Janine's cup. She didn't even glance at Janine's cup. Obviously, Kiki's message to Janine was ominous. Carlos laughed it off later that night. He said that Kiki was just flexing her feminine muscles. Kiki was a showboat. Look at her outrageous camera outfits. She was clearly defining the pecking order. Kiki wanted it very clear that she was the alpha female and wanted to be sure Janine got that message. *Ignore her*, he advised.

Janine poured cream into her own coffee mug and watched it swirl into a light brown soup. She helped herself to the biscuits and fruit. Gram loved rich creamy butter and the smooth spread made everything quite tasty. Janine stared at Gram's teacup.

"What kind of tea is that?" she asked.

"A red raspberry and green tea mix. Want some?" Gram offered the cup. Janine took a mouthful of Gram's tea.

Ugh, quite sour. She shook her head.

Gram laughed and finished the last bit as Kiki returned and sat down. Kiki retrieved the cup and tilted it around, studying the interior. She set the cup aside and smiled at Gram.

"You're definitely in for a turn of fortune," Kiki told Gram. "Major wealth is coming your way. That sounds so cliché, but the leaves say what they say. One sour note, I'm not quite sure how to put it. The return may not be worth the investment?" She shook her head and laughed.

Kiki poured more coffee into her own mug, an old University of Chicago cup, then took it as she made her way back to her room. Off to shower and get dressed, she announced. The guys were due to pick them up in a little less than an hour.

Gram beamed at Janine.

"Jaja, I'm so glad you came to visit. But does Juju need to come too? Does she need to bring the kids right now?"

"Oh Gram, you should let everyone visit more often," Janine chided her. "Juliana's kids have never seen this house, and it's a part of our family history! Juliana and I used to beg for a visit. We loved coming to California and sleeping on your back porch. Remember taking us to the ocean? Fisherman's Warf in San Francisco? Horse-riding at Gold Country? Remember taking us to ski at Homewood in Tahoe? Juliana wants the kids to experience some of those places."

A look of concern crossed Gram's eyes.

Janine continued, "Plus, you're getting a little old to tramp to Texas every year, let Juju bring the kids to you."

That sounded a little off from center, but thankfully, Gram didn't notice. Gram nervously tapped her forefinger on the nook table, deep in thought. Janine evened out the tone of her voice.

"You seem to be getting along with Kiki. Kiki never read my tea leaves. You two are really hitting it off." Gram grinned and nodded. "What exactly did you tell her yesterday? She was very hyped about your interview."

"I just told her the truth."

"You mean about my imaginary friend?" Janine asked. "Did you tell her my imaginary friend was a ghost?"

Gram poured coffee into her cup. She drank it black.

"There goes your fortune."

"Oh, that's just a bunch of nonsense. Fun nonsense," Gram said. Her mood changed to nervous. She rearranged the plate of biscuits. "Do you think those boys will be hungry?"

"I don't know, maybe. What did you tell Kiki?"

Gram's eyes met hers, "Don't you remember anything about your imaginary friend? Do you remember anything at all? That summer, you constantly rambled about her."

Janine considered that question. Yes, of course she remembered her imaginary friend. Her name was Linda, she had a funny accent, she had blond hair…but did she really remember those things? The true answer was, no. Janine did not have a single memory of that part of the summer. Anything she knew about her imaginary friend came from her older sister, Juliana. Juliana fed her the details long after Janine grew older. Juliana teased her about once having an imaginary friend. She claimed that Janine insisted Linda spoke in a funny way. Juliana said that Janine swore the girl had yellow hair and sky-blue eyes. When Janine ruminated over things, she had no personal recollection of her imaginary friend at all.

Except, trapped in the back of her mind, she did have those memories. Late the previous night, she dreamt about her phantom friend and an image of that girl hovered just below the surface of her subconscious. Maybe the house was playing tricks on her. The house definitely stirred up feelings of childhood. The atmosphere teased her memories in the dark of night, but in the light of day, she could not recall a single detail of any of them.

"I don't remember," Janine confessed. "I was too young. What, was I, five or six?"

"You were barely five that summer," Gram told her. "You drew a hundred pictures of her."

"I did?"

"Of course," Gram said. "Kiki asked me to find them, and I'm going to set about doing that later today. I kept every drawing you made. I have piles and piles of paper and such in the attic. I'm certain I saved the pictures you made of…of your imaginary friend. I wouldn't throw those away."

The doorbell rang. Janine jumped up to answer it, but Gram's maid Misty already held the door open and the guys filed in. They came early and hungry. Gram loved feeding people. She did not let them refuse her the right to cook each man eggs made to order. Fresh eggs from her free-range hens, she told them. The hens roamed all over her hill during the day and respectfully laid eggs in a coop right outside the side door. Then, they disappeared into the brush to sleep at night. There were over twenty hens in that brood. At one time, Rio Linda was famous for poultry farming.

The doctor grinned openly at Janine making her feel a bit uncomfortable. She ignored him by turning to Carlos. Carlos winked and chuckled, so she left to change into her jeans and a *Spectral Analysis* T-shirt.

When she returned to the kitchen, everyone held a plate full of eggs, bacon, fruit, and a biscuit. Scrambled with cheese for Carlos, sunny side up for Ted, not enough left to tell for Steve, and over easy for the doctor. By the time the guys finished breakfast, Kiki waltzed down the stairs ready to go.

They set off toward the bend in the Rio Linda River. Steve and Ted drove the van down a gravel path ferrying the big camera and bulky equipment. Everyone else walked. While the river access road was no more than a short drive from Gram's house, the river itself was much closer by foot. They only needed to cross over a small hill before reaching the edge of the water. A constant babble could be heard quite clearly right outside the back kitchen door.

The doctor and Kiki walked ahead, discussing last-minute details of the upcoming segment. Gram's hens clucked comically away in a large gaggle toward the brush. Kiki and the doctor spoke easily together and Janine felt something very similar to envy. Kiki seemed to chat and flirt so effortlessly with practically everyone. Janine wondered when she would excise her demons enough to flirt again.

Carlos strolled alongside her, fiddling with his portable ion wand. He had it in a plastic bag and obviously wanted to seal it with the duct tape hanging from his mouth. His eyes inquired if she'd like a similar setup for her device. Janine flipped her thermal-panger over and showed him the placard. Good for ten meters submerged. He rolled his light brown eyes.

"That's not going to work in a plastic bag." She smiled at him.

A narrow beach of pebbles came into view. Further up river, Janine spied the blackberry brambles she had forgotten about. Back there, somewhere, a narrow path led to more houses. Gram's little portion of beach had always been a popular path for the neighborhood dog walkers, but that particular morning, the river was deserted. Even though the water ran smooth and slow, manmade signs warned of a deeper, faster current hidden beneath the surface. The air progressively grew cooler as they neared the water. Janine registered the temperature drop on her gage. Even on a nice sunny day, the water could be freezing. River water in the valley came from snowmelt runoff from the mountains.

At the bend in the river, the infamous boulders glistened in the morning light. Someone had spread out a blanket where the pebbly beach met the sparse grass and put the fancy EMF box in the center of it. The big coil antenna was nowhere in sight. The doctor motioned for Carlos and Janine to stay near the blanket with the big box. At the van, Ted pulled out large, overall-looking pants from the open rear door.

"What are those?" Janine asked.

"Fishing bibs." Carlos said. "The doctor had them delivered to the hotel. It's why he didn't want to stay at your Gram's last night."

"Gram was okay with that."

"That's good," Carlos told her. "He was worried that she, you, both of you, might be insulted that we didn't stay at the house. He didn't want anyone upset that he declined the invitation."

That explained the funny look this morning, she thought. And here she imagined she may have caught the doctor's eye. Wow, Janine felt pretty stupid. She fiddled quietly with the EMF box as the doctor and Kiki slipped into the overlarge, rubber fishing bibs.

The farmer johns came with built-in boots and suspenders. Kiki and the doctor would not get wet unless they let the water rise above chest level. Kiki must have known the cut of those fishing bibs. Under the sweatshirt she ditched, she wore just the right clingy top to make her ensemble fall just this side of decent. The doctor and Kiki chuckled together as Ted joined them in tall rubber rain boots near the shoreline. The doctor's head swiveled toward Janine and Carlos.

"We're going to get started," he called to them. "Tune in at the forty to eighty Hertz range on the box and focus on the lower end. Other than that, just soak up the ambience as we venture toward the center of the bend."

"Want the thermal-panger?" Janine called to the doctor. "It's waterproof."

She jumped up as he nodded and made her way to the rocky shore. She held the thermal-panger out to the doctor. As he searched his ensemble for a place to put it, she found herself fixating on the stubble along his chin. She resisted a sudden urge to touch that roughness. He smelled nice. One of his hands fiddled unsuccessfully with the zipper pocket on the bib. He had very large hands, she noticed. Janine suddenly snapped the carabiner onto his right suspender. Then she took the silver probe and pushed it firmly into one of the belt loops on his bib. Before she could turn around, the doctor gentle grabbed her arm. There was that look of concern again and her heart skipped a beat as she gazed into his soft blue eyes. Then her eyes drifted to his lips.

Why was she reacting this way with the doctor, it couldn't just be weaning from the meds? Way back at the start of season one, when she was still a little foggy from the drugs, Carlos and Janine used to joke that Ian was a bit of a dweeb. His female fan club made them laugh. If they only knew how nerdy he was. Definitely a nervous Clark Kent hid behind his suave TV image. Now, with her mind cleared up, Janine found herself becoming one with the fans.

"Kiki says she's already feeling a tingle about this place." She zoned in on his jaw as he talked. "Just take it easy over there. According to the interview, you are linked to the spirit that haunts this river. Just concentrate on what you feel. Don't worry too much about the EM box. Just see if you feel anything."

I'm certainly feeling something, the blood pounded in her ears. *Stop it!* Her juvenile crush was beginning to get the better of her. He patted the temperature gauge.

"Thanks for the panger."

She nodded and turned. The big eye of Ted's camera lens focused directly on her as he filmed their exchange. Janine bit back a comment at the intrusion. Of course, in this episode, she was meant to be a major part of the storyline. She brushed past Ted, annoyed at him. She was not going to be part of a simulated rivalry for the doctor's attention.

Back near Carlos, she plopped down and put the EMF display tablet on her lap. They watched as the doctor and Kiki slowly waded into the river while conversing with each other, and to the camera. Kiki pointed toward the center of the river and her voice carried through the crisp air. Janine nudged Carlos.

"Did she just say baptisms?" she asked. "That this is where the early townsfolk performed baptisms?"

"Yep."

Kiki and the doctor moved out of earshot into deeper water. Janine watched as the two moved around, circling each other, smiling and chatting. Kiki said something funny, and the doctor laughed, throwing his head back. He grinned at Kiki in a pleasing way. Wouldn't it be funny if Kiki slipped under that cold surface? *Come on, little ghost, if you're out there, get her a little wet, so I command, so mote it be,* Janine joked silently to herself, mimicking Kiki's witch talk.

Kiki and the doctor turned their attention to the boulders at the bend. The rocks reflected a beautiful metallic luster. The doctor pulled out the thermal-panger and put it in the water. His large hand moved the temperature reader around, making swirls. The ends of his rolled sleeves got wet. Janine wondered if his arms and shoulders were very muscular beneath that dark blue button-down shirt. Of course they were, and she could just make out the line of his pecs against the material. *Ugh!* She should just accept that she found Ian McNally a very attractive man.

A rush of cool air blew across her neck. It felt like someone brushing her hair aside with a light touch. She instinctively shifted around, expecting to see someone, maybe Steve. No one was there. Carlos noticed her movement and gave her a questioning look before turning back to the ion detector. He adjusted the gain as he began picking up odd ticks. The cool breeze hit her neck again. Janine turned to survey the trees and tall grass. Nothing moved. There wasn't a breeze. Her vision began to tunnel and a sudden heaviness poured into her veins. Every cell in her body pinged on high alert. Her heart sped up. For whatever reason, her body began to escalate into panic mode.

She tried to focus on the action in the water but her body systems distracted her. She squinted her eyes and strained to hear. She felt something, or someone, trying to say something to her. Kiki's head suddenly snapped up and her green cat's eyes narrowed. Kiki sensed something too. Kiki's head swiveled to look around before her eyes halted on Janine. Kiki began moving toward the shore, fighting the resistance of the moving water.

A soft tickle developed deep in her ear and became a faint whistle. The whistle increased in volume and began to sound like a distant child's voice. Janine's body felt heavy, like lead, and she began to tilt over. Time decelerated into ultraslow motion. Her eyelids drooped heavily. She concentrated on Kiki and the doctor.

She watched Kiki flail, slip, and fall deeper into the river. Water crossed Kiki's bib line and her eyes registered the shock of freezing snowmelt by becoming large and round. Kiki's shirt soaked up water and started to darken and cling to her skin. At one point, the shirt passed the line into indecent. As usual, the doctor swooped in to catch her in a perfect Doctor-Kiki encounter. *So very romantic.* In that moment, Janine's eyelids slammed shut and the voice in her ear became clear.

Why did you leave me?

"Janine! Janine!" Carlos shook her.

Voices echoed in the far distance, mixed with the splashing of water. Carlos helped her sit back up. Janine blinked and opened her eyes. She felt perfectly fine; no more tunnel vision, no more leaden weight, just a bit of breathlessness. The doctor and Kiki squeaked up in wet rubber suits.

Ted pointed the big camera directly at Janine. The doctor bent down to grab her hand while Kiki shivered in front of her. Kiki's teeth chattered loudly and water dripped down her rubber suit as she bent forward.

"She was here, wasn't she? The ghost. I felt her and saw the air wavering near you. Did you see her? Did you feel her? Did you hear her? What happened over here?"

Both Kiki and Janine were shaking.

"She said something," Janine whispered.

"What? What did she say?" Kiki's green, hypnotic eyes urged her.

"She said, why did you leave me?" Janine's voice was soft.

At that moment, Steve appeared with a large towel and wrapped the top of Kiki as he helped her out of the bib. Cold water saturated the pebbles making them shine deeper colors. Kiki's voice ran a mile a minute but Janine didn't register any of it. The doctor still held her hand and she gently pulled it away, embarrassed. A blackout and a fainting. What was going on with her?

"I'm fine," she told him, avoiding his eyes.

Ian nodded and stood. He took a few steps away to remove his wet bib. He stepped toward Kiki and Ted as they set up for a parting shot with the boulders in the background. Kiki stood wrapped in the thick towel, decent again, but cozy in the one-armed embrace of the doctor.

On the walk back to Gram's house, Janine realized that they spontaneously decided to do a feature in Rio Linda. Kiki believed that the river ghost story could be flushed out more. They could be the first investigators to put it on the paranormal activity map. Excited voices brainstormed how they'd run it; as a two-part story on the Sacramento area or a standalone episode based on Rio Linda? They needed to discover the complete back story for the ghost and interview more people. There were loads of folks in that bar who wanted to help.

With their two-week break about to start, everyone discussed how to best adjust the schedule. Steve would fly back to the Texas studio to put finishing touches on the Old Town clips, then return as soon as possible, and Ian and Kiki would stay in town to research the area. They needed to develop an origin story for the ghost. The next episode in the *Spectral Analysis* lineup could easily be pushed back to make room for a closer examination of Rio Linda.

IX

The Hermit

Janine Stinger is the Hermit

Chapter 3

Sierra Nevada, 1839 Helen

Only four families remained from the dozen that forged a trail from Missouri to the top of the world. Strength comes in numbers, people said, and many advised them to travel in a later, larger group. It would be safer and easier to share supplies and share burdens. They could better help one another across the open country for the California coast and the port settlement of Yerba Buena. But they believed a larger number would prove too ripe with human disagreements and didn't listen. Also, they wanted to arrive first to the new coast and have the first pick of the land.

They set out with a count of fifty-six wagons, a small party, but full of hope with their carefully selected provisions. Now their supplies had dwindled down to three rickety wagons stripped bare of all but meager tools, a Bible, a ledger diary, and a weakened old man. Twenty souls huddled together under a frayed and sagging canvas cover. Twenty souls sat on top of a large mountain range staring at the ice-blue water of the most beautiful lake imaginable, humbled. The oldest soul being the dying old man in the wagon, and youngest being the little girl, Linda, so vivaciously alive at five years old.

A recent storm drove home the name of their jagged mountain range, the Sierra Nevada. The wind blew freezing cold over their heads making the canvas cover dance precariously between the trees. From under that cover, Helen watched Mr. Frederick Stauch limp toward the blue lake. He appeared in terrible pain. The wound he acquired during the Indian attack in the Forty Mile Desert, festered. Everyone feared he might not be able to keep that leg unless things changed for the better. Still, he got off easier than most. His wound was the only physical ail his family suffered. He could have avoided that wound altogether, had he run away from the Hansen encampment instead of toward it. Frederick only managed to save the old man by carrying the strongbox for him. The wrong box. Oh, the ire on Frederick's red face when he discovered the box was not the one safeguarding the tinder but the box with Hansen's ledger and a bottle of spirits. At least the foul liquid served to cleanse the many wounds suffered in their midst.

Helen noticed her husband, Nick, trudging into the wind toward the minister, Frederick. The two men conferred quietly as they queried the sky. Certainly, the men were afraid to tarry because the weather threatened to change. But moving forward would put a strain on the wounded. Not one of them doubted the old man in the wagon, Oscar Hansen, would die if jostled further. And the younger Miller man suffered an arrow through the arm while his wife laid miserable with the beginnings of a pregnancy. And her dear friend Irene would surely pass before the end of the night.

Thick animosity toward the dying old man streamed constantly from every circle, because the old man's sons had been their guides and led them astray. Oscar Hansen's sons were both taken in the blink of an eye and rotted in the same meadow where they had been butchered. The burden now fell on her husband and the minister to lead them to the coast. The only remaining item of the Hansen's family was the ledger book his son Stanley kept as a diary of their journey. This item passed into Helen's care. Nick and Frederick both insisted she keep up the daily record because she made very handsome letters. Some authority may ask for it as a testament to the trials of their journey.

Helen took the small bottle of black ink Mr. Hansen prized and placed it in her shirt next to her heart. It badly needed warming from the cold air.

Nicholas glanced toward her, and his gaze skirted their huddled mass. His eyes met hers for a brief moment before settling on Peter Webber. Peter recognized the summons. He and his boys stood wearily and left the protective cover to shuffle toward Frederick and Nick. The men stood close together, conferring. The wind blew their voices away, but their postures revealed tension. White flurries fluttered around them. Gustoff, who was not yet a man, stood shivering and clutched his blackened paw close to his chest. Peter Webber became more agitated. The minister, Frederick, stretched to his full height in response. Helen's husband, Nick, stepped between them, the peacemaker. His full head of sandy-brown hair blew about. It made him appear like his younger self for a moment, causing her breath to catch. Suddenly the men split up. Each moving quickly as the snow flurries grew. Nicholas entered the shelter and moved toward her.

"Grant, Ethan." Nick shook their sons awake. "Hurry now. You'll need to help Rolf and Gustoff. They are breaking down what's left of the Hansen wagon for lumber and parts. A wheel might be fit for ours."

"Are we staying another night?" Grant jumped to his feet.

"We are," Nick told him.

"The Webber boys need assistance moving Oscar Hansen and we will be erecting a more sturdy shelter. We need to better place the fire for tending."

Helen's sons, Grant and Ethan, went off quickly. Helen reached out to grab her husband before he also departed. His eyes found hers, and she noted his furrowed brow.

"It's too early for winter. Surely this flurry will cease by tomorrow," he assured her. "The old man will die soon. Moving him would unduly hasten his death, and if we rest here, Mrs. Lumen might make a recovery, if God wills it. John Miller and his wife also need the respite, and Peter Webber's own daughter is not fit to travel. I think this is best."

"What did Peter say?" she whispered.

"He urges us to keep moving. He wants to leave Hansen's father here to die and move down the pass quickly. He blames Hansen for all our troubles, but he has no means to travel. The red wagon is beyond repair and the Webbers must rely on ours, and Stauch. The oxen are near exhaustion. Peter would continue alone but knows he cannot. He believes Hansen's curse will follow us if we dally. He now believes Whitaker spoke the truth, that Hansen purposely led us astray on the trail. He believes we should have left with the Whitaker group."

Helen pressed her lips together. Deep down, she also harbored a foul feeling for their complicity with Hansen. The ledger diary was not written for eyes other than himself, and he was a devil of a man, but she did not say as much to Nicholas. The men did not bother to read the diary contents and she would not burden them with those words now, words that confirmed everything. Nicholas took her hand.

"A few days rest will give our numbers strength," he told her. "We found this rough pass and beautiful lake by the favor of God. It is not the Great Valley we hoped for, but here there are charms. With no guide, the storm fooled us in our direction. Not to fear Helen, we will likely be in the Great Valley soon."

She gazed over the blue lake. The surface acted like a perfect mirror and clouds drifted rapidly in the reflection. Tall conifers grew thick all around the lake, framing the blue waters with a luxurious green ring. Surely, they were very near to heaven. Perhaps they needed to pause and reflect on their inactions under Hansen.

The young girl, Linda, ran up as Helen prepared to write in the ledger. The child's wide and curious eyes knew not the severity of their circumstances and sparkled with amusement.

"I want to watch," Linda said.

"Of course." Helen smiled at the young girl.

Then she pulled the small vial of ink from her shirt and the turkey quill Stanley Hansen had used daily. The warmth brought the dark ink back to life and she proceeded to add her first entry into the diary. Linda smiled, fascinated.

Chapter 4

Research Janine

Spectral Analysis began with funding from Steve Hanks. Hanks, along with Ian McNally, devised a rough outline of the show the summer the doctor guest lectured at NYU. Steve became the executive producer while Ian became the main character. How Kiki came on board, Janine could only guess, but she definitely entered during the beginning stages of concept development. The three of them knew each other fairly well and envisioned the different aspects of *Spectral Analysis* as a team. Ted was a NYU film classmate of Steve's. He signed on before any recruitment went out. Carlos and Janine applied online and underwent an extensive interview process in Texas. Their actual job title was technical assistant to paranormal research doctor. Knowledge of electronics and the electromagnetic spectrum was a requirement, as well as having an open mind.

At first, Janine didn't realize she would be on camera. She thought it was a behind the scenes science gig, but Steve said there might be a tiny bit of camera time, so, just in case, they wanted a science woman to balance out the crew. Because of Kiki, they needed a "neutral female." Janine was the neutral female, whatever that meant. She guessed it meant boring and plain.

Spectral Analysis operated out of a two-room studio and a small office in Austin, Texas. Both Carlos and Janine were Austin locals, while the others moved from New York City to work on the show. Their location stemmed from the fact that Steve Hanks was originally an Austin boy. Other people involved with *Spectral Analysis* included a guy in promotions, a money manager, a lawyer, and one office person named Cheryl. It was a very low-key operation. Other than Cheryl, the main receptionist, Janine only ever dealt with Steve, Ted, Carlos, Kiki, and the doctor.

At the end of the first season, there was a little after-party, but Janine opted out. Having the job actually helped her gain enough confidence to reconnect with her family. For a long time, she alienated them through avoidance, ashamed of being on psychiatric medication and of the events that occurred during college. At the conclusion of that first season, she forced herself to attend a potentially very stressful event, her niece Sammy's fourth birthday party. It was during Sammy's party when the show's lawyer called about a second season.

Originally, she applied for the job on a lark, believing the show wouldn't really pan out. She planned to use the sign-on money to pay for her next semester at Texas A&M. But Janine didn't realize how much fun the show would be, or how well paying and popular. In fact, no one imagined *Spectral Analysis* would last past three episodes and result in the longer time commitment.

Getting a regular paycheck was nice. The college money her father set aside had been eaten away by medical bills, and Janine had no intention of asking her sister if there was anything left. For the second season, the show made her an offer she couldn't refuse. The extra season would take care of tuition for the rest of her education, if she budgeted smart. Of course, keeping the job meant delaying that very education again. Thankfully, Gram, her sister, nieces and nephew helped make the decision. As huge fans of the show, they listened when she got the call and unanimously voted for her to continue ghost hunting. Janine could see the relief in her sister's eyes, relief that she finally worked far enough past the events that landed her in the mental ward to make a solid connection with something.

Janine needed Juliana's approval to keep her momentum going. She owed it to her family to make a full recovery, and she wanted to please her young nieces and nephew. Meeting the giggling four-year-old Sammy completely melted her. She came extremely close to missing that little girl's entire childhood. So, she decided to continue with the show.

Between film locations, Carlos and Janine took a break while the others finalized plans for the next episode. For this particular break, Janine agreed to visit family in Rio Linda. She didn't anticipate visiting with her ghost-hunting coworkers, but when they switched the focus to Rio Linda, Kiki and the doctor decided to stay in town with her. They needed to conduct major research on the river ghost and develop a plausible story from scratch. Janine's grandma insisted that they stay in her large house.

*W*hy *did you leave me?* Janine tossed and turned with a mixture of vivid dreams of love wrapped inside dark nightmares of fear. In the dream, someone followed her and she was happy about it, but when he closed in behind her, fear took over. She tried to run, but the air became thick, like water. She tried to look behind her, but there was only darkness. First, she ran across the pebbly beach on a bright, sunny morning. Then the ground altered into dark woods of leaves and rocks and twisted tree roots. She stumbled through the umbrage, barefoot and fearing for her life. *Why did you leave me?*

Janine sat up in bed, breathing hard. Parts of that nightmare always crept into her dreams. An image of her niece Sammy lingered in her head. Sammy, who she only just met on her fourth birthday. Then she recalled the little girl's voice in her head saying, *why did you leave me?*

She threw a pillow across the room in frustration and guilt, then dropped her head into her hands, exhausted from all the running.

*G*ram and Janine shifted through old papers and photos as they pulled them out of a dusty attic box. It was very slow going because Gram felt the need to exclaim over almost every print. Between the photos, she pulled other useless items from the box: old bills, menus, and random advertisements. Gram insisted they would soon find the drawings Janine created of her imaginary friend. Gram saved every memento from the summers their father sent Juliana and Janine to California. Dust bunnies from the box caused Janine to sneeze uncontrollably.

"Gram," she flipped through a pile of black and white photographs of the thirties or forties. "This isn't the only box, right? Why didn't you bring down more? Or, we could go up there."

Gram gave her a look.

"It's dusty up there. Dusty and dark. I'm an old woman. Carrying down one box just about cleared me out yesterday afternoon. Want more boxes, we need to get one of those young men to carry them out. That handsome Doctor McNally will be back soon, won't he?"

The doctor was due back all right, with Kiki. The previous night, everyone except Janine gathered at the hotel to pack up. Kiki and the doctor planned to drop the crew off at the airport then drive the van to Gram's house. No sense in driving it back to Texas just to turn around and come right back. Gram graciously offered her garage to store the *Spectral Analysis* van. She probably planned on letting friends pose for pictures next to it.

"Kiki and the doctor are due back this afternoon, I suppose," Janine said.

"The doctor? Don't you call him Ian? Why so formal?"

"I don't know." There was nothing in the box after the year 1953 and Janine pushed it aside.

"Don't you think Doctor Ian McNally is a handsome fellow?" Gram smiled.

Janine grimaced at Gram.

"Now, now," Gram chastised. "Don't get into a huff. Nothing wrong with your grandma asking about you know what. Is there a man back in Austin? Maybe that cute Carlos fellow?"

"Gram," she groaned. "Carlos is happily married with twins. There is no man."

"And I don't believe that doctor-Kiki nonsense you push on the show. I have seen how everyone interacts here. Everyone agrees that there's a little something brewing between *you* and the doctor. What is he, about thirty?"

"Everyone? Who is this everyone?"

"Me and the gals. We analyze every show." She grinned excitedly. "Remember the graveyard show, the one in Savannah, where you and Doctor McNally did the lab sample thing. You know, the glowing chemical thing."

"Phospholuminescence."

"Yes, along that trail. It was very clear he was quite taken with you. I saw sparks."

"He didn't want me to start a fire," Janine told her. "Some of the stuff we were using is very flammable. Maybe those were the sparks you saw."

Gram shook her head in denial and chuckled.

Janine would chuckle too, if Gram hadn't actually hit a nerve. Truthfully, after that Savannah shoot, she also imagined something might develop with the doctor. During that shoot, they talked and laughed easily for the first time and they connected briefly on a different level. The doctor couldn't know their banter was a breakthrough event for her. Opening up to him a little bit was a huge step in her recovery.

Yet, nothing ever came from that encounter beyond Janine developing a little crush on the doctor. That, and the self-realization that she actually wanted a relationship again. Thankfully, only Carlos suspected her change in demeanor, and no one ever took anything Carlos said seriously.

"Hey, Gram, I wanted to ask you, the things you told Kiki about my imaginary friend? Did you make any of it up? Like, embellish it a bit?"

Not the right thing to say. Gram's amusement dissipated quickly. She opened her mouth to apologize, but Gram held up her hand.

"Look here, Jaja. I don't joke about that ghost girl. What you don't know is, she is a real spirit, restless, one that seeks out children. When you told me about her, described her and repeated her words, I about died of fright. Why do you think I stopped letting your father send you here? That ghost lured more than one child into the river and she was trying to lure you too. Thank goodness your sister Juliana stuck to you like glue."

Clearly, Gram believed a real spirit haunted Rio Linda.

"Did you ever see her?" Janine asked.

Gram shook her head.

"Never. Never. But I tell you, my own second cousin's sister saw her. Maple. Ma, your great-grandmother, always warned us about the little girl ghost that Maple met at the river. If I were ever to see her, I was to tell Ma immediately and nobody else. Nobody."

"You mean great-cousin Maple who died tragically in childhood?" Janine asked.

Gram nodded, "And my older brother, John. He told us the story of the mystery lady and her two daughters. Those two little girls just walked right into the river like they were following someone. The poor mother couldn't do a thing."

Gram shuffled through the box and picked up a large group photo. It was an extended family picture of about twenty people gathered together on the front lawn. The big oak tree with the tire swing was just a skinny sapling in the photograph. Gram pointed to a dark-haired woman and a baby.

"That baby is Maple. I'd like to find another picture of her. Older, near when she died. I am sure there's one somewhere in this box."

"Did she drown?"

"Of course," Gram said. "In the river."

"Did your mom ever see the ghost?"

"Oh no, not that ghost. But she did see the other one. A girl she called Mary."

"Another one! You mean there's another ghost? How many ghosts do you think are in Rio Linda?"

Gram ignored the little laugh Janine gave.

"Don't believe everything you hear," she told Janine. "Lots of folks will say there's a ghost on every street corner. That's just fantasy. There aren't any spirits except your little friend, the River Girl, and the other, Mary. Just the two of them. That old man driving a tractor out on Dreyer Road, I can't say about him, but he has nothing to do with Rio Linda. We don't generally go advertising about such things, about our ghosts. But that man from Dreyer Road has got a lot of advertising."

"Did you tell Kiki about the other ghost? Mary?"

"She didn't ask," Gram told her. "Plus, I thought it would make me look a bit looney, believing ghosts are everywhere. But she is real. Doesn't come around much. But every so often, you'll hear of a sighting different than the river ghost. It's Mary. Mary stays away from the river. She's mainly the orchard ghost. Anything else you hear, rubbish."

"Have you seen her? Any of these ghosts?"

Gram pressed her lips together and looked away.

"I won't say, so you can stop teasing me. But there is a very long history of sightings. Many have seen her." Gram found another photo. "Here she is." She held up an old black-and-white photo of a little girl.

"Maple?"

"No, your great-grandma, my mother. Looks just like Juliana, don't you think?"

Certainly. Janine trudged up to the attic for another box. Oh, the attic. Dark, dusty, and crammed with junk. Gram's description of her stacks of boxes did not do them justice. Sneezing, Janine picked the nearest, newest-looking box and headed downstairs. When she got back to the living room, Kiki had taken her spot on the couch and the doctor lounged in the recliner with a drink in his hand. He flashed a dreamy smile at her. Oh, let the fun begin, Janine thought.

They searched three more boxes of paper before finding the drawings from the summer of Janine's imaginary friend. Kiki sat cross-legged on the floor, slowly shuffling through piles of old photographs. She created three piles: one pile for people she believed saw the ghost, one pile for people she believed did not, and one undecided. Apparently, Kiki's sixth sense told her these things. *Carlos, my friend,* Janine mused silently, *you are missing some nice wisecracks here.*

The doctor departed hours earlier to take care of business. Permits and permissions were required to film in certain locations, especially if they required exclusive access to the river. Ian planned to swing by the town hall records department and copy information on river drownings and early Rio Linda history.

Janine examined the artwork she made as a child. They were simplistic drawings of a girl with a very large head, blue dress, yellow hair, with a big ribbon, or band, on top of her head. The drawings had stick arms and legs. Scribbly blue lines surrounded the girl, suggesting a windy sky or water. Unfortunately, Janine sorely lacked artistic ability at five years old.

"Here are a few better ones." Gram delivered drawings still attached to a sketchbook. "These drawings were made after you really took a shine to her. You were obsessed with your imaginary friend and drew a picture almost every day. You said you were going to be an artist someday. I didn't realize who you were drawing until a friend told me it was the river ghost. I was surprised, because everyone always agreed that the ghost only appeared at the river. Your sightings occurred in the backyard. That's why I didn't worry about the ghost at first."

There were at least twenty drawings of the same girl. The twig body didn't alter much, but the details in the face increased with each new depiction; the girl had blue eyes and red lips, her hair was quite wavy, she wore a decorative headband, her smile was lopsided and she had a mark on her chin.

"Look at the headband you drew," Kiki said. "Is that a simple three petaled flower or an attempt at a Celtic knot?"

Janine had no clue.

Suddenly, Janine flashed on a memory of her phantom friend. An image of a girl standing near the back lawn flooded her brain. She stood right along the edge of Gram's manicured yard in the middle of the day. Janine clutched her crude drawing and peered at the Crayola lines.

"What is it?" Kiki asked softly. "Do you feel her here?

"No," Janine remembered more details. "She can't come into the house."

"She can't come into the house?"

"She's not allowed inside the house," Janine mumbled. "She can't come in."

Kiki gently took hold of her hand, "Then what is it? What just happened?"

"I remember her, as clear as day," Janine said. "I know what she looks like."

Other than the soothing hum of the river over the mound, and the random clucks from hens in the brush, the night surrounding Gram's house remained quiet. Gram and Kiki ran off to visit Gram's old friends. When Gram announced that her gals always gathered for tea and cards, but wouldn't it be nice to have a tea-reading too, Kiki retrieved her signature Kiki Mellow tarot cards and suggested they do it all: tea leaves, cards, and gossip. It was Kiki's way of cleverly conducting research in Rio Linda.

After several awkward portraits of her imaginary friend, a long hot shower sounded more pleasing to Janine. Sadly, her artistic ability had not improved much in the past twenty years. She decided to relax and take in the stars on the glassed covered back porch. Being a fair distance from city lights, Gram's night sky often resembled a black star-filled universe map. Janine could even make out the faint band of the Milky Way.

Gram's home and land separated the business portion of Rio Linda from the river. At one point in history, the family property stretched to the opposite side of town and ended at I-80, the road that connects the Sierra Nevada to San Francisco. Two hundred years ago, before California's Gold Rush era, an old trail followed that same path. Janine didn't venture outside because her memories of the ghost still spooked her. She knew the imaginary girl couldn't possibly be a real ghost, but it didn't hurt to avoid the yard.

During her art session, Janine remembered other details about that girl. Very clear and definite in her mind, the girl was not allowed to enter Gram's house. She always walked at the edge of the yard, but not in the cut lawn area or near the house. Very different from most spooks. Most spirits attached themselves to a solid object, according to her experiences with *Spectral*

Analysis. Janine's imaginary friend also avoided grown-ups, she didn't trust them and would disappear whenever Janine ran off to find Gram or Juliana.

A shooting star flicked across the sky. Milky Way, Big Dipper, Man skiing, Flying squirrel. Her older sister pointed out those constellations on that back porch. Janine chuckled, remembering her sister weave imaginative tales at bedtime. Juliana always created detailed stories for the amusement her baby sister, and Janine really was a baby sister. She was more than ten years younger than Juliana.

Her sister agreed to delay her visit to avoid interfering with the *Spectral Analysis* investigation. Janine wasn't sure if she felt disappointed or slightly relieved. She was eager to see her sister and the kids again, but she was also a bit nervous. Even though she missed many years in Ashley's young life, her older niece behaved as if she hadn't disappeared at all. Would Ashley finally ask Janine why she had been so totally absent the past four years?

A slight movement in the shadows made her jump. The shadow kept moving and Janine bit back a yelp as she tensed. Then she saw the shape a little better.

"I saw the picture you drew of the ghost," Doctor McNally shifted in his seat. He cradled a tumbler as he lounged in one of Gram's wine barrel Adirondack chairs in a dark corner. He raised his glass and grinned. "I stocked your gram's bar with some nice single malt. Want a little snort?"

"How long have you been sitting there?"

"I don't know, about half an hour, maybe longer. I may have dozed off a wee bit." He yawned and stretched. "I think you were in the shower when I got back. No one else was around."

The entire time she stood musing at the stars, thinking she was all alone. He fought his way up from the deep chair and took a couple of steps toward her. His jawline fell at her eye level and she could just detect the musky aftershave he used. The top two buttons of his shirt were undone and her eyes were drawn to the indent of his jugular notch. Heat radiated from his body, drawing her to lean closer.

Janine suddenly realized that they had never been alone together besides that night in Savannah. She felt the intimacy of that fact in interesting parts of her body and the nerves along her skin woke up. Her pulse ticked faster and faster flooding her chest and torso with warmth. She hoped it was dark enough to cover the blush that must be spreading across her face. She became distinctly conscious of her flimsy outfit: thin sleeping T-shirt, no bra, short shorts, and no shoes—very underdressed for a work meeting. She resisted an urge to hug her arms to her body in a defensive stance. She didn't want the doctor to think she felt uncomfortable around him.

"Your gram has a very nice setup out here." He admired the sky view.

"Yes, it's pretty special." She made a slight move to escape into the house.

"Are you recovered then, from the river incident?" He pulled her back with the question.

"Ugh," she said, "I'm embarrassed, about fainting. I've never fainted before. I don't know what that's all about. I feel fine now. No need to worry."

"It's normal." He smiled at her. "According to Kiki. Kiki faints fairly often when she experiences a strong spirit. Nothing to be embarrassed about." He drained his glass and set it aside. "Kiki believes your gram and you are…how does she put it? Tuned in. Closet mediums. Maybe that's what attracted you to our show in the first place."

"Kiki thinks it's genetic," Janine gave him.

"It probably is. At least on the female side. Runs mostly in girls, I hear," he said.

"Well, that sounds a little sexist, don't you think?"

He smiled slowly at her, "Aye, I always thought so. Very sexist. Looks like you were having a few nice memories."

His eyes drifted down her body and she wished her shirt was tad thicker. Oh no, where was the stiff work relationship she always counted on? Her deep intake of air drew his attention and her breasts reacted when his eyes paused there, tingling from his attention. He corrected himself and his eyes snapped back to her face. His pupils were hyper dilated in the dark.

"It's not often seeing you with your hair down, smiling so sweetly. Your eyes are very golden in this light and…" He suddenly stiffened and stepped back. "Crikes. I, I'm sorry. I've had a few on an empty stomach. I get a bit buckled. I didn't mean anything by that. I just meant, you look very pleasant, enjoying the night air and all. Very, very pleasant, and even in this dim light… Crikes, am I messing up again?"

"No, no. No worries. I know what you mean." Janine smiled. How very amusing. It felt pleasantly intimate standing on the glass patio with Ian McNally in his tipsy condition. He was very cute flailing in conversation. His flustered expression was quite charming and she couldn't take her eyes off of him.

"You do? You know what I mean?" Ian's voice was low.

"Umm, yes. I do. Of course, I do. I know exactly what you mean." Not really sure what they were talking about at this point. But he looked a little apologetic, so she softly added, "It's okay, really. I don't mind at all. Really. You're not messing up."

He considered her awkwardly for a moment. In the next moment, he stepped forward and scooped her into his arms. She was overwhelmed with the contact, and the smell of him, and her body began to melt into his. Surprisingly, her arms wrapped around Ian's neck and pulled him closer. Her brain lost all command of her physical responses. Her body ignored her request for decorum as she soaked him in, welcoming and surprisingly eager. She felt a spark as their lips brushed. Then her lips parted for a deeper kiss, hungry for more. She detected a taste of his Scottish whisky as the kiss escalated. His hands moved all over her body tantalizingly bold. She was on fire! She was spinning.

In the muffled distance, her name echoed. Janine heard rustling and laughter. Ian moved away and she heard audible breathing. Every nerve pinged. The doctor's hand lingered on her shoulder as they began to realize the loud bang had been the front door slamming. Gram and Kiki called out from the living room. They must think Janine was upstairs. The doctor stared at her for a second longer.

"Crikes, lassie, all right then." His voice was low and breathless. Ian turned tail and dashed into the house.

Janine heard him greet Kiki and Gram. He offered them whisky and talked about the town records. They each sounded very excited. Janine heard Kiki say she acquired a long list of potentials and then something about Steve and Ted. Janine didn't know how to get past them without being seen. She waited a bit, felt silly for hiding, then went into the house. Ian had his back to her as he held up a folder full of paper.

"The recorded deaths go back to the start of the town. Before there even was a town," he told them. "Guess whose name is written on the very first page. You are going to shite your pants, Kiki. A five-year-old child drowned in the river during a baptism. Guess what her name was…"

But Ian no longer had their attention. Gram and Kiki both watched Janine slink into the room from the same door Ian entered not five minutes prior. Janine still felt pink from that kiss. She felt another rush of blood at the sight of him. Ian turned and slowly trained his eyes on her. He definitely appeared embarrassed. Did she really just jump him a moment ago?

"Linda," his volume diminished suddenly. "Her name was Linda Mae Stauch…" His eyes were blinking rapidly. "Janine." His voice bounced back. "Will you join us? We were just talking about…"

"Oh no," Janine cut him off rather rudely. She softened her tone and managed to look him in the eye. Her throat was dry and her voice came out odd, husky. "It was a long day and I'm going to go up to bed." She walked over and gave Gram a nice hug then buggered out of there as fast as she could.

The town of Rio Linda kept meticulous records dating from the very beginning of the settlement in the 1800s. The death of Linda Mae Stauch was noted as a back entry in a handwritten book kept by the town leaders. She died during a baptism in the *valley river* that they took as a reference to the Rio Linda River. Another line stated that *she is released from her ailments and illness*, implying that Linda had been close to death when she drowned. The doctor photocopied everything available in the city archives. Perhaps they would find more clues in the large pile of papers he stacked on the coffee table.

"Seems odd that she wasn't baptized till five years old. Wouldn't she have been baptized as an infant?" Kiki perused the stack of papers. "Some of this is unreadable. The ink is washed out."

"Perhaps her family were converts," Gram suggested. "Protestant religions don't baptize infants. They wait until a body is old enough to ask for baptism."

The doctor ordered copies of a diary from a museum in San Francisco. He discovered that the original Rio Linda settlers came off two wagon trains. The first group left the diary. The doctor put a rush request on the copy and spared no expense to have it sent to Grams house.

Gram insisted that they continue to use her home as their base of operations until Juliana's visit. The house offered plenty of space and Gram wanted to help. She even lent them her Ford F-150 with the covered bed. Gram was no fool. She hoped the house would be featured in the *Spectral Analysis* episode about the river ghost. Gram often bragged about having a historic house, now she wanted it famous too. She probably shored away bragging rights to use with her card girls. Kiki and the doctor were happy with the arrangement and made themselves right at home, choosing the rustic sitting room as a central planning area. Kiki referred to Gram as their local Rio Linda expert, their go-to guide for all things Rio Linda.

But really, Janine suspected, Gram's motives had more to do with helping Janine forge personal bonds and establish trust again.

For the next couple of days, Kiki and the doctor kept busy with interviews in town while Janine spent time with Gram. Technically, she was on her two-week break. Gram dragged her to visit friends around Rio Linda and then to different farmers markets. They went to the boarding stables at Gold Country to brushed down the patched mare Gram owned. They fed the free-range hens and delivered a flat of extra eggs to the local feed store. Gram knew just about everyone in Rio Linda and bragged to everyone about the television show being filmed from her house. Each day, Janine just missed Kiki and the doctor. She could hear them walking down the hall late at night or in the early morning, but their paths never crossed beyond that.

She finally came face-to-face with Ian two nights after their porch kiss. Gram and Janine stumbled in from a local honey vender to find Ian and Kiki lounging in the rustic sitting room. Kiki had obtained a large dry-erase board and propped it against the far wall. The doctor lounged in the recliner with the big EMF box at his feet. He glanced up quickly and Janine got the distinct feeling that he was waiting for her.

"Janine." he sprang to a standing position. "I was just about to do another low-frequency EM survey. I could use a bit of help if you care to lend a hand. Of course, it's okay if you don't, but maybe you do. Maybe you'd like to get out… I mean, come out with me, on an official errand, of course. That's what I mean. We've been running at full throttle and maybe you're thinking we're leaving you out of the loop. I just thought, you know, since you're around and about for this phase, you might want to come along. Help me with a little tech stuff. I don't know, what do you say?" He was rambling and his eyes were blinking.

"I've never seen you so smooth," Kiki smirked softly, and the doctor gave her a sour look.

Gram nudged her, "Of course she wants to go. Run along, go on, girl. I'm to bed early tonight."

In the truck, the doctor filled her in on some of the leads they were chasing. Kiki wanted to interview Janine on camera right away, before she learned too much about what they were finding out. Janine being on the crew, and in the story, could compromise things.

Ian wore a button-down, light-blue shirt with the collar open at the neck and Janine watched his Adam's apple bob. He recently shaved and smelled very nice. The muscles in his neck flexed as he turned his head and spoke. His coloring was rich, deep brown hair with bright blue eyes, *not haunting blond locks with silver eyes*. She liked it. She realized that she was staring at him and looked away.

"She wants to get your unbiased perspective. You know, not cross-pollinate your experiences with too much information from other sources. Maybe even use a little hypnosis. We're taking your story as the authentic one, your portrait of the ghost as the actual one. We will authenticate other information by what we learn from you and Gram. We're going to get your clip first off before taping anyone else."

Janine already knew all that information. His rambling voice was a far cry from the usual Doctor McNally analytical tone he used.

"Where are we going anyway?"

The doctor had steered the truck out of Rio Linda and they were heading toward Sacramento.

"Oh." He glanced nervously at her. "That was a wee ruse back there, didn't you guess? Ha-ha, I confess, I just wanted to get you out and away from everyone. You know, take you to a private dinner. Go somewhere we could be a little less, observed."

That explained the shave and cologne.

"You're taking me out to dinner?"

"That's my plan. Crikes! Is that okay?" His eyes rounded. "We could go back. I don't know. Did I cross the line? Is this unprofessional? I thought you were…I thought we were…I hope we are on the same page and about things." He appeared just as nerdy as when they first met. But somehow, she found his blinking eyes and pressed lips incredibly charming. Even quite irresistible.

He pulled the truck off the road and began navigating through a parking lot. The Malabar Restaurant appeared to be their destination.

"So, this is a date?"

"Aye. Yes, this is a date. Bollocks, I should have asked you first, right? I mean, I thought you'd want to go. But maybe you have plans. Maybe there's something I don't know. This is a bit, I don't know. I mean, I can't stop thinking about that…the moment on the porch." He parked the truck and faced her. "Tell me I haven't made a brutal mistake."

"It's just. I'm not dressed for a dinner date." She felt disappointed to be in jeans and a T-shirt and not something more girly or sexy for their first date. She imagined her hair was a total mess. That thought process definitely confused her. When in the past five years had she wanted to dress more girly or sexy, be noticed? Not once, never. How surprising. Doctor McNally looked her over. His eyes ran down her body and Janine felt every inch of his gaze.

"You look dressed just fine to me," he said. "You look fantastic." He moved toward her.

Thank you, Gram, for having a full bench seat in her F-150, she thought. They met in the middle and resumed the kiss interrupted two nights before. She went from zero to one hundred in less than a second and surprised herself at how unbashful her response was. After a bit, Ian moved away. The engine still idled and he turned off the truck.

"So, will you have dinner with me then?" He grinned at her.

"Yes," she said. "Yes."

"We need to get something straight though." Suddenly he looked serious. "You need to make me a small promise."

Panic swept in. *The last time a man asked her for a promise, bad things happened.* She tapped it back down.

"I want to go slow, you know. This is something I've been thinking about for quite a bit of time and I don't want to make any mistakes. Plus, we have the professional side of our relationship to consider."

"Are you saying, you want to keep this, thing, a secret?"

Ian looked her in the eye. "I'll leave that part up to you. You seem pretty private, reserved, and so maybe you don't want everyone to know your business. I'll follow your lead on that."

"Then what promise is this about?"

He began to blink rather rapidly again. "That you won't let me push things too quickly," he said.

"What do you mean?"

He shook his head and looked out the front windshield.

"I confess. I almost knocked on your door the past two nights. I was a bit off my head and imagined you wouldn't mind at all, that maybe you were expecting it... All because of that kiss." His voice took on a rambling tone again, and his slight accent thickened. "When you said you were to bed the other night, looking at me with those eyes of yours, I practically convinced myself it was an invitation. I've been a bit mad because we've done all these shows together, and, it's like we know each other, we're familiar, and, I guess…I admit it, I've been imagining kissing you for quite some time. But really, we know very little about each other, personally." He finally looked at her. "How do you know you even want to have a go, with me, I mean? Did you give it any thought before the other night?"

Her panic morphed into a relief of sorts.

"What I mean is, let's make an agreement."

"An agreement?"

"Let's take things slow. Not cross any major lines until the Rio Linda segment is wrapped, promise to stay a bit professional here. If we agree to this, I can concentrate and not read into things and muck things up. That way our relationship can develop more rationally over time."

"Rational sounds good."

"All right then, good." He nodded. A small smile cracked his serious expression. "So, will you have dinner with me, right now?"

She considered that nice square jaw of his, "Yes. Okay, I'll have dinner with you."

The Malabar steak house was just off highway 99 halfway between Old Town Sacramento and the international airport. The top floor consisted of a trendy bar that overlooked a dimly lit dining area. Ian requested a corner booth in the back, away from the main traffic. The young hostess instantly recognized him. After she showed them to a table, Janine heard a buzz of excitement permeate the restaurant.

They ignored the buzz and focused on their date. Ian became interested in paranormal activity at an early age. His mother, who passed away when he was a teen, saw spirits in her youth, and at one point his dad had his mum committed over her beliefs. Ian never forgave his father. Ian said he always believed in his mum. As he grew older, he wanted to obtain proof of the paranormal and found a proof of sorts; mysterious energy at the ultralow end of the electromagnetic spectrum always bounced around the more believable hauntings. But people still had doubts. Steve Hanks came along at the just right time, and had just the right proposal, to take his study to the next level.

Ian also shared past relationship history with her. He had one serious girlfriend from high school to college, a few interesting women during his graduate years, and a couple of girlfriends in the past few years, but nobody serious. Most of the brainy women he dated laughed at his paranormal beliefs. The women who were attracted to his profession tended to fall on the irrational side. He admitted that most mediums were a little off their heads.

"You think Kiki is off her head?"

"Oh no." Ian shook his head. "Kiki is the real deal. Sometimes she plays stuff up, for fun and show business, but she has a real connective link going on." He paused and opened his mouth like he wanted to say more, but didn't.

"Do you believe there's a real ghost in Rio Linda?" Janine asked. "Do you think I've seen her?"

Ian nodded, "Yes. Something real is going on in Rio Linda. The EM vortex around that river bend is enough to convince me. Plenty of high-frequency waves, perfect for misleading folks into thinking they've experienced something. That's part of the trouble. But hidden in that noise, there was unexplainable, distinct patterns in the lower than fifty Hertz range. We only detected it during your faint out, just a wee bit. It had to come from something."

Ian drank his wine. Her eyes were drawn to his very large and powerful-looking hands. Large knuckles, broad palms and long fingers. He held his glass delicately, absently caressing the curve of the bowl with his thumb. She liked how carefully he handled objects. Janine found everything about him attractive. Capable, handsome, and intelligent—a winning combination.

"I also believe you had a legitimate paranormal experience as a child. You named the ghost. You called her Linda. You drew a picture of her. Other reports, other old sightings, tell of the same spirit. We're certain it's the same Linda who died in the river in the 1800s. How would you know to call her Linda, Janine? How would you know about that?"

"Maybe I heard people talk about it," she countered. "You know, kids tell each other scary stories all the time. The river ghost is a common enough legend. People tell it to kids to scare them away from the water. The river has a real undercurrent around that bend and things get stuck in the rocks all the time. You heard that old man. People blame it on the ghost but it's just a natural trap."

"Yes, but what you may not realize is; other people have also seen your phantom friend. It's been reported and recorded. You weren't the only child to draw a picture of Linda," he told her. "We visited the old man from the pub, Henry Webber. He had a lot to say about the ghost of Linda Mae Stauch. One of his own relatives encountered the ghost many years ago and drew pictures of her. Henry Webber saved one of those pictures. Just like your portrait, her Linda had blue eyes, curly blond hair, and a clef in her chin. We're going to do a camera interview with him sometime after yours."

The waitress brought their calamari plate. Anytime Ian smiled, his eyes became blue sparkling gems. He smiled easily and often. It was contagious. He gazed at her and she felt herself melt.

"Don't take this the wrong way, but his young relative was a much better artist than you were. Her drawing at five years old looks closer to the one you made the other day. Anyway, she immediately drowned in the river after creating her portraits. Her own spirit is said to haunt one of the smaller streets in town, a Lara Lane."

"Are you supposed to be telling me all this?" she asked. "You're not afraid you might be cross-pollinating ideas or something?"

"Crikes! You're right." He knocked himself in the head. He emptied the wine bottle into both their glasses and leaned toward her. "How about you tell me more about you. I know you're from Texas. What was it, biochemistry at A&M, right? I know your parents have passed. I know your family originates from out here in California. I know you have at least one sister, with kids, in Texas. You prefer sweet tea and you read mystery novels. You like to run. And I've seen you kicking the football with Carlos. Pretty impressive moves. Gram said you played sports competitively. Any old beaus I need to worry about?" He chuckled nervously.

Oh boy. Oh brother, now she remembered why she avoided this sort of thing. Full disclosure would surely doom this new beginning with the doctor. Did she really need to answer that question right away?

At that moment, two women popped up to their table. They rudely interrupted and Janine felt relief at the pause in the conversation. She needed to think for a moment. If the date happened with a guy she barely knew, then maybe she could blow off that question. But this was Doctor McNally. They've known each other for a quite a while, not personally, but professionally. Was it okay to lie, fib a little bit, or slightly mislead him? Could Ian have at least waited a week before asking point-blank about past boyfriends?

The two women continued to chat at Ian, gushing about the show while sharing their spooky experiences. They asked for autographs and to take selfies. Ian smiled politely but kept glancing at Janine with concern.

If she couldn't just blow him off, should she tell him everything, all at once? Maybe it was better to get it out in the open sooner rather than later. But, she carried a lot of baggage, scary baggage, and most people might think her mind was messed up, broken, and her body ruined. If the truth changed his intentions with her, she'd rather it happen before she got too involved. Could she do it, tell him about her past? How would she word it? Panic bubbled under her composure. Perhaps she should just leave it and halt things right away. She probably wasn't ready to start a relationship, not if she still couldn't verbalize a little of what happened to her.

The women barely glanced at Janine. They gushed a bit more and then reluctantly slunk away when Ian reached across the table for her hand. Ian shook his head apologetically and Janine knew that she didn't want to halt whatever was brewing between them. She really liked Ian McNally and was very interested in kissing him again.

"Sorry. I still don't know how to handle that sort of thing. It's a bit like students running up after a lecture, but much more. Well, much more…"

"I get it," she said softly. "I think you handled it fine."

"Thanks," he said. "You're very easy to be with. Funny and intelligent. Delightful. You always seem so levelheaded. Reserved but also nice, open, very grounded. I love it. No games or weird hang-ups with you, just a breath of fresh air."

She suddenly blurted, "I was stabbed."

He appeared confused.

"I got involved with a psychopath."

He stared at her blankly.

"An old boyfriend tried to kill me." *He kidnapped me. He stabbed me. He left me for dead in a deserted area of woods*, she didn't add. Most of it was still hard to say out loud, even to herself. "He's currently serving a twenty-year sentence in the Illinois state pen, and I am terrified he will be released early for good behavior." *Because he's very good at pretending to be a normal person.* "I was in my fourth semester of college, the University of Chicago, when it happened."

Ian shifted uncomfortably.

"There's more." She hesitated, gripping her napkin. *Why didn't she practice saying these things out loud?* "Afterward, well, I spent some time in a hospital. A hospital for people who… It was a mental facility. It took a while getting through what happened and I only recently weaned off all my medication. It's why I didn't drink whisky with the crew the first season. It's why I kept to myself."

Ian sat frozen, eyes wide.

"And there's something else," she said. Could she really tell him? She gave birth to a baby, her niece Sammy. Her sister adopted Sammy right after she was born because Janine refused to have anything to do with the child or what happened to her. Janine had actually been infuriated with her sister for taking Sammy. Janine wanted the baby lost and forgotten in the system, forever. No, she couldn't say that. Not without becoming a blubbering idiot. She killed her wine instead.

The doctor's eyes grew serious and he fidgeted a bit.

At that moment, a different waitress came with coffee and two more fans for the doctor. The three women chatted him up, giving Janine very little notice. She almost took a sip of her coffee but stopped because there was a perfect lipstick stain on it. Did the restaurant not clean their cups properly, or had that cup been meant for the doctor as a silent message? *The doctor.* In her mind, he was the doctor again. He actually looked relieved with the interruption. *Okay*, Janine thought, *a little disappointing but survivable. Kudos for going on a date again.* That short dinner was her longest relationship in the last five years. At least she took a step. The doctor shooed the women away in a hasty way.

"All right then." His eyes met hers. "Shall we get on?"

They left quickly and silently. Outside, he stopped right in front of Gram's truck and turned to face her. He gripped her hand and stared into her eyes.

"That was a lot to take in and I don't know how to ask you about it yet," he said quietly. "I'm a bit of an idiot at saying the correct thing, and I don't want to you to get the wrong idea because I'm so lousy at expressing myself. What I mean to say is, what I want to say…"

His eyes were deep blue and just as concerned as they were in the tunnel after that electrostatic shock. Ian pulled her into a soft slow embrace and leaned toward her. He kissed her tenderly on the forehead. He felt so large and strong and safe.

"Aye, that's what I want you to know. I just want to be clear about my feelings," Ian whispered.

Chapter 5

The Ledger Diary Janine

A bulky express mail envelope sat on the front porch alongside the morning paper addressed to *Spectral Analysis*, attention Dr. Ian McNally. It came from the California History Group in San Francisco. The wagon train diary!

Janine carried the package into the house and set it on the coffee table on top of a pile of research. Kiki snatched it up and ripped open the package. She began shuffling through the pages rapidly. Gram brought Kiki and Janine mugs of coffee and sat down with multicolored yarn and thick needles. Gram settled comfortably into her chair, ready to knit, watch, and eavesdrop.

Ian McNally skipped down the stairs still damp from a morning shower, grinning from ear to ear. His intense eyes sought Janine out. Good grief, Janine thought, could he be more obvious? If they really wanted to keep their budding romance unadvertised, his huge grin was not helping matters. Janine looked away, but couldn't help smiling as she recalled their date.

"Here's a clue to our little ghost!" Kiki exclaimed. "Right here on page one. Stauch!"

From the first page of the ledger Diary of Stanley Hansen; May 22, 1839

85 souls in the Hansen virgin train from Independence, Missouri, to Yerba Buena in the Mexican territory of California.

Investing families include:

Hansen Leaders; Oscar, Stanley, Earl (2 wagons).

Stauch Group; Frederick, minster (6 wagons in this group).

Webber Family; Peter, woodworker (3 wagons).

Williams Family; Nicholas, pastor (5 wagons).

Lumen Family; Marcus, blacksmith (4 wagons).

Whitaker Family; John, farmer (6 wagons).

Miller Family; Andrew, famer (2 wagons).

Note: The Whitaker family and followers (8 wagons lost) departed our train before the desert plains. John and I were unable to come to a resolution to our disagreement and our numbers are now 63.

Signed *Stanley Hansen*

Ian sank into the easy chair with a mug of coffee. Instinctively, the girls left that seat open for him. The musky aroma of his aftershave filled the room and Janine felt him gazing in her direction again. His smug smile appeared much more conspicuous than he must imagine and she tried to ignore him. After their restaurant dinner, they drove down Marysville Boulevard with his electromagnetic energy receiver. They planned to mark distinct bands of wave energy across the old Miller almond orchard. Ian wanted a baseline of the area at night. Instead, they ended up having an old-fashioned parking session behind the trees. The memory of his large hands running over her body made him very hard to ignore.

Kiki arranged and divvied up the pages between herself, Ian, and Janine. Kiki tore blank paper out of a spiral-bound notebook for each of them. She pointed out a long list of names on her whiteboard, some already crossed off, some underlined. She asked them to cross-check connections between drowning victims and the original settlers.

"This is a list of people confirmed drowned in the river, crossed-checked with local street names. We should confirm if the streets were indeed named for the victims. Let's see if we can find any more links for my list."

"These surnames are pretty much all linked. Stauch, Miller, Webber. Here's the Williams link." Ian handed the page to Gram. Gram nodded as she surveyed the names.

"Yes, yes. These are our relatives. Great-Grandpa Nicholas Williams built this very house. There are tin types in the attic somewhere, taken when he was very old, and also one of the little boy Christopher. I remember that one well. They've mostly gone to grey and are hard to see. Old photographs of the family too, I'm sure of it. But Nicholas isn't in those pictures."

The Magician

Ian McNally is the Magician

"Where is Yerba Buena?" Kiki asked. "Is that near here? Where exactly did they want to go?"

Gram laughed, "Oh, that's San Francisco." She nodded at her face. "Back before California was a state, it was part of the Mexican territories. There are missions all up and down the California coast, built by the Spanish out of Mexico. Twenty-one, I believe. The area around San Francisco is still called Yerba Buena." Gram settled into her knitting. She seemed very pleased with the flowing script of her ancestors in the historic museum diary and glanced down at it fondly.

They spent the better part of the day sifting through the diary. The beautiful artistic script turned out to be hard to read in places. Smudged lines and random scribbles confused much of the information. Imbedded in the daily log they found crude hand-drawn maps and personal notes regarding Hansen's digestive processes.

The most fun were the scandalous sections of gossipy rantings interspersed between the regular entries. Stanley Hansen clearly disliked most of the men in his wagon train and lusted after a few of the women. He pulled no punches when writing out his personal feelings. He barely tolerated his "feeble-minded" brother, Earl, and detested his own father. Janine gasped at the bold, crude remarks regarding some of the women. Ironically, those crude words were written in dramatic cursive handwriting. They had a terrific time reading Hansen's more outrageous musings out loud to each other.

"My goodness." Kiki laughed. "He calls Mikael Stauch a whining she-goat and wonders if the little girl is really his. He's talking about Linda! Our little ghost, Linda, and her father."

"In my section, he writes that he would like to cut Mikael's throat in his sleep," Janine added. "Hansen thinks he would be doing the man's wife a favor."

"Here he claims the Webber group is hoarding the salted pork and wants to whip somebody. He's convinced someone in the Webber party is stealing food." Ian shuffled through his share of pages, attempting to put them back in order.

"Stanley wanted to knock someone else in the head, but doesn't name him. He just refers to him as that old gristle idiot far," Janine said. "Do you think he's just venting with this violent talk?"

Ian looked up, "Far? Like F-A-R? That's Danish for father. Do you think they were Danes then?"

"He wants to fine the Whitakers for disobedience. Doesn't say how they're disobedient," Janine informed them. "Did he have that kind of authority over the others? He sounds like a tyrant."

"Not sure," Ian said.

"He spied on Ingrid Stauch bathing!" Kiki looked up. "They found a pond of water and the women were washing. This occurs in an early section, and, apparently, Ingrid has the smoothest most flawless skin and very well-shaped breasts and buttocks. He writes a nice, very graphic description of how he'd like to get better acquainted with her." Kiki gave the passage to Ian. "I'm not going to say that out loud. It's no wonder they kept this diary hidden in the back room of the museum."

Ian took the passage and raised his eyebrows.

"Here's more about Ingrid." Kiki read out loud, "He writes that she is the prettiest woman he has ever seen, flaxen hair, blue eyes, tall and shapely, milky smooth skin. He wants to save her from her lazy husband. He definitely fancies Mrs. Ingrid Stauch. He actually spies on them and describes the husbands' unimaginative performance. He writes a bit of details about it." She handed it to Ian, then found another one. "He's a total peeper, now watching Mary Webber. Apparently, she was just starting to bud and quite nubile."

"He spied on all the women in this entry, where they came upon an interesting spiked rock on their journey. He tried to draw it." Janine held the drawing up for them to look at. "The Whitaker family was still part of the group and Hansen had his sights on the daughter, Elizabeth. He didn't think people would read this diary, or he didn't care. He actually describes her father as a jackass."

Kiki laughed and reached for the passage. Janine delivered the pages, then added,

"He offered to marry the daughter after kissing her, and the father refused. So, he was spurned."

"Unbelievable." Kiki scanned the section. "But don't feel sorry for him. He accuses the father of keeping him from his rightful urges by refusing a union. He offered to release her from the arrangement at the coast. He requested a handvest at the suggestion of Irene Lumen. I believe he means a handfasting, a temporary marriage. Now, that is very interesting."

"It was a hard, cruel world back then," Gram simply said. She made terrific progress in her netting. "But you say a temporary marriage, not an engagement?"

Kiki nodded. "I believe so. It's very pagan, not Christian at all, and at the suggestion of an Irene Lumen. Might we assume Irene followed a bit of the pagan ways? She is the healer of the group, and I don't believe there were many female doctors back then."

Ian blinked rather rapidly, "I guess we know what the Whitaker disagreement was about. Here's another nice comment about the Lumens. He admires Mrs. Irene Lumen as a fine woman and great cook. Apparently, Ingrid Stauch and Irene were cousins. Irene got the brains and Ingrid the beauty, it seems. Hansen also respects the Lumen men, Finn especially. Apparently, Finn is a natural blacksmith and has repaired a broken wagon wheel effortlessly." Ian looked up and chuckled.

"He disliked Frederick Stauch for praying and giving sermons all the time, said the minister felt his soul was dark. I can't say I disagree with the minister." Janine restacked her pages.

"Have you found any gossip about the Williams family?" Gram asked from her rocker and yarn ball.

"He seemed neutral on the Williams family. He just mentions them in passing in my pages," Janine conveyed. "Just notes about their wagon obligations. They carried most of the water barrels and camp supplies. Others in their group carried dry goods."

"There's a line about Nick Williams being reliable for advice and a steady voice in the masses. He calls them good, solid folk," Kiki told her.

"I'm relieved." Gram chuckled. "But coming from this rough fellow…"

"The Lumens, the Millers, and the Williams are mentioned by their workload and wagon cargo." Ian told her. "His ire seems more focused on the Stauch, Webber, and Whitaker clans. He had his eye on a female from each of those groups. He clashed the most with Frederick Stauch, a church leader. There are hints of a power struggle between them."

The diary entries end before the wagon train reached California. The last entry was dated September 6, 1839, and described a luminous red sun retiring behind the majestic Sierra Nevada Mountain chain.

"He called it the shortcut to Yerba Buena." Kiki said, "The California History Group added a note stating that the diary was delivered to San Francisco in a later group that arrived to the port city in1842." Kiki read the note out loud. "The Hansen Party was not considered an official train of the Oregon trail. They were a small collection of people who traveled before the larger migration of the Gold Rush era. A later group encountered survivors of the Hansen Party in the Great Valley. They reported that Hansen died in an Indian attack along with most of the original travelers. The survivors preserved Hansen's ledger diary out of respect for the dead, and sent it to the proper authorities in San Francisco. A section of pages were removed from the book, nobody knows why, perhaps the paper was used for kindling. The Smith Party did not leave a diary, but did create a large map of their travels instead."

The museum included a copy of the map, reproduced as a nice poster.

"Looks like a gift store item." Kiki spread the map out on the coffee table.

"So, what did we learn?" Ian asked out loud.

"Stanley Hansen was a Peeping Tom," Gram called out, initiating a laugh.

Kiki stood and stretched her legs and arms, "I'd wager it wasn't an Indian attack that led to the demise of Stanley Hansen. I'd wager one of those men killed him after he tried to seduce one of their wives. My money's on Ingrid, who happens to be Linda's mother. Do you think it was mutual? The ghost story thickens." Kiki grinned excitedly.

"That could explain why they stopped here before reaching San Francisco. Perhaps they needed to get their story straight. Perhaps someone killed him right here, next to the river." Ian added.

"Why would he stop writing in the journal before going over the pass? Maybe they killed him on the pass. Or maybe those missing pages would tell us more," Janine said. "The family surnames in the train, Webber, Stauch, and Williams all show up on the list of drowning victims. We should cross-check the other names on the wagon train with the complete city records to see if more of these people settled here. See if a Hansen stayed or left."

"You are a terrific investigative partner." Kiki flashed pleased green eyes at her. "Also, there is a Mary mentioned in the diary, Mary Webber," Kiki added. "Some folks mentioned a ghost in the orchard called Mary. Linda and Mary were the two most popular names for a little girl ghost."

"Was Mary Webber a little girl?" Janine pointed out, "If she was budding, wouldn't that make her a tween at least. Is the Mary ghost older, or younger like Linda?"

"I get the impression she's pretty young, like Linda." Kiki shuffled through the diary again. "But who knows?"

Janine glanced at her grandmother and Gram winked at her.

"I'll get the city records." Ian jumped up. "Perhaps we can develop a solid story before Steve arrives tomorrow morning. We'll want to put a few interviews on film right away." He turned his eyes on Janine. "Starting with you, Janine, okay."

She nodded.

"You know," Gram said from her knitting. "There is a pile of old books and things in the attic. Most of it stowed long before I was born and never moved an inch. Like I said before, there's an old tin plate of Great-Great-Grandpa Williams somewhere up there. You are welcome to look through it all. There might be photos of some of these other folks too."

That left them with plenty more to do. After delivering the city records to Kiki, Ian went outside to make a few phone calls to Texas. Kiki began drawing lineage trees for each of the founding families of Rio Linda. She used a very dramatic and artistic script. Gram observed her work, nodding and helping. Gram knew many of the old families and told Kiki which people in town might have old tales and even historic documents hidden away.

Janine tramped upstairs to Gram's dusty attic. She hunted for a particular box which stored tin-plated photos from the 1800s. The attic bulb was bright, but with so many boxes and furniture in the way, the light didn't do much good. Gram kept a handheld flashlight next to the door and a quick test told Janine the batteries were still good.

Gram described a specific paisley-patterned heavy-duty cardboard tub that should be near the east dove window. Janine scanned the room. There were hundreds of paisley boxes scattered everywhere, and the attic had six small oval windows. Sunlight streamed into one window which meant the opposite wall had to be east, the most cluttered and cramped side of the unfinished room. Large boxes sat trapped behind a covered desk or table. Janine managed to push the desk out a few inches and then transferred boxes one by one to the top of the covered surface. Dust bunnies leaped into the air. She felt a sneezing fit coming. A motion at the door distracted her and she discovered Ian standing there with a big grin on his face.

"Your gram sent me up to carry boxes," he said.

Ian took a quick look over his shoulder, then closed the short distance between them. Ian McNally felt like a drug to her. The moment they touched her muscles turned to Jell-O. His kiss sent a flood of fire to every private sector in her body. Then, she started to sneeze.

"Are you becoming allergic to me?" He smiled.

"It's the dust."

"Stanley Hansen and his lurid descriptions. Sorry, but my mind kept drifting to you during those diary entries. That man should have gone into the X-rated novel-writing business. I've been thinking about our agreement, that promise," he said. "Maybe it's a stupid idea. I mean, do you think it's still a good idea? Maybe Kiki and your gram already know something's up. Your gram sent me straight away up here to help you. You looked pretty cool down there, but me, they must have noticed me ogling you from across the room."

Did he imagine smooth milky-white skin under her T-shirt? Flawless skin, like the description of Ingrid? Is that what he was imagining? Janine thought about her scars, seven knife wounds across her stomach and back. *Ruined.* She could never be what he imagined. She didn't want to think about his reaction when he finally saw those marks. She pushed Ian away.

"No. No one knows anything yet. Nobody noticed. My gram just thinks I need help carrying boxes." She picked up one of the paisley boxes and put it in his hands. "I think our plan is still a good idea. We should take it slow. Slow and quiet. Keep things light while we're out here. You were right as usual."

She added a second box to his stack. She picked up a third box and turned to go.

"Have I mucked something up?" He brow had lined.

She leaned in and initiated the kiss this time. That made him very happy. She loved the way his lips moved across hers. She liked that he was so attracted to her.

"No. I just want to stick to the plan. We're in my gram's house after all. We should definitely wait until we're clear of Rio Linda and on our own time before jumping into something more serious. When we can have more privacy, don't you think?"

He nodded and followed close behind. Janine hit the light switch and stowed the flashlight on the way out the door.

I've crossed checked all the city documents." Kiki stood at the whiteboard like a school teacher and used a dry erase pen as a pointer. "Here's what I found. Of the Hansen wagon train, only the following people remained to populate the area." Kiki read them out as she pointed to the names on her board.

Janine barely paid attention as Kiki rambled off the names, she kept glancing at Ian from the corner of her eye. Would he still find her attractive when he got a good look at her mangled body? She was afraid to find out.

"No mention of Mikael, Ingrid's husband, or the three families in the minister's flock. The Millers that remained include John, Susan and a newborn baby they named Mary Elsa Miller. Nobody else."

Janine took in that information.

"What happened to the Lumens and Hansens?" Ian asked. "Where did they go?"

"No mention," Kiki said. "Most likely, they continued to San Francisco, or maybe Sacramento. There are references to a fort being built by Sutter. Although, based on the marriage list, I'm guessing Mikael died sometime between the last diary entry and the settling of Rio Linda."

"Maybe in the same Indian attack that got Stanley Hansen," Janine suggested.

"If it really was an Indian attack that got him," Kiki responded, "Perhaps they fought and mortally wounded each other over Ingrid. That's where I put my money." She continued, "There are marriages listed in the first few years. Ready for more gossip? Linda's mother married her brother-in-law! And the Whitaker family must have caught up with them, because the name Elizabeth Whitaker shows up in the Rio Linda archives. She married Ethan Williams."

Kiki set her notes aside and stretched out like a kitten on the sofa. Sometime in the recent past, she acquired a big glass of wine, and so did Gram. Kiki nodded to no one in particular.

"I may have developed a nice backstory for our ghost. Of course, I'll see what Janine here has to say first." Kiki saluted the air with her wine. "Did you know, you are the only person who has seen the ghost of Linda Stauch and lived?"

"That can't be true," Janine said. "All kinds of people say they've seen her."

Kiki shook her head, "All kinds of people know of someone who has seen her. Those eyewitnesses were kids who unfortunately drowned in the river. Have you seen her again? No, don't answer any questions or tell me anything. We're going to wait for the interview."

"Kiki means authentic sightings." Ian sat next to Gram as she rummaged through one of the paisley boxes. "Lots of times, we can rule out stories that don't fit or that are obvious rubbish. What's that?"

A map, or a blueprint, came out of the box. Gram turned it around.

"It's this house, isn't it?" Ian pointed out something to Gram. "Look here. This area is the kitchen and back porch."

"It must be when Great-Great-Grandpa Christopher built up the house. He added the first large wing and the second story. These are some of his designs. Yes, yes. See here, on the bottom, River House. That's what he called it."

"Did they build the house around a small structure?" Ian studied the rustic sitting room. "It's this room, isn't it? The original house consisted of just this room?"

"I suppose so." Gram passed him the plans.

Ian crossed to where Janine sat near Kiki. He spread the plans out in front of them and then squeezed between them on the sofa. Three pages of plans, along with a sketch of the original house, lay before them. The front porch appeared the same, but now much more house existed on either side of that porch.

"Is that a cross on top of the original building?" Kiki pointed to the sketch.

Gram spoke from across the room. "Probably. Gramma used to say the whole town started out of this very room. It was the first structure in Rio Linda. That's why Great-Great-Grandpa Christopher did not want to tear it down. He wanted to add to it and live in it."

"But why the cross?" Kiki asked.

"Why? Well, they would likely meet here for prayer on Sundays, wouldn't they? Before an actual church was built. They say the town business was executed here too. Some of those pages in the city archives probably got their start in this very room."

"This is a very historic room." Kiki mused. Her hand dropped lazily and landed against Ian. "No wonder I pick up a powerful vibe in this house."

Janine noticed Kiki's hand and fought an urge to reach over and knock it away. Kiki always flirted with whichever male happened to be around and she did not want Kiki to start flirting with Ian. Janine stared her down.

"Aha," Kiki winked and retrieved her hand.

"Aha, what?" Ian still examined the plans, oblivious to their interaction. "What?"

"Just, aha," Kiki said and stood up. "I'm going to call it a night. Steve's comes tomorrow morning and Janine and I have a date in the study with the camera, where I will ask all these little questions that are dying to pop out but need to wait. I should probably get some beauty rest."

Chapter 6

The Ghost Janine

Janine slept in. Well, it was more like hiding in. She cracked the code during a deep REM cycle and wanted to hide from her embarrassing psyche. Her shrink warned her that suppressed memories might reemerge while sleeping if triggered by daytime events or emotionally explosive stimuli. They were especially likely after weaning off the medication and her mind cleared up.

Janine was flustered, wondering what to do. She listened to the crew setting up for the interview downstairs. What would she say? She felt like a total fraud. She could honestly only affirm that she once had an imaginary friend. She no longer believed her experience at the river might be part of an actual ghost story. In fact, she felt certain it wasn't. The whisper in her ear, which felt so authentic at the river, was just more fallout from her wounded, fractured past. *Why did you leave me?* Those words had been locked away in a corner of her brain, waiting to ooze out at an inconvenient moment.

Janine hid under the covers, hoping to hide away from the demon determined to haunt her. *He* uttered those words when she completed her testimony and was forced to walk right past him. Very sternly, he said in a broken, betrayed voice, *why did you leave me?* He whispered it in the woods too, *didn't he*, after blaming her for everything and asking her to make that promise again. The memories, hazy in her mind, kept swimming to the surface. *Suppressed memories, lurking behind mentally protective layers, can spontaneously emerge if triggered*, Doctor Crisper warned her. How did Doctor Crisper instruct her to handle it? Find the trigger. *Identify the trigger, recognize it, and you'll be better able to control your responses.*

Could her new romantic feelings be the trigger? The emotions Ian stirred up when he turned the tap on her hot blood. Did that rush of passionate heat set her off. Her growing attraction to Ian McNally stirred up a flood of suppressed emotions, the exact emotions she felt with Rick when they first met, when she believed he was a normal person and fell catastrophically in love with him. Her psyche must believe it was happening all over again, and deep inside, she was scared to death.

She realized her fears were ludicrous. She knew Ian much better than she had known Richard Wilkens when she leapt into that passionate relationship. Perhaps she should call Doctor Crisper. The call was surely overdue. Almost a year passed since their last full conversation. Perhaps she shouldn't call him. How could he help anyway?

Bottom line, the river ghost was definite crap. Wasted time, wasted research, wasted money. Her little incident was nothing more than a fractured brain recalling a traumatic life experience. Should she confess her revelation to Ian? Kiki? Steve? How embarrassing. She wasn't nearly ready to tell everyone everything. The little bit she shared with Ian had been tough. Plus, the crew felt one hundred percent certain they stumbled upon an authentic, original ghost story. Janine the skeptic convinced them of that, and her wacky fun-loving grandma helped fuel that fire.

She debated coming clean or keeping quiet. Half the stories on the show turned out to be bunk and the audience still loved them. Even Kiki insisted that people wanted the stories more than the ghosts. But the team really believed in this one. Ian believed it. She could see it in his eyes. Would Kiki be able to see through her? Kiki debunked more than one fake story on camera, and not kindly. Janine lingered in bed a little longer, hiding from the world.

Steve and Ted rearranged Gram's study. They clamped the big camera to a large tripod and set it next to the piano. The winged chairs were no longer separated by Gram's country end tables, but face to face. Ted glanced up and grunted his hello. Steve greeted her with a huge hug. Both of them wore Marvel Universe shirts.

"Wow," Steve boomed. "The stuff you guys dug up, wow. We're going for a two-part episode on Sacramento now. It's the only way we can do it. Multiple camera interviews with witnesses, four or five streets to look at, and an orchard. All possibly haunted! We have a truly original, deeply rich ghost story to tell! I've even contacted my friend, Cheeky, from NYU about a reenactment segment."

He talked while attaching camera lights to a smaller tripod with a reflective umbrella. Ted hid chords and rearranged Gram's knickknacks on the piano. It looked like he wanted to get rid of some, but didn't know where to stash them. He laid a few photos flat. Steve showed her a silver sheet of metal with a faint picture of a boy on it.

"Your great-great, I don't know how many greats, but great-grandpa Christopher Williams. One of the founding fathers of Rio Linda! Your grandma found it this morning. There's another plate of the whole Williams family, but it's hard to make out the faces. This one is still nice."

Janine picked up the tin-type photo to study it. Grainy and grey, a startled boy in dress clothes stared at her.

"Not a father. According to research, he was a little boy when the town was founded," she told him.

"Close enough." Steve smiled. "We're floating the idea of staging a reenactment of the origin story for your river ghost. This is great stuff, really rich storytelling. Wagon trains, river baptisms, lust, murder. Religious undertones in a ghost story are always a major plus."

"Well, Sleeping Beauty awakes." Ian strolled into the room. He gave her a smile that sparkled to his eyes. "All set then? This'll be a snap," he said.

"Nervous about the interview?" Steve came round to massage her shoulders. "Don't worry, you come off very nice on camera. Very nice. I know it's imposing, having the camera pointed directly at you, but you're getting used to it, right? Not the monster you first imagined, that camera."

"Is it the hypnosis?" Ian asked her. "Kiki said you were hesitant but agreed to go under. Just relax, I've hypnotized lots of folks. If you really don't want to do it, we don't have to."

"She's fine." Kiki walked into the room. "Stop smothering her. You're going to make her nervous."

Kiki, channeling a sexy, gothic vampire, wore a tight, black, low-cut dress with a long slit up the skirt. A thick leather waistbelt with a small dagger formed the neck of her hourglass shape. Her outfit was bottomed with black spiked heels and topped with black spiked hair. Was it a wig? She was all black and white except for her blood red lips and brilliant green eyes. Ted whistled and Steve just gave her the up and down.

"Well," Ted grunted. "It's Elvira, Mistress of Darkness. Carlos is going to be very upset he missed this one."

"What if," Janine swallowed nervously, "What if I never really saw a ghost? My gram is a bit of an embellisher."

"Nonsense," Kiki told her. "You are connected to the spirit of Linda Mae Stauch."

Janine gave the doctor a worried look.

"Out at the river," Ted grunted again, "Can't fake that. I saw it. Something spooked you. Carlos was sitting right next to you and says he felt something too. He was totally spooked."

Janine left the room for the kitchen. Behind her, Kiki directed Ted to move the chairs back to their original positions. That entailed moving the camera and lights as well. Kiki insisted that direction was very important in an interview. Kiki needed to face west for this one. Kiki's voice carried into the kitchen.

"You know that, Ted! You too, Steve. Don't laugh, this is serious. A hypnosis subject should always face east, into the spin of the earth. I've told you plenty of times. It keeps a body from fainting, facing east. Think about Janine. What's wrong with you guys?"

Ian followed Janine into the kitchen. "Hey," he kept his voice very low. "Are you all right? Truly, hypnosis is nothing to be nervous about. Dinna worry, lass. I won't take advantage of you."

They stepped onto the back, glass-encased porch with mugs of coffee. Gram's backyard was riddled with hens. A single rooster with beautiful green and black tail feathers strutted in the center of the gaggle. Cocky Antonio strutting his stuff, Gram giggled the other day.

"What if I didn't see a ghost, Ian? What if I was just a kid with an imaginary friend?" Her voice was low. "What if that thing that happened at the river, what if that was just me fainting and hearing things? I'm nervous because everyone is so hyped about this being a real ghost story. Well, I never claimed that there was a real ghost out here. I'm worried that this story all depends on what I say, and I'm afraid I might disappoint you guys."

"Crikes." Ian set his mug aside and reached out to take hold of her shoulders. "It doesn't depend on you, Janine. You're too old to see this ghost anyway. And we're just hunting here, with this interview, like always. If you want to zero in on what happened in your childhood, let me hypnotize you. We could get a clearer picture. You could get a clearer picture of your imaginary friend. You never know, maybe we find something that links her to the historic Linda Stauch, maybe not. That's part of the fun."

In all fairness, Ian was right. They were hunting paranormal activity. They looked for evidence and clues. How could Janine rule out the ghost based on memories she could barely recall? This story was just as good as any of them. Bottom line, it was all just show business, no matter what Ian McNally studied in college or Kiki Mellow claimed to believe.

Kiki crossed one bare leg over the other as she lounged in an old-fashioned heirloom chair under the tempered beam of an umbrella lamp. She fired a series of questions at Janine regarding Gram's house and the surrounding area. Kiki urged Janine to reminisce out loud about her youthful experiences in Rio Linda. She asked specific questions about the imaginary friend, many of which Janine could not answer. Surprisingly, Kiki seemed pleased by the scant information Janine squeaked out. She leaned toward Janine with her breasts almost bursting from the deep-cut mistress of darkness dress.

"And now that you're back. How do you feel?" Kiki asked softly. "Have you seen your imaginary friend again?"

"No."

"The other day at the river, when we called for the river spirit to appear, you had an experience." Kiki drew in a breath, "Did you get the impression it was her, Linda?"

"I'm not sure." Janine glanced at Ian. "I don't know."

"You said that a voice whispered into your ear, do you still recall that voice?"

"Of course." Janine closed her eyes. "It asked, why did you leave me? It was very faint. Maybe I imagined it, but it did seem real."

"Maybe so." Kiki nodded in agreement. "Maybe yes, maybe no. Did it sound like a little girl?"

"It did."

Kiki acted very pleased with how tight-lipped Janine seemed to be. Janine appeared reluctant to participate. Well, she was, wasn't she? Kiki slowly rearranged her legs and leaned back in her chair, relaxing.

"Doctor McNally is now going to hypnotize you," Kiki dramatically extended her arm toward the doctor. "We will continue the interview shortly."

Ian wore his nerdy brown vest and rainbow *Spectral Analysis* tie. He settled into a cushiony chair and pulled a silver pen from his vest pocket. On a past show, the doctor hypnotized two different women with that silver pen. Carlos had insisted that people pretended to be hypnotized. Janine disagreed; she knew it often worked.

She followed every instruction. Ian raised the pen and she focused on it, as directed. She began to visualize the backyard in her head, as directed. She closed her eyes, as directed. At first, she felt nothing, then her muscles relaxed and her thoughts sank into a comfortable place. It felt like someone placed a heavy blanket over her, anchoring her down, keeping her warm and protected. Her body let loose some tension. She saw bright colors in jumpy, uneven images similar to an old 8mm film played against a back wall. Janine did not register Kiki's exact words, only her voice murmuring in the background. Somehow, Kiki's murmurings spurred images into Janine's mind. She answered questions automatically and periodically became aware of her own voice as the images changed.

"It's unfair that I am not allowed to leave the yard, so, I skirt the very edge of the lawn, towing my doll, Samantha. The grass men mowed and it smells very fresh. Just when I wish for someone to play with, I see another girl my age! Such bright-yellow hair, almost white. Her beautiful pearl headband makes her look like a princess, but her dress is very old and tattered. I am too shy to speak, so I walk right past, following the perimeter of Gram's yard. My boundary line is unfair! When I turn back, the girl is gone. She's free as a bird.

"Every day the girl with the pearl headband comes. All I do is wish her there, and she comes. It's a sunny day. I tell her we can be friends. I ask if she'd like to come inside, into the cool, air-conditioned house. But she is not allowed in our house or yard, so we walk along the outer edge of the boundary, back and forth, like caged animals. She asks if I found the necklace, but I don't know what she means. I never notice when she leaves. I just notice that she is gone.

"My friend comes again. Her name is Linda, and she talks funny. She's there whenever I go into the yard looking for her. She wants me to follow her home, but I am not allowed past the cut lawn, and she is not allowed into it. Juliana is always watching me, asking what I'm doing. When I go too far from the house, my sister yells at me to come back. Juliana is very bossy. Linda and I sit on the edge of the lawn until she must go home again.

"Linda wants me to follow her home. She knows where we can find wild blackberries. She wishes she had a doll like mine, like Sammy, but I will never give her my doll!"

Kiki's voice, in the distance, asks if the ghost ever encourages Janine to go to the river.

"Linda never mentions the river. She doesn't say anything about the river. She says I should not listen to the others. She knows where we can find blackberries and insists that we go back to where we belong. She says that we are forever friends and can do great things together. But I don't know how, if she can't come into my house and I can't go to hers.

"Linda refuses to meet Gram. Grown-ups get her into trouble, she says. And she isn't allowed into the house, so I shouldn't ask her to go in. I run to get Gram and Juliana so they can tell Linda that it is okay, but Linda is gone.

"Linda stays far away from the house. She always stands at the edge of Gram's yard asking if I will follow her home. She has been waiting a long time for a friend like me, but I don't go over there. Juliana tells me to stay close to the house, and Juliana is always watching. Juliana is wondering who I am always talking to."

Kiki's voice intertwines with the doctor's voice. They ask about the river.

"The voice at the river. Is it the same voice as Linda, the friend?"

The day at the river comes back. Images pop into her head of the boulders reflecting a metallic luster and breaking up the smooth surface of the water. Wavering ripples catch her attention as the doctor and Kiki wade in their rubber farmer johns.

"Kiki and the doctor are in the river, laughing again. Wouldn't it be funny if she fell into that water? Maybe the river ghost could knock her in for me. Then a voice whispers in my ear. I remember that voice. It is Linda, my funny friend. It is the same voice."

Janine opened her eyes to Kiki, the doctor, Steve, and Ted staring at her. Ian still held her hand. Kiki appeared thrilled.

"I wanted Kiki to fall into the water too," Ted said softly.

"That was a fantastic session." Kiki squeezed Janine's hand. Then Kiki suddenly rose. "I need to take this dress off and brush out of my hair. Janine, that was fantastic, just beautiful. Thank you. That was well worth the wait." Kiki flew off.

"We are going to debrief on the back patio," the doctor told the others. He helped Janine up. She felt a little heavy as he led her away.

Behind them, Ted and Steve began packing up the equipment while discussing dinner and picking up Carlos from the airport. Ian helped her into one of the deep Adirondack chairs. He knelt in front of her, holding her hand. He offered her a cool glass of ice water.

"How are you feeling?"

"I'm okay. That wasn't too bad. I think I remember some of it."

"You should," he said. "Kiki is right. You are a fantastic interview under hypnosis."

"How can you be sure I was really under?"

"You were under," he confirmed.

"Did I say anything besides my recollections of Linda? Was any of it useful?"

"You said she talked old-fashioned, dressed old-fashioned. That could be an 1840s wagon-train girl. You confirmed that her name was Linda."

Janine closed her eyes, still feeling a little dizzy.

"Why did you want the ghost to knock Kiki into the river?"

"What? Oh, that." She opened her eyes and gazed at him, thinking about it. She finally just admitted it, "I was jealous. You know, Kiki's always getting your attention. And you never noticed before; I've had a crush on you for a little while."

Ian grinned happily at her and tried kissing her, but it was awkward. Gram's wine-barrel lounge chairs were not shaped with two people kissing in mind.

"You were jealous? Let's get out of here," he whispered. "Obviously, we've both been sitting on our feelings for quite some time and we should explore it. Why wait? We should make a go of it. We could disappear for a little while and no one would miss us. The guys are going to the hotel and Kiki has her appointment. We don't have anything scheduled until tomorrow afternoon. We could find a private place and get to know each other better. A romantic getaway, alone, on our own time. You can break your promise to me." He swallowed, eyes blinking. "I'll forgive you."

Was Ian McNally the trigger? Under hypnosis, the voice at the river sounded exactly like the voice of her imaginary friend. Could the ghost story in Rio Linda have possibilities after all? The more-reasonable explanation pointed to Janine manifesting delusions because of her growing feelings for Ian, the anxiety she harbored at where it might lead physically, mentally, and emotionally; anxiety at making a terrible mistake again. Perhaps Janine needed to face her fear and follow through with Ian, it could defuse that trigger for good. Doctor Crisper said the key to her recovery would be when she finally trusted someone with everything. That someone could be the nice, considerate man she's been crushing on for months.

Gram always played cards with her girls on Wednesday night, so it was a given that she would be up late. Janine called to tell Gram not to wait up or worry. Gram didn't ask any questions, but her pause and tone of voice let Janine know that Gram suspected what she was up to.

They took the red F-150 and cruised up the granite infused mountains toward Lake Tahoe. Ian was curious to get a closer view of the mountain pass Linda crossed two hundred years ago. Ian rambled about the Sierra Nevada range. It resulted from a fault block uplifting of a gigantic igneous batholith over one hundred million years ago. Some of the giant chunks of exposed granite made up Yosemite National Park, creating the half dome monolith among other peaks. He used his lecture voice as he talked and she found him extremely cute trying to impress her.

The drive provided plenty of time to fill in the blanks of the sketchy pasts they shared. Ian finally asked the question he was afraid to voice. In the privacy of the truck, with his eyes focused on the road, she might be able to tell him everything.

"So, the bloke that's in prison…" He was hesitant. "You met him in college? So, were you young?"

"I was twenty. Young, but not too young," Janine told him. "I thought it was… I was very taken with him." She found it hard to admit that she fell head over heels for Rick and actually wanted to marry him.

"Was he a university student?"

"I thought so, at first. But then he had a house in River Forest, a small place. He never went to class." Rick seemed perfect: Easy on the eyes, athletic, considerate, funny, smart. And charming, so very charming. He drew her attention easily and filled her up with bubbly excitement. She remembered falling in love, the tumbling toward him and feeling safe in his arms. How lucky she felt. She remembered telling her roommate that it was true love, how could it be anything else? "It's still unbelievable that he is the same guy that…" her voice faltered.

Ian just drove. He let her tell the story slowly.

"It was like a switch flipped one day."

Ian nodded, then shook his head.

"Someone warned me. I don't know who. But I got a note." *Three notes that I ignored because I thought someone was jealous. I was stupid, stupid, stupid.*

Ian glanced over, and she continued,

"The note said that his last girlfriend went missing." *She disappeared from school, never to return. Someone thought I should know that. Someone thought he was dangerous. Someone I ignored.*

"She's gone?"

Janine nodded. The note writer believed Rick did something to her.

"Did the police look into it? Check him out?" Ian asked.

"She left messages to friends. She wrote a letter to her parents saying she was going to Turkey to join some mystery group. That's what people thought. That's what she wrote in the letter. That's what he said." *Rick couldn't persuade her against it. He seemed very upset that he was being unfairly blamed for her reckless behavior. People always assume the guy is at fault when women run away.*

"Is that what he told you?"

"Yes," Janine said. *And I believed him. Why wouldn't I? He seemed so normal. He was very upset that someone would write those notes. He claimed to be a victim of malicious gossip, reverse sexism. It was cruel, because she left him brokenhearted and he was blamed. Of course, I believed him. I loved him.* "When I asked about it…"

"He became violent?"

"No, not yet," she said. "Not until I broke it off." *But I didn't really break it off. Not completely. I only wanted a small break.* Janine instinctively hugged herself, reaching underneath her shirt to trace the scar near her navel. "I want to warn you. I have…I have a couple of scars." *Like seven. Seven knife marks. Mostly small, insignificant lines across her skin. But a couple of very distinct grooves, near-fatal gash marks on her back and one on her stomach. Ruined, some might say. So don't expect smooth, milky skin like Ingrid Stauch. Maybe they should turn back.*

"Dinna worry about that," Ian said. "I'm attracted to you because of you. You are so gutsy. You really make us all step up. I loved the way you just shook off that whole thing in the underground of Sacramento, like it was nothing. Ted about pissed his pants, more than once! You stay so cool, and are incredibly smart. Funny. You're always joking with Carlos. And you're a very nice person, always considering everyone's feelings." He looked back to the road. "And I bet you don't know how alluring your eyes are, lassie, bonnie golden and bright. Plus, you look spectacular in your Spectral uniform. I can tell you're smoking hot underneath. I got lots of tactile evidence to back that up. Whoops, sorry. Crikes, did I step in it?" There was a sheepish expression in his eyes. "Really, Janine, I've seen a scar, or two, before, it's okay. Don't worry about a couple of wee scars."

"There may be more than a couple," Janine said quietly. *And not so wee.*

"Dinna worry about that," he said again. "I think you're beautiful." Then after a time, "What happened?"

"I got caught up in the romance and I let things go. My grades began to slip and I needed to study. My sister became concerned about the time I spent with him. She pressed to meet him. She was wary of him. That's when the switch flipped. He turned into another guy." *He was angry. Rick did not want Juliana interfering in the relationship or influencing things. He detested anyone that questioned the time he demanded.* "I just wanted to have a little space to study, and go home for a visit. Just a break, for exams and the holidays." She stopped.

The memory overwhelmed her. She did not want to break down, but that happened to be the exact moment her bright and wonderful life altered into a nightmare. She felt a little of the love she had felt, the betrayal, and the disbelief. All those feelings were still lodged somewhere inside.

"Hey, I'm sorry. We can stop…"

"No. I want to tell you." She insisted. "I have to be able to talk about this."

"I don't want you to feel pressured and I also don't want…" He knocked himself in the head. "Crikes, I blew it, didn't I. I was hoping for full-blown romance, you know, a nice dinner, dancing, a fancy hotel, maybe bubbly. But I had to start asking these questions. I'm sorry."

"Ian, there can't be any romance if I don't tell you about this first," she said. "You need to know before we can move on, before we can go any further. So let me get it out, because, I want that romance too. Ask any questions you need right now."

He didn't say anything, just blinked at the road ahead.

"He switched personalities in a fraction of a second," Janine told him. "The man I knew was replaced by…that guy. He told me, no. No space, no break, no outside interference." *In fact, Rick would not let me leave his house until he was satisfied with my attitude. He would not let me go back to the school or anywhere.* "I tried to leave, but he stopped me."

"He struck you?"

"He beat me until I passed out."

Ian pressed his lips together.

"I woke up attached to a long chain."

Ian's brow furrowed.

"He, he…it wasn't consensual anymore. And he beat me again, when I tried to stop him. I don't know how many times because I still have a lot of missing time." *And in between those rages, Rick spoke sweetly, like everything was normal and I wasn't on a leash confined to the second story of his house. That we were just having a little tiff, a small difference of opinion, and all his actions were going to help change my mind. Make me see his point of view better.*

"Janine…"

But she cut Ian off, "I was trapped for over a week. People were looking for me. He wanted to take us on a trip, for privacy, a change of scene, to get back the romance. Back the way it was." *But maybe Rick just wanted to get me out of his house so he could kill me.* "When he unlocked the handcuffs, I ran away. Somehow, I escaped and ran into the woods. He came after me and stabbed me…a few times. He buried me with leaves." *I couldn't move. I couldn't talk. I was dying.*

Ian swallowed hard.

"A rock stymied the flow of blood. It saved me." *I lay in those leaves for what felt like hours until a guy walking his dog found me. Well, the dog found me.* "It took days until I was coherent enough to speak. I was scared out of my mind because he was in the hospital, holding my hand, acting normal." *I was confused. My brain was fuzzy. I was confused and terrified.*

"Blimey, what? How?"

"Everyone believed the story he concocted." *Even me. Even I thought it sounded reasonable and doubted my flashes of memory.* "He was actually the one to report me missing. He called my dorm, asking for me. He left messages asking me to call him while I was still chained in his house. My roommate said he was frantic. They arrested a homeless guy camping on the edge of the woods because there were handcuffs hidden in his stuff. Handcuffs that matched the marks on my wrist. I doubted my own mind at first.”

Through the meds and fuzzy haze, I thought maybe I mixed everything up. The real truth, I wanted to be mixed up. It was nicer to believe he was the Rick that I first met, the first man I ever loved, the one I fantasized about and hoped to marry. I couldn't wrap my head around what had happened. She could not admit any of that to Ian.

“That's just unbelievable. How'd they get him?”

“At the hospital. He had a disagreement with Juliana.” *Rick told her that I wanted to live with him, so she shouldn't worry about me. He planned to take me home from the hospital to care for me. Juliana did not like that idea and said as much. They argued about it.* “At one point Juliana left the room, and…” *Rick flipped the switch.* “I saw the monster again, the look in his eyes, his mumbled ranting. There was no question about it, it all happened. I was afraid he would do something to Juliana if she kept resisting him.”

“Blimey. What'd you do?”

“I could barely speak, but managed to tell a nurse. I don't remember how.” *She was great. She didn't even blink when Rick came back into the room.* “She told the police.”

One investigator never trusted Richard Wilkens. He thought Rick's truck was suspect. He had a shovel, a pick, and a tarp in the back bed. Based on that, Detective Anderson concluded that Rick planned to move my body to a more-secure location and bury me.

“They arrested him right away, right out of the hospital room. It stunned everyone: Juliana, the nurses, everyone. That's when I finally managed to give a statement. I—I still have a bit of missing time, so I don't know everything. They used that against me in court, having so many blanks. Called me unreliable, irrational, and hysterical.”

“I just… It's just…”

“I know, it's a lot. But there's more. I pretty much cracked after that. You know, total mental breakdown.”

"No one would blame you," Ian said.

"I cracked." *And had his baby,* she didn't add. *Abandoned the newborn and went back to hide in the mental ward because I feared the father. But more accurately, because I hated the mother for being so easily fooled and so completely stupid, and mostly, for still feeling in love with him. I wanted to pretend none of it ever happened and that the baby didn't exist. I couldn't look in that baby's eyes. They looked like his eyes. I worried the baby would make me go back and forgive him.* Maybe she should save that part for another day. Saying the other stuff out loud just about wiped her out.

"Anyone would crack. It's a lot to digest," Ian said.

"You'll have the rest of the drive to digest it," Janine told him. "It's a lot, I know. Does this change how you feel about me, romance wise? I'll understand if you want to turn around? Mental issues, emotional issues, relationship issues. I've got them all. This is your chance to escape. I wouldn't blame you. No harm done."

"No," he insisted. He reached over and took her hand. "No, I want this to happen. I want us to make a go of it. But are you ready? I mean, that's a lot to digest. That is a pretty heavy conversation. I suddenly feel like I'm rushing you."

"Just take the drive to digest it," she said. "I told you because I'm ready for the next step too, with you, but you should know what you're getting yourself into. I've been thinking about you for months, Ian, quite a bit. We've known each other long enough, don't you think? Already friends. There's trust, and I'm definitely attracted to you."

She watched the tree line thicken on each side of the road. Tall pines sped by in silence. They were above the cloud layer and the sun shone very bright.

They stopped at Donner Lake and checked into the resort. Patched snow still lay on the ground and the air was crisp. Beyond the pines, Janine could see the tall pole of a ski lift.

"This is on the trail the Hansen party took," was the only thing relating to the ghosts said between check-in that night and breakfast the next morning.

The aroma of coffee mixed with bacon and eggs wafted through the air. Sunlight broke through a tiny slit in the curtains and drew a bright line across the bed. Did it really happen? Did she actually begin an intimate relationship with Ian McNally? Janine kept her head down and eyes mostly closed to hold onto the feeling a while longer, but it wasn't a dream. She did it. She took a chance. Nothing in the way he looked at her changed after she told him that story, and he didn't flinch once at any of her scars. Underneath the sheet, Ian's hand caressed her lower back, right about where the near fatal wound that grazed her kidney would be. Janine tensed automatically, wondering if the deep mark repulsed him. Did he think she was ruined?

"I'm just admiring your bum," he whispered. "I've been eyeing this bum for very long time. You have no idea how long I was trying to get your attention. Hum, let's see, what would I write about this in my diary for future generations? Smooth. Aye, Janine has very nice, silky skin, very beautiful and lovely to touch. Let's not forget her ample, well-shaped breasts and buttocks, to plagiarize a phrase from Mr. Hansen. Sorry, lass, but I love the shape of you."

She playfully slapped his hand away. Then, she pulled the covers further up and firmly tucked them around her body as she turned to him. She felt a little bashful in the light of day, whereas Ian lay in all his glory on top of the bedsheets.

"How did you let room service in dressed like that?" she asked.

He just laughed and kissed her. He jumped from the bed.

"Let me fetch you a cuppa coffee, my lovely lass," he said. Ian McNally was nicely put together. His Scottish ancestry created his tall, muscular, manly build. Ripples along his abdomen drew her eyes to very well-defined obliques. She turned away, aware of the burning red blush forming on her cheeks. Did he have to look so perfect?

"I can't believe I thought you were nerdy," she said out loud.

"You thought I was nerdy?" He brought coffee and a plate of food. "Me? I'm nerdy?"

"Not anymore," she said as he slowly fed her. "Now, you're just…you're just, very, very sexy." More kissing.

"I'd like to stay here all day," Ian said. "But…we've got two interviews and a plan to shoot on a few streets tonight. Plus, I want to get pebble and soil samples from the river bed. Everyone will be at your gram's house in a couple of hours, so we should get going if we don't want to be late."

"Pebble samples from the river?"

"I want to see what's in the soil and rock," he said. "I wasn't kidding about the field lines out there. It's like a transmitter sending signals, or some sort of reflector. Maybe there's an ore or deposit picking up energy signals. I've got a theory about ghostly energy that I'm working on and want an analysis of the rocks."

He fed her the last of the toast then kissed the crumbs away. He said something softly that she couldn't quite hear, but it sounded sweet. Finally, he moved to take the breakfast plate back to the small round table with the other dishes. Janine shifted around to put her coffee mug on the nightstand and check the time. If they got moving soon, they could definitely beat the crew to Gram's house.

She sat up and quickly wound her long tresses about her hand to obtain control of the mess. Her cover suddenly slipped. She had to grab the sheet before becoming completely exposed but wasn't fast enough.

"Crikes." Ian stared at her, completely entranced. His voice was very soft. "You are going to think I'm a total animal."

Her eyes were drawn to the unmistakable fact that Ian was becoming quite aroused. As his eyes ran over her curves, they ignited every nerve imaginable. The heat spread like wildfire into her breasts and groin, teasing her. How did he manage to do that with only his eyes? He stood poised and ready to pounce, waiting for her to give him a signal.

"Let's be late," she managed to say. That was all the encouragement he needed.

On the drive back to Rio Linda they agreed to keep a low profile on their budding relationship. Janine wasn't ready to field the scrutiny, especially with her sister's family visiting so soon. Would Juliana think she was being careless? Plus, she wasn't ready to deal with ribbing from Carlos.

They found the *Spectral Analysis* crew waiting in the rustic sitting room. They were definitely late for the briefing. Every face scrutinized them when they burst through the door. Luckily, Kiki drew the attention back to her whiteboard.

"Oh, hey," Ian, a total coward in the face of his coworkers, went straight up the stairs. "Let me run up for my tie."

Gram waved Janine into the kitchen. Janine nodded to everyone before hurrying to meet Gram.

"I covered for you," Gram whispered.

"What?"

"I told everyone that you two took off early this morning to run an errand and would be back presently."

"Oh, thanks, Gram," Janine said.

"Not a problem, girl." She patted Janine's back. "Did you have a good time?"

Janine gave Gram the eye.

"Well, you look absolutely radiant, girl, absolutely radiant. Whatever you got up to, I'm going to tell you, I'm all for it."

Janine cracked a smile and hugged her grandma.

Back in the living room, Ian returned wearing his *Spectral Analysis* tie and a vest. He glanced at her and smiled conspicuously, absolutely beaming. He loitered across the room restacking Kiki's papers while shooting glances at her. *Good grief,* Janine thought, *everyone is going to guess.* Even so, she couldn't look away from his deep blue eyes, nor keep herself from smiling back and wondering when they would be alone again.

"What did you find out this morning?" Steve turned his attention from Kiki.

"Oh, well, you know," Ian uttered, "the mountain pass, rough, but nice. Very nice. Absolutely beautiful."

Steve glanced toward Janine and Carlos. "We don't need you guys until tonight, but you're welcome to come for the interviews if you want. Janine, you're probably interested in hearing what other people have to say about the ghost. Or, you can hang out with Carlos and charge up all the gear for the street shoots."

"Everything is plugged in." Carlos lounged in the easy chair, looking quite comfortable. "But I'll hang out here, I guess. I can read through Kiki's pile of stuff. Cram the info about which ghost is on which street." He tapped his head.

"I'll give you a big hint, my dear. The streets are named for the ghosts that haunt them." Kiki winked at him.

"I'll go to the interviews," Janine said.

"Maybe you can grab some samples while we're out." Ian turned to Carlos. He retrieved four collection tubes from his pocket. "I've been meaning to get to it."

A little old lady who lived on the other side of the orchard was their first interview of the day, Mrs. Caroline Govant. Several people claimed a ghost haunted her orchard and that her family kept a log of the sightings dating back almost one hundred years. Caroline's maiden name happened to be Miller. Kiki confirmed that Caroline was a direct descendant of John and Maggie Miller from the diary of wagon-train settlers. John and Maggie produced five offspring. Mary, who died very young from drowning in the river, and four boys who all lived into adulthood and sired children of their own. Only one of the boys stayed in Rio Linda, George Miller.

"Caroline is a direct descendant of George, the son that inherited the land and holdings of the Miller clan." That was as far into the history that Kiki rehashed for them.

As usual, Kiki dressed for the camera. Her hair was back to light brown and was tied into a high braided ponytail that exposed her tiny neck tattoo.

Kiki wore a tight collegiate cashmere sweater from Brown University, pearls, and a shimmery skirt with a slit all the way up her thigh.

Janine took charge of the big boom microphone. It projected from a telescoping pole. Caroline spoke very softly, so Janine would need her headset to listen in and grabbed them from the box. The Wonder Woman sticker was replaced with a Captain Marvel sticker. Janine glanced at Steve.

"After those glowing hands in the tunnel, I thought Captain Marvel was more appropriate." He chuckled.

Janine nodded and wrapped them round her neck. She had no idea what he was talking about.

Caroline Govant allowed them to prop up the camera in her living room. She was a slight old woman with snow-white hair and an unusual array of wrinkles. Although she appeared very frail, she moved easily for a woman of her advanced years. Spritely even. Caroline sank into her seat and watched them with small beady eyes.

Kiki browsed the room studying the many framed photographs along the mantel and on a small table. Kiki directed Steve to snap pictures of some of the images. Janine stood silently, holding the boom microphone and watched Caroline Govant carefully observe Kiki Mellow.

"Is this you?" Kiki held a framed photo of a young, dark-haired girl standing in the orchard.

Caroline gave a slight nod.

The doctor walked in with a mid-size electromagnetic reader and set it on the floor. He returned from conducting a perimeter check of the house. There was a chair reserved for him and also one for Kiki. After a bit more browsing, Kiki settled next to Caroline and the doctor joined them. Ted gave Janine the signal and she adjusted the boom mic.

"Tell us about your first experience with the spirit," Kiki began the interview.

It took a moment for Janine to realize Caroline was speaking. She moved the boom mic closer and adjusted the gain. The woman's voice became more pronounced in her headset.

"About the time my father died," she said. "We have always known about the spirit in the orchard. She is said to be a long-lost Miller from the olden days. Mary Miller, the lone daughter of John Miller, the founder of the Miller General and the bank. The M.G. Bank still does business over on Fifth Street, but our family no longer owns it." Caroline's quiet voice was little more than a rasp.

"Are you certain of her identity? Of who the spirit was in life?" Kiki asked.

"Positive." Caroline said. "Her father settled this land and is responsible for the orchard. Hers was the first life born in Rio Linda, and she helped plant some of those trees as a small child. We've always known about our Mary. Hers is a kindred spirit. She lingers to protects us from that other one."

"Which other spirit are you referring to?" the doctor asked.

"Why, I told you the other day." She widened her eyes at Kiki. "The one they call the River Girl. The one who preys on children."

"Yes, I remember," Kiki said gently. "We would like to record the story on camera from your lips."

"Oh my, yes, of course." Caroline nodded.

"Tell us, in your own words, how do you know of Mary?" Kiki asked.

"She watches over us," Caroline said. "My grandfather reminded us of that fact every year. We must not fear Mary. She's one of us, a Miller, and protects our bloodline. She keeps the dark spirit from seeking the Miller clan. The main road is named for her, you know. Marysville Boulevard was the first road paved in town. Rio Linda was very nearly called Marysville."

"The dark spirit being the River Girl ghost?"

"Yes."

"Have you seen the river ghost?"

"No, not her. I told you, Mary keeps her away from us Millers. We are protected."

"Of course," Kiki said. "And have you seen Mary?"

"Many times," Caroline said. "She wanders the orchard at night. Not everyone that goes out there will see her, but some do. Mostly family, and also those that…"

"And who else?" Kiki asked. "Who else can see her?"

"Those that need to." Caroline Govant shifted in her chair so that her beady eyes bore directly into Janine. "You, you would be able to see her." Her wrinkles increased with her grin.

Janine felt a chill run down her spine. She fumbled with the boom microphone and almost dropped it. The doctor jumped up and helped her steady the pole. She felt like a total idiot. Caroline's voice filtered into her headset.

"Oh, my word," the sound of the old woman's breath flowed into her ears.

"And why do you believe Janine would be able to see the spirit of Mary?" Kiki asked.

Janine got her footing back and took a firm grip of the boom microphone pole. She gave the doctor a very stern look. She hoped he realized that she was annoyed with him. What did he think, jumping up like that? He would not have done that last season. He would not have done that before last night. Do the others wonder why he ran to her rescue so quickly? The doctor gave her a little nod then stepped back toward his seat. She was instantly upset at herself for giving him that stern look. When he glanced back toward her, she offered him a little smile and watched his eyes soften again.

"She could have been the last one," Caroline Govant stared at Janine.

"The last one? What does that mean?" Kiki asked.

"I don't know what it means," Caroline mumbled. "Mary said that to me a long time ago."

"Do you know who Janine is? Do you know Janine?" Kiki asked.

"I believe she is Martha's granddaughter." Caroline smiled at Janine. "That is right, isn't it? I haven't spoken to Martha in ages, but you are the granddaughter who used to play with the river spirit, aren't you? You and Martha have the same doe-shaped brown eyes. You two look alike."

Ted swiveled the camera and trained it on Janine. Janine relaxed the boom microphone. She glanced each at Kiki, the doctor, Steve, and then Caroline. Did they plan this? No, at first Steve had told her she wasn't needed. Janine made her voice as neutral as possible.

"Yes, I'm Janine. Martha is my gram." She nodded to Caroline.

A few moments passed as she shook a very cold, fragile hand. Then Janine hoisted the boom microphone again. She glanced at Kiki and hoped she'd get the hint to continue.

"Tell us," Kiki asked, "when exactly did Mary say that to you? That she, Janine, was the last one? Did she say this directly to you?"

"Yes. Yes," Caroline said. "She revealed it in the orchard ages ago, after Henry told me about the artwork. That's a sign of seeing the river spirit, you know, making artwork of her. I went to Martha right away and she got very upset. I believe Martha eventually sent her granddaughters away, after she realized the truth."

Kiki leaned forward and crossed her legs. She gave the camera a spectacular view of one whole leg as it slipped from the slit in her skirt. Kiki teased the camera as often as she flirted with men.

"And when was the last time you spoke to Martha. Was it recently? Did you discuss this story, or anything about either the river ghost or the spirit of Mary Miller?"

"Oh no," Caroline said. "Martha refuses to speak with me since the day I shared what Mary said. She was livid. Martha does not like to hear anything I have to say about Mary. She refuses to listen anymore."

"I see." Kiki straightened up and uncrossed her legs. "At this time, would you consent to having Doctor McNally hypnotize you? We find that under hypnosis, the details of an experience are much more vivid. We would like to take you back to one of your past encounters with the ghost of Mary Miller."

Caroline consented and Doctor McNally moved forward. He reached under his vest and pulled out his silver pen. Janine closed her eyes as his hypnotic voice spoke to Caroline Govant. His instructions filtered into her headset and she reached up to take them off. She noticed Steve watching her. She gave a slight nod to let him know she was fine. Janine turned her attention back to the doctor and Caroline Govant. She moved the boom microphone closer when it was clear the old woman was under.

"Tell us about Mary." Kiki asked, "What does she look like?"

"Mary looks like me," Caroline answered, "me as a girl. Only, she plaits her hair in a single strand and has freckles across her nose. But we could be twins, her and I, that's what everyone says. The first time I saw her, it was like looking into a mirror and wondering at my new freckles."

"How does it feel when you see Mary?"

"It feels wonderful. She does not tarry long. She does not waste words. At times, she only nods. She roams the orchard, always. Sometimes she watches from very far away."

"Can you repeat anything the spirit of Mary has said?"

"She assures me that am safe. She presses me to ensure the others heed the dictum."

"The what?" Kiki whispered, looking to Ian. He shook his head.

Caroline continued, "She said that Martha's granddaughter could be the last one." Caroline became silent.

"Did she say anything else?" Kiki asked.

"Nothing. She does not waste words." Caroline's voice dropped to a very low volume.

"What do you think she meant by, *the last one*?" Kiki asked.

"I do not know," barely a whisper.

"I'd better bring her back," the doctor said out loud. "Okay, Caroline, I'm going to count back from ten. When I get to one, you are going to wake up. You will have a total recollection of our discussion and will feel very refreshed. Ten, nine, eight, seven, six, five, four, three, two, one." Ian held Caroline's hand. "Hello there. How do you feel?"

"I feel fine," she smiled with a face full of wrinkles.

"I have one final question," Kiki said.

"Yes, yes. What can I tell you?"

"Why are you speaking about the spirit now? It's my understanding that you stopped talking about this spirit a long time ago. That you refused to speak about any of it and once admitted it was a fabricated folk tale. Is that true? Is your orchard haunted, or is it a folk tale? Tell me. What's compelling you to spin this old ghost story again?"

Caroline visibly shrank into her chair. She was just a little old lady with snow-white hair and small dark eyes wearing way too much jewelry and two sweaters on a hot day. Would Caroline Govant invent a ghost story? If so, why? There didn't appear to be a reason in the world for Caroline to dream up a ghost for her orchard. Caroline turned her stone-cold eyes on Janine for a very long moment before facing Kiki.

"It's no folk tale," her voice was strong, angry. "I am the last Miller to accept and interact with the spirit of Mary and the responsibility hangs heavy on my shoulders. I didn't push the ghost on the younger generation because people now treat it like crazy talk. Things are not the way they once were. I speak to you now because the ghost must not be ignored."

Serious black eyes turned back to Janine.

"Somebody needs to accept her message and be responsible. I pass the responsibility to you. Whether you like it or not, you are a part of it."

Ted and Steve drove the van directly to Henry Webber's house while Kiki, Ian, and Janine took the truck back to Gram's. Kiki insisted on changing clothes for the next interview. Janine drove and Kiki sat in the middle of the bench seat between them. It wasn't a tight squeeze, so it irked Janine to see Kiki's bare leg pressed against Ian. Is she goading me, Janine wondered?

"So then," Kiki asked. "Was she faking it? Being under?"

"No eye flutter, no softening of facial muscles. I'd bet yes. She's a faker," Ian said.

That old woman was faking hypnosis? Janine had no idea she had been faking. No wonder they cut that session short. Why would she do that? More lying? She noticed Kiki reach up to pat Ian's forearm.

"What was that other thing she said?" Kiki asked him. "I think I missed it."

"She said dictum," Janine interjected sharply. "You know, like a pronouncement or something."

"Makes sense." Ian nodded.

"Speaking of pronouncements." Kiki's green eyes seemed irritated as they glanced briefly at Ian. "I hope nobody makes any pronouncements anytime soon."

"What are you trying to say?" Janine glared at Kiki.

"Not a thing," Kiki said sweetly. "Just being the voice of reason here. We need to focus on this job and not get distracted. We are putting together a ghost story, an original ghost story. There's something going on in this town and we need to be on high alert. Aware. Evidently, Caroline Govant believes that you are a part of it."

The drive was short and they soon pulled into Gram's driveway. Ian let Kiki out and she ran into the house to change. Janine glanced at Ian and he took her hand.

"Don't worry about her," he said, but looked a little concerned.

Kiki changed into jeans, the red cowboy boots and a tight vintage concert T-shirt. Had she really gone to a Duran Duran concert? Her hair flowed loose and wavy from her released braid. Janine could see that Kiki touched up her makeup and wore shimmery clear lip gloss. Good grief, did she take off her bra? Janine's cell phone chimed with a text from Carlos.

Kiki going on an 80s date? Followed by a winking emoji. That put her back in a good mood.

Kiki climbed into the truck and sat between them again. She took out a handwritten, folded piece of paper with directions. It was another short drive. Henry Webber lived three doors down from the Old Rio Linda Bar.

Steve and Ted already had the camera on a tripod in the small living area of Henry Webber's house. Henry was not a housekeeper. Steve quickly moved around, tidying up. Janine jumped in to help him. She gave Henry Webber a nod, but he just scowled at her.

His entire demeanor changed when Kiki Mellow walked in. He broke into a gigantic grin as he took in Kiki's appearance. He eagerly stepped forward to shake her hand. For an older man, he certainly could turn on the charm. His interest in Kiki Mellow did not seem grandfatherly in the least. His behavior was very close to being creepy.

"It is nice to see you again, Miss Mellow," he said gently. Henry guided Kiki to the chair he reserved for her and helped her settle into it. "Would you like a refreshment? A Pepsi Cola? I have beer. I bought some of that brown ale you liked. It's in the cooler."

"How very sweet," Kiki gushed. "But let's get that drink after the interview. I get a little nervous and need to be on my toes."

"Of course, of course." Henry reassured her, patting her knee. "Don't you worry at all. I'm sure we'll do just fine."

Ted waved Janine over to take the boom microphone again, then he gave Kiki a ten second signal. The doctor stood behind Janine, far out of camera shot. He carried a thermal-panger, taking readings, but Janine could tell he was just milling about. Janine tried to tune him out. His nearness distracted her. She tried to concentrated on Kiki and Henry Webber. Janine got unnerved at how Henry Webber openly leered at Kiki. His eyes seemed fixated on Kiki's tight concert T-shirt and Kiki didn't seem to care at all.

"We are here with Mr. Henry Webber of Rio Linda, California," Kiki spoke to the camera. "Mr. Webber is a direct descendant of a family who braved the Oregon-California trail in the early 1800s and settled this fertile valley just north of Sacramento. Tell us, Mr. Webber, are the stories of a haunted river relatively new, or are they as old as the town?"

"As we discussed the other day, Miss Mellow, the ghost story is as old as the town."

"Can you give us a little background on the ghost story from your perspective?"

"Well, as everyone well knows, the bend in the Rio Linda River can become a very dangerous place at certain times of the year. When the snow melt begins, the river runs deep and quick. At our bend, there are natural rock layers with crevices that feet, legs, and arms get stuck in during a fast current, a cold current. Bodies have gotten trapped underneath a small ledge. It's always been that way. Worse since farmers built the levies and redirected more water to the main channel. They did it to keep the intermittent creeks dry."

Kiki fluttered her eye lashes at Henry Webber and urged him on. He grinned at her.

"So, there are drownings. Of course, there are. People pay no mind to the warnings and take their little ones to cool off from the heat. Mainly out of towners these days, but most every year, we get drownings. It's a shame. This is well recorded information, as you no doubt discovered, since the beginning of our town. The stories go back generations. Kids are lured into the river to drown. Lured by the little river girl. She's named after the river, you know. Linda is her name. I suspect people don't want to blame kids for misbehaving when they've drowned. They'd rather blame it on a ghost. So, the ghost became a real thing around here."

"Have you ever seen the River Girl Ghost?" Kiki asked.

"I'm not sure what I saw." Henry's eyes darkened.

"Do you believe you may have seen the ghost?" Kiki asked.

Henry closed his eyes, "No. But I think I saw someone see her. Or rather, someone who thought they saw her. Or people thought she saw the ghost."

"Tell us about that."

"It was back in '71, a couple of years before the big railyard explosion. I was a young man back from my year in Nam. I come home. This house is my family home. My ma was still quite young back then. She always had my little kin, nieces and nephews, my cousin's kids running around in the summer. She always warned them to stay away from that river. She feared what people said about that ghost, that if you see the girl at the river, you are supposed to drown in the river. When I came back, she asked me to keep a look out and keep the kids away from the river. Kids love swimming in the river in the summer. It gets very hot here. They were always asking to go. Always sneaking away."

He rubbed his furrowed forehead, "I took the boys, Jim and Todd. Then little Lara wanted to go, so, I took her out too. Didn't think no harm. The river was mild. That spot at the bend, the churches will go out and do the summer baptism on that shore. It's not always dangerous."

Henry rubbed his freshly shaved chin, "I heard all the stories when I was a kid. The river ghost wanted you to drown and so on, and so forth. I was scared to go near the bend when I was a kid, but not after coming back, grown up from a war. A little ghost story wasn't going to scare me. It seemed ridiculous, my ma still trying to scare me about that. A person shouldn't be afraid of anything that isn't real, right? I didn't want to feed the nonsense."

Kiki nodded her head, "That's understandable."

"But then I saw Lara talking to herself," Henry Webber said. "Out at the river, she was talking to herself. Said she had a new friend. I watched her standing there and she was talking to the air. Never saw nothing like that in a normal girl."

"She had an imaginary friend?" Kiki asked.

Henry nodded, "She drew pictures, beautiful pictures. I showed one to you. She gave it to me. She said it was all because of me that she met her friend and she was so thankful to me. That's when my mother realized that Lara was meant to…"

Henry Webber suddenly lost his composure and his head fell into his hands. For an old guy, his head full of hair was as thick as thieves. He sobbed softly into his rough, wrinkled hands. Kiki shimmied over and touched his shoulder in a comforting way. Henry Webber pulled himself together. He sat up and leaned toward Kiki.

"Sorry about that."

"That is quite all right," Kiki said, returning to her place.

"To get to it," Henry said sternly, "she drowned in the river not too long after that. Broke my mother's heart that she had to be the one. Couldn't live with it after it happened. And my cousin couldn't bear to stay on the farm either. He blamed me. When he left, we turned his land into the bottling company. The trees had all rotted anyway and it turned things around for us." He closed his eyes again.

"I'm sorry," Kiki said, "for your loss."

Henry nodded slowly.

"Believe whatever you want," he said. "I'm not sure why she went back to the river on her own, but I don't believe in no ghosts, not no more. She was just a strange little girl talking to herself, and there's a terrible undertow with traps at that river bend."

"Of course," Kiki said. "The undertow and rocks are well documented. There are plenty of warning signs posted near the river."

"They named Lara Lane after her. A little dead end over there off Front Street. Don't quite know why. A few crazy folks say she haunts the lane." He glanced at the doctor. "You met some of them at the bar. Don't believe a bit of it. I went out there plenty of times, and there ain't no ghost. It's all just a bunch of nonsense. Every bit of it is nonsense passed down from one crazy to the next."

Henry Webber turned around and glowered at Janine.

"Course, every old woman around here pushes those ghost stories and such. Don't think I didn't have to live it down all these years. Even so, a body can be fooled once in a bit. That picture. The one Martha had on her refrigerator, the one years ago that you drew, that was a bit like what Lara made. Martha was angry at me for saying it because, well, it was quite a coincidence. She was angry at me."

Janine didn't know how to respond. Kiki calmly reached over to take his hand.

"The doctor would like to try a little hypnosis," Kiki said. "It could help you remember more clearly and—"

"I remember things just fine," Henry Webber snapped. "I think I've said all I need to say." He suddenly stood up. "I'm gonna find my way to the old bar now, if you'd like to join me. You fellows are welcome to come along. Pack up now, or later, I don't care. We don't lock our doors around here. You're welcome to take your time. But no hypnosis, and no more talk about ghosts for me. Well, Miss Mellow, are you game for that drink?"

Henry Webber held out his arm. After a moment, Kiki took it and turned to give Steve and the doctor an urgent eye so they would tag along. Ted and Janine watched them leave in a group. Janine shrugged at Ted and they began to pack up the equipment.

The entire crew met after dinner on Bradley Road. Despite Henry Webber poo-pooing the notion, they decided to investigate four streets named for drowning victims. Kiki narrowed down which streets after carefully vetting all of them.

"I chose roads named for kids documented as drowning victims who also left artwork of the ghost," Kiki told the crew. "Not real streets at all, just little stretches of road. Maybe one or two blocks at most. The street-naming system in Rio Linda mainly followed letters and numbers. But when a short, secondary street was created, the Miller family insisted they use the name of a child who died in the river. Of course, Marysville Boulevard is extremely long, which we know is named for Mary Miller, and…"

"Hold on there," Steve stopped her. "Let's get the camera rolling. Storytelling looks much better with the backdrop of ghost-hunting. Tell it again with Ted filming." Steve jumped back into the van.

The doctor lugged his big EMF box onto the back of the F-150 tailgate. He hooked it to a portable tablet monitor. He stood up and slipped into his white lab coat. As usual, Janine, Carlos, and Ted wore their purple coveralls. Ted carried the big camera on his shoulder and filmed Kiki retelling the research and justification for the streets she selected. Kiki wore a black beret on her dark-brown hair and a mustard-yellow scarf tied loosely around her neck. Her black leather boots reached to her knees and covered the bottom of her tight fit jeans.

Carlos leaned toward Janine and whispered, "If she's dressed for the French revolution, she's missing the French accent."

Janine cracked a grin and lightly punched his arm. The doctor waved them to the tailgate of the F-150. His monitor showed four indicators blinking, all potential feed-ins for his EMF box.

"These streets are short enough that I'm hoping to do a canvass cover for low-frequency electromagnetic pulses. Four channels, set to twenty, thirty, forty, and fifty hertz." The doctor adjusted the gain on his box as he spoke, "I'll need someone to set up the receiver-transmitters at four spots down the street. I'm going to monitor here so I can make minor adjustments for frequency."

"I can set them up," Janine agreed quickly, "and record thermal changes as I go."

The doctor smiled at her. "That sounds fantastic. We'll communicate on com-2. Carlos, you should trail along with Kiki so she has someone to talk to."

"Je ne parle pas francais, amigo," Carlos said in a terrible fake accent.

"What?" Ian blinked quickly.

"I'll take the ion meter and point it where she might sense something," Carlos amended. "No problem."

"Yes. Yes, excellent." The doctor stood up as Ted came around with the big camera.

"What's the set up here, Doc?" Ted asked as he filmed.

Janine and Carlos strolled away as the doctor explained the EMF box and the canvass cover he hoped to create. Carlos headed toward Kiki while Janine strolled down the block with the small receiver-transmitters. They resembled mini old-fashioned transistor radios. She reached into her sleeve pocket to reset her headset for sound from com-2. Their audio headsets operated on four communication frequencies. They could select "all" to hear all four frequencies or tune into one specific frequency on their headset. They could set their microphone to "hot" so everything they said would be transmitted or use the push to talk button to transmit intermittent messages. Kiki always used a clip-on microphone set to "hot" on com-1 and she never wore a headset. The doctor transmitted voice on com-2, occasionally using hot mic. The rest of them only used push to talk. Steve transmitted on com-4, and Ted, Carlos, and Janine shared com-3. Janine often set her speakers to "all" but decided to tune out everyone but the doctor, so set her headset to receive on com-2.

She didn't say it out loud, but she was tired of hearing Kiki prattle on about the Rio Linda ghost. Mostly, she was still a bit miffed at Kiki's earlier attitude in the truck. Could there really a rivalry for the doctor's attention on her horizon?

About a fourth of the way down the street, she flipped the switch on one of the transmitters and checked the blinking power light. She flipped open the small pudgy antenna and set it on the curb. Janine hit her push to talk button.

"Got that, Doc?"

"Affirmative."

Janine checked her thermal-panger. It registered a stable air temperature. She continued down the street activating the final three transmitters and checking the temperature. She peered down the three blocks to where the truck and van were parked. Steve shut off the van lamps, so the night turned dark. But with the moon, Janine could clearly see Kiki, Carlos, and Ted strolling toward her on the street.

When would she be able to tell Ian about Sammy? She should do it soon. It was the main thing she was most ashamed of, rejecting her own baby. She recalled sitting with Sammy as they worked out a puzzle during the visit for Sammy's birthday. She had not seen Sammy since a brief glimpse after giving birth. That small red baby had miraculously morphed into the cutest little girl. Sammy giggled constantly, and offered "tips" and advice sounding exactly like Juliana. *Look at the colors, find a nice shape*, Sammy repeated Juliana's words.

You can do it. You can find the right one. Janine remembered her sister coaching her with the same words many years ago.

"This is just a toy," Sammy suddenly announced, pointing at the puzzle pieces. Then she pointed upward, swirling her finger and said quite seriously, "All of this is the real puzzle."

"What? What's the real puzzle?" Janine had been very surprised, mesmerized.

"Life, Aunt Jaja, life is the real puzzle." Sammy nodded very seriously. Then she melted into her giggly face again and tossed her tangled hair over her shoulder.

Janine smiled at the memory and felt her heart swell up. She was going to get a second chance with Sammy. Maybe even with everything. The doctor's voice interrupted her thoughts,

"I got a nice canvas cover over the street showing nothing of interest so far."

Janine focused back on the street. The quiet of being tuned only to Ian was nice. Kiki appeared to be rambling. Carlos laughed and said something that made Kiki pause and stare at him. Janine chuckled to herself, wondering what he said. She could tell Carlos was amused even from that distance in the dark. She watched the trio move slowly toward her. The doctor spoke through the headset again.

"Not a flicker," he said, obviously responding to a question Janine could not hear. His voice continued, "I agree, we should move on to Lara Lane."

At that point, Kiki, Ted, and Carlos reached her end of the little dead-end road. Kiki turned to talk into the camera as Carlos wandered over to stand next to Janine.

"Did you hear all that?" He pulled one of his speakers off an ear. Janine did the same thing.

"I'm just tuned into the doctor," she told him. "Did something happen?"

He shook his head slowly. "Just Kiki saying this street was a waste of time in ten different ways."

Janine nodded. "I better pick up the transmitters."

"Oh, oh," Carlos touched his headset. "Steve's calling in a plan. You and me to ride with the doctor in the truck and everyone else in the van."

"Janine…" the doctor's voice came over her headset. She hit her press to talk button.

"I'll just pick up the transmitters on the walk back toward you."

"Brilliant," he said. "I'm shutting it all down here."

The crew repeated the same basic procedures on the next three streets. Jesse Street, Lara Lane, and Eloise Way were all very short, paved, dead-end roads. Kiki had higher hopes for those sites, as several people reported ghostly encounters on them, especially Eloise Way. Seven separate witnesses reported a specter on that small stretch of pavement. Unfortunately, zero indications of ghostly activity occurred for *Spectral Analysis*.

Kiki and Carlos completed walking down Eloise Way at around 3:30 a.m. The crew was disappointed and very tired. Kiki shook her head, clearly upset.

"I felt absolutely nothing, anywhere," she said. "Not one trace of any ghostly essence."

"We're going to run back to the hotel and download the footage," Steve told them. "Maybe sleep well into the afternoon. I'm beat. We'll meet at the orchard tomorrow night."

"Okay." The doctor nodded. "Don't forget the mag coil. It's in the purple case if I get tied up. We'll just head back to Gram's in the truck and see you tomorrow evening."

Gram stood anxiously on the porch waiting for them to arrive. She seemed very excited, or agitated. Janine jumped out of the truck to see what could cause her to hop about like that in the small hours of the day.

"I found something," Gram told them, "In an old book that was falling apart. A Bible with the cover torn half off. All wrapped together and buckled with a thin leather belt."

Gram is Temperance

"What, what is it?" Janine asked.

"Pages," Gram said. "Pages from the diary."

"What diary?" Kiki asked, but her eyes were wide open and she already knew.

"The wagon-train diary!" Gram exclaimed. "The pages that were torn out of the wagon-train diary. I read them. I can't believe it. You have to see them. They're in the living room on the coffee table. Oh, my lord, Janine, you will never guess about Great-Great-Grandpa Christopher Williams. And that's not the most startling part."

Chapter 7

The Lost Pages Helen

These are ledger entries made by Helen Williams. They were found hidden in a split, cracked, leather-back Bible in a cardboard box stashed in Ms. Martha Williams Stinger's attic.

September 28, 1839 Henceforth, daily entries into this ledger diary will be made by others than Mr. Stanley Hansen, as his untimely demise rendered his soul to Christ. It is now my duty to document the travails of our group. I have not the will, nor been given the leave, to recount the exact details and will simply list the restful souls that have left our numbers in the meadow of blood, fire, and death.

A long list of names followed, starting with Stanley Hansen.

September 30, 1939- The men altered our campsite. Mikael and Niels Stauch found a copse of trees that acts as a natural shelter from the elements. This, and the canvas cover from two lost wagons, make a cozy enclosure in which to shelter us from the elements. The men erected walls of fallen timber to block against winds. A sigh of relief fell over us, as this little circle of trees keeps us warmer than imagined. It is a beautiful camp, as we have sight of the deep blue lake that mirrors the blue skies. Resting was, perhaps, the better choice after all. Several of the wounded are still alive, including my friend Irene Lumen and the man, Oscar Hansen. *Gustoff Webber's burnt hand has begun to green, and we fear it may need to come off. *We lost an ox in the night. Frederick blamed the Webber boy, Rolf, for not securing the animal well and Peter Webber banished the boy from a hot dinner, though no one of us had much of a dinner as the cooking pots are lost. Dinner consisted of meager rabbit meat, on stakes, in the fire. *Nickolas tells me, we will stay until Oscar Hansen passes or one week of time. As the ground hardens, it is not clear how we will properly care for the dead when the time comes.

*October 1, 1839-*Added to the list of dead, three poor souls. *Gustoff, aged 14 years, had his hand taken. It was a messy and tragic affair, but had to be done as his hand was clearly in decay. The ax was dull from use and Gustoff was not spared a bit of it. His father, Peter, blamed Frederick. But Fred was right, my Nicholas told him. Without the hand, he could survive. If he did not lose it quick, it would rot through the rest of him in due time. What we wouldn't give for Irene Lumen to wake and tell us of her knowledge of healing. *Mary Webber found a way to bake bread in the ground, as all our cookware had been stolen away by the Indians. The young girl dug out a hole and covered it with a plank of wood. Everyone marveled at her ingenuity and warm biscuits. This is good news, as we had little thoughts on how to usefully prepare the flour without a pot or a pan. *The younger men were successful in their hunt and brought in two rabbits.

October 3- *Frederick Stauch lost his leg. Upon sight, it was further gone than the Webber boy's hand. I watched his wife, Gretel, hush him and whisper sharply to "take it like a man" when she believed no one else could hear. She used his own words against him as those were the very words he growled to Gustoff two days prior. Never have I admired her more. *Needless to say, we will reside by our lake for the ill to recover enough to travel. As the weather has turned to blue skies, we are enjoying our leisure. Our outlook is brightening. *The children, Christopher, George, and Linda laughed today. It was so startling a sound I was caught off guard. I take it as an omen of good times to come. *Oscar Hansen woke and spoke briefly. He asked of Gretel Stauch, and myself, to fetch his sons. I was dumbstruck, but Gretel just hushed him softly and said his boys were busy with the oxen and would be by presently. I was surprised at how easily the minister's wife told false. But it was the Christian thing to do. Oscar then eased back into a quiet slumber.

October 4, 1839- *Irene Lumen, wife of Finn, passed in the night. She went quietly, may she rest in peace. A beautiful girl who leaves a lone son. Meg will adopt him and we will gather around him closely. *Ingrid shows no sign that she realizes her cousin has died. Hers is a death as well. One in a living body. *Bears have been sighted in the mountains. Grant and Mikael Stauch happened upon a lair not a quarter mile from our camp. It is hibernation time for the beasts and Frederick says they should pose us no harm. The younger men were instructed to steer clear of all caves. Better to set traps for our meager meat instead of poking in the brush. *Frederick Stauch has insisted he be kept abreast of all discussions, even though he fights fatigue and blood loss. *Thank the Lord for our crystal blue lake. The purity of the water seems to have lent a healing touch to us all. Niels Stauch, and the two small boys Christopher and George, keep our barrels to the brim. Meg has done well by young George. She has kept her word and cuddles both youngsters each night, singing softly to them. *Mary Webber has made good use of her earthen oven, and the young wife Susan Miller has taken to helping forge tasty biscuits, though rough. It is Mary's biscuits that keep our bellies from growling. *The traps the young men have set yield barely a prize, split amongst us, amounts to nearly nothing. *Grant asked to take the rifle, but was set aside by Frederick. After the Indian event, it seems there is scant but 8 tried left. There was a bit of a disagreement about that with the men. When queried, Nicholas just shook his head. *Several in the party have taken ill with a bit of the runs and fever.

October 5, 1839- The ink runs low, and the men have given leave for the upkeep of this ledger to one a week. I am to write sparingly. It seems my entries are too mired in women's concerns, though I know not where they lay. Signed, Helen Williams.

Scratched out section

October 16, year of our Lord 1839, F. Stauch. The upkeep of this journal has been reassigned for the purpose of clarity and brevity. Oscar Hansen rests under a small stone pile. The ground is frozen and our efforts impotent for a proper burial. Our stores are down. The women overused supplies against better instruction. We lost another ox in the night through the delinquency of the Webbers.

October 23, the year of our Lord 1839, F. Stauch. A most unexpected storm delays our departure. The legions of snow drifts stand ten feet high. Mr. Webber is put on probation. His uncivilized tongue and acrimonious ways have made him an unpleasant companion. I have a mind to banish him from our mass, but not for the young girl, Mary, falling ill. Against my better judgement, I allowed the Webbers to stay. But only on the condition that the senior Mr. Webber aborts his tongue in all matters of decision.

October 30, the year of our Lord 1839, F. Stauch. The storm continues. Our stores shrink to alarming lows. Grant Williams and John Miller press to use the rifle for "game" of which they mean bear. They would bring wrath on us all for their young man's folly. We have not seen a live animal, except our lone ox, for days. The illness spreading through our mass has made travel impossible with but one wagon, even if the storm subsides.

November 5, the year of our Lord 1839, F. Stauch. My beloved son, Mikael Ernest Stauch, has gone to his maker. He used the fourth of our last lead bullets. Why? It is the woman he married, her family was not truly godly. Now his own brother has fallen to her bewitching. Where is the community outrage?

December 2, 1839- The care and burden of this ledger diary is entrusted to my care once more, Helen Williams. I will not attempt to recapture the many heartaches transpired. Failing this, Mr. Stauch kept scant records. My husband, Nicholas Williams, is now our leading voice on this miserable, freezing mountaintop and has tasked the book to my keeping. He keeps close counsel to Mr. Webber, as they are men still of able of mind and body. *We are starving. We are dying. We will surely perish if the tides do not change on our fortunes. In this past week, we have lost Gretel Stauch, Mary Webber, and my dear, dear grandson, little Christopher, among many others. Meg has taken to a grave illness which has protected her from the loss of her babe. She is delirious with fever, as is my son Ethan. Myself and Sue Miller tend to the infirm, with little George Lumen frantically watching over Meggie. He has taken to calling her mama, and she has called him Christopher more than once in her delirium. *Gustoff and John Miller toil day to night scavenging for wood. *Nicholas, Peter Webber, and Grant hunt the hillside for food and keep watch. Their traps yield nothing. Something dragged off the ox, Millie Mae, last week.

December 7, 1839- Peter Webber survived a bear attack, but two others did not. The men took the rifle and the last of the pellets to find meat. They went into the bear lair, as there was no other living creature to be found. The pellets did little more than anger the sleeping giant, and Peter Webber took a claw to the shoulder while Tom Merk and Carl Handling are gone. I pray Peter's wound does not infect. Daily, we melt the snow as the edges of the lake has frozen. John Miller is tireless in this task, as he knows well it is keeping our friends alive.

December 13, 1839- The last of our flour is used. We now have only a meager supply of coffee and sugar. I fear the sugar will be gone before three days. It is all I have to feed the sick. A cold sugar water mix, two teaspoons each day. The rest of us have taken to chewing pieces of the leather strap Frederick Stauch uses to fasten his Bible. It was hard to put that strap in my mouth at the first, but now I want it more and more. Our days are surely numbered. Each morning, I expect to find more of our numbers passed.

December 16, 1839- It is now clear that Frederick Stauch should have banished Peter Webber. He is a Godless man. Mr. Webber returned from a break in the storm after checking the traps. Grant asked if there was anything, dead or alive, to be found, and Mr. Webber fixed my eyes and said that the snow did preserve our dead friends well. He laughed as he took a knife to the leather cover of Frederick's Bible. He laughed as he chewed the good book until he started raining tears. When Nicholas returned, neither Grant nor I had the words to tell him why Peter Webber was crying in the corner. Nicholas crashed to the bed, exhausted and suffering a terrible cold. I fear it is turning to fever.

December 18, 1839- We have been four days without food of any kind. The last of the ill will die soon. I fear the young Stauch girl, Linda, has gone already, though no one dares to tell me and I resist adding her to the list to make it true. Webber has taken to Bible quotes. He is finally mad, I fear. I no longer have the strength to care for the infirm. This may be my last entry into this ledger journal. May God forgive us our sins and pride. This is our punishment. Whoever may find this, know that our fate is deserved for not standing against the devil when we had the chance.

December 21, 1839- It is the darkest day of the year, but there is light! Grant and Peter Webber found meat! They returned day before yesterday night with a catch and made a crude stew prepared in a wooden pot heated with rocks from the fire. They have nursed us all. I look around and see only Grant and Peter moving about, and also the child, Linda. She is alive! The child's sweet laughter woke me from a stupor. That and the food. Praise the Lord.

December 22, 1839- The infirm are making a grand recovery. The children are rays of light and Linda's giggling is a salve to our souls. The new trap Peter and Grant have set is our salvation. No rabbit, Grant tells me. He is unable to identify the animal they captured. It was mutilated before they recovered it. It spreads fear that the bear is shadowing our camp. I fear when Grant goes out again, but also hunger for the meat he brings. The rifle no longer has issue and lays useless.

December 24, 1839- The devil dwells in our house. Our fates are now destined for hell. Mine own son has damned us. Grant confessed to his father, and his father to me—There are no traps. Just the preserved flesh our dearly departed.

That is the final entry from the pages torn out of the ledger diary.

Chapter 8

Séance Janine

Steve parked the *Spectral Analysis* van on the extended section of Marysville Road alongside the almond orchard. Caroline Govant granted them permission to investigate the southeast quad of her neglected trees, the area most frequently haunted by the spirit of Mary Miller. The doctor and Carlos already disappeared into the dark to set up motion sensors and a subsonic audio recorder in the hopes of picking up ghostly vibrations. Janine hung back at the house to give Kiki more time to get ready. Kiki had a very good feeling about the orchard.

Janine and Kiki arrived in Gram's F-150 dressed for the shoot. Janine wore her purple spectral suit, red vest, and clumpy boots. Kiki came dressed like a sexy ninja without a mask. She wore black stretch pants, a form-fitting long-sleeve shirt and dark gloves. Her hair was hidden inside a black watch cap, and the small tattoo on the back of her neck was exposed. The tattoo resembled a Celtic knot. Carlos strolled over and chuckled at her. Kiki winked at him.

"Hey there, kid." Carlos flashed his dimpled smirk at Janine. "Is Kiki planning to rob a bank later?"

Janine cracked a little grin.

"Don't worry about the coil antennae." Carlos joked. "We hung it in a tree, over there. Just give it a wide berth. Unless you need another jump start or something."

"Funny." Janine pocketed an audio recorder and the silver thermal-panger.

She glanced toward the doctor. He went mysteriously missing after reading the torn-out pages of the diary. Did he go to the hotel to download data all day? His head was down fiddling with his large electromagnetic receiver box.

"The doctor's been a bit quiet," Carlos said. "He's worried about something."

I'll bet, Janine thought. *Probably thinking about the over-the-top family secrets his new girlfriend has. Just the icing on the cake to her over-the-top personal past. Damaged goods. Ruined.* And she hasn't even told him about Sammy yet.

The doctor stood up. He moved hesitantly toward her, glancing into the overgrown trees. The past year's almond husks lay on the ground covering the dirt. They crunched when the doctor stepped on them. *Does he think they moved too fast? Is he regretting things?* Kiki strolled over as well.

"We are going to go down this center, what do you call this, row or aisle, of trees?" He pointed with a hand. "I'm thinking, maybe Carlos out front with Kiki, then me and Janine."

"Janine should be out front with me," Kiki countered. "You two guys can trail behind. Caroline insisted Janine will be able to see this spirit. Us two girls need to be out front. I'm also tired of Carlos and his doty wisecracks." She fluttered lovely, green eyes at Carlos and he grinned innocently in return.

"That could work," the doctor agreed flatly. "I'm just thinking…" His voice trailed off. He tapped Janine's arm and urged her follow him. They walked to the edge of the tree line. "I'm a little concerned about you," Ian looked worried. "Are you okay with going into the orchard tonight? We're already picking up loads of activity on the EM box and there is nothing out here to create it. It's not like those dead-end streets. I don't know why I'm anxious." He glanced at Kiki. "She says things feel extremely real here, you know. There's a big possibility you may see something and not expect to. She's very hyped, and she's had real experiences and knows—"

"Caroline told us that this spirit is friendly, so I have nothing to be afraid of," Janine said softly. Did he really think they would find an actual ghost in the trees? He knew Janine didn't really believe in ghosts. "You took off pretty quickly after the diary revelations."

Ian nodded. "I thought you'd want a little space with your gram. To talk about stuff."

"The Donner party had to do the same thing," Janine said. "They were just surviving."

"I meant about your great-great grandfather," Ian said. "For some people, a name doesn't matter. For others, it does quite a bit. Knowing who you are." He leaned in. "Are you upset?"

"Gram is still working that one out. It doesn't matter to me."

His hand slipped to the small of her back as he leaned in slowly.

"I don't care about Kiki's voice of reason," he whispered. "I'm concerned with all this stuff we're learning. Crikes, you are in deep with this story. I feel like we're being pushy and I don't want you to feel compromised or something. Are we invading your privacy? Or, am I being an arse here? I feel like I should be protecting you from something. From the show? From this story? Something else? And I don't want you to feel faint again. Authentic paranormal events can make people faint."

"I'm fine," she said, relieved. "Everything's good. This is my job and it's just show business, Ian. Don't worry about the history, the ghost story. That stuff doesn't worry me."

"Hey, you two, let's huddle up." Kiki rounded them up.

They made their semicircle on the outside edge of almond trees. Ted pointed his camera and boom microphone in their direction. They passed around new clip-on microphones, one for each of them. They were foregoing their headsets to test out the new system.

"This might give us better audio," Ted told her. "I bought a complete set, five total clip-ons. All the better to get your impressions, or anything. It'll free up your heads nicely, and everyone will be on hot mic so we won't miss any wisecracks from Carlos. I got a console in the van to manage individual input. We can have nice audio of everyone this way."

"A close-up audio of Janine fainting would be nice," Carlos joked.

"Where am I going to put this?" Janine finally just clipped it onto her vest.

Kiki turned to her. "Add as much commentary as you like. Be an active part of the conversation. If you feel anything, don't hold back. Like, I'm feeling something already. Electricity in the air. What about you?"

Janine raised her eyebrows.

"If anyone's interested, I'm feeling a slight breeze," Carlos said.

"Okay, all right. Camera's set," Ted said. "Lights, and go."

The *Spectral Analysis* crew slowly wandered the orchard while discussing their interview with Caroline Govant. Kiki described a young Caroline, as seen in the photographs displayed in her sitting room. Kiki and the doctor spoke of founding town members John and Maggie Miller. They recited tales from the diary of the wagon train and the reported loss of the elder Millers during the Indian attack.

Carlos and Janine remained quiet, taking thermal readings and pointing their meters in different directions. The rising, waning, gibbous moon cast enough light to see very clearly. Aside from an owl, there was not much activity in the endless rows of crooked trees.

As the night ticked past midnight, they stopped strolling and formed a small circle. Kiki pulled a thick black candle from her ninja backpack. She lit the three wicks and placed it on the ground. A thin swirl of smoke with a spicy scent emanated from the candle. Kiki directed Janine and Carlos to free themselves of their gadgets so they could hold hands and complete a connected circle.

"Let's close our eyes and center ourselves," Kiki instructed. "Take some cleansing breaths."

Hand in hand they stood quietly, breathing. A very slight breeze rustled the leaves overhead. In the far distance, the sound of the river emerged from the darkness. The air felt clean, fresh, and charged as Kiki mentioned earlier. The temperature was very pleasant, not too warm or cold. Ian's large hand engulfed hers. His skin felt dry, rough, and warm. His thumb gently caressed her wrist and she wondered what would happen next with them. Her heart beat a little faster as she recalled Ian's protective impulse. She squeezed his hand gently as warmth flooded her system.

Kiki abruptly broke the silence, "*We seek yon souls of near to there, we call on you to us appear, reveal yourself for us to see, so I command, so mote it be.*"

Janine heard that rhyme many times from Kiki. Out of habit, she said it silently to herself as Kiki repeated it.

"*We seek yon souls of near to there, we call on you to us appear, reveal yourself for us to see, so I command, so mote it be. Mary, Mary, can you hear us? Please, Mary, reveal yourself to us.*"

An obnoxious odor wafted by.

"Anyone else smell skunk?" Carlos gasped.

"Yes," Janine said. Was the air getting cooler?

"Shh," Kiki hushed softly. "Listen for her. *Mary, I can feel you drawing near. Mary, is that you?* Do you feel it? Does anyone feel this?"

"I feel a bit of a chill," the doctor said. A cold patch of air definitely descended on them.

Janine released Carlos's hand to reach for the thermal-panger, to ensure the record function was set. At that same moment, she opened her eyes instinctively.

An angry young girl stood front and center with wisps of the candle smoke swirling around her head. Janine froze stiff with fright. Deep, dark eyes drilled into her. An eerie sensation seeped into her head and a creepy tingle snaked up her arms before sinking into her pours. Irritation, vexation, and displeasure radiated from the girl. This spirit did not have kindred feelings for Janine.

The cold that descended in the air found its way around Janine's torso and wrapped her like a tight blanket. The girl reached out with a wavering hand. Her flesh wasn't flesh at all; it appeared more like a smoky, amorphous liquid. *Was it smoke from the candle?* Smoke swirled and clung to the girl, filling in the colors of her dress. Her sketchy arms continued to stretch out. Janine instinctively shrank from her, pulse thumping rapidly. Those wavering fingers inched closer and closer and Janine felt certain the girl wanted to reach into her chest and grab her heart.

No! Janine screamed inside her head. The thermal-panger slipped from her fingers and seemed to fall in slow motion. The young girl glared at her. The girl became motionless with clasped hands in front of her body. Her head titled shyly downward but her piercing eyes remained fixed on Janine. A raspy voice floated into Janine's ear but the ghostly lips did not move. *Heed the dictum.* It was not a suggestion.

The thermal-panger hit the ground with a loud thump! Janine jumped and yelped at the same time. The apparition grinned wickedly before swiftly dissipating in a swirl of smoke. The three candle flames fluttered out one after the other. Everyone moved at once.

The cold air lingered and Janine scooped up the thermal-panger with a racing heart. She watched the numbers rapidly rise. She took deep breaths to tap down her panic. *Just calm down, just calm down,* she told herself. She felt dizzy and tried to steady herself. Carlos and the doctor turned their heads right and left, looking all around. Ted with the camera slowly circled the group and then focused in on Janine. Kiki stared at her.

"Are you okay?" Ian put a supportive hand on her arm. He asked, "What happened? You shouted."

"The temperature plunged twelve degrees in two seconds," Janine reported evenly. "It's recovering now."

"Did you see something?" Kiki's green eyes glowed in the dark.

Janine nodded, silently watching the flash of numbers slowly tick upward on the thermal-panger gage. The hair on the back of her neck still stood on end. She felt like something might be lurking in the trees, watching them, and did not want to glance outside their small circle. She drew in another slow breath in an attempt to quiet her thundering pulse. *Was she losing her mind?*

Kiki turned to Ted. "Your eyes were open the whole time. Did you see anything?"

"I saw the candle go out," he said.

"Did anyone else see something?" Kiki asked. No one did. "Me neither, my eyes were closed," she gave. "But I heard her very clearly. I heard her speak directly into my ear."

Janine met Kiki's green eyes.

"What did you hear?"

"She said, *find the dictum*. Did you hear it too?"

Unbelievable. Maybe she wasn't losing her mind after all. Janine nodded.

"I heard, *heed the dictum*."

"Let's regroup." Kiki held out her hands. "I can feel traces of her lingering around us."

Using a flip lighter, the doctor relit the candle and they reformed a linked circle. The doctor gripped her hand tightly now. Janine kept her eyes open this time, paranoid of closing them. Kiki called to the spirit. She urged Janine to call to the spirit but Janine's heart wasn't in it. Instead, she silently begged the spirit to stay away. *Stay away!*

They did not have a second encounter that evening, but they left pretty excited anyway. Janine finally verbalized exactly what she witnessed as they reached the flood lights near the van. No flashing lights or wavy, blurry air, but a full apparition. As she described the ghost on camera, their fervent jubilation could hardly be kept in check. Kiki said full apparitions were a very rare event. Usually, they only appeared to serve an important purpose, or, if called upon by a very talented witch, she smiled.

They drove to the hotel to debrief. Gram's house felt way too close for comfort and they didn't want to disturb her with their excitement. Plus, Steve's heavy software was located in the main computer in his hotel suite. Steve was eager to download and view the footage as soon as possible, in slow motion, backward, and zoomed in to catch anything they might have missed. He believed he saw something in the video. Ted, Steve, and the doctor zipped off quickly in the van, while Janine, Kiki, and Carlos followed in Gram's bright red truck.

Instead of the hotel back in Old Town, they booked rooms at the Holiday Inn Express, right off freeway 99 between downtown Sacramento and the airport. Janine gave the Malabar Restaurant a glimpse as they cruised past it and into the hotel parking lot. Carlos steered the truck around to the back lot, closer to the door they should use.

Steve sat at his computer console in the living room part of the suite working away. An open bottle of Glenmorangie single malt rested on the center coffee table and tumblers were filled. Everyone smacked Janine on the back as if seeing a ghost made her some sort of hero. Kiki took a tumbler for herself and offered one to Janine.

"No thanks," Janine said.

Janine picked up the thermal-panger to review the readings over the recorded half hour of their encounter. She watched the temperature numbers suddenly plunge, then rise. Impossible. She knew it wasn't a malfunction, or a false reading, because every person in that circle felt the cold patch that descended on them. Quite like that eerie, unexplainable encounter in Providence that spooked her. Something odd happened.

"If you see anything on video, anything at all, call me over," Kiki said from her comfortable spot on the sofa. Kiki removed her black watch cap and shook out her thick hair.

Carlos moved near Steve to watch the slowed-down action on the monitor. Kiki sipped her second whisky more leisurely, studying Janine with her striking green eyes.

"You're quite certain she said *heed the dictum* and not *find the dictum*?"

"The voice was pretty clear," Janine softly replied. "Heed the dictum."

"Was the spirit next to you, or was she next to me? I felt her essence beside me, like she was whispering in my ear." Kiki closed her eyes, remembering. "Did she whisper in your ear too? Where was she in relation to the circle?"

"The apparition stood right in front of me," Janine said, "in the center of the circle, over the candle. Her eyes held mine as she said *heed the dictum* in a very entreating way."

Kiki appeared to be thinking, "Interesting."

"What's interesting?" the doctor asked. "What did you notice?"

"The voice I heard," Kiki said. "The voice that spoke very distinctly for me too, whispered *find the dictum* directly into my ear. I felt her right next to me, her breath on my skin. Watch the clip, I actually turned sideways to look for her."

"Was that when Janine let out that, shelloch?" Ian asked. "When the temperature dropped."

"Yes." Kiki turned to Janine. "Was that shout before or after you saw her?"

"Pretty much at the same moment. Or very immediately after she spoke." Janine felt embarrassed about that yelp.

"That is interesting," Ian said. "Can we assume it was the same spirit in two places at once? Or, maybe she moved very quickly."

Kiki narrowed her eyes and sipped her drink. She stretched out and nestled further into the sofa cushions, getting comfortable.

"She said, *find the dictum*. There was a long *mm* on the end. Whew, I needed this after tonight. I was ready to faint out there. What about you, Janine, do you feel faint? Thanks for getting the eighteen-year batch." She blew a flirtatious kiss toward Steve.

Janine closed her eyes. Did she hear the same voice? What was the voice like for her?

"Mine had an *mm* too," Janine said quietly, thinking about the ghost. And she did feel weak, and in the orchard, she had felt woozy.

"Yo!" Steve pointed dramatically to the screen shot on the monitor where an odd glow hovered just above the candle. He put his finger on it. Janine could see her own startled face on the edge of the screen. Ted's camera had been focused on Kiki, but Janine's profile was clearly visible on the monitor. Her eyes were wide with terror as they stared at the light.

"Couldn't be a reflection on the lens. We used a low-contrasting polarized filter and Janine's staring right at it," Steve said. "The light pops up right at the time the temperature descends and ends when Janine shouts out and jumps. I knew I saw something. Too much of a coincidence?"

They watched the clip, a mere eight seconds, over and over. They watched Janine reach into her pocket and open her eyes as the mystery light appeared. Then, her doe-shaped eyes grew wide with fright as the light pulsed and the thermal-panger fell from her fingers. The light disappeared, along with the candle flames, as the loud thump of her panger hit the ground. Janine imagined that light hovered right about where the girl's ghostly heart would be.

"I heard a little whistling in my ear?" Carlos said. "Do you think the ghost said something to each of us? Maybe, there's a lot of stuff mixed into the tapes. I wonder if she said something to me?"

The doctor poured himself a generous portion of whisky and recharged Kiki's glass. He lounged cozily next to Kiki on the sofa, sinking comfortably into the cushions.

"She's very concerned about the dictum. She really wants us to find that dictum." He looked across the coffee table at Janine. "Or heed the dictum. Either way, we need to find out about that dictum."

"We need to go back to the orchard," Kiki enthusiastically declared, directing her attention at Ian. "We need to execute a proper séance. Maybe bring in the old girls, people with a strong connection to this place. Carol Miller believes that only certain people can see that spirit. We need to round up those people. There is a real spirit in that orchard and we've got a good shot at getting some real definitive, concrete evidence. That ghost wants to talk to somebody."

"You're right. We may already have the evidence." Ian grinned big at Kiki. They seemed positively giddy with each other. They clinked cups. "This is brilliant. Exactly what we always talked about. You should see the low frequency spikes around midnight. I'm going to check the peaks for the exact time against that little light in the video. I also need to cross-check the time on the ion detector. Apparently, a cascade of ionized oxygen moved in."

Kiki and Ian put their heads together and discussed some of the plans that drove the idea for *Spectral Analysis*. Janine watched them giggle and high five like two kids. Kiki's beautiful green eyes fell so easily on Ian and he returned her attention without reserve. Kiki poured them another round and Janine realized that the friendship between the doctor and Kiki ran deep. It was something very old, older than *Spectral Analysis*.

Carlos joined them at the coffee table and poured himself another whisky, laughing. When he set the bottle down, Janine snatched it up and poured herself one. Why not, she no longer took medication. The three of them gave her a startled look as she gulped it down. She coughed a little as she gave Ian McNally a bit of a glare.

"Whoa there, girl. Take it easy." Carlos chuckled. "I thought you didn't drink hard liquor."

"I've had a few here and there," she said simply and poured another generous helping.

"Seeing a ghost? I guess you earned it," Carlos broke out the dimples. "Hey guys, I understand what a dumb-dick is, but what the heck is a dick-dumb? Do people even use words like that? I admit it, I'm dim. But what is it?"

"Some kind of a short, little—oh, stop it, Carlos." Janine could tell he was on the verge of another rude comment. Janine put her empty glass down with a clunk. "Look, everyone, I'm going home. To Gram's house. I need to get some sleep and I'm done thinking about the ghost for the night. Does anyone want a ride?" Janine glanced at Kiki and the doctor.

The doctor's brow creased with a concerned expression, like he was trying to solve a problem. He stood up and looked around, like he still had a hundred things to do, such as check electromagnetic wave peaks against the mystery light. It would be very unusual for the doctor to leave after such an exciting, eventful investigation. Ian moved toward her. He didn't want her to go, but could see that she didn't want to stay.

"It's late, maybe we should get you a room here. You had a big night."

"She can crash out in my room," Carlos told them. "I'm not moved in yet." He indicated his suitcase on the floor next to the door.

Kiki remained lounged on the sofa like a cat, an amused expression remained fixed on her feline face as she studied their interaction. She said,

"I'm going to wait and see what else is on that video. I couldn't sleep now if you paid me. Go on, Janine. We'll Uber back when we're done."

"It's very late," Ian said again. "We really shouldn't be driving, and there are still a few things for me to do here. Go sleep in Carlos's room for now. It's right next door, right? Don't go driving back when you're tired and wired up like this. We'll take the truck back later in the morning. Also, the whisky, you don't want to drive after all that. And there's an extra bed in here for Carlos, if he needs it. He won't mind."

"That's right, no problem," Carlos gave her his plastic key card. "I'll probably fall asleep on Steve's sofa anyway. I always do."

Ian stood in the doorway of the suite to watch that she made it into the next room. Janine went inside the small room and sat on the bed, agitated and angry. She could hear murmuring through the wall. It sounded more like a party than anything else, laughing and celebrating. Why not? They were hunting paranormal activity and seemed to find just what they were looking for. Janine stayed for about three minutes before she left for Gram's house.

She found Gram, the night owl, shifting through the papers scattered in the rustic sitting room. The extra diary pages still lay on the coffee table atop the tattered Bible. Fresh photo copies of those pages lay on the very top of the pile. Gram lit up and beckoned Janine to sit next to her.

"I saw the ghost of Mary Miller in the orchard," Janine whispered. Gram nodded and patted her knee. Maybe she didn't hear. "Are you looking for more stuff?" Janine asked.

"There's nothing else here," Gram told her. "Just old bills and such. Doctor McNally asked for copies of these pages at the tear marks. See how they were torn out? He wants the museum to see if the tear patterns match the real diary." She picked up the battered Bible. "Do you think these are bite marks on this Bible?"

"He wants proof that they come from the same diary. Standard procedure, always backing things up. It usually leads to a lot of disappointment." She turned the old Bible upside down. The marks did look like bite marks; bites from someone with very uneven teeth. She handed the Bible back to Gram.

"Are you upset about Christopher Williams?" Janine asked softly.

Gram closed her eyes, then started to laugh, which turned into a fit of giggles.

"Oh my, oh my." Gram raised her hand for a moment, trying to catch her breath. Her eyes twinkled in amusement. "I tell you, I'm completely relieved."

"Relieved?" Janine was confused.

"Oh yes. I am very relieved," Gram said. "And a little ashamed."

"It isn't your fault, Gram."

"Oh no, no, you don't know what I mean." Gram patted her on the knee again. "I've been so upset at my mother. Thank God she was long passed by the time I did that DNA test. We called the company and they assured me everything was correct. Even did it a second time. I wanted to confront her, as you can imagine, but thank goodness Ma had passed away. Twenty-three and Me, how I hated those genealogy people. Leone bought me the test a couple of years ago, you know my third cousin Leone. Kiki traced her great-greats to Ethan and Elisabeth Williams." Gram chuckled as she shuffled papers and tidied up. "I swear, Leone keeps asking if I did the test and I keep saying that I didn't. She wants to share results. But not after what happened with Bertha."

"What happened with Bertha? Who's Bertha?" Janine asked.

"You know Bertha. That old gal who used to give you pennies. You called her Bertie. Leone gave Bertha a DNA test too. Leone pretty much made DNA her theme that Christmas. Everyone got one."

Janine recalled Bertha and Leone. Bertha was short and wide while Leone was tall and thin. They both went to the same Lutheran Church on Third Street with Gram. Janine imagined that they were occasionally part of the card gals too. She remembered the raucous gossip sessions when Gram's gals came to the River House. Juliana and Janine used to listen-in late at night and get quite scandalized.

"Bertha is a Williams from Christopher's side, like us, and her tests were all wrong. Leone never lets her forget that her mother was a cheating whore. Oh, she's slick about it, but I've seen her get a dig in here or there. Oh, she's backed off a bit, now that poor Bertha is not doing too well these days. Cancer."

"Gram, you took a DNA test?"

"Yep," she said. "And I really believed my mother cheated on my wonderful father. For two whole years, I believed I was the illegitimate love child of a man my mother kept a secret to her grave! It about tortured my heart thinking my mother was so thoughtless. I wanted to know who my real father was. Oh, my goodness, the anger I directed at my mother's memory!"

"Gram, what did the test show?"

"Obviously that I'm not remotely related to Leone. She was nowhere in my relatives list. Kind of another nice surprise, ha ha. Anyway, she's a true Williams and I am not. None of us are. Christopher Williams was really a Lumen. He was really George Lumen, must be. There were Lumens all over my DNA report."

"And you're not upset about that?"

"No. I'm just happy I finally have it resolved. My DNA test was not a mix-up, nor did my mother— My DNA doesn't remotely match Leone because Christopher Williams was really George Lumen, not because my mother committed the sin of adultery and kept it a secret my entire life. My poor father is my own real father and thank goodness he was never cheated on. Oh, thank goodness! I am so sorry I thought poorly of my own mother! She's likely laughing at me from heaven instead of crying from hell."

Janine didn't know what to say. They hugged and tidied up a bit more.

"Don't let me forget, I need to tell Bertha about George Lumen. I need to do it right away because she is not going to make it. She is really sitting there at the end of it all. She can go to her grave happy now." Gram closed her eyes and took a deep breath. She reached out and took Janine's face between her hands. She said, "I love you, girl."

Gram went upstairs to sleep. Janine shut off all the lights and followed her lead. But Janine couldn't sleep. The reason she left the hotel was to be alone to think. She needed to reexamine the orchard events in private. The crew had buzzed with excitement about their ghostly encounter, so thrilled they were celebrating. Janine should be excited with them, but she couldn't help feeling dread. Did she really see a little girl out there? Did she really hear a voice? *Heed the dictum.* What in the world did it mean? And the serious, ireful eyes on the girl, as if Janine had done something wrong, terribly wrong, but what? Did she break or go against the dictum, whatever the dictum was? The image of that girl, standing for only a few seconds, was worrisome. Was she going crazy, or was it conceivable that she actual saw a spirit?

The old people, Caroline and Henry, came to mind. She had a nagging feeling those two knew something more than they were letting on.

Kiki and Ian laughing together popped into her head, another nice image to keep her awake. A sour feeling welled up inside her. What was it? Jealousy? She never should have left them at the hotel drinking whisky together, flirtatious Kiki sitting cozily with Ian. Kiki with her extra-long lashes and beautiful, jade-green eyes and touchy-feely hands… And wasn't there an undercurrent of attraction between them? The show capitalized on it. *They looked good together.* Janine did not put it past Kiki to try something with the doctor, if for no other reasons than to establish the pecking order, as Carlos would say. Crap! Loads of men found Kiki Mellow totally irresistible with her voluptuous curves and startling eyes. All Kiki had to do was glance at a guy and he'd come running to do her bidding. She's seen that play out plenty of times.

Janine opened her gripe journal, a habit Doctor Crisper encouraged during her time at the hospital. A journal makes a very good listener. It can help a person work through important issues. She pushed away the image of Kiki and Ian to jot down a description of the ghost. Dark hair in a single braid resting over her shoulder. Dark round eyes, most likely brown or even black. A simple dress with a wide sash in the middle, most likely tied in the back. Protruding ears that stuck straight out, but small, without lobes. Red and pouty lips. Red cheeks, a patch of red completely covered each cheek as if the child spent time in the cold wind. *Or the cold water?* Mary came off a little sinister and her beady eyes seemed serious and angry. She was older than five, but definitely below ten years of age. Not a kindred spirit; Janine underlined it with a heavy pen.

Janine threw the journal aside and turned out the light. She started running through her checklist of things to be grateful for, another tip from Doctor Crisper. Janine needed to do something to block out the image of Kiki and Ian laughing on that sofa. She resisted reaching for her phone to call him. What if she caught him doing something she didn't want to know about? Just because her heart had open up on that mountain doesn't mean that his did too. And wasn't Janine classically terrible at reading men and their intentions?

She kept running through her checklist hoping she would fall asleep, but she couldn't and went downstairs to find something warm to drink. She found Gram awake at the kitchen nook table with coffee and the Sacramento Bee. Janine filled a mug and took her regular seat next to Gram. The gleam streaming in the window told her it was just prior to dawn. The quiet house told her Ian and Kiki were still out.

"You don't need much sleep," Janine said.

"I've never been a good sleeper," Gram said. "What about you?"

Janine shrugged. "You didn't ask me about the ghost."

Gram glanced over her reading spectacles.

"I know all about that ghost, Janine. You aren't going to tell me something I don't already know. I just don't like to talk about it much."

"Then you have seen her?"

"Oh, yes. Lots of us have seen her, long ago. I don't like to admit it, and probably won't ever again, so don't tell your friends. But Bertha and I used to sneak into that orchard, you know. We were much more friendly with the Govants back then, with Caroline even. But seeing that ghost led to our falling out, you know. Some folks think the Miller family is cursed. Lots of us stayed away from the Millers because of that ghost. They have funny ideas about their ghost."

"Don't you want to know what the ghost said to me?" Janine asked.

Gram just stared blankly at her.

"Heed the dictum," Janine said. "She told me to heed the dictum. What does that mean?"

Gram eyes darkened. Was that recognition? Fear?

"Do you know what the dictum is, Gram?"

Gram shifted her gaze to her coffee.

"No," Gram said firmly and stood up, "I'll think I'll go back to bed after all."

Janine thought that was a good idea. No one else was in the house yet. That meant everyone was still at the hotel, sleeping, planning, reviewing things, or whatever.

Janine woke from the sound of Gram speaking loudly, almost yelling. She flew down the staircase to see what was amiss. Gram stood with her back to Janine, speaking harshly into the landline telephone. It was attached to the wall with an extremely long cord. Gram slammed the phone down and turned to face Janine.

"That was Caroline Govant," Gram said calmly. Gram passed Janine a folded piece of paper. "This note was left on the coffee table for you. Kiki is upstairs, asleep."

"What was that all about? On the phone."

"Caroline has rummaged through her old rubbish for your group," Gram conveyed. "Apparently, she has some important finds for you guys. Has some story wrote about Mary Miller after she died."

"Like a short story?"

"I couldn't say. She insisted that I wake the lot of you. Convinced of her importance, as always," Gram chortled. "Do you think she'll be invited to the séance tonight? Kiki told me when she came in at noon. I'm sure Caroline will insist on it. She's very bossy. Kiki asked me to find someone else, a real Williams. I gotta go and find Leone. Oh now, look, there's some fresh lemonade in the cooler. I'm gonna run out to shop a bit. I want a nice shawl for tonight, for the camera, and I need to go get Leone and make sure she doesn't back out of this thing. I gave my assurances to Kiki. Imagine, a séance with Kiki Mellow!"

"Gram?"

"No, no, go on," Gram said as she fluttered out of the house.

Janine opened the folded note. It was from Ian. He wrote in all lowercase letters. It said, *missed you at the hotel—don't you know a ruse when you see one?* He was suddenly standing behind her on the last step of the stairs. His steady gaze was bright and cheerful.

"Got my note then?"

He strode quickly across the room. He gave off a fresh and clean aroma from a shower and shave. His skin still felt cool from the water. Somehow, he managed to wring out the sour feelings she had with a deep kiss.

"I can't believe you ran off like that. After I cleverly secured a nice private room for us."

He was not holding back. They were standing in the middle of the living room in full sight of the stairs and the front door. Yet, Janine did not push him away. She instead pulled him in. She realized she had been upset because she got jealous the night before. What had made her so jealous? Talking intimately with another woman, Kiki. Very ridiculous. She knew the crew drank whisky and stayed up late after an exciting shoot.

"Are you all right then? I was pretty worried when I found you flew the coop. That was a pretty eventful night and I wanted to check in with you, privately, to make sure you were okay. From the sound of it, your gram is going to be gone a while." Ian whispered in her ear, "Want to run upstairs and discuss things?"

He continued kissing her as they moved toward the stairs. Janine grabbed his hand and led him to her room.

Ian rested a hand on the nape of her neck gently caressing her skin with his fingertips. He lay naked atop the covers while Janine had modestly wrapped her afterglow and scars underneath a sheet. Ian possessed a smooth, muscular back and shoulders, she noticed, but his chest was quite hairy. *He looks like James Sean Connery Bond lounging at the pool in that old movie her grandma loves.*

Ian finally filled Janine in on the plan. They were returning to the orchard at midnight in an attempt to reconnect with the spirit of Mary Miller. This time Kiki planned to have a more formal séance. The crew would set up cameras at the same location as the previous evening, but they'd stay completely out of the trees. Kiki and five select others would form the séance circle. Kiki hoped for a blood descendant of each settler from the Hansen wagon train: a Stauch, a Miller, a Williams, a Webber, and a Lumen if possible. Janine might be asked to sit in if they couldn't find one of each to participate.

"So, my gram and Leone. A Williams and a Lumen."

Ian snuggled close to her on the bed. His body radiated warmth. He whispered in her ear. "Also, Mrs. Govant, a Miller, and Henry Webber. Kiki is pretty sure she can talk him into just about anything."

"Am I the only one who found that creepy?" Janine asked. "Isn't he's like sixty or seventy or something. Kiki is a terrific actress. She actually looked interested."

"Kiki's not serious there." Ian shrugged at her inquiring eyes. "Did you know, she found some history between Henry Webber and Caroline Govant. Apparently, he was the much-younger man she corrupted for several years. It was quite a scandal back in the day. Everyone except Caroline and Henry talked about it. We're also looking to find an available Stauch. We're cross-checking names against a few of the interviews we did on Tuesday. We're pretty sure most people will jump at the chance to participate."

Janine found the gossip about Henry and Caroline surprising. That must be why she put them together in the back of her mind.

"Steve pushed for you in the séance, but Kiki nixed it. Said something about six being an optimum number, divisible by three. She is set on using local folks. She'd rather have your gram at this stage. She believes the spirit of Mary Miller was vexed with you and may not appear to you again. Carlos thinks Kiki is a wee jealous of the attention you're getting?"

His hand slipped under her sheet and slowly ran down the length of her bare back, causing her to shiver. She became aware of her large scar and wondered what it felt like to him. Did he find it repulsive? She tried to ignore her marks and thought about what he just said; Kiki sensed that the spirit of Mary Miller was unhappy with her. Janine had felt the same way.

"Gram certainly wants to participate in the séance," Janine said. His warm hand became extremely distracting as he massaged her lower back and buttocks. Her pulse lurched as she felt his hand going there. "I wouldn't want to take that away from her. And I am more comfortable as a background person. I'm actually relieved to be behind the camera. Is this our final segment? Tonight?"

"Actually, actors are coming in. There's going to be a little baptism reenactment at the river to introduce characters of the ghost story through drama. Next week, a whole other group is coming. Another camera, a film crew, and a screen writer. We need to have our ghost story flushed out completely by then, for the screen writer. This story keeps getting bigger and bigger."

She wriggled away from his distracting hand and he started caressing her neck with his lips instead. Well, that was even more distracting.

"I don't know how it's going to fit into a one-hour time slot," she managed a bit breathlessly.

"We are now shooting for a two-hour special, just on Rio Linda," Ian whispered. His hand came round and found her breasts, cupping them in a warm caress, pinching the tips harshly, then kissing them soothingly. His lips left a slow trail of fire over her chest and shoulders.

"What?" She lost track of the conversation.

"A feature," Ian told her softly. "There's going to be a little kickback for everyone who participates tonight, plus for the interviewees. Steve's got it all worked out. Mike Dunn flew in this morning, prepared to create a lot of paperwork."

Mike Dunn was the show's lawyer. He drew up contracts and releases as needed. Usually, he created generically worded documents for the doctor to use, but on occasion he did a little more. Sometimes he went on location to negotiate their working conditions. If Mike Dunn came out to California, it could only mean a larger production was brewing. Ian tugged at the sheet covering her.

"My bonnie lass, I'm afraid this needs to come completely off." His eyes were very dark blue and not at all compromising. He pulled the sheet from her legs and gathered her against him. Janine could not get enough of his strong broad chest and powerful arms and legs. He kissed her deeply before turning his attention to the nape of her neck. "Let me know right away if I'm being too demanding. I know this is a quick turnaround but I can't help myself. You are too irresistible. Will you be okay?"

She rolled up to straddle him. "I think I'll be okay," she said.

Leone and Gram both wore new bright knit shawls and sported freshly styled hair with matching manicures. Angie Minnihan, the redheaded smoker from the bar, loitered in the living room, holding an iced refreshment. Apparently, they traced her lineage to Niels and Ingrid Stauch. Angie wore a ton of jewelry, and bright-red lipstick. Janine wondered if Angie or Leone knew much about their ancestors or why they were asked to participate in the séance.

The *Spectral Analysis* lawyer, Mike Dunn, walked into Gram's house to meet the players just as Janine, Ian, and Carlos departed in the truck. They were heading out to the orchard to set up remote equipment. Ted parked the van in the same spot as the previous night. He set out small cameras, audio equipment, and two large spools of coated copper wire. A big box of Kiki's séance paraphernalia sat off to the side. Carlos picked up a folded piece of paper with Kiki's handwritten instructions for the layout she required.

"She's very specific about the size of the circle." Carlos displayed the drawn plan. "She wants the candles placed on the edges with a circle radius of 126 centimeters exactly. She underlined that number two times. There's to be a candle in front of each person and three candles in the middle." Carlos held up a little bag of flour. "We're supposed to draw stuff on the ground with this." He looked around. "Is there a measuring tape somewhere? Do you think she's really going to measure and see if the radius is 126 centimeters exactly?"

The doctor disappeared into the trees to place his electromagnetic receiver-transmitters and ion detectors. Each camera could be controlled by wireless communication, but Steve insisted on two hardwired in case of interference. That meant laying down an awful lot of copper between the almond trees. Janine spooled it out right away to be sure the cables were long enough. One regular camera and one infrared were hardwired and propped on tripods. She also spooled out wire for one audio receiver. She placed a short microphone stand in the large circle Carlos chalked with the flour.

"Don't step on my lines!" Carlos warned.

Janine set up two extra cameras on tripods that swiveled by remote control. She communicated through her headset to Ted at the van and he gave her input on positioning the cameras. When she completed the setup, she went over to see how Carlos faired with the chalked circle.

Carlos drew perfect circles with flour. He spaced six candles on the larger circle and placed a little pillow behind each candle. Three thick candles were placed at each foot of a large tripod in the center of the circle. A suspended cone-shaped aqua quartz stone pointed downward from the center of the tripod. It formed a pendulum. Kiki used it on a past show. Under the pendulum bob, a smaller circle was divided into thirds with a Celtic knot design. Carlos wrote out yes in one sector, no in another sector, and nothing in the last sector. He stood over his creation with a compass in his hands. He glanced up at Janine.

"She didn't specify true north or magnetic north in the note. Think it matters?"

Janine shrugged. "I'm sure they're not too far off anyway."

"Are you kidding? Kiki will ream me. She's gotten her panties in a wad about a lot less than this. Maybe, true north. I guess I can google the variation for here. Do you add or subtract variation? That point there, that's supposed to be pointing north."

"Just go with the compass." Janine checked her watch. "We're running low on time anyway. Isn't everyone supposed to be here in, like, fifty-five minutes?"

"Think we have enough time for a Starbucks run?"

"Yes!" Janine said. "I actually saw one in Rio Linda yesterday. It's just down Marysville Boulevard a bit, five minutes. Across from a gas station with a big cow on the roof." She laughed. "I got gas there. Let's take the truck." She paused to take another look at the circle under the pendulum. "Didn't you say that point should be pointing north? Why is it pointing southeast?"

"What do you mean?" Carlos said. "That's north." He pulled out the compass. "Look, north. See."

Sure enough, the compass needle agreed with his assessment of direction. Janine shook her head.

"Carlos. The sun rises over there, toward the mountains. That's not north. It's east!" She pointed. "Earlier it set over there, west." She pointed north. "That way is north. Plus, the farmer must have planted these trees in north to south rows. Seriously, that direction is north."

Carlos shook the compass. "Crap! This compass is crap."

Janine nodded. "Come on, let's fix this quick. I really want a hot latte for tonight."

Janine and Carlos returned with fancy coffee drinks for the crew. Ted and Steve sat in the van testing the remote-control sticks where images of Kiki and the doctor walking around the séance site flashed on the main monitor. Kiki plopped down on a pillow and the doctor walked out of the camera shot.

"Looks like Kiki's checking your setup. Did I tell you, you make very well-shaped circles, not eccentric in the least," Janine complimented him.

Carlos winked as he wrapped his headset around his neck. He pulled out the old army compass and dropped it between them on the console. They watched the needle swing and twitch a moment before it stopped.

"Seems to be pointing in the right direction now," Carlos moved the compass around.

"Weird," Janine said.

Steve glanced over with a questioning expression on his face. He drank his venti hot latte in practically one gulp. He pointed at Janine.

"You may have to sit in tonight," he told Janine. "Kiki said Henry Webber did not sound receptive to participating."

Oh no, she was looking forward to a carefree time sipping coffee and watching the action on video monitor. Janine dreaded the possibility of encountering the spirit of Mary Miller with those furious eyes again. Until the orchard, she never truly believed they ever encountered a real spirit. Deep down, she always believed a rational, plausible explanation could account for every experience. The reason she could be so cool, as Ian put it, was because she didn't believe any of the stories they wove. Not until she came face-to-face with that little girl standing in the orchard. Unlike the whisper at the river, Janine couldn't fathom how she might imagine the girl in the orchard

"Wait, who is that?" Carlos pointed down the dusty road. A ghostly figure of a man emerged from the darkness. He appeared very spooky. He wore a denim jacket and a baseball cap. His hands were buried deep in his pockets and he wore a terrible scowl.

"That's Henry Webber!" Janine brightened as the old man closed the distance to the van.

The flood lights soon flushed out his features and Steve stepped out of the van to greet him. At about that same moment, Kiki and the doctor exited the trees. They both perked up at the sight of Henry. From the short distance, Janine heard Kiki gushing happily at Henry and watched as she reached out to take his hand.

"Don't know why you want a nonbeliever for your thing," Henry's voice carried. Kiki pulled him off to the side and their voices muffled out.

Kiki led a formal séance in the first season and she was dressed very similarly. She wore a flowing outfit like a movie gypsy: big hoop earrings, large jeweled rings, and a heavy chained necklace. Her wrists and hands were adorned with metals and pure minerals. *Minerals help bring out the spirits*, she claimed. The large stones in her rings included a big chunk of holly blue agate and another of white topaz. The black obsidian stone in her necklace fended against dark energy.

Ian McNally wore a thick plaid work shirt and jeans. He leaned against a tree and accepted the now-cooled coffee Janine offered. He gave her an appreciative look. They stood about three feet apart smiling surreptitiously at each other and Janine felt her pulse start to pick up. She glanced away, resisting the urge to move in closer and kiss him, only to see the spot where they "parked" after their dinner date. The flood of that memory engulfed her and she stole another wistful peek at the doctor. Carlos noticed something. He looked from Janine and back to the doctor with a puzzled, concerned expression on his face. Great, Janine thought, now Carlos has cracked the code. Teasing soon to come.

A silver Toyota Sienna rental rolled up with Mike Dunn driving. From the front passenger door, a redheaded chattering Angie Minnihan popped out. Steve hurried to open the back slider door and assisted Leone and Gram, always the gentleman, he offered his hand to steady them. Caroline Govant emerged last, springing out quite energetically. Kiki beckoned the group to form a little circle and began chatting excitedly to them.

"Better run out and give Kiki a clip mic before she says too much," Ted passed her a new blue air case. "Not sure who should have them. I only got five clip mics in there. I'll set the audio to tape everything."

Janine lugged the case to the group and stopped next to the doctor on the periphery of the circle. Ian helped Janine open and manage the electronics. Janine passed Kiki a microphone and then proceeded to clip small microphones and transmitters onto the other participants. Gram beamed with excitement and Janine just smiled at her.

"I only have five clip-on mics," Janine said out loud. "So, someone—"

"I don't need one," Henry Webber said gruffly. "Not like I'm going to say anything for this thing. I'm just here on a favor to Miss Mellow. She said my presence is all she needs."

Kiki spoke gently and put a hand on his arm. "That's right, Henry. I just need your strength and your male energy. You don't need to say, or do, anything. Thank you so much for being here. We'll all feel safer with a strong male in the circle."

Henry cleared his throat and fidgeted. Janine noticed Caroline Govant smirk as she glanced at him from the corner of her wrinkled eyes.

Just prior to eleven thirty, Kiki led her chatty group into the overgrown orchard. Low-level stratus clouds rolled in to blanket the sky. They obscured the moon causing the night to take a sudden turn to darkness. Steve worried that it might be too dark for good images on the remote cameras. He asked if they left a flashlight at the séance circle and Carlos assured him there were at least two out there. The doctor leaned against the outside of the van and glanced toward the truck.

"I'm going to monitor the EM box and my ion detectors from the truck. The van looks like a tight squeeze. I'll take the tablet and link into your main feed." He pointed to the big monitor. "I'll stay on headset if you need me. I have a little weather box sending signals, so, maybe Janine could join me in the truck." He glanced fleetingly Janine.

"Maybe Ted can join you for this one," Steve suggested. "I think we should have Janine watching the main screen on the big monitor. Maybe she sees something the rest of us can't. I want her to sit next to the control box and listen to the condenser microphone. Ted isn't an idiot. He can watch for fluctuations on your box, right?"

"Thanks for the vote of confidence," Ted said. "Maybe I'll go sit in the rental with Mike and catch a nap."

"Ted will work," the doctor said to Steve. He glanced up once more before heading to the truck.

Mike Dunn waved at them and went to sit in the rental van. He walked and tapped on his cell phone the whole way. He obviously did not believe anything of consequence was going to happen in the orchard.

Janine, Carlos, and Steve crowded into the back of the van. Steve donned his headset and pulled out the joystick controls. He flipped the feed from camera three to the large monitor and they received a nice shot of Kiki leading the group around the séance circle. Steve appeared relieved with the picture. The ambient light proved plenty adequate for clear black-and-white footage. Steve glanced at Carlos.

"You going to be able to listen to five mics?"

Carlos gave him a thumbs up.

"Janine, you focus on the condenser microphone in the circle. As long as they face it, it should pick up everyone. I want you to focus on the main monitor too. If you see anything funny, anything at all. Just watch and listen. Tap the tag as much as you need."

The tag function for their audio and video bookmarked a spot for easy reference. Steve flipped open the main switch as she donned her headset. She could hear background talk, but the group was still too far away to pick out many words. She gave Steve a thumbs up. Steve settled into his captain's chair with a big bag of potato chips and ripped it open. He leaned back balancing the bag of chips on his stomach.

On the monitor, Kiki led each person to a specific spot in the circle and explained the importance of directional placement in a séance. Janine shot Carlos a look and he shrugged. He removed one speaker pad from his ear and Janine did the same. They often wore their headsets half off so they could converse privately.

"Thanks again for pointing that out. I almost muffed that one up," Carlos said.

Kiki encouraged everyone to sit and get comfortable. Her flowing sleeves shimmered in a pleasing way on the black-and-white screen. Kiki leaned into the circle and lit the three wide candles near the pendulum. The illumination brought out the warm tones of Kiki's skin. Kiki was definitely a magnet for the eyes.

"Now, we are going to light our personal candles." The condenser microphone clearly picked up Kiki's voice. "Before lighting your candle, inhale and exhale very slowly, at least three times. Take cleansing breaths. Each time you exhale, imagine letting go of your inhibitions. Visualize letting go. Mindfully release any tension you feel. I will light my candle first, then we will go around the circle, clockwise, each taking a turn. We will use this taper stick to pass the flame. There's no rush here. We want to calm ourselves and center our cores."

Janine found herself taking three deep cleansing breaths with them, a force of habit after ghost hunting with Kiki for a year. Janine noticed Carlos taking his breaths too. They exchanged glances and giggled. Janine turned her attention back to the monitor as Kiki cleared her throat. Kiki faced Gram.

"Light the taper with the flame from my candle and then light your own candle. When you are done, blow out the taper and pass it along. It doesn't have to be exact. Just remember to take deep, cleansing breaths and relax. Steady your heart." Kiki turned to smile at Henry. "Is everybody ready?"

"Yes, yes." Henry's head bobbed.

The others also verbalized consent. Kiki lit her candle and seemed to meditate quietly. In the soft black-and-white glow of the monitor, she appeared very young and innocent. Even without the green color, her eyes stuck out as glowing orbs, drawing in attention. Maybe Kiki really was part cat. Her gypsy scarf and big hoop earrings gave her a whimsical look. Janine wondered for the first time about Kiki's real age. How old was she? Kiki always projected so much confidence that Janine imagined Kiki to be closer in age to her older sister, Juliana. Could she be in her thirties? How much of her projected confidence was real and how much of it was acting? Kiki certainly appeared much younger than Juliana, more like twenty-five, Janine's age. Janine realized she knew very little about Kiki Mellow.

Janine watched the taper move around the circle. Gram, then Angie, then Caroline, then Leone. Leone fumbled a bit. She lit the taper, seemed to remember she didn't breathe, so blew it out and apologized.

"Take your time." Kiki used a calming voice. "Breath in and then out, and let it go. It's fine. We're all friends here. Take as long as you need."

Leone's deep breaths were visibly obvious on the monitor. Gram's eyes widened as she watched Leone and it made Janine chuckle. Carlos nudged Janine, grinning enough for his dimples to show.

"Sounds like she's blowing up balloons."

Leone finally lit her candle and passed the taper to Henry. Henry quickly ignited his candle and passed the taper back to Kiki. He skipped his cleansing breaths but Kiki let it go without a word. Kiki set the taper down slowly and reached for Henry Webber's hand. Kiki smiled sweetly at the old man and he visibly softened. Kiki's movements were slow and deliberate, quite alluring, and Janine wondered again if Kiki was interested in that old man. Kiki then turned toward Gram and took her hand as well. Soon, the entire circle was connected. Three full minutes of silence passed.

"We seek yon souls of near to there. We call on you to us appear. Reveal yourself for us to see, so I command, so mote it be. We reach out to you, Mary Elsa Miller. We reach to you. We are listening for you. We desire to heed your warning. Please, come to us, Mary. Tell us what we should know." Kiki used a soothing, silky voice. Another long silence passed as the group sat motionless.

The obnoxious crunch of Steve's potato chips filled the van. Janine and Carlos both shot him looks, but he was oblivious with his eyes glued to the screen. Carlos opened his mouth to make a wisecrack, but froze. He slipped his second headphone speaker over his ear and adjusted the volume knobs for one of the microphones.

"She's whispering something," Carlos said softly. "Caroline Govant."

Janine adjusted the gain on the condenser microphone, then the volume. Nothing.

"She's saying, one each for redemption." The moment Carlos verbalized that phrase, Janine heard it softly through the condenser microphone. But it was Angie Minnihan who spoke. Angie repeated it. Then Angie joined by Caroline. Then joined by Leone and even Henry. Each of them repeated it in unison, *one each for redemption*, over and over again. Gram's eyes darted around the circle before settling on Kiki.

"What's going on?" Gram asked softly.

"Is this the spirit of Mary Miller," Kiki addressed the center of the circle. "Is this Mary speaking?"

The others stopped chanting. Angie ventured hesitantly, "She wanted us to repeat it."

"Did you hear her say this?"

"I felt compelled to repeat it," Angie told Kiki.

Muttering agreement permeated the circle.

"Let's center our energy," Kiki said. "Let's all breathe. Slowly."

Kiki called for another moment of silence and Steve crunched loudly on his chips again. Janine blocked him out by putting her headset over both ears. On the main monitor, Kiki leaned forward and touched the pendulum bob. Janine noticed Steve zoom in on the crystal with the second camera. The pasty white *yes* and *no* were both clearly visible against the dark ground. Kiki's voice filtered into her headset.

"Are you here, Mary Elsa Miller? Did you, Mary Miller, send the message *one of each for redemption*? Is that message from you?"

Kiki set the pendulum in motion with a tap of her finger. Everyone in the circle watched the bob move rhythmically back and forth along the line separating yes from no.

"Move the pendulum to yes, Mary Elsa Miller. Let us know that it is you."

No apparent change in the pendulum motion.

"Tell us, Mary, what is the dictum? Are those words the dictum?" Kiki asked.

Nothing.

"Is one each for redemption the dictum?"

Nothing.

"What's that?" Kiki asked "What are you trying to say?"

"Four-lend-day?" Gram said suddenly. "I feel like she might be trying to say, for Linda."

The pendulum suddenly shifted to swing in the northwest sector, to the yes.

"Is this Linda then? Is this Linda Stauch? Are we speaking to Linda Stauch?"

The pendulum came to an abrupt stop.

"I don't like this." Leone's voice?

"Don't break the circle," Kiki stressed sternly. Kiki rose on her knees and scanned around like a river otter. Janine heard static begin to build in her headset.

"It's getting cold," Angie declared, and Janine felt it getting cold inside the van too.

"This is a load of crap!" Henry snapped very loudly.

In the next second, Caroline Govant released Leone's hand. She slowly stood and pointed dramatically toward Kiki. The candles flames began to waver, as if a breeze passed over the circle. Caroline calmly uttered in her scratchy voice,

"She's standing right behind you."

Every other person on the monitor turned in unison to look toward Kiki. Kiki spun and rose in the same movement. Her gypsy outfit flowed beautifully around her as the candles extinguished one by one. For a brief moment, the image on the screen went pitch black and the audio remained silent. In the crackling static of Janine's headset, very faintly, a child's voice said, *she can be the last one.*

Someone in the darkness screeched.

Someone repeated, "Oh my god, oh my god, oh my god."

Henry Webber cursed loudly.

Suddenly, Kiki waved a bright flashlight.

Everyone began talking at once. Gram and Leone gathered together in a huddle. Someone had kicked over the pendulum and a few of the candles. Caroline stood near Kiki and appeared as calm as a statue. Angie fidgeted behind them. Henry Webber found another flashlight and aimed it toward the trees behind Kiki.

"Who is that?" he shouted. "Someone is out there." Henry glowered toward Caroline Govant and Kiki. "I'll not participate in this nonsense anymore!"

"I can hear someone running," Angie said to no one in particular.

"What's that back there?" Leone pointed in the opposite direction, south.

Henry Webber turned and trained his light on the south end of the orchard. From the third camera, they saw a form running toward the séance circle.

"It's only the doctor," Kiki told them.

A bright light filled the séance clearing, followed by Doctor McNally. He stopped beside Gram and Leone. He politely asked if everyone was brilliant while putting a hand out to calm each of the ladies. He took Kiki's hand and leaned toward her.

"Had a bit of a scare?" he asked in an upbeat tone.

Henry redirected his flashlight back toward the north sector of trees. Janine couldn't hear him clearly, but he spoke in very harsh tones. Ian gave his camp light to Gram and the women started moving away. Ian said something to Kiki and then turned to step closer to Henry Webber.

"We're done here," Kiki announced. "She's gone."

Kiki led the ladies away from the circle. The condenser microphone did not pick up the conversation as everyone moved further away. Janine watched the ladies exit the main camera shot. Ian remained with Henry

Webber, staring into the trees. Ian turned toward the circle and Janine heard him say,

"You are welcome to go have a look. Take the flashlight."

Mike Dunn suddenly appeared on the screen. He dropped a camp light and a big box in the circle, all while staring down at his cell phone. He turned and followed Kiki and the women. The doctor reached down for the condenser microphone and Janine swept off her headset as he handled it.

On the monitor, she watched Henry Webber suddenly turn and follow the others out. Janine and Carlos silently watched the black and-white scene of the abandoned séance circle.

Ted popped open the back door of the van and reached for his large camera. He hoisted it on his shoulder and quickly turned toward the line of trees. Janine could see light from a flashlight flicker on the ground and then the gaggle emerged from the orchard. Carlos sighed and looked at Janine. They both turned to Steve. Steve was holding his empty bag of chips with a strange expression on his face.

"Did it get extremely cold in here?" he asked.

It did feel extremely cold in the van. Very cold. Janine glanced at the newly open door. The night air was warmer than the inside of the van. The three of them exchanged glances and then they all shrugged. Carlos started to stand.

"Round up the gear?" he asked.

"Let's go," she said.

Janine was anxious to head directly to Gram's house after the equipment was stowed in the van. She knew that Kiki, Mike Dunn, and Ted with his camera were there, but she wanted to make sure the old gal was okay. She stood next to the truck wondering where Ian disappeared to. The keys to the F-150 were in his pocket.

Carlos meandered over and stood beside her. He surveyed the stars and moon in the rapidly clearing sky.

"We're about to take the van back to the hotel," Carlos told her. "The doctor called on walkie-talkie and said he'd ride with you in the truck."

"Does he know I'm going to Gram's?" Janine asked.

"He does. He said he'd debrief and download later, or catch a ride with Mike if they were still there."

Janine nodded and sat on the tailgate of the truck. Carlos stood with his hands in his pockets, facing her. He rubbed the top of his thick mop head.

"I can wait with you if you'd like," he said.

"I'm not afraid of the dark, Carlos," Janine told him. "Go on."

"Are you sure?" Carlos crossed his arms in front of his chest, not budging.

"What is it?"

"What was going on with the doctor earlier? That did not look like your little crush thing. I'm concerned that he might cross a line. You need to be careful, kid. Look, Janine, I've seen him give a girl the wrong impression and then get too embarrassed to admit it. Keep that in mind. He can give a girl the wrong impression. That last girl, he didn't want to hurt her feelings and it went on for a month because he couldn't tell her he wasn't interested."

Wow. Was Carlos really giving her the big-brother talk? She knew, for all his wisecracks, Carlos cared about her. He treated her like a little sister. He once tried to set her up with one of his brothers. Carlos also knew more than most people about her past. Not as informed as Ian, but Carlos knew an old boyfriend stabbed her at least once. She gave Carlos a little push.

"Don't worry about me. I'm not getting the wrong impression," she said. "Just go."

Carlos hesitated before returning to the *Spectral Analysis* van. Janine watched them drive away, waving and beeping. When the van disappeared from sight, the night became very dark and quiet.

She can be the last one. Did she really hear that wispy voice? Why did Janine think of Sammy in that moment? She pictured Sammy running, with her long hair trailing behind her.

When she met on Sammy at her fourth birthday party, Janine nearly fell over from the impact of her emotions. Sammy was a sweet and funny girl and could already dribble a soccer ball well. Then, there were those precious moments when she echoed Juliana, trying to be serious, like with the puzzle. Sammy resembled Juliana's other children so closely she could easily pass as their real sibling, except she inherited Rick's pale eyes, eyes that induced complicated feelings in her. Eyes that haunted her dreams. Janine wondered if she would ever stop thinking of them as Rick's eyes. He was sure to get out of prison, sooner rather than later, on good behavior. Would he try to find Sammy?

Ian McNally snuck up and engulfed her in his arms. The heat of his embrace was a welcome change from the cold. He kissed her, holding her head in the palm of his hands. Her mind flashed to images of him in the hotel on the mountain and then during their afternoon tryst. The memories caused a delightful flash of heat in her groin. She didn't want to get too caught up in the moment and pushed him aside.

"I'm worried about Gram," she told him. "I need to go home and check on her."

"Sorry, of course." He opened the door for her and she slid onto the bench seat. "I saw Carlos talking to you. I hid in the trees so I could drive with you. I couldn't think up an excuse not to go back to the hotel in the van. What were you talking about, with Carlos?"

"He was worried you might be giving me the wrong impression," Janine told him.

"Really? Crikes. Has he caught on then?" He started the truck and leaned over to kiss her. "Maybe we should come out with it, us, I don't think anyone would be upset. Then, I could kiss you all the time and not have to duck in the trees in order to ride in the truck with you. I could hold your hand whenever I want." He put the truck in gear and they headed off to Gram's house.

Kiki and Gram lounged in the sitting room with a box full of manila folders between them. Gram did not appear upset in the least. She actually seemed a bit excited. Janine noticed the near empty bottle of wine on the coffee table. Kiki and Gram relaxed on the sofa sipping and chatting like old girlfriends.

"Where is everybody?" Janine asked.

"You just missed them," Kiki said. "Mike Dunn is running Leone and Angie home. We dropped Caroline off before coming back here. That Caroline Govant is one cool cucumber. She gave us this box. Apparently, it has a story about Mary Miller in here somewhere. Some old relative wrote down her history or something. Caroline insists there's something very interesting in this box."

"Why don't you two join us for a glass of wine," Gram invited.

"I thought you'd be upset about the séance," Janine said. "You look fine."

"Oh, it was loads of fun." Gram sipped her wine.

"What exactly happened out there? Did you see something?" Janine asked.

"Not me," Gram said. "I didn't see a thing. I just heard a tiny whispered voice say, *for Linda*, but with a very funny accent, like Lind-day."

Kiki lounged on the sofa like a cat again.

"I didn't see anything either, but the air was very thick with her presence. Very thick. Caroline swears the spirit was standing right behind me. Ted got her on tape describing what she saw; definitely Mary and not Linda. Dark hair in a braid, very like your description last night. Angie and Leone both saw something like a child shape just before the candles went out, but they never really described anything. They basically concurred with everything Caroline said."

"There was a cluster of ions in the area, just like the other night, I'd almost venture to say plasma but that'd be crazy." Ian told them. "Webber looked troubled. What'd he have to say?"

Kiki Mellow is the Star.

Kiki and Gram exchanged a look.

"That man needs to learn his age." Gram chuckled.

Kiki shook her head sadly.

"He saw something, but wouldn't admit it. He accused me of, how did he put it? Cheap-ass shenanigans and in cahoots with Caroline for attention. I don't know what that means. Says we rigged the pendulum to move and had something to blow out the candles. That we pumped in the voice of a child with a hidden speaker. He even accused us of hiding a little girl in the trees to spook people. I'm certain Henry saw her, the spirit."

"He mentioned something like that in the orchard," Ian said. "I suggested he go and look for himself, but he seemed too petrified to go out there. He definitely saw something."

Kiki drained her wine and appeared a little shaken, "He started yelling at me, cursing. Mike had to forcefully escort him outside."

"Crikes." Ian rushed over to Kiki and gave her a comforting hug. He rubbed her shoulder a little, very concerned. "He felt that strongly? Are you okay?"

Kiki nodded.

"And," Gram added, "Kiki has lost her chance with him. There's no way he could be involved with such a deceitful woman."

That lightened the mood a bit, but Janine also felt bad for Henry Webber. She witnessed how Kiki flirted with the old man. What was it he said out there? Janine thought back. Had he been speaking to Caroline or to Kiki? What nonsense did he believe he was participating in?

Gram poured both Ian and Janine a little wine and they toasted the success of the séance. Kiki felt eager to see the film, but she wasn't in a mad rush to get back to the hotel. She wanted to shuffle through Caroline Govant's box of papers first.

"Let's split this up and see what we can find," Kiki suggested. Ian took his standard place in the easy chair. Janine plopped next to Gram on the settee while Kiki stretched out on the sofa. Her green cat eyes bore into

Janine. "We didn't get a chance to talk out there," Kiki said. "Did anyone see anything strange on the monitor? Any hovering lights?"

"No, nothing that I noticed."

"Any weird things on audio? Anything other than us talking? I heard a few things. All very faint. I felt her mostly."

"No." She thought about that little wisp of a voice at the end. "Well, I heard a little static," Janine said. "If there's anything mixed in there, the guys will find it on playback. I tagged it." Janine didn't want to own up to the wispy voice she might have heard. She wondered if she only imagined it. In fact, she was sure she only imagined it.

"Poor Leone," Gram said. "She is fit to be tied. Believes we should all go to church on Sunday and ask forgiveness for participating in the séance. Says we stirred up dark, sleeping forces. Don't you worry. She'll be bragging about it for years to come. And I'll go with her on Sunday. Which reminds me, Jaja, Juliana flies in Sunday morning. She insists on renting a car from the airport but I want her to use my Accord. Adam took off work and is coming with them. With the three kids, they want to rent a van. What do you think?"

"They're coming on Sunday, already? Just let them do whatever they want, Gram."

Kiki perked up and looked at Ian. "That means you and me better clear out so this young lady can get her house in order."

Gram laughed at the young-lady remark. Kiki shot a nice smile at her.

"You have been an incredible host, just brilliant Thank you so much for everything, Gram."

"It's been a wonderful adventure for me. An eye-opener on our ancestors. I never would have found out this important information if not for you." She must be thinking about George Lumen and the DNA test.

"If your family, or any of the séance players want to watch the reenactment shoot, that offer is still on the table," Kiki told her. "It's a sure bet Angie Minnihan will be there."

"Don't worry about us," Gram said. "We won't likely go down to the river." Gram found another bottle of wine and Ian opened it.

"Did you come to a consensus about what it all means? One each for redemption? Did people say what they thought it meant?" Janine asked. "Are the ghosts of Linda and Mary connected then?"

"Everybody must give something to be forgiven," Gram said. "That's what Leone thought. And Angie agreed."

"Bingo!" Kiki cheered. "That is exactly what I think too. The two spirits are most definitely connected. And that phrase, *one each for redemption*, that phrase has to be the dictum. Has to be. But what must they give for redemption? Both girls drowned in the river, right? It's in the city log. Maybe the spirit of Mary is angry because she died in the river? Something wasn't given and she went to her death, like Linda. She wants to warn others. But what needs to be given? I'm going to work it out soon."

"Another reason Leone insists we go to church," Gram said.

"Hey, look at this," Ian spoke up. "Apparently, there was an official group that kept track of ghostly sightings and drownings. Looks like it was part of an actual town council meeting. The local governing body discussed summoning the ghost to determine what it wanted."

"That must be a joke." Janine couldn't believe it and took the typed pages to have a look.

"Dated 1923," Ian added. "Ghosts, séances, and magic became quite popular during that era.

"Maybe that's why the Mary ghost began to appear." Kiki waited for her turn to look at the document. Janine handed it over.

"Here it is." Ian found a short story titled, The Story of Mary Miller. It fit on one side of a piece of thick white paper, typed. He handed it to Kiki and she read it out loud.

"The Story of Mary Miller. Mary Miller was the first child born in our settlement along the river and the first child born of John and Susan Miller. Her birth, long considered a blessing from God, gave our founder reason to pause near the river and test the fertility of the soil. As a child, Mary planted many of the trees that flourish along Marysvilles road, the path that led leads to the river. The river, giving both the blessings of salvation and the curse of danger, took Mary at the tender age of seven. Her life sparked a town in this unlikely place and her name must never be forgotten."

How disappointing. They sat silently, digesting the short story.

"That's the big story Caroline Govant wanted us to find?" Janine voiced out loud.

"I've seen that story before," Gram said. "Long ago. Caroline showed it to all of us. Her father was very set at changing the name of the town to Marysville, or even Millersville, instead of Rio Linda, back when the city of Sacramento required an official name for our area. He pressed hard and I think that story was written for the paper to persuade folks. The Govants had quite a little cult back then. Obviously, Caroline would like to press for the name change and hopes your show will help. Don't fall for it. She wants attention. Caroline always wants attention."

Gram gathered up the wine bottles and nodded at the group with a slight flush to her features.

"This old gal is going to bed. Don't stay up too late looking through that pile of nonsense from Caroline. Those Millers have always been a bit loose in the head. Ask anyone."

Kiki helped Gram ferry the wine glasses to the kitchen and begged off to bed as well. Kiki appeared dog tired. The adrenal excitement of the past two nights must have finally caught up to her.

As soon as Kiki and Gram disappeared at the top of the stairs, Ian grabbed Janine and guided her to the couch. They had a kissing session on her gram's sofa, just like a couple of teenagers, giggling. Then his kisses turned hungry and slow. His body crushed hers but she still wanted him closer. Janine became intensely aroused, but hesitant, because Gram and Kiki were right upstairs and Gram was a very light sleeper. Ian pulled himself to a sitting position.

"Maybe I should take the EM box to the hotel," he said. "They're probably wondering where I got to, and Carlos is probably worried I'm dishonoring your virtue."

"Really, you're thinking about Carlos right now?"

"You're thinking about your gram," he accused. "I know you are. So then, lass, are you going to sneak me upstairs or should I go to the hotel? I'm afraid it'll be tough sleeping here with you right down the hall. Imagining you on that bed, I wouldn't be able to stay away from your door. Are we still playing it quiet?"

"My sister comes this weekend," Janine whispered. "I still want to keep things quiet a little longer."

Ian kissed her grudgingly before standing up.

"Good night then, my sweet lass. Let's finish this after the thing on Saturday."

The next morning, Janine crept down the stairs to peek at the driveway hoping the truck with Ian was back. No. The house was still quiet. The aroma of coffee fresh in the pot wafted from the kitchen. Someone had been up and about already. Mysterious Misty, most likely. Janine found fresh homemade biscuits cooling on the stove. She grabbed a cup of coffee and smothered a biscuit in Gram's rich creamy butter, then went to sit on the recliner and muse about Ian.

The coffee table was still a mess with the old papers from Caroline Govant's box. Janine shift through them, organizing and putting them back into folders as she worked. Old photos of men in army uniforms, the Miller Bank front, aerial shots of the orchard and river. Letters from an APO address. Grade reports from the Rio Linda Elementary School. Pages of handwritten fluff Janine already skimmed the night before.

As she crammed the items into the box, she spotted a piece of paper against the side of the box. This one had not been in one of the manila folders and the paper looked similar to a brown paper bag. It blended in with the interior cardboard and was pressed flush along the inside wall. Janine felt a shiver run down her spine as she fished it out. It was written in beautiful old spidery script not unlike the writing and paper from the torn-out pages of the wagon diary. How did they miss it the previous night? Too much wine and not enough sleep. Tired eyes.

There was no date and no signature.

For days in her delirium, she spoke of a girl and urged me to write this down, and I do so to quiet her hysteria. The darkness will rest if one of each will go with her. Linda believes it unfair that she alone was tasked for this punishment. Everyone sat at the same table. Why did the elders blame only her? She was obedient. All must be redeemed together, or none will be. It will never end until there is one of each for redemption. Then all can go into the house of God, together. Riches will be rewarded as each acquiesces. Resisting will bring despair and death.

Mary said she will go willingly to set the example. She will be the first. Better to settle this debt quickly else there be too many called.

There was a postscript, written in a shakier hand.

Everyone failed to grasp her meaning. After her fever broke, she went to the river. Her body was found between the rocks.

Her cell phone chimed.

"She can be the last one!" Steve's excited voice burst in her ear. "Did you hear that last night? You tagged it for review. Regular speed, very faint, from the condenser microphone, along with some static. We cross-checked it with the clip-on recordings and no one said anything like that. Unless Henry Webber can sound like a little girl."

"I don't know, maybe," Janine said. "There was a lot of static."

"Believe me, it's there. Sounds like a little girl saying, 'She can be the last one." Steve chuckled. "This is proof! Proof positive. Look, Kiki is not answering her phone. It might be dead, but I need you to wake her up and get down here. We want to run through it with both of you and then get the story straight. I've got a writer working on putting together some scenes."

"Yeah, okay, I'll wake her and bring her out."

"ASAP," Steve said. "ASAP. We've had zero sleep out here and I've got some calls to make. Lots of stuff going on. I want to punch this out for the writer."

"ASAP. We're on the way," Janine told him.

Chapter 9

Rio Linda, 1840 Helen

The Hansen wagon party survived the winter by committing a most atrocious sin. Her husband and her son tried to comfort her, but nothing could ease her shame. Helen would never confess the deepest despair resting in her heart; she eventually ate more than needed to survive. Her tastes adjusted and she closed her mind to the meal's origin. She ate to thrive. Other women, like Meg, weak Ingrid, and frail Nancy were forcefully fed throughout the entire winter. Less sinful women either died, or remained ill in their sunny valley below the mountain ridge.

Only one wagon with movable wheels remained, and the Webber boys pulled that wagon like oxen. Their father, Peter, acted as the leader. The minister and the infirm rode in the back buckboard. Sue Miller, large with her startling pregnancy, rode in the coach seat, radiant, like a queen. Helen wondered if that seed had been planted in the meadow during the last days of the Hansen rule. John Miller cared not, so neither did the rest of them. Susan's pregnancy was their only miracle, and when Sue's water broke, the travelers stopped moving for the birth of the baby.

They found a rather-large branch of the watershed snaking near their path. Beautiful boulders marked a gentle bend in the river and the stone glittered a rainbow of colors in a metallic luster. Surprisingly, almond trees and wild blackberry bushes populated the area. The past season's almonds lay on the ground in husks. The vegetation provided sustenance and the river provided water enough to make camp. After days of walking in silence, the group welcomed the respite. Not one of them desired to reach their original destination of the port city yet. Helen did not know what they would convey about their trials.

Collectively, they took the birth as a good reason to delay their journey. Helen's daughter-in-law, Meggie, still festered with a confusion from the fever she suffered, but she was able in body enough to help with the birthing. They gathered pregnant Susan to the edge of the flowing river, away from the others. A natural hill blocked the view of their camp from the pebbly shore. Helen tasked her son Grant with the keeping of Sue's husband, John Miller.

In all the birthings Helen had seen, Susan Miller's proved the easiest. After near starvation, trials of life and limb, want of shelter and comfort of cloth, her baby eased into the world with very little fuss. Susan herself made not a peep. Only the small baby squeaked when they cleansed her in the cool water, but quieted as they swaddled her in the cleanest blanket left in their supplies. When they placed the babe in Susan's arms, silent tears streamed down the mother's face.

"Do you think we are coming back into the light of God?" she asked.

Helen and Meg both nodded, they did.

John Miller and Grant discovered that the almond shells showed signs of cracking. They reasoned the husks would give good fruit in the next week or two. The young men sat together discussing the possibility of propagating the trees into an orchard. The land beyond the river proved flat and rich in dark minerals, and the wild trees looked plenty healthy. A positive glint in the eyes of her older son soothed Helen's fragile heart.

Further in their scavenging, the men made an interesting discovery; lumber. New, but a little weathered, a broken flatboat full of cut boards had run aground upstream. Their excitement, coupled with the easy birth of the baby, lifted the spirits of each member in the small group as they pondered what to do with the treasure.

Lately, they shared one large community fire. No more secrets lingered between them. The infirm, pulled from the wagon, thrived on the wild berries and rabbit meat. The new baby woke Ingrid and Meg from their melancholy stupor as they took an interest in the infant, and the men spoke amiably for once. Frederick found a water smooth log and he took the ax-head to try to fashion himself a new leg. Young Gustoff Webber hovered near, itching to help, but waiting to be asked.

In the western distance, along the flat line of the horizon, the sky glowed a beautiful burnt amber in the wake of the setting sun. The clear California sky rarely held a cloud in that direction. But the opposite view, in the east, grey water-filled shadows congregated over the mountains of their heartbreak. Helen kept her back to those mountains as much as possible, angry at the losses they endured and ashamed of what they had done.

Her daughter-in-law walked with young George Lumen over the mound toward the river. They took the water bucket. Meg still called the boy Christopher and not one of them had a heart to correct her. Not even George himself. Everyone called the boy Christopher near her ears.

"Fred," Grant spoke quietly across the fire to the minister. "We want to ask if it is possible. George does not want to be called George anymore. And we are going to raise him as our son. He has asked to be renamed before the eyes of God. Already, we each call him Christopher." Grant had tears running down his cheeks. "I'll never forget my son, but this would be for Meg and George, for their peace of mind. Can he be baptized again? Can we name him in honor of our Christopher?"

Murmuring went around the campfire. Everyone desired to be cleansed of sins. The prospect offered hope. Little Linda abruptly stood up. She startled them with her announcement.

"I like the berries but I hate this kind of meat." She threw her rabbit piece back into the fire. Then, the little girl skipped down to the river to help Meg and George with the water. So young and innocent, Linda was free from the burdens of a grownup heart.

The next morning, the men dismantled the wagon for the spare parts and the metal. Grant decided to use scraps from the wagon and the scavenged lumber to erect a permanent structure. All the men wanted to help. It was her son's wagon, so perhaps it would become a William's structure, a house shared with the community. Both Grant and her husband Nicholas desired to stay in the area longer. Even John Miller wished to stay for the almonds. Each of them felt something positive growing in that valley near the river bend. The birth of a healthy baby girl delivered hope to all of them.

The Webber boys had been trained in woodwork by their grandfather and offered to make a sturdy frame by way of hewed, notched fittings. They could easily make the notches with the ax. Half dovetail ends on the boards would keep the walls firm. River rock might be used to help stabilize the base. It would hold well enough, they believed, until someone could go for more supplies.

Frederick Stauch prepared a big Sunday service. He retrieved his cover-chewed Bible and slowly turned the pages. Everyone would be invited to ask for redemption through a confession, and then the group would put all the foulness behind them for good. They would be free to move forward, unburdened by what they endured.

But did Frederick mean all of their sins? The collective sins that had rained the wrath of God on them in the high Sierras? By turning a blind eye, they condoned everything that transpired under the shadow of one Mr. Stanley Hansen. Not one of them stood up with the Whitakers when Hansen's true colors emerged. The lot of them kept their pact with that devil and followed their government notes. Whitaker and his group left empty-handed, invalidated, in the cloak of night.

Hanson had charmed them easily with his confident talk. When he finally took liberty with Ingrid, everyone quietly minded their own business. When he preyed upon young Mrs. Miller, no one said a thing because John enjoyed his new status with the leader, relishing the favors and power bestowed on him. They separated their wagons a little further after that, wondering who else might fall from grace.

Then came the native family. By not addressing the evil inclinations of Stanley Hansen, they each carried blame for the treatment of the Indians and the subsequent destruction of the Lumens the night the Indians sought revenge. Would Frederick allow any of them to admit those sins? If they acknowledged such things, each of them could never pretend ignorance again.

No, he was only interested in the one sin; breaking their fast by consuming flesh of the dead and forcing the meal on the sick without their full knowledge or consent. Little Linda continues to ask for it again and again even in their sunny valley. Frederick's furrowed brow creases deeply when he stares at his grandchild. His fear mirrors each of their hearts. They desperately need the girl to forget, so that they can forget. Helen fears that Linda might speak of their transgression near outsiders. Who, besides their group, could ever understand it?

After the first day of building, the size of the small structure became clear. It might be used as a small home or a small meeting place. The men worked day to night, happy for a positive project with results they could see. After two full days, the Webber boys, Nicholas, Grant, and John Miller completed a rough square building. The addition of a cross above the door was a sign of coming home. They completed that touch in time for Sunday morning. Frederick nodded his approval. The children, Linda and George, very much desired to go inside the structure, but Frederick stayed them with an outstretched hand.

"After we are cleansed of our sins, we will come to fellowship in this fine house of God," he announced. "But we must first be redeemed and reborn."

Everyone dressed as fine as they could muster. Torn clothes, but clean faces. Young Linda and George watched Susan feed her baby as they broke their own fast. The girl Linda was prone to giggles, and she adored the baby who would soon be christened Mary.

Then, the small group filed to the river as Frederick preached about redemption. He mentioned naught the trials with Stanley Hansen, and that worried Helen. He solely mentioned their unholy transgression to survive. Peter Webber quaked with fury. In his sermon, Fred directly blamed Peter for the unholy meals. Frederick grasped his staff in one hand, steadying himself. He refrained from moving about, as he was unpracticed with the wooden leg.

"Forgive us our unholy appetite." He shouted to the sky. "Rid Linda of this sickness!"

Linda giggled at the sound of her own name.

Frederick Stauch glared at the child. Ingrid pulled her daughter close, afraid of the minister. Niels Stauch hovered near Ingrid and her daughter, offering what scant protection he could offer. For all his holiness, Frederick Stauch proved a hard man to live with. He summoned the Millers first, to baptize the baby and then the parents.

"Mary Miller," Frederick announced. "The savior of our hope. Your birth signifies the redemption of this community. May God bless you and keep you."

He baptized each member of the community in the ice-cold water of the river. He pushed heads beneath the water with a strong, firm hand. Everyone accepted the watery renewal without fuss. Then, they each strolled over the mound to the small square meeting house. Their new church and home stood proudly in the small clearing. The fire, with their Sunday meal of duck, roasted several yards away. People tarried shyly outside the house, choosing to drip the river near the fire instead. The aroma informed them that the duck was ready to eat.

"Oh no, not that again," Little Linda's voice carried loudly. "Why can't we have the other food? Why do we no longer eat the other meat? I like it much better than this greasy duck!"

Frederick Stauch screeched in vexation. His uneven hopping on one leg startled each of them. He moved at top speed, finally dropping his staff to the ground. His face flushed a livid red of anger and his wood leg had dislodged in his scurrying about.

"Do not say such things!" he screamed and spittle flew from his lips. "You are baptized and cleansed of that foul event! Put it away from you!"

Linda giggled nervously at his red face. She half hid between her uncle and her mother. Frederick fidgeted. His unkind grimace stared down on Linda.

"Look at you!" he chastised the little girl. "You are plump with the unholy meals you've eaten. Where most only ate to survive, you ate for pleasure. I watched you!"

"Oh now." Helen ran over to stand beside a trembling Ingrid. She hugged the mother then reached out to cradle Linda's head in the nook of her arm. "Look here, Frederick Stauch. This here is only a child. Children have plumpness in their cheeks naturally. She has not done anything anyone else has not done."

"There is a vast difference in our actions," Frederick insisted. He searched the lot of them. "Does any among us still hunger for that which we ate on the mountain? If so, do not enter that holy house. You will proceed to soil it."

One of the Webber boys, Rolf, retrieved the wooden leg. He offered it to Frederick then took a step back. Peter Webber stepped forward as Fred reattached the appendage.

"Here now, Fred, keep with your accusing eyes! We saved you on that mountain." Peter Webber spat on the ground. He might never agree with Frederick's ways. Peter helped his wife to a seat near the roasting duck, cussing under his breath. His sons followed. The Webbers all turned their backs to Frederick.

Niels Stauch began moving toward the house with Ingrid, but Fred hobbled in front of them. He spread his arms wide.

"No!" They flinched at his shout. "Mine will not go into that circle. Not yet. This family is still in need of reflection and acceptance of our sins. Saved us, Mr. Webber? Maybe our fleshly body, but our souls are condemned!" Frederick's gaze bore down at the small girl and she looked terrified. "You will not go into that house until you are redeemed. Until you rid yourself of your foul illness, you will not enter that house. Do you hear me! You and your mother! Not until you both truly repent for what you did. You are my burden now, and I will fix you!"

Linda ran away. She disappeared over the mound toward the river. Ingrid nearly fainted. Niels tried to hold her up but needed help. Grant stepped forward to help him and they carried Ingrid into the camp circle near the fire.

"Can you please attempt to control your temper," Nicholas whispered harshly to Fred. "We experienced a lovely gesture out in the river, but our day is now ruined. Each of us are trying to cope with the memory of our ordeal."

"Gesture?" Fred shoved his Bible into Nicholas's chest. "Take this book and pray. If I am ever free of my filial burdens, if my family ever repents, I will fetch it again. I vow to rid that child of her illness and our family of the evil stain brought by that woman!" Fred turned and began to carefully step away.

"Where do you go?" Nicholas called after him.

"We will set up a camp nearer the river. A camp for sinners." Frederick waved in the direction of the mound. He awkwardly hobbled away. He shouted to the circle, where his son Niels cradled Ingrid. Fred's voice carried crisply through the air. "Niels! You will bring what little is our own and join me," he ordered.

For two nights, Frederick Stauch kept his small family separated from the rest of the party. They spied him on their daily water run but gave him a wide berth. Shouted prayers could be heard over the hill, day and night, as well as his reprimands toward the poor child. Helen found it increasingly difficult to sit at the fire and do nothing for the child or her mother. Fred loudly accused Ingrid of being a witch and her daughter too.

Nancy Webber, still quite frail, lamented that someone should fetch Ingrid and Linda into safety. But the men urged the women not to meddle in the Stauch family affair. Nicholas fairly ordered Helen to let that family work through their problems in peace.

"They'll return," Nicholas said.

"He's a tyrant," Helen told him. "That poor woman and her child are being tortured."

"Niels will keep him at bay," Nicholas said. "Frederick speaks correctly about the illness. It is unnatural for the child to keep asking for the meat she ate. It is an unnatural illness and he is doing his best to correct it, and her mother is not helping. We must respect his efforts."

Peter Webber suggested that someone should continue to the coast. He wanted to go, but his wife refused to travel so soon and claimed he couldn't fetch supplies anyway, they had no money. All their tender had burned in the Hansen wagon. They had nothing to barter except the scant personal jewelry in Helen's small box, the silver rings and trinkets from the Lumens.

Helen strolled to the top of the mound to check on the girl and her mother. Linda stood facing her grandfather with her blond waves fluttering in the breeze. They each leaned toward the other with hands on hips. If it were not so heartbreaking, it would have been comical. The child definitely inherited Frederick's anger and stubborn attitude.

"I want to camp with the others. I want to go into the house," Linda demanded, stamping her foot.

"You are not allowed in that house or anywhere near it!" Fred shouted.

Niels and Ingrid remained huddled together under a tree, cowed by the girl and the old man. Helen decided something right then; she didn't care what her husband had commanded. The Stauch family needed help. Helen no longer cared that Fred was a man of God and delivered the wisdom they all needed to heed. She could no longer tolerate watching and hearing his unbridled anger at Ingrid and her child.

"You! You ate it too. You told me to eat it!" Linda stamped her little foot.

"And now I'm telling you not to speak of it!"

Helen marched down the slope. She waved and shouted a greeting.

"Here now! I'm coming down there!" She made haste toward their little camp.

Ingrid and Niels rose, expectant and hopeful.

"You mind your own business! This is a family matter." Frederick glared at her.

He was a frightful man, tall and powerful-looking, and more menacing with the wooden leg. He swooped down to grab Linda up and she railed in his arms. He hobbled into the river, spewing holy words in a vile tone. In contrast, the water ran smooth and kind behind him, murmuring quietly with a tinkling melody.

"You will be redeemed! You will repent! You will rid yourself of this sickness and your unholy appetite! Each of us must go willingly toward redemption!"

They splashed into the water disturbing the tranquil surface. Helen glanced at Niels and Ingrid. They were hopeless. The poor woman appeared ready to faint again. Her eyes were glassed over with grief. Where once there had been striking beauty, now lay an empty wasteland. She lost her virtue, her husband, her cousin, her vitality, and she was now trapped in the clutches of Frederick Stauch. He was almost as bad as Hansen, maybe worse. Helen gestured for Niels to take Ingrid over the mound. He did not need coaxing.

"Why are you in that freezing water, Fred?" Helen reached the river shore as Niels passed with Ingrid. The pebbles of the beach crunched under her feet.

"He baptizes her daily," Niels managed as they went by, "hoping to cleanse Linda of her sins."

"He's crazy," Helen mumbled mostly to herself.

Frederick waded waist deep with a squirming Linda wriggling in his grasp. He was growling and she was screaming. Her flailing arms hit him repeatedly and he slipped. They both plunged under the smooth surface of the water and the yelling and screaming suddenly halted. A momentary peaceful silence filled the air. Then, hands slapped the water surface. The old man's head popped out and swiveled all around. Linda popped to the surface once before smacking into the boulder at the bend in the river.

Helen waded into the frigid water seeking the girl under the surface. She could see the colors of Linda moving rhythmically with the current. Somehow, the girl got stuck in that beautiful rock. Frederick splashed up next to her and pushed her aside. He hurried to fetch his granddaughter. His hand pressed against the rock for support and he balanced on his one real leg. His arm reached out. His head bobbed under and over the water. From behind Helen, Niels splashed into the river. He went right past his father but the current instantly caught him and pushed him hard against the rock. He slipped around the outer edge and disappeared downstream followed by Fred's wooden leg. Frederick gasped for breath but kept bobbing back down.

Already, Linda was under the water too long.

Frederick kept dipping back under the surface. Helen reached out to stop him but he shoved her hand away with a snarl. Niels came back, huffing and puffing, dripping from head to toe. As he reentered the water, Helen slowly backed completely out. She retreated toward Ingrid, who stood motionless on the slope of the hill. Ingrid's empty eyes certainly did not understand what was happening. Helen took Ingrid into her arms anyway, for her own comfort. Hot tears dribbled down her cheeks. From over the hill top, Nicholas and Peter Webber emerged to see what the fuss was about. They ran quickly down the hill.

"It's Linda. She's stuck in the rock," Helen managed to say.

Both men plunged into the icy river to help. Each grappled against the rock but were unable to free Linda. Webber called loudly for his sons and the younger men came down the hill. No one could free the child. After a time, the water-soaked shivering men huddled on the beach, defeated. Hours had passed and their efforts had been fruitless.

Frederick crouched alone, up river, under his tree. His hands covered his face and Helen thought he might be crying. Niels sat close to the water's edge, breathing loudly. His brother's widow, Ingrid, sat behind him, patting his back in a comforting manner. She did not seem to understand that her daughter remained underwater. She instead seemed relieved that the screaming had ended and the valley was peaceful.

The men were never able to free Linda's body. Sometime during the second night, she freed herself. Her body was no longer in the rock. Webber's sons walked the whole day downstream, hoping to find her washed on the shore, but she was gone, never to be seen again.

The second gathering in the small structure was a memorial for Linda. Her grandfather's Bible provided the words, but her grandfather steered clear of the camp. Frederick chose a place even further upstream to reside. He disappeared alone.

Peter Webber still wished to find supplies for the building of more structures, yet he was wary of Frederick Stauch. He feared the old man had gone mad in the head. Peter was torn between going for provisions and remaining to guard the fledgling settlement. Two days after their memorial for Linda, he no longer needed to fret. The supplies came to them.

Long before they met the group, they felt them, given away by vibrations on the earth. A very large train of wagons neared. Wagon after wagon after wagon passed on the main trail, much larger than their group had ever been. The men walked out to greet them. Their leader, a man named Archie Smith, halted his horse and jumped down as the entire train stopped to set up camp for the night.

A few ill people in their party needed tending, one of whom was Archie Smith's mother. Helen offered them respite in their small shelter. It was cool and pleasant in the house, protected from the dust, and comforting. Helen also led them to the river for fresh water and shared the wild blackberries. John Miller harvested early almonds from several trees and they proved good to eat. There were piles of fruit in their empty shelter that the travelers were welcome to taste. Their new friends were charmed with the small settled area and several folks were fascinated at the solid build of the cabin walls. Archie Smith knew the source of the found lumber.

"John Sutter sent men into the mountains to mill trees, way up river. This batch surely took a wrong turn at the fork. He built a saw mill up yonder. I'll have more lumber sent your way when I speak to him," he offered. Archie carried a supply of real nails which he used on their meager structure. He gave them a sturdy hammer and an ax.

"We can't pay for this metal," Peter Webber told him.

"No payment necessary," Archie said. "I'm grateful that you built this house and it's here. My mother has been ill for most a month and begged for a roof over her head before she dies. She is done with the natural elements. I believe, if these are her final days, you have provided her last wish. I am forever grateful."

The travelers shared many provisions, pots and dishes, cloth and clothes to spare. Every item on Peter Webber's wish list dropped into their laps. Throughout the day, different folks arrived to see the small square structure and brought a housewarming gift along with their curiosity. They donated old chairs, a clock, candle holders and an old iron stove.

Another miracle emerged from that large train. One early afternoon, a familiar family meandered near, the Whitakers. John and his wife walked hand in hand, followed by their daughter, Elizabeth. Helen watched her younger son Ethan rush to meet them. He stood fast in a mixture of happiness and disbelief. Elizabeth appeared just as stunned. Then, the two young people sprang forward into each other's arms. Tears of joy streamed down Helen's face. The Whitakers! Delivered to their laps for them to seek amends. Nicholas stood beside her.

"Did you know of this?" he asked, watching their son embrace Elizabeth.

Only the men never saw it. "I suspect we may have a new daughter soon."

The next day, Archie Smith sent the bulk of his party ahead to the coast. He was delighted to see his mother return from the edge of death, but she refused to continue on his wagon train. She didn't want to leave the quaint house in the middle of nowhere. Their group agreed to welcome the elder Mrs. Smith indefinitely and Archie vowed to spare no expense in sending provisions to add to the house and build an entire community. Although the Whitaker family would press on with Smith, everyone realized Elizabeth wished to stay behind and a small wedding ceremony was planned for Etan and Elizabeth.

The morning of the ceremony, John Whitaker inquired about Hansen's ledger diary. He asked if it still existed. He wanted to take the extended Hansen family to task for his wagon-train losses and thought it was possible, if he could deliver proof of their investments. Nicholas informed him of its continued existence and said he was most welcome to take the diary. Nicholas only saved it as a document to release to authorities upon reaching the port city.

Helen went into the small house to retrieve the ledger. Nicholas never looked with his own eyes into the diary and did not know what had been written by Stanley, or Frederick, or Helen. As she fetched the book, Helen hesitated. Giving that diary would out them all for what transpired on the mountain. Would Whitaker still acquiesce to his daughter marrying Ethan? Whitaker was a hard, religious man. Ethan would not fare well in losing Elizabeth a second time. Most of all, Helen was ashamed and did not want the world to know what they ate to survive. Weren't they cleansed of that sin, in the river? Why did anyone else need to know of it?

Helen tore the pages out, each page back to Stanley Hansen's last entry. It was not a lie to take those pages from the book. In truth, the Hansen ledger dairy ended with Hansen's hand. Helen unbuckled Frederick's Bible and stowed the loose pages within, then fastened it up again. The Bible and her pages would wait in the house for Frederick to fetch. He could decide what should happen to them when he returned for his book. Hopefully, he'd never return and they could put that past to rest forever.

Chapter 10

The Curse Janine

Janine couldn't wait for her sister to bring the kids to Rio Linda, but at the same time, she was anxious too. She wondered if the kids would feel free to ask her the questions they politely avoided at Sammy's birthday party. Such as, why has their aunt been missing all these years? Surely, Ashley must wonder why her aunt dropped out of their lives so completely. Did Ashley know what happened in Chicago, or did Juliana protect her daughter from that story? Janine imagined an easy visit with Juliana, but with her fledgling relationship with Ian included into the mix, her anxiety level rose astronomically. Juliana's radar would surely detect something and she didn't want to field the questions her sister might ask.

Then, there was Sammy. She still didn't know how to act around Sammy. In Texas, she found herself staring at Sammy with a mixture of yearning and guilt. Would Sammy begin to notice her aunt acting weird around her?

In the back of her mind, Janine also harbored fear that the spirits of Mary and Linda might actually be real. After everything she experienced, she was practically convinced something paranormal existed in Rio Linda. Surely, her post-traumatic brain couldn't conjure the girl she encountered in the orchard, could it? And although Caroline Govant might pretend to see a ghost, she wondered about the others chanting together. Did they really hear something in the trees, or did they get caught up in the excitement? Collective hysteria? Leone would never pretend like that, would she? And Henry Webber's rage pointed to him seeing something he did not want to admit. What nonsense did he think he was participating in? Janine found Gram in the kitchen with the Saturday edition of the newspaper and a pen. Gram smiled up from her crossword puzzle.

"Are you worried about Juliana's kids coming here?"

"Of course," Gram said. "For years you girls have poo-pooed me and called me a silly old woman. Of course, I'm worried."

"Shouldn't we warn Juliana about the ghost?"

Gram looked at her wryly. "Good luck, Jaja. Don't you think I've been warning her about that ghost for years? You yourself have chastised me about my warnings."

"I know." Janine sat down hard in her usual spot. "It's just, I might believe you now. Juliana should not bring those kids here. What if the River Girl Ghost tries to get one of them to go to the river?"

Gram set her Sacramento Bee down in a wrinkled pile. "Really, Jaja. No one has mentioned the river ghost in many years. Your imaginary friend was probably the last we saw of her. The more I think about it, she was probably just an imaginary friend, or an echo of the original ghost. Kiki and I had a long discussion about it and we believe the river ghost might be a faded spirit."

"A faded spirit?"

"One that used to haunt a place, but their purpose is gone, and so the spirit slowly fades away. Kiki says it often takes a very long time for a spirit to fade completely. Even today I get a little upset at Henry for scaring me like that. He had everyone convinced the river ghost wanted you to drown, but she never asked you to go to the river, did she?"

"No, she never asked me to go to the river."

"Well, that ghost is known for luring children into the river. We haven't heard of any drownings blamed on that ghost in over twenty years. No sightings. Henry's niece was the last drowning blamed on that ghost. Maybe all the signs and precautions have helped, or maybe the ghost has lost her purpose, which is what we think." Gram nodded to herself. "Fact is, drownings are not what they once were. Perhaps folks should just let that ghost rest. Also, you know Juliana as well as I do. Those children will not leave her sight for a second. The river has always been off limits to Williams kids, and I'm sure Juliana will put her foot down hard about that."

"I swear I saw a ghost the other night," Janine insisted. "In the orchard. You say your mother saw that same spirit and even you saw her once."

Gram's worried brow aged her.

Janine quietly added, "Maybe Juliana and the kids should stay in Sac, just to keep them away from the river."

Gram chuckled. "I'm not the one you have to convince, Jaja. Juliana would never hear of any such thing. If you want her to stay in a hotel in Sacramento, you need to be the one to convince her. She doesn't listen to me about my paranoia."

Gram was right, of course. When Janine was under ten, Juliana and Janine tried unsuccessfully to petitioned Gram into letting them visit Rio Linda. *Rio Linda is not for young children*, Gram would say. It was a miracle when Gram consented to the Rio Linda visit at Sammy's birthday party. Janine realized that it was probably her own fault. Gram and Juliana would consent to almost anything to keep Janine from disappearing from their lives again.

"I have to go shop." Gram began to gather up her large purse and new shawl. "I am going to make a large roast for dinner tomorrow night. Well, Misty is cooking it. I hope you don't mind, but I've invited Kiki and Doctor McNally to join us. Your niece is a huge fan of your show, you know."

"Gram!"

"This gets you off the hook," Gram told her. "I invited him, you didn't. You can keep your secret a little longer and still have your sister size him up for you. Now, don't rain on my parade, girl. And I know you have that thing tonight, so don't worry about me."

The "thing" was a cocktail party with the *Spectral Analysis* staff and the reenactment actors at the Malabar Restaurant. The entire upstairs area was reserved for the party. A few of the show sponsors would be there, as well as some other high-ups, whatever that meant. Steve told her that some very important people were interested in meeting her, and although Janine was technically on her break, she should come.

Janine had not seen anyone on the crew for days. Carlos flew home to Texas, Kiki and Ted were working closely with the reenactment crew, and

Ian and Steve were analyzing the séance footage. Ian hadn't been able to break loose at all. They were working eighteen-hour days, cleaning up clips and putting together some sort of last-minute presentation for someone. Janine spent the time childproofing Gram's house for Juliana and the kids. Janine replaced a broken electrical outlet, a light fixture, plastered wall holes and oiled squeaky doors. She also swept out the henhouse. The yard men usually managed the henhouse, but it didn't hurt to sweep it out again if the kids were going to fetch eggs. Gram and Janine even went to the stables to brush down Gram's painted mare and polish the tack in case Juliana wanted to go riding. Juliana always wanted to go riding and always scrutinized the state of the saddle.

Cheryl, the *Spectral Analysis* office manager, planned the entire party from Texas. Cheryl called Janine to schedule her transportation to the party but Janine said she'd take the truck. A dress came to the house, by courier, from Kiki. Kiki wrote a short note that said she recommended Janine dress up a bit, as the party leaned on the semi-formal side. Kiki's note said there'd be many pretty wannabe actresses and they needed to exert their status as the real stars of the show.

Come confident, Kiki wrote.

Janine stared at the dress, which was definitely a Kiki choice. She didn't know how she could wear such a revealing, sexy dress and not look totally self-conscious. Come confident? In that dress? How? Most of her scars would be visible: the X graze mark near her breasts that he made to be cruel, the jagged scar under her right armpit that looked worse than it had been, the deep gash on her right shoulder blade, and just a peak of the near fatal kidney scar. People would definitely stare and wonder. Questions would fly around about those scars. Did she have time to shop for an alternate? Janine glanced at her own wardrobe, jeans, T-shirts, sweatshirts. Nothing there for a fancy cocktail party.

Her cell phone chimed. Ian.

"Hi, Janine, I've got a few moments here and just wanted to check base with you." There were a lot of voices in the background, so he was still in some sort of meeting.

"Check base?"

"I wanted to hear your voice again." He said softly, "I miss you. I really miss you. I cannot stop thinking about you and your lovely lips. You're coming tonight, right? Remember, we have unfinished business. I had a wonderful dream about you last night. Shall I come fetch you?"

"Don't you have to be out there extra early?"

"Yes, yes, but I can come now. In half an hour. We can get ready together at the hotel. I have a private room. We can have a preparty cocktail or… Hey, what…" Janine could hear Kiki speaking to Ian. She obviously took the phone away from him.

"Janine?" Kiki asked but didn't wait. "I think you should come to the hotel right now. Bring the dress. We'll get ready together. In my room. Ian and I will come get you, or, if you prefer, meet us there in half an hour. But come now, right now. We should get ready together."

"Kiki, that dress…"

"Is going to be gorgeous on you. Bring it."

"I don't know. You just don't realize…"

"I don't think you know what's happening out here," Kiki said. "Things are getting bigger than we expected. There's talk about a feature film documentary for the big screen, Janine, the silver screen. We had a terrific presentation and people are very interested. This party is extremely important. It's not just Ian and me people want to meet. Carlos flew back this afternoon and will be there too. Shall we come get you?"

"I'll come in the truck."

"Good, room 335." Ian said something behind her, but Kiki repeated, "Room 335. They'll give you a key at the front desk, but there should be someone there waiting. I hired a stylist to do our hair. Don't forget the dress."

Beatrice had lopsided pink and frost-colored hair. Her big bag of tools sat half open and three curling irons were lined up on the vanity. When Janine arrived, she smiled, introduced herself as the beautician and invited Janine into the chair in front of the mirror. Beatrice studied Janine in the mirror.

"Let's get started," Beatrice said. "Your hair is very nice, very long." She pulled the ponytail out. "Let's go with flowing ringlets. It looks like it'll take a curl easily. Kiki mentioned that she thought large ringlets would look nice and I agree." She started brushing Janine's hair. "Light on the makeup, just a bit of lips and lashes, although, I want to clean up your brows if that's okay?"

"Whatever you need to do. Where's Kiki?"

"She's in the shower."

Beatrice somehow made Janine look glamorous. All it took was pulling out a few overgrown brows, applying a light touch of color to her lips, and adding large soft waves to her hair. She resembled the old Janine, from long ago. The college girl. No, not quite. She was just a little more defined and harder around the edges. No baby fat lingering along her chin line.

Janine recalled the last time she wore lipstick, in Chicago, before going out on that last date. Kiki stood behind her, looking with approval at Janine's reflection. Kiki wore a blood-red ruffle and lace dress, which was even more revealing than the ice-blue sparkly dress lined up for Janine. But then, Kiki often wore over-the-top outfits. She easily morphed into whichever character she wished to create.

"If I can wear this," Kiki said to her reflection, "you can surely wear the lovely dress on that chair without complaint. We need to be as glamorous as possible without looking like we're trying too hard. The studio is coming to the party. We want to stamp the seal on this deal."

"Kiki, that dress, it's just too…sparse. I'm going to need more dress."

"Just put it on." Kiki took the hairdresser's seat as Janine stood up. "I'll come see it in a minute. Think of it this way, Janine. It's just a costume, and sex sells. Why do you think I dress the way I do on the show? Because I enjoy it? Because ghosts like it? No. To make the ratings and get the sponsors. It helps fund what we do. I chose that dress specifically for you. The color, the cut. And it really is kind of modest, you'll see. I thought about that for you. The least you can do is try it on."

Modest? Okay. Janine could see what Kiki meant. It was modest compared to some of the stuff Kiki wore. But Kiki did not know about the scars Janine needed to hide.

"Could you just try it and then we'll discuss it."

"Fine." Janine took the dress into the other room.

Might as well just come out with it. Let Kiki see for herself. That'll shut Kiki up for life when it comes to dressing her up again. Let Kiki see the scars and she'll want to cover them up herself. She kicked off her jeans and T-shirt and began pulling up the dress. There were two very thin satin straps and she could see there was no hiding her bra under there. Luckily, the dress was designed to support her with a reinforced spandex type of material. When she pulled it up, she clearly saw that Kiki was right. The dress was very sexy, but also kind of modest in a classy sort of way. Kiki chose a gorgeous dress for her. A perfect color against her skin. Where Kiki's red dressed screamed devil, this dress sang angel. Kiki must be going for that message, they're opposites. Surely, Kiki didn't expect the angel to have such deep, angry scars. Janine could not get the zipper up all the way. She was about to zip it back down when Kiki walked in. Kiki gasped and then stepped over.

"Let me do that." Kiki turned her around to face the mirror and finished zipping the dress. It fit perfectly to every curve of her body. Janine noticed Beatrice standing in the doorway, staring at her.

"You look incredible in that dress," Beatrice said.

"She's right," Kiki told her. "You must wear it."

Couldn't they see her scars? The knife marks? Janine turned and looked over her own shoulder. Yes, there they were, glaring gash marks across her shoulder blade and one down her back. The near-fatal mark peeked ominously over the edge of the dress near the zipper. Dark and ugly. Surely, Kiki saw that entire scar before she zipped up the dress.

"They just make you look more badass than ever." Kiki stared solemnly at her shoulder blade, then turned her jade-green eyes on Janine in the mirror. "They go with your badass image, it's so right. And they don't take away one ounce from how beautiful you are in this dress."

Beatrice at the door nodded her head. "You look incredible," she repeated.

Janine shook her head. "You think people want to see this? Those?"

"Let me tell you what people, our audience, see when they look at you, Janine. For the first few shows, you and Carlos were just kind of there, barely in the background. Then you guys started with the wisecracks. You were the voice of reason, keeping us honest. People see you as the calm, cool chick that doesn't quite believe all the nonsense. Nobody scripted that. It just happened."

Beatrice continued nodding. "That's right."

"Remember Sacramento, in the tunnel. You were glowing and didn't blink an eye. You just shoved the doctor aside. You practically dared Ian and Ted to go into the room with all those ominous noises. *You're a badass.* That's what people see. And what's better, the badass nonbeliever now seems to have seen and spoken with a real spirit. You are a major key to our being taken seriously with this story. If you're convinced, the audience is convinced. The studio is convinced. This thing is going to be big. Nobody planned it this way, but there it is."

Janine looked in the mirror. The dark angry X over her left breast stood out glaringly. How many times did people tell her the scars were barely noticeable and to ignore them, and she knew they were always lying. Her scars were startling and frightening.

"Wear them proudly," Kiki said softly. "They just confirm once again that you are a badass. Those scars are terrifying, and yet, you're still standing here looking absolutely beautiful. You don't fall for any nonsense. Really, Janine, just keep reminding yourself that you are a badass, and you'll be fine."

Kiki spontaneously hugged her tightly.

"I'm so sorry for what happened to you," Kiki whispered in her ear. "It all makes sense now, this dark aura. I was afraid to look at your fortune, your future, but it was your past I feared. I think I know who you are." Kiki peered into her eyes and said very softly, "You're Jane Doe from Chicago, aren't you?"

You are a badass, you are a badass, you are a badass. Janine repeated it over and over to herself as Kiki directed. Carlos showed up to escort her to the party, the two sidekicks. Kiki suggested they make an entrance together. Kiki said that if they played their cards right, they would not only be on the silver screen, but on every screen from sea to shining sea. And they were the authors of this little ghost story, with all the rights involved. Kiki said that the little taste of success they've had was about to overflow.

But for Kiki, the best part of the media attention was providing proof that the mysterious door to the spiritual world, once closed fast to the world, would be opened. Kiki insisted that they were on the cutting edge of revealing a new dimension. Good grief, Janine thought.

Janine opened the door of Kiki's hotel room and observed a very uncomfortable version of Carlos standing in a jacket and open collared shirt. His eyes popped open when he saw her.

"Oh my god," he exclaimed, "you really are a girl."

"Is it too much?"

"Depends on who's looking."

"What do you mean?"

"The other girls are going to hate you." He chuckled.

Carlos offered his arm, and they started walking. Out the back door of the hotel, the Malabar steak house was in the next building over. The parking lot overflowed with fancy cars. Two limousines parked side by side in the back told them they were fashionably late.

"Did your wife get upset that you got called back so soon?"

"Maria's a little excited about the possibility of us being backed by a big studio. She already calls me a TV star for walking around in the background, now she thinks I could be a movie star too. The bonus didn't hurt either." He chuckled.

Carlos opened the door for her and the hostess directed them toward the stairs. They moved past a jam-packed bar and a restaurant full of a glamorous-looking crowd. Excitement buzzed throughout the entire building. When they reached the top of the stairs, Janine could see that it was basically a cocktail party with a buffet. Carlos pointed to the bar.

"I'm going to need a drink to get through this," he said. "Want one?"

"Go on," she told him. "I'm going to stroll around."

What she really meant was search around for Ian or Kiki. Mike Dunn stood in the corner, talking to a small group of men in suits. Lawyers circle, Janine guessed. Ted sat uncomfortably at a far table, eating by himself and ignoring the people, introvert's circle of one. Pretty girls fluttered everywhere, pretty men too, most likely all actors. Janine spotted Steve at a table, speaking intimately with three men and an older woman. Kiki stood in the middle of the room surrounded by a small crowd. She chatted and laughed in a flirtatious way with the people around her, right at home being the center of attention. How did she do it? Doctor McNally stood in the center of his own small circle. Mostly women surrounded him. They all resembled models or actresses. Ian appeared very pleased with the attention and not at all concerned about finding her. She felt a little heat of anger well up that she realized was jealousy. You are a badass, she told herself.

"Hey there, miss. Can I get you a drink? You look like you might be a little thirsty." A nice-looking man moved up next to her. He wore black rimmed glasses and a nice suit and tie. "Are you an actress?"

Good question. Was she an actress? Maybe she was. She was wearing a costume. She worked on a TV show.

"I noticed your scar, is that a…"

"Knife wound," she said in a matter-of-fact voice.

She noticed his eyes staring at her cleavage. Her X. He glanced into her eyes. He was captivated, she realized. Weird. Another man came up and said hello to the first guy while sizing Janine up. Their little trio chatted about the

Spectral Analysis show. They pondered if ghosts were truly real. By their conversation, the two men knew Kiki Mellow and Ian McNally pretty well. It dawned on her that they might be trying to impress her with their associations.

Holy crap, she thought, are these guys connected to the show? Janine knew there were people connected to *Spectral Analysis* that she had never met, like silent sponsors and producers. The black rimmed glasses guy apparently had connections to many of the people in the room. He flashed his nice even teeth and was not shy about flirting with her or touching her arm.

Janine glanced toward Ian's small group and noticed that he finally spotted her. He stared at her with a concerned expression. When she moved to face him, she watched his eyes grow wide as he realized who she was with. Janine turned to the man in glasses as he handed her a fruity cocktail that she didn't plan to drink. She thanked him nicely and was about to move away when Steve suddenly stepped up.

"Janine, I've been waiting for you." Steve nodded to the two men. "Guys, I see you've finally met our tech specialist, Janine Stinger." Why did Steve get to wear a T-shirt and jeans to this fancy party?

"Wait, this is Janine Stinger from the show?" Black Rims asked. He gave her another look up and down. "Wow, you're totally different out of that, what is it, a jumpsuit?"

"Sorry, I didn't recognize you." The other man smiled at her and shook her hand. Janine gave him a small nod. He seemed nice enough.

"Really." Black Rims grinned and felt free to touch her shoulder again. "You should think about wearing your hair like this on camera. I mean, you're cute in the uniform and all, and whatever it is you do with your hair."

"Ponytail."

"Ponytail, yes. But like this, wow. Very pretty. Sexy. I like it."

"Put a sock in it, Max," Steve told him. "Come on, Janine. Someone wants to meet you." Steve led her back toward his table. "Don't worry about those guys. They're old buddies. Contributing, silent partners. If they bug you, let me know. I want you to meet Mr. Dixon and Ms. Stammers. They're with the studio. Don't worry, you just need to say hello for a minute."

"Okay," she said.

"You look awesome, by the way," Steve said.

"So do you. Awesomely comfortable," she said, and Steve laughed.

Mr. Dixon and Ms. Stammers rose slightly when Steve introduced her. She shook hands and smiled politely. They exchanged a few pleasantries. No, Janine told them, the X did not have a specific meaning. Then, their actual question came.

"You saw a ghost out there?" Ms. Stammers asked.

"I am almost certain of it," Janine said evenly.

"Just like that? Were you scared?" Ms. Stammers asked.

Steve cut in, "Why don't we have our little question-and-answer session now. We're all set up right over here." The other side of the table had reserve placards. Steve helped Janine to a chair. He turned to wave others over and then left suddenly to fetch them. Janine turned to Ms. Stammers on the other side of the table.

"I was scared," Janine said evenly. "In fact. I'm still a little scared."

A glimmer flashed in her eye and a small smile creased her lips. That was exactly what Mrs. Stammers wanted to hear.

Steve returned with Carlos and Ian and a few others, including Black Rimmed Glasses. Eventually Kiki strolled over and was helped to a seat. Mr. Dixon, Ms. Stammers, Black Rimmed Glasses, and two other men sat on one side of the table. Ted, Kiki, Ian, Janine, and finally Carlos sat on the other side. Most of the party people gathered around to watch. Steve introduced the crew and then the questioners; Dixon and Stammers from the studio, Black Rimmed Glasses was Max Colliers, then John Buckley and Guy Montague, all producers or sponsors, Janine didn't pay too close attention. Steve summoned a waiter to bring out tumblers and whisky. He poured for the crew and offered shots to the questioners.

"This how we debrief after a shoot," Steve spoke to the crowd. "With single malt whisky to cool our nerves." People laughed. "We review the material, analyze all the data, and discuss our findings. At this time, we'll take questions from the panel." Steve opened his hand, indicating they could start.

Mr. Dixon asked the first question. "How many unexplained encounters did you experience in, is it, Rio Linda, for this ghost story?"

Ian answered, "We investigated multiple sites, one site twice. At two of those locations, we believe we experienced true paranormal activity."

"With proof to back it up?"

"Yes," Ian confirmed.

"Can you elaborate on the proof," Ms. Stammers asked.

Steve spoke up, "We'd like to wait for the show to make those items public. But we are talking about undeniable recorded proof here. Backed by scientific evidence."

There was an elevated murmur from the crowd.

"Of course," Ms. Stammers said. "I was also told that you know the identity of the spirits you encountered. That there is a detailed story behind them. Is that true?"

Kiki answered, "Yes. We know the names of each spirit, there are two, and we know a little bit of their life story. The blood lines of the population in Rio Linda run deep. We have oral history passed down from generations. We found written notes saved in private homes as well as official documents and news clippings. Together, all of the information, and the very real psychic energy, helped us reveal a rich story line for these hauntings."

"Official documents?" one of the other men asked.

"The official city log and a vetted document from the California History Group in San Francisco. They each corroborate the history of the spirits we discovered," Ian told them.

Many questions flew at him about the science side of things. The doctor spoke about very low-frequency electromagnetic disturbances and what they could mean. He explained precautions he took to crosscheck possible causes, other than ghostly, for oddities of temperature and energy disturbances. Someone asked Carlos about the technical setup and if he believed they actually encountered a real spirit.

"Oh yes!" Carlos dramatically tugged on his collar and gulped down his whisky, drawing lots of laughter. He flashed his dimples at the crowd.

The panel was extremely curious about the ghosts. Beyond revealing that they were both young girls who lived in the 1800s, the crew didn't reveal much. Janine was encouraged to give a brief description of each apparition. She confirmed that she encountered the river ghost as a young child and mistook her for an imaginary friend. Kiki told them that several drawings by kids who drowned in the river matched Janine's description and artwork perfectly.

"As far as we know," Kiki said, "only children can see the river ghost, and every one of those children met a watery death. Except, Janine Stinger."

"Did the doctor hypnotize you?" someone asked.

"Yes, he did." Janine glanced at Ian. His eyes lingered on her and she felt an instant stirring. She hoped she wasn't beginning to blush at his smoky eyes. *You are a badass*, she told herself.

Kiki fielded questions about psychic energy and the séance in the orchard. She kept it strictly on séance setup and how best to orient a circle, only saying that the séance was a huge success but they would have to wait for the film. Janine learned that Kiki hailed from Scotland, like the doctor. Did the two go back that far? Nobody asked. Then the questions started to get more personal. Someone asked if the doctor and Kiki were secretly a couple, and everyone chuckled.

"I could never limit myself to just one fellow." Kiki purred, and that got a bigger laugh. Clearly, a few fellows were encouraged by her statement.

"I've got a question for Janine Stinger." Max with the black rimmed glassed peered directly at her. "Would you be free for a few quiet words later? I'm hoping so. I'm in town through Monday morning and hope we could have dinner tomorrow night?"

Before she could answer, Ian McNally cut in rather sharply, "Unfortunately, Janine's been called to a dinner engagement tomorrow night." As soon as he said it, he realized how he must look. He glanced at her and leaned back. "Sorry, I just know that she can't get out of it. Kiki, myself, and Janine. We're meeting with one of the main subjects for dinner. It's a pretty solid commitment." He made it sound all business.

Max was not put off, "Maybe before dinner then." He passed his card across the table confidently, clearly establishing his interest. He grinned in a charming way. His overconfidence made him very attractive. "Please, let me know if you're free. I'd love to hear more from you."

At that point, Steve stepped in and made a few toasts. The crowd closed in and random people asked their own question of the *Spectral Analysis* cast members. Carlos stood abruptly and went behind Janine to help with her chair. Together Janine and Carlos headed out of the crowd to the far side of the room.

"That guy that wants to take you to dinner. That's Max Colliers, the oil guy."

Colliers Oil? Texas oil and petroleum? No way.

"He's like a billionaire or something. I heard they might buy the Spurs. Can you imagine that kind of money? Woohoo. Last season he was all about Kiki. He likes his pretty women. Dressing like a girl pays off, hey? I need to find me a dress like that. That kind of money, how can anyone say no? Think about the courtside seats you could get me."

"You are such a jerk, Carlos…" but she stopped immediately. Max Colliers appeared behind them, clearly hoping to take her away.

"I'm sorry to interrupt." He smiled and patted Carlos on the back. "I feel compelled to chat with Miss Stinger. Do you think we can we have a private word together?"

Max had very kind eyes behind his glasses, light brown with long lashes, and he carried himself like a gentleman. He glanced at Carlos, and Carlos looked at her, then shrugged and went away with a grin. Clearly, Carlos approved of Max.

But they weren't alone for long. Ian caught up to them. The two men seemed annoyed with each other and Janine guessed that she was the reason why. She felt guilty and thrilled at the same time. The flash of emotion in the doctor's eye tugged at her heart and the anticipation of a private reunion got her blood pumping. She glanced at his large hands and imagined a rough, warm exploration from them in the near future.

"Hi there," Ian said stiffly. "I'm going to steal Janine away for a moment."

"This is a party, Doctor. Save that work stuff for office hours. Miss Stinger, Janine and I, are just getting acquainted here. Plus, looks like you have a fan behind you."

Sure enough, there were a couple of girls standing right behind the doctor. When he turned, they instantly began chatting to him. Janine saw his flustered, blinking eyes. Ian didn't know how to be impolite. They insisted on taking a photo with him. Max leaned in to speak softly. He attempted to lead her away, but she didn't budge.

"Can we find a less busy spot? Downstairs. Or, I have a car out back. We could disappear somewhere quiet for a coffee, lose this crowd. I'm very interested in learning more about you." His eyes seemed very interested in her X knife scar.

Ian suddenly reached out and put his arm around Janine in a clearly protective embrace. He rudely ignored the fans. His sudden passionate hug was tantalizing.

"This can't wait." He glared at Max Colliers and whispered to Janine, "Come along with me."

Ian led her down the stairs, ignoring people as they went by. They snaked around the booths to the small L hallway that led them toward the facilities. As soon as they turned the corner, Ian kissed her full on. His hand went over her near naked shoulders and then lightly traced her X. Her body instantly reacted and she pressed herself against him. For a moment, the noise and activity in the restaurant ceased. She was breathless, happy, and extremely hot for him. She was right where she wanted to be. She had waited two long days for that kiss.

"Do you want to wear my jacket?" he asked.

"What? Why?"

"Well, you look absolutely beautiful, stunning. But you in that dress is getting a lot of attention. The way some of those guys were looking at you, especially that pretentious prick, Max. The nerve of him asking you for a date in front of that crowd. What did he expect you to say on the spot like that?" He looked down at her and drew in his breath. "This has to be Kiki's handiwork. I don't know whether to thank her or curse her." He caressed her shoulder again, then bent down and kissed it lightly. "Did you find Max interesting? I about had a panic attack seeing him and Dave swarm you. Those two are notorious playboys. You should stay away from them."

"You don't think I can handle myself? What about you? You have a lot of female fans flocking around you and they don't appear very shy." Her hands pressed against his chest, to push him away, but he didn't yield. He kept her solidly in his embrace, not letting her budge.

A sudden wave of ice-cold fear coarse through her veins.

"I'd like to get you out of here right now." He kissed her again. People walked past, clearly noticing, but Ian didn't seem to care. "Do you think we'll be missed? Probably. I'm afraid you might get propositioned if you stay. By more than just Max Colliers. Crikes, why aren't you sticking next to Carlos or Ted?"

"Why aren't you?" *Was it anger she felt developing?*

"Okay, fair. You're having a good time." Ian was a little upset. "But if you're not careful, you are going to make me clock some poor lout."

"I'm not making you do anything." *Or just fear?*

He considered her for a moment.

"I've got an idea," he said. "Let's go back upstairs together, like this." He held her hand up in his. "And maybe, some of the time, I can slip my hand around your waist, like this." His arm went down to pull her even closer. "And just to make sure nobody has a question about what it all means, perhaps I can kiss you once or twice, like this." He leaned in and pecked her lightly on the cheek and behind her ear. He whispered softly into her ear, "I want it to be crystal clear to everyone that you are taken, that you're mine."

This blood flow was different than the heated response to his kiss earlier. Something felt completely out of phase, lopsided. A familiar and very frightening feeling flooded her chest. She imagined Ian pulling her away and confining her somewhere until she agreed to behave the way he wanted. She knew that was crazy, but she couldn't get the thought out of her head or tamp down the panic building in her chest. *What would he do if she refused?*

Janine forcefully pushed Ian away and looked into his eyes. A worried expression crossed his face.

"I think you need to trust me," she said very softly, blood pounding, moving away. *Good grief, was she afraid of him?*

"I do. I do trust you," he countered quickly.

"Well then, Max Colliers or any of those other men upstairs shouldn't matter, should they? So what if I talk with any of them. It's a cocktail party." *She definitely felt fear.*

"I guess I'm a wee bit jealous," he said. "I did not enjoy seeing him ogle you like that, or pulling on your arm. Talking to a guy like Max encourages him. He's got a considerable reputation and, somehow, lots of women actually prefer him." His eyes began to blink, and he was clearly upset.

"I understand jealousy." Janine tried to suppress her growing emotions. "I get jealous watching girls flirt with you but I don't try to dictate your movements, or hide you away, or act like I own you."

"Blimey," he cursed. "That's not what I meant. I don't think I own you. I just don't want—"

"I won't have a controlling, possessive man in my life ever again. Never. I won't do it. Do you understand? As much as I really want you, I'm afraid to leave with you right now."

Immediately, she wanted to take it back. He appeared slapped in the face. And why wouldn't he? Didn't she just equate his possessive impulse with the man who made all the marks on her body?

He moved away from her. His eyes were blinking rapidly, his sign that he was trying to sort things out in his mind. He looked everywhere but at her.

"I didn't mean it the way it sounded," she said softly, slowly. "I'm sorry. I'm just…I just missed you, and I'm self-conscious in this dress, and I don't really drink, and I'm afraid of…I don't know what I'm afraid of."

Ian nodded. He still did not look her in the eye.

"No need to explain, we're just a little anxious, that's all. There's a lot going on, and this thing, with us, we got…interrupted." He gave her a stiff little smile, still blinking. "Let's just go up and finish out the party. We'll work this out later."

She nodded, "You go first. I'll meet you. I'm just going to step into the ladies room for a bit."

She watched him meander away before she beelined out the door. She found the truck in the lot between the hotel and the restaurant and pulled out her phone. She woke Doctor Crisper, she could tell by his groggy voice. But the good doctor always said to call day or night, rain or shine. So far, she managed to avoid calling Doctor Crisper for ten months.

Cool as always, the doctor did not act surprised at her phone call. He spoke as if their last conversation happened earlier that week. She told him about finally visiting her sister and Sammy. She told him about her job, the friends she made, and her plan to finish college. She told him about taking a chance with Ian McNally and then becoming frightened.

"Janine," he said over the phone, "you realize that the first relationship may not be the one that lasts. There's bound to be a minefield of these flashes of feelings and memories to work through. Just take it one day at a time. I am proud of you. You sound like you are doing great. But give yourself permission to make a mistake here or there and move on if needed."

Doctor Crisper asked her about Sammy and more about how that meeting went. The entire conversation lasted about half an hour. Mostly just Janine talking. She ended the call and stared at the restaurant. She debated whether she should go back inside. It didn't seem to be a good idea. She no longer felt like such a badass.

She noticed three new messages. All from Ian. *Where are you? Are you all right? I'm sorry, are you still downstairs?* Then he was there, standing outside the door of the Malabar, searching everywhere. His eyes, like heat seeking missiles, zeroed in on the truck. Spotted!

Janine quickly turned over the engine and drove out of the parking lot. She texted with one hand, I'm tired, it's late, my sis comes in the morning. See you tomorrow. Then she completely shut her phone down as she drove away.

Why did you leave me? One each for redemption. Where are you? Heed the dictum. She can be the last one. Are you all right? The first relationship may not be the one that lasts.

Voices echoed in her head and tumbled together in her sleep. Janine remained stuck in a vivid nightmare. Loads of kids frolicked along the river edge as the current raged dangerously behind them. A voice kept whispering, *why did you leave me?* She tried to call out, to warn the children, but only static emerged. A young Henry Webber stood on the shoreline encouraging everyone to play in the water. She began to panic. Suddenly, she was running through the dark woods, familiar woods, worried she'd turn wrong again. She felt his footsteps right behind her. Miraculously, she turned right and relief flooded her system, but only for a second, because she was back on the pebbly shore moving obediently toward the river.

"Wake up!" Someone shook her.

Janine opened her groggy eyes and felt dizzy. Jumbled images of Henry near the river remained behind her eyes. Was that a memory or a dream? Her heartbeat pounded in her ears. Juliana smiled down at her. Janine sat up in bed and hugged her sister. Beautiful, capable, levelheaded Juliana.

"We're all downstairs," Juliana said. "Gram told me not to wake you. You had some sort of big-deal party last night?" She noticed the shimmery blue dress slung over a chair. She walked over and picked it up, admiring it. "You wore this? Must have looked gorgeous."

Janine checked the time. Noon!

"Oh no, Gram should have woke me. When did you guys get in?"

"Don't worry about it, we were running late," Juliana said. "We've only been here for about half an hour. The kids are not going to let you sleep. They all want to go to Fairy Tale Town. Gram is feeding them a little snack right now and we're going to head out in about twenty minutes. Think you can be ready by then?"

"Of course."

They wandered around Fairy Tale Town, a little storybook village filled with playground equipment across from the Sacramento Zoo. Ashley was nearly a teenager but still had fun with her smaller siblings. Jack was eight, and Sammy just turned four. Janine watched the kids run into the crooked mile attraction, a short, raised, winding pathway painted bright yellow. It wound through a jungle of trees and bushes in a twisting, turning circuit. Janine remembered the fun she used to have with her older sister on that narrow trail.

"Juju, Jaja, Juju, Jaja," Sammy and Jack chanted together, taunting their mother and aunt.

Gram laughed with them. She followed the children into the crooked mile walk.

"Let me get this straight, your imaginary friend is now a ghost." Juliana said. It sounded ridiculous coming out of Juliana's mouth.

"So it seems," Janine said.

"Gram says you guys are digging up real ghosts out here," Juliana said. "She seems to think your show is going to make a movie out of her river ghost." Juliana was laughing. It sounded incredibly ridiculous when Juliana said it.

"Don't tease, Juju, it's my job. We really got some interesting stuff out here."

"Didn't you just tell me, at Sammy's birthday, that this show was all fun and games for you?" Juliana asked. "Now tell the truth, do you really think you've seen a ghost?"

Janine hugged her sister. "I'm not sure what I believe. But believe me, at least there's talk of a real movie here. And there's a good story for a ghost out here. And we've got some nice unexplainable footage that people are really going to love. Better than anything we've taped before."

"Gram says this is going to be big for you." Juliana hugged her back. "I'm just really happy that things have turned around, and you're doing so, so fantastic. I'm proud of you, Janine. Truthfully, the kids, Ashley especially, love the show. Ashley is always bragging about her aunt Janine. She loves having you back. And she's super excited to meet Kiki Mellow and that dreamy Scottish doctor tonight."

Just worry about one thing at a time, Janine told herself. They watched the kids emerge from the crocked mile then turn to go right back in again. Janine's eyes were drawn to Sammy.

Juliana called out, "Where's Gram?"

"We're going back in to get her," Ashley told her.

Sammy and Jack sang, "Juju, Jaja, Juju, Jaja."

Jack held Sammy's hand as they ran past, grinning wildly at Juliana and Janine. Sammy's hair flew all over the place. Her ringlets were probably a nightmare to detangle. Sammy's laughing bright eyes locked right onto Janine's, causing her heart to skip a beat. *Oh my god, she's so beautiful*, Janine thought.

"Juliana," Janine got her sister's attention. "I never thanked you properly for taking Sammy. After everything I said and did. How horrible I was. I'm so sorry. Thank you. I'm so grateful you took her. I can't believe how beautiful she is."

Juliana embraced her for a very long time. They both ended up crying a bit.

"She really is a terrific girl. She's a lot like you. She's the most adorable little imp imaginable."

"I wasn't kidding when I said I might be a believer. Gram may not totally be off her rocker about these ghosts. I think I've seen something?"

"Like a real ghost?" Juliana's eyes creased.

"It doesn't hurt to keep the kids in sight when we're so close to the river, right."

"Oh Janine, are you going to pull a Gram?" Juliana looked worried. Janine didn't like that distressed face. She caused more stress in Juliana's life than she cared to admit. "Ghost or no ghost, my kids won't run around unsupervised. We'll restrict them to the cut lawn, like you were. Please don't press Gram's ghost on us, okay. We want a nice, no-nonsense visit. Gram already urged me to tell your Kiki about what happened way back then, and I'm not participating," Juliana said.

"Kiki wants an interview?"

"I don't think that request is coming from anyone but Gram." She turned her big sister, scrutiny eyes on her. "Look, Janine. You had an imaginary friend, okay. I watched you. You would get bored in the house and run around talking and singing to yourself. There was nothing there but you, Janine. It was broad daylight. I was too old to play kid games all the time, I'm sorry. I was a bit of a preoccupied teen."

"They say other kids saw the same girl I did. I knew her name."

"That may be my fault too." Juliana shook her head. "You always wanted to stay up and roast marshmallows when my friends came over. You heard plenty of tales about that river ghost. Me, Chrissy, and Tanya, we told you the stories. I was responsible for babysitting you, remember? Gram often ran off to play cards and put me in charge. I didn't want you running down to the river on my watch."

"But, I actually remember seeing her."

"Janine, the first time I asked you what your friend looked like, you couldn't tell me. I suggested blond hair. I suggested blue eyes because that's what the river ghost is supposed to look like. I didn't know it was so taboo for you to see that ghost. I didn't realize that Gram would take it so seriously."

Juliana nodded at her disbelief.

"You see, there is no ghost." Juliana said firmly, "There is only a ghost story."

Gram loved hosting large dinner parties created by her mysterious roommate, Misty. Janine realized that Misty must also be responsible for the biscuits and coffee each morning. Misty, who people hardly ever encountered, was like a ghost herself. When they got back from Sacramento, Janine noted that Misty prepared easy-to-serve food and set the table. Then Misty pulled her disappearing act and hid in her room from the commotion.

Adam, Juliana's husband, relaxed in the doctor's easy chair with the newspaper. He remained at the house to repair a rain gutter for Gram and must have completed his task quickly, as, he appeared pretty comfortable in the lounge chair. He also discovered Ian's single malt Scottish whisky and enjoyed an early cocktail. He smiled as Sammy ran over to jump on him. Sammy adored her father.

"Your Misty says it's all ready to go. She's done for the night and doesn't want to be disturbed." Adam managed to relay his message from under Sammy's little bear hug.

"Such an introvert," Gram said. "She abhors any type of socializing. Even when it's just the two of us. She refuses to eat or even watch TV with me sometimes. She's so sour."

"How long has Misty been here?" Adam asked.

Gram just waved the question away and hurried into the kitchen. Juliana and Ashley rushed upstairs to freshen up. Janine plopped on the couch and Sammy ran over to bear hug her next. Janine still felt overwhelmed around her little niece. She hugged the little body tightly, soaking her in. What did Juliana plan on telling Sammy about the past? Surely, Ashley knew something, but how much? She obviously knew Sammy was adopted, but did she know how that adoption came to pass? This was a subject Janine feared to bring up.

Sammy grabbed Janine's face with her little hands and looked directly into her eyes.

"I love you, girl," Sammy said, stunning her with an echo of Gram's voice. Then she jumped down and ran off.

"Jaja!" Gram called from the kitchen, "Are you setting up the cocktail bar?"

Janine jumped up, still a little touched from Sammy's spontaneous declaration. She felt very lucky to get a second chance with Sammy. She went to Gram's minibar area.

"I didn't know I was supposed to!" she yelled back, looking for the ice bucket.

Adam strolled over to help. Her brother-in-law was a Texas A&M grad who worked as an accountant in a large company. Adam and Juliana's relationship went back to their high school days and Janine first met Adam when she was Jack's age. Through the years, Adam always managed to stay out of the drama between the sisters. Janine knew that Adam harbored guilt for encouraging Janine to go so far away to college against Juliana's advice. He shouldn't. How could anyone know what would happen?

The doorbell rang. Both Adam and Janine looked toward the front door. Adam glanced her way but Janine remained frozen in place. This was it. What would she do? Doctor Crisper's wise words put things in perspective. Maybe she should just tell herself, *nice try*, and move on. Maybe Ian decided not to come after all and it was only Kiki. Crap, she wished she didn't have so many fears haunting her. Once upon a time, she had been the opposite of insecure.

"Should I get that? Or do you want to?"

"You go," she said quietly.

But Ashley leaped down the stairs and beat them to the door. She flung it open and instantly gasped and did a little jump.

"Oh my god! Hello, hello, come right in." Ashly's wide eyes were excited as she waved Kiki and Ian into the house. "Mom, Mom! Gram, they're here. The guests are here!" Ashley announced loudly.

Kiki was dressed like a normal person. She wore a simple, pretty, fairly modest, calf-length dress with low heeled, neutral-toned shoes. Her hair, now a dark-brown color, flowed naturally in a very feminine, conservative style. But there was no way to tone down her striking green eyes, and she still drew all the attention in the room instantly.

Ian carried a bottle of wine, which Adam took off his hands. He also carried two bunches of flowers. He briefly nodded to Ashley and Adam before fixing his attention on Janine. He seemed on edge, and his eyes were blinking.

"Can I get a picture? Would you take a picture with me?" Ashly pulled her cell phone out. "Dad, Dad, take one with my camera."

"Ash. Let them come in and get settled a bit. Maybe they'd like a refreshment. We have a nice batch of single malt Scottish whisky," Adam told them.

Kiki smiled and winked at the teen. "Let's take a few now while we're fresh, and we'll take a few later when we're old friends."

She glided over to Ashley, took her phone, and passed it to Adam. Kiki and Ashley were very close to the same height. Adam appeared a bit bashful with Kiki. He probably imagined Kiki in one of her revealing show outfits. She did have a sex-symbol reputation and was striking no matter what she wore. Kiki passed Adam her own phone as well.

"Call me Kiki, by the way. And this fine fellow is Ian McNally."

Ian greeted Adam and joined Kiki and Ashley. Ian still clutched his two bunches of flowers. He gave Janine a brief smile under his blinking eyes. She instantly felt bad about turning her phone off to avoid talking to him. She really just wanted to walk over and embrace him. But Doctor Crisper's warning, *the first relationship may not be the one that lasts*, hovered in the back of her mind, keeping her frozen in place.

"I'm Ashley," the teen said a little meekly.

"We know who you are," Kiki told her. "I've heard a lot about you from your grandma, great-grandma, Gram." she corrected. "You remind me a bit of your Auntie Janine over there."

Gram entered the room, as did Juliana, Sammy, and Jack. Gram conducted formal introductions while Janine stood like a statue as quiet as a mouse. Ian and Kiki shook hands with each small child. Sammy stared into Kiki's eyes and wondered how they got so very green. Sammy giggled contagiously and Kiki fell into the giggles with her. Then, Kiki fixed those very green eyes directly on Janine and it was clear that she knew exactly who Sammy was. Thankfully, Adam began pouring drinks. Janine snapped out of it enough to help open the bottle of wine Ian brought. Kiki strolled over and gave her a very warm hug and accepted a glass of wine.

"These are for you," Ian presented Gram with one bunch of flowers. "A spring mix, to liven up the table." Gram smiled, very pleased. Ian turned to Janine, he hesitated a moment, unsure of himself with blinking eyes. "And these are for you." He passed her a bunch of red, long-stem roses. He gave her a nervous smile. Janine accepted them shyly, melting all over again. She managed not to leap into his arms and bashfully returned his smile instead.

"Thank you," she said. "They're beautiful."

Ian appeared very relieved. His eyes calmed down.

"Come on girl," Gram nudged her toward the kitchen. "Let's find a couple of vases for these beauties."

Misty prepared the perfect roast with stewed potatoes, steamed carrots, and a nice pumpkin soup to start. Juliana and Janine served. They were seated on the kitchen side of the table, facing Kiki, Ashley, and Ian. Adam carved the roast at the head of the table and Sammy and Jack were seated together at the tail. The kids were in their own little world, ignoring the grown-ups and giggling about something. Juliana, Ashley, and Adam asked loads of questions about ghosts and the show. Janine realized that though she knew much of the Rio Linda story, she did not know how they planned to tell the story.

"I'd like to read the wagon-train diary, if that's possible." Juliana cut roast and potatoes into very small pieces for Sammy. Sammy's eyes stared adoringly at her mother. "Are there copies here?"

"I've got a set in the office," Gram said, "as well as the pages found in the old Bible. The torn-out, secret pages. Although, Doctor McNally asked to borrow some of them for something, what was it, an authentication check?"

"I won't need them till Tuesday," Ian said across the table. "I'll bring them right back, of course. I'm afraid the history group will be interested in buying them, all the torn-out pages, eventually. They were pretty excited on the phone." He turned his pretty blue eyes on Janine and Juliana. "The tear marks on the pages found in your gram's old Bible appear to match tear marks in the wagon-train diary. They want to see a couple of actual pages to confirm and agreed to do a little low-key interview this week."

"If you can get away," Kiki spoke across the table toward Janine, "Maybe you can go and help the doctor with that. Take one of the handheld cameras. Better than a tripod. Everyone else is pretty booked with the river shoot. I'm sure Ian would love the help."

Was this another ruse? Was Kiki helping him now? Janine glanced between Kiki and Ian, suspicious. She changed the subject.

"Be careful reading that diary, Juju." Janine glanced at Gram. "It has some upsetting revelations in there."

"You mean the Donner Party type stuff?" Juliana asked. "I know about that."

"Ooh, a party!" Sammy perked up with bright eyes.

"Not that type of party, honey." Juliana stroked Sammy's wild hair. She chuckled and then Sammy and Jack went back to their private, quiet chatter.

Everyone focused on their meal for a few moments. Ashley told Kiki her friends in Texas tried to conjure a ghost during a slumber party. They used Kiki's summoning charm and freaked themselves out, but nothing happened.

"What's the Donner Party?" Ashley suddenly asked.

"The Donner Party," her father Adam grinned wickedly, "not the best dinner conversation, but you asked for it. Back in the Old West days, a group of travelers got stuck in the High Sierras during a snowstorm. They nearly starved to death at Donner Lake, right up Interstate 80. They survived by resorting to…" He looked around, then dramatically turned to Ashley. "Cannibalism!"

"That's so gross, Dad!" Ashley pushed her plate away.

"Cannon balls!" Sammy giggled across the table at her father. "Cannon balls!"

"Want me to take her to the glass patio to watch a movie?" Jack asked his mother.

Juliana nodded. "Are you two done here?"

The kids nodded and flew from the table, but not before running around and giving everyone a little hug and kiss or a handshake.

"That's not what I meant about the revelation. This one is a little more personal," Janine said.

"You mean about Great-Grandma Williams?" Juliana and Gram exchanged a glance with each other and then burst into laughter. "Gram already told me. How did you put it? Grandma Williams is no longer a sorry sinner. Gram has solid proof that exonerates her completely. What's the name again? Not Christopher but…" Juliana started snapping her fingers and looked to Gram.

"George Lumen," Gram said.

"You already know about this?" Janine asked Juliana.

"I called Juliana when you were out doing your street filming, as soon as I read that thing. What was I supposed to do?" Gram told Janine. "I had to tell somebody, and Juju has always known about my mistake blaming my mother. You know, thinking she was hiding that terrible secret."

"What secret?" Ashley asked.

"Juliana knows about the DNA test too?" Janine asked. Was Janine always the last to know everything?

"Who do you think helped me contact the DNA people?" Gram said. "I'm a little old lady. I can barely use a computer."

"What DNA test?" Ashley asked.

They spent the next several minutes reviewing their family lineage and how Leone, with her obsession with her online DNA family tree, opened up a whole can of worms. The real Christopher Williams was buried somewhere near Lake Tahoe, which meant half their ancestors were really not their ancestors at all. Gram proposed a road trip to see the lakes, Tahoe and

Donner. They could check out the history museum at Donner Lake and get a better idea of what must have happened in 1840.

"Plus, it is really beautiful up there," Adam said.

"I agree." Ian stared directly at Janine. "Very bonnie landscape up there."

Janine felt that moment in the hotel at Donner Lake again. The moment when she woke up in bed with his hand caressing the scar on her back; when her past didn't seem to matter at all; when she no longer felt completely ruined. Ian's soft eyes warmed her heart.

"I got an idea," Ashley said. "When Aunt Jaja goes to San Francisco for work, we should do a day trip to Tahoe. I want to see some of the history stuff."

"That's a good idea," Gram said.

"I am up for that," Adam said.

"I still don't understand where the ghosts come in," Juliana said. "Who are they? Were they kids in the wagon train? Did they die on the wagon train? Where do the ghosts come in? Why would one haunt an orchard and one haunt the river? Are they connected in any way?"

Kiki leaned toward Ashley.

"I'm going to tell you the whole story. We didn't even tell the movie people, but I'm going to tell you, because you're family." Her green eyes flashed excitedly. "The Hansen wagon train was cursed. Terrible things happened, and they were cursed."

Ashley looked thrilled.

Kiki continued, "The River Girl Ghost is the spirit of Linda Stauch, the youngest survivor of a wagon train led by the Hansen brothers out of Missouri. In life, Linda had a sunny disposition and loved to giggle and play. She died of an unnamed illness on the same day they baptized her in that river over the hill. The baptism was likely a rushed event, in order to beat her impending death. Maybe they didn't do it in time, and thus, she is cursed to wander the surrounding area forever.

"As a spirit, Linda is a restless child, always hoping to find other children to keep her company. She lures them to the water in an attempt to get them to share her fate of drowning. She promises to be their friend forever. Unfortunately, the spirits of other children don't hang around long and she keeps searching for new friends."

"Linda was your imaginary friend, right?" Ashley peered at Janine.

"Apparently so." Janine nodded.

"Was she trying to lure Aunt Jaja to the river?" Ashley asked Kiki.

"I'm not absolutely sure," Kiki said. "You see, I believe Linda stopped luring children to the river around 1970. That's when the final part of the dictum was met and the curse was broken. Not many drownings since then, but her spirit still appears now and again because she became a part of this place. Her spirit has walked this area long enough for her essence to linger, but her original purpose, luring kids to drown, is complete."

"What's the dictum?" Adam asked.

"One each for redemption," Kiki told him. "I'll explain it in a moment."

Ashley appeared confused.

"In the first two years of the settlement, child drownings in the river were a common occurrence. People didn't realize the danger of the undertow or the catch in the rocks," Kiki continued. "In as early as the mid-1800s, many drownings were connected to the river ghost. We have those facts backed up with documentation. The town even had a special council that met about the ghost. Folks really took it seriously."

Gram brought out hot apple pie and steamy coffee; the aromas were sweet and enticing. Fresh from Apple Hill, Gram bragged. She informed Julianna and Adam that the kids appeared ready to fall asleep. With all the excitement and the time change, they were wiped out. She set up the sleeping roll outs on the back glassed-in porch for them. Juliana smiled gratefully.

"The second spirit is the essence of Mary Miller, a girl born very near the time Linda Stauch died. According to our sources, she was well aware of the River Girl Ghost. Perhaps she felt lured by the ghost or saw the ghost. It's very likely both happened. We found, or rather, your auntie found a little handwritten note buried in a collection of important documents from the ancestors of Mary Miller. A note that indicates Mary drowned herself, on purpose, at an extremely young age."

"Suicide?" Ashley gasped with wide scandalized eyes.

Kiki nodded, mirroring Ashley's shocked expression.

"We also discovered that Mary Miller is not buried in the consecrated grounds of the cemetery, but on the outside edge of the orchard."

"I didn't know that," Janine said. "Is there a family plot out there?"

Kiki shook her head. "Just Mary. The rest of the family is in the cemetery. Mary was banned from the cemetery because of her suicide. We're going to film a little clip at her grave marker with the actors this week."

"I bet that's why she haunts the orchard," Ashley said, and Kiki nodded agreement.

"Her headstone rock is flush with the ground," Ian added. "It's a chunk of river rock, similar to the big boulder in the water. I can't quite identify all of it, but it has a bit of magnetite and hematite, minerals with lots of iron, and maybe some other choice elements that I'm studying. It shows signs of magnetism, you know. A closer inspection of that river boulder suggests that a section was cut from it. Mary's marker is the right size for that missing piece."

"The Mary spirit warns people to follow the dictum," Kiki said.

"What was that again?" Ashley asked.

"One each for redemption," Kiki told her. "We're pretty sure those exact words are the dictum that she wants followed."

"What does it mean?" Juliana asked. "One each for redemption."

"It took a while to figure it all out," Kiki told her, "but, I think we've cracked the code." Kiki nodded toward Gram. "*One each*, refers to each of the original survivors of the wagon train. *For redemption*, means that the survivors must seek forgiveness for a grave sin. They want to be redeemed. But what grave sin has been committed? That's the fun part, guessing. Perhaps for killing their wagon-train leader and blaming it on the Indians. Or maybe for the cannibalism in the mountains. Or maybe something else. Either way, they're cursed until the dictum is fulfilled."

"Why would they kill the wagon-train leader?" Adam furrowed his brow.

"Read the diary." Ian patted him on the shoulder.

"What is it they must do for redemption? What do they give?" Juliana asked. "How is it tied to the river or the orchard?"

Kiki leaned in. "I think it means death. One descendent from each survivor in the wagon train must drown a watery death. Just like Linda during her baptism. That's how they will be saved. Perhaps it's some weird baptism of their lineage. Mary's written note states that riches will follow if they go willingly to their death. Hardship and death, senseless death, will occur if they resist. And that is exactly what happened here. Come on, let me show you the connections we've made."

They moved into Gram's old-fashioned rustic study. Much of the preliminary research still lay in large piles between the wingback, antique chairs. Kiki rummaged through the written notes she created. Her whiteboard still sat propped in the corner against the bookcase and Kiki retrieved it. She turned to her audience and waited as they settled into separate chairs. Kiki's eyes flashed excitedly as she spoke,

"Only a small group survived the Sierra Nevada winter of 1839 to 1840, maybe sixteen or so, a fraction of the original travelers listed in the Hansen wagon train. Parts of the Williams family, the Stauch, Miller, and Webber families made it. They decided to stop here, near the beautiful river bend instead of pushing to their final destination of San Francisco. Why? Maybe to get their story straight: To cover for the murder of Hansen, or the ordeal in the mountains, or because they have a few sick folks to care for. Linda, for instance. Or maybe something else. Whatever their reason, the cursed survivors must sacrifice one soul from each family to be redeemed. Death and struggle will befall them if they resist, riches awarded if they follow the dictum.

"The first to succumb is little Linda Stauch. Her death may have sparked the dictum, *one each for redemption*. Following her death, what happened? Riches appear. Practically overnight. The town surges in size and money drops on the vagabond survivors in the form of goods, tools, and all kinds of wealth. It's a mystery how they got it. The Millers and Webbers manage to build a successful hotel and store. The new outpost is touted as a stopping place for travelers on their way to San Francisco and the town thrives all through the1840's. But the wagon train survivors fail to feed another soul into the river.

"A whole slew of other people drown instead. An average of fifteen drownings the first few years. That's incredibly high. And we found documentation that tells of a ghostly girl haunting the river in 1843. The River Girl Ghost has made her debut. Linda is desperately seeking souls to share in her watery fate. Unfortunately, she requires souls from the wagon train, not the others, and she keeps hunting for the right victims. The town begins to falter due to a bad reputation and a better route over the mountains is created."

"The route near highway 50, on the other side of Sacramento?" Adam asked.

Kiki gave him an approving smile.

"Possibly. Mary Miller is the next link from the wagon train to drown. In a delirium, Mary dictates the secrets of the curse. She gives the guide book, so to speak, and explains the rewards and punishments of the dictum. Mary sneaks into the river willingly to set an example, to demonstrate the truth of her words. The year following her death is the first spectacular year for the new orchard. A local almond industry is born, creating the riches. Wealth from the orchard saves the community and the town grows exponentially. An added bonus, not a single child drowning for the next three years.

"But people fail to follow Mary's instructions, and the dictum is ignored. As a result, tree rot descends on Rio Linda with a fury. Much of the orchard is ruined, only the Miller trees are saved, and child drownings begin again. Four kids are swept away in 1851 alone. The River Girl Ghost is blamed for every one of them. People believe that any child who sees the ghost will surely find their way into the river. That belief stays with the town to this very day. That a death must follow an encounter with the ghost, and if it doesn't, a more terrible loss, like a disaster will happen."

"Wow. That is quite creepy," Adam said.

Kiki winked at him and flamboyantly wrote the name Sarah Williams on the board.

"Then Sarah Williams drowns in 1853. One of your relatives. I tracked her back to Ethan and Elizabeth Williams." Kiki turned to Ashley. "Sarah spoke of a girl named Linda before drowning in the river. It's reported from oral history. Almost immediately following her death, the Southern Pacific train company built a major junction a few miles from Rio Linda. It's a boom town all over again, and the hotel business flourishes. The economy thrives like never before and the local descendants of the wagon train reap the benefits, the riches. Then another kid, Bradley Monte, drowns. He descends from Ingrid and Niels Stauch. His death keeps the momentum going on the local growth of wealth. Plus, there are no child drownings for the next three years."

"All this is documented?" Juliana's brow was raised.

"City history on drowning victims and of the local economy," Ian told her. "Personal notes and letters cover the ghostly sightings. We even found two old articles from the local Herald mentioning a river ghost. One printed back in 1840 something, 1843, and another printed a couple of decades later. There are copies in those piles." He pointed to Gram's copy of the research. "There is an implication that a committee once managed the ghost sightings and was tasked with authenticating them. There are actual meeting minutes from the early days that mention a river ghost task force."

Kiki wrote the name Bradley Monte and Eloise Webber on the board. She tapped the dry erase pen in her hand as she spoke.

"More drownings occur three years after the rail junction opened. Mostly kids without links to the wagon train. Child drownings increased drastically with the increased population. The River Girl Ghost is clearly an established myth by this time. Lots of oral history reports of her. Many of the victims make artwork right before their demise." Kiki glanced at Janine. "The dictum is not being fulfilled, so disaster hits again. Flood water covers the entire valley. Even downtown Sacramento near Sutter's Fort wallows in water. The lucrative train junction is completely destroyed and Rio Linda descends into ruins once more.

"That is, until 1865 when young Eloise Webber drowns. I traced Eloise back to Gustoff Webber, another founding member off the wagon train. Miraculously, Rio Linda recovers with poultry farms. Following the valley flood, thousands of chickens descended on Rio Linda. The new and very profitable poultry business saved Rio Linda for several years, more of the riches. The new upswing in wealth and downswing in drownings lasted almost a decade. There is only one new drowning during that entire time period, a small child named Timothy Williams, a descendant of Christopher Williams. No new wealth with this one, but the community didn't really need it as things were going well.

"Eventually more and more kids are lost to the river. More hard luck followed as well. Sometime in the early 1900s, a fowl illness, a chicken disease, wiped out the local poultry farms. The local economy suffered again."

Ashley glanced at Gram, "Do you think the free-range hens are related to those old chickens?"

Gram nodded, "I bet they are."

Kiki continued, "The population is riddled with ghostly sightings during this era. People are terrified of the ghost. The river ghost is blamed for any death near the water. At the same time, there are reports of a different ghost, one in the orchard. Each sighting mentions an urging to heed the dictum. Many believe the new ghost knows which children must be sent to the river. Perhaps the dictum was a known secret in certain circles. The Miller family has always had Mary's written instructions hidden away."

Kiki wrote Maple on the whiteboard and moved toward Gram's collection of photographs on the piano. She tapped a framed group photo.

"Next to drown is Maple Williams in 1931. Your gram has a picture of her over here. A direct descendent of Grant and Meg Williams. That's when the military base breathed life back into community. Between 1931 and the 1971 the river averaged one to two victims a year. The Mary spirit is very prominent during this period. The Miller family kept an extensive log of documented sightings of the orchard ghost." Kiki wrote the name Lara Webber and underlined it.

"The last significant victim was Lara Webber in 1972, directly linked to Rolf Webber, the last of the founding fathers on our list of survivors. Lara's death was followed by the erection of the Pepsi Bottling Company. Money pumped back into the economy and provided many of the remaining descendants the ability to make a good living, especially the Webber clan since the factory was built on their once barren plot of land. It happens to be where a section of the original orchard rotted away years ago. The most interesting fact to note, since 1972 there have been only two drownings in the river. A normal number for a river like Rio Linda. Actually, a pretty good number considering the rocks and undertow."

"Do you think the curse is broken?" Ashley asked.

"It's very likely." Kiki nodded. "The curse is fulfilled and the dictum is met. One descendant of each founding survivor has met their murky end."

"Then why would the ghost still haunt this place?" Ashley asked. "Why is she still around? Why did Aunt Janine see the river ghost?"

"Echoes. The spirit has been here for a very long time, as I mentioned earlier. Although her purpose is met, the spirit stays in a familiar spot. She lurks near the river, but no longer entices anyone into the water. Under hypnosis, your auntie said that the spirit never tried to lure her to the river. She never even mentioned the river. And your auntie was really the last one to see her. Perhaps the River Girl Ghost has finally faded away and now she is only a whisper on the wind. Soon, she'll be nothing at all."

They were interrupted by Sammy standing in the doorway.

"I need juice!" Juliana moved to rise, but Janine jumped to her feet first.

"I'll take care of this one," Janine told her sister. Janine took Sammy's hand and led her back toward the kitchen. Behind her, the conversation went on. It was a little disappointing to miss what came next, but Janine would hear it soon enough. She was more interested in tucking Sammy into bed; she hadn't got to do that yet.

"What happened to Jack?" Janine asked.

"He fell asleep," Sammy said.

Janine poured a small glass of apple juice and watched Sammy drink it down in one gulp. Sammy indicated she wanted more.

"Maybe you should drink a little water," Janine suggested. "That's a lot of juice."

"Juice!" Sammy ordered with an irresistible smile.

"Okay." She poured a little more for Sammy. "Did Jack fall asleep on the porch?"

"Gram is letting us sleep on the porch," Sammy told her. "We can see stars when we sleep. It's like we are outside but it's not outside. You can see every star in the world, Aunt Jaja. I have stars in my room, but Gram's stars are real. Really real. Real stars from outer space. I'm going to go to bed now. Thank you, Aunt Jaja."

Good grief, she was absolutely precious. Janine gave Sammy a tight hug. Little hands patted the back of her head in a comforting manner and Janine's breath caught in her throat. Little Sammy felt so nice. She had grown so much since their first brief meeting in the delivery room. She had turned away when they brought the baby over, because the grey eyes that locked onto hers were exactly like his. But not any longer. Janine could only see Sammy in those eyes now. *This is the baby I abandoned*, she thought. *Will she ever forgive me?*

She walked Sammy to the screened-in porch. Jack snored softly on one of the rollout cots and Sammy crawled into the other one. Janine tucked the blankets around the little girl and hummed softly. Janine was rewarded with one last smile. The kids slept in the rollouts Juliana and Janine used many years ago. Janine eased away and lingered at the propped open kitchen door to watch silently. She tried to resolve her tumbling emotions by breathing slowly. Sammy tossed a bit before settling in. After a moment, Sammy's breathing became slow and even.

Ian moved up behind her and her entire body felt his presence.

"That wee lassie is pretty cute. Looks just like her beautiful auntie," Ian whispered softly near her ear.

"I'm sorry about last night." Janine didn't turn around.

"Oh no, that was all me." He stepped closer, "I got stupid, jealous. I'm not used to feeling this way." His hand just barely touched hers, diffusing some of her nervous energy.

Janine glanced toward the den. Voices floated out in a lively discussion. Any one of them could come looking for her at any moment and she didn't know how to have the conversation they needed in a quiet way. Janine silently led him through the glass porch and out the back door. They stood in the fresh night air under a dark star-filled sky. *Every star in the world*, Janine silently chuckled. The river burbled in the distance. They shared a long hug. She felt herself start to breathe easier and relax, he fit her so perfectly. She debated what to say. Doctor Crisper's warning echoed in her ear, *the first relationship may not be the one that lasts*. The problem with Doctor Crisper and his friendly warning was; she wanted the relationship to last. Ian's voice broke their silence.

"Janine, I have to tell you something, about what I feel for you. Maybe we went a little too far, too fast, I don't know. I just got very swept away, overexcited. I was worried about that, you know, that I would push things too fast and scare you off. But I need to tell you…" Ian paused, and Janine could feel the anxious energy he emitted. She felt nervous too. He hesitated a moment longer, then inhaled a deep breath. "I'm pretty sure I may have fallen in love with you."

Why did you leave me?

She froze, suddenly frightened. Did she actually hear that whispered voice? Something caught her eye. In the distance, at the edge of the manicured lawn, where Linda used to stand, shadows moved in the darkness.

Were her eyes playing tricks on her? Were the stories in the den catching up to her? She took a hesitant step toward the shadow.

"Crikes. Too fast again?"

"Shh." She grabbed his warm hand and hushed him. She pointed to the far lawn, heart thumping. "Something's out there. I just saw, or sensed, something out there."

Slowly, silently, they inched toward the far edge of the green. The ghost was not supposed to come out at night, Janine reassured herself. Linda was a daytime spirit. But the air temperature dipped as they moved farther from the house. The river flowed just beyond the small mound in front of them and the sounds of moving water grew louder. A very faint breeze stirred her hair and it felt like the whisper from the river that day. Did she detect another movement in the corner of her eye, in her periphery? Janine turned quickly but saw nothing.

Her heart hammered in her chest. She could hear herself breathing.

"Do you see something?" Ian whispered.

"No."

"Did you hear something?"

"Maybe."

"Does this feel familiar, like the ghost?" he asked.

"A little."

"Are you scared?" he whispered.

"Yes." But she wasn't sure what she was scared of. *Identify the trigger.*

"Should we go back inside?"

"Yes."

He stood very close, protectively close.

"About what I said a minute ago…" He hesitated again.

Identify the trigger.

Her hand shot up to stop him from speaking.

Fixating on the firm line of his jaw, she realized the meaning behind her out of control pulse, the panic attacks, the sensations haunting her, everything. Like pieces of a jigsaw, they all snapped together dispelling the mystery. Beyond a shadow of a doubt, *he was the trigger!*

She felt like such an idiot.

"I may have fallen in love with you too." Her voice was barely a whisper.

He stopped moving.

She nodded. "And I'm a little scared about that."

His eyes stared at her in the darkness. He pulled her into a close embrace and they kissed passionately, then desperately. Janine entertained the idea of getting a bit indecent with him on Gram's back lawn. The yard was completely sheltered from the road and other houses, she reasoned. As long as everyone stayed inside, they could get away with it. It could work. It would be so nice. The voice of a little girl interrupted them. They both jumped at the same time.

"Is somebody out there?" Sammy's voice floated from the house. They could see her silhouette poking above the screened door window. "I see you!"

"It's just us, Sammy," Janine called to her, "Aunt Jaja and the doctor. We're coming in." Janine turned to Ian. "Let's not discuss what happened out here, with them in there. I don't want to freak anyone out tonight. After Kiki's story, poor Ashley is going to start seeing ghosts."

"Are you coming with me to San Francisco?"

"Yes."

"Good." He took a firm grip of her hand as they approached the porch door.

They entered into the little glass covered room as quietly as possible. Jack still snored in the corner. Sammy stood poised with her hands on her hips and a critical look in her eye. All Juliana, Janine thought.

"What were you doing out there?" Again, just like Juliana.

"Nothing," Janine told her. "Why are you still awake?"

"I heard somebody talking," Sammy critically sized up Doctor McNally then gave him the cutest smile. Sammy giggled a bit.

"Sorry Sammy, it was us," he said.

"Are you going back to sleep?" Janine asked.

"I need another kiss good night."

Janine urged Ian to go ahead to the den. Then she kissed Sammy on the forehead and tucked the small girl into the rollout bedding.

"I love you, girl." Sammy wriggled into her cot.

"I love *you*, girl," Janine said back softly, heart pounding.

Sammy closed her eyes instantly and settled into her pillow with her golden-brown hair splayed this way and that way. It will surely be a tangled mess in the morning, Janine thought. *He thinks she looks just like me.* Janine touched one of Sammy's curls before standing up. She made certain the back screen and the actual door were both locked and bolted shut. Linda is not allowed to enter the house. She glanced toward the edge of Gram's yard and only saw a quiet night. Definitely her mind playing tricks out there. That shadow was likely one of Gram's hens. *There is no ghost. There is just a ghost story.* And she didn't care what Doctor Crisper said.

Apparently, Kiki, Juliana, Gram, Ashley, and Adam had gotten into a nice discussion on the differences between pagan practices, wiccan belief, and witchcraft. Kiki had her signature tarot cards spread out on the table and was in the process of explaining the meaning behind them to Ashley. Kiki told Ashley that a dear friend back in Scotland made the art on those cards. The images came from dreams, and Kiki has had similar images in her own dreams.

Ian was beaming. He wore a giant grin and was conspicuously in a terrific mood. He stood off to the side, conversing with Adam in an animated way, sharing the last of the whisky. Juliana flipped through the photocopied pages of the wagon train diary. After another half hour of tarot lessons, Kiki and Ian declared it time to leave. They had an early morning at the river. The actors were going to film a scene in the water. They would be able to see the whole thing from the top of the mound on the edge of Gram's property.

After the door finally closed, Ashley turned her big brown doe eyes on Janine.

"Oh, my goodness, Aunt Jaja. Doctor McNally is totally trying to date you!" Ashley exclaimed.

"Where in the world did that come from?" Janine laughed.

"He gave you flowers. Did that not clue you in?" Ashley said.

"He gave Gram flowers too," Adam pointed out.

"Dad," Ashley rolled her eyes. "What do you think long-stemmed red roses mean? Love. Love, Dad. Doctor McNally is such a dreamy romantic with a cool accent. Are going to go for it, Aunt Ja? You should. All my friends will be so excited." Ashley did a little jump.

"Yes." Juliana laughed. "Do it for Ashley's friends. They will be so excited."

Janine just waved them away and went into the den to help Gram clean up. Gram sat on the piano bench looking at the photographs lined up on the baby grand. She inspected the old tin type of Christopher Williams. She motioned for Janine to sit near and handed the tin-plated photo to her.

"That Kiki is a character," Gram said. "I enjoy her company. She went out of her way with Ashley, you know."

Janine studied the photo, grainy and dark, a boy stood stiffly. He was dressed in a plain shirt, string tie and short pants. There were buckles on his shoes. His hair was slicked to the side in an unnatural way. Most likely, he had an unmanageable cowlick, like Jack, and they used a lot of hair grease, or water, to try to tamp it down.

"She knows all about me, everything," Janine confided in hushed tones. "Last night. She saw some of my scars and guessed, *Jane Doe from Chicago*. On her first try. She instantly knew who I was."

"It's a scary story, Janine. And Kiki makes a lot of good guesses. She's a real spiritual medium. Kiki is someone who can see things other people can't. I don't think anyone else would be able to guess. I also don't think Kiki is the type to talk about it. Gossip about it."

"I agree with you," Janine said. She held the tin plate photo. "So, is this Christopher Williams or George Lumen?"

XVIII
The Moon

"I think Christopher Williams," Gram's said. "This boy looks blond, and Christopher Williams, our Christopher, George, had brown hair."

"Hard to tell in this photo, a grainy black and white. Plus, hair often darkens with age. But it could still be our Christopher, George."

Chapter 11

River Girl Janine

Janine's family enjoyed the morning sunshine on the top of the small hill that separated Gram's house from the calm Rio Linda River and watched the film crew set up along the small sparse beach. The boulders responsible for so many deaths jutted out of the water reflecting the morning light with sparkles of different colors. A small group of actors dressed in old-time clothes were gathered in a group drinking coffee and chatting.

"I see Kiki!" Ashley said. Kiki turned at that moment and waved. Her sixth sense?

"What are they doing with those huge tripods?" Juliana wondered.

"Looks like their rigging a cable across the river. Maybe they're going to suspend a camera," Adam said. "Anyone want to get a closer look?"

"Me!" Jack could barely sit still.

"Me too." Ashley stood up.

"You're not going to get past those two guys," Juliana said. "Plus, Gram wants to go to the market up in Roseville."

Two policemen stood on the outer edge of the roped-off area where they recently turned a dog walker away. Adam stood up and motioned for Ashley and Jack to start moving toward the river. Sammy sat in Janine's lap, humming and blowing on dandelions. Janine was in absolute heaven cuddling her.

"Well, okay. We'll see you three later. Stay away from the water!" Juliana yelled after them.

Ashley turned and waved. They watched as the policemen stopped Adam, Ashley, and Jack at the perimeter line. The small group talked a bit, then Kiki strolled toward them. She reached over the line and hugged Ashley. The trio crossed over with Kiki and joined the group of actors.

"They got in." Juliana smiled. She nodded to Janine and Sammy. "Come on, girls, let's take Gram to that farmer's market. Somebody told me we can get some local almond butter there."

There was a close call at the river. One of the actors, a little kid, went beyond the safety zone placed in the water. He purposely waded toward the center of the river and then slipped into the quick rip stream along the bottom. The river grabbed him and swept him quickly toward the rocks. For a couple of terrifying moments, the water forcefully pressed his body against the boulders as the current tried to pull him under. Thankfully, rescue personnel were standing by for just such an event. Two men with air tanks moved fast.

"The water seemed absolutely calm," Adam said. "You'd never imagine it could sweep someone away that fast, but apparently there's a drop-off and a narrow slip stream where the water rushes by. It can knock a grown man off his feet, they say."

Juliana handed a sleeping Sammy to Adam.

"Can you put this one to bed?"

"Sure." He lugged Sammy away with Jack following.

"And where were you and Jack during this near-drowning?" Juliana crossed her arms over her chest. "Were you scared? Are you okay?"

"Oh mom," Ashley said. "We were sitting on the beach. We hung out with Kiki and the director. But it was pretty scary, I mean, it didn't look like there was a current at all."

"Just stay away from that river bend," Gram told her. "You heard the history of drownings. There doesn't need to be a ghost to make it dangerous."

"We definitely saw that," Ashley said. "One of the rescuers got stuck in the rock during the rescue. When he came out, he told us that the water pushed his foot into an opening. He had to fight the current and twist his foot to get out."

Juliana shook her head. "They should remove those rocks if they're so dangerous."

"Well, there's no swimming in that part of the river. You've seen the signs," Gram said. "A while back the city looked at giant boulder removal and it would cost a pretty sum. The city planners argued that moving the rocks would shift the placement of the river downstream. They figured it would flood Marysville Boulevard at least once a year, all the way down to where it connects to Elverta Road. Kind of a busy place. There are houses down there. Lots of people live down there."

Early Tuesday morning Ian McNally came round in a BMW rental car with an extra warm latte from Starbucks. Janine carried the lost diary pages under her arm. They were stowed inside the old Bible again and strapped together with a narrow leather belt. She double checked the equipment in the trunk to ensure they had everything needed to film an impromptu interview at the museum. Everyone in the house was still asleep when they left and the sun peeked just above the horizon. They talked and joked on the drive. Ian filled her in on what was keeping him occupied.

"I've been pretty busy with the underground stuff. I've been working with the satellite trackers to see if we can detect anything in the deeper layers of earth. There's too much high-frequency wave action to write off as ambient. They're directional. I want to rule out anything that could have caused the low frequency spikes we got."

Ian met with tech geeks from UC Davis and borrowed their ELF dish antennae. The folks at the university were very pleasant and accommodating. One professor urged him to consider being a guest lecturer in the future. He thought he'd give it a go between the seasons, what did she think of that? Ian and a few graduate students spent all day drawing lines of flux around the river and Caroline's old orchard. Something emitted, or reflected, signals with similar energy to a LORAN navigation station. It might be the river rock. Those rocks were slightly magnetic and their magnetic field did not match the direction of the earth's magnetic field. Janine found it amazing, the lengths Ian went to disprove something he wanted to prove. If he could find the source of the low-frequency electromagnetic waves, then they couldn't come from a ghost. Ian missed the reenactment shoot, so he missed the excitement.

He heard the same basic story Ashley told, but with an extra bit of information. Kiki's internal radar detected a strong presence at the river. It was similar in feeling to when Janine heard the whisper, but much stronger. Kiki claimed the river ghost was there, watching the film crew, interested in somebody.

"Kiki's worried there's something missing in her interpretation of the ghost story." Ian said. "We know plenty of spirits hang out in a familiar spot, but Kiki believes this one is getting stronger. She felt more energy than with the Mary spirit."

"She's changing the story?" Janine asked.

"Not really, just running through it again. She mentioned hypnotizing you again. Afraid we didn't ask the right questions. She's going through all her notes and pondering another séance but isn't sold on it yet. Kiki has always been a fantastic receptor for paranormal energy, but she can't summon a ghost at will. She would like to contact the river spirit, but doesn't think that particular entity would respond to an adult."

"Did you tell her about what happened out on the lawn?"

He gave her a sly smile. "You mean what almost happened?"

"Not that." She punched his arm. "I mean that I may have felt something out there. Something watching, or listening."

"I didn't say anything," he said. Then, after a moment, "I want you to know that I meant what I said out on that lawn."

"I did too," she told him. "Do you really think we took things too fast?"

"Not too fast for me. This feeling I have for you, it's not out of the blue, or a flighty fancy." He confessed, "I fell for you the first time you looked at me. Do you believe in love at first sight? Truthfully, this is something I've been carrying around for months." Ian seemed deep in thought. "When we first met, you definitely grabbed my attention, but I didn't want to be unprofessional. Who knew if there'd be more than one show? Then you got that boyfriend you seemed very serious about. You were always running off with him. I was trying to be very cool about it."

"A boyfriend? What are you talking about?"

"Back in Austin, at the end of the first season. You know, that guy you were with at the end of last season. I was certain he's the reason you didn't want to come to the after party. I was a very disappointed because…because I was going to woo you away from him."

"I had Sammy's birthday," Janine reminded him. "I told everyone that. But who is the guy you think was my boyfriend?"

He stared at her. "Oh, come on, Janine. I watched him drop you off every day at work and then come back to fetch you. It seemed like he never let you out of his sight."

"Did he drive a blue Toyota?"

"Yes, that's the one. He had that little goatee. Very hip." He looked annoyed with her. "He showed up right about the time I was working up the nerve to ask you out. You know, after the cemetery in Savannah. I thought we finally connected and you might consider socializing with me, away from the show, I mean. You don't have to laugh about it, that guy showing up is not a fond memory for me. I thought maybe I missed my chance."

Janine laughed so hard she could barely breathe.

"I'm glad you're having fun at my expense and I'm glad he's out of the picture. When I asked about an old boyfriend on our dinner date, he's the one I was worried about. Who was he anyway? Is he totally out of the picture now?"

She caught her breath. "My Uber driver."

He was stunned. "What?"

"He was my Uber driver for a couple of weeks. My car was in the shop. It finally completely died and I didn't have the money for something else." Her amusement finally calmed down. "Not until our final checks came through. He lived in my building, Mike, very nice. Only charged me one way. I felt silly sitting in the backseat because we were neighbors and quite friendly. I guess, he did hang around a lot, but we never dated or anything."

Ian shook his head. "Crikes. No kidding? I'm such an idiot."

"You're not an idiot," Janine said softly, becoming serious. "You're actually pretty terrific. You're romantic and sweet. The flowers, thank you. And I want to make sure to tell you, that night at the party, wanting to go upstairs and announce your feelings for me, any normal girl would think that was pretty romantic. A normal girl would have been pleased with you. The problem is me. I'm making things hard."

"No, no. You're perfect," he said.

"I wish that was true," she said.

"I wish you told me you were leaving that party. I was very worried."

"I didn't know I was going to leave," she said softly. "I only went outside to make a phone call. The truck seemed like a good place for the call I needed to make. I was upset at how I was reacting to you, so I called my shrink. It's been a while since I talked to him. This relationship has triggered some deep buried fears, automatic responses. Things I can't control."

"It's PTSD. Post-traumatic stress disorder." He nodded. "Kiki believes that you must suffer terribly from PTSD from time to time. She said I needed to be patient and—"

"You're discussing me with Kiki?" Just like that, her anger button was pushed. "You're discussing me with Kiki Mellow? Really?"

"We, no! Not really. Not everything. But Kiki guessed."

"Did you fill her in on the details of our trip to Donner Lake? Just how much does she know? Did you tell her the things I told you about… Did you tell the things I shared about… What did you tell her about me? How long have you been discussing my personal life with another woman? What kind of details did you discuss, Ian?" Her heart pounded in her chest, in her ears.

"I didn't discuss any of those things with her. I just told her about my feelings for you. You don't understand, Kiki knows me like a book. She can see right through me. There's no pretending around her."

She recalled a vivid image of Kiki stumbling in the Biltmore Hotel basement and falling into Ian McNally's arms. His overly concerned face flashed into her mind. She remembered being disappointed, thinking, there's no use competing with Kiki Mellow. Kiki always gets her man. Didn't it always seem like Ian was Kiki's man? He has always been very protective of Kiki, shooing off guys who got too chummy with her, almost punching that fellow who cornered her in New Orleans.

"Why is that, Ian?" Janine asked. "Is there something you haven't told me? Is there some history I don't know about? I opened up my past up to you, Ian McNally, I spilled my guts out to you and you're hiding something from me. What is it? You and Kiki are both from Scotland, Ian, what is it that you're not telling me?"

"Crikes," he said, eyes blinking. "Look, we wanted to keep it under wraps. You know, for the show's sake."

Kiki's hand on Ian's leg flashed into her mind, a gesture so familiar to him that he didn't even notice. The way they bent their heads together in private intimate discussions. The way they always seemed to understand what the other was thinking, laughing together with their cryptic inside jokes. Picking up each other's tabs or dry-cleaning. Kiki and Ian drinking whisky together, buying whisky for each other. They were so familiar with each other they could have been married.

"Keep what under wraps? What are you hiding? Do you keep all your past girlfriends a secret? Were you and Kiki an item? Is that it? Were you engaged or even married? What is it?"

"Janine, Kiki is my cousin."

"Kiki is your cousin?"

"Aye, my cousin. You know, our mothers, sisters," he said.

"Kiki is your cousin."

"Yes, my cousin," he repeated. "We're cousins."

They were cousins. It was her turned to be stunned. She would never have guessed on her own, but suddenly it seemed obvious. Ian's mother and aunt belonged to the same coven. Kiki and Ian spent their young summers on the island of Skye in a community of pagan women of the arts. That is, until Ian's father had enough. His father disliked the influence from his mother's side of the family. Too many spirits, faeries, and witches in their history. Regular people wondered why he allowed his son to intermingle with such nonsense. He forbade Ian and his mother from further visits to Skye as Ian grew older. So, while Kiki continued being instructed in a world rich in mysticism and spirituality, Ian got shut out. He pursued his interest in a scientific manner after finally breaking with his father.

Kiki still belonged to the same community of spiritualist. They consider themselves a coven of witches, but not like Janine might think. It's more like an ancient school of learning, where mothers pass down an old philosophy and crude science to their daughters. Ian's mother had been an important leader in the group and had a following of young lassies. Ian always felt a bit teased by the girls, because as a lad, he found the teachings very sexist. Of course, many of those girls turned out to be his very best friends. Did Janine notice, he got on with girls very well? She may have noticed that.

Ian and Kiki didn't advertise their family bond because they wanted to approach ghosts from two independent perspectives. They wanted to prove that the opposites, science and mysticism, could support each other in the middle, with proof of spiritual energy. They believed it would distract from that message if people knew they came from the same roots. Their main goal was to find authentic, paranormal activity and document it.

Steve's backers were more interested in ratings. When the fans responded to the doctor catching Kiki in that hotel basement, they latched onto the possible romance as an ongoing side narrative. It boosted the numbers and made the sponsors happy. It's what got them the funding to keep the show alive. To reach their goal of researching hauntings, they were willing to include some harmless acting here and there.

"You and Kiki. You two truly believe in these ghosts. This is not just another ghost story to you?"

"Well, yes." Ian glanced at her. "Aren't you beginning to believe? You're the one who heard them. You saw them. What are you telling me?"

"If I had to swear on a stack of Bibles, I'd say I heard and saw everything that happened," Janine said. "And I did. But even though I did, I can't help feeling a little unsure. I mean, ghosts? Spirits? Could it be something else? A trick of the mind?"

"You mean like that PTSD you mentioned."

"Yes. My therapist, Doctor Crisper, told me I might have some reactions. Spontaneous memories, flash backs, as this, our relationship, progresses. Deep buried emotions might be triggered. I'm sorry about this, but…"

"It's okay," he said.

"This is hard for me to say. Especially to you. I don't want you to take this the wrong way because you're very important to me," Janine said. "But you need to know. I loved him. Rick, I mean. It was a head over heels, passionate, euphoric love, and this, with you, feels similar. Different, but basically the same out of control feeling. Doctor Crisper says it could trigger psychosomatic delusions."

"Like a ghost?"

"Like deep buried flashes, repressed memories, or something. Deep fear and denial creating protective impulses. I'm sorry, but this feeling I have for you is mixed with… It's mixed with real fear. You saw a little of that," she reminded him. "Maybe my mind has played tricks on me. Think about it. Every time I started thinking about you, like at the river, in the backyard, in the orchard, one of these encounters occurred. Maybe my mind distracted me out of fear. It makes more sense than a ghost, doesn't it?"

Ian stared straight ahead. His eyes were rapidly blinking. She continued, quietly,

"Mary Miller, the ghost. She looked exactly like Caroline Govant in that photo of her as a kid. I saw the photo before the séance. Kiki held it up for us. I went back to look at it again. The girl in the orchard stood in the exact same spot, in a similar pose. *Heed the dictum?* Caroline said that to us in the interview. I reviewed the tape."

"What about the event at the river? You heard, *why did you leave me?* No one said that to you first," Ian argued.

But someone did say that to her. She turned away.

Should she dare to tell him what she thought of those old people, Henry and Caroline, that they were hiding something? That they were part of a secret group, a lingering variation of the city committee that once existed. *Somebody needs to accept her message and be responsible.* Caroline had said. *I pass the responsibility to you.* And lately, Janine remembers seeing a man on the back lawn, a young Henry Webber. He had encouraged her go look at the river. *What nonsense did he think he was participating in?* She was certain those two old people had been tangled in more than just a scandalous love affair in the past.

No, saying all that would make her sound paranoid as well as crazy.

They drove in silence for a time. Ian finally spoke up.

"Maybe so, but I've recorded real, unexplainable energy out there. Measured energy. We taped a faint voice that had no apparent source and Kiki feels these spirits. I totally believe in Kiki. Sure, she will embellish a story now and again, but Kiki has an inherent gift. Most of the women on my mother's side have it. Goes back for generations."

Janine agreed that Kiki had a gift. "She told me I had a dark aura."

"She just meant she can see something dark surrounding you. When we first met, she didn't know if it was in your past or future or what. She was a little scared about it, you know."

"You talked about me?"

"We're cousins! We discussed everyone at the beginning. Brainstormed what a good team would look like. We needed a neutral backup team, people with doubts, not easy believers. It was your dark aura that sold Kiki. She found it fascinating. Fascinating and scary because it can mean so many things."

"Did Kiki also tell you she figured out my past?"

"No," he said. "Did she? How'd she do that? She figured out everything?"

"The knife marks. My scars. The dress she insisted on. I thought I was going to shock her into backing off on that dress, but instead, she knew exactly who I was. She pretty much knows everything that happened to me, everything. Did she tell you about that?"

He shook his head. "What do you mean everything that happened to you? Obviously, you took a knife in the back, but Kiki was able to figure out all the rest?"

"Jane Doe from Chicago," she said quietly. Finally, all her cards were on the table. "It was a pretty big news story four, five years ago. Kiki instantly knew it was me." She watched his eyes grow wide as he remembered the story.

"Crikes, I am a complete idiot. You told me the whole story and I didn't put two and two together. Wait…" He looked at her. "Wasn't Jane Doe from Chicago with child?"

She nodded and said softly, "Sammy."

He took it in. "She's a cute one, that Sammy."

The California History Group in San Francisco housed an extensive collection of photographs and documents chronicling California's history. The archive section of emigration to the Wild West was on the basement floor. They needed to go to that level of the museum to find the Hansen Ledger diary. Doctor McNally and Janine greeted the museum guide, a tall, lanky man with an overly large mustache. He led them down a narrow staircase to where they kept documents unfit for display. He rambled as he walked.

"We have more than fifty thousand volumes of books and pamphlets, four thousand manuscripts and in excess of five hundred thousand photographs. The library is home to five thousand other works of art, including paintings, drawings, and lithographs. The most popular items are upstairs for easy access." He quoted right from their website. "But your diary is down here due to the fragility of the binding."

They entered an extremely small room. A large table dwarfed the room even more and created narrow aisles on all four sides. Three tall stools were placed randomly about and a dissecting microscope and a handheld magnifying glass sat on top of the table with the Hansen Ledger resting next to them. Their guide's name was James Monroe, like the president. His large handlebar mustache called to mind the Old West. James Monroe pushed a box of disposable rubber gloves their way and they each donned a pair. Ian quickly took a closer look at the ledger and started flipping through the pages. The ink-paper contrast on the actual pages made them harder to read than the photocopies. The ledger paper was a bit oxidized and matched the lost pages Gram found in color and texture. Ian turned to the middle of the ledger and found the torn-out section. Janine pulled out the old Bible and unstrapped it. She handed loose pages to James and Ian.

"I think it's absolutely crazy fantastic that you found these lost pages in some basement somewhere," James said. "I never really looked at this one before, but when you ordered a copy, I got very curious. Hansen was a colorful personality, to say the least."

"Wait till you read the removed pages," Janine said.

"More good stuff?"

"It's going to blow your mind," she told him.

"Look at this, Janine. It's a perfect match." Ian pointed to the line of tear marks in the binding of the diary and a page from Gram's collection. "Is it all right if we take a little video clip of this?" he asked James.

"Oh, yes." James nodded. "We got an okay for your project. Film and snap away. We're at your disposal. If you need us to copy or officially document something, we're ready."

They spent the next few hours matching each page in Gram's pile with torn edges in the ledger diary. Janine snapped pictures of each match. They also filmed a nice fifteen-minute interview session with the museum guide. James pulled out other historic documents from the wagon-train era. He showed them a letter that suggested witches from the east traveled to California and settled in Santa Cruz. Ian thought Kiki would find that letter interesting. James also spread out a large, hand-drawn map that traced possible routes over the mountains. By the time they emerged from the museum, it was midafternoon.

"I hope you don't mind, but I made reservations at the Bix restaurant for dinner. They have live jazz and it's a little fancy." Ian grinned. "It's a very pleasant setting, and it'll just be the two of us, no one to bother. We could explore other places, but we could dance together at the Bix." He turned his expressive eyes on her and smiled shyly. "Remember that night in New Orleans with the street musicians and that old guy that claimed you right away? You were nice enough to play along. You were very sweet. You danced to that slow jazz with him. You don't know how badly I wanted to be that old man. What do you say?"

She watched the muscled chords in his neck flex as he glanced up and down Market Street. She loved his height. Ian obviously hoped for a romantic excursion in the city. She felt a surge of happiness staring at him. Apparently, Ian McNally might truly be in love with her. He wasn't put off by her scars, or her muddled emotions, or her dark past.

"How fancy is this place? Will we go dressed like this? If I agree to another date with you, I want to be dressed nicely."

They happened to be very near the fashion district on South Market Street and decided to splurge on fancy new outfits for their dinner date. They also made a pact to turn off their cell phones and spend the evening offline and off the grid. Their planned few hours turned into the rest of the night. They stayed at the Hyatt Fisherman's Warf and did not leave San Francisco until well into the afternoon on the next day. Janine reactivated her phone when they entered I-80 heading east toward Sacramento.

The sky glowed reddish orange and the sun hung low in the sky behind them. Multiple messages from Juliana, Gram, and Kiki immediately popped up in her alerts. She read a few out loud to Ian.

"Juliana is done with all the ghost talk. Gram is driving her crazy. They're taking a road trip back to Texas, probably starting tomorrow. I don't know what happened."

"Oh no, sorry I monopolized you," he said.

"This is normal Juju-Gram behavior. After a couple of days of bliss, they start attacking each other. Two hardheaded women who like to be in charge."

Yet, there was something in the wording of Juliana's messages, worry? Should she call? She checked Gram's message first.

"Gram says you got some sort of FedEx package from a lab called ALS. It came to the house by currier."

"Oh yes," he said. "Rock sample results. Curious to see what's in there."

"Gram is wondering when we plan on returning. She says Juliana needs to be convinced of the facts."

"What does that mean?" he asked.

"Not sure," she told him. "Kiki says the filming in the orchard went well. The grave is very near her séance site, just east of it. And the headstone is definitely magnetic. Says Carlos blathered on and on about his compass? She also says that Timothy was adopted."

"Who's Timothy?" Ian asked.

"A grandson, or something, of Christopher Williams," Janine continued reading. "She double-checked the records. He was adopted from a neighbor. You remember, he was one of the drowning victims Kiki mentioned the other night."

Timothy was their Christopher Williams link. If he was adopted, then his death would have no effect on the dictum or any curse. There were no riches with his death. Kiki assumed his death continued some other windfall. Apparently, she was having second thoughts about that conclusion. Janine called her sister.

"What's going on?" she asked.

"Gram and her ghost again," Juliana told her. "We were having a very nice visit for once in our lives and now she wants to ban us from Rio Linda.

She insists the ghost may go after one of the kids. Kiki Mellow called her and said the curse may not be complete after all. What a loon, what a complete loon! She got Gram in a fit. Plus, Gram found the drawings the kids did on the back porch. All of a blond little girl."

"They drew the ghost! They saw her?"

"No, Janine," Juliana said calmly. "They copied your old drawings. Jack said they liked the painting you did of your imaginary friend and they each copied it pretending to have an old-fashioned imaginary friend. Kids do that sort of thing, pretend. Gram about had a fit when she saw the pictures. Don't worry, we're not going anywhere till you get back."

"Good grief, I can't believe this," Janine said. "We should have come back yesterday."

"No, Janine, you did exactly what I hoped you would do," Juliana said softly. "I'm happy you stayed in the city with that nice man. I hope you had a very pleasant time. You can tell me every single detail when you get here. I feel like you're finally, finally coming back to us now. All of you. Ashley's friends are going to be so thrilled." She laughed softly.

Janine didn't know what to say. Ian gave her an anxious look.

"Is Gram there?" She asked.

"At the zoo, with Adam and the kids. I'm stuck here, packing stuff. Gram is pretty adamant the kids are in danger and wanted them away from Rio Linda during the day. Afraid some ghost is going entice them to the river. If I see Kiki Mellow anytime soon, I may just give her a nice, sharp, slap to the face. I know everyone loves her, but really, does she need to play an old lady like that?"

After they broke the connection, Janine called Kiki.

"It's the only thing that makes sense," Kiki said. "These spirits, they're too strong to be echoes. They still have purpose. Why else would she seek you out that afternoon?"

"But she never asked me to go to the river," Janine reminded her. "Under hypnosis, we determine that she never even mention the river. And the drownings have stopped."

"I'm not trying to be mean, Janine," Kiki told her. "Every part of my being tells me that these two spirits are strong and active. This is my curse, Janine. I can't help feeling the wants and needs and desires of the spirits I encounter. In the orchard, I got a very strong sense that Mary was urging us to complete the dictum and annoyed the hell at you. Probably for not completing the dictum when you were young. Out at the river, I got the very strong feeling that Linda was trying to take that boy. It was unnatural. He said he felt something urging him to go out further into the water. I felt her there! That feeling was not an echo."

Janine gave Ian a worried look.

"*You can be the last one*," Kiki quoted. "Remember that. Caroline Govant told us the spirit said that about you. *She can be the last one*, remember that? We have it recorded, regular speed, clear as crystal. Who said it? Who said those words? They were whispered right into the condenser microphone. To you, Janine. Who do you think Mary was talking about?"

Janine felt her blood start to race.

"We're worried about the same little girl, Janine. Your gram thinks she knows a way to end the curse. I don't know what she was talking about, but she started rambling about someone named Bertha."

Janine relayed everything to Ian. He decided to pull off the road and call Kiki himself. They hit the next exit and coasted the car into an Exon station then parked in one of the empty spaces. Janine called Gram.

"Are you coming back today? We have some bad news about the curse."

"I spoke with Kiki," Janine said, "And Juliana."

"Juliana will never believe us about the river ghost," Gram told her. "Even when her own children drew pictures of her. She didn't listen. We are not going to tell anyone that they drew those pictures. No one. And I have an idea. A terrible idea, but it might be a solution. For more than one problem."

Janine waited for Gram to continue.

"Remember Bertha. I told you about her DNA test and what Leone did. Bertha has decided to stop her chemo. It isn't working anyway and she just feels tortured by it all. They say with or without chemo, she only has days, a month at most. So, she left the hospital. They won't help her out there. Oh yes, they give her stuff for the pain, but they won't really help her do what she wants to do."

"Gram, what the hell are you talking about?"

"She's considering it," Gram said.

"She's considering what?"

"Going willingly. Like Mary Miller did. To the river," Gram said.

"You're trying to talk this woman, Bertha, into drowning herself in the river?"

"Better than a child," Gram said. "Better than one of those beautiful children. And no one is talking anyone into anything. I told Bertha about George Lumen. She was grateful to find out she wasn't living a lie. I told her about everything days ago, and Bertha wants to die. She begged the doctor to give her something to end her life. She's already decided that she wants to die and was looking for help. It's just cruel that they insist on making her suffer out her last few days. She's in pain!"

"Gram, you stay out of whatever it is Bertha wants to do," Janine said in hushed tones.

Gram begged off at that point. She said something about being needed and ended the call. Janine looked at Ian. He came round to hug her.

Bertha walked to the river. It wasn't too far from her worn-down armchair, only a couple of blocks away. She waited until just after her TV show and for her nurse to run an errand. One last game of Jeopardy, one last iced tea with crackers. She couldn't drink the tea and she could barely stomach the crackers. It was no way to live out her last few days. The river could offer her a better purpose. All her life she knew she was destined for something great. She lived years and years of disappointment, never seeing or knowing what it could be.

Then Martha told her the story again. It was all so simple. They always wondered if they really saw a ghost in the orchard when they were young girls. A ghost who urged Bertha to *heed the dictum*. When Caroline dared her take a dip in the river to see if it was true, she called Caroline crazy. But maybe crazy Caroline always knew something the rest of them didn't; that Bertha was meant to go into the river and join the ghost. She could have altered everyone's lives by going to the river. The financial woes her family suffered could have been eliminated. They can still be eliminated. She could redeem them all, save their souls, pay their bills, and end her pain with one decisive event. Perhaps the cancer was God's gift to make her sacrifice easier.

Bertha removed her slippers at the river edge and stepped into the water. She waded slowly and did not notice the ice-cold temperature until she got waist deep. The cancer not only took her fear away, it took the feelings in her legs as well. She admired the metallic luster of the large rocks. She inched further into the water and felt the slip stream. She willingly slipped under that surface.

The current swept her rapidly to the boulders. Water pressed her firmly against the rocks. She couldn't move. She was weak from chemotherapy. Water flowed over her head and washed her scarf away. She gasped for breath but could neither move up to breath, nor down to drown.

An old man walking his dog spotted her in the water. He called 911 on his cell phone and then waded in to get closer. The current pushed him over and he stumbled. Luckily, he regained his footing and made it back to shore. His dog jumped up and down, yelping at him. The dog knew better than to go into the water. Then others gathered around. A human chain was made to reach Bertha.

They got to her! Bertha was pulled to the safety of the shore. The witnesses heard her say something as she laid soaking wet on the pebbles. Soft and woeful and broken.

"She didn't want me."

An ambulance took Bertha away. The human chain dispersed to share the story of the woman they saved and the heartbreaking thing she said. Poor old lady. Shameful that the old and sick are no longer wanted by the young. Whoever *she* is, she should be ashamed.

Traffic through Davis made them very late getting back to Rio Linda. Ian dropped her off at Gram's and greeted her family again, this time as her boyfriend. The smaller kids were already asleep and Gram was mysteriously missing. Ashley and Juliana seemed very approving of Ian. Ian retrieved the FedEx package and turned to head back to the hotel. He needed to pack to make an early morning flight. They were flying back to the main studio in Texas to start putting the movie together. Janine walked him out to the porch to say goodbye.

"Please let your Gram know I said thanks."

"I will. I wish I knew where she was. I'm a little worried about her," Janine held his hand. Even though they were due to see each other by the end of the week, she didn't want to let him go. She had an uneasy feeling about parting with him.

"Are you sure you don't want to fly back with us?" Ian hugged her tightly. "Five days is a long time. I miss you already."

"I need to drive back with Juliana and the kids," Janine told him. "I've got more catching up to do. But I know how you feel. I'm going to miss you too."

Back inside, Juliana stood waiting for her. They went into the study to talk. Piles of ghost research laid conspicuously stacked next to two of Gram's attic boxes. Adam must have lugged the other boxes to the attic. Janine put the Bible with the torn-out diary pages on top of one of Gram's paisley boxes.

"You have no idea where Gram is?" Janine asked.

"We had a little tiff," Juliana said. "She won't answer my phone calls."

"She doesn't answer her cell phone often," Janine told her. "She accidently mutes it a lot."

"There was another near-drowning at the river today. All the neighbors were talking about it. Adam got the story from the man next door," Juliana told her. "They made a human chain to reach an old lady at the rock. She was very lucky."

Two near-drownings in less than three days.

"Do you know who it was?"

Juliana shook her head.

"Are you going to tell me about this doctor of yours?" Juliana asked.

In the midst of telling Juliana about her San Francisco adventure with Ian, her phone pinged with a text from him. Gram and Kiki were both at Caroline Govant's house. The three of them planned an impromptu séance in the orchard at midnight. That's probably why Gram didn't answer the phone. Juliana became visibly agitated at the mention of Kiki Mellow.

"I'm going to try calling Kiki," Janine said.

"You go right ahead," Juliana told her. "I'm going to bed. I am so done with Gram's ghost nonsense."

Kiki picked up on the first ring.

"Gram is fine," Kiki assured her. "She called me this afternoon. These ladies are both very anxious to summon Mary again. Gram seems to believe that Caroline speaks for Mary. Don't worry about anything, I'll drive her back myself after our thing. We'll give it a go and see if the spirit will answer any questions. Three is a very good number for contacting spirits. Now that we have a better idea of what Mary was trying to tell us, we may be able to ask the right things. These two women seem to be insisting."

Juliana was right, that did sound looney. What was Gram up to? *Janine's suspicions about Caroline and Henry popped into her head.* Was Gram trying to convince the ghost or Caroline?

Janine stole through the kitchen and checked the enclosed patio. Jack and Sammy snored in the rollouts. Janine quietly snuck in to check the lock and bolt on the door. The inside kitchen door was propped open, as always, and Janine eased between the two sleepers where the rollouts met in the middle. They looked so much alike, Jack and Sammy. Same color hair, same pink lips, same little nose. Jack stirred. His eyes fluttered.

"Aunt Jaja. You're back."

"Shh, Jack. Yes, I'm back," she whispered.

"Did you fall in love? Ashley said you were out falling in love."

"I guess I was." She petted his head. "Do you mind if I sleep in here with you for a bit?"

He nodded and closed his eyes again. Janine reminisced about the day Jack was born. Her father allowed her to ditch high school to visit her new nephew. Her sister had been exhausted in a hospital bed, radiant with happiness, and Adam beamed with pride. Ashley, who only turned five years old, made it very clear to everyone that the new baby belonged to her. Janine smiled at that memory. Ashley sitting between her parents, clutching the swaddled baby and making that loud declaration to everyone in earshot. There was so much love welcoming baby Jack into the world.

Very different from the day Sammy was born. Janine turned to the little girl. Her hair was wild and loose across the pillow. Janine touched a stray curl. Sammy took a deep breath. Once again, Janine couldn't believe that beautiful little girl was the baby she gave away; the baby she refused to hold; the baby she refused to acknowledge with more than one brief glance; the baby Juliana and Adam saved from being lost to the unknown. Deep down, Janine wanted her back. She wanted to take Sammy home and love her. She knew that she didn't deserve Sammy after abandoning her at birth and it was wrong to even imagine disrupting her family like that. Juliana was Sammy's real mother. Janine should just be grateful to get a chance to be her aunt.

Sammy shifted and Janine settled down next to her. Janine closed her eyes and cuddled the little girl. A silent tear trickled onto the pillow they shared. What would life have been like if Sammy's father had been the man she first met, and not the one she constantly tried to forget? Sammy's breaths came deep and regular and soon put Janine into a deep sleep.

She woke to Sammy's grey eyes boring into hers. There was a burst of giggles. By the light from the window, it was just after dawn. The porch felt cold and damp. Sammy held Janine's face firmly between her two little hands. Sammy was inspecting her. Janine blinked and stretched, sore from the thin roll out bed.

"You snore, Aunt Jaja," Sammy said.

"I do?"

"Yes. I knew you would sleep with us, but I didn't think you would snore."

"Really, and how did you know that?" Janine asked.

"I heard you last night," Sammy said.

"I thought I was being quiet. Did I wake you?"

"You were being silly."

"I was?" Janine noticed Jack had gotten up. He was not in his rollout.

"You said to follow you home. We are home."

Janine sat up and stared at Sammy's laughing eyes.

"What did I say?" she asked.

"You said to follow you home, silly."

Did she say that? Last night. Did she say something out loud? She didn't think so. Janine felt her pulse start to pick up. *Follow me home.* Where had she heard that before?

"I said that last night?" Janine asked. "Right here?"

"You were outside again," Sammy said. "Out on the lawn, like always."

Janine suddenly felt weighed down, sinking.

There is no ghost. There is just a ghost story!

"You heard me on the lawn, last night?"

"Are you okay, Aunt Jaja?" Sammy asked.

Heed the dictum.

Janine's eyes shot around the room. The back porch door was cracked open and cool damp air trickled in. Janine stood up too quickly. She was instantly dizzy and put a hand out to catch herself. Sammy giggled at her.

"Jack?" Janine called.

She pushed the door open a bit and looked out into the backyard. "Jack?"

She turned to Sammy. "Where's Jack. Did he go outside?" She called into the house, "Jack!"

She looked back at Sammy.

"I don't know," Sammy said.

Janine flung the back door wide and ran outside. "Jack!" *Where was Jack?* Janine turned to Sammy. "Stay inside. Go upstairs and wake your mom and dad. Tell them Jack's missing. Can you do that, Sammy?"

Sammy nodded.

One each for redemption.

"Now go. Go! Tell them. I'm going to the river."

Sammy disappeared into the house.

She can be the last one.

She or he? Janine started running toward the mound and the river. She never, ever thought it could be Jack. Not Jack!

The grass felt cold and damp on the manicured lawn. She reached the edge of the cut lawn, her old boundary line, and crossed over into the rough where smooth grass became prickly weeds. Then she was atop the mound and looking at the river. The water sparkled in the light of a beautiful morning. The shoreline appeared deserted. She kept moving, head swiveling right, then left.

"Jack! Jack!"

Janine could see tire marks on the pebbly beach where someone drove up to the water's edge. She ran to the water and searched all around. Nothing. She ran toward the large boulders at the bend in the river. It was impossible to see under the rippling water.

"Jack! Jack!"

She looked up and down stream. No one, nothing. She waded into the water, knee deep. The freezing snow melt assaulted her legs. Her toes curled in protest. She hesitated and strained to see into the water. Something was down there. Something colorful moved under the water near the rock. Something flowed with the current. *Oh my god, Oh my god, Oh my god,* she thought, *Jack.*

Janine waded further. As she neared the large boulder, the current flowed against her, pushing her around. Her hand passed over a flattened section of rock and she immediately thought of Mary Millers' headstone. The river fought hard to kick the feet out from under her, but she took sure steps, she kept a flat palm on the rock for support. The water was up to her chest and she began to shiver from cold and fright. The sun was not yet high enough to cast any direct light on the river bend. She reached out to grab the flowing object. She had to completely submerge to reach it. She pulled and pulled and got it loose.

Juliana was yelling behind her. Janine slowly backed out of the river. She turned her head and saw Juliana running down the mound toward the shoreline. Cold wet hair hindered her tunnel vision. Juliana, wrapped in a housecoat, looked just out of bed and furious.

"What in the world are you doing!" Juliana yelled. Janine only waded back to waist deep. She thought she might go for another look. "Janine, get out of there!" Juliana demanded.

"Jack's missing," Janine shouted through chattering teeth. "Jack's missing. What if he's in the river!"

"Jack is not missing," Juliana fumed. "Get out of there right now!"

"Jack could be in the water! The door was open and he could be out here!"

"Jack is not in the water! Jack is fine!" Juliana confirmed again.

Janine moved toward shore. She was freezing wet and confused. She shivered. Scowling, Juliana removed her robe and covered Janine with it. Scowling, Juliana took the soaking wet cloth Janine recovered and held it up. A blue-and-orange head scarf. Not Jack's.

"Jack is with Adam. They went out to get us donuts and bagels for breakfast," Juliana calmly told her. "They're at Raley's right now. I just spoke to Adam *and Jack* a moment ago on the phone."

Jack was all right and Janine was all wet. Juliana no longer scowled, but her eyes screamed *complete moron*. Poor Juliana, always dealing with her crazy sister.

They walked back to the house silently. Janine felt a little guilty for using her sister's robe on that crisp morning, but it was too late to give it back now, the robe was soaked through.

Gram stood at the kitchen door with a large beach towel. She seemed in an awful mood with Juliana. Both ladies glowered at each other. Juliana silently implied that Gram should accept some blame for Janine jumping into the river that morning. Janine just wanted to disappear into a warm bath before Jack and Adam returned. She was too embarrassed to face her brother-in-law just yet. She truly believed the river ghost had gotten young Jack.

Though she was sopping wet, Juliana hugged her and said not to worry about it. Ashley hugged her and said she was her hero. Gram hugged her and said everything would be all right. Sammy hugged her and giggled at her silliness.

Then, Janine slunk upstairs to draw a warm bath and hide. Gram disappeared into Misty's room to complain about her granddaughters. Juliana and Ashley strolled to the front room to organize the luggage. Ashley pumped her mother for information regarding her aunt and the dreamy Doctor McNally. What did she find out about their wild adventure in San Francisco?

Nobody noticed when Sammy slipped out into the backyard. Nobody saw her go to the edge of Gram's cut lawn, talking to the air like children do. Nobody observed Sammy run up and over the mound, giggling to no one in particular. Nobody watched her pick up the blue-and-orange head scarf and swing it into the air. Nobody witnessed her drag it into the water, going deeper and deeper and deeper. And nobody ever saw Sammy again, alive or dead.

Most of the town helped search the river and trails around Gram's house. People stayed out all day and night looking for Sammy. The police brought in dogs who scented Sammy's clothes and led them right to the river edge, barking. Lots of voices began to whisper about the River Girl

Ghost. Most locals agreed that the small girl probably went into the river and got washed away. Someone saw a man at the river that morning and thought he might know something. Downstream in Sacramento, they dredged areas of stagnant water and found nothing. All the usual catches for miles down the river were searched to no avail.

Janine kept reviewing that first afternoon on the river shore. Henry Webber stood inside the police tape with his dog on a leash. He pointed to some discarded slippers with an angry frown. Why had he walked his dog so far from home? Why had he assumed those slippers meant a small child had drowned? Was he the man someone had mentioned? Why did he purposely avoid turning in her direction.

She suddenly recalled when Henry stood there before and her heart pounded manically. She noticed who he kept glancing at in the small crowd at the river, Caroline Govant. The white-haired old woman watched the action with an expressionless face. Her head swiveled around as she listened to murmurs in the crowd. At one point, Caroline faced Janine and stared right into her eyes. Caroline mouthed something, something that looked like, *heed the dictum.* Janine rushed down the pebbly shore but was stopped by one of the policemen just prior to reaching Henry Webber.

"What did you do!" she screamed at him. "Did you tell her to go into the river!"

Henry Webber turned away and someone dragged Janine off. A tight-lipped frown twisted Henry's face as his eyes refused to meet hers. The police ordered Janine to stay away from Henry Webber.

When Ian called, she finally revealed the theory formed in the back of her mind. They needed to include it in the documentary so that no one would get away with anything. It made more sense than a ghost, didn't it? *A secret cult simmering in Rio Linda, a cult of people who believed in the dictum.*

"It isn't a ghost luring kids, but a human cult of the ghost!" Janine insisted into the phone. "We cannot let them get away with this, Ian. We need to flush them out and expose them if no one else will. The police think it's crazy talk, so we need to include it in the documentary. It all makes sense now. Henry Webber and Caroline Govant and who knows who else!"

There was a very long pause before Ian spoke. His voice was calm and soft.

"Janine, be careful. You're really emotional right now, and, and you're reaching wild conclusions in an attempt to come to grips with what happened."

Oh no, no. He did not just say that. She went completely cold. Her vision began to tunnel as his soft, rational voice, continued,

"It's not uncommon to become hysterical or even irrational as your mind tries to cope with something like this. This is your grief working on you, misplacing blame. We can't blame innocent people of…"

All the soft rational voices came flooding back.

"…*enhanced by pregnancy hormones, combined to cause her hysteria. Plainly, her mind altered the images to cope with what happened to her. She spent a week acting normal, before she became irrational with these wild conclusions and falsely accused an innocent man. Why didn't she speak up sooner? Her mind is misplacing the blame because of their argument, spurred on by a surprise pregnancy…*"

Rick and his legal team nearly convinced everyone with those words, even herself.

She let the phone drop from her hands.

A dark omen.

Janine could barely breath. Her gut tightened into a tense knot. She was dizzy. She would never be able to look at Ian McNally again. She felt so incredibly stupid.

Castle Ewen is the Tower.

Epilogue

The Riches Janine

The boulders in the river turned out to be mostly made of quartz, feldspar, hematite, and magnetite. Yet, they contained a significant mix of neodymium and the rare earth metals europium, terbium, and dysprosium. The cost of removing the boulders was less than one percent of their net worth on the world market. The town of Rio Linda and all the local citizens would share the wealth of the boulders. Under the mound between Gram's house and the river, another pocket of the same mineral mix lay buried. The rare earth elements alone were estimated to be worth millions.

The extraction of the boulders removed the dangerous catch that trapped so many victims in the past. The river flattened out and grew wide, slowing the rip current in the center of the stream. The predicted flooding of Marysville Boulevard never happened. Instead, the river bend became a popular cooling-off spot in the summer and an unlikely place for a water emergency. Tourism boomed in Rio Linda, sparked by the film documentary on ghosts. People flocked to the pebbly shore to get a glimpse of the river ghost and the orchard ghost. Séances became regular events in Caroline Miller's orchard. A popular walking tour visited the river, the orchard, the grave site of Mary Miller, and a couple of the streets named for drowning victims. Plans for a museum to highlight the history of wagon trains were discussed at a city council meeting.

Janine sat stiffly in the back of a stretch limousine with Kiki, the doctor, Steve, Ted, and Carlos. She sat right across from Ian but was still unable to completely meet his eye or even to speak to him. She felt furious, ashamed, and sad at the same time. *Doctor Crisper had been right after all.* The car picked them up at the Ritz-Carlton and they followed a long line of limos to the theatre in Los Angeles. Although the February clouds were holding their water, the air felt quite cool outside and anything could happen. Unfair that the guys were fully clothed in tuxedos and protective footwear. The girls wore glamourous heels and fancy dresses designed to expose as many of their scars as possible. Don't worry about it, Kiki told her. A million eyes could stare directly at you and never guess what is in your head, or your heart. This time Kiki wore the light-blue angel color and Janine wore the dark-red devil.

Their documentary proved to be a huge financial success, grossing in the twenty-million-plus category even before the end of the rushed initial run. By the second weekend, the film topped the box office in cities across the country. It grossed even more in theaters in Asia and the European market. People love a good ghost story. The Rio Linda Ghost film earned a nomination for best documentary feature film. Steve laughed about the sheer success of a film thrown together in a single room studio and in the back of a van on a shoestring budget. His main goal from film school had been met. He became a hero in his personal circle and favored to win the Academy Award. He wore a superhero T-shirt under his tuxedo coat and grinned constantly.

The rest of crew, as on-screen stars of the film, experienced an entirely different form of attention. Photo shoots and talk show offers came their way. Their images mysteriously popped up in magazines. The WB considered picking up the rights to the *Spectral Analysis* TV show with a rumor that the production might be moved to a giant new facility in Arizona and flooded with money. A new managing producer would fill in as Steve stepped away. Max Colliers with the black glasses wanted to step in.

Those old people back in Rio Linda always knew the elements of the dictum, she realized. Poor Gram never wanted to accept it or admit it. Gram's denial led to her animosity with Caroline Govant all those years ago. There were still lots of unanswered questions but nobody was talking. Janine felt completely cold about all of it and about everyone. It was karma, she realized. She did not deserve a second chance with anything.

Once again, Kiki suggested the mantra, *I am a badass*, to get across the red carpet. But Janine no longer needed that mantra. For the past months, she went through the motions expected of her under a bright spotlight instead of hiding in the shadows and she realized that it worked just the same. Kiki was right, no one could guess what was in her heart or in her head. Only an intimate few knew how she really felt about their success. It had been in the tea leaves…

The return was not worth the investment.

End of Part One

Part Two

Spectral Voices

Speaking To Spirits

Star Tarot SV
Story Arc
the problem 1
past influence 4
Future 6
XII
The Hanged Man
Ian McNally is the Hanged Man
II
The High Priestess
V
The Hierophant
VI
the outcome 7
The Lovers
XIX
The Sun
XV
The Devil
pos+ influence 2
XI
Strength
neg-Influence 3
present 5

Prologue *Randy*

n excess of stars, and an engorged yellow moon, shimmered behind a veil of wispy clouds, making a spectacular night sky for the city. It was the perfect night for possibilities. It took Randy twenty-five minutes to drive from the university to the edge of Thatcher Woods. That included his quick stop into CVS for a six pack of Icehouse Ale. He parked his Chevy Malibu under the soft glow of a streetlamp along the road edging the south side of the meadow. He fingered the written instructions Melissa had scratched on the back of a torn envelope.

If you really want to see me on Friday the thirteenth, Melissa had eyed him coyly, *meet me here at midnight.* Soft giggles escaped her lips, then, she gathered her books and walked away in a protected clump of girlfriends.

He totally wanted to see her. He'd dropped hundreds of hints during Ancient Native American History study group about getting together after midterms. He thought she never noticed. Then, she slipped that note atop his book and fluttered her mascara thick eyelashes at him. His heart pounded as he wondered if she could be the one. He read the note again.

Go down the Blue Prim trail and cut straight north toward the pond. There will be a dim light marking our spot. Come with an open mind.

Thatcher Glen Pond was really a bog. This early in the season the ground felt soft and mushy from deep layers of waterlogged soil. Luckily, the cool air kept the insects away. The entire River Forest area probably flooded due to a meandering river, hence the name River Forest, Randy guessed.

Randy climbed out of his vintage Chevy with the package of cheap beer under an arm. He guessed the girls planned an after-party to celebrate their first milestone in Ancient Native American History. Everyone warned them that the midterm would consist of a kazillion questions about absolutely nothing mentioned in class, and the warnings had mostly been right. He fished a blanket and flashlight from the trunk, they might come in handy, then turned toward the woods, picked out a landmark directly north and started walking.

Large oak trees peppered the area and the air suddenly became very cold away from the street. He could smell the acrid earth wafting through the weeds. He kept a towering tree front and center, and marched on. The elevation dipped to the right, and he surmised that it led to the pond. Soon enough, he spotted a twinkling light through the brush, a beacon guiding him in. As he drew closer, a soft rumble of voices carried through the cold air. That husky voice definitely belonged to Melissa. He smiled.

"You found us!" Melissa sprang to a stand, her eyes dropped to his blanket and bag.

"I brought beer," he said.

Her friend laughed while Melissa's eyes remained fixed on his. She smiled at him.

"Hush, Trish." Melissa gave her friend a little push with her foot. "I wasn't sure you'd really come."

Randy tossed the blanket to the ground and reached into his bag to pull out bottles of Icehouse Ale to offer. Melissa accepted a beer and stepped back, waving a hand at the third chair.

"I brought an extra chair for you," she said, "And Trish made brownies."

Randy crossed into their circle and offered a beer to Trish before dropping into the extra-fold out camp chair. *She brought him a chair!* He noticed the open bottle of wine between their seats and the brown grocery bag with a baguette sticking out. He helped Trish unscrew the tight top of her beer bottle before taking a sip of his own cool ale. They sat quietly for a moment and Randy glanced between the girls. He noticed Melissa giving him a shy survey as her plump lips bowed sweetly. He returned the smile feeling more and more confident. Trish leaned back, head tilted up, perusing the sky.

"That was a brutal test," Randy said to break the silence.

"Uh, no. No test out here," Trish blurted, "No school talk out here, not tonight."

"What are we doing out here?" Randy asked.

"There's a ghost—" Melissa started, but Trish quickly interrupted.

All term, Trish had interrupted consistently during their study group, one of the reasons Randy always sat far, far, away and never remembered her name. She never said anything about Native American History, but what she did say was always more important than what anyone else had to say, or so Trish seemed to think. Very different than considerate, careful Melissa. He wondered how such opposite girls became so connected in friendship.

"We heard it from one of the girls on our floor," Trish prattled on. "A ghost that only comes out on the full moon. An angry woman searching for something near Thatcher Pond wearing a U of C sweatshirt, that's why we wore the colors." Both girls wore school spirit shirts and threw their arms up in a cheer. "Everyone insisted we'd see a ghost out here on the full moon, and it's Friday the thirteenth, the perfect night for a ghost. She's is supposed to be so scary nobody dared come back."

"You two are roomies?" Randy asked.

Melissa and Trish both nodded. That explained it.

Sometime after they killed three bottles of cheap ale and one bottle of wine, Randy found himself stretched out on the blanket between Trish and Melissa gazing at the stars. Insects, frogs, and Trish eked out a steady stream of quiet noise. Randy now smiled openly at Melissa and she seemed to get over her shyness to return his undivided attention. With Trish chatting softly in the background, Randy sent Melissa silent messages. He stretched out his fingers until they touched hers and she didn't move her hand away. After a short pause, his fingers enclosed hers and he felt her gently return his clutch. They were definitely speaking the same language.

"What is that?" Trish abruptly sat up and her hand flew to her head. "Ooh. Blood rush."

Randy attempted to ignore Trish and concentrate on the silent messages between him and Melissa.

"I see something out there, look! What is that?" Trish's voice became high and sharp.

That sharp voice broke the spell and killed the mood. Melissa shifted to a sitting position, taking her hand far away. Randy moved quickly, also wriggling to a sitting position. He glanced in the direction Trish indicated.

"Oh yes, I can see her," Melissa said. "It's a person."

A very long way off, toward the pond, a person stood still as a statue. Or, perhaps, it was a tree. No, it was a person standing about a football field away. She stood bent at the waist, hand on a hip, hair hanging limp. Randy stretched his neck up to get a better look.

"She isn't moving," Melissa whispered.

The moment the words left her mouth, the person moved so startlingly fast that Randy felt his heart lurch, then plummet. Dread filled the place his heart had been. She had moved way too fast to be real, first one hundred yards away and then in the blink of an eye only fifty yards between them. Every muscle in his body tensed as he rose to his feet with the girls.

"Shit!" Trish snapped. "Did I miss something? Did she move?"

Melissa's breathing slowly warped into panting gasps. Her fear was contagious. He felt her inch closer to him, full of tense energy, while the person, a woman who now stood fifty yards away, slowly turned to face them. Had she really moved superfast a moment ago? He must have consumed more alcohol than he thought, or more likely, Trish spiked those brownies with something.

"She's trying to say something. I think she sees us," Trish's slurred voice broke the silence. "Hello there!" Trish waved. "Are you here to see the ghost?" Trish turned toward Randy and Melissa, "I think it's that one girl from our floor, the one down the hall. I didn't think she wanted to come. Do you recognize her?" Her voice had a pleading quality in the question.

They turned back toward the girl. She stood absolutely still, but startlingly closer again, maybe twenty-five yards away. Melissa took a small step backward, poised to spring away. The mystery woman wore a college sweatshirt with an old University of Chicago logo across the chest. Her long dark hair hung in perfect straight strands on either side of her narrow face, and her large eyes gazed at them, expressionless and dark.

Was she the ghost? Ridiculous!

At that moment, the woman seemed to register him and her eyes bore right into Randy's.

He turned his head slightly toward Trish, but snapped it back in the next moment. In the blink of an eye, the woman stood directly in front of him, and Melissa was gone. The pitter patter of her footsteps quickly dimmed as she receded into the brush behind him. Trish became unusually quiet and Randy felt frozen. He could not move. Petrified with fear, he stared into two dark pools of emotionless abyss. He barely felt capable of drawing in air and heard himself gasping. White skin stretched the surface of the woman's face and her thin lips moved ever so slightly. She leaned toward him, like she hoped to kiss him.

"Find it," she hissed.

Randy regained control of his muscles and ran. He stumbled into the same brush Melissa disappeared into and heard Trish screaming behind him, but he didn't care. He only cared about getting away. He ran haphazardly through the oak trees in a sprint, stopped when he realized he left the key to his car back on the blanket and he wanted to cry. It was on a simple little ring with only the one key. If anyone moved that blanket it would be lost in the grass for sure.

He cursed and kept running until he reached the road. He could see light in the far distance and moved toward it. His mind flashed briefly on Melissa and Trish, but he dismissed them quickly because he could only think of one thing: keep moving away from that woman.

Chapter 1

Season Three Begins *Kiki*

Spectral Analysis completed season two of their television program near the top of the ratings list. After an academy award for their feature length documentary on ghosts in a rural town, their popularity skyrocketed. The small group of paranormal investigators became tabloid favorites and household names. Hundreds of fan letters flooded their inboxes. People urged them to investigate ghosts in different corners of the country, but tired of traveling, and reeling from the effects of their success, they chose a ghost story near their own back yard to kick off the third season. Now, the night before cameras rolled for the season three opener, the *Spectral Analysis* crew found themselves in the city center of San Antonio along the famous river walk.

The new producer, Max Colliers, insisted on a new tradition; start each shoot with a casual dinner party on location, with the entire staff, for bonding purposes. *A good idea*, Kiki agreed, due to the changing aspects of the show, and the extra crew. They hired a replacement cameraman and master control panel operator, along with their replacement executive producer. Plus, behind the scenes helpers, gofers, hair dressers, and production assistants were all part of the team now. Everyone met briefly in Austin, but they hadn't gotten a chance to bond as a group until the dinner.

Kiki Mellow, the spiritual medium and a star of the show, wore a floral head scarf and overlarge vintage black sunglasses like a 1950s movie star. The dark lenses allowed her to covertly glance around. Carlos Fuentes, one of the tech specialists, brought his wife Maria. Apparently, his family hailed from San Antonio and their kids were tucked away with grandparents in town. Kiki met Maria several times and was always startled by her dark beauty and intense aura. Carlos doted on his wife, and Kiki couldn't help being amused at how the wise-cracking Carlos kept seeking spousal approval any time Maria turned her head.

She worried about her cousin, Paranormal Physics Professor Doctor Ian McNally. He shifted uncomfortably in his chair and hunched down with a Longhorns baseball cap pulled snuggly over his head. A thick, curly, three month old beard covered his lower face. After the last season, he grew the dark beard in an attempt to hide from a very public image. He assured them the beard would disappear before the taping at the Alamo. His attempts at hiding seemed fairly successful, as, no one recognized him outside of their small group. Ian had begun the evening quite chipper, but grew progressively low spirited as it became clear that Janine Stinger, the missing link, was not going to show up and "bond" with them.

The new executive producer called most of the preseason shots, and that came with pros and cons. For instance, they were booked into a very nice hotel and had a very swanky new office set up in Austin. He hired lots of extra help, but demanded the final word on film sites, story development, and their on screen images. Max focused on the money making aspect of the show more than the old producer. He pushed his fancy glasses up and plopped into the chair next to Ian. He arrived fashionably late and hadn't eaten dinner with them. He immediately sent several of the extra staff back to the hotel to prepare the newly reserved boardroom for the next day. The extra helpers were very excited to get started and went away happily. Only the primary investigative players, and Maria, lingered in the restaurant.

"Did everybody mingle well?" Max asked, and they all nodded happily.

Max hired the replacement cameraman and control board operator by outbidding other programs. The new cameraman, Don, came with years of experience behind a studio camera and Max "stole" him out from under one of the big stations in Austin. Don was a little older than the rest of the crew, perhaps in his mid-thirties by the look of him. By contrast, the control board operator, Ben, appeared to be a kid. He wore a Star Wars T-shirt with jeans and sneakers and was bright-eyed and bushy-tailed. He kept glancing toward Kiki from the corner of his eye and she pretended not to notice. He seemed curious and harmless. She remembered someone mention that Ben had just turned nineteen years old and already had a degree in computer science. He received numerous job offers out of college, but his big dream was to hunt ghosts with *Spectral Analysis*.

"I can't believe Ted ditched us," Carlos griped, then glanced at Don. "Of course, we're happy to have you Donny, it's just so unexpected to lose Ted too."

Max laughed, "Oh, come on, Ted wasn't going to leave Steve. They've been a team for a long time." Max grinned at him.

"I'm a little concerned," Carlos continued. "Has Janine contacted anyone? It's getting very close to show time and I wonder if she's checked in with anyone? I'm pretty excited to see her and hoped she would be here tonight."

Janine Stinger had been the missing piece of their puzzle for months. Toward the end of the last season, after the award winning documentary, she took an emergency leave of absence. A family tragedy hit. She touched base a couple times but had been impossible to reach since the night they won the academy award. Kiki glanced at Ian and watched him lapse into a deeper grey as he recharged his glass with the margarita from the pitcher. Janine skipping out of this get-together would surely rile all his sensitive spots. He'd take her absence as a personal avoidance of him due to her continuing hard feelings. He obviously felt the sting of rejection all over again.

"We've been in constant contact with her," Max assured them. "It's no secret that she wants out of her contract, but she will definitely show on time for the taping tomorrow night. She owes us several episodes before she can walk, and I made sure she can't walk early. To alleviate your immediate concerns, I did get confirmation that she checked into the hotel yesterday." His sparkling brown eyes fell on Kiki, and he paused. He loosened his tie a bit. "Have you spoken with Janine, Kiki? Do you know why she skipped this get-together? Maybe we should have stressed that it was mandatory."

"No." Kiki didn't move her head, but watched Ian to see his reaction. The idiot perked up. He appeared very drunk and not slowing down a bit on the booze. Kiki noticed several shot glasses between Carlos and Ian, most belonged to Ian. Maria seemed to have a modifying effect on Carlos and his consumption of alcohol. Hearing that Janine actually made it into town perked everyone up. For the past week, each of them harbored real concern that they'd be short one person for the season premiere taping, and no one wanted to start the season short one player.

"We finally get to meet Janine Stinger!" Ben grinned.

"Got a little crush on her?" Carlos laughed. "Get in line. After the feature, her fan mail skyrocketed."

"Did she drop out of last season because she got scared of the ghosts?" Ben asked.

Carlos shook his head. That was a common question. Carlos recapped the tale of the Biltmore Hotel, their first successful spectral connection, and Maria took the opportunity to move closer to Kiki. Both women noticed the waiter deliver more shots of tequila to the table. *Poison*, Kiki thought. Unbelievable that Ian continued drinking that vile liquid. As a nice Scottish lad, he usually stuck to single malt whisky or dark ale beer. Maria rolled her eyes at the shots.

"Kiki." Maria took her hands. Maria was a very tactile woman and beautifully dramatic. She projected a bright, bluish, happy aura. Not unusual for a woman with beautiful babies to love. "My niece Isabella is planning to visit soon. She is coming to stay with us in Austin for a visit. She is young, but not so young. My sister's husband says that she is different."

Kiki could guess where this was going, many young girls wanted to meet Kiki Mellow. As a famous spiritual medium and self-proclaimed witch, Kiki's considerable following of fans included people interested in the pagan arts. Most of her fan mail came from girls wanting to know more about the occult and ancient teachings. Most were bored, imaginative youths, but mixed into the letters were some gifted vessels, girls floating through life without a proper spiritual teacher. *Wasted talent*, Kiki thought. She already pondered her own transition from the ghost chasing TV show. *When I finally birth a baby girl,* she mused, *I'll focus on mentoring*. Kiki knew her time for reproduction was on the horizon and it excited her to imagine mothering her own daughter, her *Next* as the women in the coven called a first born.

"She's gifted," Maria hesitated, "and has asked if it would be an imposition to meet you sometime."

"Of course," Kiki said, "I would love to meet her."

The growing volume of the men interrupted their conversation. Rowdy laugher drew their attention. Apparently, the new cameraman had said something lewd. Young Ben appeared bright pink in the face and Ian wore a smirk, but Carlos appeared a tad upset. Kiki felt that something may have been said about their missing colleague, Janine, and Ian relished the snide remark as a patch on his damaged ego.

"Oh, come on, Carlos," Max Colliers shifted to the edge of his chair, closer to Ian. He seemed very interested in what Ian would say.

Since when did those two get on, Kiki wondered. Ian could barely stand Max Colliers and knew very well about Max and his inappropriate bad boy behavior. Max had quite the reputation.

"I'm sure you noticed the intriguing marks on her body," Max said. "On her chest even. She has an X carved over her heart, I've seen it. What does it mean? Does anyone know why it's there? I'm told it's body art. A symbol that means her heart is off limits. Like she's only interested in other things. I couldn't take my eyes off the…"

"Hey now." Carlos stood a little wobbly out of his chair. He glanced over at Kiki and Maria and seemed a bit startled that the women were actually listening in. He got his footing straightened out and turned to the other men. "Let's be respectful now, my wife is sitting right over there, and Kiki too. They don't want to hear this type of talk."

Max waved his hand as if to say they were all grown-ups.

Don grinned at Max. "Are you saying she's a wildcat then?"

"Guys." Carlos implored.

Max ignored Carlos and pointed to Ian. "He's the one to ask. Snatched her right out from under my nose, didn't you, McNally?" He chuckled. "Come on, what's the verdict? Don't hold back now, at that party, she was very hot and ready for something, I could smell it on her. I have a feeling her quiet exterior is camouflaging a dangerous, adventurous woman, if you know what I mean."

Kiki watched Ian open his mouth and knew he was about to say something incredibly stupid in his drunken, upset state. No one else could possibly guess what was going on in his head, and he would never admit it, but he fell for Janine Stinger like a ton of bricks and jumped in way too fast at her slightest encouragement. Janine proved to be a complicated girl for an idiot like Ian. She was dark, broken, and confused. Too many skeletons stumbled out of her closet, and thick headed Ian wasn't prepared to handle them. Kiki had warned him, but he didn't listen.

"Aye indeed, she's very sexy, and hiding quite a passionate side," Ian slurred to Don and Max, "She can seem very unassuming and uninterested, but, *wildcat* is an accurate description when you get her behind a closed door and…"

Smack! With a closed fist, Carlos flat out punched Ian in the eye and Ian nearly fell over in his chair. Of the scant people left in the restaurant, everyone turned to watch. She witnessed Ian get socked more than once and was afraid of what would happen. Those times were long gone, but he seemed to be in state of regression lately. Kiki watched Ian tense up and fought the urge to run over and placate him.

"Respect!" Carlos said sternly and pounded the table with his punching fist. He glowered at Max, who flinched with a respectable fear behind his glasses. Don scooted back and Ben appeared terrified of Carlos. Carlos shook out the hand he used to punch Ian, stretching his fingers. His voice became very calm and his typical joking tone came back. "Respect to the ladies please. I don't want my wife thinking this is common talk. She'll never let me go on site again. Ian, my brother, your stiff eye has made mush of my poor hand."

Ian managed to stand up and Kiki could see by his posture that he was not going to punch Carlos back. She let out a sigh of relief. Ian slumped over to hug Carlos quite heavily.

"I'm so, so sorry Carlos," Ian slurred. "Can you forgive me about your hand?" He pulled back from the hug, holding his own hand over his right eye. His good eye searched out Kiki and Maria. "I'm an arse. A bloody, idiot arse. Please forgive my mouth." Ian pointed at Max with his free hand. "And you're an arse too, a true bloody arse. And you too." He pointed at Don, then Ian looked at Ben. "And you, don't be an bloody arse. Don't be like us."

At that point, Ian and Carlos began laughing at each other and Max joined a little hesitantly, adjusting his glasses, but Don and Ben sat stiffly, unsure of what to do. Clearly, Ian and Carlos were still a little shell shocked from how things ended the past season. Only the three of them knew how tough it was to film the final episodes of season two after what happened in California.

"I'm going to get those fools some ice." Maria slipped around her. Kiki could see the boyish grin Carlos shot at his wife in response to her very stern eye. Soon, Maria returned with bags of ice for each of them and then fussed over Carlos and his hand. When Ian's good eye found Kiki, all she could do was shake her head at him, the poor bugger.

Max Colliers reserved the hotel boardroom as the *Spectral Analysis* prep area. He was throwing a pot of money on their little television enterprise, so they'd no longer be squeezed into small rooms in affordable roadside inns. Only a very fancy and elegant hotel along the San Antonio river walk proved suitable for the new executive producer. Not only did Max hire an award winning cameraman and a brainy control board operator, he added two image coordinators, a make-up artist and a hair stylist to prep them for the camera, just like a real TV show. Kiki looked forward to that positive change.

Kiki snuck into the board room well before the scheduled shoot and felt the buzz of excitement. Along with makeup and hair chairs in the corner, a short garment rack of zipped up items was propped in the opposite corner. Max Colliers must have hired a costume designer without consulting any of them. Kiki knew Max pretty well and expected the garments in those bags were likely on the suggestive side. Racy items that Kiki wouldn't mind, but the conservative crew might. Out from behind the rack, a tall athletic woman with long auburn hair stepped back as she unzipped one of the bags. She glowed with a nice tan, which made her light brown eyes appear golden. Janine noticed Kiki right away and instantly brightened as Kiki strolled over.

One glance told Kiki everything she needed to know. Janine had made it through the doldrums, not smooth sailing yet, but gliding slowly forward at least. She seemed heathy and strong, and her dark aura was not so thick it was frightening. When Kiki hugged Janine, she held on long enough to allowed Janine's residual grief to touch her. Kiki let out a sigh of relief that Janine had actually showed up.

Carlos jumped in on their reunion and the three of them huddled with their energies mixing for several minutes, then they turned to the garment rack and the bag Janine had unzipped. Her name was written on a card in the name placard. It appeared to be a full body suit in deep purple with flashes of bright colors as useless pockets on the sleeves, legs, and chest. It was made of a very thin stretchy material and cut with a low V-neckline. *Certainly not something Janine would choose*, Kiki thought.

"What is that?" Carlos asked. "Are you filming an episode of Star Trek, or are you ghost hunting with us?"

They all laughed as Janine zipped the bag back up. Carlos flipped through the rack.

"Whoa, look. There's a *Star Trek* suit for me too." Carlos opened the bag wide. The male version zipped all the way up to a crew neck but appeared just as form fitting. Carlos could barely contain his amusement. "I'm not shy about showing off my guns, but I'm afraid this material will reveal too much of the family jewels. I don't want to offend anyone with my overabundant gems, Maria would kill me." They laughed again, and it felt like they were right back where they left off many months ago.

"At least the new producer doesn't sexually discriminate in his exploitation," Janine said. "Is he's requesting we wear these suits or demanding it?"

Carlos pointed out three bags with Kiki's name on them. "Hey look, Kiki. Colliers has three outfits for you. Should we take a look at them? Should be interesting."

Kiki shook her head, the nerve of Max Colliers. Did he really imagine he could dress her up without discussion? More and more she felt like strangling the old producer for leaving them in a compromised position with Max. He proved over bearing and over controlling, sticking his foot into every aspect of the production without even considering the original vision of the show. Kiki and Ian McNally dreamt up *Spectral Analysis* for the sole purpose of investigating and revealing authentic paranormal activity. Max seemed to think the show was just spoofy fluff entertainment.

A mood change overcame the group and Kiki turned to see Ian standing near the main door staring at them. Clean shaven again, Ian managed to appeared chipper while chatting with the new guy, Ben. When he turned sideways, they got a good glimpse of his eye. *Ouch*, he would be bruised for weeks. A deep purple patch had developed over his right eye and a portion of his cheek. His eyelids began to flutter as he moved toward their small group. Ben followed closely behind him.

Kiki's cousin had once been a nervous kid. Extremely shy as a youth, Ian struggled through a stutter in his earlier years. Unlike the stutter, he was never able to completely get over his signature blinking, Ian's tell-tale sign of nervousness. Other than that little tic, he appeared calm and cool, ever the suave Doctor Ian McNally, paranormal investigative researcher and author.

"Look at this." He joined them and stiffly patted Janine's arm. "She's back. Ben, this is Janine Stinger. Janine, Ben is going to man the console. He's a wiz with computers."

A distinct dent lightened the dark aura surrounding Janine, but the tension in the air grew thick enough to cut with a knife. Ian and Janine avoided looking directly at one another. Ian was the easiest person in the world to read with those colorful expectant streams radiating from his head, so why did Janine have such a hard time seeing how happy he was to see her?

What appeared quite clear to Kiki was obviously a cryptic puzzle to the two of them.

Janine noticed Ian's shiner and her expression turned tender. "Are you okay? That looks pretty painful. What happened?"

"Oh, you know, rugby and all." Ian glanced quickly at Carlos. "It's nothing, just a wee bruise, I hardly notice it. You look very well. Very nice. It's nice to see you looking so… so fit."

As always, Mr. Smooth. Kiki wondered how her bumbling cousin managed to attract so many girls. As if on cue, one of the beauticians, Lauren, crashed the group. Lauren bounced with excitement and everyone paused to consider her. She turned a tad red at the sudden undivided attention.

"Hello, Ian, I mean, Doctor McNally," she giggled. "Hello, Miss Mellow."

Oh dear God, Kiki thought, *he went and did it again*. Ian had a habit of befriending women and more times than she could remember, they always came off with the wrong idea. Many times, Ian became so guilt ridden for leading them on, he actually dated them. This little exchange would not help him close any divides with Janine.

"I'm Lauren." Her blonde head nodded all around and she beamed at Janine. "You're Janine Stinger, right? We're supposed to prep you and Miss Mellow for the show. I'm supposed to do your hair."

"I usually just pull it up into a ponytail," Janine told her. "It takes, like, two seconds."

"Oh no, Mr. Colliers asked for a set style on you. He instructed me to create a cascade of flowing ringlets. He hoped your hair was still long, it's very lovely. Miss Mellow, he said you would let us know what you wanted. I'm not supposed to let either of you out of here without some prepping."

There was an awkward silence.

Lauren's nervousness began to escalate and Kiki wondered if Janine could read the poor girl. Clearly, Lauren feared muffing up her first real workday on the show. Max had given her distinct instructions and Lauren definitely wanted to please the boss. Pushy Max, first the new outfit and now the girly hair. What would Janine do? Would she walk off and leave Lauren standing there, or would she play nice? Would she follow Max Collier's clear instructions or thumb her nose at him? Kiki wasn't sure what to expect. Janine's reactions had never been easy to predict.

"Sure, no problem," Janine said softly to Lauren. "But, please, call me Janine."

Lauren became visibly relieved as Janine followed her to the hair chair where Guy, the makeup artist, stood smiling at Kiki. He waited patiently for her to come to him. Kiki wondered if Janine might wear that new outfit. *Not a chance*, she thought as she followed Janine toward Guy and Lauren. Carlos called after them as they walked away,

"What about my hair? Doesn't anyone think my hair needs a curl?"

As they rotated through the makeup and hair chairs, Kiki briefed Carlos and Janine on the plan. During the past week, she interviewed several people who claimed to have spectral encounters in the Alamo complex. While she tracked down the stories, Ian scouted the entire five acres of Alamo grounds for hot spots with his EMF box. He found unusual energy inside the chapel, along the soldier's barracks, and near the wall between the Alamo and the Menger Hotel. Those locations were also cited by Kiki's witnesses.

Max managed to have the large planters blocking the plaza relocated, so they could park the van along the walkway in front of the chapel. He also reserved the entire Alamo for a single night of exclusive filming. Nobody would be in the complex except the *Spectral Analysis* crew.

Ben and Ian had gone ahead to meet Max and Don with the van. Kiki, Janine, and Carlos were delayed by the prep crew and followed half an hour behind in a hired car.

"The Alamo was originally known as the Mission San Antonio de Valero," Kiki informed Carlos and Janine. "It was built it in the early 1700s as part of a religious outreach program to indigenous people, to convert them. I felt a distinct presence in the chapel, the original structure. That presence may be residual energy from the Spanish Franciscan friars who built the church, it had a holy feel. Those friars may also be the six diablos that saved the building from destruction after the battle of the Alamo. It's a famous folk story that one of my interviewees tells very nicely. Then, out near the barracks, I experienced a strong melancholy energy, perhaps from one, or maybe from several spirits, it was hard to determine. I believe it came from someone who fought in that Alamo battle over 100 years ago."

"You think the spirit of James Bowie or Davy Crockett or even Santa Ana himself is wandering around in there?" Carlos asked excitedly, eyes wide open.

"Why would Santa Ana be a ghost at the Alamo, Carlos? He lived through that battle and had a long and successful career." Janine smirked, and Carlos creased his brow and frowned.

"People report three types of spectral energy," Kiki added. "A youthful energy that befriends children, fully formed spectral masses that resemble men dressed in old time clothes near the barracks wall, and ghostly whispers that emanate along the outer wall. I'm told the fully formed spectral masses are often mistaken for real people, and three separate witnesses have sworn to have seen one of them."

It was a short drive from their hotel to the old mission. As the car pulled onto East Crockett bend, Kiki spotted the newly painted *Spectral Analysis* Van on the wide stone-paved walkway. Instead of a simple decal, the entire van was airbrushed with a colorful rainbow. The rear doors were splayed open and they could see young Ben sitting in Steve's old captain's chair. Max stood outside the back door speaking to Ian.

Kiki, Janine, and Carlos jumped out of the car and made their way to the van. Kiki adjusted her overlarge Aztec poncho as they traipsed down the street. Something just snapped when she saw the ridiculous outfits set out for Janine and Carlos and she decided to go fully drab at first sight to freak Max out. She knew he expected her to be in a sexy outfit, but instead, she came covered from head to toe in bulky woven layers. Even Carlos couldn't think of a wisecrack for her oversized poncho. As they drew closer, Kiki delighted in Max's surprised, upset face.

Carlos started laughing when the new cameraman emerged from behind the van. He wore one of the *Star Trek* outfits and, unlike Carlos, Don's physique was not quite cut out for such a tight ensemble. His middle aged pouch was very well pronounced. Ian grinned at their approach, pleased with their costume decisions. The doctor wore a new version of his signature multicolored *Spectral Analysis* tie paired with a very nice form fitting shirt under his standard white lab coat.

"You look so sexy, Don," Carlos teased. "Ready to be beamed up, are you?"

Don visibly fidgeted.

"Didn't you guys find the suits I left for you?" Max stomped over and surveyed them. "Kiki, I left you three choices. What are you supposed to be dressed as?"

"I'm sure I have no idea what you mean." Kiki fluttered her eyes at him.

Max put his phone up to his ear and immediately began talking. He ordered someone, somewhere, to bring the garment bags from the hotel. He stared at Janine and Carlos. They both had donned their traditional gear, purple coveralls with red fishing vests and black work boots. Carlos pulled a pack of gum from an arm pocket and offered Max a stick. Max didn't take it. Their new executive producer did not appear amused at having his plan ignored.

"You're telling me you didn't see those designer new outfits?" he growled at Carlos.

"Oh, we saw them." Carlos chewed his gum. "They were very interesting. Were we supposed to wear them? I thought it was optional."

"Do you get that I am the executive producer here? I'm not sure you get it." Max inhaled slowly, then continued in a calmer voice. "The plan is to start the season with a new look. It's not unusual to tweak costumes for a new season, even the doctor has new ties and better tailored shirts."

"We get it," Janine stepped up. "We know you're in charge, it's my fault. I just didn't think I could get the zipper all the way up. It seemed to stop right about here." She pointed to a spot about mid-chest and stared straight at him. "It's an extremely revealing outfit and I'm not going to be able to wear it, ever. And Carlos and I always match, so he couldn't wear it, either."

Kiki relished the expression on Max Collier's face. Finally, he was at a loss for words. Over the past month he had hinted about his many plans regarding Janine Stinger. He wanted to take her under his executive producer wing and convince her to sign the contract by elevating her from the second fiddle chair. The fan mail pouring in proved the public wanted more of her, and Max planned to highlight her activity on the show. He wanted to polish her screen image and create a more alluring "character" for her. Obviously, being cast as the dowdy girl alongside Kiki's sexy image must be the reason she wanted to ditch the show. He felt certain she'd be thrilled with the changes and be appropriately thankful. Moving up in the hierarchy must be what Janine desired.

Max paused and studied them. Smart fellow, Kiki could see him backing away from this particular battle. He set his jaw and nodded. He put on a pleasant face.

"Okay, we'll figure out a fix for the next time," he smiled at Janine, but gave Carlos a critical gaze. "You hair looks wonderful, beautiful. That's a good update at least. I take it you girls are happy with the new stylist and makeup artist? Our plan is to up the ante a few notches this season and get the band out of the garage, so to speak."

"Lauren is terrific," Janine said sweetly, then she reached into her arm pocket to retrieve one of the many hair bands she always had stashed. She casually drew her lovely amber ringlets up and banded them into her standard ponytail. Max appeared both mesmerized and flabbergasted. Janine barely noticed his reaction as she moved toward the air cases to gather her gadgets.

Max turned his attention to Kiki and she winked at him. "Thank you, Max. The extra attention and effort you put into the show is amazing. Those outfits were such a nice surprise, but I have a plan for tonight. Right now, I need to step away for a moment and get centered. I usually center my core as the crew gathers their trinkets, so no chit chatting for a few minutes, okay?"

Just as Max opened his mouth to exert his authority, Kiki whipped the large Aztec shawl up over her head and handed it to him. His eyes bulged at her cleavage and his mouth dropped open. Kiki knew her outfit was another over the top success story. She wore a very tight, skin toned, swede leather dress over her generous curves. It was extremely small and short enough that someone else might wear it as a long shirt. Her arms were adorned with intricate beaded bands. Then, she shed the overlarge sweatpants to reveal leather moccasins with straps crisscrossing all the way up her legs to finally tie together at her lower thigh. A small ornate knife was strapped to the outside of her right thigh in a dark leather sheath. She stuffed the sweat pants on top of the shawl in Max Collier's arms and leaned toward him.

"Be a dear and put those in the van for me." She purred, then sashayed away, consciously soaking up his undivided attention.

"Oh my God," Carlos's chuckle echoed over the pavement. "It's the real Poca-haunt-us."

Chapter 2

Inside the Alamo *Janine*

The *Spectral Analysis* team stood in a semi-circle outside the main entrance to the world famous Alamo Chapel. At a nod from the doctor, Don activated the main camera and began panning from left to right.

Carlos pulled open the doors of the centuries old façade as Kiki recapped the history of the chapel. They entered the building one after another. Inside, Carlos quickly crossed to a far corner of the room to set up a low-spectrum infrared camera on a tripod. That camera had a wide angle lens designed to capture the entire room. Janine retrieved the spare thermal-panger from her side pocket and snapped it on. The thermal-panger was an elongated metal gage that recorded micro changes in air temperature. Over her arm, she carried the heavy coil of copper wire for the ultrasensitive large EMF box.

Janine remembered the last time she helped set up the magnetic antenna for that box, something went wrong and she took on quite an electric shock.

"We're setting the EMF box in the chapel to take readings while we wander the grounds," Ian spoke toward Janine, but he was really talking to the big camera. Don pointed the lens in their direction. "We'll try to tap into low frequency electromagnetic waves and see what happens. That large coil is a magnetic antenna. It's not feasible to capture electric pulses at ultralow frequencies, so we'll tap into the magnetic part of the wave instead. I'll place a monitor just outside that door and our backup recorder is in the *Spectral Analysis* van."

"Kiki says we might sense the six diablos in here, known to carry fire swords or something like that. Shall I leave my nice new thermal-panger right here, set to record?" Janine continued screwing the ends of the copper antennae to the box.

"Good thinking," Ian gave Don a signal to follow Kiki with the camera.

Kiki currently walked the perimeter of the room feeling out the energy. Don meandered away in his tight outfit and Janine almost giggled at the sight of his backside stretching the material. She noticed Ian rub the side of his face and wondered if the bruised eye bothered him. She watched him play rugby before and wondered why he loved such a brutal contact sport.

"Is the swelling giving you problems?" she asked softly.

He turned to meet her gaze. It was the first time, in long while, that they properly met each other's eyes. She felt a sudden shift in her chest at the full impact of it. She stayed stuck there for a moment, before dragging her attention back down to wrap the leads completely.

"Oh, no. I had a bit of a beard before this morning and it's a little getting used to. Itchy." His Scottish accent came thicker than normal. "I was a right, rough bloke there for a little while. You wouldn't have recognized me."

"I saw the beard," she told him, keeping her eyes down on her work. "I thought it looked nice."

Truth be told, when Janine spotted him at the hotel bar in his thick curly beard, all she could think about was running her fingers through it while kissing him. Her heart had been pounding and she felt very happy to see him. She almost ran to him, but hesitated, wondering how he felt. Was he still upset with her? Sad, or maybe angry? Or even worse, did he no longer care? Almost a year had passed since their very short fling. He was probably well past it, and maybe that was for the best, as she didn't plan on hanging around. Right when that thought crossed her mind, she realized he wasn't alone. He sat cozily with a very pretty woman, flirting, and so, Janine consciously hid from his view.

"You saw my beard? When, where?"

"I'll admit it, I spied on you for a little while right after I arrived. The beard looked very nice on you." She took a step back from the antenna. "Nothing's turned on yet, right? I want to stand clear before you flip the switch."

"Of course." He stood when she stood. His eyes intently watched her and she began to feel like she should have just kept quiet. Ian kept his voice low. "Why didn't you come say hello? I was hoping to see you sooner, and talk before we got busy here."

"I didn't want to interrupt your lunch." Janine avoided his gaze by looking across the room at Don and Kiki in the far corner. Ian kept staring at her and she lowered her voice even more. "You were with Lauren. I wasn't sure who she was until today, but you appeared a little busy."

Oh, the blinking eyes on Doctor Ian McNally. He stiffened and straightened and pressed his lips together.

"I know she shaved your beard this morning, because she told us all about it. Said she was nervous about hurting your black eye, but was glad you

Ian McNally is the Hanged Man

were ditching the beard, it got in the way with…well, she had a lot of nice things to say about you."

Lauren had chit chatted her way through styling Janine's hair and hadn't been the least concerned about throwing gossip around about herself, or Ian. She insinuated things without outright saying them, implying intimacy, confirming that she "socialized" with the doctor outside of work. Kiki grimaced through it all and got quite short speaking with Lauren, but that was Kiki's way. Janine just listened quietly and admonished herself, what did she expect after slamming the door so solidly in his face?

Ian was close to blinking his way into a coma and she became angry at herself for making him feel guilty. She was out of bounds here, being very unfair. Why did she say anything at all? Perhaps, she didn't expect her feelings to flare up so dramatically, not after her entire world had felt so completely dead just a few short weeks ago. It surprised her, the intense jealousy zinging through her veins. She could barely look him in the eye without wanting to either slap him or kiss him.

"Don't worry about it, Ian," she insisted. "It's all right, really. I'm not, I'm not upset at you about that, not at all. I'm okay with it, she seems like a very nice person."

He looked at his hands, "Crikes."

Kiki's loud voice urged them to the door, the haunted barracks awaited. Janine set the new updated thermal-panger next to the EMF box and set it to record. Unlike the original version, the new gadget was the size of a fat marker and able to record temperature readings for hours instead of one thirty minutes clump.

They trailed one by one out the rear door onto a nice paved path. The sweet fragrance of jasmine welcomed them into the night and Carlos, Janine, and the doctor finally inserted their ear pieces. Janine instantly heard Max Colliers giving instructions over the airways. He insisted everyone switch to hot-mic because he wanted to hear everything. He wondered out loud why they weren't already tuned in. His voice sounded impatient.

Throughout the first season, the *Spectral Analysis* crew wore bulky headsets to communicate with the control van. Over time, their communication equipment upgraded into better and better audio transmitters. Now, they each wore a minimal ear piece with an attached microphone. Both Janine and Carlos rarely selected hot mic. They always opted for the press to talk function, to ensure they didn't muddy the airways or accidently speak on top of the doctor or Kiki.

"Colliers, you may want to use the press to talk function," Doctor McNally's voice transmitted clearly through her receiver. "We can hear all the ambient noise in that van and it's quite distracting. We need to be able to hear each other out here. Don, you should turn your hot-mic off. Not sure why yours needs to be up."

"I want to hear him acknowledge my instructions, and I know his hands are tied to the camera. We're going to tighten things up this season. I'm committed to participating as your full producer/director here," Max came back. "I'm turning my transmitter down two notches so it should be a bit better for you. There, are the ambient noises gone?"

"Aye," the doctor answered him. "Are you insisting on constantly transmitting on hot-mic? Steve rarely transmitted during an active shoot."

"Get used to it," Max's voice came across the wire. "I'm running this thing now, McNally. Steve was a laissez-faire kind of guy, but that's not me. I've got a brain and know how to run a dynamic battle plan. Don't worry, I'll only give instructions as needed. You'll get used to me. Your first focus is near the long barracks, to your left."

"All right then," Ian responded. He glanced at Don. "Are you on com three or four?"

"Three," Don told him. "That's correct, right? Janine, Carlos, and I are supposed to be on com three. Kiki on one, you on two, and Mr. Colliers on four."

"Yes, that's perfect," the doctor told him. "Head over that way and stand just outside the courtyard entry, the one that leads to the mission well, next to that history wall. We are going to walk toward you and you can film us heading that way. Kiki and I will review the nature of the ghosts reported near the long barracks as we walk. Then, we'll…"

"Yes, yes. That's a nice idea," Max's voice interrupted through Janine's headset. "And don't forget to point out the history wall when you approach it. You'll want to mention James Bowie or Crockett, perhaps, and hint that their ghosts may be lingering about…" Max continued with his suggestions and Janine pulled the earpiece from her ear. Carlos laughed silently, holding his sounds in with a hand over his amused mouth.

The doctor shooed Don around the corner and then turned to Kiki, Carlos, and Janine. He held up two fingers and pointed to his earpiece, then to his microphone. Janine reset her transmitter and receiver for communications restricted to channel two.

The doctor covered the microphone with his hand.

"We're going to send and receive on com two, all of us." He whispered. "They will hear our chatter, but we won't hear them. I'll give a signal if we need to switch around. We'll do it as often as needed until he gets the message."

They each adjusted their settings and reinserted their earpieces. Carlos grinned, pleasantly amused by the power struggled playing out. Janine found it funny as well, but Kiki rolled her eyes.

"The long barracks proved very interesting from an electromagnetic standpoint," the doctor started walking ahead with Kiki. Carlos and Janine followed. Carlos had his low IR camera out and Janine monitored the air with an ion detector. Back to familiar ground, they grinned at each other.

She had to admit, it was a little fun to be looking for ghosts again. *Come out, come out, wherever you are,* Janine silently called to the ghosts. They could see Don in the distance filming their approach.

"There are several spectral masses haunting the long barracks," Kiki said to the doctor. "From my interviews this week, several witnesses spoke of general feelings of sadness flooding the area. Could those feelings belong to the ghosts of weary soldiers, Mexicans and Texans alike, wandering the area of their untimely death?"

"I measured distinct pulsing energy bands surrounding…" the doctor stopped talking when Kiki suddenly stopped walking. "What is it, Kiki?"

Kiki turned in a different direction, to face a small building, one made of light colored stones similar to the chapel. From the map she surveyed earlier, Janine knew it was the gift shop.

"Do we have access to that building?" Kiki asked. "Is somebody in there?"

"All the buildings are unlocked," the doctor told her, "and empty. Security is outside the walls, so we should be the only people on the premises. We have exclusive access until four in the morning. A contact man is at the Menger Hotel, if we need him, Reed something, remember? What is it?"

"There's somebody in there, or something," Kiki said. "It's calling to us. Urging us over."

Kiki stepped gingerly toward the gift shop building.

"Carlos?" the doctor pointed him toward Kiki.

"I'm rolling. Want me to go regular or keep it IR?"

"Keep it IR. Don, join us here, quickly," the doctor spoke calmly over the wire. "We are changing direction and heading into the gift shop. I can see you standing there, not moving. If you don't bring that camera this way, you are going to miss everything. We're following Kiki."

Don hurriedly toward them, balancing the camera on his shoulder, scowling. He must be listening to alternate chatter from Max on channel four. Janine turned back to follow Kiki into the gift shop and a cascade of pings went off on her ion detector. Ian and Carlos paused near the door to watch it pop off wildly. The doctor traded his portable blinking EMF box for her ion wand.

Kiki forged a path through the merchandise toward a back hallway. As she passed a table display, Janine noticed a book titled *Haunted Alamo* right in the middle of the souvenirs. Kiki always led them into unexplainable encounters when she ran off like this. Janine kept an eye on the portable EMF box for more blinking lights. Carlos skirted around the tables to catch up with Kiki.

"Tell me someone else feels this," Kiki tiptoed up a staircase to the second floor. "He's urging us to hurry. *We're coming.*"

Don finally caught up, huffing and puffing, balancing his camera on his shoulder. His angry eyes searched out the doctor.

"I heard loud knocking out there by the barracks," Don announced loudly. "Are we going to go back out there? Who do I listen to?"

"Hey, there, Max." The doctor calmly raised a hand up for Don to be quiet. "Max, just relax a minute. We're going to follow this up first, then we'll head to the barracks. When Kiki senses something, it is usually wise for us to follow her."

Kiki's voice came over the wire, "He's young. I think it's the boy. The boy ghost a couple of witnesses reported. I can't quite place him, but I sense him up here, in this general area."

The doctor smiled and made a motion for Don to remove his ear piece, which he did. His shoulders instantly relaxed. The doctor pointed up the stairs for Don to follow Kiki and Carlos. Janine followed next.

"*Where are you? Who are you?* Carlos, do you feel anything at all, I sense that he's right here, standing right here."

"I don't feel anything," Carlos said softly.

Janine did. She felt a temperature drop near the stairs and her stomach automatically clenched in response. Temperature drops often came with unsettling encounters. Janine slipped the portable EMF box into her front pocket and retrieved her silver thermal-panger, the original temperature sensing device they used in the first two seasons. Very large compared to the updated version in the chapel, this gadget was embarrassingly shaped like a phallic device. She flipped the on switch and the silver panger confirmed a temperature drop with every upward step on the stairs. Kiki's voice continued rambling over the airwaves.

"*Are you in this room? No? Over here?*" Kiki's voice lowered in tone, a sign that she now addressed the crew. "He's very young. He prefers to watch people from afar, from out this window. I think, somebody here is making him nervous, one of us." Kiki's voice switched back to a higher tone. *"It's alright, dear, we just want to say hello."*

"Kiki," Carlos said softly. "I'm picking up a nice blip of heat near your left hand."

"I can feel him there," Kiki said. "Don, be sure you've got an angle. I'm going to pull out a little mirror here, to look for a reflection."

The doctor crowded Janine in the close quarters of the dark stairwell and spied the readout on her thermal device. Did he notice her hesitation to continue up the stairs? She stopped one step ahead of him and her eyes fell right in line with his.

"Are you okay?" he whispered. He sounded concerned.

"Of course," Janine said sharply, then she shook it off, because what did it matter if she was a little spooked? Or, more honestly, off keel at being there again and acting like everything was normal. She probably should have met them earlier, at the get-together the previous night. They could have gotten this awkward reunion out of the way in a less busy situation, without worrying about ghosts. *Don't let procrastination and avoidance become your middle name in uncomfortable emotional situations*, her old shrink's voice echoed in her ear.

Suddenly, the ion detector popped off like a fireworks finale, startling them, followed by total silence. Shuffling sounds occurred upstairs and Kiki appeared on the top step with Don and Carlos right behind her. Kiki started down, cutting in between the doctor and Janine.

"He's gone. Just like that, he left," Kiki said. "He was a very strong presence, a very strong energy. He felt very young, only a kid, and he wasn't very sure what was going on."

Doctor McNally nodded and glanced at Don. He pointed to the earpiece dangling from his lobe.

"Don, your receiver is hanging. Let's head out to the long barracks now," Ian said.

Steady noise streamed from the long barracks. Shuffling footsteps and eerie voice-like sounds floated out the door. The crew stood just under the stone overhang, listening. The doctor glanced at Kiki and she shrugged, rolling her eyes in the opposite direction. Carlos peered downward, adjusting his camera controls. Don huffed, agitated, but his lens stayed on Kiki and the doctor. He openly glared at the doctor. Max must be trying to get their attention, Janine imagined.

"Doctor McNally, why don't you answer him?" Don appeared stressed about the whole situation and Janine felt sorry for him in that ridiculous outfit, shifting his weight from foot to foot. Don still didn't realize he was the only one listening to Max Colliers. This was his first night filming a live investigation and he was caught in the middle of a silly power struggle, and unlike Janine, he probably didn't want to lose his job.

"Oh, hey, Max," Ian stepped toward the overhang and glanced down the dark corridor. "We're tied up with our equipment here. Why don't you use Don as your go between so we don't all step on each other?" It was not typical for Ian to let a joke go this far, and Janine wondered what was really going on.

Don shook his head. He could see that Doctor McNally was not fiddling with any equipment. He opened his mouth, but Ian held his hand up.

"I'm just thinking here," the doctor told him.

"That was a pretty ominous moan," Carlos inspected the top of the stone overhang. "Could some of those noises be the wind rushing through the rafters? It almost sounds like a recording, doesn't it?" He angled the infrared camera to the top of the wall even though he knew full well it couldn't pick up anything through the stones. Perhaps he was looking for cracks.

Kiki's attention was not on the long barracks, "Where does that opening lead, that one over there? That's another little courtyard, isn't it?" Kiki didn't seem interested in the long barracks at all.

"It goes to the Calvary Courtyard," Janine told her.

"I admit that there are fabulous noises in there," Kiki said. "But I am very drawn to that little opening over there, to the Calvary Courtyard, and I have zero feelings about that place in there. Maybe we should split up. There's a very sad energy coming from the courtyard, much stronger than it was during the day. I don't want to ignore it."

"Okay," the doctor agreed. "Kiki will follow her nose with maybe, Don. Yes, Don, you should trail Kiki and get everything on the big camera. Janine, Carlos, and I will check out the noises in here, and then meander around to meet you at the tail end of the yard. I believe there's an opening at the far end of this hall, one that empties into your courtyard."

Don shook his head and glared anxiously. He pushed his microphone away from his mouth and leaned toward the doctor.

"No one is going to answer that question?" Don asked. "I'm not sure whose instructions to follow, who's the boss? Aren't you going to take that order into account?"

"Have you watched the show, Don?" Ian didn't cover his microphone. "I'm the boss here. During any investigative shoot, I'm the boss. I am the main scientist conducting an investigation of paranormal activity. That's what *Spectral Analysis* is, a paranormal investigation. Kiki is my spiritual medium, Carlos and Janine are my tech assistants, and you are my cameraman, for documentation. Do you hear that, Max? We are conducting a scientific investigation here, this is not a sitcom. Sit tight and see what happens. We are going to cover everything."

The doctor watched as Don flinched at whatever was coming through his earpiece.

The doctor continued, "I'm insisting, Max, that Don follow Kiki with the camera. The rest of us are going to walk down this hall and meet them at the other end. Carlos is going to record us on his camcorder, but right now, there is no script. Kiki always follows her nose and the big camera always follows Kiki."

They watched Don nod hesitantly, then nod to Kiki as they broke off. Janine trailed Carlos and the doctor into the dark museum while listening to

Kiki prattle on to Don about the soldier spirits of the Alamo. She kept asking him if he could feel the sadness.

"*Oh yes,*" they heard Don say, "*I'm definitely feeling the sadness.*"

Faint, whispery, echolike sounds engulfed them inside the door of the long barracks. *Air flowing through a small opening would not sound like that*, Janine thought. Janine dug into a pocket to retrieve her audio recorder and set it for sounds in the lower sonic to subsonic range, then reinserted it with the microphone sticking out.

They watched their many gadgets silently. Carlos noted a very tiny hot spot down the hall and they slowly made their way toward it. Before the shoot, the doctor insisted that all the electricity on the premises be shut down. That small hot spot should not be an outlet or an electronic of any kind.

Kiki's voice suddenly turned to a higher pitch, a pitch she used when directly addressing a spirit. Janine focused on Kiki's voice for a moment.

"Sadness. *I feel you.* Overwhelming grief." Her voice changed a bit. "What are you filming? He's going over there." Her voice stopped for several seconds. "*Just calm down. I can feel you standing there.* Don, point your camera over there. Point it at… at him. *Oh my. Hello there.*"

The doctor turned toward Janine and Carlos with wide eyes.

"Kiki, what do you see? Is there somebody out there?" the doctor asked softly.

"I thought it was just a shadow," Kiki whispered. "But it's a man. He's moving in slow circles. Get up here and film this." She must be speaking to Don again. Her voice dropped lower. "Ian, get out here. There's man out here, and he's strange. He's looking all around, confused and so, so sad. He's becoming quite clear."

Ian muffled his microphone and pointed to the corner with the heat blip. "Carlos, check that out and then come over to the Cavalry Courtyard immediately. See if you can pinpoint that whispering sound. I'm going out there. There's something fishy going on." The doctor grabbed Janine's hand and pulled her along. They exited the museum and sprinted to the path Kiki and Don had disappeared into.

"Can you hear me?" Kiki used her higher pitch again. *"I can feel your sorrow. My goodness, you're energy is like a flood. You're in pain, I can feel that. Will you speak to me?"*

Don stood at the western end of the courtyard with the camera on his shoulder. Kiki stood just beyond him, facing the trees near an old cannon that was cemented to the ground. The foliage lay just beyond the cannon. Janine peered into that extremely dark corner, and, as they drew near, the figure of a man emerge from the shadows.

He meandered in a slow circle staring fondly into the sky. He wore an old military uniform which appeared weathered and torn. The edges of his sleeves were frayed at the wrists and the lower button on his breast was missing. That man was not a ghost at all, he appeared completely solid. His slicked back hair framed a dirty face and a pencil thin mustache lay crooked above his lip. The doctor's ion detector began to pop off and both Janine and the doctor stared down at it, startled.

"Can you tell us your name?" Kiki asked the fellow. He seemed completely unaware of Kiki, searching around in a spaced out manner. As they drew nearer, Kiki held out her arm to stop them. She waved at them to stay behind her.

There is something very strange about that man, Janine thought. A chill ran down her spine. If he was an actor, he was doing a terrific job. Janine glanced toward Don. His face wore an expression of absolute terror. His terror sent another chill down her spine. Don's eyes shot to the doctor, seeking him out. He waved the doctor over with an agitated hand.

"There is a very strong energy coming from this fellow, and he seems completely unaware of us," Kiki whispered. "I swear to you, earlier, he was not as solid as he is right now, granted, he was in the shadows, but look at him. I know what you're thinking, but this is not just some bloke standing in the trees, I don't think he's really there."

"Hey, buddy," Janine called out to the man, upset that he was trying to scare them. "Who are you? What are you doing out here? You can stop pretending now."

The man suddenly turned and his eyes went directly toward Janine, yet he behaved as if he couldn't quite see her. Kiki also glanced at Janine, surprised that the man responded to her.

"Do you need help?" the doctor asked, but the man didn't move.

"Do you need help?" Janine demanded firmly.

The man began to nod at her. He opened his mouth but no sounds emerged. He changed direction and moved slowly toward the wall of the barracks. The doctor moved closer to Don.

"What happened? Did he do something? Why are you shaking?" Ian asked softly, as he kept an eye on the strange man.

"He's not in the camera," Don said. "The camera's not picking him up."

They always shut down the digital display during investigative shoots, too much ambient light could spoil their night vision, so it wasn't easy to see what Don was talking about. The doctor bent to look through the eye piece and his body visibly tensed. Ian snapped his head back up to stare at the man. Ignoring Kiki's outstretched hand, Ian walked directly toward the soldier and just when he reached him, the soldier turned into the long barracks wall and disappeared into thin air. Janine inched forward to see better. *Did he go through an opening?* The wall was solid stone. While their mouths hung open, Carlos emerged from an escape door to the left of where the man disappeared. Carlos almost bumped into the doctor. He noted their shocked expressions.

"Yeah, yeah." Carlos nodded at them. "You guys figure it out too?"

"Did a man just pass you in there?" the doctor asked him.

Carlos glanced over his shoulder, confused. "A man, like a person? No." He hesitated, then turned his back on Don's camera and opened his hand. A small cube, the size of a die, lay in his palm. He handed it to the doctor.

The doctor inspected it closely, while at the same time keeping an eye on the long barracks wall. The doctor took his audio headset off and completely switched off his transmitter. Everyone else did the same thing. The doctor motioned for Don to keep the camera pointed at the bushes, then Ian tossed the cube back to Carlos.

"Is it a micro speaker?"

Carlos nodded. "The heat sig lead to it. The minute I handled it the whispering noises cut out. It's a pretty awesome sound system, wouldn't you say?"

"Son of a bitch!" Don muttered, he let out a huge sigh of relief. "I about had an accident over here. Who do you think did this?"

"Max." The doctor shook his head. "It has to be Colliers. He's planted some ghosts for us to find."

"Maybe the Alamo people did it," Don suggested.

Kiki took a few steps toward the foliage. "I don't understand. I got a very strong feeling out here, intense spectral energy, and in that gift shop too. I don't see how Max, or anybody, could do that. That can't be faked. How do you explain the man? His energy?"

"I don't know, a hologram?" Ian searched around the trees. "A projection device could be anywhere."

"A really incredible hologram that moved all over and seemed to respond?" Janine said. No one had any answers. "What's the plan?" They still had two other destinations to investigate, the battle cannon walk and the main chapel.

"Shall we go out there and confront Max?" the doctor raised his eyebrows at Kiki.

"Maybe we should play along with his little charade and toy with him before unmasking him." Kiki narrowed her emerald eyes. "See what he has in store for us in that chapel, he seemed insistent that we have our finale in there. Let's see how far he's willing to go."

They all agreed. The doctor put his audio back in his ear.

"Audio all now. We'll want to hear everything Colliers has to say, where he urges us, and such," the doctor said.

Janine tuned in to hear Max rambling about their failure to follow direction and wasting the camera. He informed them sternly that he was not just the executive producer, but he was also the director. He reminded them that a director directs and they needed to listen to him.

"Yes, Doctor, I get that this is an investigation, but to film it and present the story nicely, you need the direct input from your director. I am the eyes of Oz, so to speak, and can see things you don't. More direction would have helped you at the end of last season. Let's not let our egos keep us from getting the good stuff."

"Kiki talking to a ghost wasn't good stuff?" the doctor interjected.

"Oh good. You're no longer ignoring me," Max snapped back. "From my angle, Kiki appeared to be talking to a bush. Now we lost what happened in the long barracks with the ghostly noises. Those were super spooky sounds. I don't want to lose anything else. Do not give Don any more conflicting orders. I want Don pointing that camera in the right directions, especially in the chapel. Can we agree on that, McNally?"

"Aye, absolutely," Ian grinned. "Perhaps we should head straight away to the chapel. Carlos is a little shaken up about the long barracks."

"Oh yes," Carlos said. "Very unexplainable voices and footsteps echoing in there. I had to get out of there fast. I almost freaked out."

Kiki shot Carlos a look and he just gave her his dimpled grin. Max's voice filtered through the airwaves again.

"Let's put that behind us. I will say, I was hoping to get the Doctor-Kiki moment, the catch, in the long barracks. Maybe we can get something dramatic in the chapel. Don, get that camera up. I want everyone to head over to the chapel now. Don, this time film the group walking away from you. I'd like Kiki at the tail end, center shot. I love that outfit Kiki, very, very… well, very Kiki. Don, you know the angle I'm looking for."

They entered the chapel through the same door they exited earlier. Carlos disappeared into the chapel first, followed by Kiki, and then Don. Janine hung back with the doctor to look over the display for the EMF box. Nothing of note showed on the readouts. As soon as she entered the chapel, they noticed the interior felt extremely cold, as if someone ran the air conditioner on full blast. *Tricky to do without electricity*, she thought, *and an obvious stunt*. A room of cool air was not the pocket of coldness that preceded an interesting encounter.

"It's very cold in here," Kiki announced. "Do you guys feel it? Very cold."

"Let's check the thermal-panger you left and see what it tells us." The doctor nodded at Janine.

Max came over the wire. "Excellent idea. Don, you'll want a close up on those read outs."

Don rushed over to Janine and pointed the camera over her shoulder as she checked the panger. She skipped back over the past couple of hours to when she placed it on the ground, then set it to play back in quick-time.

"It recorded a steady drop in temperature that began soon after we left. It's roughly twelve degrees cooler than when we started the night."

"Must be a ghost on the horizon," Carlos said, "And do you hear that sound? Is that a clicking noise?"

"It is. It seems to be coming from the roof," the doctor looked up.

All eyes turned to the rafters. Then, the shuttered windows suddenly burst open, startling them, and the flutter of wings roared deafeningly. Hundreds of bats zig zagged manically overhead. The crew calmly gathered in the center of the main shrine room, crouching in a huddle. They watched as bats swooped up and down searching for a way out, but the shutters had closed, trapping them in. Several of the winged rats came to rest in the rafters.

"My word," Kiki gazed at the hanging bats. "There is definitely something afoot in this building." Her green eyes flashed irritably.

Max came over the wire, "Wow, you guys handled that pretty calmly. It looked scary as shit on the camera."

"We're professionals here," Carlos said. "Bats don't scare us. I'm getting warm bands coming from that room over there." He hit the playback on his infrared camera and showed the doctor his digital display where a definite human heat signature had moved.

Kiki added, "I also sense a strong feeling seeping from that room, like some sort of menace might be there. What is that room again? The monks' burial chamber if I remember correctly. The diablos were thought to be the men who built this chapel. Do you think we'll find six ghostly holy men lounging in there?"

"I detect a flame," the doctor said. Janine noticed a faint glow of light coming from the next room, pulsing, and the faint scent of vanilla finally reached her nose. Kiki narrowed her green eyes and shook her head.

Carlos tapped Janine on the shoulder. "It just hit me. Doesn't this feel like we're on an episode of *Scooby Doo*? Would you say I'm more like Shaggy or Scooby?"

"With your mop head, definitely Shaggy," Janine said.

Max Collier's voice cut in.

"What is going on in there? What is Carlos rambling about? Is anyone going to investigate that glowing light or are you just going to sit around? We only have the grounds exclusively for a couple more hours, and we need to get some good footage, spectacular footage. It was a big price tag, so don't fool around in there. If you guys don't start getting serious—"

"Oh, I'll go investigate it!" Kiki huffed as she stood up.

She reached dramatically down to draw the small dagger from the sheath on her thigh, giving the camera a nice shot of one near naked leg. She displayed the ornate grip for Don's camera lens. She held it by the silver blade and grinned wickedly. The wood handle was carved with an intricate Celtic knot.

"This is my witch's knife," she told the camera. "If the spirit of a holy man is trapped on Earth, I can release him with this dagger. I only need to be sure it passes cleanly through his heart essence. Come along with me and we'll try to release the holy devil from his earthly prison."

Everyone exchanged amused grins. Kiki strolled purposely toward the entrance of the monks' burial room and Don followed her with the camera. Janine, Carlos, and Ian all hung back, watching her swagger away. Was Kiki really planning to do something with that dagger?

Ian bent toward Carlos and Janine, "She's an expert at throwing the Sgian-dubh, she hardly ever misses her mark."

Kiki suddenly moved fast. She shifted her weight and planted her feet firmly on the ground. In one swift, graceful motion, she threw the knife into the next room, yelling, "Be free, ye devil!"

"Fuck!" an angry male voice echoed from the room. "That was a real knife!"

Kiki strolled backward, laughing. She smirked at Don's camera with her emerald eyes flashing impishly. "Well, kids, it's time to go out to the mystery machine and reveal the true identity behind the spectral madness we've witnessed here tonight. Hey, in there," she called into the chamber, turning her voice silky sweet. "Be a dear and bring my dagger with you."

Chapter 3

Debrief *Kiki*

Max Colliers admitted ordering the miniature sized speaker for the long barracks and the bats in the chapel. The chapel was super-cooled per his instructions and he directed somebody to place another small speaker in the amphitheater. Max also admitted to hiring three actors to hide on the grounds, the guy in the chapel dressed like a monk, and two guys dressed as soldiers poised to shadow them in the garden near the arcade. Max would not own up to a hologram or other projection, or any other types of disturbances. He swore that nothing was placed in the gift store and never expected them to go into that building.

"Think about what made this show popular, the strange noises, the glimpses of a possible phantom, sexy costumes on a sexy woman," Max crossed his arms over his chest, defending his decisions. "Speaking truthfully, the last two episodes of the second season were duds without one spooky encounter of note. A terrible way to follow up your fantastic feature documentary and the very entertaining Old Town Sacramento episode. We need to jump start the enthusiasm right out the gate, or this show may die a slow and painful death. Those bats were very expensive and hard to do. You lost a golden opportunity tonight."

Ian, Kiki, and Max huddled in a corner of the hotel conference room, debriefing quietly. Everyone else in the room kept shooting them worried looks from afar. The extras stood near Lauren and the makeup guy. Before they changed clothes, Kiki noted that their costumes were very convincing, but new, clean, and pristine. Where was the guy from the courtyard in the tattered uniform? Her anger flared up just thinking about that fellow. Had it been a spoof or a spook? Kiki wondered how Ian managed to keep so calm.

Carlos sipped single malt whisky near the tech equipment watching Ben download different footage into the main computer. Every now, and again, he laughed loudly at things on the monitor. Janine was long gone. She ignored everybody to disappear straight to her room without a word about any of it. The man who played the monk glared across the room at Kiki. So what if her knife poked him in the shoulder a wee bit. It was his own fault for moving. Plus, his wound wasn't so large that a couple of Band-aids didn't cover it. She reached down to touch the returned dagger and smiled sweetly at him, then turned back to Max.

"That was over the top nonsense with the bats, Max. Messy, dangerous, and inhumane to the poor creatures," Kiki admonished. "And those guys over there, were we supposed to mistake them for ghosts just because you dressed them in old fashioned uniforms? Ridiculous."

"I don't see the man from the courtyard," Ian surveyed the room, "Are you still insisting you didn't have some sort of optical illusion out there?"

Max smirked at them. "It's not going to work McNally. You are not pulling my chain like that. I realize you caught onto my plan somewhere between the gift shop and the chapel, and decided to play a joke on me. You could have at least squeezed in the romantic Kiki catch at some point. In the middle of those bats would have been a nice place. Why you two are so riled up, just admit it, I threw some good stuff at you, stuff that could have been top notch entertainment. It's not any different than that catch you like to do, audiences love it. People want to be entertained. And those baggy outfits on Janine and Carlos, those two have assets we can use, they could be more appealing."

Kiki and Ian exchanged glances. They silently admitted that Max made a small point. When Kiki fainted into the doctor's arms on an early episode of *Spectral Analysis*, the audience loved it because nobody knew Kiki and Ian were cousins. They often questioned their decision to allow that romantic tease to continue from episode to episode. It certainly proved valuable at making the show more successful. They realized the audience needed more than just the hunt for paranormal activity to keep them interested. Max was only guilty of exaggerating what they had already introduced into the show. It burned Kiki to have Max point it out to her. She watched Ian blow a deep sign out of his pressed lips.

"Okay, I get your point," Ian admitted. "But tonight was way over staged. We need to have a serious discussion about which direction we want things to go. We clearly have a difference of opinion here."

Max pushed his glasses into place and patted Ian's shoulder, "I agree. We'll tackle it in the Austin meeting this week. Right now, why don't we have a nice whisky and see if there's anything to salvage in those tapes? Let's mingle with the troops, they seem a bit nervous. We need to calm our people down and project a united front."

Kiki didn't like to admit they almost sold out on being taken seriously back in season one, when they were desperate for success. That little bit of play acting just about cost them their reputations. Their feature documentary undoubtedly saved them, but they were right back on the fence again. How they dealt with the next few adventures would either mark them as real paranormal investigators, or just plain entertainers.

Chapter 4

The Office *Janine*

The Austin office and studio relocated and expanded to include a dedicated sound stage with green screen, a conference room, a full workshop, and several offices in a suite of rooms. They occupied a lower floor of the First Bank Tower, to make it convenient for Max Colliers. The main Colliers business offices were fifteen floors above the less fancy *Spectral Analysis* space. It meant Janine and Carlos was expected to work between shoot sites and take on an expanded role before filming. Max asked them to keep regular hours at the new facilities, especially on Tuesdays and Thursdays, to attend meetings. Janine ignored that request, as she never signed the new contract and didn't intend to.

The *Spectral Analysis* reception area appeared larger than the entire old office had been. Cheryl, their original receptionist, squealed with delight when Janine strolled into the foyer. She hurried around her island desk to envelop Janine in long arms.

"It's so nice to see you," Cheryl gushed. "Let me show you to your office. You're sharing with Carlos, of course, but it's very spacious and has a nice view of river. I'm so glad you came a little early, you can get acclimated to your space before the big meeting. Everybody has been dying to meet you!"

Cheryl led her down a wide hall to a spacious room with two desks and a bookshelf. Carlos hadn't done a single thing to make the place homey. Clearly, he claimed the area in front of the shelves. Packages of his favorite gum littered the desk and random electronic gadgets were thrown haphazardly into the bookshelf. The desk closer to the window appeared to be a junk area with two cardboard boxes of papers on the desktop with another box in the chair. *J. Stinger* was scrawled across each of the boxes. Cheryl smiled from the open door.

"Reminds me, there are a more up front. I'll have someone run them down, pronto."

"What is it?" Janine asked.

"Fan mail," Cheryl told her. "You've gotten a steady stream of letters since the movie. Well, since the electric shock." She nodded and smiled. "I've had the reader sorting them. They're the usual; adoring fans, concerned mothers, kids. Your fan mail actually rivals the doctor's now. I'm not sure how you want to handle it, but the reader, Kristine, drew up a few form letters you can approve. The doctor does things that way, except, I'm told he writes a personal note on the rare occasion."

"What does Kiki do?" Janine asked.

"She does the same thing, only, she pulls a few out to answer *personally*. It's a little spooky how she chooses them. Her hand hovers over the pile, then she reaches in and clutches an envelope for a few seconds, then she either throws it back for Kristine or runs off with it. I think she's does it to spook us." Cheryl laughed.

"Wow, three boxes of fan mail." Janine stared at them. "Crazy, I think I only received about ten total letters the first season, and one was from my niece."

"Well, you came across very nice in the movie," Cheryl nodded. "People trust you. And you and Carlos have gotten much more air time than in that first season."

Carlos popped into the shared office a few minutes shy of the big meeting, or, more accurately, he had been in the studio with Ben and Ian watching Alamo footage while Janine sat reading letters from fans. If she had known those guys were in the building, she would have looked for them. She arrived early with the intention of seeing Ian. She finally felt like she might be able to chat with him, and she wanted to completely bury the hatchet so they could part ways as friends. Instead, a chattering Carlos guided her to the spacious board room. They plopped into seats at the large wooden table. Janine could hear Ben and Ian in the back room setting up the audio visual equipment. She debated running back to say hello, but the room began to fill in with people who stopped to greet her. In between the introductions, Carlos occupied her with photos on his cell phone, all of his wife, his toddler twins, and his long list of athletic brothers. Carlos shared photos of the house he purchased for his parents.

"We closed escrow on it last week," Carlos declared proudly. "It's down the street from mine, so Mama and Pop can live here instead of San Antonio. They need a big yard, cause they're gonna have so many grandkids. I'm telling you, Janine, you should consider staying on this season. Max is very generous in the new contract. Yes, we have office hours, but really, I just hang out in the green room, or in the doc's workshop, just joking around and smiling at people."

Lauren glided into the room like a ray of sunshine, followed by Guy, the makeup guy. Lauren flashed an over large smile at everyone and ferried two cups of coffee. She placed one cup on the table across from Janine. She gazed sweetly and said hello in a bright happy voice. She touched hands with several people before finally settling next to Guy in a chair against the wall. Another young woman joined them. Carlos identified her as the costume person, Sally, and the three, Lauren, Guy, and Sally chatted together in an fun way. Lauren seemed very popular.

Mike Dunn, the old lawyer, carried a briefcase in his hand and hurried to the far side of the table. He gave Janine a little nod before shuffling through papers. She wondered if any of that paperwork involved her contract. She doubted it. Management had been very flexible about her emergency leave of absence, but they were not so flexible about letting her out of the contract. Mike was probably tired of her queries. Over the past six months, she had called to insistently review her legal obligations to the show, and he took on the task of disappointing her over and over again. Janine finally came to terms with it, she owed *Spectral Analysis* payback time or a ton of money.

More people filed in and took seats against the wall. Carlos whispered, *he's in production, he's the graphic designer, she does something with the mail.* Don sat against the wall before someone reminded him to sit at the table. He blinked at Carlos and Janine but didn't really say hello. *Just like their old camera man, Ted,* Janine thought. Cameramen must be a grumpy bunch. An older woman with white hair and thick glasses turned out to be the letter reader, Kristine, who had been sorting Janine's mail. She carried a pile of papers in her arms and seemed preoccupied with them. Carlos could not identify a few others that strolled in, including another lawyer type who sat next to Mike.

Ben and Ian finally emerged from the back room and slipped into the seats across from Janine and Carlos. Ben smiled brightly at her. He seemed to get along terrifically with the doctor. The doctor noticed her and nodded. His bruised eye was now rimmed with a tinge of yellow skin and his jaw appeared very scruffy. He must not have shaved the past couple of days and looked a little like a pirate, rough and dangerous, very cute. She couldn't help smiling at the sight of him. He noticed and smiled back. The cup of coffee got his attention and he spun quickly around toward Lauren.

Lauren winked at him with bright, happy eyes. *How very thoughtful of her,* Janine mused. Janine watched Ian mouth a *thank you* and then he spun back to the table. His eyes met hers, but quickly darted away again. Janine watched his eyes begin to blink. Obviously, Ian had a beautiful new girlfriend and was worried that fact might hurt her feelings.

Boy, did it, but she decided she was going to just eat it. Being supportive and happy for Ian was the least she could do. She would soon be away from *Spectral Analysis,* and she could put that past behind her, with all the other stuff. She could hear her shrink virtually tsking in the distance, *Running away from uncomfortable situations just exasperates a problem, Janine.*

Oh, shut up, she wanted to tell him.

Cheryl followed Max Colliers into the room and flopped into the seat behind him with her computer pad out. Max beamed and personally greeted several people. He gave Janine an approving smile as he introduced her to the group. The season started weeks ago for most of them, and Janine got the impression that they were pleasantly surprised that she actually showed up to the office building. Max proceeded to give a very nice speech recapping recent events, including the shoot in San Antonio. There wasn't a hint of the disagreement during that shoot. Max glanced at the empty chair next to him, and shrugged. *Where was Kiki,* Janine thought.

"More things to focus on, promotions: We need to update everything with the new logo, everything. Nothing old out there, that includes the old ties and work suits. We have a few critical fixes in wardrobe to consider," Max glanced briefly at Janine. "Sally, your period costumes were very nice, and although everyone raved about the crew uniforms, Don tells me the new suit is a tad uncomfortable. He says it hinders his range of motion in the lower extremities. Perhaps we need a slight redesign, the crew will give you input on what they'd like. We've got a couple of solid weeks before our next shoot to work it out."

Though she just met him, Janine could not imagine Don using the phrase *range of motion*. She wondered if Max said that to keep the designer from knowing that she refused to wear the costume.

Max continued, "Now that Miss Stinger is here, perhaps she can make herself available for measurements. All of you, Don, Carlos, Janine, please see Sally sometime today so she can get your updated numbers. We're throwing out the old jump suits and need to make appropriate replacements."

The young brunette next to Ian's girlfriend raised her hand and waved.

"I'm down the opposite hall on the left, the middle door. It's always open." Sally smiled.

Max gave her an approving nod, "Thanks Sally. Please run your design ideas by the crew as well, we want to get their input so there are no surprises on location." Max gave Janine a handsome smile, all teeth. "We're also developing a plan for hair styles, and grooming. Carlos, how do you feel about growing some sideburns?"

Carlos laughed, "If you think sideburns are important for the ratings, why not."

"And what about you, Doctor? Lauren believes sideburns on the crew might be a nice touch this season, it'll jazz up your style in a subtle way."

Ian dragged his hand over his whiskery jaw. "I'm going to grow the beard back, I kind of miss it. Believe it or not, I've gotten a nice compliment or two about it, and it jazzes me up a bit, I think." He glanced fleetingly at Janine, then spun his chair to face Lauren. "I'll agree on a beard, and Carlos and Don can do the side burns. How about that?"

Max glanced at Lauren, "Beard on the doctor, chops on Carlos and Don, that sounds fun. Will that do, Lauren?" A little disappointment crossed her face, but she nodded and smiled. She must not prefer the pirate look for Ian. Then, Max rapped his knuckles on the table.

"I'm told, we have a little preview before breaking off into just the crew meeting." Max nodded at Ian.

"Yes, right." Ian straightened up as Ben disappeared into the back room. "After reviewing the material from our Alamo investigation, we were pleasantly surprised to discover startling evidence of a spectral entity haunting the mission grounds. What you're about to witness is film of Kiki speaking to a ghost. A ghost that everyone in the courtyard could see, but the camera could not." Ian pointed to Don. "Don here can attest to that, right Don?"

"Well, yes," Don wobbled as he adjusted his lounging position. "The man in the courtyard was not recorded on film. It was very scary."

People murmured around the room.

"But who's going to take our word for that?" Ian wondered out loud. "Nobody. At first glance, Kiki appears to be addressing the bushes, as Mr. Colliers first pointed out."

There were giggles and Max flashed his perfect smile again.

"But then, we put the video together with a subsonic audio recording." Ian waved an open hand at Janine, "Janine Stinger will often record encounters on her audio device. This time she set the device to record in a frequency band including the lowest range of human hearing down to an area in the subsonic zone. Ben noticed that the subsonic peaks matched patterns very similar to human speech. We decided to raise the pulses by a common multiplier so that they just reached the sonic zone. Sure enough, we heard an eerie voice."

The excited murmurs escalated. Janine recalled turning her audio device on in the long barracks, but had forgotten all about it.

"What you are about to see is footage of Kiki talking to the bushes. Superimposed on top of those images is the recorded subsonic voice, all time hacked together. So, you are going to hear the mystery voice in common time with our film clip."

Ben's head poked from the back room door and Ian gave him a thumbs up.

The conference room came with a supersized television and a surround sound system. In the next moment, the screen came alive with a still shot of Kiki standing next to the cannon.

Good lord, Janine observed, *Kiki's dress really was over the top*. It blended magically with her flesh and only the dagger sheath and bands of beads stood out against her skin. An excited murmur permeated the room.

Kiki always knew how to pose in a striking way on film. Her head swiveled from the background trees back toward the camera and her voice was very clear, "I swear, earlier, he wasn't as solid as he is now. Granted, he was in the shadows, but look at him. And I know what you're thinking, but this is not just some bloke standing in the trees. I don't think he's really there." Heavy breathing noises reverberated under her voice. With an outstretched hand, Kiki presented the bushes for the camera and the picture had just a hint of fuzziness in front of the foliage.

"Hey, buddy," Janine's sharp voice came from out of camera shot. "Who are you? What are you doing out here? You can stop pretending now."

A low-pitched, eerie response suddenly emerged from the breathing noises. "I am here on my watch. Women must congregate in the chapel, you shouldn't…"

"Do you need help?" the doctor spoke over the low-toned voice. The doctor's voice had been much louder, and it was hard to decipher what they just missed. Then, Janine's voice came in again, "Do you need help?" On the screen, Kiki's glowing eyes turned toward the camera, then her head swiveled toward the darkness again.

"Help is not coming." The low tone created an ominous voice that slowly began to fade. "There is no one to help us. Women must return to the chapel, and I must return to my wall."

Doctor McNally passed quickly in front of the camera and then the screen froze again. After a short silence, the room burst with excited chatter. Janine had to admit, that was a very spooky clip, wavering dark shadows behind an aesthetically pleasing Kiki, with a spooky low-toned voice answering her questions. It was spookier than when she actually saw the man standing in the bushes.

She glanced at Don and he appeared very unnerved. Ben reentered from the back room and Ian stood up to smack him on the back. The room continued to buzz with chatter.

"It was a brilliant, innovative idea from Ben here, and so simple really, pulling that pattern of energy into an audible range by increasing the frequency. Keep in mind, it was not a real voice, but energy transposed into a section in the human hearing range. Typically, we'd hear nothing but static, but in this case, the noise made words. Unexplainable, yes, but we believe we captured the energy of a spectral voice."

The room clapped for Ben.

"Fantastic work, Ben!" Max Colliers grinned at him. "Everybody, fantastic work! We are getting off to a fine start. Before I cut the support team loose, are there any questions? Anyone have something they'd like to add or ask?"

The reader, Kristine, raised a shaky hand and Max nodded to her.

"I think I'm asking for a lot of us here," Kristine grinned at Ian while peering over her square reading glasses, "but I'd like to know how Doctor McNally got that nice shiner. Was it during the investigation? Will it be in the upcoming Alamo episode?"

Good hearted chuckling permeated the room, from everyone except Carlos, Ian, and Max. That question appeared to stump Max for the first time. He glanced quickly at Ian, then at Carlos, then at Janine, then back to Ian. The room fell silent as everyone waited for an answer. Finally, Don spoke up to fill in the silence.

"It was Carlos," Don said. "He punched the doctor right in the eye during dinner."

As they began to review the season line up, Kiki finally waltzed into the meeting and sunk into the empty seat next to Max. She fluttered her eyes at him, then turned her attention to the lawyer, Mike Dunn. A few snags with local governing bodies had created last minute changes to the schedule. Janine realized that Mike's paper mess was about filming on location, not her personnel issues.

Kiki wore a pink sparkly track suit. She had rushed directly from her personal trainer and had to cut short her session with a metaphysical reflexology therapist. She advised Max that he needed to schedule meetings at least a day in advance if he required her presence. Lately, her life was a busy labyrinth of important obligations, and she couldn't just alter her appointments because he got a wild hair and wanted to meet at the last minute.

"You missed the meeting for a massage?" Max asked her. "This is hardly last minute, Kiki, we talked about this meeting days ago in San Antonio. It's a regularly scheduled event now. Between locations, we'll all be here."

"You didn't set an exact time," Kiki rebuffed, but she smiled sweetly at him. "And it wasn't just a massage. It happens to be very crucial recuperative therapy, vital for my well-being. Tuning in to spectral energy takes concentrated effort. It takes quite a toll physically, mentally and emotionally. You wouldn't want me to have an on the job injury, would you?"

Max couldn't help grinning as he readjusted his designer tie. "Okay, I get the picture. There's a diva around and I wouldn't choose anyone else to be that diva, Kiki. Mike, do you want to tell everyone the good news?"

Mike Dunn restacked his papers. "Seattle, Florida, Chicago, and Toronto quickly rubber stamped the show plans. We're still waiting for Santa Fe to decide, so you'll need to push that plan later in your lineup. Another little glitch, although Chicago approved everything, they won't guarantee exclusive access to Fort Dearborn Park and that other little park, not unless you guys go in the next month when the metro station is closed for reconstruction. They can do it then. Of course, they say you can access those parks anytime, but they won't close them off for you. You'll be part of the public parade."

"Okay, we push Santa Fe further back into the schedule and move something else up," Max said. "Kiki, Ian, where to next? Seattle? Janine, you're only obligated to film the next few shows, unless I can talk you into staying longer. Do any of those places strike your fancy? Personally, I like the idea of Chicago, I have some business that I can take care of out there, and we can take advantage of the exclusive access to that park. Why did we want that area again?"

"The Fort Dearborn massacre occurred on that spot," Ian said. "Lots of spectral activity in the area. Several years ago, I did a bit of research into the odd electromagnetic waves seeping from the Dearborn Massacre sites. I devoted a chapter in my book to the energy in that smaller park down the street. I'm excited to take Kiki there, for her take on it."

"We don't need exclusive access to any park." Kiki flipped through a thick planner, seemingly absentmindedly. "Chicago can wait, Seattle sounds nice."

"Exclusive access anywhere would be pretty nice, in Chicago. Chicago is a very busy, crowded city," Carlos said. "People are going to be stopping us, and talking, and butting in while we're filming. Have you been to Chicago? People are wandering around at all hours of the night. I don't think people know what dawn to dusk means in Chicago, it's crazy there."

"Carlos has a point," Max tapped his thick ballpoint pen on the table. "Think of the security problems we could avoid."

"We can hit Chicago later in the season." Ian rubbed his scruff.

Ian and Kiki hoped to avoid Chicago for her sake, because Chicago held traumatic memories for Janine. Back when she attended the University of Chicago, she was knifed in one of the wooded areas of the windy city and nearly killed. Recovering from that experience took several years of expensive therapy. Her therapist warned her that she might never completely recover, but she didn't want to be so fragile she couldn't go into the city again. If she went back to Chicago, she could prove to herself that she was finally past it. A *Spectral Analysis* shoot might give her the only excuse to ever go back.

"I vote for Chicago," Janine murmured softly. "Exclusive access to an open public area is surely a good reason to move it up in the schedule, rather than wait. Why would we wait? There's no reason to wait."

"Thank you," Carlos interjected.

"Are you sure about that?" Ian's soft blue eyes were focused on her. "It isn't a big deal for us to go later in the season. The small park I'm interested in is not a busy area."

Janine ignored those eyes and turned to Max. His eyes were equally soft, studying her. Did he sense the tension in the air?

"I vote for Chicago," she said firmly. "If you really want to make me happy, I think Chicago would be fun."

"I definitely want to make you happy." Max slowly removed his glasses. His attention flickered around the table. "We all want to make you happy, right, guys?" They all agreed. "I'm hoping you become so happy, you'll choose to sign on for the rest of the season, and more."

Max proved to be a savvy boss. Evidently, his goal was to make things so nice for Janine that she would change her mind about leaving the show. For months, Janine didn't understand why he wouldn't cut her loose, and then those boxes of fan mail provided a pile of enlightenment for her. People felt a direct connection to her experiences in the last season, and many of her fans confessed to having paranormal encounters of their own. Janine's obvious skepticism, followed by her very reluctant acceptance, liberated a number of viewers. They no longer felt the need to hide a ghostly encounter at the risk of being labeled a nut job. She unexpectedly developed a critical following that might be instrumental in the show's continued success.

Carlos distracted her by opening and closing the drawers on his desk. He appeared to be moving paper, pens, and other office supplies from drawer to drawer. He noticed her scrutiny.

"I'm organizing," he explained. "I never had a desk before, at a job, I mean. I'm going to figure out the perfect arrangement to streamline my access to things."

"You're streamlining office supplies, in case you need them in a hurry? Like in an office emergency? Like, maybe, important papers will need to be stapled quickly and you don't want to drop the ball on getting it done in a timely manner. Is that what you're thinking?"

Carlos flashed his dimpled grin and they both started laughing. They spun around in their very fancy, swivel and roll, bonded leather office chairs. Carlos grasped a three hole punch in his large hand.

"Why do I need this? Am I going to be punching holes in something soon?" He pointed to other supplies. "And this stapler with five thousand staples, five thousand! I don't think I've stapled fifty things in my life. And this set of highlighters, and look at this tape dispenser, and these paperclips. Why do I need all this stuff? I mean, how many paper clips does it take to do my job?" His eyes rolled to the ceiling, "Okay, I've summed it up, not one."

"This is definitely a different gig without Steve. Max is so much more…business. I admit, this place is tons nicer than that box of an office on Stone Oak Parkway, but it was fun. Remember how hot it got in the summer? Remember that time Cheryl's makeup melted, poor girl, she must be in heaven here. Was that a cappuccino machine by her desk? Even that hotel in San Antonio was nice with the private suites and fresh fruit, and real coffee after the shoot. People running around carrying the air cases for us, and that guy, Guy, powdering my nose and such."

Carlos nodded. "All the extra help is nice. Did you know, Max hired two tech guys from one of his other ventures to help in the doctor's workshop? They're down there perfecting and developing all kinds of meters and stuff.

The big box is shrinking and the doctor's workshop is not lacking for tools. You should come down and see it, it's so cool. It's down two floors, next to the computers and green room. We call it the dungeon, but it's cool. The doctor is a happy man down there. He's having a hard time staying upset at Colliers for nosing-in during the Alamo shoot."

Should she ask? She wanted to know, so she asked, "Did you actually punch him in the eye at dinner? Is that how he got the black eye, or did Don make that up?"

Carlos widened his light brown eyes and blew the dimples out of his cheeks before tilting his head at her. "Yes, I punched him. There was a little too much tequila flying around that evening and it was sort of a reflex action, an accident. Don't worry about it. Everybody's good here." Carlos shrugged at her, "Guys punch each other sometimes. That's the way we are."

She wasn't buying that, something happened that they didn't want her know about. Carlos spun back toward his desk, and she decided to drop it. The older woman, the reader, popped her head in the door. Kristine wore her hair in a short beehive hair style, and thick glasses attached to a bright purple lanyard were propped in the hive. She exuded primary colors with a bright yellow shirt, navy blue pants, and a red scarf. She delivered three more letters for Janine. Carlos took the opportunity to slink out of the room as Kristine fully entered.

"Have you decided on putting a personal note in any of your fan letters?" Kristine asked. "If so, just take them out of the box and I'll have Keith pick up the rest so we can send out your responses, the generic responses. I wrote three samples for you to sign, one signature on each will do, and we'll keep a copy on file for the future. If you tell me the type of letters you'd like to personally read, I can set them aside for you. The doctor enjoys letters with science questions from kids, for example."

"Thank you," Janine touched one of the boxes. "I can't believe the pile of mail you've already sorted through."

"I've gone through them little by little since you've been gone. The first few months, I hope you don't mind, but we sent responses without asking.

Back when Steve called the shots, he said you'd be happy we sent out those responses."

"Yes, yes," Janine agreed, "I'm happy you did it. I'm sure the generic response is fine, and recycling is fine. I don't need to see anything."

"We'd like to get an updated photo, a head shot and others. They can take them in the green room downstairs. Also, there are a few with no return addresses, or sender names. I rubber banded them together and stuck them in the miscellaneous box. I meant to point out a couple of them. That long one in your hand might be from the same sender, I daresay. No name, unit, or whatever, but stamped from the Stateville Correctional facility." Kristine paused and glanced out the open door. She turned back and spoke in a hushed, excited voice. "Do you know somebody in the clink? Sorry, but I was tasked to read your fan mail and a couple of them made me curious. I assure you, I'll keep those letters strictly confidential, I'm like a priest in that regard. But is there an old boyfriend in prison perhaps?"

Janine plopped down in her swivel and roll, soft leather chair. Did *he* send her a fan letter? She shuffled through the five envelopes in her hand and found the one stamped in red, *Stateville Corrections*. She stared at it. He loved to write her notes, almost every day. He'd leave them on her pillow, or dorm door, or tapped to the soccer post on the practice field. They always made her feel special, loved, *adored*. She felt a bit of panic bubbling and tamped it down with a slow breath.

"Lots of inmates write to Kiki, from all over, nothing to get nervous about. She gets very raunchy letters from the inside. I've saved a few that I like to read on a cold night." Kristine giggled and adjusted the glasses in her beehive. "I banded your more amorous letters together and placed them in that box over there, good reading, you might want to save a few, but there were two others like that one. They're in the anonymous pile, and the wording led me to believe that you might know him, so I saved them for you to look at. Perhaps that one finally has a name on it."

"Hello ladies," Kiki suddenly stood in the doorway. "Hey, Janine, they're screaming for you over there in design. Sally wants your measurements." Kiki turned to Kristine. "Kristine, I need your help. I've got some new things for fan response that I'd like to run by you. Are you done here?"

"Yes," Janine said quickly. She smiled at Kristine but wasn't sure if it was convincing. "You know, I don't need to read anything, you seem to have it handled." Then, she threw the five envelopes onto the top of the pile as if none of them meant anything to her.

"Janine," Kiki stepped into the room and touched her arm. "Right after Sally measures you, can we meet? We haven't had a chance to catch up and I've got some stuff on the horizon that I'm planning. We can get out of this hell hole and go for a nice girl's cocktail or something. There's an important topic we need to discuss."

Janine nodded. "Sure."

As soon as Kiki pulled Kristine away, Janine fished out the Stateville letter from the box. She then rummaged in the miscellaneous pile and found the banded pile with no return addresses. She shuffled through to find the other two Stateville letters. They were each opened at the top with a single slit along the seam and she noticed a single folded piece of bonded white paper in each. She opened the lower drawer of her new desk and tossed the letters in for safe keeping.

Not because she wanted to read anything *he* had to say, but because she needed to confirm for certain that he really did send them. Janine closed her eyes. It would be very nice if they turned out to be written from someone else, but she doubted it.

Then, she went off to get measured by Sally.

Chapter 5

Rosemount Room *Kiki*

Kiki could kick herself for not handling Janine's fan mail in her absence. She would have discovered those letters from the Illinois state penitentiary and kept Kristine from reading them, but things got busy and it never occurred to her. Kristine wasn't just a fast and thorough reader, she was quick to grasp the difference between a regular fan letter and a message from an actual acquaintance. Kristine might easily figure out Janine's carefully kept secret, and what a media frenzy there would be if people found out the identity of *Jane Doe from Chicago*!

Kiki and Janine chose the Rosemount Room to take advantage of the plush private lounge and the fancy drinks. Kiki avoided the Twelve Grand because most of the *Spectral Analysis* staff found themselves in that whisky establishment after hours. Someone from the office always dropped in and Kiki wanted a private chat with Janine.

They found a spot behind two large potted plants and Kiki ordered a couple of old fashions right off the bat. She didn't ask because Janine normally said no to a stiff drink. She also knew Janine would love the Rosemount Room's version of the old fashion. They claimed the furthest leather sofa in the balcony area, in a spot secluded from most of the room.

"I'm guessing you want to talk to me about Ian," Janine said after the drinks arrived.

"Yes, a little about Ian," Kiki said. "But there's other stuff too. I want a good solid chat and to catch up." Kiki gave the waiter a signal for two more, best to have one waiting in the bull pen to keep the conversation pleasantly flowing. "You probably know that Gram and I keep in touch. She's kept me up to date with the goings on in California, and with your family, and with you."

The High Priestess

Kiki Mellow is the High Priestess

Janine drained a healthy amount from her glass and nodded. Sure enough, their reinforcements arrived promptly. The waiter, Jeff, recognized them and Kiki laughed at a joke he made about ghosts. Kiki decided to go ahead and order ahead again. Even though she only took two sips of her first drink, she could see Janine was surprisingly ready to let loose.

"Let's try the fish house punch next," Kiki eyed the waiter. He was very bright eyed at her attention. "As long as you keep us a secret out here, we'll stay as long as you like." Kiki winked at him. "When you see these old fashions getting low, we'd like that punch? And how about a nice cheese board to nibble." Off he went.

"Kiki," Janine started, "I'm a little ashamed about the way I behaved. I put everyone on the spot and I need to apologize. Asking you to take sides…" She sipped her drink carefully. Her large doe eyes made her appear like a princess in a fairy tale, the kind that always needed saving. "Now that I've gone over things rationally, it was out of line to expect the show to accuse Caroline and Henry Webber of—"

Kiki reached out and grasped her hand. "That's behind you Janine. No one here blames you, and frankly, Henry Webber was not hurt. Caroline Govant was not hurt. Believing they were behind Sammy's loss was your need to solve things in a way that made sense to you. I don't blame you for pressing it so hard. You were grieved, anyone could see that, and everyone could certainly see the logic in your theory. It wasn't farfetched with the history in that town. I wish Ian could have been more understanding when you proposed it and handled it better. But he has his own issues."

Janine nodded, "What I'm trying to say is, I realize why Ian flat out refused to consider my theory for the movie, the legal ramifications, and, I'm sorry that I put you and Carlos in the middle of it when I reacted so harshly to him."

Janine blinked her emotions away and Kiki hugged her. Sammy had been Janine's very young niece, a bright eyed, beautiful little girl. Really, Janine's older sister adopted Sammy right after Janine had given birth to her. Sammy had been part of the aftermath of that life threatening relationship she survived in Chicago, and she disappeared mysteriously during one of their spectral investigations. People believed a ghost took her, the one from the award winning documentary. They believed the ghost lured Sammy into the river, like all the other victims in the river ghost story. That's what Kiki believed.

The official verdict stated that Sammy accidently drowned and her body was washed away, lost to the river, forever.

Janine argued against an accident or a ghost. She accused two old people in the town of directly participating in Sammy's disappearance. Janine proposed that the kids weren't lured by a ghost, but by a living group of crazy people who believed they needed to sacrifice children to the river, a cult that possibly existed for years, generations. The authorities disagreed. Janine pushed to include her conspiracy theory in the documentary, but Ian wouldn't have it. He put his foot down hard at her suggestions, and said it was irresponsible to accuse people with absolutely no proof. Ian told Janine that she was not being rational. *She was being hysterical.*

Janine had been accused of hysteria before, back in the courtroom, after she had been stabbed. Her attacker nearly got away with everything by insisting she was irrational, hysterical, delusional. So, Janine stopped speaking to Ian completely. She wouldn't even acknowledge him. Then, she took that extended leave of absence.

"I know you felt helpless," Kiki held her hand. "Everybody felt helpless. We weren't careful, and it was just an awful, shit situation, Janine. A terrible loss."

They quieted down as Jeff brought out the cheese plate.

"Your Gram says you've been taking classes, at a university."

Janine laughed softly, "You think I'm crazy? I don't know what got into me, but I had to fill up my waking hours with something. I took an overloaded semester on top of a winter session. I actually have two more exams, one coming next week, so not quite completely done. It feels good to get caught up on the education I put off."

"It sounds like pure torture," Kiki said.

"It helps me. I feel like I'm doing something right. I stopped thinking about everything and just pressed right through. I guess it's my new therapy, no medication needed. I'd like to get back as soon as possible, but Mike Dunn tells me I'm bound by my contract to *Spectral Analysis*. Max could let me go, if he wanted, don't you think? I offered to buy out my contract, but he put a million dollar price tag on it. Can you believe that?"

Kiki nodded. "Oh yes, adorable Mr. Max, he is quite a little dobber. He certainly could let you out of the contract, very easily. I wouldn't like to see you go, but you have some compelling personal reasons for wanting to leave. I don't blame you one bit for wanting out of your contract."

Oh my, Kiki thought, *what was the look Janine gave her?*

"Is that why we're here? Are you worried about Ian? You said, you wanted to talk about him," Janine gulped her drink nervously. "Before you say anything, I want to repeat that I've accepted that Ian was right about what shouldn't go into the documentary, and I'm sorry for the way I reacted, for how harsh I was to him. To put your mind at ease, I'm not going to mess with Ian while I'm here. I realize I broke his heart back there and can see that he's moved on, so you don't have to worry. You can tell him…"

She stopped talking because Jeff came around with their new drinks. He could see that he interrupted and quickly left. Kiki touched Janine's hand to keep her from continuing.

"No, this talk has nothing to do with any of that," Kiki said. "Ian and you, and, well, it's none of my business. Anything you want Ian to know, you'll have to tell him yourself. That's not what I wanted to talk about."

"Then, what did you want to talk to me about? In regards to Ian?"

"His birthday," Kiki told her. "I'm planning his thirtieth and I think he would be very pleased if you were there. Steve and Ted and those two guys that used to fix the van. Current cast, crew and office staff will be there, also some of our past interviewees, the Savannah caretaker, Paul, and that crazy chicken girl, Foxy, from New Orleans, the one that scared the shit out of Carlos. Plus, Gram, maybe. I wanted to make sure it was alright with you. I'm setting a date and I don't want you to miss it." Kiki drained her drink.

"Go ahead and invite Gram. I'll come to the party. I want to end things as friends with Ian," Janine assured her. "I won't ditch it. Gram and I are good now. I'm not sure what she's said to you, but I can't very well drive to her house every weekend, not with the load of classes I took. Gram and I are talking again."

Kiki nodded. "Good. There is one more thing," she hesitated.

Janine was a terrible skeptic to almost everything Kiki believed. She and Carlos often laughed at Kiki and her witchy practices, and although Janine had come around to accepting some of Kiki's extrasensory perceptions, Janine would dismiss her own similar gifts. Kiki had itched to broach the subject for quite some time. Now that they were both a little tipsy, perhaps the subject would not be too brazen for Janine.

"Janine, I believe you're a *dragoma*," Kiki said bluntly. "In the spiritual sense, that's a person who can easily get their point across to spirits. Spirits listen and often obey a *dragoma,* and a strong *dragoma* can actually converse with a spirit."

Janine's eyes opened just a little wider. Amusement hovered in her expression and her shoulders finally relaxed with the change of subject. She downed the rest of her drink.

Kiki smiled back, "Laugh all you want, but I'm pretty certain of it."

Janine chuckled. "I'm taking this as a compliment, coming from you, Kiki, but I'm not into the psychic or medium thing. There's no longer a doubt in my mind that you have an uncanny ability to tap into that world, but I think I'm probably like most people, clueless. I don't even know what that is, a *dragoma.*"

"Ian's mother, my Auntie Celeste, was a very talented *dragoma*," Kiki told her. "She was a true mystic seer, her callings were legend, and she taught many of us. She was the most gifted witch I have ever known. She spoke to many restless spirits, helping them find peace. Only a mystic who communicates easily with the spirits can do that, a natural speaker. I believe speaking to spirits might come easily for you too."

Kiki didn't mention that Celeste often spoke to ghosts as a child. It seemed to be the mark of a *dragoma*. Children could see and hear spirits easier than adults, perhaps due to unspoiled sensory receptors and an unbiased mind. Partnered with early learning, a child could carry certain talents into adulthood, like learning new sounds and training the ear, or training the tongue. If they're not practiced in youth, they could be lost to a person for life.

Janine laughed, "Only, I don't speak to spirits."

"That's not true," Kiki said. "You've communicated very successfully to spirits, and they've listened to you. They've obeyed you. Think back, Janine."

Janine stopped laughing because she could see Kiki was serious.

"You watched the playback of the soldier at the meeting, with the audio? He heard you, Janine, and apparently answered you. It didn't take any effort from you at all. Back in Rio Linda, you asked the river ghost to pull me under water, and she did, I felt her. She listened to you. When I slipped in the Biltmore Hotel and you made that wisecrack to Carlos about taking me to a party, directly after you said that, the ghost invited me to a party in room 1404. I know you think I made that bit up, but I didn't. You may have been doing it all along. I assumed it was me, getting better at projecting into the spirit world, but now, I realize, it was you. You were helping me. You whispered to them during our little excursions, haven't you? Calling them out."

Janine listened silently, her brow creasing. Kiki could see Janine trying to be open minded and that gave Kiki some hope.

Janine asked. "What if I have? What would it mean?"

"Not a whole lot," Kiki said. "Unless you want to develop your talent and explore it. I could help you there, or…" she hesitated.

"Or what?"

"Gwen. One of my coven sisters. She's the real teacher." Kiki watched Janine's smile grow. That was why she needed the drinks. Kiki was proud of her background, but knew Janine would not understand and make light of it.

"You're laughing at me, but the sisters in my coven are also very nice girls of the Kirk. Gwen's father is actually our pastor, so, we're all very normal. Anyway, Gwen is coming for Ian's birthday and wants to meet you. An actual *dragoma* is rare to find. I shared my suspicions, and now she insists on seeing for herself. Gwen can be a bit much, and intends to bend your ear extensively about speaking to spirits."

"I don't care," Janine smirked. "She can ask me about anything she wants. I'm very curious to meet any of your friends. She's coming for Ian's party? Does she know Ian too?"

"Well, that's another thing," Kiki sighed. "There is a little history between Gwen and Ian. History long past, but history none-the-less. That's the most I'm going to say about it because I don't like to poke my nose in there, but it's only fair to let you know. So, Gwen might gossip with you about Ian too."

Kiki had a difficult time reading Janine. It was both unsettling and refreshing. There were rare people that Kiki could not read well and Janine was one of them. Janine's aura was just too dark to penetrate much.

"I'll be okay with your friend," Janine said.

"Are you also going to be okay with Chicago?" Kiki asked. "I don't understand why you did that; told Max Colliers you wanted to go to Chicago. Unless, you're ready to face the city again,"

Janine nodded. "Only, I'm beginning to wonder if I made a mistake, if I'm really ready to go back there. I've been scared of Chicago for years."

Kiki hugged her. "This is something you can do. And I'll be there with you, Ian too. You know you'll have our support."

Janine reached for her purse. With a shaky hand, she extracted three envelopes, the fan letters. She passed them to Kiki. Interesting sensations seeped through the paper, dark and intense energy.

"They're from the Illinois state pen," Janine told her. "I believe Rick sent them. Kristine said they weren't signed, but she guessed they were from…a friend."

Kiki ran her hand over the envelopes. "Do you want me to read them?"

"I need to know if Rick sent them, but I'm afraid find out."

Kiki would bet money that Richard Wilkens sent those letters. Who else would stamp dark energy onto a piece of paper addressed to Janine Stinger? But Janine the skeptic would not be satisfied with a psychic assessment. Janine needed to read the actual words for definitive proof.

"Let's read them together," Kiki suggested.

She pulled each letter from their covers and laid them in chronological order.

"We'll read them silently, one, two, three, and deal with it at the end," Kiki suggested.

Janine nodded and they both bent over the typed letters. None had a salutation, no dates, and no named writer. Only one short paragraph on each page, centered, giving them a similar appearance and indicating they came from the same source.

Letter one.

Your image popped up in the movie tonight. You look well, beautiful, not ruined at all. You did this so that I could see you again. Maybe you wonder if a second chance is possible. Forgiveness? I want it too. We're soul mates, after all. I miss you, and now know that you miss me too.

Letter two.

I found your first season. You appeared fragile, but getting stronger. Were you sorry? Why didn't you trust me? And, why am I still incarcerated? You realize, you're the one who broke your promise and caused everything to fall apart. You could fix it all with a word. Come see me. Speak for me. We can start again.

Letter Three.

Sometimes I wonder about our baby. I am not allowed to ask about it, but that doesn't seem right. No one will tell me, boy or girl. When we meet again, you can tell me what you did. I won't be angry. I know what went wrong now. You were haunted, and it mixed you up. You weren't ready to believe in us. I forgive you. Come speak for me.

Good Lord Kiki thought. Richard Wilkens still enjoyed scaring the shit out of Janine. Did he really think she would recant her testimony and get him out of jail, *just because he asked her to?* Kiki drained the rest of her fish house punch in one gulp. She moved the letters to the sofa between them. She did not want them in her hands any longer. Janine folded them over and stuffed them back into her purse. Instead of fear on her face, Kiki detected a flash of anger in her eyes.

"He's clever, don't you think," Janine said. "Didn't use my name or his name, and he typed them. There's no way to prove he violated his order to leave me alone. He's still covering his bases to keep from getting caught. Not admitting anything and still trying to play with my mind."

"Are you okay?" Kiki asked.

Janine fidgeted. "I'll be fine. I think, I need to go, if we're done here. I want to sleep and then start studying. I'd like to get back to UC Davis before the end of the week. Thanks for reading these with me, Kiki, you are a good friend."

Janine stood up and appeared unusually sober for a girl who never drinks. They hugged briefly and Janine left. Kiki plopped back down to finish the cocktails and cheese. *Good Lord*, she thought again. Then, she picked up her cell phone to ring Gwen.

Chapter 6

Chicago *Kiki*

They booked everyone into the Lincoln House hotel near Millennium Park. As usual, Kiki and Ian arrived a week early to scout out the area. Aside from a plan to investigate the site of the Fort Dearborn Massacre, Chicago was a city teaming with reported paranormal activity. Criminals, disaster victims, and civil war prisons were all part of the city ghost stories. Kiki and Ian spent the week visiting possible haunted sites and conducting preliminary interviews to get a sense for where they could find authentic spectral activity.

They sat in a lounge finishing their notes while waiting for the *Spectral Analysis* team to show. They reserved the roof top restaurant for a pre-shoot dinner party, but planned on greeting people with drinks as they arrived. They also procured the Whistler Ballroom as their command center. Ben and another techie had arrived with the van the previous night and set up equipment in the ballroom. Kiki and the doctor conducted three camera interviews earlier that day. They interviewed the caretaker of the Graceland Cemetery, a maid from the Congress Hotel, and a gentleman who claimed to have photographic evidence of specters near the Dearborn Massacre site. Kiki and Ian found a comfortable spot in the lobby bar to enjoy a cocktail and wait for the others.

"I know it's popular with the ghost tours," Kiki tapped her pen on the paper, "but this Krill House devil child, I want to skip it. It's so clearly a farce and didn't you find that curator a bit over the top?"

Ian nodded, "I agree. We have equipment for four sites. We need to weed out one or two places."

"The post office," Kiki said. "You know, the Holmes Murder Castle. The building isn't really there anymore, except that one wall. I admit, it was an interesting wall in that basement, but I couldn't get a definite feeling about it. It came across like static energy more than anything focused. And the Valentine Day Massacre site, there's nothing there."

Ian agreed. "But let's definitely hit the water tower. It's one of the oldest structures in the city and quite garish in style, it'll look good on film. Who knows, maybe there really is a ghost in there. And I liked that wall too, the post office wall. I just wish there was more of the original structure. I wonder what the wall's composition is."

"You still gathering evidence for your theory on elements that take on a ghostly stamp?" Kiki watched Ian. He began developing his theory years ago.

"Magnesium and phosphorous," Ian said. "Those are prime energy elements. Gram hasn't detected a trace of that river ghost, has she? The boulders in the river not only contained rare earth elements, but the magnetite in the rock was jam packed full of magnesium and phosphorus in a slightly higher ratio than usual. I truly believe those elements absorbed the spirit of the girl who became the river ghost."

Doctor Ian McNally's theory about ghostly energy developed over years of research. He first noticed that spectral energy was connected to solid objects, like bone, wood, or stone. The doctor analyzed those objects for mineral content and found that tombstones associated with ghosts contained more traces of the elements magnesium and phosphorus. The foundations of haunted houses and old castles were rich in those elements, as well as the hydroxyapatite in bone found near paranormal activity.

Doctor McNally also noticed that when the material was destroyed, the ghostly encounters waned and disappeared. Ian and Kiki always accepted that spirits weakened over time, eventually fading from existence, Ian now theorized that it was due to the natural weathering and erosion of his trace elements.

Ian once attempted to entice the essence of a spirit to move from one tombstone to another. He used a concentrated mix of phosphorus and magnesium in the haunted Savannah graveyard. Kiki remembered that night well. Kiki told him he was being a nut and didn't want to participate. If a spirit "stamped" itself into things, as Ian suggested, Kiki believed it would take a very traumatic, emotional event to do it, not just some bloke with a few flammable chemicals.

"I've checked with Gram, and she says there's still nothing," Kiki told him. "She's happy to help with your theory development, and always asks after you."

When the boulders from her river were removed, Janine's grandmother no longer sensed the river ghost. Gram never realized that she always sensed the ghost, until the ghost was no longer there. When Kiki returned to Rio Linda for a short visit in November, she no longer felt the ghost, either."

Ian rubbed his new beard. "I'm going to go out on a limb and put the theory in my new book."

"You need to be careful of your reputation," Kiki told him. "You're the serious one."

Ian made a face. "I know. Okay, on day one, the crew sets up remote monitors at the Dearborn sites, the water tower, and the theater alley. After dusk, we film in those areas until midnight or so, then we head over to film your séance at the Congress Plaza. You want a two AM séance?"

"Two sounds good. Your mother always said two at two bells will fast the two heads," Kiki said. "It's midway between the change of day and the witching hour."

"I never knew what she meant by that," Ian said.

"A reference to the thinning of the veil," Kiki told him. "It's why two in the morning was her favorite hour for a séance."

"Day two," Ian continued, "We sleep during day, and then at nightfall, we run out to the Graceland Cemetery and Lincoln Park. We need to flesh out the area for the historic society. I owe them. If there's a need for any follow up interviews, we can stay for a day three."

Kiki added, "At that graveyard, we should both gaze directly into the face of that statue, the *Statue of Death*, to see if there's anything to see. It'll make for nice drama. That caretaker was pretty convincing and we can highlight his interview with the footage."

Ian agreed. He glanced into the lobby expectantly. Lots of activity occurred as folks arrived. "Looks like our people are here. Why don't you order some drinks and I'll wave them over?"

The lobby bar soon housed most of the *Spectral Analysis* staff. Everyone enjoyed a welcome cocktail and socialized nicely. They were no longer just six people in a van traipsing from place to place checking into affordable hotels. The money making machine behind the Colliers business empire treated them very well. Fancy hotels and a long list of extra helpers were nice improvements to their working conditions.

Kiki noticed the image people, Lauren and Guy. At first glance they seemed like peas in a pod, but Guy's aura was a tad murky. He must be working through something difficult in his life. Sally also came on location, in case someone needed to modify their new wardrobe. She carried a sewing machine into the lounge. She must not trust anybody with that valuable thing. Ben and his tech crew grabbed drinks and left for the ballroom. A few of the gofers sat together, laughing with the new van driver.

Kiki hoped Max and Ian got their control differences worked out. She detested how males loved to clash with each other. Everyone knew Max Colliers did not believe in ghosts and he probably thought they faked the subsonic voice, but he was happy to hear it and use it in the show. Luckily, the Alamo provided plenty of fun film to pull off a nice premier episode. The bats and knife throwing were funny, and Carlos's humor added a nice touch. Still, Kiki didn't completely trust Max. His aura broadcasted all ego and she imagined he'd try to exert himself somewhere during the course of the shoot. She hoped it wouldn't be in the guise of fake paranormal activity again.

Kiki lounged between Carlos and Don at the bar, admiring photos Carlos shared on his phone. Apparently, Milo Fuente, no more than four years, already showed signs of soccer superstardom and would soon be on the Olympic team playing alongside his Uncle Lonzo. At least, that's how Milo's father saw things. Kiki found Milo completely adorable. Same light brown eyes and dimpled grin as his father and uncles.

"He looks very sweet," Kiki sighed.

"Sweet? He's a world class, bruising, toe tipping second Cristiano. He's a monster!" Carlos shouted.

"And very sweet," Kiki insisted. *Carlos had the right focus in life*, Kiki thought; love your wife and adore your children. Perhaps she should take another look at that eligible brother of his.

The doctor came around to say hello and Carlos showed the pee wee soccer photos all over again. Kiki noticed Lauren and Sally eyeing their little group. Just how involved had Ian gotten with Lauren? Lauren certainly wasn't shy about chasing after the doctor. Business trips in hotels were the worst for creating sticky situations and Kiki hoped Ian chose to be careful about getting involved. An entanglement with a coworker was a sure fire way to create a whole mess of trouble, did he need to learn that lesson all over again?

"Anyone seen Janine or Max?" Ian asked. "Our dinner reservation is in fifteen minutes."

"Max didn't fly in with us," Carlos told him. "He had some other stuff, upstairs work, to take care of. He has to manage the profitable business first, right? Said he'd try to make it out tonight, but not to expect him until tomorrow."

"As for Janine, well, she is flying out of Sacramento, isn't she? Maybe her flight gets in later, who knows," Kiki reminded him.

"Crikes, she's going to come at the last minute and ignore everybody again." Ian's eyes flashed around the bar but nobody had an answer. Kiki could hear it in his tone, he was certain Janine Stinger was avoiding him. "She's bloody planning to do the bare minimum, isn't she? Show up at the last second and fly the coop as soon as the camera's off, brilliant."

"Isn't that what she's always done? Maybe she doesn't know this season is being run differently, with welcome dinners and mandatory socializing." Carlos smiled at him. "Just relax, she'll be here."

Don patted Ian on the back. "Yes, relax. In the meantime, how about you get me in good with your friend's friend over there?" Don waved at Sally sitting next to Lauren. As soon as Ian looked their way, Lauren gave him a one thousand megawatt smile.

Kiki watched Ian consider Lauren a moment, then nod and motion Don over to the two women on the sofa. The girls made room for them, and when Ian hesitated, Lauren reached up and pulled him down. The grouped all had a laugh about the way he plopped into the sofa. It drew the attention of the entire room. Ian just smiled and stayed put. Kiki, along with everyone else, watched Lauren feed Ian one of the fresh strawberries from the coffee table platter. *The idiot*, Kiki thought, *he could at least be discreet*. She walked over and leaned down to whisper in his ear.

"Do I need to say it again? You need to be careful of your reputation." Then, she skipped out the back door to go find Ben and his crew. She wanted to remind them about the dinner upstairs.

Chapter 7

The Negotiation *Janine*

Janine's big mistake was calling a Lyft to transfer from the airport to the hotel. Actually, she called two Lyfts. The first car's engine cut out at a stop sign and she called for another driver. The first driver begged the second driver for a jump start and Janine found herself teaching two Lyft drivers the proper sequence for safely jumping a car, *unbelievable*. The driver who had the jumper cables in his dead car also had a flat spare tire, a forward thinker. Long story short, she was more than an hour late getting to the hotel. She noticed everyone already mingling in the lobby floor bar and she hesitated.

Janine found herself spying on Ian McNally again. He seemed much more at ease when she wasn't in the room. She enjoyed watching him interact with other people. The way he moved and flashed his smile fascinated her. His new beard was growing in nicely, not yet long enough to grab, but a thick dark mess never-the-less, and his hurt eye appeared practically back to normal. She watched him stroll to the sofa and grin down at the stylist, Lauren. Lauren playfully pulled him down next to her. He soaked up her flirty attention, appraising her with his soft blue eyes. *Ouch.* Then, Lauren feed Ian something in a very sensual interchange. They made a very nice looking, *sexy*, couple.

Janine flashed back to a time Ian had fed her food by hand. He did that on more than one occasion, in bed, after very starling nights of love making. A sudden heat flooded her body at the memory.

She watched Lauren run her hand along Ian's arm and remembered exactly how that arm felt, solid and corded with muscle, warm. Ian loved to wear silky, stretchable button down shirts and Janine imagined unbuttoning the dark green shirt he wore and seeing his broad, powerful chest emerge slowly under her fingertips as she climbed into his lap. She felt her heart rev up and sensations below moved in like a flash flood. Her eyes were drawn to the thick muscles of his neck as he chatted and laughed. Then, she watched his large hand rub the hair on his jaw and she imagined rubbing parts of her body in that curly mess.

She was startled out of her illicit musings by someone standing next to her, spying on the *Spectral Analysis* staff with her.

"Are you debating whether to go in there?" Max Colliers appeared amused. He wore a suit and tie and had a brief case in his hand. He watched the staff mingle a moment more before looking back at her. He must have noticed her flushed cheeks because he was taken aback slightly.

"You scared me." She let out the breath she had been holding.

"The fearless Janine Stinger? No way." He said softly. Max glanced into the room again. "I'm not going in. I've had a very long day and I'm not ready to be jolly right now. I hear they reserved the roof top restaurant for dinner. You are going to love it, enjoy."

"Wait a minute. You're not joining us for dinner?" Janine stopped him with a hand on his sleeve. Her heart was still racing and she took a deep breath to calm herself down. "We were supposed to talk at dinner tonight. Your secretary assured me."

He clearly did not want to have that conversation with her, he looked away and set his jaw. His eyes seemed weary. He had a bad day, she could see it.

"I'm beat, and I just had them send my dinner to my room. I'm not up for a crowd. I'm supposed to be backing off on location and allowing Doctor McNally to run the show. I'm afraid if I go in there, I'll start making speeches and…" He shrugged at her. "Unless you'd consider having a private dinner in my room. I have a suite. Very spacious."

"Okay, sure." Mostly because she didn't want to enter the scene in the bar, either.

"Yes?" Max perked up and his eyes lock on hers. "Wow, that would be very nice. I'll have them send something for you, what would you like? This will be a nice treat. A quiet, private dinner with a beautiful woman. Lately, all my dinners are either quick bites alone or big parties. This will be a very pleasant change. I like this idea. What shall I have them send for you? Got any preferences?"

"Just, whatever you're having, I don't need much. Just, anything, a salad, bread and butter." She found his giddiness amusing.

Max skipped over to the front desk and spoke to the desk manager, then he beckoned her to the elevators pulling his suitcase behind him. Janine picked up her backpack and got into the elevator wondering if a private dinner with Max Colliers was a good idea. He smiled like she just agreed to go on a date with him. Did he realize she wanted to talk about getting out of her contract? Of course he did, that's all she ever mentioned.

Max stayed at the Lincoln House in Chicago many times before. He raved about the spa on the fourth floor and wondered who might be up for getting a spa treatment. Kiki for sure, but did Janine think Carlos, Don, or Ian would go for a massage? He highly recommended the hot stone treatment. Then, he complained about the meeting back in Texas that made him late. Max had a brother that loved to foul things up and create messes for Max to clean up. Then, his uncle started questioning whether the company should be involved in show business.

"*Spectral Analysis* is my fun project," Max said. "I'm the one who actually got Steve Hanks interested in making movies when we were kids, we used super eight film for the fun of it. Steve studied whatever he wanted in college and he never grew out of it. My parents insisted on business and, here I am. Steve has all the fun, while I'm stuck funding the fun for everyone else. Work, work, work. I deserve to have a little fun too, right?" He noticed her silence. "Sorry, am I venting?"

"It's fine," Janine said.

Max's room was on the twenty-first floor. They stepped out of the elevator to see a flurry of hotel staff in the hall. The door was open and people were moving in and out of the room. They created a cozy romantic dining area in the suite, with candles, crystal glassware, and fancy folded napkins. Max let one of the workers take charge of his luggage while he slipped out of his jacket and tie. He handed those over and then hurried to the table and filled two glasses with the open bottle of wine. He ferried one to Janine.

"To a quiet dinner," he said.

"To a quiet dinner." Janine clinked her glass with his and took a sip of the wine. It was an incredible buttery smooth chardonnay and she took another sip, very easy to drink, very tasty. Max noticed her approval and was pleased that she liked the wine he chose. He slipped the waiter a tip.

"Shall I serve dinner, sir?" the waiter asked.

"I'll take care of serving," Max told him. "Maybe, send down another bottle of that wine, but don't knock, just set it right outside the door. I'll get it when I need it. On ice."

Janine set her backpack down and looked at the table.

"How in the world did they beat us with the dinner?"

Max laughed. "It's the same dinner they catered upstairs for the party, I had them bring down two plates. They only had one floor to go down, while we had twenty floors with four stops to go up. It's lobster and steak. The alternate was French chicken. Shall I have them send a sample of the chicken?" She shook her head.

Max positioned himself directly in front of her. He moved so close that a whiff of his cologne infiltrated her nose. His trimmed brown hair framed a manly face, and his brown eyes glittered behind his designer eyewear. He stared intently at her eyes. He was just as broad in the shoulders as Ian, slightly taller, and quite physically fit. She felt the heat radiating off his chest and it succeeded in keeping her blood stirred up. She didn't move away. His nice white teeth lined up perfectly in his grin.

"I want to get this out on the table before anything else is said." He kept his eyes on hers, and moved a tab bit closer. "I am very attracted to you. I don't mean to put you on the spot, or anything, but you should know; I consider you a very beautiful woman." Max sipped his wine, watching for her reaction.

Janine didn't know how to respond. Standing so close to Max after just spying on Ian, was confusing. Her nerves were all revved up and his aftershave kept invading her nostrils, egging things on. The first time she met Max she found him handsome. She excused his pushy attitude as a symptom of his success. She had been distracted with Ian back then too, but this time things were different, Janine was determined to let Ian be, and Ian had definitely moved on. Janine stared back at Max, considering him. She hadn't thought much about him in the past year, not until he became their acting producer. She took a deep sip of her wine, fully aware that her nerves were tingling from her clandestine musings downstairs.

"I'm here to discuss my contract."

Max nodded, "I know, and we'll discuss it, I promise. But first, let's get this out of the way, because I can see we're both thinking about it." He took her wine glass and set it on the table next to his. Then, he moved even closer. His hand brushed the hair away from her shoulder, surprising her. She didn't know what she wanted. Did she want Max Colliers to kiss her? Well, she wanted somebody to kiss her, she knew that. So, she didn't move when Max bent down to brush his lips lightly on hers.

Max grew bolder, and Janine closed her eyes. Not mind blowing, or earth shattering, but pleasant. It was very nice, she decided, and kissed him back a bit. Her hand touched his jaw and it suddenly felt terribly wrong. She pushed him away and Max grinned happily at her. He reached down and took her hand.

"Shall we eat?"

Like a perfect gentleman, he pulled out her chair and helped her get settled. He removed the silver domed cloches from their dinners and recharged the glasses with the buttery wine. *Crap*, Janine thought, *why did she kiss Max Colliers?* She was there to talk about her contract.

"I know you could let me out of my contract right now, if you wanted." She decided to be direct and get right to the point. "I can buy the contract out, if you put a reasonable sum on it."

"You don't want me to let you out of the contract yet," Max softly said.

"Of course I do, why would you say that?"

Max chewed quietly, "Carlos. I don't feel right about letting him go."

"What do you mean? What does that mean?"

"You and Carlos are two parts of a duo," Max said. "When you were absent last season, Carlos didn't fit anymore. It was an awkward dynamic. There was no one for him to joke with. If I let you go, I'll have to drop Carlos as well. We haven't found anyone to fill your shoes and play off Carlos the way you do. We would need to create a whole new backup team for the doctor and Kiki."

"You're saying, when I leave the show, you plan on firing Carlos?"

Max shook his head. "You're taking this the wrong way. Look at it from the business point of view. Did you catch the final episodes of last season, after you went off on your emergency break? Did you see what happened? Boring flops. We can't have Carlos by himself as a support team."

"You're telling me, that unless I stay with the show, you are going to get rid of Carlos too?" Janine stood up, sizzling with anger.

"I'm saying that you being on the show is the easiest way to keep Carlos." Max didn't raise his voice, but his brow tightened. "It's going to be very easy for you to cast me as the bad guy right now, and that upsets me, because I have nothing but positive, glowing, thoughts about you, and of Carlos too. I think you two are fantastic. An original dynamic that's hard to match. I don't want to see either of you go. Believe me, we've tried to find a Janine Stinger replacement but you are one of a kind. Have you seen your fan letters? This won't make me popular, but that's one of the evils of running a business and being the boss, making the hard, unpopular decisions."

"I see your mind is already made up," Janine accused. "You're going to fire Carlos the day I leave. You're not even going to give him a chance to find a-a dynamic with another partner."

Max leaned back wearily. He looked just as tired as he had in the lobby. He rubbed his brow with a hand.

"It's hard to imagine him in a light other than the one you guys have painted," Max said softly. "Our attempts at changing his image have been flat out rejected. He's keeping loyal to you and won't bend from the image you two have created. I've got zero evidence Carlos can be flexible enough to fit with a new partner. Both of you were pretty hard headed about some of the simple changes I tried at that last shoot."

"Are you talking about those costumes?" Janine shook her head and searched for her backpack. She grabbed it up. "To me, that looked like you wanting to exploit us."

Max shot up and stepped around the table to block her exit. He pressed his lips together. She wondered if he would physically try to stop her. He was tall and appeared quite strong, the muscles on his forearms flexed as he stuck his hands in his pockets. He had a determined personality, and might be hard to fight. His eyes said that she was being unreasonable and unfair, causing trouble, when all he wanted was a pleasant dinner with her. *Would he stop her, or grab her, if she tried to leave, like Rick had?* She took a measured breath to tamp down the deep seated fear rising to the surface. *Was she reacting to him, or was she reacting to Chicago?*

"Work with me here," he said gently. "Wait a moment and listen to what I have to say." He took a small step back and relaxed his shoulders. *Did he register her fear?* "I made a mistake. Both you and Carlos have very nice physiques and I was trying for a different image. Truly, if we see Carlos in a different way, then maybe we'll have an easier time fitting him with a new partner. There is a distinct direction I envision taking this show."

Janine stared toward him, focusing on the air between them, trying to stop the panic attack simmering. *Was this always going to be a problem for her, reading men this way?*

"I realize the new outfit is revealing. You have a valid grievance with me about that, and I'm sorry. Believe me when I say that I never imagined you would be insulted. After all, I've seen you dressed very sexy and looking quite comfortable. I can't unsee what I've seen. You have very nice curves, and the marks on your body are intriguing. I thought we could enhance your screen image and give you a sexy, dangerous look. With the way Kiki dresses, your reaction completely surprised me. You never came around for us to run it by you, nor did you respond to the queries. I took your silence, your disinterest, to mean that anything was okay with you."

There was some truth in there. The show sent her plenty of invites to participate in meetings before San Antonio. She deleted them all.

"Please, let's sit back down." Max stepped further away. He put on his perfect smile again. He peered at her from under his lashes. His voice was calm, nice. "Let's negotiate a plan we can both be happy with. I'm not kidding," he put a hand over his heart, "I want you happy with me. I don't like being the bad guy, especially with an lovely woman. We can negotiate and eat this nice dinner and become friends. Let's be friends."

Janine sat down grumpily. She couldn't just run off without knowing what would happen. How many chances would she get to speak directly with Max Colliers about her contract? And now she had Carlos to worry about. Didn't he recently buy a gigantic house for his parents? He couldn't lose his job now.

"If you want me so happy with you," her voice was low, "Why are you playing hardball? Forcing me to return and now threatening Carlos. You want to know what would make me happy? Let me out of my contract, right now, and give Carlos time to mesh with a new partner before writing him off."

Max nodded, sipping his wine.

"Your wishes are noted," he matched her low tone. "But, speaking from the executive producer's seat, the CEO trying to keep a business afloat, I forced you back to save the show. The audience needs to see you. If all we get are a few episodes, then I need to take them. Hopefully, the ratings and popularity get back on track, and losing you will not hurt us as much as I think it will." Max took a deep breath. "Right now, the best replacement option for you appears to be a replacement of the entire back up team, which doesn't thrill me, I don't enjoy letting people go. If I can talk you into staying the rest of the season, those worries will disappear, but I can see that's not going to happen."

Janine shook her head, "It's not going to happen."

"We vetted potential partners for Carlos. We screen tested and personality checked many candidates. He rubs people the wrong way. Look at how he grates on Don. Don is an award winning cameraman with an incredible reputation, we're lucky to have him. So, a new partner for Carlos, we haven't found the right chemistry yet. He tears everyone apart, and it's not always funny. But we do have an alternate backup plan. We found one potential replacement team that might work."

"Does Carlos know about this?"

Max's brown eyes shifted down. "Nobody knows. I hoped to change your mind; charm you into staying."

"What will it take to give Carlos a fighting chance?" Janine asked.

Max leaned forward. Carlos needed to show Max that he could be flexible and mold into a new image. Max planned on pushing a sexier back up team, but didn't think Carlos would follow through with that angle. If Janine wanted to help Carlos, she might take the wardrobe and image team seriously, and encourage Carlos to do the same thing. If Janine jumped on board with a few of his modifications, then Carlos might too, and if Carlos could pull it off, Max might be able to find a fit for him when she left. If he found that fit sooner, he could cut her loose from her contract early.

"You mean, let me out of my contract now? Like, right after this shoot?"

Max nodded.

"Why would you do that?" She didn't trust his complete change of heart. It was too easy.

Max poured out the rest of the wine.

"I now see how important it is to you. I misread you. I truly believed that you were tired of being the girl in the background," he said. "But, I want something in return." By the way his eyes flickered over her, Janine could guess exactly what he wanted in return. She picked up her crystal of expensive buttery wine. If he propositioned her, she was going to throw it in his face.

"And what would that be?" she asked.

He reached to the dining trolley and ferried two smaller plates to the table.

"That you allow me dibs on the carrot parsnip cake and let me believe the chocolate mouse is exactly what you would have gone for." He set the deserts in front of them. "I'm sorry, but I love the carrot cake."

That completely disarmed her. Janine drained the tasty wine and regarded him silently. She kept expecting Max to be more nefarious but he was actually quite nice, and though she didn't like to admit it, his explanation made a little sense to her. He chatted about his disaster of a brother who always took more of the cake than the standard lot when they were kids, always trying to steal things right from under his nose. Then, he insisted she have a bite of his carrot cake to see why he preferred it.

"I also, humbly, request a do-over," he added softly.

"A do-over?"

"Dinner. Promise to have dinner with me again, maybe, back in Austin, on a real date." He stared at her with his steady brown eyes and she could see that he wasn't joking. "Just dinner. To give me a chance to win you over, not for the show, but for me. I'd like to get to know you. That's not too much to ask, is it?"

Just dinner? Max was a handsome, wealthy, confident man, and she was very single. Why not? She even felt somewhat attracted to him. What woman wouldn't be a little attracted to him? And he seemed to be trying very hard to be nice to her.

"Okay," she agreed.

Max smiled. Then, he jumped up to retrieve the wine outside the door. He insisted she stay to toast their upcoming date and put the seal of approval on their agreement. He felt certain everything would turn out terrific for everybody; win, win, win. In the middle of opening the bottle of chardonnay, his cell phone began buzzing. He glanced at it and his eyes widened slightly.

"It's Doctor McNally," he picked up the phone, "Hello, Ian, how are you?"

Janine could hear the cadence of Ian's voice, but not the words. Why did she feel like she just got caught doing something wrong? Max poured the wine as he listened to Ian on the phone. Janine was limited to hearing a one sided conversation.

"No worries, I got room service."

"Is that right?" Max glanced at her.

"Let me put your mind at ease, she's here, she made it, no need to worry."

"Because…because, we're having dinner together. Don't worry, I'm sure she'll be on time tomorrow."

"Yes, okay. See you then."

He chuckled when he ended the call. He raised his glass to her.

"To our upcoming dinner date," he said, and she returned the salute. Max chuckled again. "He's keeping tabs on you. The doctor wanted to put out a search party for you. I'm not sure where he planned to look, but he was worried something may have happened to you between the airport and the hotel." Max zoned in on her small backpack. "He said you haven't check in yet."

She shook her head. "I haven't, not yet."

"Where's your luggage?"

She pointed to her backpack and watched his eyebrows shoot up.

"That's it? Wow, you travel light. I feel like a prima donna with my bags. Want me to call the front desk and have them change your room to one up here? I can have them send up a key."

Janine stood slowly, shaking her head. She needed to get out there, the wine was making her feel too comfortable, warm, and careless. She grabbed her backpack. Max followed her to the door and, like the perfect gentleman, he kissed her hand and said he had a wonderful time. He looked forward to seeing her again, the next day, and in Austin for their date.

When Janine finally checked in, she retrieved a note informing her to meet in the Whistler ballroom no later than nine in the morning. She recognized Ian's blocky letters. *Did they look angry?* Ian expected her to help set up remote cameras, audio, and other equipment in the morning.

Janine found Carlos in the small ballroom joking with compact blond Ben and another young man. They were loading audio and visual equipment into different air cases for protection. Carlos introduced the other guy as Mike, the van driver. Janine wore her standard *Spectral Analysis* T-shirt and saw that Carlos wore his too. From across the room, the image team, Lauren, Guy, and Sally, eyed them warily. After San Antonio, Janine didn't blame them for being hesitant of approaching her.

Janine waved and the trio instantly perked up, surprised at her spontaneous greeting. Janine nudged Carlos.

"Let's go over there and see what they have in store for us," Janine said.

"Did you give input to Sally when you got measured?" Carlos asked.

Janine gave no input. She hadn't planned on wearing anything new and assumed Carlos had a similar mind. Janine studied the thick and messy sideburns on his face. Those giant pork chops could not be what Lauren had imagined, they completely covered his adorable dimples. Janine suspected they were his way of following orders while rebelling at the same time.

"Are you going to let her trim those?" Janine asked him.

Carlos chuckled. "I found the design sketch they planned for me. They're going to transform me into an anime character."

"What if we cooperate with their design plans and see what happens?" Janine said.

"You mean, go Hollywood? Seriously? Or in your case, playmate of the month. I happened to see the design sketch for you, and they're going to outdo Kiki with the outfits, Janine. Are you sure about this?"

"I don't think it's going to be that bad," she hoped. "I had a conversation with Max and he gave some convincing reasons for the design ideas. Why don't we give one or two of them a try? We can ham things up to make it fun."

Carlos studied her. "The doctor said you were with Colliers last night instead of at the dinner party. I'm not going to say I totally object, because Maria says that he is an awesome catch for some girl, and he's filthy rich, insanely rich, and they might buy the Spurs. I just want to make sure you're being careful. Don't squander the milk, Janine, girls often squander the milk with guys like him. My mama always said, why buy the cow if you can get the milk for free. That's sound wisdom, from my mom!" Carlos raised his finger to drive the point home. "Even more important, don't give your heart away too fast, okay."

"No chance of that," Janine giggled at Carlos and his clumsy big brother advice. "I don't think my heart is very keen on him." A thought just struck her, "I guess, that might make Max Colliers the perfect man for me."

"Hi!" Lauren and her gigantic smile had snuck up behind them. She glanced between them expectantly. "Are you two ready to get prepped for the morning segment?"

Janine nudged Carlos. She could see him hesitate.

"We're really going to do this?" He stared at her.

"I am," Janine told him. "I'm going to go all in with this." She turned to Lauren. "I'm all yours."

They crammed into the van with a plan to hit four sites. Don would film the crew setting up the remote sensors, and the footage would be used as backdrop and filler. They packed regular and low IR cameras, audio recorders, and a mini weather station that could record data on temperature, pressure, and humidity. Most of the information would be sent via wireless communication to their control center in the ballroom. Ian instructed Ben to have someone remotely monitor each site over a twenty-four hour period. The doctor settled next to the driver and Janine rode in the rear with Carlos and Don. Ian hardly said two words to her before jumping into the van. He barely glanced her way. *Well, hello to you too*, she thought.

Their new *Spectral Analysis* shirts were athletic, form-fitting, moisture-wicking, long sleeved shirts. They were brightly colored in the visible bands of the electromagnetic spectrum, starting with a red left sleeve and ending with a deep violet right sleeve. A small logo was stitched into the fabric along with their first names over the left breast. The female version of the shirt had a generous scoop neck to show off her cleavage. They paired their colorful shirts with dark stone-washed jeans and heavy duty work boots. They looked a bit like comic book characters. Everyone wore the outfit, except the doctor, he wore another nice shirt with his updated tie.

"The plan for this morning," the doctor read from his clip board. "We are going to set up remotes at the old water tower, the alley behind the theatre, Fort Dearborn Park, and also that little park near 16th street and Indiana Avenue. All, hopefully, before taking an afternoon lunch at the hotel where we will touch base with Kiki and Colliers before getting in a good sleep. After sunset, we'll head back to those sites and film segments with Kiki and mix in a little ghost theory. We'll conduct an onsite investigation in the smaller park before our séance at the Congress Plaza, so it'll be an all-nighter. The more we do tonight, the less we worry about tomorrow."

The old tower in Chicago was a historic water landmark on Michigan Avenue in the shopping district. It happened to be the second oldest water tower in the United States, built in 1869, and was originally constructed from limestone blocks. As one of the only surviving structures of the Chicago Fire, it represented an important event in the city's history. Periodically, the police received reports of a hanging man in the tower, only to investigate and find nothing at all. The hanging man ghost was rumored to be a victim of the Great Chicago Fire. A lone man who refused to abandon his post during the blaze, and later hung himself in the 154 foot tower rather than succumb to the flames.

Doctor McNally stood just inside the entrance with their point of contact, a short man with a thick neck and round, bulging eyes. His bulging eyes kept returning to scan over Janine and she felt self-conscious in the skin tight shirt and push up bra Sally dressed her in. She silently repeated "you are a badass" to herself over and over again, the mantra Kiki once suggested to pull off a racy outfit. Janine found it worked well at boosting her confidence. Don filmed the doctor's conversation with their bug-eyed contact man while Carlos and Janine posed stiffly, like bad asses, next to the equipment cases. Carlos's biceps bulged quite nicely in his form fitting shirt and she doubted she looked even remotely as tough.

"Can you point out which of these blocks in the building are of the original limestone pillars?" the doctor asked.

Their contact pointed out the different columns and talked about the past renovations with the doctor. After the short interview, the crew filed into the main stairwell of the tower and climbed the spiral steps into the top dome. The doctor and their contact man led the way.

"You go ahead," Don said to Carlos. "I'll film from the rear following after Stinger."

"Oh, come on, Don," Carlos chided him. "My ass is going to look ten times better on film than hers." Carlos pushed Janine up ahead of him. "No offense, Janine, but I doubt you do any squats in your spare time? I really doubt it. Let me tell you, Don, I do squats from all around the world. Bulgarian squats, DMZ landmine squats, Japanese sumo squats, Donny dumbbell squats. You probably do those. Believe me, this is the ass you want in the shot. I've been working for this opportunity, I deserve it."

Max was right, Janine noted, *Carlos didn't try to get along with anyone.*

At the top of the tower, they rigged a remote infrared camera, a regular camera, a small weather box, and an ion detector. The doctor seemed uncertain about the audio recorder and then decided it wasn't needed. A hanging man wasn't going to say anything.

"We'll save it for the alley." He gave Don the signal to start moving down the stairs. Janine and Carlos snapped the gear boxes closed and gathered them up. The doctor moved closer to them, keeping an eye on the bug-eyed contact man.

"Carlos, do you think we can swipe a sample of that wall on the way down? Just a wee chip? Maybe at a corner, low. I'll tell you where," the doctor whispered.

"Yeah, sure. I've got a little tool." Carlos glanced at the bug-eyed man.

The doctor softly added. "He's not going to give us much of a chance, unless…" the doctor didn't quite look at her, "Janine could distract him a wee bit."

"How do you suggest I do that?"

"You're distracting him already without even trying." Ian's eyes avoided hers, then they aimed downward and scanned her skin-tight, low-cut, moisture-wicking shirt. "You could easily get him to start walking down the stairs with you, right now. If he resists, stand up nice and straight and look him in the eye. He'll easily follow you. You know, lure him ahead and be flirty."

"Fine," she snapped, knowing she sounded very pissed off.

Their next stop was a pathetic little patch of grass near the 18th Street metro station named the Battle of Dearborn Park. The entire park was corded off and reserved for them. They quickly set up a camera on a lamppost before driving a couple of blocks away to a smaller patch of grass on the corner of Mark Twain Parkway. Again, the police marked the area as reserved for the *Spectral Analysis* TV show. Those signs were sure to attract a late night audience, so Ian removed them and threw them into the back of the van.

The patch of the park the doctor directed them toward was separated from the main play area by a set of railroad tracks and fencing. Several mature trees stretched across the grass, shading the area nicely. A few of the trees had low, thick branches and looked very easy to climb. When Janine had been in Chicago for college, her soccer teammates often had climbing contests to see who could get up a tree first, or go the highest, or brave the thinnest branch. The trees reminded her of that nice memory.

"That park back there," Ian told them. "That's where the massacre occurred. But this place right here, this is where they buried the dead, on this little triangle of land, especially in this patch of trees here. In the past, I recorded some eerie low frequency electromagnetic pulses on this spot. We're going to bring the magnetic antennae and the big box tonight. Right now let's get the remote audio and cameras in the trees. Maybe higher up, then angle them down at that spot. Kiki wants us to suspend small mirrors from the branches as well."

"Why did you want a piece of the wall from the water tower?" Carlos asked him.

"It's part of the original stone," Ian said. "No worries, the historic society said it was okay to take a wee sample, but that guy wanted to give us a problem and I wanted to avoid a long discussion about it. I'm going to have it analyzed. The tower was constructed from limestone, you know. Some limestones are more dolomite than calcite. Calcium magnesium carbonate. I'm interested to see the amount of magnesium in the minerals."

Janine listened in. Why was the doctor concerned about levels of magnesium in limestone? That seemed random. Janine stared up at the trees and really wanted to climb one. Maybe this was one of those places they could ham things up and have a little fun.

"Hey, Carlos, think you can climb that tree before I can get up this one?" Janine called over. "I'll put the audio in mine and you can put the camera in yours."

Mike brought out a ladder but Janine and Carlos waved him away. They started climbing and Don started filming. Janine grabbed a low branch, then swung her legs up to curl around a higher limb. She pulled herself easily up to a standing position. She was about seven feet off the ground looking down at the doctor.

"How high would you like the audio recorder, Doctor?" she asked.

He unexpectedly turned his soft blue eyes on her. "About that high." Ian smiled at her and she melted a bit. "You make a very lovely monkey."

"Thank you, Doctor." Then thought, *That's the first time he's looked directly at me today.* She turned to start strapping the audio device to the tree, feeling suddenly sad. A whisper of a breeze blew through the trees that sent a chill down her spine. It felt familiar, like a ghost from the past. She glanced at Carlos and noticed that he had climbed much higher than her.

"My camera is just a little harder to attach," Carlos said. "I've got this swivel attachment to hook up."

"You win." She told him, gripping the tree because she felt slightly dizzy. "Just be careful going down."

Janine moved to a lower branch then jumped dramatically to the ground. She gave Don a little gymnastics end salute as Ben delivered the small mirrors.

The alley behind the Nederlander Theater was their final destination before lunch. Back in 1903, a fire broke out in the theater killing more than six hundred people. Most of the victims fell to their death on the back alley ground. That event was still considered the deadliest single building fire in United States history. The doctor said that many people claimed the *Alley of Death* was haunted and reported hearing whispered voices when walking that stretch of pavement.

Doctor McNally directed them to set up remote cameras on both sides of the alley with audio recorders tuned to cover the sonic range. They finished rather quickly and were happy to know they were a couple of blocks away from their lunch. Although, the doctor suggested they might swing around to the river to set up the extra camera. Apparently, that intersection was the actual site of Fort Dearborn. He checked his watch and saw the time.

"Tell you what," he surveyed the crew. "You lot pack up and go back to the hotel. Have lunch, then take a nap so you'll be fresh tonight. I'll set this one up on my own. Just tell Kiki and Colliers that I'll be straight away, and that we're on schedule." The doctor ran down the street with the camera and soon disappeared around the corner.

As they began loading the gear into the van, Janine noticed one of the small wire connectors used for attaching antennae to cameras or audio devices. It could be one of the many extras, but it also might have fallen off the camera the doctor took. It lay on the ground, right outside the van door. Janine picked it up and looked at Carlos and Don.

"Did the doctor drop this?"

Nobody knew. They debated calling him, but Janine volunteered to run after him. If he didn't drop it, then no problem, but if he needed it, he'd have it right away. Mike suggested they drive around as soon as they got the van packed, but Janine insisted that she could get there sooner if she started running immediately. The doctor obviously wanted everyone to go eat and then sleep all afternoon.

In the corner of her mind, she knew there was a different reason she wanted to run out alone to Doctor McNally. A reason she refused to formulate in her head just yet. She imagined that little connector as some sort of cosmic sign urging her along.

Janine ran in her clumpy new boots as her lovely curls flew all around. It didn't take long to catch up to Ian. She'd been running the track regularly and had gotten into top shape. She closed in on him, just as he reached the corner of Michigan Avenue and East Wacker Street. His was surprised to see her right behind him, and she held up the little connector. The doctor paused, examined his camera, flipped it around, then shook his head.

"Not mine," he said.

They stood quietly, catching their breath. He watched her with eyes that blinked a little quicker than normal, probably wondering why she ran after him like that. *Why did she run after him like that? Damn you*, she cursed herself. *What are you doing here? You told Kiki you were going to leave him alone.* Janine reminded herself that she wasn't planning to hang around Texas or *Spectral Analysis*. Her plans were separate from his plans and she needed to let him move on in peace, with someone who didn't have the issues she had. She straightened up and brushed the tangled hair out of her face. He waited patiently for her to speak.

"Ian, I want us to be friends," she said softly. "I know it may take some time to completely forgive each other, but maybe we can try to forget some of what happened and be friends again."

Janine Stinger is Strength

After an excruciating long moment the doctor nodded. He gave her a weak smile. Of course, he wanted to be friends too. He stepped over and hugged her briefly. Then, Ian took a step back and eyed the tall lamp post.

"Since you're here, we could attach it up higher. That would be the optimum placement. Come on, I'll give you a boost."

She unlaced her boots and took them off. The doctor readied the camera and flexible clamp for easy attachment. Then, using the post for balance, she stepped into his hand and he easily propelled her up.

"Stand on my shoulders?" he said.

She stepped up and was soon on his shoulders using the lamppost to steady herself. She reached down and took the camera from him. She quickly wrapped the clamp around the post and began tightening all the loose ends. Ian started talking.

"People report seeing spirits out here and along the river walk down there. I doubt it, but since we're investigating the massacre site, we may as well monitor out here as well. We've got the extra camera and all. Don't forget to adjust the panoramic lens horizontally." His warm hand patted her foot. "You really do make a brilliant monkey."

When she finished attaching the camera, Ian tried to squat to make her descent less dangerous, because she couldn't jump to the pavement without her shoes. She grabbed the lamppost.

"Don't do that. You're going to break your back. I'm going to slide down this pole fireman style, no problem," she said.

"Too bad Don's not here to get this on camera. It would go nicely with your new sex kitten image."

They started laughing, shaking with the giggles. She slid down safely and let go of the post, but she wasn't paying attention to the ground. The lamppost was on a little pedestal and her first step was a misstep that set her balance off and she stumbled. The pavement was going to be a very hard landing.

But she needn't have worried, because Ian happened to be a world class catcher of falling women. The show definitely capitalized on that skill during the first season. The doctor saved Kiki from one nasty fall after another. He even caught Janine once on the show. The Doctor-Kiki catch provided a little side event the audience always looked forward to. The human drama of a possible romantic interaction was the first thing the audience latched onto. True to form, the doctor did not let her hit the pavement.

It was a perfect catch. Janine felt his strong, solid arms embrace her as he spun a bit. She remembered him once explain, in his doctor voice, that he spun in order to slow the fall, which lessened the force of impact between them. More collision time, less force, same impulse, basic physics, he had explained to the camera. *Yep*, Carlos had chuckled, *he's a real nerd.* Janine felt Ian's hand move slightly along her back and the base of her neck. She got her balance back quickly but her arms moved up automatically to hold him in a loose embrace. One hand reached over to steal a feel of his curly beard. *It was so soft!*

Ian released her and they quickly separated, but he still faced her. He stared into her eyes. Her pulse raced. There was no way to hide what was in her heart as she looked at him. She desperately wanted to move closer.

A car honked. And honked again. Janine realized that someone called out her name and a man stood a few feet away snapping photos with a cell phone. Then, a deep voice, that Janine instantly recognized, called her name again. She turned her attention quickly toward that voice.

"All right, that's enough. Run along," the deep voice ordered the photographer.

An extremely thin man in an oversized crumpled suit shooed away a man with a cell phone. The cell phone guy raised his hand and said, "Nice catch Doctor," before moving away. The thin man walked toward Janine and Ian. He had wiry brown hair and thick, light-sensitive glasses. Janine wondered if that man would know she had returned to the city. She wondered if he would visit her. She was very happy to see him.

"Detective Anderson," she said.

"Janine Stinger," he responded.

Detective Anderson smiled his toothy smile and nodded with a very pleased expression on his face. He glanced at Ian.

"Do you mind?" He held his hands out like he wanted to hug Janine.

"What?" Ian appeared confused. He saw that she was happy and turned back to the detective. "No. Aye, go ahead."

Detective Robert Anderson stepped in to give her a giant hug. Even though she was a tad taller than him, she felt very safe in the presence of his quiet, solid strength. Once upon a time, Janine and the detective spent the better part of a year getting to know each other. After Janine survived a brutal knife attack in a section of Chicago woods, Robert Anderson was the lead detective tasked to investigate, solve, and see the case to conviction. There had been an extended period of time when she only felt safe in the vicinity of Bob Anderson and his crumbled suits.

"I dropped in at your hotel," Detective Anderson said, "looking for you."

"We were setting stuff up," she smiled at him. Janine glanced at Ian. "Ian, this is Detective Robert Anderson. Detective, this is Doctor Ian McNally."

The two men shook hands and exchanges pleasantries. Detective Anderson informed Ian that he read his book on paranormal electromagnetic energy. He was curious after watching the show, but hardly understood any of it.

"Do you mind catching up?" Detective Anderson asked Janine. "Maybe over lunch?"

"Why don't you join us at the hotel," Ian suggested. "We have a generous spread and you can meet the rest of our team. If you need a private spot, there's plenty of room."

"Thank you. I think I'll take you up on that offer." The detective waved away the car parked on the side of the road. Was it his partner? After Janine got her boots back on, the three of them started the short walk around the corner to the Lincoln House Hotel.

Chapter 8

The Detective *Kiki*

A local catering service provided a large spread of various salads and sandwiches. The hotel often sponsored groups in the ballrooms and pulled out nice dining tables for one corner of the conference room, creating a lunch area. Apparently, Max Colliers often booked the Lincoln House for his business trips. In fact, Kiki discovered that he reserved a smaller boardroom to meet with folks the next day, for business unrelated to *Spectral Analysis*. Kiki watched Max stroll toward her table with his lunch plate.

"Well, hello, Kiki Mellow. You look very fetching. May I have lunch you? I promise to behave."

"Please, sit down."

"I saw Carlos and Don, but what happened to the doctor and Stinger?"

"They're setting up one last camera around the corner," Kiki told him.

Most of the team ate, socialized, and left before Janine and Ian returned. Just a few stragglers hung out in different corners, chatting. When the doctor and Janine entered the ballroom, Kiki noticed an unfamiliar man following along. That man joined them at the buffet table. He projected a very strong and interesting energy. Kiki was delighted to see such a fascinating array.

The man's aura blended pink and radiated out of his trunk, hands, and head, which was an incredibly rare thing. There was further light around his crown, and Kiki concentrated to pick it up. Yellow and orange and a bit of emerald green intermingled. Definitely a peaceful shade of green, not the darker shade of envy more often seen in a halo. The yellows resonated confidence, while the orange tint hinted at perception. Kiki knew the man must be analytical. Ian vibrated some of those same patterns. But mostly, the mystery man exuded a gentle pink energy with open and loving vibrations in all directions. His aura fascinated her. Masculine, but certainly not a typical man's aura at all.

Kiki suddenly felt nervous as the trio turned toward her table. She felt as if this would be momentous meeting. She wore a very snug, low-cut shirt, no bra, and a flashy gaudy belt, like a rock groupie. She knew it was a very tantalizing ensemble, a Kiki Mellow ensemble, and now she wished she had change clothes after setting up for the séance. Ben had filmed the setup, which included a little banter with the manager of the Congress Plaza. The buzz of sexual tension always made an interview more fun, and helped Kiki tune into the energy around her. Now she just felt silly, and she certainly didn't want the man with the pink aura to presume she was frivolous.

"Who's that man?" Max asked.

"I haven't the faintest," Kiki said. "But he's absolutely gorgeous."

Max laughed softly. "Yes, that's a gorgeous wrinkled suit he's wearing. And look at that curly wiry hair, and those safety glasses. He winked at her. "I never knew you to be so sarcastic, Kiki."

"I wasn't being sarcastic."

Max rose to greet the trio as they reached the table. Janine introduced the man as Detective Robert Anderson, an old friend. *Her detective!* Max insisted that Janine and her old friend join them to eat. Kiki could see that Max's curiosity was as piqued as hers. Of course, he had no idea about Janine's past in Chicago. Max arranged things so that Janine took the chair next to him, and he make a big point of helping Janine get comfortably seated. Max seemed obvious about what he was after. Kiki wondered how Janine was handling the Max Colliers seduction experience. Kiki admitted that she enjoyed watching Max in action, he tended to be quite successful and always ended up on good terms with each of his conquests.

"Are you part of the park security the city is providing tonight?" Max asked.

Detective Anderson shook his head slightly. "That's a special job, not really my area of expertise as a detective." He smiled at Janine, "If I get a chance, I might drop in on one of your shoots to see you in action. We've plenty of interesting ghosts here in Chicago."

They all agreed that he should come out, anytime. Ian recited their rough timeline and gave him his cell number in case he wanted to call ahead. The detective whipped out his little book to jot it all down. Kiki gave him her personal number.

"In case Ian doesn't answer," she said.

He glanced at her and she could see that he understood her completely. In regards to Janine and Chicago, Kiki was the confidant. Kiki asked if he had any paranormal experiences.

"I might not have been paying attention properly," the detective admitted to her, "but I've been to a few places that give me the feeling someone hasn't quite left. That back alley you're visiting is one of them. It's a very cold stretch of pavement, I would say."

"How did you and Janine become old friends?" Max asked. "It's kind of unusual, isn't it? A young Texas gal and an old city detective. How do you know each other?"

Janine answered quickly. "I went to the University of Chicago my first two years of college. I met the detective back then."

Kiki noticed that Janine's aura had altered into softer hues under the influence of Detective Anderson's pink pulse. *Wow, his energy proved powerful enough to brighten Janine's dark cloud.*

"That's right," Max said. "I remember seeing U of C in your personnel file. That's a pretty impressive school. Did the detective break up a frat party or something? Is Janine hiding a party girl past from us, Detective? Or did she get into some other type of mischief?" His attempts at light hearted teasing were falling flat.

"Well," the detective smiled calmly. "It's nothing like that at all. I just happened to be in a position to help Miss Stinger one day and we became fast friends. If it was a story worth telling, I'm sure she would have told you by now."

The detective pegged Max pretty quickly, Kiki thought. The detective gave Max an even look. His big brown eyes were firm, but not mean in the least. *He's likely a terrific detective*, she thought. He'd probably make a terrific father as well, and Kiki wondered if he already was a father. He looked to be in his late thirties, or older. The thought of him being married with children caused a little flutter of panic to rise in her chest.

"Are you married, Detective? Do you have children?" Kiki blurted. After a stunned moment, everyone chuckled.

"Why, no, Miss Mellow. I've never had that pleasure." He gave her a generous smile. "Of course, I love the idea of marriage and raising children. How do you feel about it?"

"I love the idea of having children. With the right man." Kiki smiled at him. She absolutely enjoyed gazing into his eyes. "Very much so."

Max Colliers let out a big laugh. "Be careful." Max patted the detective on the shoulder. "Kiki's a bit of a man-eater. A real ball-buster, some would say. You can't be too keen on marriage, Kiki. I know two guys, who very recently came calling with outlandish diamond rings, only to be sent away with their tail between their legs."

"Feel free to air all my dirty laundry whenever it strikes your fancy, Max," Kiki said sweetly to him. "Not that any of it is your business."

Kiki didn't think there was anything wrong with dating men she found interesting. She loved being in the company of attentive male energy and often channeled that attention into honing her mystic senses, and she never, ever, promised anybody anything she wasn't willing to give. That last fellow wasn't interested in a real marriage anyway. He only wanted to prolong the illusion of their flashy romance for the sake of his reputation and growing fan base. It had been a mutually beneficial arrangement for them. Date and have fun in front of the media without the pressure of a real relationship. Her vow of chastity and his homosexuality would cleverly stay hidden. But then he wanted to up the ante in their game. He believed the extra payout for Kiki would be in obtaining citizenship. He imagined she would jump at that offer.

She didn't and broke it off immediately. Fake or no, she did not plan on marrying anyone, ever.

"Perhaps you misinterpret Miss Mellow," the detective said. "I believe she is what one might call a coquette. A lovely woman only having a little fun, but means no harm."

"Who was the other bloke?" Ian raised an eyebrow at her. He only knew about the basketball player who wanted to improve his second string reputation by dating a TV personality. Kiki waved the question away, miffed, because Ian likely agreed with Max regarding what he once called her "callous" treatment of men.

The detective stood and excused himself from the table. He begged their pardon but desired to privately catch up with Janine. They moved across the room to sit in the plush chairs near the coffee dispenser. Kiki wondered if the detective could see auras. He must be able to see something, because he seemed to understand her perfectly.

Kiki, Ian, and Max quickly reconfirmed the plan for the evening and Max requested a spot in the séance. Kiki anticipated his request and agreed rather quickly. Max could provide some vital male energy to the table. They were going to attempt to contact several famous spirits at the Congress Plaza, but Kiki believed the room 441 ghost might be the only real specter they'd encounter. That ghost was notorious for waking guests with noises and moving objects. Many people even reported the manifestation of a dark shadow in the shape of a woman in that room.

Lauren suddenly plopped into the chair beside the doctor. She gave him a bright smile and casually placed her hand on his arm. They each said hello, then turned back to their personal notes. Max turned his attention across the room to Janine and the detective. In truth, all of them covertly watched Janine and the detective, Max was just very obvious about it.

Lauren already knew the man was a police officer, she spoke to him earlier in the day. Guy, Sally, and Lauren were very curious when he popped into the ball room looking for Janine Stinger. They wondered if she witnessed a crime, guessing it was the reason she missed the welcome dinner the night before.

"She's quite the mystery lady, isn't she? I wonder how they know each other, a windy city detective, no less. She's hiding a notorious, dangerous past. That's my guess. Maybe she ran with the wrong crowd once upon a time," Max grinned. "I wish she'd let on more. We had dinner last night and she doesn't give away much. Think I can crack her shell and discover all her dark secrets?"

"I think so," Lauren nodded brightly. "I probably shouldn't say this, but I overheard her and Carlos. Guess what she said?" She beamed at Max, "She thinks *you* might be the perfect man for her."

"Really?" Max grinned back at Lauren. "Finally, someone on my side. The perfect man for her, how about that, Doctor, Kiki, I might be the perfect man for Janine Stinger."

Max enjoyed pushing Ian's buttons. Kiki glanced at Ian and his blinking eyes.

"Max, obviously, that was sarcasm," Kiki purred. Lauren gasped, shocked.

"Come on, Kiki," Max smiled at her. "Why can't you be nice to me? Are you jealous?"

"Of course I'm jealous. You know how I like being the one to bust your balls." She winked at him, reminded Lauren about their hair plan, then excused herself to go start her beauty rest.

Kiki couldn't sleep. She was waiting for Janine to respond to her text. She insisted Janine message when she finished with the detective to confirm that everything was all right, or if she needed to talk. Kiki texted that she would not go to sleep until she heard back. Then, a soft knock came at her door.

Janine stood in the bright hall and Kiki ushered her in. Janine carried a bottle of wine.

"What's that for?" Kiki asked.

"It was sent to my room, from Max Colliers," Janine said. "We had dinner together last night and he noticed I liked this wine. Kind of a sweet of him, don't you think? Do you have an opener?"

"Careful with Max, he's quite a player." Kiki found a cork screw and handed it over. Then, she checked the cabinets in the suite and found a couple of very nice wine glasses. She held them while Janine poured.

"Are we celebrating or medicating?" Kiki asked.

"Just drinking," Janine said.

Kiki took a taste of the wine. Oh yes, a very elegant, creamy, full-bodied papaya taste. It slipped down very easily. Kiki could see why Janine preferred it. They sat silently enjoying the wine. That was one of the nice things about Janine Stinger, she was a quiet girl. Many of the women Kiki knew needed to chatter. Not Janine. They could sit and enjoy a quiet room and soak up some calm vibes.

"Detective Anderson wanted to tell me in person that Rick has his first parole board soon, in a couple of weeks," Janine said softly. "He's been the perfect prisoner and has a better chance of being released than most. Prisons are overcrowded and all, and it's not like he successfully killed anyone. The local politicians love him, I hear, especially the new governor."

Kiki sat up. Janine did not seem very upset.

"I've been anticipating it," Janine said softly. "He's very good at acting normal. He can be very convincing, likable, appealing. He even made me doubt my own memory at first."

"I remember that," Kiki said. "It was part of his main defense; That you didn't accuse him right away. That you must have been coerced into blaming him, by some detective."

Kiki knew the story from news features that referred to Janine as Jane Doe from Chicago to protect her identity. While Janine was a student at the university, she fell head over heels for a charming psychopath. Sometime during that relationship, she tried to leave him, but he didn't let her and held her prisoner in his house. When she finally escaped, he caught up to her and stabbed her multiple times. Janine had garish knife wounds on her back, stomach, and chest. She almost died. Later, in the hospital, it took more than a week for her to tell people that the man holding vigil at her bedside happened to be her attacker. A notorious trial followed, one in which the defense harshly questioned Janine's state of mind and memory. The defense claimed that she was irrational, hysterical, and in a hormone-induced emotional state. She was an unreliable witness. Her reckless defamatory allegations slandered their client, and she was accused of spreading false testimony. Different media outlets took opposing sides in the scandalous case, mostly because her identity was kept locked tight.

"Did you tell the detective about the letters?" Kiki asked. "They may be enough to keep him locked away."

Janine nodded. "He has them."

They polished off more than half the bottle of wine and Janine poured herself a little more.

"I really like your Detective Anderson," Kiki said out loud. "I mean, I *really* like him."

Janine smiled at her. "I think he really likes you too."

They started giggling about the detective. Janine told Kiki that the detective always came off very gentle and sweet, but once, she watched him take down a large burly drunk, completely immobilizing him in a matter of minutes. Then, he talked the man into being calm and quiet without further need of force.

Kiki described his aura and Janine had a hard time believing that it was pink. 'Crusty Detective Anderson with a pink aura, no way,' Janine said. Kiki also described the hues of yellow she found so attractive in his halo, and the little touch of tan that was similar to Ian's aura.

"Kiki, I know we need to get some sleep, to be fresh for tonight, but I have a favor." Janine stared into her glass of wine. "There were flowers with the bottle from Max, and a note. And then there's Ian. I'm sorry to say, I may have looked at Ian in a suggestive way on the street today."

Kiki shook her head. "You're afraid someone might come knocking on your door?"

"Does that sound arrogant?"

"You can just say no, Janine. Or you leave the door unanswered," Kiki told her.

"If a certain doctor shows up, I don't think I can just say no," Janine confessed. "I don't know what's wrong with me that I don't think I can say no to him. But I won't do that again. Would you let me nap in here with you?"

"It's part of that dark aura of yours. There is a streak of pure red underneath, the passion speaking. You thrive on the physical plane. Some of it is the trauma you're holding onto, but mostly, it's just your sensuality. Yes, you can nap in here. I've got plenty of room on that king size bed."

It was Ian that Janine was wary of, but Kiki would be worried about Max. After what Lauren said in the ball-room, she doubted Ian would be knocking on Janine's door. Especially after those conclusions he jumped to the night before, and the fact that he hadn't broken it off with Lauren yet. But that fantastic bottle of wine was a different story. It shouted that Max certainly would come knocking and expected to share that sweet chardonnay. Kiki knew very well Max's modus operandi, his notorious reputation, and the pride he took in it.

They were on a strict schedule for the evening shoots. They would walk down the alley at nine, visit the water tower at ten, and be in the parks by eleven. Then, they would meet Sally, Guy, and Lauren at the Congress Plaza for a touchup before her séance. Kiki planned a wardrobe change between the street investigations and the séance. If everything flowed smoothly, they'd be back in bed before dawn.

The guys already left for the alley and a fancy car waited to ferry Kiki, Janine, and Max after the girls were prepped. Max lounged in a chair completing paperwork and sipping an evening cocktail. True to his word, he planned to watch the filming from afar, from his limousine. Janine rushed into the conference room and did a double take of Kiki's hair.

"Wow, that's quite a red," Janine said. "I didn't know they could dye hair down here."

"Lauren colored it in my room. There's no plumbing down here," Kiki shook it around. "You were pretty conked out and slept through the whole thing." Then, Kiki leaned in and lowered her voice. "I want to try something tonight, in regards to you being a *dragoma*. Will you try a little experiment with me?"

"What kind of experiment?"

"Just one in which you mimic what I say on purpose, with concentrated intent, when I call out with my summons," Kiki said. "Speak to the spirits with me. Come on, I'll give you some insights while Lauren curls your hair."

More than a century ago, hundreds of people lost their lives right here on this spot. The Nederlander Theater replaced an earlier theater called the Iroquois, which burned down, tragically," Kiki spoke to Ian in front of the camera. "It occurred during the opening night of a show called Mr. Bluebeard in 1901, a show for children, so, many of the dead were very young. Today, people claim to hear whispered voices echoing down this alley, youthful voices. Perhaps they hear the ghostly cries of victims who tried to escape through a door on the upper level, a door that opened into nothing; no fire escape, no balcony, just open air. It wasn't the fire, but the fall, a plummet of over three stories, that led to their untimely demise," Kiki pointed to the top of the building. "An unknowing crowd pushed victims out the door as the flames closed in behind them."

Ian fiddled with his subsonic audio detector and monitored the needle swings. They sent Carlos and Janine down the alley with a small EMF box and a thermal-panger, but being in a paved back alley between two active buildings was not an optimum site for many of his gadgets. They gradually moved toward Carlos and Janine while Don filmed their conversation.

"We've been monitoring this alley for close to six hours, remotely," the doctor continued. "So far, we've detected nothing out of the ordinary. It doesn't help being in such an active area of the city."

"I do feel a deep hum back here," Kiki said. "A buzz of excitement that could be the energy from the people surrounding the area. Perhaps we should come back to the *Alley of Death* in the dead of night, when we know all the actors in this building have dispersed."

"Let's attempt something before we move on," the doctor said. "In our last investigation, we discovered one specter speaking on a subsonic level, in a range inaudible to the human ear."

"We've been told that people hear their own names being whispered in this alley," Kiki added.

"Yes. Let's see if we can mark a discernable pattern with our names, and then see if any matching patterns pop up in the subsonic range."

They finally reached Janine and Carlos. Their new *Spectral Analysis* investigative suits were very similar to the ones Max proposed at the Alamo. The main difference was in the trouser area. Sally added more leg room and added large cargo pockets to give them a military flavor. She also topped them with a thick web belt of clips and carabiners for attaching gear. Janine's outfit was cut low enough to expose most of the dark knife marks on her left breast. Those marks were in an X pattern and Kiki knew that Janine preferred to hide them. Many people mistook that scar as body art and tended to stare when it was exposed.

Carlos raised his eyebrows at Kiki's ensemble. He often teased her about her outrageous show costumes, but this time he didn't say a word. Her skintight, zipper up the front suit happened to be a knock off of the crew's new uniform. Only, she did not have the cargo pockets or the web belt.

The doctor tasked everyone with saying their names into the audio recorder. He then saved the pattern and set his device to beep for any slower, similar wave fluctuations in the subsonic zone.

They huddled in a circle watching the meter. After a few moments, the doctor let out his breath.

"It was worth a try. Wait a minute, maybe I should reset it before we give up." The doctor studied the bottom of the meter. "I need something small, like a pin or something." His hands were searching his pockets.

"I've got it." Carlos frantically patted around his own pockets. "I've got what you need!" He handed his camcorder to Janine and dug in deep on his arm pocket. Then, he pulled out a paper clip, which got Janine and Carlos to laugh hysterically as he unbent the small metal loop.

"Let's try something else as well," Kiki turned to Janine. "Let's have Janine summon the ghosts this time. Speak as if you're calling through a tunnel. Your voice needs to echo to the end of that tunnel. It can be a whisper, or just thoughts in your head, but you need to project it. Ask any spirits to speak to us, and really feel the words while you ask."

Janine took a few slow breaths. "Speak to us," she whispered.

A series of pings went off on the doctor's meter startling them. They all stared at the meter. Did Janine or the paperclip set it off? Then, it went silent. Kiki wasn't surprised at all. Now, she knew the secret to their success. *Her poor ego*! Kiki had been convinced she was becoming better at sending messages to the other side. She had been pumped up with her own importance and even bragged about it to a couple of the sisters back home, *there's a new* dragoma *in town*. Now she knew, all along it had been Janine whispering to the spirits.

"What was that?" Carlos said. "What just happened?"

"A lot of subsonic noise," the doctor said. "It was a burst of energy. Mixed, so it's hard to see a pattern. The machine believes there were some matches, but we'll get this back to Ben and see what he comes up with." He glanced around. "To the water tower?"

"To the water tower," Kiki agreed.

Don and Ben rode in the van with the driver, while the rest of the crew piled into Max Collier's hired car, a very roomy and comfortable short Limousine. Carlos and Ian took the rear facing seats, while Janine and Kiki sat on either side of Max on the forward facing seat. Max seemed very pleased with his spot in the car. He made no attempt to be discrete in gaping at both Janine and Kiki in their near matching *Spectral Analysis* suits.

"You girls look fantastic," Max gushed. "Do you guys see what I'm trying to do here? Now, this is top rated stuff. We are going to have the audience going bonkers over this episode, I can't keep my eyes off of these girls!" He glanced at Carlos. "And you look like a god, Carlos, aren't you glad you let the image people do their stuff?"

"My kids say I look like Astro Boy," Carlos laughed lightly. "I admit, I like this batman utility belt. I will give wardrobe an A plus on the bat belt."

"Can we focus on this shoot?" Ian sounded very irritated and they all went silent for a moment.

Poor bloke, he was blinking again. Kiki noticed Max casually resting his hand on Janine's thigh. He was doing the same to her, so it was nothing for Ian to get overexcited about. He must be upset because Janine and Carlos fell in line with Max's design ideas. Kiki knew Ian had been pleased when they refused to comply back at the Alamo. She could see the tension rising from Ian's corner of the car, green and orange sparks streamed from his halo. Max tossed his cell phone at Carlos.

"I want a picture with these sexy women." He put his arms around Kiki and Janine and pulled them in close.

Carlos feigned having trouble working the camera, he kept muffing things up, like he wasn't sure what to do, or maybe, there was something wrong with the phone. Whoops, another failed attempt. He asked the doctor to assist, but the doctor snapped at him and didn't look up from this computer pad. Carlos's attempts at creating a lighter atmosphere were not working.

"Just take the picture, Carlos," Janine said irritably. "It's fine."

And then they were at the water tower.

The tower consisted of a gothic building made of rough faced rock that the doctor told them was carved limestone blocks. It no longer pumped water because the main sand pipe had been removed years ago. When Kiki spotted the winding staircase that led to the top of the tower, she wondered if they actually needed to climb those stairs. Had the remote sensors picked anything up? She definitely did not get any sense of paranormal energy in that direction. They only included the tower because it was such a historic landmark.

They made the decision to skip the climb and gathered on the steps where Kiki briefly spoke with the bug-eyed point-man regarding the hanging man ghost. Don filmed with a single camera and boom microphone set up. The doctor planned an experiment on those front steps with a substance he called sodium thiosulfate. Ben delivered a tray of materials. Everyone gather on the steps to watch the doctor with the looming tower providing a nice backdrop behind them.

"I want you to remember this," the doctor said to the camera. "A wee lesson on the absorption of energy, the storing of energy, and the release of energy. Understanding energy exchanges like this can help us understand what may be happening with spectral or ghostly energy. Perhaps we can begin to understand why ghosts are attached to certain locations, and how they migrate from life energy into something else."

He added a few drops of water to a small vessel of the crystal pellets and then proceeded to warm the mixture with a small blow torch.

"Are you melting it?" Carlos said.

"Aye, but I will quick-cool the crystals below the melting point, so they shouldn't remain a liquid. I'm only heating them now to allow them to better dissolve in that wee bit of water. The absorbed heat will allow them to remain dissolved in what is known as a supersaturated solution. This is the energy absorption phase."

"That's not enough water to dissolve that much stuff," Carlos observed.

"Not unless the crystals absorb and retain this heat," the doctor told him.

The crystals and water soon appeared to be a clear fluid. The doctor transferred his mixture into a small bucket of ice. It was dry ice, so the solution cooled very quickly. The doctor carefully retrieved the container of clear liquid and set it on the steps, propped up in a test tube holder.

"Go ahead and feel the outside of the test tube," the doctor invited them.

"Cold," Kiki said. "Very cold."

Janine used a thermal-panger to get a reading of the cold temperature, well below zero Celsius.

"Aye," the doctor said. "Much colder than when we first began. If those pellets were not dissolved in those few drops of water, they would have solidified, froze into a solid, as soon as the temperature reached their normal freezing point of forty-eight degrees. They can only stay dissolved in those drops if they retain the heat used to melt them. This is an example of a substance storing enormous amounts of heat energy. It's hard to tell, because it's so cold, but believe me, the heat that melted those crystals is trapped inside that cold, clear solution waiting to be released."

"How do you get the solution to release the energy?" Kiki asked.

"A simple disturbance. Like adding a seed crystal," the doctor said. "Keep this in mind for later, when we talk about paranormal energy. The science behind this energy exchange may mirror a similar process that happens in ghostly events. Most substances will absorb energy, store it, and then release it, but supersaturation is a little different. Not every substance can hide this much energy, nor do they require a trigger to release the energy."

Then, the doctor added one small seed crystal to the supersaturated solution and the sodium thiosulfate instantly began to crystallize. The entire container appeared to turn from a clear liquid into a solid block of ice in a matter of seconds.

"Go ahead and touch the outside of the container," the doctor invited. "You will feel the heat those crystals had been storing."

"That's crazy!" Carlos touched the container. Janine used her thermal-panger to get a readout of the temperature again, forty-eight degrees and rising.

Kiki also felt the container and it was indeed very hot. A moment ago, as a liquid, it was freezing cold, now frozen solid, it radiated ample amounts of heat. Clever Ian, he was setting things up nicely to reveal a bit of this theory. Janine volunteered to help Ben clean up. She gave the doctor a very nice compliment on his presentation and Kiki watched him nod stiffly before walking away.

This time Janine jumped in the van with Ben and Don. She surprised them with her last minute decision. Kiki imagined she wanted a break from Max and Ian.

"I don't understand why you're not using the earphone microphones. It's a state of the art audio system," Max said. "I could listen in while I make my phone calls. And why does eight o'clock in Moscow have to be so late at night here?" Max chuckled. He was enjoying a large drink and offered one to Kiki.

"We don't drink until the night is over," Kiki told him. "We don't want to impair our perceptions or put them into question."

Max quickly set the drink down. "Sorry, I didn't know." He grinned mischievously, then glanced at the doctor. "Why don't you guys go on audio for this next stop? I'd like to hear everything. I promise to only use push to talk. I'm on the phone anyway."

The doctor agreed that was a good idea. He planned on separating the crew in the second park, so being hooked up made sense. He had fetched the crazy coil of copper wire that he used as a magnetic antennae and was checking to make sure the wires weren't crossed. Kiki could see the animosity emanating back and forth between Ian and Max, their clashing auras. Carlos flipped through the messages on his cell phone, trying not to look up. Clearly, he felt it too.

Then, Kiki felt Max's hand. His warm fingers caressed the small of her back. Max pulled that maneuver before. She caught him scanning over her scanty outfit, so she leaned forward to give him a better view, then pulled his hand away to let him know that looking was about all he'd be doing. He grinned and had a little more of his drink. He must be compensating for being brushed aside by Janine. Max gambled that Kiki would flirt back, because she often did. He was very good at focusing his energy, and at that moment, he focused directly on her.

A group of people were gathered outside the police tape at the Battle of Dearborn Park. A squad car and two uniformed police officers stood near the crowd and people carried signs with *Welcome, Spectral Analysis* drawn on them.

"Terrific," Ian grimaced at the crowd of about twenty spectators.

"Don't be a grouch," Kiki purred. "We'll go out and mingle before we get to work. Good thing we skipped a climb up that tower."

Janine and Ben were already chatting with people on the sidewalk. Carlos filed out first, then the doctor, but Max held her back with a firm grip on her wrist. He pulled the door closed and the dome light dimmed.

"Wait a moment and make an entrance. They're eagerly waiting for you, Kiki." He was staring at her cleavage again. "You're about to burst out of that thing, are you sure you won't give me a quick peek? I love that you asked Sally make you one, and just the way I designed it." He moved his hand down her thigh. "We think alike, Kiki. We know what it takes to make things happen. We could be a good team."

"How much were you drinking?" Kiki asked.

"Don't be coy with me. We understand each other, and I believe you were jealous earlier today. Do you miss being the object of my attention?" He ran his hand up and got a nice feel of her buttocks. "She may be athletic, but you are all woman. Are you going to change your mind about us?"

"Let's not revisit that old conversation." Kiki slowly removed his hand from her body. "I love flirting with you, Max, but we need to work together, so let's not mix things up."

Kiki popped out of the car. She actually relished the flirty sparring match with Max because it came at a very opportune time. Having him shower her with that stream of desire energized her. She could turn that verve to her advantage. Male erotic energy was a powerful stimulus for mystic receptors. It was an age old practice, well known to the sisters of her coven, and people didn't realized that her show outfits weren't just for show. It wasn't anything that hadn't happened before, with Max. She'd bet money that he propositioned almost every woman on his staff at one time or another. Feeding off his desire was harmless to a player like him.

The small crowd immediately encircled her, snapping photos and asking for autographs. Kiki noticed the doctor and Carlos speaking to three young women, while Janine spoke with an older couple, Kiki attracted everyone else, including the burly policeman hovering behind her. Her core energy well would not be waning anytime soon.

After the fan meet and greet, the doctor rallied the crew toward a single tree in a round area of grass. It was surrounded by a cement walkway and three benches in an arc gave them a place to gather. Kiki and the doctor took one bench, while Janine and Carlos settled on another. Don filmed their conversation from a standing position. The doctor handed a computer pad of digital controls to Carlos. On the small screen, Carlos could zoom in on their group through the camera they planted earlier that day. The doctor encouraged them to hunt for ghostly images on the screen. Spectral reports regarding the Dearborn massacre always involved ghostly images on camera.

"The Potawatomi may have been acting in retribution for broken promises from the US government on that August day in 1815. It's pretty safe to say that the natives were caught between the British, the Americans, and other native nations, and choosing sides was likely very chancy and incurred dangers from multiple angles. The possibility of being double crossed, high," the doctor told them. "Whatever the reason for the attack, whatever caused them to target the people in the fort, it resulted in a terrible loss of life for the United States troops and their families. It was mainly the young men of the tribe that attacked, so no one can blame the entire Potawatomi nation."

"This must have been a quiet spot, beautiful, very close to the lake like this," Kiki said. "It's hard to imagine such a savage event occurring in this serene location."

"Savage it was. The records state that native warriors bludgeoned twelve children on this very spot in a brutal and senseless act. The history of the entire tragedy is commemorated as a star in the city flag. The Chicago flag has four red stars. The first represents Fort Dearborn, marking it as an intensely emotional event." He held up his hand. "But, was it intense enough for a part of their life energy to be absorbed into something? I think, yes."

"That's fascinating," Kiki said. "Usually in areas of traumatic loss, especially involving children, I feel an abundance of psychic energy. But I don't feel anything here. Do you think there's a possibility that this isn't the massacre site? That perhaps the historians got it wrong?"

"Not a chance, Kiki," the doctor said. "I believe you don't feel anything here because this place is missing the elements needed for a ghostly stamp. Remember, not every chemical can trap heat and become a supersaturated solution. Perhaps it takes a key substance to absorb and retain that intense psychic energy you often feel. Something in bones and wood, or in certain minerals found in some types of stone, such as—"

"Such as boulders in the river?" Janine's voice interrupted sharply. "Like the mineral deposits in those boulders in the river? Is that the theory you've been hoping to push? It is, isn't it? Why you so adamantly refused to even consider…" Janine closed her eyes and stopped herself. She stood abruptly and everyone stood with her. Janine pressed her lips together and shook her head. "I need to take a little break," she moved quickly down the path, away from them.

"I'll go." Carlos set the computer pad on the metal bench and took off after her.

Don raised an eyebrow at the doctor. The doctor gave him a ten minute break and he meandered toward the van as Max emerge from his car. Max hurried down the path to where Carlos and Janine stood under a lamp. Kiki couldn't hear what was being said but watched them talk. The group of spectators also watched. Both Max and Carlos stood very close to Janine and she wiped her eyes, but held herself pretty solidly. She was not accepting any hugs. A slow moving train rumbled behind the park, shaking up the atmosphere. Ian dropped a fisted hand on the bench.

"Crikes. Maybe I should go over and apologize or something." Ian's voice sounded perturbed. "What would I be apologizing for? We've been through this one. Even if I didn't have a theory, she knows—"

Kiki stopped him with a hand on his arm. "Hush, Ian. You don't need to go over there, just give her a minute. She'll be fine."

"She's fallen for Max Collier's game," he spat under his breath. "I'm certain of it, and it's burning me up. I thought she was smarter than that," he shook his head. "I'm such an idiot. This morning, I almost thought…I went to check on her, you know, after the detective, I was worried about her. It turns out, she wasn't even in her room, and she was definitely with Max, because he wasn't answering his phone either. Both of them indisposed, and look how giddy he's behaving and how he keeps touching her. She doesn't seem to mind it at all. Can you believe it? Do you think she's trying to rub my nose in it?"

"I knew you were jealous, but that's why you've been so hostile?" Kiki patted his hand. "No worries, Ian, she was not with Max Colliers. She's not rubbing anyone's nose in anything."

"How can you be so sure? Look at her over there. She's totally playing into his hands, letting him dress her like that." He glanced at Kiki's outfit and pressed his lips together. "Sorry," he said.

"Ian, Janine slept in my room this afternoon," she nodded at him. Kiki watched his aggravation begin to break down into pieces. "I'm not going to go into detail, but she wanted to hide in my room to take an undisturbed nap. She was actually avoiding both of you blokes." She noticed Carlos and Janine heading back and stood up. "Here they come."

Kiki gave Janine a quick hug and the doctor nodded at them.

"I'm sorry about that," Janine said. "It just hit me unexpectedly. The mention of innocent children must have set off my emotions, I guess. Obviously, I still harbor reservations about things, but I'm fine, everything is good. I'm sorry. Let's continue."

They went back to the benches. This time the doctor switched with Carlos. He hovered over Janine, full of concern, but she glared at him until he backed off. Don trotted up with the camera.

"We don't need to talk about my theory, we can change the plan. I can talk about it in the green room later," the doctor said softly. "We can wrap things here and go to the small park. That's where we have the best likelihood of getting some odd stuff."

"Nonsense," Janine snapped. "Keep going with your theory." She eyeballed Don. "You're rolling, right? So, energy absorbed, stored, and released. Different substances absorb differently, like having a different specific heat capacity, or something? But it's not just heat energy, even light can be stored, right, Doctor? Like a fluorescent mineral or glow in the dark stickers. You're thinking some kind of special psychic energy is being stored. In what? You mentioned magnesium earlier today. Magnesium in those limestone pillars at the water station."

"Aye," the doctor said softly. "There may be something I've missed, but magnesium seems to be one of the elements that absorb spiritual energy, phosphorus as well, maybe others. Those elements are found in bone, wood, and rock forming minerals."

"Then why don't we see ghosts everywhere? Those are pretty common elements," Janine asked him.

"I'm still working on that answer. Perhaps there's a specific ratio, or an isotope, or a key arrangement involving other substances. Sodium thiosulfate needs to be in a solution to store energy, mixed in a small quantity of water."

"You would need a traumatic event to stamp in that kind of energy, don't you think?" Kiki added. "Like when the doctor added heat to get the sodium thiosulfate to dissolve in the first place. Spirits are associated with tragic events. Murder, sorrow, disasters."

"What kind of energy are we talking about here?" Carlos asked. "What type of energy is being stamped into these elements?"

"Aether, life energy," Kiki said. "Psychic, spiritual, the energy that's part of what we call our feelings, our souls, I would imagine. Think of this, who hasn't felt the presence of another person standing behind you? Maybe that energy. Or the intensity of being observed from afar? Everyone projects an aura. It's part of the energy of life, but it isn't really alive."

"A mystery energy we haven't yet discovered," the doctor nodded, "Or found a way to measure. Quintessence, maybe? Or something else. Aether might be the right word for now. Those low frequency EM waves I always get excited about, that's not it. Those low frequency pulses result when our mystery energy is transformed from one medium to another. Like a friction of sorts, it's not a completely efficient transformation when the energy is released and we get leaks resulting in low frequency electromagnetic waves. The mystery energy is not going to be electric or magnetic. We are not going to measure that mystery energy on the EM spectrum. It's on some other plane, some other dimension. Right now, all we can do is measure the whispers of when that energy seeps into parts of the world we understand."

"Okay," Janine asked, "then wouldn't the energy, the aether, be released sometimes… spontaneously, similar to radioactivity for instance? We've been monitoring this place for hours now, with very little to look at, according to Ben. Why would we expect to see a ghost right now, just because we decided to go looking for one?"

"There needs to be a trigger to release some of the energy," the doctor explained. "Perhaps something inside a living person, living energy is the trigger. But, not all people can see or hear ghosts, perhaps it takes a certain type of person, projecting the right type of vibe, to be a trigger. The correct type of disturbance on the surface of the solution, so to speak. Like a seed crystal or a catalyst. A person like Kiki probably provides a bigger disturbance than most."

"I would agree that Kiki provides a pretty big disturbance everywhere she goes." Carlos nodded thoughtfully.

Kiki flashed her cats eyes at Carlos as they chuckled.

"Very interesting," Kiki said. "Now earlier, you mentioned that this place is missing the elements for the ghostly stamp of aether. Where do you suggest we find that stamp of energy?"

"In the small park a few blocks from here," the doctor said. "That's where they buried the massacre victims, and some of those bones are still trapped in that plot of land. Bones don't just store calcium, you know. Traces of magnesium and phosphorus are mixed in as well. I believe, if we show up with our lovely trigger here, we may see some interesting things." He glanced around. "Shall we head out to the small park?"

They all nodded and said in unison, "To the small park."

This time Carlos snagged the extra seat in the van. Kiki, the doctor, Max and Janine all piled into the back of the hired car, with Kiki and Max on one side, the doctor and Janine on the other. The doctor picked up his large copper coil to inspect it again. Max had another drink in his hand and his brief case in his lap.

"If you don't stop drinking, I'm not going to let you sit in on the séance," Kiki chided him. Max just smiled pleasantly at her.

It was a short drive to the next park, just down South Prairie Street and then a turn onto 16th Street. They hopped out of the car pretty quickly and had to wait for the van. There wasn't a crowd at their little triangle of the park, but Kiki noticed a squad car with a small gathering on the other side of the railroad tracks near the playground.

"Someone should run over and greet that crowd," Ian said. "Pass out stickers or something, placate them so they don't head this way. This is our critical location, where we want a little privacy."

Max volunteered to run over in the limousine. Would the doctor object if he took a little speaker and hooked up the audio? He could divert the folks with a little preview and give them a listen in on the investigation, a reward for being dedicated fans, and the way he said it, he'd already made up his mind. To Kiki's surprise, the doctor agreed with him. Ian shrugged at her.

The van rolled up and Ben jumped out. He rigged an audio set up pretty quickly. Max grabbed Kiki's hand and pulled her toward the car, then he grabbed Janine's hand as well.

"I'll take the girls with me," Max said. "Just for a few minutes, to greet your fans and take a pictures while you set up." Max grinned at the doctor. "You don't need Kiki or Janine for anything, do you? I'll send them right back."

Kiki could see a confrontation on the horizon, so she moved closer to Max and slid her arm into his. Max smiled at her. Kiki glanced at Janine and winked, then looked into the doctor's stern face.

"We should go," Kiki said. "Those fellows won't stay over there unless we give them some attention. Don't worry, Ian, it's going to take time for you to connect that big box of yours, and we'll be back in fifteen minutes. Twenty, tops."

Max was positively delighted with her, and a little drunk. He must have completed his long distance phone calls and was winding down. His tie was gone and his smile constant. He lounged across from them for the short drive around the corner. His eyes gleamed in a devilish way.

"I'm sorry I've been drinking so much, Kiki," Max said. "I don't want to worry you about my behavior in the séance later, so I've lined up my replacement."

"No kidding?" Kiki asked. "And who will be replacing you?"

"Lauren." He grinned wickedly. "She's quite pretty, don't you think? That's natural blonde hair on her, you know, gorgeous lips, and smile. Gets along well with Doctor McNally. She's been hinting at the possibility of being on camera for quite some time. Did you know, she did a screen test with Carlos a couple of weeks ago and looks good on film, natural? We're vetting her to possibly replace Janine if she leaves. When she leaves." He shot a look at Janine. "This could be a continuation of that screen test. So, is it alright with you, that Lauren takes my seat in the séance tonight?"

Well, that was a lot of information, unusual for Max to share so much. Kiki imagined it was spurred on by whatever he'd been drinking and to get a reaction out of Janine. *Which button was he trying to push*, Kiki wondered. Janine didn't budge and inch. Good for her.

"She'll make a terrific replacement in the séance, Max," Kiki told him. Janine agreed with a nod.

Then, they pulled up to the curb to greet their fans.

Chapter 9

Ghosts In the Park *Janine*

A flurry of flashes blinded her, setting her nerves off and irritating her. Kiki, on the other hand, relished the rowdy attention. She strutted in her racy costume and flashed her glowing eyes at everyone. Janine couldn't fathom how she managed to feel comfortable in that crowd of boisterous young men. Then, Kiki suddenly rushed away. She beelined toward a woman with a baby carriage leaving Janine abandoned in a laughing group of frat boys. They were university students and Max lost no time in telling them that Janine once attended the University of Chicago as a student. They became over excited and squeezed in to take photos while shouting "U of C, U of C!"

Max carried a bottle from the limousine bar to share, definitely in a party mood. A few of the men told her that a guy named Randy knew where to find *Spectral Analysis* that night, a ghost had whispered the location in his ear. Kiki, still speaking to the woman with the baby, must have heard that talk, because she perked up and faced them at that very moment. Kiki finally started moving back toward Janine when a young man decided to grab Janine's hand. Max instantly jumped to the rescue and shot the guy a scrutinizing look.

"Here there," Max admonished, "hands to yourself now," which Janine found very ironic. Max had barely keep his own hands to himself in the car, with her and with Kiki. He appeared quite drunk and was acting extremely strange. Perhaps he really had knocked on her door expecting to share that bottle of wine with her. Janine had no idea what type of women Max was used to. Either way, she felt a touch of agoraphobia in that crowd of university students and couldn't wait to escape into the car.

Max instructed the driver to set up the speaker system at a table in the playground. That drew most of the attention away and she breathed a sigh of relief. Kiki ran up gushing about the baby. They drifted closer to the car, but a small group blocked their path. It included the same grabby young man from earlier. His wild hair half hid his eyes, and his mouth was pressed into a tight line.

"Randy saw a ghost," one of the fellows announced. "A real ghost. He's totally possessed. The ghost talks to him in his sleep." He indicated the man who had grabbed Janine's hand.

"How interesting," Kiki's glowing green eyes narrowed on the young man. "In his sleep?"

"Go on, Randy," the friend pushed the nervous one forward. "Did you bring it? Give it to her. He has something for you, for Janine Stinger."

"Come here, handsome." Kiki pulled him closer, and he relaxed a bit. "You say a ghost is haunting you? How do you know it's a ghost?"

"I saw her by the pond." His bloodshot eyes briefly landed on Janine, but darted away quickly. "She comes back in my dreams."

"You poor dear." Kiki reached up and stroked his hair. His friends got a kick out of that and snickered, but Kiki ignored them. Her voice was soft, soothing. "You say you have something for Janine?"

"I don't need anything," Janine continued moving away. She avoided contact with the mystery guy and nodded toward the car. "Come on, Kiki, we need to get back to the other side." Janine waved to the other college guys. "Sorry, but we need to go."

Kiki nodded reassuringly at her, then turned back to Randy. He seemed transfixed by her attention. "I certainly believe you, Randy. Come around to the Lincoln House to see me, if you like. Day after tomorrow would be best, in the afternoon. I want to hear all about your ghost." Kiki smiled flirtatiously at the other guys and Janine was never more irritated at her unending quest for male attention.

Randy gave a jerky nod before glancing at Janine. Finally, Kiki climbed into the limousine. After the door closed, Janine turned an angry face to Kiki, perturbed that she needed to flirt with every male that crossed her path, and now, she was trying to drag Janine into it. Janine regretted wearing that ridiculous, stupid jumpsuit.

"Why did you invite that guy to the hotel? He was beyond creepy and I don't want to talk to him."

"He's haunted, Janine." Kiki ignored her upset attitude. "I could feel it all around him. You could feel it too, it was that creepy feeling you noticed. Haunted people have a very distinct aura." Then, Kiki took Janine's hands. "Let's talk about what we're going to do in the park. We have different talents, you know. While you may be a natural *dragoma*, a sender, I'm a natural receiver. I can focus my energy on receiving if you can do the summoning. Ian thinks I'm the only trigger out here, but I believe it's really you."

"I'm still not certain what you mean by talking from my core," Janine snapped, still irritated.

"Just repeat what I say out loud, or silently if you prefer, but not passively like you do, but with determination. When you hear me speaking to the spirits, recite it and try to *feel* the words, Janine, *in your core,* your heart. Direct your intent and project it to where you feel a soul might receive it. I'll vocalize as much as possible out there, but you will need to open your heart and really feel like you're talking to them."

The doctor placed the copper antennae on a branch and the large EMF box along the edge of the tree line. He planned to man the box and communicate over the wire on channel two. Anything they wanted people in the park to hear, they'd transmit on channel one. Carlos would trail them into the trees and record low spectrum IR images with his camera, and Don would film the normal stuff with the big camera. Janine clipped a thermal-panger, ion detector, and portable audio recorder onto her web belt.

Kiki wanted to meander toward the mirrors hanging from the trees. The doctor aimed his magnetic antennae in that direction. As Kiki stepped away to center herself, Janine turned to the doctor and found him quietly regarding her. Whatever had been bugging him earlier had passed. *Out of sympathy regarding her little outburst?* She didn't want to know and turned back toward Kiki. She simmered thinking about it. Her conspiracy theory was no more lunatic than a ghost, did he need to be so harsh about it, calling her hysterical and irrational? *No, no, don't get upset again*, she told herself. *He had been right to shut her accusation down quickly.* Luckily, Kiki became "centered," and they began a slow stroll into the trees.

The atmosphere transformed the moment they crossed under the canopy and the trees obscured the sky. Kiki reached for Janine's hand and pulled her close. She insisted on walking hand in hand. She whispered something about sharing their gifts. *When witches hold hands, their gifts are shared,* Kiki conveyed. Kiki spoke in a soft voice, a whisper.

"*We seek yon souls of near to there, we call on you to us appear, reveal yourself for us to see, so I command, so mote it be.* Project that, repeat it, open your heart," Kiki instructed Janine, then turned to the spirits, "*Hello, hello. We wish to speak with you. You can trust us. We want to help.*" Janine concentrated on repeating all of Kiki's words, but she felt very silly hearing her voice muttering that witch talk.

The doctor's voice came softly over the audio, "We're getting definite ultralow frequency pulses. I've seen those here before."

"*We seek yon souls of near to there, we call on you to us appear,*" Kiki continued softly. "*We come to help you.*"

Janine grabbed her thermal-panger and clicked the button to record. She felt the temperature begin to drop. The ion detector on her web belt popped off a couple of times.

"*I can hear you,*" Kiki said. "*I hear you. You're fine now, please calm down, it's all right. Don't be afraid.*" Then, the tone of her voice changed, "Janine, are you focusing? We need to talk to these spirits. Are you repeating this?"

"Yes, sorry, I'll focus. Go on."

"*Please calm down. You are fine now, it's over.* They're afraid, Janine. I sense that they are afraid. We need to let them know that they no longer need to be afraid," Kiki whispered, but changed her voice for the spirits again. "*Your ordeal is over, and we want to help you.*" Janine very softy whispered a repeat of most of that, feeling completely idiotic.

"My camera is picking up a cold spot," Carlos's whispered voice came over the audio. He stood six feet behind them. "To your right, beside that tree. The one you climbed today."

"Tell me about it, the panger is picking it up too," Janine told Carlos.

Kiki gripped Janine's hand firmly and pulled her toward the tree.

"*Don't cry.* They're crying." Kiki said. "I feel scared children, several children, Janine, they're frightened, can you feel them? We need to help them calm down. Maybe we can sing them a song. Do you sense them at all?"

The doctor's voice came over the line. "Do you think you sense kids from Fort Dearborn? Maybe try to ask. Ben says the audio receiver is getting flashes with speech patterns across the sonic zone, but just faintly. Do you hear anything?"

Kiki squeezed her hand. It was too dark to clearly see under the trees. "Really feel the words now. Open your heart and communicate this." Kiki took a deep breath, and Janine did too. "*We are here to help you. You're no longer in danger. We come to help. Sing with us now, sing a little nursery rhyme to calm down.* What's something old?" Then, Kiki recited, "*Pat-a-cake, pat-a-cake, bakers man, bake me a cake as fast as you can. Pat it, prick it, mark it with a 'B,' and put it in the oven for baby and me.*"

Janine joined her. An eerie feeling cascaded all around and Janine could feel movement in the air, gentle swirls of molecules. It felt as if someone moved passed and the pressure fluttered on her skin. Someone kept moving past. It couldn't be a breeze. The feeling barely stirred in every direction, circling them.

"Do you hear them?" Kiki asked, chuckling softly.

Janine concentrated. *Was it her imagination? The power of suggestion?* She heard a faint, almost imperceptible giggle. Childish giggles and then the rhyme. More giggles from a little girl. *Could it only be in her mind?* The pounding of her own pulse made it hard to determine. The air took on a heavier feel. Then came a burst of giggles, sudden and strong, and her heart pounded loudly in her temple. *She did not just hear that!* A warm pocket of air pressed into her ear and Janine barely heard the whisper of a voice say, *I love you, girl.* Her heart bottomed out. She broke away from Kiki and her eyes flew wide open. Janine searched frantically around.

She called, "Sammy? Sammy?"

Faces were everywhere, flickering in the trees. Young faces, smiling, frowning, confused. Janine spun around, scouring those faces as every eye bore down on her, waiting. They wanted her to say something to them, imploring, earnest, attentive young faces, watching her. She hunted for a familiar face, but couldn't find it. Her chest felt very heavy, and she couldn't breathe. Her pulse flooded her head and she no longer heard the giggling. She turned to Kiki, seeking direction. *What should she say? What should she say to them?* Kiki's mouth moved, but Janine could no longer hear anything. And then, the world turned black.

Kiki also saw the faces. She always insisted that spirits were more easily seen as reflections than directly. Kiki also detected faint ghostly forms moving under the shelter of trees. Ben planned to zoom into the footage later, to see if any camera picked up the impressions she described. Janines' blackout only lasted a few moments, but she felt very sluggish. Kiki was usually the sluggish one, but she seemed just fine. She wished Janine had not let go of her hand.

"Just drink this tea and rehydrate," Kiki advised. They relaxed in the back of the limousine while the guys stood outside talking to the fans that drifted over. Janine could hear Ian's voice as he explained his electromagnetic box to someone.

"I don't get it," Janine said. "I'm not a fainter. Is this how you usually feel?"

Kiki smiled at her. "Don't worry, it'll pass."

"I feel like total crap. Are you going to do the séance without me? I heard some talk out there about rescheduling it or sending me back to the hotel. I can't believe I feel this sluggish, like I just ran ten miles or something." *Why did Kiki appear unfazed?* Usually, she was all droopy after an extreme encounter.

Kiki shook her head. "I don't want to do it without you, so we'll try the séance another time, if needed. Maybe, it's not needed."

Janine became the weak link, the runt of the team. She didn't want to be the reason the entire schedule got wrecked. Didn't they invite guests to participate in the séance? Would a delay add another day to the schedule? She needed to fulfill all of her obligations for it to count for the contract. If she bailed on part of her duties, Mike Dunn warned that she could be strung along to make up for it later. Janine sat up and drank the tea.

"I'm going to be okay," Janine insisted. "I just need a few more minutes, then you can tell the guys we can proceed. There's going to be food at the plaza, right? Carlos said there would be a late night snack while we mingle with your séance guests. It'll give me more time to rest and get some sugar into my system. I don't want to be sent back to the hotel, Kiki, I'm okay. You always recover just fine, so I'll be fine too. You're back to normal already."

"You did the sending out there," Kiki told her. "I kept my focus to receiving those spirits. Janine, I don't believe this energy drain is from sending. I believe you were trying too hard to see and hear them, and it taxed you. I should not have asked if you could hear them, because it encouraged you to focus on receiving." Kiki watched her curiously, then reached to the limousine bar and poured a very short touch of whisky into a nice crystal tumbler. She handed it to Janine. "Just drink that."

They never drank alcohol unless they were done for the night. Kiki must not think Janine would be much help at the plaza and Janine had to agree with her. She could barely sit up without feeling achy in the head.

"Want to know how I can bounce back so easily?" Kiki pushed her blood red hair behind her ears. "How I can manage to go from one encounter to another some nights? Why I have so much energy right now, tonight? You'll need to keep an open mind. You could try it, if you want to feel better."

"Of course I want to try it," Janine pushed herself to a better sitting position. "I'll try anything, what do I need to do?" She was willing to try whatever ritual Kiki was about to come up with. She had plenty of positive results using Kiki's methods. Where she once used to laugh at Kiki's antics, she now believed Kiki possessed effective mystical knowledge. Crazy things always happened around Kiki Mellow.

"Male sexual energy is a powerful thing, Janine. It's one of the quickest, most powerful resources for a witch," Kiki said. "If you want to recover quickly, you could tap into some of the testosterone driven energy out there."

Did Kiki just flip her lid? "Are you suggesting I have sex with someone right now?"

"No, absolutely not." Kiki burst out laughing. "Now keep an open mind, every witch in my coven knows this trick. When male sexual energy is directed at you, you can soak it in and use it to feed your core. The momentum can open and fuel your psychic receptors. You have to be careful, though. You can't think about where it usually leads for you, physically, I mean. Try not to slip down that slope or the energy won't make it to your core. It'll seep in your Base Well, and then you'll be up a creek. Just welcome the energy in, accept it openly, and send it to your core. Then, use it for psychic purposes. It can be very restorative."

Janine was at a loss for words.

"I do it all the time. When you think I'm flirting with a fellow, it's not real flirting. And I can use any male. Old, young, all that matters is the energy. Don is a terrific cameraman in this regard, and Carlos is another nice source in a pinch, but that might be a bit awkward for you."

"You want me to flirt with one of them? The guys?"

"You don't need to actually flirt," Kiki said. "Just be open and receptive to any passion energy that's directed your way. Let the fellows admire your womanly form without reproof. Flirting accelerates the process and focuses the energy on you, which is a must. You'll need the energy aimed directly at you. This suggestive outfit can do the flirting for you. That crowd of fraternity boys was a powerhouse of energy. If you had opened up to their attention, instead of blocking them out, you wouldn't be in the position you're in right now. Those men provided a ton of sexual energy and you completely shunned it. Some would have naturally seeped into your core and kept you from feeling this way. Next time, absorb it, like I did, and use it. Many women do it without even realizing what they're doing."

Janine agreed to give it a try, as long as the plan didn't include Ian or Carlos. Kiki insisted she needn't to do anything beyond openly receive the energy directed toward her, and that didn't require anything physical on her part. In fact, Kiki instructed her to avoid any sexual thoughts at all. If she did, the energy might get trapped in the wrong well.

Kiki opened the limo door and waved to Ian. She informed the doctor that they were feeling better and wanted to start moving toward the plaza. Kiki insisted that the doctor and Carlos give Don a break from the van and let him ride in the limousine with Max, Janine, and Kiki. Then, Kiki slipped into the rear facing seat and pulled Janine with her.

"Just relax," Kiki said. "I'll get things ramped up. Be open and receptive, none of your normal deflecting, okay? I'll get them focused directly on you as quickly as possible. This isn't a long drive, so we'll have to get straight to the point." Kiki urged Janine to lay across the seat with her head in Kiki's lap.

Don scooted in first. His eyes darted around the interior of the fancy car and noted the small bar and the stereo controls. He fiddled with the overhead lights, then nodded at Kiki and Janine.

"I hope she's okay," Don said to Kiki. "That was quite a tumble. Mr. Colliers said it was a missed opportunity. He wants me to film the doctor catching one of you."

Kiki broke into a sly smile. "No worries, Don, we'll get that catch in the graveyard tomorrow night."

Max jumped in, still chuckling at something said outside the car. His eyes skirted over Kiki and Janine, then he set his empty tumbler on the bar.

He gave Janine a concerned closed lipped grin. Janine could tell he was still quite intoxicated.

"How are you doing over there, Janine? Are you up for the séance? I'm told you're only needed to monitor stuff in the background. Carlos can do it all if you want to sit this one out," He said gently. "I think it would be fine if you'd like to sit out and the doctor agrees."

"Janine doesn't like to sit out, she's always all in." Kiki used her super silky voice, almost purring like a cat. She often used that voice during interviews when she wanted to woo information out of someone. *She certainly could change the mood with that voice*, Janine thought.

Kiki stroked Janine's long auburn hair with a slow hand. Her fingers paused to play with the curls at the end, and though Kiki was hamming it up for the men in the car, her caress delivered a nice healing touch to Janine's pounding head and a soft sigh escaped Janine's lips. She noticed that both Don and Max were trying not to stare at her, and failing. A buzz of intense energy streamed off them.

"Just relax, sweet girl," Kiki murmured in that silky voice. "Don, you were right about these outfits, they are very constricting. I better loosen her up a tad, don't you agree?" Kiki's hand dropped to the zipper on her outfit. *What was she doing?* "Let me help you, my sweet girl. Give you more room to breathe." Kiki gently tugged at the zipper and gave Janine strikingly more cleavage, so much more that she felt almost completely exposed. Certainly, that lacy red push-up bra was no longer hidden. Kiki leaned down and whispered in her ear. "Accept it, and soak it in. Stop deflecting. Breathe deep and open your core."

There was indeed an energy spike directed at her from the men. Dons mouth gaped and Max eased back into the leather seat. His arms crossed over his chest as his eyes fixed on her exposed lace. Janine had his undivided attention, but he also appeared a little confused. *Kiki was right*, Janine thought, the buzz of desire got her blood flowing, and she no longer felt as sluggish. Kiki removed her hand and helped Janine sit up. Kiki whispered into her ear so that the men couldn't quite hear.

"Channel it to your core, Janine." Then, she turned to Max, "Switch with me, Max."

"What?" he asked sharply.

"Switch seats with me, she might get faint again and need to lean against you, or something." Kiki reached over and took his hand. "I want to make a short drink for Don, I've seen some of the playbacks and Don is making me look very nice on film. He has a good eye for accentuation. I haven't gotten the chance to tell him how happy I am at having such a talented cameraman on staff." Don actually appeared scared of Kiki.

Kiki pretty much forced Max to switch seats with her. Don dribbled off a stream of words to Kiki that Janine couldn't quite analyze because Max had moved very close to her. He stared down at the X knife scar and she watched the bulge in his pants grow. His proximity made her very uncomfortable, hot. She could hear him take in air and she wanted to zip back up, but that zipper would take a little fight to get started and she was afraid the fight would draw even more attention. Max opened up his arm and offered his chest as a pillow. She wasn't sure what she should do, so she leaned in and lay against him. She could feel the hard muscles underneath his shirt and the warmth radiating from him. Her body responded to his proximity, and she was afraid to move. She glanced at Kiki and those green eyes held a warning. Kiki sharply shook her head.

"Direct it to your core," Kiki said evenly, her brow creased with worried.

"Direct what to her core?" Max asked.

"The tea," Kiki said. "She needs a little more tea." She passed Max the tea cup and clearly meant for him to feed it to Janine. "It looks like we're here. Can you manage her, Max, help her out of the car, and make sure she drinks that tea. I'm going to run to the ladies' room."

Max stretched out his legs after Kiki and Don departed. Janine shakily turned away from him and zipped up her front. She felt a whole lot better physically, but was very embarrassed at the same time. She couldn't quite meet Max's eye. He held the tea cup for her, then set it aside when she didn't take it.

"I'm not sure what Kiki's up to; teaching me a lesson, maybe? That short drive sobered me up quick," Max said. "Before you run off to do the séance, I want to apologize for my behavior earlier. I haven't been acting exactly a gentleman. Is that why you participated in this? Is it because I was being a sore sport about it?"

"A sore sport about what?"

Max pulled out his cell phone. He called up a GIF of the doctor catching her by the lamppost. Somebody, that man, posted it, and it apparently caused quite a stir. People were very excited about the *Spectral Analysis* team being in Chicago. It certainly painted a romantic scene as Janine gazed so fondly at the doctor. The clip gave the impression that a very differently ending had occurred.

"It started popping up right after lunch. Our lawyer contacted the fellow to have him take it down." He glanced at her from under his eyelashes. "Look, I admit, I was a juvenile tonight. I was excited to make a little headway with you at our dinner, and then very disappointed when I saw that clip. You got the flowers, right? I actually imagined us sharing that bottle over a romantic conversation." Max raised his eyebrows, "And then that showed up and I can guess why you were unavailable. He outplayed me again, I assume." He studied her. "I completely understand, he did mention that you two can be very hot at times, very physical, so he must be hard for you to pass up. I get it."

"What are you talking about?"

Max glanced at her body again, focusing on her marked chest. *What was his obsession with the scars about?* "I'll be honest with you. I imagine that's a message that means your heart is off limits, and I can respect that, if that's what you want. But maybe you can give me a chance next time. I'm getting the message that you might be open to it. I know you two aren't exclusive. I mean, there's Lauren, and…"

Max Colliers is the Devil

"Ian talked about me? To you? What exactly did he say?"

"Not much. He was very complimentary, of course, and it was entirely my fault. I've always been curious about you, since that thing in Sacramento, and I probably pumped him for the information. You know how men talk when they've had a few." Max indicated himself as an example. "Maybe I filled in the blanks, after his wildcat comment. Don't worry, Carlos stopped him from going too far with that punch in the eye, but, the conversation did reboot my curiosity. I'm very interested in getting to know you better."

Wow, so those guys had some type of sordid discussion about her. No wonder Max Colliers presumed she'd be open to his advances. At least now he was being up front about his motive. He gave her a nice smile and a little more room.

"I'm headed back to the hotel. I've got a board meeting at ten in the morning, so you probably won't see me again, until Texas. I'm jetting home tomorrow evening. I want you to know that I'm looking forward to our date in Austin. We still have a deal, right? You give me a fair shot at impressing you, and I'll take a good look at the contract. I'll take it any way you want to play it."

Chapter 10

The Séance *Kiki*

They secured room 441 in the Congress Plaza hotel for an early morning séance. The haunting in that room included a mystery woman who assaulted sleeping guests. Kiki invited five participants, because six was an optimum number for a séance table: Agatha, a maid who cleaned 441 regularly, an elderly couple named Walter and Emily Croager who once stayed in room 441, Lauren, and Doctor McNally. Kiki touched base with

Lauren to see if she'd ever participated in a séance before, and other than teenaged fooling around, she hadn't. Lauren's aura burst with bright, happy energy. All that life force would surely attract curious spirits.

"I'm happy Max asked you to sit in for him," Kiki told her.

It wasn't the best set up for a séance. Kiki usually included a virile male for the energy they provided, and the doctor didn't count for her. She had actually been banking on Max Colliers to provide that small service. Kiki might need to tap the spectators for supplemental energy, or, she could only pretend to call on the spirits and bank on Janine to send the messages. Kiki needed to discuss it with Ian, why calling to spirits completely drained her of energy, but tuning into them did not.

Lauren, the old couple, and Agatha mingled near the refreshment table and Kiki glided toward them. She had changed into a flowing outfit with beautiful silk scarves and accented her outfit with jewelry laden with precious stones. Sally had made a stretch lace tie-up top with dangling coins that she wore under a sheer shirt. Compared to the *Spectral Analysis* suit, her gypsy attire came off more modest. Still sexy, but not blatantly so. Kiki preferred the more sensual profile the translucent material created. She always enjoyed a subtle feminine mystique when conducting a séance. At the moment, they waited for the second hour to draw nearer and the doctor meandered over. She retied the silk strip in her red hair.

"I sent Ben to the hotel to start processing the earlier tapes," he whispered to her. "We're going to be wiped out at the end of tonight and will want to see things fast. I'm not sure anyone got any shuteye earlier."

"We've tried the mirror trick before," Kiki said. "All we can do is cross our fingers. I'm interested to see what the audio picks up."

"You and me both." The doctor spotted Janine and a smile creased his lips, his eyes tracked her movement across the room.

How did Janine manage to capture Ian so completely with all that dark energy? Was it because her physical shape was copy of what Gwen's had been? Or, perhaps, it was because her aura mirrored the streams his mother often projected? Janine had an underlying array of pink below the murk, and

Ian's mother had similar layers. Could he detect it? He always claimed he couldn't see an aura, but maybe he didn't realize that he could.

Ian interrupted her thoughts, "She seems quite recovered. Max didn't take her back to the Lincoln House after all."

Kiki patted his hand, she didn't dare tell him what they attempted in the limousine earlier. Ian knew her coven tricks and always frowned upon her using them. He chided her more than once about the sexist teaching in her pagan education. She walked toward Janine, who was standing by the snack table eating fruit. Janine looked up at her.

"I feel a tons better. I guess your method actually works. Although, I'm not sure I can do that on a regular basis, and it may have backfired on me. I can't believe you left me alone in the car with him after that." Janine banded her long hair into a loose pony tail as they stepped away from the group.

"I genuinely needed to pee, sorry," Kiki said, then scolded softly, "You know, you would feel ten times better if you would have channeled that energy properly. You should be buzzing, receptors on fire, tuning into everything on heightened alert. Max sends some extremely good vibes." Kiki mused. "You may need help on finding your core. You feel better because sexual energy accidentally leaks into the core. It always happens that way for women, mixing love and sex energy, but most of Max's efforts went straight into all the wrong places, Janine. Oh well, no worries, we'll work on it."

Janine appeared miffed, but Kiki didn't have time to worry about her hurt feelings. At the moment, she needed Janine to focus and pay attention. She was a smart girl with natural talents. If she could get past her passion energy, and over active analytical mind, she could be quite powerful in the spiritual realm.

"I need you to go around and rally the spirits in this building. Tempt them into coming to the séance. This is a very old hotel and may be haunted by more than just that woman in room 441. Remember, they will obey you if you direct your intentions properly. Open your heart and feel the words."

"I'm not sure I understand," Janine's face erupted into a smirky grin. "You want me to wander around the hotel and whole heartedly invite ghosts to come to the séance?"

After everything that happened that night, Kiki expected a more tempered response. She waited for the chuckling to end.

"Sorry, it just sounds a little comical, crazy to me. I guess I'm not as convinced that I'm speaking to ghosts."

"You speak to them. And it's no more crazy than glimpsing those faces in the mirrors, and you saw them," Kiki felt a little angry. "Why do you refuse to accept your own perceptions? You need to get out of your head for a little minute and get out of your skin too. Try to sense with your core, your heart, pretend if you have to. Pretend until you believe it."

"Can I just whisper to the ghosts, softly? Maybe even, not say anything out loud. It makes me feel a little conspicuous, speaking out loud to ghosts."

"Whatever you need to do, just do it, and then get to 441 right after," Kiki snapped. "And don't try to see anything, Janine, just transmit. I've got a theory that your energy drain is on the receiving end. And remember, whatever you say, or think, you should end it with: *as I command, so mote it be.* For instance, *you will come to the séance in 441, as I command, so mote it be.*"

Janine trudged off and took Mike the van driver with her. Janine didn't want to do it alone. Kiki turned to her séance guest and guided them to room 441.

They had rearranged the room earlier that day. A round table had been placed in the center of things, and salt lamps glowed in the corners. Kiki arranged a crystal grid on the table with a quartz ball dead center and six trails of colored minerals radiating out of it. Each radiating line led to a heavily cushioned chair. Most pieces in the grid were smooth, tumbled gemstones, but she included purple amethyst pyramids for protection.

Kiki placed Agatha, the maid, in the chair on her left and invited Walter Croager to sit in the one on her right. Lauren came next, on the left, and Walter's wife Emily sat next to him, on the right. The doctor took the spot directly across the table from her. A small white candle, a silver tray, a small square pad of paper, and an old fashioned fountain pen flanked each of the six mineral lines. After settling into their seats, Kiki dictated a series of breathing exercises to calm their nerves.

"At times during the ritual," Kiki touched each item in front of her, "I'm going to ask that you use the pen to write a word, just one word, on a little square of paper. It's called automatic writing. It's critical that you don't dwell on what you write, just do it, no matter what the word is. No matter how crude, grotesque, embarrassing, or if the word makes no sense at all. Those words won't be coming from you. Write them down immediately, when you hear the command *write*." Kiki reached for a long taper. "We're going to light our candles now. Mindfully, take three cleansing breaths before igniting your flame, then pass the taper to your left."

Kiki illuminated her candle and passed the taper to Agatha. As Agatha lit her candle, Janine slunk into the room and settled herself against the far wall directly behind the doctor. The taper soon made its way around the table and Kiki blew it out, then, she reached for the hands of both Agatha and Mr. Croager. Everyone joined hands at that signal.

"*Hear us now.*" She used a voice to cross the veil. "*Speak to us, bring us light, in this dark night, and we will listen and heed your voice, your choice.*" Kiki stared at Janine, willing her to repeat the words. Janine dipped her head slightly in acknowledgement, but rolled her eyes.

"Hear us now, speak to us now, bring us light, in this dark night and we will listen, and heed your voice, make your choice." Kiki repeated those words over and over until the air had become heavy and thick.

A faint flutter descended on the room and a faint hint of lavender wafted in the air. Kiki hadn't detected that scent before. She felt a buzz of energy skirt the edge of the table.

"I feel a woman in this room," Kiki said aloud. "Are you the woman who haunts this place?" She paused to give Janine time repeat her questions. A faint haze descended on the table and Kiki felt a momentary pressure against her shoulder. Lauren visually fidgeted and she locked eyes with Kiki.

Kiki tilted her head and focused on the crystal in the center of the table. "What do you desire to tell us?" A buzz hummed in her ear. The crystal began to shimmer. Kiki commanded, "Write."

She put the pen atop the stack of paper and allowed her hand to move freely, unaware of what she scribbled, ignoring her hand until the pen dropped. Kiki noticed the others writing. Janine's brown doe eyes bore directly into hers and Kiki shook her head slightly. She hoped Janine understood that she should not *tune in to the ghost, just transmit*. Kiki felt certain Janine's energy drain occurred when she tuned in. They were like opposite sides of a coin.

"We will each read aloud our words," Kiki told her séance participants. "And, after you've read your message, you shall burn it. Obliterate it in your candle flame and place the burning paper on the small silver tray. If you're feeling taxed, breathe deeply, to calm yourself. I'll read first. We'll go around the table in the same direction that we lit the candles. That will be how the message was given."

"Why do we need to burn them?" Lauren asked softly.

"To cleanse us of this communication," Kiki told her. "Burning the words will release us of this message and sever our link with this spirit. Automatic writing can cause an essence to feel powerful, like they can control you, because, for a brief moment, they controlled one little part of you. Don't be surprised if you don't recognize the handwriting."

Mrs. Croager glanced at her paper and gasped. Kiki locked eyes on the woman, and sent her a friendly smile.

"No worries, the crystal grid will contain her ambient energy. Only your hand is in that realm."

"Are you sure?" the old woman asked. Kiki nodded at her.

"Let's read our messages. *Intrusion*." Kiki touched the corner of the paper to her candle flame before placing it on her silver tray to burn away.

"Privacy," Agatha mumbled and lit her note and placed it into her own tray.

"Silence," Lauren added softly, and burned her note.

"Annoying," the doctor said, and burned his note.

"Quiet," Emily Croager's shaky hand lit her post-it, then moved it to the tray.

"Uncomfortable," Walter Croager huffed before burning his note.

Their words hung in the air as they quietly waited. Kiki closed her eyes and used each word to create a mental picture, a picture that *somebody* wanted her to have. Random colors spun behind her eyes as the jigsaw snapped together. Kiki could feel her, an introverted woman, upset and unnerved.

"She feels annoyed with the guests here. This is her domain and people keep invading her peace. Living energy is too loud for her." Kiki stared at Janine. "We should assure this spirit that we'll be out of her space soon. We apologize for the intrusion."

Kiki retrieved the hands of Agatha and Walter, and instructed the circle to take three deep breaths to clear their cores. The density of air had gotten very thick and she focused on the movement of energy that circled the table. She could detect sparks of spectral energy along the crystal grid. Kiki wondered if anyone else could see it, but no one else seemed to notice. Several souls competed for their attention and she studied the central orb closely for signs of life.

"I feel others here, many others. I feel a young man lingering near. Please, tell us why you have come," Kiki said. The orb in the center of the table changed faintly. "Write."

Each person gripped their pens and scribbled. Starting with Kiki, they read their words out loud again.

"Music."

"Booze."

"Party."

"Smokes."

"Party."

"Crazy."

They each went through the ritual of burning their written words. This spirit felt confused and eager. Kiki felt spirits like this before, a whiff of life energy completely unaware that their life was gone. They always attempted to mingle with the living.

"He's looking for entertainment," Kiki said. "He came searching for a group of people having fun, but he's leaving. I feel another woman, a different woman. Look!" The orb in the center of the table glowed dimly. Someone in the circle let out a startled sound. "Quick, write." Kiki ordered. They wrote swiftly, then read them out.

"Forsaken."

"Terrified."

"Sorrow."

"Empty."

"Regret."

"Helpless."

This spirit had commanded the table easily, and felt powerful. It had purpose and a very dark center. But the spirit did not show Kiki any images, just confusing feelings. This particular spectral voice was eager to tell them something, while at the same time, it desired to stay hidden.

"She is very sad and may have done something regrettable. She's afraid of what she has done. Her actions came from a place of deep sorrow and feelings of… abandonment," Kiki whispered.

"What has she done?" Emily Croager's scratchy whisper hung in the air.

"She may have killed herself," Kiki said softly. "And someone else. A child, yes, her child. That's it, I think that's exactly it. She wants to take it back. She's desperate to take it back." Kiki stared at Janine and locked onto those glittering brown eyes. "A *dragoma* might counsel a spirit like this one, find words to ease her guilt. She yearns to find peace and needs solace. Sometimes, people act from terrible grief and regret rash actions that cannot be undone. This poor soul carries a burden past her own death and feels that she can never right it."

Maybe Janine would know what to say to that spirit. Commiserate on regrets. Janine once abandoned a newborn. Kiki knew that she had awful regrets about it, but she would never be able to make amends, because Sammy was gone. Janine shut her eyes on Kiki. Kiki glanced around the table.

"I think I feel her sorrow," Lauren whispered. Agatha and Emily nodded.

"You probably do," Kiki said.

"I also feel weary," Lauren said. "Exhausted."

"Me too," Agatha chimed in. Emily Croager nodded.

Kiki felt the quiver of energy intensify. There were several conflicting vibes bouncing inside the room, most were weak, but there was one focused point of energy hovering near the table edge and running along the lines of the crystal grid. It was an insistent voice demanding to speak through the void, a very impatient presence bearing down.

"We'll try one more," Kiki said. "But first, rearrange the stones in front of you. Take the nearest stone and trade it with the pyramid in your line. Place that pyramid at the end, closest to your seat."

She watched as they rearranged the stones. Kiki approved, and they all joined hands. She searched out Janine but did not think anyone needed to help this spirit. This spirit wanted to talk without encouragement, and that scared her a little.

"Okay, three cleansing breaths," Kiki began, but the orb was already glowing. "Write!" This was definitely an aggressive spirit, but their distraction had a moderating effect on its vitality, and the orb pulsed. The group seemed a little unnerved and Kiki saw why. Her hand had written in a distinctive spidery thin cursive.

"Ignored."

"Misunderstood."

"Disregard."

"Entitled."

"Respect."

"Bad."

Kiki nodded. "He's angry. He isn't held in the esteem he believes he's due and feels overlooked. He wishes violence on those who would dismiss him. Perhaps, he is a violent criminal."

"Al Capone?" Walter Croager asked timidly.

The table vibrated suddenly and Agatha almost jumped out of her chair. Both Lauren and Emily Croager pushed their seats away from the table. The tension in the room skyrocketed.

"No, no," Kiki slowly stood. "Not him, this spirit is someone else," *or something else?* "Someone who feels very important." *Someone who feels important to Kiki? Or to one of the others in the room?* The spirit felt animosity and it still had a message. The orb began to glow again. Kiki stared at it.

"Write," she said softly. Her pen began to move on that square paper, deliberately and forcefully guiding her hand.

"Curse."

"Souls."

"Irene."

"Vengeance."

"Control."

"Nothing."

"I feel an overwhelming dread," Emily Croager squeaked suddenly. The age lines around her eyes were etched deeper. "My hand is weak."

Kiki locked eyes with Janine. "We ask this spirit to leave at once. To be gone! Make sure you mean it. Tell it to be gone! We ask all the spirits to leave. Please go." Kiki reached out to grip Agatha's hand to calm her. "We are going to block ourselves from any lingering souls. Snuff out your candle, then touch the tip of the small pyramid with your index finger. Breathe, and try to connect within yourself. Close your eyes if needed and stay quiet. Stay connected to that pyramid. Keep your connection until you've completely calmed your heart."

Kiki shut her eyes and retreated inside herself. She listened to the spectral sounds echoing as they faded away. So many voices wanted to speak.

On her earlier survey, she had no clue the old building contained so many restless souls. After a moment, she asked Carlos to activate the lights.

"Oh my goodness, I can't believe that happened, ghosts were in here." Emily Croager clutched her husband's arm. "They touched me."

All the participants buzzed as they recovered. The doctor held Lauren's hand, and he had moved closer to reassure her. Janine walked around the table to Kiki. She appeared in fairly good shape.

"Good job, Janine," Kiki told her. "This room was jam packed with energy. I couldn't tell how many life forces were here, but more than I could count. Whatever you communicated in the halls worked." Kiki shook her hand, "What exactly did you say? It might be worth writing it down for future use. You can begin your own grimoire. We need to get you a diary, soon, so you can chronicle your charms."

Janine rolled her eyes. "I had a hard time thinking séance, so I projected party. I projected that there was a party in room 441 and everyone should come. It just seemed easier, and I felt less silly."

Kiki stared at her, then laughed. Okay, probably not a spell for a true grimoire. *That explained the party ghost.* Who would have guessed, even spirits have a hard time resisting a good shindig. Yet, that last spirit confused her. It was a strong, angry energy that felt slightly familiar. It easily controlled her hand, and those extra words didn't spark anything but dark shadows in her mind.

Chapter 11

Debrief *Janine*

There was an hour left till dawn when they returned to the Lincoln House ballroom. Janine and Carlos helped unload the van, then changed into their normal clothes. Carlos vigorously combed his hair down, no longer an anime knock-off. He had been a good sport about it, so Max couldn't say Carlos was inflexible after all that. Four nice varieties of alcohol waited on the refreshment table and Janine wasn't shy about pouring a generous helping of the Macallan bottle. Kiki came around and handed her a slip of paper.

"Max left you a note," she whispered. Janine opened it, skimmed it quickly, then crumbled the paper and tossed it into the small garbage bin next to the refreshment table. Kiki gave her a questioning look.

"He can't stop thinking about the limousine ride and hopes to meet for an early breakfast before he's in meetings and I'm asleep all day. He suggests breakfast in my room in about," Janine glanced at her watch, "an hour. I think that energy boost you suggested is coming back to haunt me."

Kiki chuckled, "You weren't ready to try that yet, sorry."

"I'll just hide in your room again," Janine said irritably.

"Fine," Kiki said. "I'm going to check if there's anything worth waiting for."

Janine didn't know how long Kiki wanted to stay, but hoped she would be quick. Between the long day and the chattering Lauren, Janine itched to disappear as soon as possible. It wasn't like the old days. They weren't actually putting anything together in the debrief. That would happen back in Texas now. Janine caught up with Carlos in the back of the room. They lounged in the nice leather chairs clinking their glasses of whisky. Janine ferried the expensive bottle over, so they were set for a nice draw down to their long night. Up near Ben and his console of electronics, Kiki and Ian kept nodding at a very animated Lauren.

Stop judging her, Janine admonished herself. She just participated in an exciting paranormal event that will soon be on television. And, who wouldn't flirt with handsome doctor McNally given the chance? *Plus, they were a thing, right?* Yet, the way Lauren kept touching Ian's arm and flashing her mega-smile irked her. She just wished Lauren would stop lighting up the room in her upbeat, peppy way and act like a normal person. *Jealous much?*

"Lauren worked out well in the séance, don't you think?" Carlos noticed who she was staring at. "Don says she's very photogenic. Comes off nice on camera. Doesn't have a bad angle."

"Do you think she could be my replacement?" Janine asked.

"Oh no, she could never replace you." Carlos smirked. "You are the least photogenic person I know. We would have to mess up her hair and wipe off that perfect lipstick, and maybe teach her a little sarcasm and slouchy posture."

"Jerk." Janine kicked at Carlos. "At least I'm not a cartoon."

Carlos chuckled and poured them more whisky.

"I don't have slouchy posture. So, was Lauren there when you punched Ian in the eye, in San Antonio?" Janine asked.

"Oh, no. Most everyone took off by then," Carlos shook his head. "It was just the guys, and Kiki. It was nothing important, just guy stuff."

"You mean like— just you and Ian and Max? Or, was Don there too?"

"Well, Don and Ben. I think that was it. It was nothing," Carlos said. "What put that in your head?"

So then, Ian McNally boasted to all the men she worked with that she was a wildcat, or something, in bed. No wonder Don leered at her and Ben acted so shy, and Max believed she would be interested in getting together in hotel rooms.

"Just something Max said earlier," Janine told him.

Kiki and Lauen appeared next to them. Ben did not have anything for them to see on film, but did confirm that the pattern on the alley's subsonic recordings matched the sound signature of their names. It felt like years since they were in that alley. Kiki grabbed her hand and pulled her up.

"Come on, lets walk up together. Lauren is going to get my color back before bed," Kiki told her. "We can have a girls only debrief in my room."

Wow, Lauren offered to correct Kiki's hair before going to sleep. Not just totally adorable, but over the top nice too. Nice, pretty, positive, shiny and bright as a new penny. Definitely an upgraded replacement for quiet, morose, messy, marked up Janine. Lauren likely lacked all the complicated relationship issues too.

"Sure thing," Janine snatched the bottle of whisky to bring along.

Kiki prattled on about the séance while Lauren used a special cleanser to wash the temporary red from her hair. Kiki complimented Lauren on her ability to open up during the séance. She showed a natural ability to use her *core* to channel psychic energy. Kiki flashed her emerald eyes toward Janine when she said that. Janine lounged on the bed, glaring, not adding much to the conversation. Kiki winked at her, then grew serious and asked Lauren about the last word she had written.

"What was it," Kiki's brow creased. "Was it a name or a word?"

"I think it was a name, Irene." Lauren said.

"Odd," Kiki said. "A name."

After Kiki's rinse out was complete, the three of them had a celebratory shot to conclude the night's success. As Lauren made her way to the door, she glanced back at Janine.

"Are you sleeping in here again?" she asked Janine.

"We still have a few things to go over," Kiki told her. After Lauren left, Kiki refilled their tumblers. "We probably shouldn't, but why not. I can see you're pretty far gone already, so what will one more hurt? Self-medicating again, I see." Then, she turned and peered deeply into Janine's eyes. "Shall we talk about the park? Do you need to talk?"

"No, I'm too tired and intoxicated." Janine shied away from Kiki's penetrating gaze. She definitely did not want to talk about the park. She pointed to the door instead. "You realize that girl is putting two and two together and coming up with five."

"She probably is," Kiki chuckled, then purred. "It'll just add to our mystique. Let's not worry about it and get some sleep. By the way, your detective messaged me when we were out tonight. I have an early dinner date with him tomorrow. What do you think about that?" Kiki beamed at her.

ery hot. Physical. Wildcat. Carlos had to punch him before he said more. So, what did he say before that punch? What exactly did Ian McNally say about her? Never in her wildest imagination would she believe that Ian McNally would speak ignominiously about her to Carlos, or Max, or to two guys she hadn't even met yet. Janine lay in bed, still very drunk, and growing angry that Ian would betray her so casually. She was terribly tired, but she couldn't sleep. Kiki had no problems and snored softly beside her.

Janine thought about that voice in the park. Did she really hear a little girl's voice say, *I love you, girl?* She was half afraid Ben would have visual playback of the park, that Don's camera had picked up the faces in the mirrors and that one of those faces would be Sammy's, calling from the other side. *Crap!* She could not let those thoughts spin out of control. She should go back to the anger instead. *Grab onto the anger!* Just what did Ian say to those fellows? Did he get super explicit? Is that why Carlos hit him?

A thin layer of whisky lined the bottom of the bottle and Janine eased out of the bed to reach it. It always helped on a sleepless night and it stopped the dreams when she did sleep. She was afraid of those dreams. Why were so many restless ghosts children? It was heartbreaking. Was Sammy's ghost out there somewhere, restless and lost, abandoned? *No, no, no, focus!* Janine told herself. *Don't think about that.* Focus on that dammed asshole, Ian McNally, running off his mouth and getting Don, and Max, and probably even Ben, to objectify her before she even showed up to meet them. They were all probably passing around the stories and *imagining things.* She was not going to wear that *Spectral Analysis* outfit again. Perhaps she should go across the hall and tell Ian off. She should pound on his door and just do it, get it off her chest, and then she'd be able to sleep. But what if Lauren was in there with him? *Even better.* Maybe he needed a dose of his own medicine. She could gossip about him for a change. She could out him good with some uncensored talk. She would tell Lauren that Ian was so... so incredibly tender, sweet, and unbelievably satisfying? So irresistible? *Crap*! No, she would think of something else. Like, he was a blinking idiot. *Ha ha, that's it.* That's exactly what she'd say, that was funny. She drained the last of the Macallan whisky.

Janine searched around, then remembered her clothes were sent to the laundry, all except the thin T-shirt Kiki lent her and the panties she wore. Her jeans and shirt would be cleaned and delivered back by noon, before she planned to wake up. She needed it done, because she only brought the one small backpack, with one change of pants, two shirts, and extra undergarments. She barely packed anything because she didn't really want to be there. The extras must be down the hall in her own room, cleaned the previous night and returned. *Crap again*! Wait! There were perfectly luxurious hotel robes in the closet. Janine snagged a plush robe and wrapped it around herself, then, she quietly snuck out the door and went directly across the hall.

She stumbled over and knocked hard. She immediately regretted it. The bright hallway was unforgiving, and she suddenly didn't want to see Ian, or especially Lauren, on the other side of that door. She turned back and realized that she didn't bring the key, any key. Not to her room, or to Kiki's. She would have to wake Kiki up. *Crap,* Janine thought. She'd rather sleep in the hall than wake Kiki up.

Then, Ian McNally's door opened and he stood there staring at her, bleary eyed. He wore pajama bottoms, but his top was bare. Janine's eyes drank in the muscles of his chest and stomach. The sight of his muscular hairy torso felt more intoxicating than the whisky. Her eyes drifted to the base of his throat and over his broad shoulders. Clearly, he'd been working out in the past year. *No, he had always looked that good. Good lord, was she actually salivating?* She swallowed.

"What are you doing out here?" He searched up and down the hall. He reached out, grabbed her wrist, and pulled her into the room. "Come in here."

They stood just inside his room, but he didn't close the door all the way. He took a step away and stared at her in a confused manner.

"Why are you wandering around in a bathrobe? Are you drunk?" he asked. "You are. Are you alright? Shall I walk you to your door? Or, are you staying in Kiki's room again?"

"I'm locked out," she muttered. "I didn't bring a key. Kiki's sound asleep."

"Where were you going?"

"Here," she confessed. Then, she reminded herself of why she was there. She tried to call up the anger, but it wasn't quite catching. She peered deeper into his room to see if anyone was in there. She lowered her voice, "So, is she in here? Do you have someone back there?"

"No, no one is here." He shut the door completely. "Do you need to talk about something? Something bothering you?" His voice became very soft and his eyes were so tender, she felt like she was melting in them. Was he doing that on purpose? "I heard who you called out to, in the trees," he whispered.

"Oh, no, I don't want to talk about that." Now that she knew no one was there, she went all the way in. Right to the bottle she knew would be on his night table. She needed a touch more to help fire up her nerves and squash that voice from the trees. "I want to talk about you, and why Carlos had to punch you in the eye." *Yes. Yes, think about how he called you a wildcat, providing him with hot sex that he must have described to tons of random guys, probably hundreds.* "I heard that you were talking about me. That you were having a nice time giving out explicit details of—of our past. Putting ideas into people's heads. To all the fellows, Max, Ben, Don, anyone I left out?"

"Crikes, you're completely drunk." His eyes were blinking up a storm. "Maybe we should talk about this another time."

Janine laughed. "Fancy that. Did I disturb your sleep? I'm so sorry. Why isn't your girlfriend here disturbing your sleep? Is she not wild enough for you? Do you talk about her with the guys as well, or is it only me you discussed? Are you going to deny it?"

"Crikes, Janine. I, I'm sorry. You, you have every right to be angry. Did somebody s-say something to you?"

My goodness, was he stuttering, Janine thought. It was not right of him, to look so sorry and sad when she wanted to be angry at him. He was in the wrong here! She stared at him, fully aware that she was very, very drunk and wobbly. She saw that he was getting his blinking back under control, but he still wore a flush of shame. *My goodness,* the thought struck her, *his eyes were absolutely beautiful.* Blue and surrounded by thick lashes and his curly black beard was so dark and crying out to be touched. And his hair was all mushed up from sleeping. He crossed his arms in front of his chest like he was protecting himself from her. *From her!*

He shook his head. "I, I was a complete arse that night, I won't deny it. Totally drunk, and an idiot, waiting to see you. I was disappointed. I, I felt like you were personally ignoring me by avoiding that dinner. Snubbing me. I just wanted to hurt you back, lass. I'm sorry."

She wanted him to look at her. Not with those eyes he wore at moment, all sad and sorry, but with the eyes he wore on the street, full of desire. Like he couldn't wait to draw her in and make love to her. If he could talk about her like that, then he should look at her like that, shouldn't he? Maybe a little flesh would change his attitude. Let the outfit do the flirting, as Kiki advised. Janine untied the Lincoln House hotel robe and let it fall to the ground. She knew she was practically naked in front of him. *Crap!* She was pretty far drunk and in the back of her head some part of her did not agree with her actions here. Well, fuck that part of her! She needed to feel Ian's male sexual energy and channel it into her core properly. As his eyes changed to the smoky ones she desired, she stepped toward him.

Then, she had him like she had fantasized, running her fingers through his dark beard as she kissed him. It was overwhelming and so, so satisfying. That electric charge was still very much alive everywhere they touched. His taunt muscles felt so nice. They sunk onto the bed as his large hands left a hot trail all over her. He was just as eager, until… he suddenly stopped. Ian pushed her away. He was moving further away from her and holding her at arms' length. She couldn't believe he had stopped kissing her. She was infuriated. What was this? Her entire body burned for him and he was pushing her away.

"We can't do this," he gasped. He stood up from the bed, and stepped away. "You're totally drunk. You're upset. We can't do this. I know what you're upset about and I don't want you this way."

"What do you mean?" *Was he kidding?* He could talk about having sex with her to everyone she worked with, but he couldn't do it when she needed it? "What are you talking about? You don't want me?" Janine stood up and she slapped him, hard. Ian just took it, and she was instantly ashamed of herself. She reached over to grab his bottle of whisky.

"Why are you drinking so much?" He took the bottle away from her.

"Give that back! It helps me sleep," she added softly. "It helps me forget." And then she burst into tears. Cold, dark, desolate tears.

Ian instantly engulfed her in a tight embrace. He held her close, taking in her grief. He didn't let her push him away. He radiated a comforting sphere all around her. He was whispering things she couldn't understand in his thick Scottish accent and it sounded so sweet.

She'd never forget, she knew, but at night, it was always worse. Her dreams gave her hope that things could be changed, that events could be undone.

If she wished hard enough, then Sammy would return. She'd emerge from a hiding place, giggling that everyone thought she washed away in the river, how silly- *and that oppressive weight would blissfully be gone.*

Sometimes, Rick was still the man she first met and she had been mistaken about things. His kisses were filled with love, *love, love,* and he, and her, and that little girl were a happy family- *relief would flood her chest.*

Or, she made a silly blunder believing such a horrible thing happened. There were no knife wounds to hide, no scars, and her body was nice again, smooth, normal. She had never been a victim, or stupid, or powerless. She was whole- *the pressure in her head would ease.*

In some dreams, Sammy turned out to be Ian's daughter, how lucky was that? *A sliver of hope would dribble in.*

Happy images invaded her sleep, giving her peace, such peace…but then, she'd wake, and fully realize her folly, and gravity would yank her back down, *down, down*…and she'd have to face her harsh reality all over again.

Ian put her in his bed and covered her with his sheets and blanket. He brought back something and made her drink it, all of it. It was some sort of sports drink. He sat on the edge of the bed and stroked her head like she was a baby. It was already very cold being out of his embrace. Did he notice that she had slapped him really hard a moment ago?

"Go to sleep, lass." He didn't look upset at her. "You'll be better after you sleep it off."

Janine sat up. She was past the sobbing wreck phase of her tantrum. It had cleared her head a little.

"No. I'm not going to kick you out of your bed," she said. "Hand me my robe. I'll go back to Kiki's, or to my own room, you need to sleep too."

He pushed her gently back down and tucked the sheets in firmly, all around her, like a mummy.

"You're going to stay right here, where I can keep an eye on you," he ordered. "No arguments about that." He climbed over her, onto the bed, and lay on top of the covers next to her. "You see, I'll sleep right here." He lay very close to her and draped his arm across her body. He whispered into her ear, "I do want you, lass. I want you right here." And that's how she was finally able to fall asleep.

Thick blackout curtains kept the room dark and everything seemed turned around. Then, she remembered. She had been totally drunk and went into Ian's room. She sat up and looked around. The room was quiet and deserted. The hotel clock blinked the time, four forty-three in the afternoon. She had slept soundly for eight hours, a world's record. She actually felt very good. She spotted a note at the foot of the bed next to a small folded pile of her clothes, a room key, and an extra toothbrush. She picked up the note. It was written in Ian's blocky square letters, which happened to match the blocky L and H on the hotel stationary paper.

The hotel sent up an extra key, so I fetched some things from your room. There's water by the bed. Crew dinner at six upstairs. We get started at seven thirty. Hope you feel better. Ian.

Janine slipped her jeans and shirt on to make the short trip down the hall to her own room. She needed to shower and get ready. She was embarrassed. She wanted to skip the dinner, but somehow, she felt like Ian would be insulted if she skipped it. She made it to her room without bumping into anyone, but then she saw what Ian must have seen when he came to get her things.

Now there were two vases of flowers, violets and roses, *very lovely*, another bottle of wine, and a small bowl of strawberries. She spotted another handwritten written note and picked it up.

Thinking of our kiss and that ride in the limo. Sorry I missed you this morning, Max.

Ugh! Fine. Good. There were worse things in life than having a handsome, wealthy man shower her with flowers and attention, but she couldn't think of one just then. She decided to get cleaned up fast and run upstairs for the dinner. She didn't want anyone to think she was ignoring them.

Most of the *Spectral Analysis* staff sat outside on the terrace overlooking the Chicago River. Janine glanced around and spotted everyone except Kiki. Ian lounged at a table with Ben, Carlos, and Lauren. *Why did that woman have to be so pretty and perfect?* Max was there and brightened up when he saw her. He wore a very nice designer suit and tie. Janine wore a faded old *Spectral Analysis* T-shirt and jeans.

"Hello there, we meet again," he said.

"Are you coming from one of your board meetings?" she asked.

"No, I'm about to catch my flight," he said. "Sorry to say, I've got a few fires to put out back home and you guys will be on your own for the rest of this outing. I think the doctor prefers it that way. If last night is any indication of what goes on during the shoots, then I think we're going to have a successful episode."

"And, you got a good look at Carlos in a different light, right? It's easier to imagine him teaming up with someone new. A more glamourous girl, maybe, like Lauren, even."

A tiny flicker of caution passed through Max's eye as he smiled at her.

"Why don't we save that conversation for our date in Austin? I've got a few things to nail down first, but I think you'll be happy with the outcome. I have a feeling you'll find it a celebratory date." He lowered his voice. "I missed you this morning, for our early breakfast," he smiled at her.

Janine glanced away, embarrassed.

"You're just more alluring than ever. I enjoy that, believe it or not, a challenge," he smiled. "Part of the fun is in the chase."

She didn't answer him. Other people came around, and the conversation turned to other things. Max Colliers was in high demand. Most everyone wanted to curry his favor. Janine grabbed salad and bread from the buffet, then settled at an empty table. It didn't stay empty for long. Soon, Ben and Carlos and the doctor plopped down next to her. The doctor gave her an amused smile that she definitely deserved.

"Guess what," Carlos said. "We found images in the mirrors. On the IR clips anyway, not on the regular camera."

"There appear to be thermal images on Carlos's camera," Ben chimed in. His big bright eyes beamed at her.

"Ben fine-tuned the infrared clips and found patterns captured in the mirrors. They appear very face like," the doctor patted Ben on the back. "But there was nothing on the audio, just crackling noises under the voice tape of you and Kiki."

"Are they recognizable faces?" Janine asked. "Do they look like anyone?"

Ben and Carlos shook their heads.

"Did you do your subsonic trick?" Janine asked Ben. "For the audio in the park?"

"Not yet," Ben said. "The camera doesn't pick it up well. I'll have to analyze the audio recorder you attached to that tree when we recover it." Ben saluted and said he needed to run downstairs to make sure everything was loaded into the van correctly. Carlos took another trip to the buffet.

"You look remarkably recovered," Ian said when they were alone.

"I'm sorry about… " Janine briefly met his eye, then glanced to where Lauren sat spying on them from a corner table. She wondered if Lauren knew what Janine had done that morning, if Ian told her. "Did I make a total fool out of myself?"

Ian shook his head slowly. "You were very charming, no worries. I'm just glad to see you looking yourself again. Before I head downstairs, I want to apologize for the jack-ass things I said behind your back in San Antonio, and for any problems it's caused you. I'm very sorry," he said. "See you downstairs."

Kiki perched in the makeup chair chatting to Guy. Apparently, Kiki was going goth for the graveyard shoot. Her eyes were outlined with thick, dark, smoky liner which always made the green pop, and she paired it with jet black lipstick, and Lauren had succeeded in getting her dark brown hair back. Janine sat on a stool to watch. Carlos came around and sat next to them. He gave Janine an interesting look. His brow was furrowed and, for once, he was not smiling.

"Don't worry, we're not going goth," Carlos said. "I got a look at tonight's outfits and we're basically going to be dressed as Kiki's biker back-up squad. Why isn't the doctor being dressed up like this? I never thought I'd say it, but, I want to wear a rainbow tie and button down shirt like the doc."

Guy smiled at his remarks, "I'm still supposed to blacken your eyes. Doctor McNally doesn't like anything that isn't casual conservative and he won't wear makeup. Sally's been buying him nice shirts, though. His rainbow ties match everything, and I love the statement they make."

Very nice shirts, Janine silently agreed. Kiki gave her a small manila envelope. A silver chain snaked out of it followed by a pendant of a *patron saint?* She didn't recognize the saint. *Saint Comba* appeared to be a naked woman, *very Lady Godiva-ish*, with an animal at her side. There was something odd about that darkened silver metal, it repulsed her. Very ornate and old, it felt cold and heavy, an unwelcome weight in her hand. Was it lead? No, it wasn't soft. Janine poured it back into the envelope and returned it to Kiki.

"That guy," Kiki told her, "from last night, the haunted one. When I was running out to dinner, he was standing out on the steps. Poor dear, he looked confused, like he didn't know what he wanted to do. He begged me to give that to you."

Janine remembered the haunted one. He had been very creepy. "I don't want it."

"Are you sure?" Kiki took the envelope and flipped it over. "That's his name and number. I'm going to meet him tomorrow and ask about his ghost. He's eager to get things off his chest. That woman is Saint Comba, on the pendant, you know. My auntie had a similar charm, maybe even, exactly like it, and she wore it on a special occasion. I often wonder where it went. Saint Comba was a witch and a Christian saint, Janine. Some insist that she's the patron saint of witches. She's important to my coven. Isn't it strange that he said a ghost wanted you to have it? Do you mind if I wear it tonight? I feel streams of interesting energy seeping out of it."

"Go ahead," Janine told her. "It's all yours."

"I'm not going keep it," Kiki said. "I'm going to hold onto it for you."

Janine decided to check out the garment rack and see why Carlos was so upset. Carlos followed on her heels. His garment bag already lay open and his outfit spilled across the table; black leather chaps and a silky see-through netted shirt. Over the top, he'd wear the bat belt. *Good grief, that was quite a getup*, she thought.

"And look, silver metal wrist bands like I'm some sort of slave, or something, and is this a metal collar?" Carlos laughed without humor. "The doctor doesn't care what we wear, but said there was an agreement that Colliers called the shots for design changes, like our onscreen images, which includes costumes and such."

They unzipped the garment bag for Janine as Sally wandered in. Sally smiled, excited to see them examining her creations.

"Want me to help you get suited up?" Sally asked. She pulled out the female version of the sexy biker gang outfit and it was quite a sight. Leather chaps again, but where were the pants for underneath? All Janine could see was a very small leather bikini bottom. Then, the top, leather again, with a lace up back. Or was it the front? They couldn't be serious about that outfit.

"It's the front," Sally said. "Very tricky to hide everything, but I'll show you how to lace it up so nothing important gets exposed. Mr. Colliers designed this costume for the graveyard scene, he's actually a very good artist. He said you guys might go for it after last night." She smiled proudly. "Of course, there's a toned down version I can pull out, but this is the ensemble he hoped you'd choose tonight. So, how about it, feeling brave?"

"I'm not going to ask what type of film you made costumes for before this show," Carlos said.

Sally didn't seem to understand his comment, then Kiki appeared. Her eyes popped open at the leather outfits and she let out a startled laugh. She gave Janine an amused eye. Was Kiki daring her to wear it? Janine spun to Sally.

"Can we have the room to ourselves for a minute? I'll call you, if I need help."

Sally shrugged and walked off with a frown. Kiki raise her eyebrow and caressed the skimpy leather top.

"If you're not going to wear this," Kiki said, "I think I'll give it a try. It looks like one size fits all. It's much better than the top I had planned. My goodness, this is absolutely wicked. I'll want those chaps in the future as well." Kiki laughed, apparently happy there was someone dreaming up crazier outfits than her. "Max is going to get us a more risky rating, and maybe a later time slot as well."

"Tell me we're not going to wear this stuff, am I right?" Carlos appeared relieved. "I gotta say, last night was incredibly awkward, I only did it for you, Janine, but this leather stuff is not okay. Maria would not understand this. Maybe we should just wear those stretch shirts from yesterday, they weren't too bad, just a little form fitting."

"Look, Carlos," Janine started, "Max Colliers is having trouble finding a replacement, for when I leave. The only reason I wanted to dress up was, well, because he wanted to see you in a new light, to better match you with a new partner. Otherwise, he's thinking of replacing both of us at the same time."

"You mean, like firing me?" His eyes widened.

Janine nodded, "But he said something just now, upstairs, that made me think he's seen what he needs to see, and you'll be okay. But, for tonight, I'll be frank with you, I can't wear this either. I don't want to wear any of it anymore. I'm thinking, this T-shirt and jeans for tonight, it's the type of uniform I signed up to wear. I never agreed to wear this type of stuff." Janine pointed to the leather chaps.

Kiki shook her head. "That arse! I was wondering what got into you. You should have come to us with this right away."

"What good would that have done?" Janine said. "He was pretty convincing."

"We've got a package contract, Janine," Kiki nodded her head. "Ian insisted on it. None of us are officially signed, until you sign. We've been waiting for you, you're the final signature on the block. If you don't sign the contract, then they have to draft a whole new document with whoever the new person is going to be." Kiki patted Carlos on the shoulder, "We could all jump ship on Max if he tried to pull something like that. He would shite his pants."

"You would do that for me?" Carlos asked.

"Of course, sweetie," Kiki said.

"Are you sure about that, Kiki?" Janine asked.

"Absolutely."

If she wanted, she could check with the doctor, or better yet, give Mike Dunn, the original show's lawyer, a call. But Kiki knew, beyond a doubt, that if Janine did not sign the contract soon, and they wanted to include someone new, then everyone would have to sign again.

"He cannot spontaneously drop Carlos," Kiki said. "Seriously, Janine, Max threatened all those things to either convince you to dress in his outrageous outfits, or to get you into bed. That's how he operates, and he's clever at getting his way. Carlos is a big part of this show and we could not do without him. Max knows that."

"Thank you, Kiki," Carlos hugged her. Kiki pushed him away and took the scandalous black leather lace-up body shirt off Janine's rack. "Very soft lamb's leather, very witchy. So, I guess you won't be needing this sultry thing." She winked at them before running off to change.

"She's in a fantastic mood," Carlos watched Kiki skip away. "Someone at dinner said she had a hot date. Only Kiki Mellow can reel in a fish on such short notice in Chicago. Who do you think it was? Another athlete? Maybe she had a connection through the last guy. I wonder how she juggles her suiters so smoothly without them killing each other? My brother Lonzo has a terrible crush on Kiki, he begged me to set them up, but I am not going to let that happen. She would eat him alive."

"If we're going to go grunge tonight," Janine interrupted, "we should probably bring an extra shirt for Don. They already took off and I bet he's dressed in something like this. You have an extra *Spectral Analysis* tee, right?"

Carlos laughed, "But Don loves dressing sexy. Sometimes, I wonder if Sally and Don came off the same show before this one."

They were scheduled to hit the Graceland Cemetery first, then head over to Lincoln Park during the wee hours of the morning. If things flowed smoothly, they'd rap up filming on location before dawn. Then, they'd gather the remote equipment the next day and fly back to Texas the next evening, just in time for the birthday bash Kiki planned.

The doctor, Ben, and Don drove ahead in the van, while Janine and Carlos would follow after Kiki was ready. Max left the limousine for them. Sally was visibly upset that they did not wear any of her designs. She sat on the other side of the room, next to Lauren, pressing her lips together and feigned reading a magazine. She snapped the pages audibly. Janine turned away from them and pulled her hair into her standard pony tail. The only new items they allowed was the dark eye makeup and the bat belts over their jeans.

"Well," Carlos lounged in the limousine, "this is more like it. So, Kiki, are you going to tell us who your date was with? Was he perhaps a Bull, or a Bear?"

Kiki smiled demurely at him. Her hooded cape draped all the way down to the bottom of her black boots. The boots stretched all the way up to her knees and she wore a dagger strapped on her thigh. Janine wondered if Kiki also wore that silver ornament with the witches' saint. As if in answer, Kiki opened her cloak a fraction and fingered the silver accessory. It dangled between plump breasts which were scarcely contained under that laced up leather shirt. *Oh my goodness,* Janine thought, *is she's trying to recharge her receptive batteries using Carlos?*

"You are so astute, Carlos, how did you know?" Kiki gazed at him in wonder, shifting suggestively so that most of one leg escaped from the cloak. She used her sultry voice on him. "He's a definite bull, very strong, very powerful, and very virile. In Celtic beliefs, the bull is the symbol of fertility. Don't laugh at me, but I think it's a sign, the heavens throwing a powerful bull at me, less than a year before my twenty-eighth birthday, when I need to start making good use of my eggs. I need a virile male, don't you agree, for that activity? Next spring, as the delicate blooms bud, I'll be free to enjoy all the fruits of the Beltane festival for once in my life. That's a fertility festival, you know. Yes, that date of mine was a definite bull."

Carlos glanced at Janine, and she could tell he was a little flustered. "What are we talking about here? When I said bull, I was asking if he was one of the Chicago Bulls?"

"He's definitely a Chicago *bull*," Kiki purred. Then, her entire demeanor changed and she smirked at Janine. "But even better than that, he's got the prettiest aura, head aura mind you, that I have ever seen. I have never been in the presence of a man so, so in touch with his entire triquetra, his body, soul, and spirit in perfect harmony. You know, we often use the word spirit incorrectly on our show. We use it referring to a ghost. What we should really say is soul, because that's the essence of a person." Kiki's green gems glowed out of the dark black eye powder. "I have never met such a soul, Janine. If you believe in soulmates, then you could probably bet that I met mine. Detective Robert Anderson is my idea male. Our cores connect, and I'm convinced he can see my aura."

Carlos and Janine exchanged glances. They both tried not to laugh, because Kiki came off very seriously. This was something new, Kiki never gushed about anyone she dated before, and Kiki had gone on dates with very attractive, eligible men.

"Is Kiki telling us she's in love?" Carlos asked. "With a detective? Have I seen him? Was it the big guy at the park last night? He was very interested in speaking with you, Kiki, but I didn't think he had the guts to do it. I have to tell you, he did not, exactly, come off as a brain. But he did look a little like a bull. Did you see him, Janine? He was a giant, I'll give you that."

"No, no, not that bloke," Kiki giggled. "Janine already knows the detective. He is much more powerful than that fellow in the park. Imagine a cosmic burst of solar energy. Like, an extreme coronal mass ejection that creates an aurora so spectacular it lights up the entire northern hemisphere."

Now they were all laughing and Kiki held up her hand.

"Okay, okay, that may be a wee bit of exaggeration," she grinned playfully. "Let's just say, I adore Bob Anderson."

On the corner of Clark and Irving Park was Graceland, a classic example of a decorative garden cemetery. Their main goal in the graveyard was to film clips in front of varied tombstones and monuments. They wanted to use the footage as a backdrop for Kiki's voice overs. Many of the *Alley of Death* victims happened to be buried in that patch of land. Markers from Lincoln Park had also been transplanted to Graceland, though, it was rumored that many of the remains had been left behind.

"If you're so gaga about Detective Anderson, why didn't you recharge your receptors off him instead?" Janine whispered as they walked toward the *Spectral Analysis* van. The van sat in front of the Getty Tomb, an ugly box-like mausoleum with an ornate iron door. "You shouldn't use Carlos like that."

"It's because you misdirect the energy, Janine. Man is of the sun and woman of the earth, even Plato knew that. We'd wither without the constant radiant energy men shower on us, and, admit it or not, Carlos is a very red blooded, masculine man. He directs his energy at every girl he sees, and does it in a very nice way, all of the time. What do you imagine his humor is covering up? He tries to disguise it, so he doesn't offend, but believe me, his wiseass comments are a projection of admiration. I use his energy often, but I never do anything naughty with it. His energy never touches my passion zone." Kiki rolled her eyes. "And, if I ever did return some of that energy, Carlos would never, ever, stray from Maria, not for me or anyone else. He isn't molded that way."

"I feel like you just threw feminism right into the trash can somewhere in that speech," Janine huffed. "I'm just saying, couldn't you have reset your batteries on your date, instead of on our friend?"

"Well, Janine, I was like you were last night. I had problems redirecting Bob's energy to my core. It took me by surprise, and frankly, I didn't want to redirect it, he is so genuine. Gosh, if that's what happens to you all the time, no wonder you need to hide in my room." Kiki patted her hand, then went over to meet the doctor at the van to discuss the shoot.

Don emerged from the van as they approached. He took one look at Janine and Carlos, stamped his foot and cursed. Carlos shook as a slow rumble of laughter rolled from his chest. Don wore the chaps. He wore the sheer, tight, muscle shirt. He wore the metal collar and clumpy wrist bands. His eyes were dark colored cavities of blackness.

"This is not happening," Don spat out. "Why aren't you two in costume?"

Carlos pressed his lips together. "I didn't think I could pull off that outfit the way you do." Carlos grabbed Janine and pulled her aside. "Don, I have to hold this girl back, you're so sexy! Maybe you should cut her a break and change into something more toned down." Carlos laughed at his own antics. He let go of Janine and pulled out a first generation *Spectral Analysis* T-shirt from his backpack. It was a basic black cotton shirt with the electromagnetic spectrum stamped across the chest.

"Sorry we didn't get to you sooner," Janine said to him. "We decided to go grunge for tonight's shoot, back to basics. You would rather wear a regular T-shirt than that outfit, right?"

"Isn't that going to get us into some kind of trouble with management, the producer, Mr. Colliers?" Don still wore a scowl. Carlos held the T-shirt out and, after a pause, Don grabbed it and stomped behind the van to change. The doctor noticed the commotion and joined them.

"You two look very nice, very retro, I like it." His eyes smiled at her, and Janine felt herself blush.

Kiki and the doctor posed in front of different grave markers discussing his theory regarding elements that store ghostly energy. They began the conversation at the Getty Tomb, then changed locations as they continued the discussion.

They next moved toward the Shoenhofen marker, which was basically a small pyramid and sphinx. The doctor theorized that the stone composition of the pyramids were perfect for absorbing paranormal energy, because they were composed of limestones and granites, with a generous helping of micas. No doubt many workers were killed during the construction, under harsh conditions, Kiki added. She said that the shape of the pyramids lent to the focusing of cosmic energy. She often used stone pyramids to focus energy during a séance.

The Greek temple of Potter Palmer was another extravagant burial chamber. Kiki elaborated on the mystic oracles and lamented the loss of that ancient knowledge.

They filmed short clips at smaller tombstones, all victims of the fire who died in the *Alley of Death*, and discussed the unusual whispery recordings they gathered from the sensors planted behind the theater. Finally, they congregated at the Dexter Graves site where an ominous life-sized figure loomed before a black granite backdrop, the "Eternal Silence" statue. The figure appeared to be oxidized bronze, or copper, and wore a metallic cloak very similar to Kiki's velvet one.

"Dexter Graves was originally buried in the old City Cemetery," the doctor told the camera. "Which is now Lincoln Park. People from all walks of life were laid to rest in that old cemetery. For political or financial reasons, the city closed that burial ground to accommodate a surging population. Many bodies were exhumed and sent to other places, like this one, Graceland. That movement didn't happen overnight, it took years. The final graves scheduled for relocation had markers made of wood, and when the Great Chicago Fire hit, those markers were reduced to ash, which made it near impossible to locate graves to be moved. Basically, unaccounted for remains are rumored to still be in Lincoln Park, our next destination.

"The curator shared something interesting with us," Kiki reminded him. "This monument is also known as the *statue of death*. Many people have stared into the face of this monument and received a vision of their own death. Shall we try it?"

Don filmed as the doctor and Kiki strolled up to the statue from different angles, from the front, from the rear, and in slow motion. Kiki allowed her cloak to drift open, just enough to show off her racy suggestive outfit, and she pulled her hood up for the start of each clip. As she lifted her face to the statue, the hood always drifted dramatically back, exposing her startled, glowing eyes. Carlos filmed one take in infrared for a spooky effect. After a few clips, the doctor nodded at Kiki, apparently done.

"I guess that's a rap here. To Lincoln Park?"

"Oh, no," Kiki pulled him back. "Now, we must peer into the face of that statue, seriously, and seek a vision of our deaths. I'll use a prophesy charm, and we'll give it at least three minutes." Three again, her witching number, Janine recalled, all things divisible by three.

Carlos and Janine strolled toward the van to stow their equipment, one small EMF box, a thermal-panger, and an infrared camera. Behind them, Don shouted. Janine turned just in time to see the famous Doctor-Kiki catch.

The doctor spun round and caught Kiki in one fluid motion. *Was it a staged fainting?* Kiki mentioned a *graveyard catch* in the limousine the night before. Yet, Kiki appeared very limp and drooped dramatically. Her cloak hung open, scandalously exposing the lace up shirt. Max Colliers was going to love that shot. Ian lowered Kiki to the grass and knelt beside her. Janine and Carlos double-timed back to the Dexter Graves monument.

"Kiki, Kiki?" The doctor rubbed her hand as Don hovered over them with the camera.

The statue of death loomed in the background. Janine didn't dare move her eyes to that figure. *Did Kiki see something in that stone face?* Kiki's lashes fluttered as the doctor helped her to a sitting position. Kiki's trembling hand reached up to grasp the pendant hanging from her neck. Her bosom heaved against the laces of her shirt, and her legs peeked haphazardly from her cloak, creating another great shot for Max. Kiki's brilliant green eyes glowed like cat eyes in the dark.

"Someone killed me with their bare hands," Kiki breathlessly declared. "I was choked to death. That's how I die."

Janine, Kiki, and Don rode in the limousine. Janine managed that combination by insisting Kiki needed to stretch out across one of the seats. She insisted that Kiki might need Don to recount exactly what he saw when she fainted. It sounded ridiculous, but if Kiki needed to soak up some male sexual energy, Janine did not want young Ben or her friend Carlos to be the sacrificial lambs providing it. The doctor raise his eyebrow when she proposed that seating arrangement, but didn't say a word and went along with her suggestion. *Did Ian know about the witches' trick?* She would be incredibly embarrassed if he found out she tried it on Max the night before. They made a plan to meet at Clark Street, near the old Couch Tomb in Lincoln Park.

Kiki stretched across the rear facing seat with Janine and Don across from her. Janine assured Don that Kiki fainted regularly and snapped back quickly. Kiki smiled at him.

"Don't worry, Don, sometimes the mystic world takes a toll on a girl."

"Did you actually see your death in that statue? By strangulation?" Don asked.

"Yes, I did. My killer felt familiar, like someone I knew, but he isn't someone I've met yet. He strangled me with his bare hands," Kiki whispered. "Could you be a dear and pour me a bit of water? I'll tell you exactly what I saw. I'll need to recite it for the green screen later, but let's hear how it sounds out loud, right now."

Don poured the water. He added a cube of ice to it, and Kiki released a little sound of appreciation with her breath. She glanced through fluttering eyelashes as he handed the tumbler to her.

"Thank you." She sat up straighter and was quite a sight. Under the cloak, in that lace up shirt, she looked like a character from a racy vampire movie. Dark, dangerous, and unpredictable.

Kiki tilted her head back and closed her eyes. "The vision commenced with me hiding from someone. Someone who felt like my lover, but I couldn't quite decide. Was he, or wasn't he? That was in question. One thing was clear, I had no doubt that he wanted to kill me. The sky was dark, definitely night, and a full moon reflected on a body of water, or, perhaps the moon was low in the sky? The image seemed to waffle and the moon went from horizon to water. The grass beneath my feet felt cool, smooth, then scratchy. Again, I couldn't decide. The images were very tricky, because it felt like I was in two places at once. One place was cool and breezy, while the other was more stagnant. Heather bloomed everywhere, but then, the heather morphed into cattails, very confusing. A gentle breeze stirred my hair, and for a moment, it felt a wee bit like Scotland on a warmer winter's night, peaceful. For some reason, I wasn't afraid to die. I realized that being killed wouldn't matter at all and that it was somehow needed." Kiki fingered the silver charm with a far-away look in her eye. "But then, I turned around and he was there, and I was terrified, and his hand felt hot with passion and tight on my throat. It began as a caress but turned into anger as he squeezed." Kiki ran her hand along her own neck. "He smiled lovingly at me, squeezing tighter and tighter, and the world around me dimmed until there were only pinpricks of light before there was nothing at all."

"Jesus Christ," Don exclaimed. "Did you get a good look at him? Maybe you can avoid him. You can watch out for him. I don't believe the future is fixed, Kiki. You can change things. You don't have to date him if you know what he looks like."

"The darkness made him hard to see," Kiki glanced from the corner of her eyes at him. "But I noticed that he had strong arms."

"There you go," Don said. "You can avoid him. If you believe all this psychic stuff, maybe this prediction is a 'maybe,' right? Has anyone ever died after looking at that statue? It's got to be an old wives' tale."

Kiki shrugged, "The images point to a definite strangulation, but I think you're right, Don. I don't think the future is fixed. The environment kept changing, so nothing was fixed. You are a very observant man."

"Could you identify anything else, other than his arms?" Janine asked.

"He was a devil," Kiki stated. "Or a demon. A man with no soul, no aura radiating from his core. I just need to be sure that I don't cross paths with a demon." She inhaled deeply, and accidently spilled the water. Droplets dribbled into the crevice of her chest starling her. Kiki attempted to pat down the drops through the laces of her shirt in a very ineffective way. *Good, grief,* Janine couldn't believe she had participated in that behavior the previous night.

Ian and Janine are the Lovers

Of the tombstones left in Lincoln Park, the largest was the Couch Mausoleum next to the Lincoln memorial, near the final resting place of one David Kennison, their spectral focus for the night. Although a plaque annotating Kennison's life lay blocks away from where they stood, the doctor's research suggested his original burial site lay near the Couch tomb.

"It's believed that David Kennison's bones were never exhumed and moved with his marker," the doctor rambled as they drifted through the park. "He was a larger than life figure who live well past one hundred years old. One hundred and fifteen, people insist. He didn't want to leave this world, and many reports suggest that he never did. His ghost wanders this area regularly."

The doctor carried his ion detector and waved it around. Carlos carried the infrared recorder, and Janine clipped a thermal-panger and subsonic audio recorder to her bat belt. The doctor anticipated too much ambient electromagnetic noise for the big box, so they basically followed Kiki, hoping she'd pick up a hint of paranormal energy and lead them to David Kennison's ghost.

"Ghost sightings have waned in recent years, so there's a possibility that the spirit has faded away," Kiki said, still dressed in her gothic cloak. She struck quite a pose on that grassy mound. "Well, Doctor, care to elaborate on your theory regarding a fading spirit?"

"Of course," the doctor said. "When the substance a spirit has locked into is broken down, weathered and eroded, scattered, the energy is lost. Burn down a haunted house and the ghost leaves too. Pulverize and scatter the minerals of a rock or bone, and the energy becomes dispersed. Over years of erosion, a spirit can fade away as the tainted elements are reabsorbed into nature."

"You believe this ghost was stamped into the bones themselves?" Janine asked him.

"Yes," he answered. "Probably the best material for trapping the energy of a soul, as bones are likely stamped from the inside, very deep. It would take years to erode bone down to the particles that store ghostly energy, perhaps centuries. This particular soil is very moist, due to the proximity of the lake, and with the excavation of the cemetery, and the building of this lovely park, the remains were disturbed, bones possibly broken. Any fragments left behind would decompose at a much quicker rate than in a dryer, more neutral environment. I'd wager that this soil is also quite acidic, due to the fertilization of the gardens and grass."

"Who was David Kennison?" Carlos interjected. "Anyone of note?"

"Heard of the Boston Tea Party? Well, David was one of those guys," the doctor told him. "He fought in the revolutionary war and the War of 1812. He was a busy, active man, larger than life. One historian said that Kennison was too busy to learn how to sign his own name, until he was sixty. His exact resting place is unknown and the city office asked…" The doctor continued rambling to Carlos and the camera.

Kiki came close and slipped her arm through Janine's. The silver necklace reflected in the darkness, dangling back and forth under the laces of her shirt. *Why did that pendant bother her?* They walked together, like they were casually strolling through the park.

"Let's see if you can call him out," Kiki whispered. "I'm feeling a buzz of energy radiating from an area up ahead, but it could be a lot of things. It's very faint. Do you feel anything?"

"Not a thing," Janine confessed.

"Remember my favorite summons? *We seek yon souls of near to there, we call on you to us appear, reveal yourself for us to see, so I command, so mote it be.* Say that."

Janine whispered it, barely audible.

"Be direct, Janine. Be nice, but be direct. Say it again, and this time don't ask, order him to talk to us. Demand that he tell us why he's here. My Auntie Celeste always tried to release trapped spirits, instead of expecting some erosion process to occur. Maybe we can help him find peace sooner rather than later. We need to know what's keeping him in this realm to do that."

The doctor stopped talking, and all three of the men turned back. Don pointed his camera at them as Janine silently requested that David Kennison reveal himself and speak out. Janine pulled her thermal-panger from her pocket and watched the temperature drop minutely, not unusual for a night near a large lake.

"What are you two up to?" The doctor straightened the lower portion of his tie. "Do you feel something?"

"I do," Kiki said. "Something over here."

Kiki's long cloak trailed in a wake as she directed them to a nice patch of grass and stopped. As they drew closer to her destination, the temperature took a severe nose dive.

"Whoa," Carlos said. "There is a major cold pocket of air right here. Just a bubble of cold air."

"It's him," Kiki said. "He's here, and he's upset."

"Tell us why you're upset." Janine spoke toward the air surrounding them. The doctor gave her a surprised look. It was usually Kiki saying such things. "What do you want us to know?"

They shifted and formed a small circle. The ion detector popped off, the thermal-panger temperature numbers still decreased.

"He's missing his head." Kiki touched her own head. She allowed one sleek leg to slip from her cloak. "And his left thigh, and a few fingers, but he's not worried about those. How large is this cold patch, Carlos?"

"I would estimate about ten feet in diameter," Carlos said. "Give or take, a little."

"Well, he's scattered all around." Kiki spread her hands out and spun slowly. "And he's very anxious about his head and thigh. He's upset that someone took his head away."

The doctor pulled a collection of small survey flags from the pocket of his lab coat, the type workmen use to mark underground water lines. They set about marking the edge of the cold patch using the IR camera as a guide. Kiki stood directly in their intended circle with her eyes closed, listening.

"He's very faint," Kiki said, as they positioned the flags. "Barely here."

The city was very interested in finding the remains of David Kennison. Kiki spent the next ten minutes trying to confirm who she was communicating with, but never got a definite answer. The spirit kept insisting he cared more than three straw for his head, she chuckled. After they marked the site for the Historical Survey, Don snapped off his camera, rapping the Chicago shoot.

I made it, Janine felt a mass lifted off her back. *I made it through Chicago without begging out anywhere.* It was so simple, really. A near fatal knife attack paled in comparison to losing a child. She was the only one scarred in Chicago, whereas, the loss of Sammy scarred everyone she loved.

Chapter 12

U of C *Kiki*

Ben, Don, and Mike drove the van back to the hotel, while Janine, Kiki, Carlos, and the doctor cruised around in the small limousine. They hit up the small bar and took the scenic route to the Lincoln House. They discussed the contract and Max Colliers, and the doctor confirmed everything Kiki told them. They had a little leverage on Max, if he tried to release one of them, but he could levy some hefty fines if they jumped ship. At the moment, they were in a compromised position.

"Don't worry about me," Carlos suddenly said. "Pay wise and fun wise, this job is hard to beat, but I have other prospects, you know."

Kiki wanted to discuss the fainting spells, and why it drained her of energy to summon a spirit. If spectral energy, the aether, was stamped into an inanimate object, why would her personal energy be sapped at all? She requested the doctor's scientific explanation. He considered her question as he removed his multicolored *Spectral Analysis* tie and loosened the top buttons of his shirt.

"The doctor inferred that you were like a catalyst," Janine interjected gently. "Using that analogy, a catalyst implies that activation energy is required to initiate a reaction, the disturbance on his supersaturated solution, for instance. Perhaps your energy sap is the activation energy needed."

"That's an idea worth considering," the doctor poured the drinks. "Or, perhaps it's in the translation of the messages that take the energy."

Ian offered a dram of whisky to Carlos and Kiki, but he offered Janine an iced soda. Janine's light brown eyes flashed, but she took the cola without a word, glancing at him from under her lashes. *Those two seemed to be getting on much better than the previous evening, but not easy friends yet,* Kiki noted. Janine's dark aura waned considerably any time Ian fixed his eyes on her. Then, Kiki witnessed something she never thought she'd see: Ian poured himself an iced cola too. When had that man ever passed up a wee dram? Never. When they arrived at the hotel, Ian and Carlos ran off to the ballroom to see how the download was progressing, while Janine and Kiki escaped to their separate rooms to sleep. So, Kiki noticed, no more hiding.

The next day, while the gofers were busy packing up the ballroom, Janine and Carlos took the van to retrieve the static recorders left around the city. Kiki recorded a voice over for her vision of death clip and conducted a short interview with Lauren regarding the séance, then she was off for a mid-afternoon rendezvous on the other side of the city. She agreed to meet Randy Ivy, the haunted college guy, at a coffee shop near the university. The limousine driver waited outside the main entrance, and Carlos and Janine happened to roll up as Kiki exited the hotel. Carlos stuck his head out of the van's driver's window.

"Where do you think you're going, young lady?" Carlos demanded, all dimples. "Not another date with the mystery man, is it?"

"Not the fellow you're thinking of." Kiki told him. "But mysterious he is."

"Not the bull?" Carlos asked.

"Not the bull," Kiki winked at him. Janine popped out the passenger door wearing a scowl. "Come with me, Janine, just a little coffee run, it'll be fun. I'm meeting your creepy, haunted college man for a latte."

She shook her head grumpily, "Count me out."

"I feel like you need to come," Kiki urged her. "This fellow needs to talk to you more than me. He's haunted. He's been hexed by a ghost to do their bidding and we might be able to help him. He claims that it's you he needs to talk to. You're the one he delivered the charm to."

"Fine," Janine's doe eyes softened as she reluctantly climbed into the limousine. "But I'm going to need a stiff shot of something to get through it."

Kiki poured them both two fingers of whisky as the car pulled away from the hotel. She passed the tumbler to Janine. They clinked their cups but neither of them tasted the golden liquid. Kiki worried about that sullen attitude and itched ask.

"Anything interesting to tell? Last night, I noticed you weren't hiding anymore," Kiki said softly. Her Aunt Celeste always demanded the girls steer clear of matters of the heart, but Kiki worried about her thick skulled cousin. Until meeting Detective Anderson, she had no idea what was at stake.

"Well, after being denied the traditional whisky after our shoot, I had a whole bottle of Max's wine waiting in my room, and I didn't have to share it with anyone, if that's what you're asking." Janine sunk into the limo seat. "I guess, I'm pretty arrogant after all. It doesn't matter, everything is as it should be. I don't know what I expected."

Too bad, Kiki thought, *no wonder she's in such a foul mood.*

She's surely avoiding dreams with all that alcohol. Janine hadn't taken one sip of the whisky in her hand. She only drank near bedtime, and then she really poured it on, medicating herself into a stupor. It just prolonged the pain, avoiding dreams. Dreams play a crucial role in putting the pieces of a fragmented soul back together. People needed to endure their night visions, painful as they may be, so that the jigsaw could be worked out and the pieces replaced correctly. Nightmares included. But try suggesting that to a wounded soul and they might snap your head off.

"Are you going to advise me not to drink so much," Janine challenged. "To find my core, stay away from Max, and try to make things up with Ian? Advise me what is, or isn't, best for me?"

"No," Kiki said slowly. "You already know what's best for you." She set her whisky down. "If I'm going to tune into this fellow properly, I'd better save this for later."

Janine set hers down too and stared at Kiki. "So, how exactly do I find my core?"

Randy Ivy crouched in the back of Build Coffee, a little shop on the south side of campus, with hair falling over his eyes and a gloomy frown on his lips. The skinny barista was the only other soul in the place. His eyes grew wide when they entered, then darted to where Randy slunk in his corner.

Randy scrambled to his feet and stared through blood shot eyes.

Kiki nodded at Randy, then chatted with the barista as she ordered coffee drinks. He gaped at her from under his lopsided bangs, but quickly worked the espresso machine, steaming milk and mixing drinks, grinning nervously and trying not to stare at Kiki's bosom. When the drinks were done, he quickly returned to his counter and hid behind a book. He clearly meant to listen to their conversation. Kiki and Janine moved toward Randy and they all sat down simultaneously.

"Tell us about your ghost," Kiki got right to the point.

"She moved without moving," Randy mumbled, examining his own dry hands. "She moved fast."

"Are you describing things in a dreams?" Kiki asked.

"No. This happened in the park, at night, that night," he mumbled softly. "We were partying after our midterms. The girls heard a rumor of a ghost that only comes out on the full moon, so, we went to check it out. At around midnight, we saw the ghost. She appeared far away, and, at first, I thought she was a tree." An odd laugh sputtered out of him and he shook. "Then, she was right next to us. She didn't move at all, but she moved real fast."

"So, she appeared in the distance, then she moved closer?" Kiki said. "Was she transparent? Shimmery? Floating? An odd size? Anything you can add?"

Randy's eyes darted all around. "She was real. Like a real person, only intense, very intense. She commanded me to find the necklace, right up in my face. It was terrifying, only, I didn't know what she meant. But when I found it, I knew. The necklace… " His eyes rolled haphazardly, then stopped suddenly on Janine. "She wanted you to have that necklace. She demanded I find it and bring it to you."

Janine glowered, she scowled at the poor guy, but Kiki gently gathered Randy's hands into hers. She could see that he was shaken through to his core and guessed that the spirit had touched his heart. He must have been feeling love when the ghost appeared. Only a heart feeling love could open sufficiently for a spirit to enter. Randy visibly calmed with Kiki's hands covering his.

"Did she guide you to the necklace?" Kiki asked. "Did she lead you to it?"

Randy shook his head. "I found it with a metal detector. My key got lost in the meadow that night and I took the detector out to search for it. I found the necklace instead, buried beneath the soil. It was dirty and I cleaned it, polished it, I felt compelled to prepare it. The saint is chained to the wall on that pendant. I've never heard of that saint."

"Why do you believe the ghost wanted Janine to have the necklace? Did she mention Janine by name?" Kiki asked.

Randy shook his head again, then glanced at Janine.

"That part came in a dream." He lowered his voice. "She kept entering my dreams, over and over again, and hounding me to find you." He stared unblinkingly at Janine. "She screamed, find her, find her. FIND HER!" His fist slammed on the table, hard. Kiki took his hands again and asked him to calm down. He nodded, red eyes fixed on Janine, voice firm and harsh. "At first, I wasn't sure who she was talking about, and she kept insisting that I deliver the necklace, because you needed it. Or, you needed to do something with it, or, something."

"Janine needs to do something for the ghost?" Kiki asked.

"That's the feeling I got," Randy conveyed. "I got the feeling that she needs something done, that someone owes her. You owe her, and you would know what to do."

Kiki nodded. "Then, we probably will know what to do, if you got that distinct feeling. We just need to figure out what that is."

"You didn't tell us how you came up with my name, from the ghost." Janine clipped in sharply. "How did you determined that it's me the ghost is interested in."

"I knew it when I saw you," Randy said. "On the TV. When we were watching the ghost documentary. You were in the movie, talking, and I knew instantly, you were *HER*. The ghost meant you. You need to take that necklace and do what she wants."

"Well, what does she want?" Janine snapped.

"I don't know," Randy finally seemed calmer. "You're the ghost experts. You can figure it out, I just want out of it. I delivered the necklace, I delivered the message. I should be out of the loop now. I did my part. One of the girls, a girl who saw the ghost with me, who went out there that night, well, she dropped out of school at the break. She went home and doesn't contact anyone anymore. Nobody. The other girl won't talk to me and acts like I'm a leper. Most people say I'm cursed." He stared at Kiki. His eyes pleaded with her. "Am I cursed?"

"Do you still feel that way?" Kiki asked softly. "After passing on the necklace?"

"I feel better." He blinked. "I feel more better now that we've talked. Maybe, after you figure out what needs to be done, maybe, I can get back to normal again. You'll let me know, right?"

"Of course," Kiki assured him. "Perhaps you're on your way to being back to normal already. I don't believe you're cursed at all, Randy. You were tasked with a message to deliver, and you did it. You delivered. You can move on now."

Randy let out a long sigh and his shoulders relaxed.

"Could you give us a complete description of the ghost? It might help us figure out who she was," Kiki requested.

Randy described the vision in his dreams, and the one in the park. Tall and slender, but solid, with long dark hair. She appeared much prettier in the dreams, alluring, and alternately much scarier and sinister. In the park, her large oval eyes were bottomless and dark, while in his dreams they resembled kaleidoscopes of dark shadows. She wore a University of Chicago sweatshirt, but it changed styles in the dream. Her face was narrow and thin, and her voice sounded painful, scratchy, surreal. From a distance, at the very first, he mistook her for one of the girls in his dorm, but he was sadly mistaken. He couldn't describe her main feature, it wasn't something visual. It was a feeling, *like cold despair?* He had no words to do it justice.

"Would you be willing to accompany us to the park where you had your encounter?" Kiki asked. "Show us where you found the charm?"

Randy jerked his head side to side, no question about it. "I'm never going back there."

Kiki's eyes softened and she patted his hand. "Of course not, but would you draw us a map? A rough sketch of the park with marks where you found the necklace and where you met the ghost."

"Okay," Randy agreed.

Janine remained quiet, observant, frowning. The barista delivered complimentary scones with the pen and paper, and he joined them. While Randy took up the pen with a shaky hand, Kiki examined the barista's palmar flexion creases and allowed him to stare into her eyes. Kiki gushed over all the lines that indicated his good characteristics and ignored all the bad ones. Janine kept her own eyes on Randy's pen as he scribbled faint lines for streets and a squashed circle for a pond. He added small dots that he labeled with wobbly letters. Randy explained that the "G" was where he first saw the ghost. The "M" was where the ghost came upon him, and the "N" is where he found the necklace. He forgot the park's name, but one of the streets along the edge of the woods was very easy to remember. He wrote it in severely slanted script, and Janine's doe eyes narrowed more and more with each letter that emerged from the pen; *Edgewood Street.*

"Edgewood Street or Edgewood Place?" Janine asked in a soft, sad voice.

"I don't know," Randy answered just as softly. "I could show you on a real map, if you like. It's not around here, it's a little drive away."

Janine rose and Kiki realized she meant to leave quite abruptly.

"It was nice meeting the two of you." Janine gave the two men a brief smile before turning her head away. "I'm going to wait in the car."

"I'm coming with you," Kiki accepted the map drawing and thanked Randy for his bravery. She left the barista a huge tip and hurried after Janine. She slipped into the limousine just as Janine drained her tumbler of whisky. Janine pressed her palms into her eyes. Kiki told the driver to start rolling and unfolded the drawn map. "He didn't write the name of the park, but I guess he didn't have to, did he?" Kiki said. "You know exactly where this is." She held up the drawing.

"Yes," Janine told her. "And I'm not going to tell you where it is until we get back to Texas. Don't even think about driving past that park, it's not going to happen, not with me in the car. Just, let me get out of Chicago before we talk about it. Okay, Kiki, please? Let's wait until we're out of Chicago to talk about this."

I an chose to drive back to Austin in the van with Ben and Mike. He wanted to meet the historic society in the park near his survey flags and chat with the director. He assured Kiki that they would get to Texas in no time, driving in shifts, if needed. Kiki wanted to kill him. He very possibly might miss his own thirtieth birthday bash if they got delayed. On the bright side, she could finalize the party plans without Ian butting his nose in. Their own flight was delayed a few hours due to thunderstorms, and they did not get into the air until just prior to midnight. Most of the crew fell asleep after liftoff, but not Janine. She sat doing the crossword puzzle in the inflight magazine.

"Okay, we're out of Chicago," Kiki said when the plane leveled off at altitude. "People will project, Janine. Just because that fellow tied you to his ghost doesn't mean you're really tied to it. People observe us on the show and they add us into their own stories, it's not uncommon. Even if that park is where I think it is, it could just be a coincidence."

"It's a map of my woods, Kiki, of Thatcher Woods, but his map is of the south side of Chicago Avenue and my side is the north. I know exactly where that pond is and all of his dots. I used to go on early morning jogs in that park." Janine stopped working on the puzzle and eyed the sleeping people in the dimly lit cabin. Back, two rows behind them, Sally and Lauren chatted quietly. "There's something else I want to talk to you about, something Randy mentioned, but not here, okay? Maybe tomorrow. I'm trying not to think about it right now. This isn't the place to talk about it."

Kiki nodded. "I'm supposed to fetch Gwen tomorrow afternoon, so maybe we can meet in the morning, or for an early lunch. I can run by your place before fetching her. Where are you in Austin these days?"

Janine stared at the crossword puzzle and shook her head.

"Janine, where are you staying in Austin?"

Janine sighed. "I haven't decided. Last time, I stayed at the Holiday Inn, and I'll probably stay at the Holiday Inn again. I don't really have it worked out yet. My home is in Davis and I'm not planning to stay in Austin very long. If things go according to plan, I'll probably be back home in Davis this weekend."

She planned to disappear that quickly, unfortunate, just when Kiki figured out why they were good at summoning ghosts. She'd miss having a sister witch around, even one that didn't consider herself a witch.

"Stay at my house. I have two extra rooms. That way I can sleep in and go to church before picking up Gwen. I should get it out of the way before seeing her. We can iron everything out and settle all our questions before you leave. We won't have to rush our way through any conversations if you stay at my house."

Chapter 13

Witchy Ways *Janine*

Kiki lived in the luxurious Westgate community of Austin in a million dollar home on the banks of the Colorado River. She claimed to have two spare rooms, but didn't mention that the other three bedrooms belonged to her cousin Ian. They shared a large kitchen, dining room, den, pool, playroom, and living area. No worries, Kiki told her, sometimes days passed without her bumping into the bloke on the other side of the house. Besides, Ian was in the van, driving back from Chicago at the moment. It would be at least another day before he made it home. The girls would have the house all to themselves in the meantime.

The décor was surprisingly normal, conservative, urban. A display of large minerals in the living room was definitely the doctor's doing. It was a spectacular showcase of pure specimen, each crystalized in a different geometric pattern, each the size of a cobble, and each nested in their own lit up cubby of a wooden shelf system that spanned the entire wall. Very nice, Janine admired the collection of crystals. The only item in the common area that appeared remotely Wiccan was a round table with a carved Triquetra under the glass top. Even the guest room was void of mystic influence. Just a regular queen size canopy bed and a generic empty dresser. Janine didn't know what she had been expecting. Luckily, the room also had a private bathroom. Kiki confessed that there were more bathrooms than bedrooms in that house.

Janine slept until just after noon and woke after Kiki had already left for church and the airport. She was curious to learn what type of church Kiki attended. Was it Wiccan? She did mention that her coven were girls of the kirk, was that Catholic? Kiki left a note and an extremely small string bikini if she wanted to go for a swim. *Fat chance wearing that.* Instead, Janine lounged on the plush sofa admiring the mineral wall, reading, and enjoying coffee with a bagel. Kiki's house was much nicer than a hotel, and more serene. Janine noticed several messages on her phone, most came from California, but two were Texas numbers.

Ian McNally texted; *Just checking to see if you got in okay. I know you're planning to leave soon, but please stay for my birthday party. And let me know where you're staying.* Janine texted that they made it just fine and that she would be at his party. She wasn't sure about letting him know where she was staying, in case she wanted to clear out before he got back.

Max Colliers also texted; *Lets have that date tonight or tomorrow.* She texted that she would get back to him soon, she didn't have anything appropriate to wear for a fancy date. Then, her phone rang, Max.

"I'm glad you're back. You aren't still living out of that back-pack, are you? No roots in Austin?"

"Well, if it's good news for me, then I might only need what's in that back-pack," she said.

"Except for our date. I can have Sally leave something for you in the office, or she can deliver, she has your measurements." He paused. "Not like the show stuff, I promise. Sally told me you didn't go for the chaps." He chuckled, "Can't blame me for trying to up the ratings."

She told him that he didn't need to send anything. She would drop by the office and decide if she'd wear any of it, or find something on her own. Not to worry, she wouldn't be in jeans and a T-shirt and promised it'd be a real date. They could go out the next night, if he liked. She'd meet him somewhere, *the sooner, the better*, she thought. The day after that was Ian's party, then she could head back to California and get back to her real life.

She texted back and forth to her grandmother Gram, her next door neighbor in Davis, and her niece Ashley. Kiki had groceries delivered and Janine carried them to the kitchen. She noticed fruit, vegetables, pasta, chicken, and a box with a dessert inside. So then, Kiki planned on cooking. The large kitchen window had a nice view of the backyard pool and river. Janine watched the speed boats pass by as she put the groceries away.

Kiki soon returned with her friend from home, Gwen. Janine came out of the kitchen to greet them and was surprised to see that Gwen was just as tall as Janine, at least five foot nine. Flowing red hair framed the spectacular freckled face that greeted her. If Kiki's eyes were a glowing emerald, then Gwen's eyes were a sparkling sapphire, and Janine sensed an analytical mind behind those eyes. No generous womanly curves on Gwen, but a strong, muscular, athletic build, flat chested, yet still feminine. Gwen gave Janine a good dose of scrutiny before smiling.

"Gwen, this is Janine Stinger," Kiki formally introduced them. "Janine, this is my oldest friend, Gwendolyn Allina Murphy, Gwen."

"Oh, the tales I've heard about you." Gwen hugged her.

It turned out that Kiki was not doing the cooking, Gwen insisted on preparing the feast. She insisted they relax in the kitchen and get better acquainted while she prepared a chicken scaloppini for dinner. She poured three large glasses of wine as she made herself at home in Kiki's kitchen. Kiki and Janine sat at the breakfast bar to watch her chop everything up.

"Kiera knows well that I unwind by cooking," Gwen said as she delivered the wine glasses. "Nothing is as relaxing as creating a culinary masterpiece, and then enjoying it with a pair of common allies such as yerselves."

"Unwind by cooking!" Kiki giggled. "Can you believe she said it? It's a witch's ploy, Janine, feeding you. Gwen is using her kitchen magic to open your heart to her ministrations. She wants to hear what you have to say about that guy's ghost."

"Ho, ho," Gwen laughed back at her. "Listen to this wee yin, cryin' about how one needs to tread lightly and then go spillin' the beans." Gwen turned her amused freckled face to Janine. "I mean no harm here, lassie. Kiera tells me you have something important to talk about and a little wine and spice can only help. My cooking is a wee attempt at coaxing me into the conversation, and I really do love to cook. Of course, I understand if you girls need to take it off in private."

Wow, Kiki discussed the creepy college guy with Gwen. Did she mention the woods? Janine wasn't upset, it was very hard not to like Gwen, she exuded warmth. Janine wondered what else Gwen knew.

"How much do you know already?" Janine asked.

"Only that a haunted lad gave you a charm of Saint Comba. Tis a very rare charm to be had, indeed, and very similar to a dear charm we once admired. And that you're familiar with the area he found said charm," Gwen told her. "And you had something mysterious to add, something you wanted to save for private. So, maybe, I'll need to entertain myself for a wee bit later? Or maybe not?"

"She doesn't know anything else," Kiki told Janine. "Nothing."

"That's not true." Gwen was busy mixing things. "I know that you may be a *dragoma* and that you made good use of sweet Ian not too long ago." They all shared a little light hearted chatter about Ian. "It's likely none of my business, but I'm always curious, and Kiera, sorry Kiki, keeps a tight lip. Perhaps I can just listen in then?"

Janine really liked Gwen. She needed to tell Kiki about the ghost, because Kiki would understand, and if Gwen was like Kiki, wouldn't her insights be valuable too? There didn't seem to be any harm in Gwen knowing everything.

"The woods, where that college guy saw a ghost and found the charm, it's the same woods where I was brutally stabbed and left for dead some years ago," Janine told her. "Maybe you heard of the story. The news called it the Coed Captive case, and they referred to me as Jane Doe from Chicago."

Gwen glanced over, and Kiki nodded slightly to Gwen.

"I heard of it," Gwen said slowly. "One of the reasons I argued against Kiera moving to America. The guns and violence, and incredibly, that story in particular."

"Good, then you know what happened to me," Janine said. She sought out Kiki's green eyes. "That description the college guy, Randy, gave of the ghost. Long dark hair, slender, strong looking. I think, I saw her, the ghost." Janine drained her wine and Gwen refilled it. They waited patiently for her to continue. "When I was being attacked, she came. Only, I didn't notice a university sweatshirt."

In the past year, Janine no longer needed to suppress memories of that ordeal and she analyzed them all over again in her solitude. When her captor unlocked the tether that kept her restricted to the upstairs area of his house, she automatically bolted. It startled both of them, as evidently, they both assumed she had no fight left inside of her. She was the one who carried the hunting knife into the woods. She snatched it off a side table near the door as she ran by. She remembers wondering why it had been there. Janine ran, or hobbled more accurately, directly into Thatcher Woods in the dead of night. Terrified and weak, bruised from his abuse, she didn't really believe she could outrun him, or fight him off. It didn't take long for him to catch up and push her to the ground. Her weak arms were feeble, and her spirit was nearly broken. When he noticed the knife, he slapped it out of her hand and snatched it up. He stabbed her in the back more than once, to teach her a lesson. *Her fault,* he growled, *for bringing it. Did she mean to stab him with it? Consider it karma.* He flipped her over and she remembers begging for her life, apologizing, promising never to run away again. She'd stay as long as he wanted. Anything. But he kicked leaves and rocks over the top of her, saying he was going to bury her in the park. He wasn't angry, Janine recalled, but disappointed. She felt warm blood pooling underneath her and wondered if she was already dead. He leaned in close and demanded that she say it one more time, *that she really loved him,* and to promise they could start again and that she'd stay forever. And so, she promised, still hoping he would go get help. He glared at her and asked, *cross your heart and hope to die?* Then, he carved that X on her chest and called her a liar, finally looking angry. He continued placing rocks on top of her, saying it was too late, she was ruined. *Ruined.* And that's exactly what she believed, for a very long time.

"At the moment I realized he meant for me to die, I called for help, but it was only a whisper. No one would have heard me. Deep inside of me, I was screaming for help, but I could barely make a sound. And then I saw her, standing in the shadows, absolutely still, frozen in place, staring, with dark, indefinite eyes. I wondered if she was really there."

Janine certainly had their undivided attention. She pointed to the simmering chicken and Gwen moved it off the burner, then turned back to face her.

"The ghost heard you," Kiki softly said, "And listened, because you're a *dragoma.*"

Janine nodded. "Maybe. She stopped Rick, because she startled him and he was instantly terrified of her, like he recognized her. She appeared exactly as that college guy described. She commanded him to stop, *she used his name*, that's why I thought she was real. I remember wondering how she could scare him so easily. Who was she? But I didn't care, because he ran away."

"Did she say anything to you?" Kiki asked.

Janine hugged her arms to her chest as the images materialized in her mind. "No. I passed out staring at her eyes, deep and dark. I wondered why she didn't go for help. I wanted her to find help, begged her silently, but she remained a statue. For years I believed I only imagined the woman in the woods."

Janine initially told the police about the woman, but no witness ever came forward. They concluded that she imagined someone, because there was no physical evidence that anyone stood at the spot she described; no footprints, no damaged vegetation, nothing. A dog found her in that tucked-in back cluster of trees. If that dog had been five minutes later, she would have bleed to death.

"Kiki, do you believe animals can hear ghosts? Animals, like dogs?" Janine wondered.

"Oh, absolutely," Kiki nodded.

Gwen agreed. "Some dogs have a talent for sensing spirits, like humans. Why do you ask?"

"The dog that found me. The owner said he acted strange the moment they got on the trail and became antsy. He only let the lab off the leash to have a dip in the river, but the dog ran straight to me instead, in the opposite direction, at least a quarter of a mile through the woods. He'd never done that before. He knew right where to find me. Would it be pure conjecture to say the ghost sent that dog and now she wants me to do something for her, in return? What would she want?"

"Finding out who she is and why she haunts those woods would help," Gwen said. "Let's eat while we talk about it. This is best hot off the stove, and I'm famished."

Gwen prepared their plates and Kiki quickly mixed up a salad. They all helped cart the meal and wine to the large dining table. Kiki fully opened the blinds to reveal an orange tinted sky of setting sunbeams over the river. Gwen asked Janine about her family and her studies at UC Davis. Janine discovered that Gwen worked as a nurse specializing in pediatric oncology.

"It's all very crude medicine, chemotherapy," Gwen told them. "Gruesome, but miraculously gentler on the youngsters. Adults are barely able to endure the same treatment. It breaks the heart. The children are always so brave, and the parents sit helplessly watching as it's done to their child. The kids rarely get stirred up unless their parents are stirred up. I find myself praying for those parents as often as the kids. Dark energy can have a negative effect on healing, you know. It can eat away at a healthy person and jump from soul to soul. Those kids need their parents to be strong, and prayer works. Prayer brings positive energy to everyone involved. It nurtures the soul."

"Praying, like to God? How does that work with claiming to be a witch?" Janine asked. "Kiki ran off to church today. What kind of church? A Christian church?"

"It's a Presbyterian church, very like our kirk back in Scotland. You just don't understand what a witch is, Janine. It's someone who follows a type of practice. Our pagan beliefs are shared with most modern religions. In our coven, we each made a vow to attend regular services at least once a month. To stay connected to the male aspects," Kiki told her.

Gwen considered them both for a moment.

"Most modern religions are very similar at the deepest level," Gwen told Janine. "That symbol on the coffee table out there. The Triquetra or the Trinity knot. A nice Christian would say it represents the Father, the Son and the Holy Ghost, while the original meaning is the Mother, Maiden, and Crone from the roots of our pagan practice. Many Christian symbols come from pagan roots with the meaning altered to accommodate a masculine ego. Very simply put, most modern religions are just the old ways, rewritten from a male point of view."

"Women naturally follow a path of empathy and caring and community, generally speaking. Spirituality is a natural facet of a female aura and men have a much harder time. It's all ego with men and base instinct," Kiki interjected. She was startled to see Gwen giving her a stern look. Gwen turned back to Janine.

"The masculine end of the spectrum is not naturally tethered to the nurturing Earth like the feminine. Masculine energy, and a vivacity for the physical, make it very difficult for a male dominated personality to recognize and grasp a world outside of themselves. Modern religions strive to bring those with a masculine nature closer to the center, to embrace their spiritual side. Now dinna think we're just a bunch of sexist females, thinking we're all that. A feminine soul needs a good dose of physical pleasures to bring them closer to the center as well. It's impossible to grow spiritually without experiencing the physical world, and each needs a little of the other to become whole."

"Male energy is very animal, whereas female energy is very spiritual," Kiki interrupted again.

Gwen grew red as she gave Kiki another stern look.

"A theological discussion such as this conversation should take days," Gwen grimaced. "In a nutshell, male dominated religions were created to help men, or rather the masculine dominated personality, to stretch beyond their base tendencies and experience a spiritual side. Over the years, like any good plan, the details got muddled in the misinterpretation. People often tweak the rules to suit themselves and many male religious leaders did the same. Kiera's a terrible teacher of coven principles, tossing around generalities so loosely. And it's nae exactly men versus women, but masculine and feminine, or more like the concept of yin and yang."

Kiki threw a napkin at her, "I beg your pardon, but who is the more gifted witch here?"

"Ho, ho. You've heard the saying, *those who can, do, and those who can't, teach?*" Gwen said to Kiki. "It should be, *those who can do, because they can't teach.* Seriously, Kiera, you *do* because you are the more gifted witch, but those who *do* are sometimes the worst teachers of all. It all comes so naturally, and easily, for you, and you have no clue how to help someone over a hurdle, as you dinna recognize what a hurdle is yourself."

"She's taught me a little about speaking to spirits, being a *dragoma*," Janine said softly. "I think that's how I put things together, that I must have called that ghost in the woods when I needed her. And she's taught me a little about absorbing—" Janine felt herself flush as she recalled the experience, "Absorbing male energy to recover from... Kiki says it recharges the receptive batteries."

Gwen's eyes were round balls of shock. She soon dissolved into laugher, along with Kiki, and then Janine. Apparently, Gwen knew the exact practice Janine tried to describe. Kiki did say that every witch in the coven used the trick.

"So, lassie, tell us how that went," Gwen requested.

"I felt better right away," Janine confessed. "But it was very uncomfortable."

"She failed to divert the energy to her core," Kiki told Gwen. "Most of it went straight into to her Base Well."

"Did Kiki give you any direction on finding your core? Or how to divert passion into your core?" Gwen watched her confused expression and gave Kiki another stern look. "Seriously, Kiera, you really are the world's worst teacher. Not everyone knows the Triad of Wells, and even so, not everyone naturally absorbs passion into their core, like you. You think everybody has the skills of a Core Master? None of the rest of the sisters are even close. Most of us girls naturally allow sex energy to flow where it belongs, into the Base Well."

Gwen seemed truly miffed at Kiki, then turned to Janine and reached for her hand.

"Don't try it again," Gwen advised. "Not until you can solidly find your core. It'll be playing with fire, I know. Unlike our perfect little witch over there, it took me a very long time to learn how to divert passion energy into my core, because typically, it doesn't flow that way. Also, better to practice on a fellow you won't mind slipping up on, in case it leads to a nice coupling. Kiera never had a problem sending any type of energy into her core. She's a bit of a savant, she is. Lacking any understanding of the passions, but a gifted Core Master. That's why she's still a coven vestal," Gwen shrugged at Kiki. "What, she dinna know this? You try to have her brim the well, but leave out any foundational information?"

"Janine is a classic skeptic," Kiki defended herself. "She needs a concrete experience before hearing, or considering, what she thinks is silly nonsense."

Janine shook her head, "It's alright, I don't want to cause a stir."

"No stir," They both chimed in unison, then laughed.

Kiki confessed, "Gwen is quite right about a lot of things. I truly don't understand where the hurdles pop up for most people. For instance, when we're on an investigation in the presence of an extremely strong spirit with a very obvious buzzing of energy, and not one of you feel anything at all. Sometimes I think, *you're kidding me*! As if you're ignoring a glaring light in front of your faces."

Gwen came around to give Kiki a hug. Her bright blue eyes fell on Janine.

"This should be another long conversation," Gwen said. "Kiera should have begun by telling you of the three wells, or caldrons. What we call the head, base, and core. Those are the wells from which we create and take in the universe. The aether flows easiest between like wells, but energy can always leak in every direction. That's why we feel love when there's passion. It has mixed up more than one person in the world. If you're aware of your wells, you can divert or alter energy from one to the other. Each person has their distinct strengths. Kiera is definitely tuned into her core, that's the heart, or soul well. It's why she can hear ghosts easily and can see auras. Most ghostly aether is of the core. I'm nae kidding about her being a savant. Most folks are more focused in their heads and the passions. And it's true, one of the quickest most intense sources of energy is testosterone driven sexual passion, from the base. Most will go directly into your own passion center, unless you divert it. Energy doesn't divert or change without effort, you know. Learning to redirect passion is a tricky process that usually takes years to develop." Gwen gave Kiki a look.

"I thought she'd be a natural," Kiki said simply.

Gwen and Kiki both displayed the tattoos on the back of their necks, a small, simplistic Triquetra, or Trinity knot. Most witches in their coven had one in the same spot. The three wells, or cauldrons, that every witch hoped to fill equally. Janine had seen Kiki's tattoo before and always wondered about it. Now she knew.

"Three is a sacred number in the universe," Gwen told her. "You study science, right? Think about those building blocks of matter. The nucleons that make up atoms. What are they made of? It's a trio too, right?"

"You mean protons and neutrons?" Janine said.

"What are they made of?" Kiki asked.

"Quarks," Janine said. "Three quarks a piece."

"A Triquetra of quarks. And quarks have distinct orientations, right? Opposite orientations, just like the feminine-masculine dichotomy, but it's a trio that make up the whole. Two up and one down make a proton, if I remember correctly. And it's a trio of wells that make up a person, each with opposing aspects. Three is a very sacred number. The Triquetra happens to be one of the oldest symbols known to humankind."

Gwen offered to keep in contact with Janine and answer any questions she might have regarding their coven belief system. Gwen and Kiki were excited that Janine was interested in the ancient teachings. Janine admitted that she had many odd experiences around Kiki and was truly curious. Then, they cleared the dinner plates, and Gwen asked to see the charm. Janine disappeared to find it. Kiki had placed it in Janine's room earlier that morning, because Randy insisted the charm was meant for Janine.

Chapter 14

Detective work *Kiki*

Kiki could see Gwen's emotions had gotten stirred up at her for encouraging Janine to practice coven secrets without any sort of education, but it wasn't like open heart surgery, was it? Either a girl had the talent, or she didn't. Janine definitely possessed some talent, and it was perfectly natural to assume a *dragoma* could find her own core. Spiritual communication emanated from the core, didn't it?

"Well, Kiera," Gwen craned her long neck to spy down the hall. "You said she had a dark aura, you didn't mention she had that dark past."

"She's working through it. She might be close to being over it."

"Maybe," Gwen gave the opposite hall a glance. "So, tis Ian's lair back there, is it?" Gwen took two steps toward Ian's side of the house. "Maybe I'll just pop over and do a little snooping. He knows I've come, doesn't he? He would be truly insulted if I didn't care to invade his privacy a wee bit."

Gwen disappeared down Ian's dark corridor. Kiki didn't put up a fuss because it would do no good, Gwen would sneak back there eventually and she had a valid point, Ian would expect it. Janine returned, and they moved into the den with the comfortable sofa. Kiki prepared a tea pot and cups, and Janine put the creased envelope containing the charm on the coffee table next to the pot. They lounged quietly, observing the early evening stars through the back windows. Kiki checked her messages.

"Gram isn't coming to the party." Kiki studied Janine, who gave a small nod. "Says she's too busy. We rented this house because of the windows. It's a little like your Gram's back patio. Ian loved her big sky."

"She texted me."

"The detective messaged me," Kiki showed her the text. "His words declare that he cares deeply for me. I believe he's feeling love. This is an *I love you text*, look at it."

Janine examined the text. Her eyebrows went up in amusement. "He asked you to let him know that your flight made it in okay."

"It's a very blatant *I love you* text," Kiki declared. "It must be. Clearly, Janine, you need to learn to read between the lines. Detective Anderson is thinking about me, and his concern about my whereabouts speak volumes. He reached over a great distance to stay connected after only just meeting. He's visualizing me in his mind, tracking my movements in the world. Those words are definitely a message of love."

Gwen emerge from Ian's hall sporting a little smirk.

"You're cousin is a neat freak," Gwen squeezed between them brushing her red curls behind her ears. She poured the tea. "He doesn't have a single photograph of me back there. The nerve of him, after all the effort I put into Ian McNally in my youth. The fun we had with me trying to divert his energy to my core and failing so miserably." Gwen winked at Janine. "Dinna worry yourself, that's all ancient history by now. He's all yours."

Kiki couldn't help laughing at the face Janine made; wrinkled nose and pouty lips. Janine shifted around to face Gwen. She shook her head.

"What do you mean by that?" Janine asked. "We're not— Ian and I are also ancient history. It ended a long time ago. In fact, it was barely anything at all, just a very short fling. So, if you've come to reconnect with him, go right ahead, it's perfectly fine with me. Although, he may have a new girl, right Kiki? He's with Lauren now."

"Nae danger of a reconnection for me. I've got a very nice pediatric oncologist back home, but let me divulge a little secret. Ian has several photos on display in his office and bedroom, only three with people in them. One of his dear mother, and two images of you." She nodded at Janine. "Anybody wonder what that means?" Gwen didn't wait for an answer, she pointed to the manila envelope instead. "Is this the necklace?"

Janine grinned after that secret and the beautiful undertones in her aura sparked dramatically. Would Auntie Celeste have considered that meddling? Gwen definitely approved of Janine Stinger for Ian, even with the dark past. Kiki noted the similarities between Janine and Gwen; both tall, same hips, similar manner of movement, and radiating the same red undertone in their auras. Janine tipped the envelope and they watched the charm and chain spill onto the coffee table. Gwen's hand hovered over it and Kiki knew that Gwen felt energy radiating off the charm.

"This is a very old medallion," Gwen said.

Kiki agreed. "I sense that as well."

"Is it haunted?" Janine asked. "Is that ghost in it? I wonder what type of metal this is?"

"No ghost or a spirit here," Gwen cupped the charm in her palm and studied the raised image. "This is more akin to an ambient emotion. Nae different than the way a musical instrument takes on the character of a musician and gets flooded with a taste of their soul. This trinket has had a number of musicians. Faithful owners who gave part of their heart to it. It must be centuries old."

"Does this image of Saint Comba seem familiar? It's an uncommon one," Kiki asked.

Gwen narrowed her bright blue eyes and raised her ginger brows. "It is exactly like hers, you're right about that, though it was years ago when I last saw one. Meg had one too."

Kiki nodded. Gwen confirmed it. Her Auntie Celeste often wore the same ornament. She would have to ask Ian's father if it still existed.

The image depicted a woman with long flowing hair, naked, and her left wrist was chained to a wall. An unidentifiable beast lay near her feet. The words "Saint Comba" was stamped across the bottom in clumpy letters. Kiki noticed Janine eyeing the image through narrowed lids. *What was she thinking?* Janine had been chained by the left wrist as well, and still bore a scar from the handcuffs. *Was she thinking about that?* Did Janine know any of Saint Comba's story? Imprisoned, raped, saved by an animal. Did she draw parallels between Saint Comba's story and her own?

"Was the woman, Randy's ghost, a witch?" Janine asked.

"Hard to tell," Kiki told her. "But I would wager more than one of the women who wore that charm practiced something of the arts. I sense four owners, maybe more. The freshest vibe reeks of anger, and the metal radiates... guilt?"

Gwen wrinkled her speckled nose, and nodded. "We have a few clues. She wore a university shirt, was tall, with long dark hair. Anger such as this might come from a young woman in the heat of her passion years, or an older woman, severely betrayed by life. One thing is certain, she was dead long before Janine ever went into that park."

"I'm going to go to bed," Janine rose suddenly, her dark aura thick again. "There was a girl before me, with Rick, a track star. Someone warned me about her. She's supposed to be living abroad, but someone didn't think so and flat out accused Rick of doing something to her. Could it be her? The ghost? Back in the woods, the ghost called him by name and he was startled. And, she may have attended the University of Chicago, at least that's what Randy implied."

Kiki nodded. "I can contact the detective and confirm if she's is still missing, he probably knows about her. It's a lead, at least."

They watched Janine retreat to her room, and Gwen slipped the charm back into the manila envelope.

"Here, finish your tea, Kiera… sorry, Kiki. How am I going to remember that? Everyone calls you by your baby name? Brilliant. It's absolutely comical, this TV personality you've invented. Now drink that up, I want to see if the person you were whispering about is in there."

Kiki did as she was told and handed the cup over. Gwen was a gifted psychic, a prophesier, able to detect how energy swirled around a person and to work out how the currents might spin. Kiki felt a little nervous at what her leaves might reveal. Would there be a death mixed into the sediments? A strangling? Gwen flipped the cup and peered into the dish. She glanced at Kiki with a small smile.

"Nice, I see him here," Gwen said. "And you're thinking about a baby. Please assure me, Kiera, that you haven't jumped the gun on that one. We intend to arrange a proper coming out for you, a true awakening. You've been focusing on babies, I can see it. It's also obvious your Base Well has begun to shimmer and swell. You want this fellow to be the father?"

No hint of a strangulation, Kiki sighed. Perhaps the vision in the cemetery belonged to a soul connected to that charm. It had hung next to her heart when she saw those images, and her heart had been vulnerable, unlocked, *feeling love*. Gwen's blue eyes bore into her inquisitively, waiting, likely worried the prime vestal had fallen off the pedestal.

"I only just met him," Kiki told her. "He has a pink aura and he's the detective Janine mentioned."

Gwen chuckled. "A pink aura? This ghost and the mystery charm is a reason to call him. Maybe we'll see you finally get flustered over a nice lad. Of course, there's a few bets running round the girls that you've already done as much."

Kiki waved that comment away as she watched Gwen peek into Janine's cup. Gwen flipped the cup once, then gazed at the leaves with a creased brow.

"I'll be honest, there's a lot of darkness in there," Gwen set the cup down. "But, it might belong to that monster who chased her. Those shapes could be in the past, but indications imply that darkness still follows her. I'm going to add her to my prayer chain tonight, I can have a hundred of devoted mothers directing their positive energy to eradicating the darkness on her back. It'll fade before we know it. We need to help that lass, for Ian's sake."

Kiki researched Thatcher Woods after Gwen finally collapsed for the night. She matched up the marks on Randy's crude drawing to a real map. She googled the Coed Captive story. No photos of Janine, but there were several of Richard Wilkens. He was quite handsome, angelic. Kiki often had difficulty recognizing acquaintances in photographs, because she required their energy to really *see* them. She suffered from a condition called partial prosopagnosia, or face blindness, according to one doctor. Kiki recalled the day she realized most folks couldn't see an aura. It stunned her. Kiki assumed everyone identified people by analyzing their energy. She stared at the photos and wondered what type of colors he emitted, a man who could brutalized the woman he loved. How were his sacred wells intertwined? For Janine to misinterpret him so completely, his energy must be a twisted knot of contradictions. Either that, or he was a true devil without a core, perhaps the soulless demon from her vision.

Kiki studied the contours of Thatcher Woods. It encompassed a very large area. Too large for a typical ghost to wander. Perhaps the woods contained more than one ghost, or perhaps, Janine's summons was so compelling the ghost couldn't resist. Several hiking trails snaked through the area and it would be near impossible to hide a body for any length of time. Kiki left a message for the detective because the midnight hour had already passed. Detective Anderson was a rare gem, very in touch with his feminine side. Kiki wondered how he became a police officer. She sent him a photo of the charm with a short message about the ghost.

Kiki and Gwen spent the day preparing for Ian's thirtieth birthday party. Gwen insisted they bake a birthday cake from scratch and hand-whip the icing. To ensure a cake filled with love, they needed to use raw ingredients, so they spent the better half of the morning baking and mixing up a delicious frosting. Luckily, Gwen didn't eliminate the caterer too. Kiki was not fond of kitchen magic.

The party would take place in the common kitchen, living room, game room, and pool area, and Kiki hired a service to clean and set up the premises. A caterer brought several small tables with nice cutlery, and a dance troupe set up a small square floor on the far lawn. There'd be Irish dance instruction and a drum heavy Scottish band. Lauren arrived partway through the day with decorations. She seemed very eager to put her stamp on Ian's birthday and flittered about adding nice touches to the party layout. After Gwen transferred the cake to the cooler, they all lounged on the pool deck watching the dance floor being snapped together.

"Thanks for finding that troupe," Kiki said to Lauren.

Gwen crinkled her nose when Lauren turned away. She seemed irritated with Lauren's dazzling smile and bright chatter, and Gwen's eyes kept drifting to Lauren's petite feet, ogling them in their strappy high heels. Lauren grew curious about Ian's side of the house, but Gwen put a stop to her snooping. Better let Ian show people around at his own pace, Gwen suggested firmly. Lauren then proposed ordering a professional cake, raving about some designer bakery and Gwen finally snapped at her. Lauren just giggled at the outburst, surprised and amused.

"It can be an extra cake," Lauren beamed. "Marino Brother's makes a *to die for* three layered Chocolate Decadence."

Kiki patted her arm. "We've got it covered with the caterer, but thanks."

"Sally delivered dresses to your office," Lauren gushed toward Janine. "They're there right now. I would have brought them if I knew you were staying here. I can drive you to the office to pick them up, if you'd like. I go right by that area on my way home."

Kiki gave Janine a questioning look. Sally made dresses for her? Janine appeared caught in a tight spot as she avoided eye contact. Did it have something to do with Max Colliers? Before she could ask the question, Kiki received a text from Chicago. She scanned it quickly.

"Her name is Miranda Daily and she lives in Turkey. Her family insists she's alive and well," Kiki read it out loud. "But when he mentioned the charm, they were very interested in seeing it. He's going to meet with them soon, to show them the picture. He wants to see their faces when they look at it."

"Maybe we can look her up, do an internet search," Gwen suggested.

Janine turned away from the conversation, frowning. The previous night, she had left the charm in the living room. It lay abandoned on a side table. Why did she find that necklace so repulsive? Kiki felt positively attracted to it.

"I'll take that ride if you're ready to go," Janine said softy to Lauren, then turned to Kiki. "I'll be back late. I've got a dinner date, so don't wait for me. And don't worry about anything, I know what I'm doing."

"Be careful, Janine." Kiki noticed Lauren's curious gaze, but couldn't be bothered with what she might think. She pulled Janine into the house for more privacy. "You think Max plays fair, but not all the time, not when he feels dismissed. He can be quite a brat, I've seen it. He's going to make sure he wins something. I wish you could record exactly what he says about the contract so we can find the loopholes later. And Carlos isn't going to like it, if you try to save him by agreeing to something you wouldn't normally do. Like wearing the costumes."

"Okay. Don't worry about me, I won't be fooled again. Worse case, I miss the summer session at Davis and move in with you for a month or so," Janine said. "Or until you get tired of me. I think, I only owe two more shows."

Lauren caught up to them and Janine ran off with her. Gwen raised her ginger eyebrows as she watched them run away.

"We've got an hour before we can ice the cake," Gwen said. "Shall we have a go at finding Miranda Daily?"

They searched her name first. With a name like Miranda Daily, they could see that tactic wouldn't work. Mostly, they found photos of a celebrity named Miranda in her daily routines. Then, they tried Facebook. Several accounts for Miranda Daily popped up and they perused them carefully, but, none of the Mirandas lived in Turkey. They found a few old accounts that had been abandoned, none with a connection to Chicago. They did find one Miranda Daily from Boston.

"Look at this," Gwen pointed to a woman in her family photo. "This old lady is wearing a charm necklace. Too small to tell which saint is on it, but, it's the right size and color. Let's click through her friends and see what we find."

Although Miranda Daily halted all activity on her Facebook account several years ago, her friends were alive and well, and posting up a storm. Most of them limited their personal information, but a few of her old friends were not shy about listing their phone numbers for the world to see. Kiki and Gwen jotted down two promising numbers to call. Both women listed the University of Chicago as their alma mater. The first number went directly to voicemail. Kiki left her name and number.

They meandered into the kitchen to make the next call. Gwen needed to frost the cake and declared that it was late enough to open a bottle of wine.

"Hello," Kiki said when the phone picked up. "Hello, I'm trying to contact Lisa Welks, a University of Chicago Alumni."

"I'm not interested in donating," the woman on other end snapped. "Please don't call…"

"Don't hang up, I'm not looking for a donation," Kiki said quickly. "I'm calling about something personal, about someone you might know."

"This better not be a sales call," the woman said. "Who is this?"

"My name is Kiki Mellow. And I'm calling about —"

"Kiki Mellow? Like the TV ghost whisperer? From that show, *Spectral Analysis*? Is that who you think you are?"

"That's exactly who I am," Kiki said. "Can I ask you a few questions?"

Lisa Welks informed Kiki that Miranda Daily moved to Turkey, or somewhere close to Turkey, in the wilderness. She left unexpectedly during their final semester at college and never returned. They had been roommates for three years and Miranda always talked about living abroad. Lisa felt certain that Miranda was in Europe, because she still received cards from Miranda, always around Christmas and on her birthday. But, Miranda no longer engaged on social media, and it was against her beliefs to be photographed or to use a phone.

"This may sound funny," Kiki said. "But, what does she look like?"

"Right now? I have no idea, but in college, she was on the tall side, with dark hair, very long, tall and thin, and she was a runner. She was on the varsity track team, I don't think she would ever give that up. Smart too, she completed her requirements early, that's why she left early."

"Was she religious? Have a favorite patron Saint?" Kiki asked.

"I assume she's pretty religious now. She converted to some sort of cult out there, but back in school she never went to church or anything. I don't think she was very religious."

"Do you remember if she had a boyfriend?"

The woman laughed, "She had several boyfriends. She liked them handsome, blond, ripped, and tall. Other than that, I don't remember much about them."

"I see," Kiki said. "Well, thank you for talking to me."

Gwen gave a little smile. "Sorry you hit a dead end. It looks like this Miranda girl really is in Turkey. That ghost must be someone else."

They enjoyed another home cooked dinner by Gwen and discussed Kiki's future. There were several new sisters in the coven and Kiki had missed a few important pagan events. She felt like she was losing touch with her roots. Close to three years away was an awful long time, and things had not gone as she expected with *Spectral Analysis*. Regardless of how much film footage they shot, the world was not ready to believe in paranormal activity. All Kiki really accomplished was obtaining a mountain of money and a popular persona that some of the sisters teased her about. She may have gone overboard as Kiki Mellow, she admitted, but had a lot of fun doing it. Suddenly, a text pinged.

Kiki and Gwen read the text together. *Miranda Daily is dead. And your friend is lucky to be alive. I warned her. Don't contact me again, I'm going to block your number.*

"That was the number for who? The Lisa Welks number? Or the Mary Kline?"

"Mary Kline," Kiki said. "I wonder if Detective Anderson knows about Mary. Mary certainly knows about Janine Stinger."

Chapter 15

Men *Janine*

Janine learned a few things on the drive to the office building. Sally believed that Janine and Carlos wanted to get her fired, Guy petitioned for the company medical plan to cover his transition, and Lauren hoped to compare notes on Ian McNally. *Sorry*, Lauren grinned impishly, *but it was common office gossip that there was history between Janine and Ian.* Don had confirmed that information for them. Janine learned that Lauren and Ian hadn't yet transitioned from a casual dating relationship into something more serious and exclusive. Lauren felt ready to jump all in, but like most men, Ian seemed hesitant. *Sorry*, Janine thought, *but I may be a little happy with that information.* Lauren also considered Max Colliers a fantastic boss. She never understood why Kiki Mellow always derided him. From her perspective, Max created opportunity after opportunity for everyone in his employment. So what if he came across a little flirty? He always behaved like a gentleman around Lauren.

Janine decided to wear one of Sally's dresses, a cute sundress. It was perfectly acceptable and it would save her shopping for something else. All she needed to do was sit through a nice dinner, make polite conversation, and get out of her contract. She would stay cool, reserved, and soon be home free. She would not ignore Max and be a nice date. She'd keep an open mind, or at least try to. Janine noticed that Carlos left a couple of small audio recorders on his desk and wondered if she should borrow one. She slipped it into the small pocket on the cute sundress Sally provided.

Max Colliers chose a fancy seafood place called Bobby D's for their date. A live piano played in a far corner and Max hovered near the entrance waiting for her. He broke out in a broad smile and delivered a glass of wine as she walked in the door. A tiny bit of his aftershave infiltrated her nose as he leaned in to pecked her on the cheek. He was acquainted with three or four people in the vicinity and introduced her to each of them, all while holding her hand in his. A steady stream of soft jazz floated out of the lounge. It felt nice to be on a date again. She didn't know why she had been so apprehensive.

"I can order a semiprivate table, or we can become part of the scene near the piano and people watch," he whispered. "What does the lady prefer?"

"Either way is fine."

He eyed her critically. "You are going to give me a fair chance here? Before we start our date, you should know that you're officially cut loose from the show, if that's what you want. Scot-free, no penalty fee, no more obligations to *Spectral Analysis*. We might ask for a few promo photos, and maybe an appearance at a future press function, but that would be the limit. And, don't worry about Carlos, we're going to make it work. He stays as long as he wants." His eyes softened and he squeezed her hand. "Admit it, I just put my pretty date in a very good mood. You're happy with me now."

A long envelope emerged from his inside breast pocket, which he handed over. "Here's the official copy, all you have to do is add your signature. We can do that right now, or wait till later. Hopefully, it'll put your mind at ease, and you can relax. We can focus on getting to know each other, something I've wanted to do since the first time we met. Do you remember?"

Janine read through the short document while they sat at a semiprivate table. They were shielded with a shimmery canopy and the table was set with crystal flutes, sparkling silver, and napkins bended into the shape of mini-swans. It was a very fancy, romantic setting. Max took her hand again, and caressed her palm. He suggested she sign the document later, then send it to Mike Dunn. Max already signed it, so it was official on his part, unless she ripped it up or delayed acting on it.

"I'm not asking you to rip it up," he said. "I actually prefer that you're not in my employ tonight. This way nobody has an upper hand or feels pressured in any way." Max poured them both a little more wine. "Let's put this part of the conversation aside, shall we? I'd like to focus on finding out what makes Janine Stinger tick."

Max turned out to be an intelligent and entertaining date. He was quite funny and Janine found herself enjoying his conversation despite herself. He studied at Columbia University, then at Wharton for his upper degree in business. Steve Hanks, the last producer, was his cousin and they lived next door to each other growing up, although, next door for them meant a couple of miles between houses.

Did she know, Max had always been the main contributor to *Spectral Analysis,* since its conception? He admitted to chasing after Kiki quite ardently at the beginning, but soon realized he was no competition for the professional athletes she preferred. He told her about his family and a past fiancé that had been arranged, a thing he never wanted, and thank god, she didn't either.

He tried to tease information out of her. He charmingly tip toed his way around personal questions he could see she avoided, but he pressed her anyway, trying to be light-hearted about it. He pried for the sordid details regarding her knife scars. Her quiet, shy demeanor didn't fool him, he *knew* she was into *interesting* things. Max clearly believed her chest X was a self-inflected personal statement. Her marks seemed to excite him. She didn't know what to say, so she let him believe whatever he liked.

After dinner, they migrated to the lounge area to listen to the jazz pianist and bass. They slow danced. Several people stopped to say hello and Janine felt envy from a few of the women in the room. Max charmed every pretty woman that chatted with him, but that wasn't so strange for a bachelor like him. She questioned why Kiki was so wary of Max Colliers, he seemed pretty typical of his station. She tried to imagine how a romance with a wealthy sophisticated playboy might play out. Too many fancy dinners and uncomfortable situations, she imagined, and his fascination with her scars felt very odd, a major red flag. Although he talked nice, she sensed a sinister goal underneath his surface. She wondered why he put so much effort into a girl who was not interested in hanging around.

Janine originally planned to call a taxi, but Max appeared hurt that she didn't assume he would drop her off, especially as his car and driver were waiting in the parking lot. It seemed silly to say no to that very nice chauffeured Mercedes sitting in front of her. Max helped her into the back of his car and then climbed in beside her.

"Mind if we take a scenic route? Are you staying somewhere nearby?" he asked.

"I'm staying with Kiki," Janine said. "Do you know where that is?"

Max chuckled and nodded. "Yes, I've been there a few times, it's actually one of my rentals. Let me tell the driver." Max opened a little window to give their destination and then closed it. His driver was partitioned off from the rear by a thick tinted barrier. When that barrier shut him out, she noticed a distinct change in Max's demeanor. He shifted closer and cozied up to her. He reached over to touch the very top edge of her scar and Janine brushed his hand away.

"Don't do that."

"Why won't you tell me about this cut mark and why you did it?" He considered her angry eyes and narrowed his own. "Don't be like that, I know you're attracted to me, I can feel it. You've been having a good time and you've been sending me signals since we bumped into each other at the Lincoln House. I'm not sure what you and Kiki were cooking up in that limousine, but you led me to believe that getting physical is not out of bounds for you."

Janine shook her head slowly and Max stiffened slightly. His calm, cool, unpredictable behavior had a unsettling effect on her.

"Have you been toying with me?" he asked. "That isn't nice. I've been more than fair with you, out of my way accommodating some would say, and I know you're leaving as soon as you can, so…I'm not asking for a lengthy commitment," he touched her scar again, "Just a chance to play. I'm interested in why a nice girl gravitates to this type of harmful behavior. Is it something you still do? This dark, dangerous stuff? Would you do it with me? I want to understand it, I'm curious. We could go somewhere private and you could tell me all about it."

"I'm not going to sleep with you," Janine told him.

Max nodded. "You sound sure about that. That's okay, but I know you've considered it." His eyes made a pass over her body. "How about showing me everything, as a thank you, a parting gift? Would you be willing to show me all your scars? That entire blemish between your breasts and the one on your back, it went pretty far down. I'm just imagining how far. Are there many more? Someone told me there were lots more, all over. Did you let different guys make them, or was it the same man? Does it turn you on before it happens, or when it happens? I'm dying to know."

"You want to see a body riddled with knife scars, as a thank you?" Janine glanced at the driver to see if he could hear any of it. So, this was what Kiki sensed, some kind of odd, creepy fetish. It didn't cross his mind that her scars were the result of a life threatening, violent attack. He seemed convinced that she invited them on purpose, *for fun.*

"You let your beautiful body get marked up, more than once. That's fascinating? I want to know what type of play precedes them, and why you wanted it. Did anyone go too far and get carried away? What harm would it do, to show me and tell me about it? Not here, but somewhere private. We can get a dual massage, I can easily arrange it, it's the polite thing to do, return the nice favor from me, with a harmless favor from you. You're the only woman I know who's done anything like this, this Marquis de Sade stuff. I admit, it excites me."

"Are you making this a condition, for that document?"

"No," Max said. He shook his head. "No, I already signed those papers and I always keep my word, guaranteed. I'm only asking for a small favor, yours to give freely, just to be nice. What would it hurt? Haven't I been extremely nice? Very fair? I'd settle for just seeing the scars and hearing the stories, but if you wanted to give more than a look, that would be very appreciated. You could tell me what to do."

"I don't think so," Janine said softly. She couldn't look at him.

"Or, you girls could let me watch. I know what you and Kiki were up to in Chicago. I got it all wrong, didn't I? Someone told me, but I should have guessed. Did Kiki make one of those marks with her special dagger? Did you let him watch? I wonder how that dynamic works for the three of you. Did you know that they're related? Cousins. Did they tell you that? Kiki's extremely sexy, isn't she? Did he worm his way in and burn a bridge somewhere? Is that what happened?"

Janine stared at Max in his tailored suit and expensive designer eye glasses. He was so polite and nice in public, always behaving like a perfect gentleman, keeping his distance and not overstepping social boundaries. What did he really want? Did he really expect a response from her? Did he expect her to seriously participate in this conversation? She glanced out the window. At least they were driving in the right direction, in another ten minutes she would be free of him.

"He's making quite a few messes, wouldn't you say?" Max settled back comfortably, studying her. "Has one girl fleeing due to his harassing behavior while he works on another. I'm told quite a few young women find him a little too friendly, and it might be prudent to start an investigation. It's the responsible thing to do."

What was he talking about? Where was he going with this? What was he up to?

"Sexual harassment in the workplace is a multimillion dollar problem these days." Max stared at her. "I could back him up, of course, because I don't believe he harassed you. Or, I could flush him out and question his reputation. Not a hard stretch to assume he forced you to flee a promising career. Did he? Is he the reason you're leaving?"

"I haven't accused anyone of sexual harassment," Janine said.

"You don't have to, there's already a fair amount of gossip about it. Everyone is wondering why you avoid him and are hell bent on leaving," His light brown eyes smiled at her. "I can always ignore it. Loose talk usually fades with time, but what do I get for going out on that limb?"

Max Colliers was a snake, who didn't think he was a snake. Kiki warned her, but she didn't see it coming. His charming and accommodating demeanor fooled her. She needed to learn from this and not play into his hands.

If Max investigated the doctor for sexual harassment, he could make it stick. A minefield of pretty women worked in that building and would say just about anything Max asked. After months of ignoring her requests to be released from the contract, she should have realized that he wouldn't just give in. Not without a triumph in the end, or some way of making it clear he controlled the outcome. She needed to *reveal his true nature with undeniable proof.* She reached into that small pocket on her dress.

"You don't think that this, what you're doing right now, is sexual harassment?"

"You no longer work for me," Max smiled. "You owe me nothing and I owe you nothing. This is just talk, and we're on a date. If I do you a favor, or you do me a favor, we're just friends, doing each other favors. You don't have any obligations here and there are no direct repercussions on you, no matter what you do. And I always keep my word."

"You're asking for a favor then, to keep a target off the doctor? Exactly what type of favor, so I can think about it?"

"Nothing harmful. My top choice: you come on a private weekend with me. It'll be very nice. We can take my jet to a warm, exotic location. We can keep it private, no one needs to know." He grinned and raised his eyebrows. "You and I could have a lot of fun. I'm not squeamish. Maybe, you'd let me add my mark, I would love to see what that's like."

He waited, but she didn't say anything.

"Okay, second choice, you can invite me over and allow me watch you and Kiki. Just three friends hanging out, I would be quietly respectful. That's fair, after the game you two played in the limo."

He waited to see her reaction to that.

He smiled, "Fine, that's just wishful thinking. Last choice, but one you might find easiest, you allow me to see everything and tell me the story behind each of your interesting scars. Why you allowed each of them, who did them, and how you felt when it happened. Fair choices, don't you think, harmless really?"

Harmless, wow, what a delusional fool. Why was he so upset at her? Janine noticed Kiki's driveway and was relieved when the car pulled in. Janine didn't know how to respond to Max Colliers other than saying, *get the fuck away from me.* How clever of him to invent this tough spot for her. Using her departure as evidence that Ian harassed her. Was this another trick, like the one he pulled with Carlos and the contract? Was he really expecting her to do one of those things, or was he only being mean because she wasn't interested in him? Was Janine that easily fooled?

"Let me know by the end of the week, or when you turn in that paperwork. We wouldn't want rumors surrounding your departure to spark an investigation." The driver came around to open the door for her. "I could be your date to the party tomorrow," Max offered.

"No thank you." She couldn't get away from him fast enough. She stood in the driveway and watched his car fly off, then Janine reached into her pocket to turn off the audio recorder.

She searched around the front porch for the spare key. Kiki said it was under a rock, but a garden full of rocks speckled the beds around the porch. She could ring the bell. She noticed it was half past midnight and the house appeared quiet. Maybe Kiki and Gwen were still out on the town. Janine rolled over a few of the rocks and found the key by chance. She opened the door and slipped into the house. A tall shadow stood in the foyer and she jumped. Ian McNally.

"Kiki messaged that you were staying here," He grinned at her. "You're back early. Where is everybody? Kiki and Gwen with you?"

"No, I was with Max. He let me out of my contract." She waved the long envelope. "When did you get back?"

"Just a bit ago. We drove for twelve hours straight on that last stretch, taking turns." He rubbed his head. "I guess Kiki and Gwen are out tearing it up, just as well. I couldn't stay awake for the grilling Gwen has for me," His eyes perked up. "So, did you two get on?"

Janine nodded, "She's very nice."

"Did Gwen tell you that I proposed marriage when we were both eight years old?"

"No." Janine had a good laugh with him about that.

"It's not like Max, caving in. I guess, he had to accept you wanted out." He shrugged. "I'm glad things went your way."

Janine debated telling him about Max, but she still wasn't sure how she was going to respond. Then, she decided to let Ian relax and enjoy his birthday. He appeared exhausted in his T-shirt and sweats. He must have already been in bed when he heard the car in the driveway. His hair was mushed up and his beautiful eyes were rimmed.

"I guess, you're pretty tired." Janine inched toward Kiki's side of the house.

"I'm glad you decided to stay for the party," Ian said. "It means a lot to me."

"It's really no problem. I wanted to wish you a happy birthday, in person," she said. "Only, I didn't get you a gift. That's pretty lame of me."

"I don't need anything," he moved his arms casually across his chest as he watched her. What was he thinking? He was beginning to make her nervous. Could he read her mind? See right through her?

"Okay, that's a lie," she confessed. "I did get you something, a bottle of Glenmorangie Signet. It's supposed to be one of the best, and it is, very smooth. But I opened it last night to help me sleep. It's still pretty full, but… I should have come out here to get something from the bar, but Kiki and Gwen were still up, and I was," she closed her eyes a moment, "Embarrassed. So, I ruined your birthday gift. Would you like it anyway, the rest of it?"

"Do you know what I want for my birthday?" Ian spoke softly and his eyes started slowly blinking. "I want what we did in Chicago. You know, where I got to hold you and help you fall asleep. You didn't let me do any of it last year when I should have been there, helping you get through things. I wasn't allowed. That could be your birthday present to me, let me be there for you tonight. You're still having trouble sleeping, you just admitted it. I could be there tonight, and every night, until you leave."

She felt sudden hot tears behind her eyes that she had to blink back. He still wanted to comfort her, after she had shut him out so brutally and broke his heart. She had to admit, she slept very deeply under his arm in Chicago, and loved it. Just the thought of being cocooned in his protective sphere felt peaceful. She dreaded going off to bed with her wandering mind and wanted nothing more than to lay under Ian's arm and listen to him breathe. But wouldn't that open up an old wound?

"Ian, I'm leaving," her voice was very soft. "For good. I don't want to lead you on about anything."

"This is not about trying to win you back," his voice was also soft. "It's hard to describe how I feel, like I was robbed of something. A role that should have been mine. One that I really wanted. I really wanted to be there for you, even, just as a friend. You could give that back to me, like you did in Chicago. What do you say? It would mean a great deal to me. I really liked being there for you in Chicago. It would be the finest birthday gift you could give me. Just let me hold you and see you through the night, that's all I ask. No funny business, I promise."

Chapter 16

Birthday Party *Kiki*

Kiki stumbled out of bed halfway through the day. That's what a visiting Gwendolyn Murphy will do to a girl. Gwen insisted on visiting some real Austin hotspots, and they spent a fair amount of time in the warehouse district taking in the up and coming music from local bands. Gwen begged to visit a real Texas honkytonk and twostep with real cowboys. So, they found themselves at the Patient Pony and danced around a track the rest of the night. One thing Kiki loved about Austin, she could run around an entire night and not be recognized. Her secret was to dress, and talk, as Austin Texas as possible, and use her real name. No one was ever the wiser. The funniest moments were when someone accused her of trying to look like Kiki Mellow but didn't the quite make the mark.

She stumbled into the kitchen and found Gwen and Janine at the table drinking coffee and eating fresh scones. Did Gwen wake early and do another kitchen magic trick? Oh yes, one bite of the scone and Kiki could detect a certain witch behind them. Perhaps she should practice more in the kitchen. Kiki wondered if Detective Anderson enjoyed a domestic type of girl. Surely, all men admired a woman who could cook. To think she could have been practicing all these years.

Kiki searched for her purse. Good, on the counter. She pulled out her cell phone and saw that it was dead. One of the problems with coming home tired and tipsy, no one cared about charging a cell phone. She plugged it in.

"What are we talking about?" Kiki drank her coffee black.

"Just a little of this and that," Gwen told her. "You missed your handsome cousin by a wee bit. He ran off to work, got in late, I hear. You didn't tell me he grew a beard! He looks very tough. I forgot how cute his blinking eyes were," Gwen chuckled.

"Did you tell Janine what she missed last night? The two-stepping cowboy and his rodeo winning friend? Did I invite them to the party tonight?" Kiki and Gwen went into fits of laughter. "And did I see you trying to teach those girls an Irish jig?"

"Ho, ho, don't try to push that one on me," Gwen said. "Couldn't blame me anyway, they were very lovely."

"Well, you missed quite a girls' night," Kiki told Janine. "I'm sure your night came off well?"

"Max let me out of my contract," Janine told her. "I'm going to meet with Mike Dunn in an hour to have him look over the paperwork, in his downtown office. I want to run something by him."

Kiki spontaneously hugged her. Too bad seeing her go, but it was what she wanted. She wondered how Ian would take that news.

Janine said, "Summer session doesn't start for couple of weeks, so I might linger a few days, if that's okay?"

"Stay as long as you like," Kiki told her. "Gwen's here for two weeks and you could pick her brain about the Trio of Wells and get things straight." Kiki glanced at Gwen's freckled face. "Have you mentioned our little research project?"

Gwen shook her red head. "Oh no, we were too busy harassing Ian." Gwen retrieved the coffee pot and came around to refill everyone's cups. Kiki stretched her phone to the table and tuned it on. It should have enough of a charge to show Janine the texts.

"We did a little sleuthing on our own, and found a thing or two about Miranda Daily. She has a Facebook account that hasn't seen business for eight or nine years. We got a hold of two people from her friend list. One friend places her in Turkey, still gets letters and such, but no photos or phone calls. The other insists that she's dead and says she warned you. Wait, here it is." Kiki showed Janine the message from Mary Kline. "She knows who you are and that we work together."

Janine studied the message and number, then pulled her own phone out. She punched in the number for Mary Kline. Kiki and Gwen exchanged quick glances.

"Hello, Mary?" Janine said into the phone. "This is Janine Stinger, don't hang up. I want to thank you for trying to warn me. I should have taken your notes seriously." Then, Janine just listened, her brow took on a very worried crease. After a moment, she put the phone face down on the counter.

Wow, what did Mary have to say, Kiki wondered. Nothing good by the look of it.

Janine carefully sipped her coffee. "She doesn't want anything more to do with it and I think we should respect her wishes."

"She said something else," Kiki could see the caution coming off Janine. "What did she say?"

"She's terrified. Expects he'll come after her if he ever gets out." Janine covered her eyes with her hand. "He always suspected she sent those warnings and has harassed her for years over it. At least now he seems to have forgiven her, so she doesn't want to be involved. She has a family and she doesn't want anyone to call back. If she gets another call, she's going to change her number."

"Do we have any idea how she knows him, or Miranda," Gwen said. "I wonder if the other one, the roommate, Lisa, knows Mary Kline. Maybe Lisa knows all of them."

Kiki called Lisa Welks again. Lisa might recall a Mary Kline, but couldn't be sure. Lisa railed at Kiki for calling and pumping her for information. If the questions were for the ghost show, shouldn't she be compensated in some way? If they needed her input, why didn't Kiki interview her? She's seen the show and watched Kiki interview people all the time on TV. Lisa would be happy to help, but she didn't want to be used. Kiki thanked her for her time and said she'd call back soon for a more formal interview, then set the phone down.

Kiki lent Janine her car for the meeting with Mike Dunn. Kiki trusted Mike. He would ensure the paperwork was in order with no funny business from Max. Mike would certainly make sure Max worded things correctly in that document he gave Janine.

"Looks like my prayer chain is working wonders already." Gwen said after Janine left. "She's looking well."

Kiki did notice. Janine's dark aura had definitely lightened and her undertones were amazingly bright. Perhaps getting out of that contract was exactly what she needed.

Ian's birthday party turned out to be a spectacular bash. The entire *Spectral Analysis* staff, the old producer, cameraman, neighbors, a smattering of friends, and a few gate crashers crowded around the pool and party room. Several of Ian's rugby mates stumbled in, and Carlos brought his wife, Maria. Kiki noticed Max arrive with a familiar female executive from the upper floors. Kiki watched all the mingling with satisfaction, Texas horseshoes around the corner, Irish dance across the pool, food and drink under the awning. When Janine finally returned, they found a quiet corner to chat.

"You must have good news," Kiki said.

Janine slipped Kiki a copy of an audio on thumb drive and disclosed what she discussed with Mike Dunn. She floated suing Max for harassment, unless he completely backed off on anything to do with *Spectral Analysis*. She asked Kiki to be the one to talk to Ian about it. Janine wondered why she wasn't surprised, and Kiki said she's warned her plenty of times about Max Colliers. He did not play fair in love, and Kiki suspected it was mostly idle talk to get what he wanted.

"Why do women believed any of his nonsense. Max only wants to win the game. He must be bluffing about whatever he threatened to make you squirm and give in." Kiki told her.

Carlos quickly insinuated himself into their conversation. He left his wife in the company of Gwen and they appeared to be laughing hysterically. Was Gwen flirting again? She always became very flirty at parties.

"I'm officially jobless," Janine gushed to Carlos. "I mean, I'm going to miss you, but I'm pretty happy about it. We'll keep in touch, right? And I got confirmation that you'll stay on the show through the end of the season, if you want."

Carlos nodded and then shot them a funny grin. "I already know about it, and I may not stay on, either." He flashed guilty eyes at Kiki, he shrugged. "I confronted Colliers when we got back from Chicago. He asked me to finish the season, but I've been offered the weather job at KVUE and decided to take it instead of signing again. This is something Maria and I have been discussing since last year. There's too much traveling with the ghost show. At KVUE, I can stay at home and coach peewee soccer year round. Meteorology was my original plan before I got sidetracked with you guys. Mimi and Milo already notice when I'm not at their games. I can't have that."

That news was not unexpected. Kiki hugged him.

"With those wee bairns, I don't blame you."

"You're sounding more and more Scottish with your friend around." Carlos laughed. "She's hilarious by the way, telling some funny stories about your friend Kiera Lovett, a gal who's gotten into a brawl over sports. She may be perfect for my brother, Lonzo. If she ever comes to visit, let me know, 'cause I want them to meet."

"I believe she's already met your sweet brother, a few times." Kiki winked at him and walked away. She heard Janine explain it to him as she wove through people toward Gwen and Maria. She smiled when she heard Carlos laugh out loud. If Gwen continued running off at the mouth, Kiki's mysterious image would be lost forever.

Kiki asked the Celtic Lads rock band to stop playing and help shoo people away at two in the morning. She did not plan to party till dawn. Unfortunately, the Celtic Lads were not big on leaving themselves. She should not have fetched her collection of daggers for a little target practice, but couldn't resist when she bumped into the guy who had dressed as a monk in San Antonio. He stared at her with a mix of hostility and lust, so Kiki coaxed him over to show him how to throw a knife properly. Most people probably imagined she was flirting with that group of hunky blokes, but she really just wanted that one fellow to realize she didn't have to miss in San Antonio. The band also took turns throwing knives at the target and Ian rushed over.

"Kiki, are you sure it's wise to encourage a bunch of drinking Scotsmen to throw knives back here?" Ian asked.

Lauren tagged along after him, holding his hand and staking her claim. Ian seemed a mite perturbed with Lauren, especially after the very spirited and public kiss she landed on him when he blew out the candles. Apparently, Lauren was tired of waiting for him to make a move and decided to go for it.

"Someone is going to get skewered," Ian said, but he grabbed a dagger and had a go at the target himself. "I'll get these lads under control if you can start clearing out the rest of the crowd."

It took an effort, but soon folks cleared out. The last of their guests gathered in the den for a final drink. Gwen engaged Max in an intimate discussion near the kitchen, and the others sat along the sofa, chatting. Apparently, Janine had hidden a nice single malt scotch in her room for Ian's birthday and shared it for the nightcap. They toasted Ian's thirty years one last time.

"I got a message from the parole board earlier," Janine quietly confessed to Kiki. "The letters are inadmissible without proof that they came from Rick."

The small group shift around when Carlos and Maria left. Then, Lauren succeeded in convincing Ian to give her a tour of his side of the house. Everyone watched them walk down his dark hall wondering if they were gone for the night. Ben shifted to chat with the woman Max brought to the party.

"I can make another statement to the parole board," Janine continued softly. "In writing, or in person. At first, I wasn't even considering being there."

"Are you considering it now?" Kiki asked.

"It's early next week," Janine said. "I've another favor to ask. I can bring someone with me, as support, Rick might be in the room. My sister, Juliana, and I are still in a rough place. I spoke to her, earlier, but I couldn't bring myself to ask her to come. I know you have Gwen in town, so it's okay to say no. I think, I can go by myself, but… "

Kiki took her hand and squeezed it, Janine never asked for Kiki's help with anything before. "I think Gwen would enjoy Chicago. She can come with us." Kiki hugged her. "It's no problem, I could introduce her to my detective and we could go to the Congress Plaza and have another little séance." Kiki also wanted to see Rick Wilkens in person, to get a good look at him.

"Your detective?" Janine smiled, very relieved. "You mean my detective."

"We'll see about that," Kiki pulled her in for another soft embrace. She whispered, "You're not alone, Janine."

Max noticed their interaction with a devilish gleam in his eye, so Kiki gave him a sly smile. Ian and Lauren retuned to break up the group again. Ian babbled idiotically and Lauren appeared a bit stung. Things must not have gone her way back there. People shifted again, and Gwen migrated to Janine and Kiki.

"She's even more beautiful when she's upset," Gwen whispered, glancing at Lauren. "Her smile tries way too hard, but her pout is positively captivating. It makes me want to cheer her up."

"How did you enjoy Max Colliers?" Kiki asked.

"He's a charmer," Gwen grinned. "I felt like he was wooing me. Did you know, a huge part of his parent company invests in the direct research and production of cancer therapies? His family hosts a local fundraiser for the Saint Jude Society every summer. He's a real philanthropist, that one, and he knows his stuff. Sorry, girls, I can't help it, I like him. Part of my rebellious nature, fancying the naughty ones. He even offered to show me some of the Austin sights, if you were too busy."

"Am I too busy?" Kiki asked, and Gwen laughed softly. She obviously found Max a harmless flirt.

After a while, their final guests began to depart and Ian stood at the door thanking everyone who came. Max offered rides to anyone who needed one, ever the gentleman. An uncomfortable moment occurred when Ian hugged Lauren in a stiff way, then they closed the door on the last guest. Kiki felt relieved, but happy. Throwing large parties always got on her nerves.

"I guess, I'm off to bed," Ian said. "That was a brilliant party, thank you all."

Kiki hugged him generously, then Gwen came around to embrace him and slipped in a nice peck on the lips. She laughed when he shooed her away.

"That's a fine thank you after the cake I slaved over." Then, she pushed Janine toward Ian and his side of the house. "Go along then, nae need to tip toe around us. Everyone here already knows everything anyway."

Ian and Janine exchanged guilty looks; caught red handed. Then, without a word, Janine followed Ian into his lair. Kiki gaped at Gwen's amused flush face.

"I didn't know about that," Kiki said.

"Why else would he send that gorgeous girl, Lauren, away?" Gwen smirked. "Shall we tidy up now or leave it for the morning?"

Kiki listened to the thumb drive recording after cleaning up a bit. Max Colliers had a very vivid imagination and quite an ambitious playlist. He was a complete and total brat. If Janine believed for a second that he was serious about investigating Ian for sexual harassment, then she didn't know Max. He would never destroy the primary character in his entertainment investment and have it all implode. Max was smarting because unassuming Janine didn't care for his advances, and no amount of wealth, charm, or romantic overtures worked. She shut him down cold without explanation or apology. He probably felt like a fool and wanted her to squirm a bit. He was smart and leaned in the right direction, Janine would definitely protect a friend. But his big mistake was not understanding Janine Stinger. She was not the kind of girl to call a bluff, or to cave in, or play his silly games. She was the type to quietly access the situation and then counterattack. That's probably how she survived that brutal episode in Chicago.

Kiki rang Mike Dunn and got the run down on everything. Janine planned to go full public on Max Colliers with that audio tape. It could spoil the future in politics he always talked about. Janine might even sue the greater company, if he continued to stick his nose into *Spectral Analysis*. Max was on his way to becoming a very silent producer once again. Kiki wasn't sure how things would play out, but if a senior Colliers, his uncle or father, caught whiff the tape, Max would be knee deep in shite. Poor Max, all he probably wanted was another notch on his bedpost.

Chapter 17

Parole Board *Janine*

It was the second time Janine woke since falling asleep. The first time followed a semisweet dream that left her crying softly. Ian stirred beside her, then embraced her until she drifted off again. It was the third night she slept with Ian in his bed. Kiki and Gwen assumed more was going on, but Ian was very clear about what he wanted. He only wanted to cuddle and help her get through the night. He was right, as usual, she could bear the dreams better with him embracing her when she stirred. The past night had been the easiest, but, it was also the final night for them. She needed to fly to Chicago for the parole hearing and then return to Davis. The past two mornings, Ian woke first and was already up and about before she opened her eyes, but this last morning, she woke before him, so she got a chance to study him without him interfering with her scrutiny.

His brow furled and he murmured in his sleep. His eyes moved beneath his lids in a dream. His lips bent up in a momentary smile The previous evening, she watched him draw diagrams in his journal and type out a paragraph for his new book. Along with his ghostly theories, he studied basic energy exchanges in common minerals. He made mapping the difference between rocks with more or less feldspar versus quartz sound very exciting, and Gwen enjoyed his discourse regarding the large mineral collection as much as she did. Then, he spoke excitedly about elemental allotropes and the possibility of a fourth phosphorus or second magnesium. He wondered if there was an unknown crystalline shape that hadn't been discovered. *C60, the buckyball for carbon, wasn't discovered until the 1980s*, Janine had mentioned. Then, Ian pulled out his collection of rock slices, gathered from ghostly sites, and slid one under his binocular dissecting scope to show her. It was fun. She could definitely see why he had been a popular professor.

She was going to miss listening to him speak in his Doctor McNally voice about small details in objects that he found so fascinating, and then how his eyes began to blink when he couldn't find the right word. She'd also miss the way he grinned when those two witches teased him unmercifully over their morning coffee, trying to embarrass him, and his smooth crawl, as she spied him swimming laps in the pool through the kitchen window, and then those whispers in bed before he fell asleep about something amusing that happened earlier in the day. But mostly, she'd miss being cocooned under his arm as she slept. His nearness generated a peaceful feeling, and she was glad they had become friends again.

His hair was all mushed up and his beard needed a bush. He must be uncomfortable, because he slept on top of the covers in a sweatshirt and sweat pants. Not the most comfortable sleeping attire, but it was part of their unspoken agreement, padding to tamp down any simmering flames that might develop. She knew she wrecked things for him, with Lauren. That picture of herself on pier 39 in San Francisco was propped right on his dresser, and there was a second photo in his office, tacked haphazardly to the wall. Sure, it was part of a sea of photographs, but she was the only person in any of them. Mountains, valleys, shorelines, rocks, the aurora, and then Janine. He didn't seem to realize the message those pictures sent out. No way Lauren missed them on her tour the other night. Here she was, messing with his love life without even trying. *Maybe he wants it messed with*, she thought.

She reached over to touch his beard and found that she couldn't stop herself. Her fingers slipped right into the curls and she found his jaw. His whiskers were soft and silky. She felt a tad guilty for invading his space, but he did grow the beard because she liked it, didn't he? His eyes fluttered open and he stared right at her. They were beautifully blue and so clear and happy. She realized both her hands were in his beard and she quickly pulled them back.

"What are you doing?" He yawned.

She didn't know. She didn't know what she was doing. He watched her closely and she became embarrassed.

"I'm sorry about that. Your beard just looks so… so soft. It is soft. Very soft. I just wanted to, you know, it was a little out of sorts there." That sounded very stupid. "It was my last chance to see how it felt, sorry."

Ian shifted around to give her his full attention, but keep a space between them. He propped himself on one elbow, silently attentive.

"You should put that photo away." Janine couldn't maintain eye contact with him. His constant steady stare and his wall of space aroused her senses despite the padding. "You might not realize it, but if you bring a girl back here, the photo on the dresser is not going to help you. It's going to cramp your style. I'm afraid it may have already messed things up for you, in regards to Lauren."

Ian turned his head and spotted the photo she was referring to. "I like that picture. It's a very nice sunset over the San Francisco Bay, look at the colors in the sky." He squinted at it. It was not male sexual energy he directed at her. It was something else, but it had a similar effect, causing a blanket of warmth to flood her core. *Did she just realize her core?* Was that the sensation she'd been noticing each night? Ian feeding her core, but not with sex energy, with something else, something better. She should share this breakthrough with Kiki and Gwen. She moved to rise from the bed, but he took her hand and tugged on it a little, so she turned back to him.

"Were you going to kiss me? The way you did in Chicago when you were drunk?" He looked amused.

She let out a soft laugh and pulled her hand away. "I guess, I was considering it. You don't have to tease me about it."

His hand fell to her hip now, and he deliberately pulled her closer, bridging the gap. The heat from his fingers seemed to penetrate right through the heavy net cotton of her track pants. Janine watched his gaze change, and her heart started beating faster. *Was he shifting his energy, or was it only her?* He slowly guided her hand back up, toward his jaw, and his attention went to her lips. The sparks in his eyes lit fuses on her nerves as she vividly remembered that kiss. Her fingers sank back into his soft curly beard again. His eyes locked onto hers and he let down his guard. *He had guarded himself from this!* And now, his eyes had altered to a deeper shade of blue.

"So then, lass, what will it be?" he dared her.

What will it be indeed? Her heart pounded in her ears. *What would one little kiss hurt?* She leaned in to brush her lips to his and felt a thousand tingling points start right there and shoot all the way down to her toes and everywhere in between. It was a sweet kiss that turned into a passionate, urgent need very fast. They had slept in close quarters for three nights, just simmering, but this heat was searing. She flashed on fantasies she secretly had about him, thoughts of rubbing suntan lotion over his muscular shoulders after he rose dripping from the pool, or kissing his thick chorded neck when he bent over his dissecting scope, or climbing into his lap as he drank his morning coffee, or rubbing her breasts into the soft curls on his chin. Before she knew what she was doing, she tore off her sweatshirt and straddled him, practically attacking him. Ian removed his sweats too, all of them, and she saw that he was fully aroused. Then, he took over and pinned her down, kissing her neck and running his hands everywhere, speeding her up and slowing her down at the same time. He meant to take his time with her, she could tell. And, he was right again, as usual.

She lay spent in his arms, embarrassed for tearing up. His kisses were slow and sensual, and he held her close. His scent was intoxicating, musky and arousing. They both knew it was getting very late in the morning and her phone pinged with a message from Kiki. They were due to leave soon, to catch their flight to Illinois.

"I don't want you to go," Ian whispered. "Tell me that we'll see each other as often as possible, between your terms and whenever I can go out there. You'll finish up out there soon, right?"

"I'm never coming back to this TV world, Ian. And I'll want to go to graduate school too, maybe. I'm going to be in school for a very long time, who knows where." Her head lay against his chest, so she couldn't see his face. Janine worried if making love with Ian had been the wisest thing for them. Deep inside, it certainly felt like the most natural thing. She whispered softly, "I certainly will visit you, when I can. And I'll welcome your visits too, anytime. But, I don't want you to put your life on hold for me, okay? Promise me that you'll do what you need to be happy. I'll totally support whatever you do and whoever you end up with. I realize I have a lot of issues. But if, eventually, we find ourselves in the same place, and it works out in the end, then that would be very nice."

He didn't say a word. He just held her close until she absolutely needed to go.

Janine and Kiki rode the train to the parole meeting with Detective Anderson. He would submit her taped statement as Janine waited in the wings in case they invited her in. Janine's hands shook in her lap. She had not seen Richard Wilkens since the day he was found guilty of aggravated assault, battery, and unlawful imprisonment, the only three, from a slew of charges he had faced.

Kiki and the detective chatted quietly together for most of the train ride, then, the detective moved next to Janine and took up her shaking hands. The detective shared news regarding Miranda Daily. She resided in a mountain village in Turkey and posted letters home at regular intervals during the year. Her family recognized the Saint Comba charm and were surprised that Miranda never mentioned losing it. They sought its return, as it was an old family heirloom. They could prove the charm was theirs, and shared many photographs of their last matriarch wearing the pendant.

"Have they spoken with her lately? Can we get her phone number?" Kiki asked.

Detective Anderson shook his head. "She only corresponds through the mail with very little telecommunications. The family got the feeling that her cult frowns on modern technology. They implied that she's called in the past, but not very often."

"So, it's a strange situation." Kiki tapped her own chin. "Have you ever heard the name Mary Kline?"

"Kiki!" Janine interjected. "She doesn't want to be part of this."

Detective Anderson patted her hand again. "I won't bother her," he assured her. "I know about Mary. I know she wants nothing more to do with Richard Wilkens. I met her many years ago. You may not know this, but Mary is his sister."

His sister? "He claimed to be an only child," Janine said.

Richard Wilkens had both an older brother and an older sister. His brother went MIA years ago, likely killed, during a skirmish in the middle east. At the time, his sister lived near the university, as a student, and his parents resided in the house on Thatcher Road with a very young Richard Wilkens. Within a year, the father had an unexpected heart attack. Curiously, the mother was missing. No one knew where she went, or when, but the younger Richard Wilkens says it was soon after his brother was reported killed in action. Mary Kline became the guardian of her minor brother for the next few years. It was not an easy situation for the two siblings with the parents gone so unexpectedly and the sister recently out of college. Their relationship turned extremely sour, and a few odd accusations were made by the sister." The detective double checked the details when he investigated Janine's case.

"That's a lot of mystery," Kiki said.

Detective Anderson nodded. "An unusual amount of mystery, I would say."

The parole board did not have questions for Janine Stinger. They reviewed her filmed statement and sent out a thank you for her input. The detective disclosed that Richard Wilkens had not been in the room. The detective was scheduled to give his own statement after the lunch hour, and then they would leave. If they preferred, he could have someone drive them to the town center to wait, and they could hop on an earlier train back to Chicago. Then, an announcement for visitors blared over the loud speaker and Janine stared at Kiki. Kiki knew exactly what she was thinking.

"Are you sure about this?" Kiki asked. "It's the one thing you were dreading."

Exactly, and it was the reason Janine dragged Kiki to Chicago with her; to hold her hand in case she had to face him. For days, Janine psyched herself up for that meeting. She wanted to look Rick in the eye and show him that she was no longer afraid of him. *She wanted to see him.* Detective Anderson said he could pull some strings, it wouldn't be hard. Rick waited in a nearby room, very available, and it was not unusual for a prisoner to have visitors on a hearing day.

He sat chained to a table on a much shorter leash than the one he used on her. He appeared undamaged by prison and actually thriving. Two suits sat near, clearly part of his legal representation. When Janine entered the room, his eyes lit up as he tracked her motion. It used to put a flutter in her chest when he reacted that way. He looked the same. *It was going to be harder than she thought.* But, she didn't waver, or run from the room. She continued steadily to take the seat across from him. Kiki followed, along with a prison representative, and they sat somewhere behind her. Rick didn't even glance at them. He silently beamed at Janine, as a his handsome smile stretched across his face. Janine forced herself to breathe easy.

"You have no idea how happy I am to see you," he gushed. "I'm overwhelmed. You look absolutely beautiful, wonderful, Janine. Have you come to speak for me? You have, haven't you?"

"Are you still claiming innocence? That I misidentified you as my attacker?" Her voice was shaky. She forced herself to meet his eyes. Pale, grey, clear and pretty, just like Sammy's eyes, and she quickly glanced away. She forced her emotions down and turned back to face him. He used that same expression in so many different situations with her: after a tender kiss, when she a cooked meal for him, the night she lost her virginity. She swallowed down the lump in her throat, because those had once been happy memories.

His eyes filled with concern. "I forgive you, for saying that, for thinking it. Deep down, somewhere inside, you know that it wasn't me." His voice wavered with emotion. "That attack traumatized you, and I'll never forgive myself for not protecting you better, and for the stupid argument that sent you out of the house. I've studied in here, about how the brain changes images in the mind after a disturbing event. I understand how your mind transferred those actions to me, because you were angry with me. I made you angry the day you left. Someday, I hope, when you realize your mistake, you can forgive yourself. I already forgave you, long ago, and I don't blame you at all, Janine. I'm just happy to see you looking so well."

Janine realized that his lawyers believed whatever bullshit he'd been feeding them over the years. Their stern eyes bore into her. Even Janine felt herself wavering. He appeared so earnest, open, and full of concern, sweet. But, she wasn't fooled. She was prepared for this duplicity after experiencing a similar game with Max Colliers. *Thank you, Max, for that warm up round.*

"You're so full of crap," Janine hissed softly. "I came to tell you, and whoever will listen, that we both know there's no misunderstanding. Stop lying, Rick."

When the parole board questioned him, they very likely might believe every word out of his mouth. His handsome features and perfect smile were pleasant and disarming. He certainly came across as innocent. Did she really think she would find a chink in his façade after those letters? It infuriated her, this overconfident smugness that he could get away with anything. And they were going to let him get away with it too, she could feel it in the air. *Okay, okay, think! There must be some way to expose his true nature with undeniable proof, so he could never fool anyone again.*

"People realize a mistake was made," Rick told her softly. "It's not your fault, you were traumatized, but others are starting to listen and accept the *truth*. Actions speak louder than words, Janine, I could never harm anyone. Not many people continue to believe that I could do the things you accused me of. I wish you were not so clouded. I still love you, you know, and I always will. We made a vow to each other, do you remember? And, you're the mother of my child, I will never forget that."

He paired his soft voice with a tender smile and resembled the Rick she fell for in the very beginning. Janine felt herself fidget because the visit was not going the way she wanted. She needed an admission from him, no matter how small. She needed to eliminate the last little bit of self-doubt that she might be unreliable or irrational. *Prone to delusions, ghosts, and conspiracy theories.* But how could she get an admission when he wanted her confused? Needed her confused. *Don't fall for his nonsense. Don't fall for it!*

"What about Miranda Daily?" Janine asked softly. "What would Miranda say?"

His lips tweaked almost imperceptibly. "Miranda? I don't know. I assume, she would be concerned about you. She would definitely speak on my behalf."

"You think so?" Janine continued softly. "I'm planning to meet her later, and speak with her again. We'll see what she has to say."

His face relaxed a fraction. His mouth bent in a near imperceptible sneer. Did he allowed his real thoughts to peek through, *did he slip?* She spotted amusement behind his expression. He didn't believe there was any chance in hell that Miranda Daily would speak with her. *Because she was dead?*

"Again?" He shifted in his seat. "I didn't know that you two ever met."

"Again," Janine confirmed. "We're meeting *again*, in Thatcher Woods, where we first met. You remember? When you were burying me in those leaves, that was Miranda, wasn't it? Standing there, watching. The woman near that tree, the one who told you to stop."

Ah, now that smug expression melted off his face. A shadow of stark fear passed over his eyes. It was that recognition of the truth she wanted. *He remembered the ghost in the woods!* She felt something loosen from her chest. It was the last little thing she needed for closure, even if he didn't say it out loud, his eyes said it all, she wasn't delusional.

"She haunts the woods, Rick, because you left her there." Janine leaned forward, speaking softly. "And she knows everything."

One lawyer stood up and took a step toward him. He could see the fear in Rick's eyes, the rapid breathing. The lawyer meant to protect him, but didn't know what caused his fear. *Only someone who has seen the ghost would understand this fear, ask Randy.* Janine relished watching the confidence drain from his face. He glanced down and tried to rebuild his façade.

"I have her Saint Comba pendant, found in those woods." She watched his eyes flicker toward her at the mention of the pendant. *He knew the necklace she meant!* "And when I summon her tonight, I'm going to find out where you left her, and when I do, her remains will tell everyone here exactly what you're capable of." Janine glanced at the two lawyers, "All these people you've been working, they'll turn on you, and if they're smart, they'll make sure you never get out of here."

They ended the visit after that statement. Janine didn't care, seeing the smug confidence drain out of him was enough for her, and she was convinced, beyond a doubt, that Miranda Daily was buried in Thatcher Woods. They needed to find her, *for that undeniable proof,* before the Illinois parole board concluded anything. Kiki remained unusually quiet on the walk back to the waiting area.

"Kiki? Kiki, what did you think?"

"He's a true demon," Kiki told her. "That man, Richard Wilkens, has no core aura, no soul. It's scary to see a missing core, Janine. He's a demon," Kiki repeated. "A very charming and dangerous one. The other people in the room, they all had positive feelings for him."

On the train back to Chicago, Detective Anderson recapped his own statement in the parole hearing, then asked about their prisoner visit. He filled them in on what he remembered of the investigation regarding

Miranda Daily. He didn't work the case, but read about it when Janine's case came up. Cadaver dogs canvased every inch of Thatcher Woods and found nothing. Before the family began receiving letters from Miranda, someone accused Richard Wilkens of duplicity. The investigators later discovered that it was his sister, Mary Kline, and found that bad blood had existed between the siblings, for years. When their father passed away, all the assets went directly to Richard and Mary felt her brother was not capable of managing the sizable estate. Mary developed a pattern of accusing her bother of different crimes in an attempt to make him ineligible to collect the family assets. Stealing the mother's jewelry, for instance, and hiding the heirlooms. She even accused him of killing their parents, both her father and her mother. Mary always claimed her mother either "escaped" or she was dead. Apparently, the father had been a very controlling individual and passed that characteristic on to his namesake son. Mary warned them not to listen to people on the block who found both the senior and junior Richard Wilkens personable and nice. Those people had no clue what occurred behind closed doors.

Bob Anderson's large brown eyes focused intently on Janine. "Miranda's family is satisfied with the letters from Europe. They claim that Miranda always threatened to run off to exactly where she went. They insist she is alive."

Kiki watched the detective offer assurance without making false promises. He felt the parole board leaned toward forgiving Rick Wilkens, especially as they approved of his conduct in prison. Even Kiki observed how easily Rick charmed people. The board believed a different inmate was responsible for the letters Janine received and that Rick had no knowledge of them. Although her identity had been protected, it wasn't top secret information. They advised her to be prepared, in case there was a media revelation. Perhaps, she shouldn't have taken such a highly visible job.

The Hierophant

Gwen Murphy is the Hierophant.

Chapter 18

The Woods Ghost *Kiki*

Gwen had devoted her day to exploring The Art Institute of Chicago with an old friend who happened to be a nurse at one of the pediatric cancer hospitals in the city. She listed all the pros of being a tourist when they met for a late dinner. Gwen's bright chatter improved their mood.

Kiki soon tuned them out, in order to revisit her death vision again. Something about it tugged at her; did that vision seep out of the charm? The charm reeked with the auras of many powerful people, but those conflicting images of the strangulation unsettled her. Did cattails or heather litter the landscape? Wind or no wind? Kiki worried that perhaps more than one vision had been intermingled. The heather definitely reminded Kiki of Scotland, and though the image of the man was very dark, he definitely resembled the Rick Wilkens she'd seen in the flesh. *Could he have killed more than one person?* Gwen pulled her from those thoughts by asking a question.

"So then, Kiera, did you invite Detective Anderson to the summer solstice?"

"I didn't quite get the chance as of yet," she answered.

"Did you lose your nerve?" Gwen giggled.

That wicked witch, Kiki thought. "Of course not!" Kiki lied. "But he's likely very busy being a detective, isn't he? And though he's quite an understanding fellow, I worry the ways of our solstice festival, and especially the other ritual, is not something he has encountered before. I hesitate to broach it with him because, frankly, I'm not sure how to word such a thing. Will I will shock him with the invitation? I mean, to my awakening?"

"Nae doubt he will be shocked." Gwen chuckled. "Many fellows would be shocked at such an invitation. But, he may be delighted as well."

"If you're inviting Detective Anderson to a pagan festival, I'm sure he'd take it in stride," Janine told Kiki. "He's very open minded and I get the sense that he's a bit enamored with you. Good gracious, I never imagined you could be nervous about inviting a man anywhere, and it's only Detective Anderson. I'm positive he'd be beyond flattered that you're asking him to go anywhere."

Gwen continued laughing up a storm. The skin between her freckles became so red that her complexion appeared to smooth out, yet Janine remained completely clueless. Well, this subject proved a bit mortifying for Kiki. She assumed that Janine had caught on in earlier discussions, but perhaps she hadn't. Kiki planned to have coitus for the first time in her life during an awakening ritual after the solstice. Because the detective was a powerful man, in the cosmic energy sense, he'd make a special partner. He could possibly be the perfect man to sire Kiki's future child. A baby conceived during an awakening came with a special blessing.

Kiki waved Gwen away from the subject, feeling a dreadful conversation in the making. There was nowhere near enough time to go into all the nuances of the coven hierarchy, the traditions, or the importance of practicing celibacy to master the Core Well. Plus, Kiki didn't think she could survive explaining it to a skeptic like Janine.

"Let's focus on tonight," Kiki said. "Since Gwen is here, and is a *master teacher*, she can give you tips on finding your core. You'll need to beckon from your core when engaging this spirit. It'll be interesting to see what happens when you exert your full center into calling a ghost. If you can manage to reach from your core, that is."

"I may have found my core," Janine mumbled shyly. "With Ian. I felt light, weightless, and Ian was being so sweet and caring. The entire weekend, I felt him all around my heart, leaving his love. Not passion, better than that. This feeling was light and pure, and went to the center of my body. That's my core, right?"

Kiki and Gwen nodded at her.

"I'm sorry, Kiki, I told you that I would let him be, but I couldn't help it. I think, I love him. You two probably believe I should return to Texas.

Think I'm making a huge mistake for going off on my own. But I need to do something first, to find my purpose, and it's not being on a TV show. And before I can accept what Ian was offering me, I need to get my issues settled."

Kiki nodded and patted her hand, happy she figured that out.

Gwen said, "I don't think you're making a mistake. People have it all wrong these days. Women following a man's ego and becoming lost spirits in the process, it's the downfall of humankind. You're right to go out and find your own purpose. Never forget, woman is of the earth, Janine, the fertile soil, the cradle of life, the home. If it's meant to be, Ian will find his way to you, he won't be able to resist. All you need to do is open up your world to him when he does, and bask in his sunlight."

They parked the rental car on Thatcher Avenue in front of the Wilkens house. Janine stood motionless as she stared at the structure, the front yard ran deep, at least 30 yards from the curb. Light streamed from two windows and it felt occupied. Did it still belong to Rick Wilkens? Perhaps a service rented it out while he was incarcerated. The neighborhood was well cared for and nice. Quiet. No one would guess that such a normal house owned that notorious past. Janine quietly turned away with a pensive expression on her face.

"I ran this way," Janine abruptly crossed the street and walked into the woods. They each carried an electric torch and Kiki snapped hers on.

The lack of lunar light created a very dark woods. The college guy, Randy, claimed that the ghost only emerged on a full moon, but Kiki knew that the moon affected spirits similarly to the tides, and the new moon pulled on the aether just as vigorously as a full moon. Just in case, Kiki carried a special candle to woo the spirit. She also brought the mystery charm. Three strong witches performing a traditional séance could surely summon Miranda Daily from the void, especially since the ghost specifically sent for one of them.

Janine kept a quick pace, so it was hard to keep up. She had long legs and she was a runner, while Kiki was mainly a yoga girl. Gwen glanced at

Kiki. *Did Gwen sense the tension streaming off Janine?* The twigs and leafy debris crunched beneath their feet as they veered off the regular path. Janine turned to enter a small clearing, just a small open circle hidden between the oak trees. She stopped to glance around. Kiki met her eyes through the dark shadows.

"This is where he caught up to me." Janine aimed her torch at the ground to reveal fallen leaves, twigs, and stones. She moved the light around, searching. "I almost bled to death right here." She sounded winded and far away, as if she was talking to herself. "A stone, maybe like that one there, lodged into my back and slowed the bleeding, saving me." Her light hovered over a large stone. Then, Janine turned her light to the left and illuminated a tall tree, her expression was expectant, "She stood next to that tree."

They meandered around the clearing, but Kiki couldn't detect anything unusual, not even a hint of a presence.

"Have you tried calling to her?" Kiki asked.

"Not yet," Janine said. Her doe eyes shone in the dim light. "I didn't think I could ever come back here, but this place means nothing to me now. It's just the woods." But when Gwen came around to hug her, the tears came fast. *When would Janine realize that she didn't need to play brave with them?*

"Go on then, get it out," Gwen urged softly. "It'll empty the murk so you can think clearly. Never fight your tears, lassie, or be ashamed of them. Crying is a sign of strength. It's a fallacy to believe holding your emotions proves you valiant. It's the exact opposite."

They moved south, toward Chicago Avenue and the pond. They searched for the spot Randy first spotted the ghost. They followed his crude map. The pond emerged from behind several trees under a blanket of stars. They traced the water's edge to a less weed covered spot. The quiet was broken by croaking frogs. Kiki noticed the serene surface of the water and the many cattails poking through the liquid. Goosebumps trickle down her arms as they gravitated toward two fallen weathered tree trunks.

Kiki felt certain they entered the climatic location in her vision of death. The smell of the air, the soft grass, the call of the insects added to her memory, but it wasn't the right night. The glass surface of the pond reflected a moonless, cloudless sky, and unlike the vision, no gentle breeze stirred her hair. Kiki drew in a breath to calm herself. *Don't worry, the strangling devil is still in jail,* she told herself.

"Kiera, is something amiss?" Gwen noticed her distraction.

Kiki nodded. "What time is it?"

"Well after midnight, and the veil thins." Gwen turned to Janine. "Do you recall the hour you faced the ghost?"

Janine shook her head. "I was disoriented. All I know is that it was night."

"Randy's encounter occurred around midnight, but well before the witching hour," Kiki said. "Let's set up a candle." Kiki's inner meter sensed a scant energy brewing in the air.

"I thought the witching hour was at midnight," Janine said.

"Only in Hollywood, Janine," Kiki told her. "The actual witching hour is on the third bell, when the curtain thins and the spirits swirl, transcending the void as they seep into our world."

Janine found a rock. She insisted they not place a burning candle directly on the dry grass. She hunted for a good spot to place the stone and Gwen gave Kiki a raised eyebrow. Did she wonder if that was instinct on Janine's part, delivering the needed alter and placing it? Traditionally, the *dragoma* always placed the altar.

Kiki pulled out a thick candle of bay leaves and cinnamon, a perfect summoning aroma, and she handed out the small pouches Gwen put together. Each contained a sample of brittle black tourmaline, smoky quartz, and jet, a petrified wood, to help guard against dark spirits and negative energy. Mixed with the minerals, Gwen had added anise and cloves to complete the protective sachets.

"Petrified wood and tourmaline would have some of Ian's elements in them," Janine whispered. "And so would the anise."

Kiki smiled at her. "Your science grew out of alchemy, which first grew out of pagan practices. Trial and error, it's how the ancient sisters did things. What is that really? Experimentation without the male ego. What Ian doesn't understand about his theory is, that it already exists, just not in a man's scientific terms. He likes to narrow it down to a few elements, but I wonder if he's missed something in the combination of things."

Kiki could see Janine become a little miffed about that. Good for her, smarting on Ian's behalf. A woman needed a man in the world, and a powerful witch needed a powerful man, and very powerful men had attempted to attach themselves to this girl, that devil in the prison and then her cousin. Surely, Gwen would agree that a powerful witch lurked in this friend of theirs.

Kiki passed the candle and matches to Gwen, but Gwen relayed them to Janine to place on the rock. *Let the* dragoma *build the altar.* Kiki retrieved the charm and gave it to Janine. They each tucked one of the sachets into their shirts, next to their hearts. Kiki waited for Gwen's signal. As the senior sister, it was Gwen who should dictate the evening's events.

"We should leave a place in our circle." Gwen nodded at the space closest to the pond, and they shifted to make room. "If Miranda Daily is a witch, she'll want to join our ring."

"If she isn't a witch?" Janine asked.

"Then, she'll do whatever it is that she wants, I suppose," Gwen said.

They giggled nervously on that for a moment. Gwen turned to Janine.

"Ian's mother was one of our spiritual teachers," Gwen told her. "A powerful speaker, a *dragoma* like no other. She spoke special spells and charms that only a *dragoma* would use. There exists a book, back home, which contain many of her writings and it was placed into my care. It's meant for our next coven *dragoma,* or for Ian's future daughter. Celeste believed they would be one and the same. I memorized many of the summoning charms in that grimoire, but I am nae speaker to spirits. The charms were brilliant successes for her, but not for me. Would you consider trying one?"

Janine nodded and looked down at her hands. "Of course, I'll try one. But will you tell me something first, Gwen? Did Ian's mother give you that book because she hoped," Janine hesitated. "This may be none of my business, but I'd like to know. Did she give you her book because she believed you would be the mother of Ian's daughter?"

Well, Kiki thought, *now here it comes*. She wondered when Janine would ask more about Gwen and Ian. Janine had seen how well they got on. They could not hide their deep bond, anyone could see it. Gwen gave Kiki a brief look before turning to Janine.

"Of course it's your business, lass," Gwen told her. "You know, the Triquetra encompass many meanings, Janine. In marriage, it means to love, honor, and protect. In our coven, it also symbolizes the perfect union of spheres, when head, heart, and passions are linked in a person, or linked each from you to your mate. It's a rare thing indeed, to find the lad whose Trio of Wells are linked each to your own. From the look of things, I'd say you found it with our Ian. That didn't happen for me. Dinna worry yourself about me, lassie, that's the way it is." Gwen nodded. "Even my beloved teacher knew it was never meant to be. My dalliance with Ian was just foolish child's play."

So then, that was how Gwen wanted to tell it. Janine looked to Kiki, for her take, and Kiki nodded in agreement, it was true enough.

"Is that what you have with Detective Anderson?" she asked Kiki.

"I'm not sure yet," Kiki confessed.

"So," Janine asked, "how did I get so confused with Rick? I feel so stupid, because to be honest, I fell completely head over heels in love with him. Sometimes, I can still feel it, and it scares me."

"No one taught you to be wary of a demon, Janine," Kiki told her. "I told you, he was a true devil. I could see it easily because I'm not ruled by my passions, my base, like most. I can see his aura and that he lacks essential parts to his aura, like his core. There isn't a core for the aether to latch onto in that one, and his soul is empty, vacant. Most people can't see these things."

"It's her curse, being a savant and all." Gwen grinned.

"It's my strength," Kiki countered. "It allows me to see and hear spirits. It allows me to see people clearly too. The colors of one's aura never lie, or the lack of part of an aura. It's the interpretation that can be tricky. I wanted to tell you, your aura has brightened considerably in recent days. Darkness isn't a true part of a person's essence. That muddied light is a response to something crushing it. It's very scary, that darkness, because it's not nice to see someone's soul being crushed."

"For most, it can be difficult to recognize a demon or a devil," Gwen told her. "Demons are drawn to certain women of the realm. They sense their strong core and seek to devour it, to fill their own empty void. It feels like love, because that's what they're taking. They use their intellect, charm, and good looks to weasel their way in. Most do this through the passion zone, because it's the easiest to penetrate and the easiest to confuse. Use care regarding people who seek you out, Janine, dinna allow your passions to drive your decisions. There's a huge difference between a Max Colliers and a Richard Wilkens, though they use similar manners. Max is only an ordinary rogue, one who resists developing his core, while Richard is a true devil, a person without a soul. If Miranda Daily was also a girl possessing strong spiritual energy, then that's the reason he latched onto her. She was tricked by the demon as well. The Comba charm points to her being from a witching family, and the nature runs deep, even if she dinna practice the arts herself."

Gwen signaled for Janine to light the candle, then Gwen and Kiki each took one of Janine's hands. Their free hand lay palm up, in offer for a fourth witch to enter the circle. Gwen explained that sisters in a circle could transfer their talents to each other, if they joined hands. So maybe, Kiki could transfer her sight to them and Janine could transfer her voice. But that takes practice too, so she shouldn't worry about sharing her talent right away.

They closed their eyes to take cleansing breaths. Gwen told her that the cleansing breaths were really a moment to pause in prayer and open their cores. Gwen would recite the summoning poem aloud and repeat it, over and over. Janine should join in when she felt ready. Kiki could also join, if she wished, but as Janine learned the words, both of them would go silent. They would let the *dragoma* call to the spirit alone, so the message would be clear.

"I'm a little nervous," Gwen admitted. "Putting the control to a novice, but you've participated with Kiki many times before, so we'll do it." Gwen instructed Janine, "When you recite the words to the spirit, remember to speak as if you're calling to someone you love. Reach into that core you found and speak from there. You cannot expect this spirit to respond if you are nae open hearted to her. Also, remember not to break our circle. Keep hold of our hands." Gwen began reciting the charm in a steady voice.

"Sister come, complete our ring, tis assist and ease we bring. Meet us now and reap your meed, a sister's oath we do concede, accept our vow to set ye free. So commanded, so mote it be."

Kiki remembered the words right away and joined in. They repeated it slowly for Janine.

"Sister come, complete our ring, tis assist and ease we bring. Meet us now and reap your meed, a sister's oath we do concede, accept our vow to set ye free. So commanded, so mote it be."

After Janine joined once, the air suddenly cooled, and Kiki's eyes flew open and met Gwen's wide blue gaze. The chilled air did not come with a breeze attached, and Kiki's pulse quickened. Spirits that brought the cold were usually unhappy ones. The candle flickered in a soft dance, and Kiki and Gwen both went silent as Janine repeated the words alone. Janine's voice took on a much surer tone than the one she used on their *Spectral Analysis* quests and sounded very American to Kiki's ears, not like Gwen's voice or that of her late Auntie Celeste.

"Sister come, complete our ring," Janine said loudly. *"It's assist and ease we bring. Meet us now, and reap your meed. A sister's oath we do concede. Accept our vow to set you free. So I command. So mote it be."* She repeated it confidently.

The night descended into blackness as the candle fluttered out. Only the stars above cast their meager light upon them. Kiki felt a sliver of burning cold move tangent to her empty hand. *Was it a cold finger touching her?* Kiki tried to turn her head, but couldn't. Her neck felt like a solid stiff pillar. She could not move at all, but she could sense another presence there, right next to her. She tried to remain calm by inhaling and exhaling slowly, but her body had become a frozen paralyzed prison with only her eyes as small windows. *Oh no, they should not have let a novice call on this one.* She felt more cold fingers moving. They were slowly adjusting and perfecting their grip, encircling her hand to grasp it. The cold seeped through her skin and crept deep into the tissue.

Across from her, Gwen's eyes were round circles in the dark, rimmed with her white sclera, her blue irises strained to the empty spot in the circle and her skin reddened. Kiki forced her own eyes to strain in that direction as well. She could just make out a shadowed form in the darkness, sitting quietly, hunched over. A slender woman, motionless, limp limbs, yet vibrating with intensity.

Straight hair hung past the specter's waist, skirting the ground. The dark night caused her hair to appear very black, and a few strands flowed in a breeze that wasn't there. Her icy hand gripped Kiki's, sealing them together like the cold metal of a vise. Cold continued to seep into Kiki's hand and inched toward her wrist. Her appendage felt like it was lodged in a frozen block of ice.

Kiki had never been in such a situation before, immobile and at the mercy of an angry spirit. She could not make a sound and tried to calm herself with gentle breaths, *never let a spirit feel your fear.* She was frightened and could feel her heart beating faster and faster, running out of her control. She could neither move, nor speak, to break the spell, and that unnerved her. On her other side, Janine's warm grip was a comfort and she hoped Janine would not let go. Janine's hand felt like life, while the other hand felt like death.

"Who are you?" Janine asked the question in a strong voice.

A soft raspy voice answered. "A sister."

The cold continued to creep up her arm, and Kiki was happy for the sachets Gwen insisted on making for their séance. Placed over her chest, the sachet would surely keep her heart warm and beating. The old sisters told tales such as this and they always came out okay. Janine asked another question.

"Did Richard Wilkens kill you?"

There was no answer, but Kiki watched from the corner of her eye, straining to see. The woman gave a slow meticulous nod. Her head drooped all the way down, chin to chest, then snapped back up rapidly. *Yikes!* The woman repositioned her head slightly toward Kiki. Did she hear Kiki's silent outburst?

Kiki noticed dark patches of abyss for eyes. She remembered Randy saying they were like kaleidoscopes of shadows in his dreams and Kiki could see what he meant. She reminded herself that this spirit wanted their help, she wasn't there to terrorize them. The cold grip tightened. *In response to her thoughts?* They tightened again. *Yes.*

"What is it we can do for you?" Janine's voice still came strong and steady.

"Find me." Her voice trickled out, then increased in volume. "Find me. FIND ME!" The voice increased in pitch, almost to a screeching, but also slowed down like a warped record. "Help me go where I belong. There is an empty place to be filled. Fill it!"

"Are you here? In this spot? Will we find you right here?" Janine asked quickly.

Kiki could detect a frightened pitch in Janine's voice, and her warm hand loosened. Kiki could feel her own panic. *No! Don't let go*, Kiki thought, but she had no voice to speak.

"Where are you?" Janine sounded desperate.

No, no, Janine, calm down. You must speak from the core here. This ghost will only answer if you speak from your core. Kiki wanted to advise her, but her lips were sealed.

"An empty place needs to be filled." Rasped into the air. "Fill it!"

"Tell us what happened to you," Janine demanded. "Where to find you."

Kiki felt the cold grip tighten again as a cackling laugh swirled in the air. She happened to glimpse Gwen and saw the blue rolling behind red lashed lids. If she passed out now, the ghost would leave as well, but Kiki had no voice or ability to move, no way to tell Janine to tighten her grip and pour her warmth into them, they needed her. Kiki felt completely helpless. The raspy voice whispered in such a way that it seemed like the words meandered about, passing into and out of her ears. Janine suddenly tightened her hold, and Kiki's own eyes rolled up into her head, where she entered the vision of death again.

She crept down a hall in her bare feet, careful not to make a sound. She left him in the bedroom sound asleep, breathing deeply, and his faint snoring followed down the hallway. She felt afraid to sneak away, even though she desperately wanted to leave. Old habits die hard. Where did he hide her shoes? He was always hiding her shoes. She worked her way to the front door, silently clutching the key that she took from his pocket. The key to the deadbolt. He hadn't used that key in ages before suddenly bringing it out again.

The house was a prison, locked down to keep her in her place. The thick double paned windows were sealed shut, unable to open. The deadbolts all required a key on each side of the door, and there were deadbolts on every door, even the inside doors, so he could control who entered and exited the house.

He revealed himself again, and she could no longer deny it. She'd hoped he might change, that she could change him, but not anymore. He didn't lift a hand during their disagreement, didn't say a harsh word when she confronted him. He just quietly locked her inside the house with a familiar steely expression in his grey eyes. That was all it took to silence her, and she felt the violence hovering just below the surface of his skin. What she once took for undying, dedicated, passionate love was always something else. Something just as intense. Something malevolent. An incubi, a demon. Something that followed her and enslaved her. Now she was terrified, and upset for being complicit and blind. Guilty. Weak. She would no longer be the his woman, she would no longer be his victim. She wondered what they had created together.

She tiptoed toward the door wearing sweat pants and a university sweatshirt. The key slipped easily into the deadbolt, and she turned the knob silently. Relief flooded her chest. She felt tears form behind her eyes. She would be free again, and maybe she could set everything right. She would run down Thatcher Street, and then down Chicago Avenue to the all night diner. She would call Mary at the University to fetch her. As she pulled the front door open, it made a sucking sound that echoed in her ears. Then, she felt the air stir. Someone was watching. She turned to look up the stairs.

He stood silently in the shadows, casually regarding her. In the next moment, he bound down the stairs vaulting over three steps at a time. She flung the door wildly, stubbing her toe in the process. But there was no time to acknowledge that shooting pain. Tears flooded her eyes, blurring her vision. She sprung into the night. She could feel his silent pursuit.

She sprinted onto the deserted street and turned to follow her planned route. But that plan was no good, she realized. He would tail her all the way to the diner and then he would drag her back before anyone was the wiser. If she ducked onto a porch, he would surely grab her before she could knock on a door or get anyone's attention. She needed to run somewhere she could hide, somewhere people didn't think he was so charming. She bee-lined across the street into Thatcher Woods. The trees would give her cover and she could dart around quickly, losing him in the brush. She could give him the slip with a little help from the trees.

The ground became rough with twigs and uneven little rocks as she zig zagged through the oaks. She moved toward the softer grass of the glen, toward the pond. The snapping branches from behind helped her ignore the piercing pokes of the weeds. She didn't bother to turn around to see if the gap between them was closing, that was always a surefire way to lose a race. She bent forward and sprinted faster, away from the sounds of him following. She could never pretend she didn't understand him now. Pretend she didn't realize she had been a prisoner all this time. His reaction to her fear would not be nice. She cracked the shell open on the polite world they created, and she gave away all her cards by running out that door. He knew she would never go back into the house again, not willingly.

Her feet naturally avoided the rough ground and sought out the soft grasses of the pond glen. The cushioned earth drew her bare feet further and further from the oaks, and she knew it was a mistake. As the tall grasses and cattails reached her shoulders, she hunched into the flapping blades hoping to hide. She should not have let her feet decide the direction. Every now and again, she felt a little slice as the thick grass cut her. Suddenly, the edge of the pond appeared and she stopped.

She tilted her head to listen. Nothing, just the buzz of insects and the croak of a frog. Did she lose him? She took slow deep breaths and carefully walked the edge of the water. She spied a few large logs on one end of the pond. A place to hide and wait for dawn. She strained to listen for his movements but felt plugged up with the sound of pulsing blood thumping in her head. She crept toward the logs and sunk between their protective cover. Her eyes darted in every direction until they were finally drawn to the glass surface of the pond.

The flat water reflected a perfect sky. Clouds shrouded most of the full moon, and the stars played peek-a-boo through the haze of the strato-layers. It was a breathtaking sight. Calm. Beautiful. Quiet. She did it, didn't she? She lost him. She would lay low for a few minutes to be sure. Perhaps she should wait until daylight to move. Early morning joggers and dog walkers loved Thatcher Woods. Another soul would make it safer. A movement in the water startled her. It was only a turtle swimming in the moonlight. She loved turtles, once had a stuffed turtle to cuddle in her sleep. She let out a very long, slow breath. Her breathing came quieter and softer. The drum of her pulse ebbed off and her vision widened. The beautiful night easily distracted her from her predicament. Was she really running from the man she loved and their spawn?

As if on cue, she suddenly felt his eyes on the back of her head.

"Did you think you got away?" he whispered. "The breeze carried your scent."

She twisted around and glimpsed his displeased grimace. The devil her grandmamma always warned her about.

How had he moved so quietly? His hand shot out and grabbed her by the neck, shockingly swift, choking her, but not completely. Under his strong fingers, her rare, silver, Saint Comba pendant necklace cut into her. His free hand reached out and tore the chain from her, rubbing her skin raw in a painful line. He flung the precious keepsake into the distant grass, a treasured item she never removed, not even to bathe. That pendant had always irked him. Would she ever be able to find it in those weeds? Forget everything else, she would never forgive him for throwing her charm away.

"Devil!" she gasped and glared at him. She began to fight.

He answered with a tightened squeeze on her windpipe, shutting off any further protest. He slapped her hands down easily with the muscular arms she once found so attractive. She realized his plan. She could see it in his eyes. He planned to leave that necklace in the tall grass, forgotten forever.

And her as well…

"Tell us where you are!" Janine's voice broke the spell of the vision. "Tell me now!"

The ghost cackled. Her voice became a soft lullaby.

"The turtle turns. The turtle turns and gently crawls into these arms."

The voice faded as she cackled into the night. Kiki felt the cold grip on her hand disintegrate. The spirit was departing, she could feel it. Her chest released a tight contraction and open up in relief. Kiki watched Gwen go limp.

"Wait," Janine called out. "Wait! I want to thank you. Thank you for saving me."

And in just the softest whisper of an echo, "Thank you for saving me."

And just like that, the paralysis was broken. Kiki's body slumped down. She felt exhausted, as if she had held the plank position in yoga for a very long time and sweat dripped down her brow. She swung her head around and saw nothing in the empty spot. She could have imagined it all. But that vivid death vision was too terrifying to be imagined. Across from her, Gwen also had slumped over, eyes closed. Had she seen it too? Janine had tears on her cheeks. They both scooted across the grass to check on Gwen. Gwen's ginger eyelashes fluttered and then she slowly straightened up flexing her hand. Kiki glance at her own hand and flipped on her electric torch. The ghost had bruised them both.

"Why didn't either of you say anything?" Janine asked, still panicked and upset, wiping the tears from her cheeks. "Didn't you see her? Hear her? Feel her? For crying out loud, you were each holding her hand!"

Kiki couldn't help smiling a bit. How ironic was this?

"I was a bit frozen," Kiki told her. "Completely paralyzed. I couldn't speak, but I heard it all and saw her from the corner of my eye. Did you see the death vision? It was very vivid and more complete than the one at the statue. Not as confusing. She was strangled."

"Aye." Gwen took in several deep breaths. "I could nae move a muscle as well. It was a brilliant summoning. Amazing and terrifying. I dinna see a vision of death, but something very different. Perhaps a future. A collection of women gathered hand in hand, joining in a circle one after the other. You did very well, Janine. That one was definitely the spirit of a witch. I'm just happy you held onto my hand. I felt the cold might have gone to my heart."

Janine admitted, "I almost let go. Your hands were so limp and very hot, but I didn't see a death, or a circle of women, I only saw the ghost. You both saw a vision? Something more than the ghost?"

Kiki and Gwen both nodded. They would go over it together, but somewhere else. Kiki was quite certain it had been Richard Wilkens in her vision, though he did appear different in the darkness. The moonlight cast harsh shadows across his face, warping it slightly and deepening his faults. Their altar sat on the very spot of the spirit's death. How did Janine manage that trick?

"'Twas exactly like the tales the old ladies tell." Gwen stared over to Kiki. "Unbelievable. Now you know what it's like when she really tries." Gwen gazed proudly at Janine.

"I thought it was me, all this time. Gaining a talent," Kiki said.

"We still don't know where she's buried." Janine's brow furrowed. "Where her bones are. The detective said the cadaver dogs sniffed all around this park and found nothing. I don't know how we're supposed to find her. Do you think she's right here, in this spot?" Janine moved the rock alter. "What if we dig right here?"

"She told you where she is." Gwen shifted and sat up straighter. "She said the turtle turns and turns, then crawls into her arms. That's where she is."

They each looked at one another, then slowly stood and searched around, but only blackness and the sound of frogs could be detected. Kiki steadied herself and noticed Janine was a little wobbly as well. Then, Janine snatched up a torch and snapped it on. She pointed it in every direction, illuminating the vegetation around them. All they saw were trees, trees, and more trees and a small meadow. Janine stared into the distance.

"These trails all have names. I can't remember if one is named after a turtle? Didn't Randy find the medallion in that direction, somewhere. Maybe that's where she is. The trails wind around, they turn. Maybe that's what it means," Janine said. "Kiki, do you think you would feel her presence if we got closer? We can follow that map to where he found the charm and feel out the area."

Gwen added her light to their sphere, but she pointed it in the opposite direction. "Before we go hiking into the brush, take a gander at this."

Their eyes followed the beam of Gwen's torch over the black flat surface of the lake. A multitude of stars reflected off the water as wavering points of light, because the surface wasn't serene. Something made gentle ripples. Janine added her own light to increase the luminosity along the surface of the water and Kiki suddenly saw it, something sticking it's head up in the center of the pond. It turned. It turned again. Then, it disappeared below the surface. *Diving down to crawl into somebody's arms, perhaps?*

They stumbled into a pub to search out a stiff drink and meet with Detective Anderson. For the early hours, a fair number of burly men hunched against the bar watching late night television. As usual, Gwen and her flaming hair attracted attention. She volunteered to fetch the drinks and sauntered over to flirt with the barkeep. Kiki wonder if Janine realized what Gwen was up to, feeling out a little male attention to replenish her energy. When Gwen returned to the table, they each shared their visions.

Detective Anderson appeared sometime later, tired, but happy to see them. He waved away the offered whisky and asked the bartender to send unsweetened black coffee instead. He gave Kiki a nice smile and she felt very pleased to see his large brown eyes. Janine told the detective where she believed someone might find Miranda Daily. He didn't balk at all that they summoned a spirit to reveal the location. He only nodded and smiled as his pink aura sent out a blanket of understanding. He could probably have the pond searched without too much difficulty. He had a buddy who liked to dive in murky water. Kiki didn't know if he said that to make Janine feel better, or to show support for their mystic endeavors, but she didn't care. She was just happy to see him.

"Bob," Kiki interrupted the conversation. "Would you consider attending a pagan ceremony with me, over the solstice, in Scotland. Perhaps, you could take a vacation. I'd enjoy showing you around the island."

His face opened in surprise for the first time. "That sounds interesting," he beamed.

"Be careful of my invitation," Kiki warned. "I might ask you to participate in a ceremony, or ritual, of sorts. Nothing illegal, but you would need to keep an open mind."

"Let's make a deal," Detective Anderson said. "No matter what, I will definitely attend any festival you have in mind, and, if my diver finds Miranda Daily on the bottom of that pond, it'd make a firm believer out of me, and I'll participate in any ritual or ceremony you want." He smiled, "No questions asked."

Well, Kiki thought, *perhaps she would now embark on the next chapter of her trilogy, from maiden to mother, she certainly waited long enough.* That last summoning put a fright into her and she needed to get on with it. She had no doubts that they would find someone in that pond, and that she was a strangulation victim. If it wasn't Miranda Daily, she would be very surprised. After chatting a while longer, they bid farewell to the detective, Janine was due to the airport for her flight back to California.

True to his word, the detective asked a friend to explore the bottom of Thatcher Pond and scour for debris. The bones were easily found, still pretty much intact. Eight kettlebell weights marked the location and were used keep the body from floating. The divers noted that the turtles were using the bones for their nightly rest, almost as if they were lying in the arms of the skeleton to sleep. They couldn't positively identify the skeleton, that would take a few weeks, but a rough examination of the neck area showed the hyoid bone had been snapped, a sign of strangulation. It was enough to delay the parole board's decision.

Carlos Fuente is the Sun.

Epilogue *Janine*

*S*oon after Janine returned to Davis, Kiki messaged that she met with Miranda's family and returned the charm necklace. Kiki hoped to buy the charm, but they refused to part with it. It originally belonged to Miranda's grandmother and had been passed down for generations. No current witches, Kiki said, but she could feel a wee bit of the ancient blood in the air. The family planned to send someone to Turkey, to return the charm to Miranda and personally check on her. They were not willing to accept that the skeleton in the pond was their girl.

On a personal note, Detective Anderson attended the solstice festival. Kiki felt hope that he might even agree to participate in her upcoming awakening under the Harvest Moon, but she was still apprehensive about fully describing it to him.

Then came a text from Carlos, full of photos of his twins playing soccer and an obviously pregnant Maria. They waited to announce it. Carlos already started at a local news station as one of the weather men. He finally got his suit and tie. And, did she know, all weather-men were expected to be funny and crack random jokes? So, it was his dream job.

Ian never messaged her, he always called, but she let every call go to voicemail and listened to them late at night. She was afraid she would break down, or beg him to come to her, that she would hinder him from getting on with his life. He was always sweet, missed her, and looked forward to when they would be in the same place again. He hoped that she was sleeping well. She always sent a text back to him, well thought out, upbeat, and noncommittal.

Then, Kiki sent a startling message in August. She was moving back to Scotland. The show shifted with a serious turn, focusing on the science and gadgets more, and they planned to film from a research laboratory point of view. Ian finagled the changes after the audio tape debacle involving Max

Colliers, and Max agreed to everything. Kiki would not be needed until the culmination feature, when they went ghost hunting for the season finale.

Perhaps the most frequent messenger was Gwen. She sent short, one sentence messages that Janine suspected was the beginning of her education into the coven. A salt lamp could help tamp down her passion urges. August first was the Lugnasad, a good day to make an oath of change, and embarrassing visualization exercises that would help her quickly find her core, or base, or head.

At the end of the summer session, she found herself with two weeks to spare before the start of the fall term. She debated a visit to her sister, to work through their issues. If she flew all the way to Texas, perhaps she could also visit Ian, but she wasn't sure where he was, or if she should interfere with his life. His messages indicated that they were going to film and work out of a research lab somewhere, but where? Perhaps, they were expanding the workshop in that Texas building. After the fallout with Max Colliers, she didn't think they'd want to work that closely anymore. But men were different than women. They let go of their hard feelings much more easily. She decided to ruminate the pros and cons of going to Texas on her morning run, but when she opened the door, she found a surprise waiting on her door step.

Ian McNally stood just outside, looking unsure if he was going to knock on her door or not. Luggage rested at his feet, and he gave her a sheepish smile. Janine jumped out and hugged him on the doorstep, then invited him in, because he felt stiff with her public display of affection.

"Are you here for a visit?" she gushed. "I was just thinking of visiting you."

Something felt wrong because he was blinking, a sure sign that he was uncomfortable. He glanced around her small living room.

"I'm not here to visit," he said.

"Oh, are you passing through?" She glanced at his bags. Where was he going? "Is everything all right?"

"Everything is fine," he said stiffly, his demeanor scared her. Did he stop by to tell her in person something she might find hard to bear? Something he could have done on the phone if she would have answered his phone calls? He must have seen her worried expression, because his blinking slowed down and he gave her a reassuring smile. "I'm not visiting, I'm moving here. I'm going to teach two classes at your university as a guest lecturer this fall, and, we are going to be filming out of a lab on the Berkeley campus, so I'll commute back and forth."

She pulled his crossed arms apart and slipped into them and hugged him firmly. He still felt hesitant and stiff? Was he unsure about dropping in without notice, that she'd feel her privacy was invaded?

"It's okay with me," she assured him, "if you're thinking of staying here for when you need to be in Davis. I've been aloof, I'm sorry. Maybe you're afraid you're overstepping your bounds? Don't think that, Ian. I want to be with you. I would love it. It's exactly what I want. Don't you think it's perfect?"

"Aye, lass, I do." He finally smiled at her. "I do believe it's perfect. Here we are, in the same place, right?" But his eyes were still blinking and speeding up slightly. "We should come to an agreement first, don't you think? I want to have an agreement." That sounded very familiar. He had asked for an agreement once before. *To move slow in their relationship and take things rationally.* "You allow me stay here on the days I need to be in Davis, and I can… I can… Perhaps, I can get you a discount on your tuition, if you agree to be…"

She started giggling. What was he talking about? "Ian, I want you to stay with me, and you know I don't need a discount on my tuition. How would you even manage that anyway? Do you want me to be a research assistant? I'm too busy, and how would that look? Living with your research assistant? But, we can go as slow as you like. It's what you asked for at the beginning, and you were right, as usual. I have an extra room that I use as an office. It won't be any trouble to set it up properly and make it a private bedroom for you."

"That's not what I meant." He pulled something out of his pocket. Was it a ring box? What was he doing? What was this? She suddenly felt out of breath, weak in the knees. Ian helped her sit on the sofa and settled next to her. He held her hand in his. His blinking stopped and he stared into her eyes with that steady melting gaze of his, bright eyed and sure of what he meant to say. He was definitely holding a ring in his hand. It had a central diamond linking two Celtic Triquetra knots.

"Ian, what are you doing?" she whispered.

"There's no moving slow with you, lass, so I'm asking you for an oath." Ian took her hands. "And soon. Maybe on the equinox, that's a good day for joining two halves, right? Will you marry me? I want no misunderstanding about what we are to each other. I know that I want you, and I want you to wear my ring. I've been thinking on this for a very long time. We belong together, don't you think? A perfect fit. You advised me to do what I needed to be happy, and said you'd support whatever I needed to do. This is it." He used the smoky blue eyes that always melted her into a wobbly mess, and in his voice, there was just a touch of a dare. "So then lass, what will it be?"

What will it be indeed?

End of Part Two

Part Three

Spectral Redemption

The Comba Coven Curse

Star Tarot SR
Story Arc
the problem 1
past influence 4
Future 6
IV
The Emperor
X
The Wheel of Fortune
VIII
Justice
III
The Empress
XIII
the outcome 7
Death
VII
The Chariot
pos+ influence 2
XX
Judgement
neg-Influence 3
present 5

Prologue

Skye *Celeste*

On a clear moonlit night, a girl with the right attitude might spy a faery, or even a spirit, while peering through the window of a hagstone.

Celeste and Trinity crept out of the old cottage right under Auntie Meg's sleeping nose, to give it a go. The gibbous moon cast plenty of light and they hoped to glimpse something in the glen before morning. Every summer at Auntie Meg's, their mother took them for at least one midnight hike. *We can spy on those that live in the glen*, she'd wink, but this particular night their mum wasn't there. She was summoned away for a grown up endeavor on one of the other isles.

Celeste, three years older than Trinity, recently turned twelve. Both sisters had long dark hair, ivory skin, and light colored eyes, Trinity green and Celeste blue. Celeste felt plenty old enough to lead her sister into the Faerie Glen. It lay only a scant walk past the far end of the stone wall. They needed to sneak into the glen, if they wanted a tale to tell their mum. She'd delight in hearing about their risky adventure when she fetched them later that week.

"Will Dad let us stay the rest of the summer with Auntie Meg?" Trinity asked.

"Who knows what's in his head." Celeste used a hushed voice. "He doesn't approve of Auntie Meg and the talking of faeries and the like. I heard him call Auntie a silly old bat, and look at how he begged Mum to the lower isle instead. Have you got your hagstone?"

Trinity nodded and held the stone between two fingers. She peeked at her sister through the jagged hole in its center. They followed a border of rocks that snaked gently up the green mound. Most of the land had gone wild since Auntie Meg's companion passed, only the garden near the house stayed presentable. Meg couldn't be bothered with a real crop, she only cared about her herbs. Celeste often wondered about Meg's age. She looked well over a hundred years to young eyes and couldn't be Mum's true sister. Maybe she was a great auntie or other distant relative. Somehow, their true relationship to Auntie Meg was never quite clear to Celeste.

On that dark night, the breeze felt cool and Celeste worried that they left their coats by the entry door. They followed the moss covered wall as it slowly descended into the ground and came upon a large rock preceding the glen. Earlier that day, they left an offering in the nook of that giving rock. They slipped past it and climbed to a higher vantage point.

Never let the wee folk see you, their mother warned, *for they are mischievous and should never be trusted.*

"Stones," Celeste whispered. They each peered through a hagstone.

The waning moon illuminated the entire glen, but not bright enough to wash out the other lights flickering in the grass. Small, luminous, blue-green specks blinked on the far side of the clearing. Will-o-the-Wisps, some called those lights, but Trinity and Celeste knew them as faeries. That's what their mother and auntie insisted. Celeste heard her dad poo-poo that notion, saying they must have seen glow worms or fireflies, but their Mum had admonished him sharply and he never said it again.

Never insult the fae, she warned, *their feelings are sensitive.*

On those former visits, their mother always advised them to stay a distance away and zip their lips near certain areas in the glen. If faeries caught a whiff of a body, they'd flit off for cover or do something to make you pay. So, Celeste and Trinity remained silent as they watched the blue pinpoints dart about, hoping one might pass close enough to see.

Celeste recited a faerie charm in her head, *Come, little faeries, no cause for alarm. We vow to protect you and keep you from harm.*

They observed the flickering lights for nearly an hour before trying to inch closer to the glen floor, but they were too loud. The last of the lights faded into darkness. They waited, but the fair folk must have gone to slumber. Celeste noticed the moon was well past its apex and in a descent. They needed to head back to the cottage. No telling if the old gal would wake in the night. Celeste grasped Trinity's hand and realized the night had gotten very cold, a faint fog hung in the air.

"Come now, Trin," Celeste whispered. "Let's hurry, it's getting cold."

"Maybe we'll glimpse the ghost of the upper wall," Trinity whispered. "Auntie said the old hag can be felt on a cold full moon with the faeries. The moon is mostly full."

Well, that would be something, wouldn't it? Not many have seen the ghost of the wall. Their mum always recited a charm to keep that ghost away, because that one carried the burden of a curse.

Spirits hide, we dare not see, as I command, so mote it be.

No need to scare her wee daughters with such a serious spirit, she always said. Celeste thought about that. At eight and twelve they weren't exactly babes anymore. Pretty soon, Celeste would have her first moon cycle of womanhood and be free to begin a serious study of the ancient feminine teachings.

She might try a little summoning charm to practice. She'd done it before with a bit of success. She had seen ghosts many times. Meg claimed the old spirit belonged to an ancient witch, an old hag who would only manifest for a special charm. Wouldn't that be a tale! Perhaps she could woo the old ghost to appear with a rhyme, so she spun up a clever charm in her head. The air cooled considerably, and the fog grew thicker.

"Say this with me," Celeste whispered to her sister. "*Come, wise soul, to us appear. Show yourself as we come near. Draw us in to make us three, so I command, so mote it be.*"

As Celeste and Trinity strolled along the stone wall, they recited the short summons multiple times. Celeste enjoyed dreaming up the rhymes. She wrote the better ones in her diary, hoping to perfect them later, convinced each would work with a wee bit of fine tuning. Her mum once believed in such things as strongly as Celeste, but like most adults, she developed other concerns to occupy her mind. That was the main reason they always begged to visit Auntie Meg. Meg remained one old lady who took the old beliefs very seriously. As a lifelong practitioner of the old ways, she taught many girls the ancient secrets.

"Look up there, is that a person?" Celeste stopped reciting the poem and pointed into the distant fog where something gathered at the bend in the wall. It sat hunched under the old tree. Through the wet air, Celeste could make out a distinct shadow. Auntie Meg did not bend in a similar way, so clearly this was somebody else. *Could it be the spirit of the wall?*

"Hello?" Celeste called out tentatively. She slowed their pace.

Don't show a spirit fear, her mum always warned, *a spirit will freeze you solid if you show fear.*

Celeste drew a long breath, then let it slowly escape. Perhaps that shadow only resembled a sitting woman, she told herself. As they drew closer and the fog cleared, the woman appeared quite solid, not ghostly at all.

"Hello," Celeste said again. "Are you looking for Auntie Meg?"

The woman's head swiveled, but her body did not sway an inch. Her face met theirs squarely, yet there was something odd about the position of her head and body. It was an unnatural angle to accommodate their face to face situation. This was no regular old woman, Celeste realized, and stopped her sister from moving closer. She calmed herself with another slow breath.

"Who do you see?" Trinity asked, raising the hagstone to her eye, then froze and gasped. Celeste realized that Trinity could not see the old hag, not without her stone.

Celeste turned back to the woman and found that she wasn't old at all. From the distance, she appeared ancient, perhaps due to her hunched posture, but on closer inspection, she looked much younger than their mother. Her hair stuck out in a wild mess, but her luminous skin stretched smooth as porcelain over delicate bones and was creamy white in the moonlight, beautiful. Her eyes hid under that mess of hair, and her hair magically straightened and glossed over the more Celeste peered at it.

Her bulk, Celeste realized, was not due to a thick body, but to the many layers of clothing she wore. The woman might actually be slender. A long thin neck like hers would not be attached to a heavy woman. An elegant hand extended out of a wide sleeve to move flowing wisps from her eyes. Celeste became instantly enchanted. Those eyes glowed like twinkling stars, emerald green, bright and glittering. Plump, pink lips opened over delicate white teeth. She was a very lovely young woman. Then, she arched up, sitting straighter, and Celeste could see her graceful physique.

"Is she the spirit of the wall?" Trinity whispered while peering through her hagstone.

"I don't know." Celeste let out a nervous giggle. Then, she nodded to the woman. "I'm Celeste, and this is my sister, Trinity. We're staying with Auntie Meg. Are you a ghost, or are you one of the sisters? Are you here to see Auntie Meg?"

The woman finally turned her body to align with her head and that suddenly seemed much better, a relief. The woman gave the slightest nod and closed her generous lips. Trinity's hand tightened. Celeste realized her sister was very frightened.

"Shall we go wake Meg?" Celeste asked. "Auntie is sleeping near the hearth, inside." Would Auntie Meg wish to be woken for a guest or a ghost?

"Dinna wake the auld witch." Her voice sounded like a soothing melody. "Lest ye risk the wrath of Caer Ibormieth."

"Why are you here?" Celeste asked weakly.

"A *dragoma* called," her green eyes peered intensely and untamed hair flowed in a luxurious wave in the air. "One to wrest a curse from the demon's grasp."

Celeste felt a cold tickle run up her back.

"A curse, which bids *one each for redemption*, over and over." Her melodic voice warped midsentence into a scratchy hiss, "Lest it be wrested away, it shall play out forever, over and over, into eternity."

The woman turned slowly and became tall and straight, beautifully framed by the star filled sky. How did she become so tall? A lone owl hooted in the far distance and the woman began to chuckle softly. Celeste felt Trinity's hand shake with fright. The tallness of the woman disturbed Celeste, her dimensions seemed out of bounds, too tall, too thin, too beautiful. Then, her melody emerged in discordant tones as her glowing green eyes held fast to the girls.

"Beware, wee lassie, the demon preys on one such as you."

An undertone of woe whistled through the air and Celeste realized that it came from her sister. Trinity stood wide-eyed with terror. Then, the light in Trinity's eyes fluctuated and she knew it meant the woman was moving. Celeste glanced back and nearly jumped from her own skin.

The woman shrank before their eyes. Her tall frame inched shorter and shorter, and her round shoulders began to hunch forward into the posture of a crone. That black silky hair withered into a charred grey wiry mess, and her once luminous skin dulled and wrinkled while her plump lips contracted into a parched tightness. Worst of all, her eyes lost the green glow of life and became dark orbs of blackness.

All the while, her mouth remained open in a small O as she seemed to shrivel and burn with no flame. As the woman dried and charred before their eyes, her arms reached out. Did she wish to embrace them? Celeste pulled her sister further away, but the woman's long arms kept stretching toward them, closer and closer.

Celeste could barely breathe, but managed to squeak out, "Leave us!"

Then came the thump of footsteps, fast and loud on the crunchy ground. As the mystery woman deteriorated into fine particles, Auntie Meg stepped into her spot. Sleepy eyes blinked at them. Meg, in her night dress, looked just out of a deep dream. Her soft pudges were a sight for scared eyes.

There was no longer a trace of the other woman. Meg stepped forward to catch up a teetering Trinity. As Meg held Trinity, her eyes sought out Celeste, searching for an answer.

"To whom were you speaking?" Meg asked, but anyone could see that she did not need telling.

Meg nodded. They remained a moment longer before heading for the farm house. Meg insisted they tell her everything and then add it to the big book locked away in her cabinet, the coven *Book of Happenings*, where everything worth noting was written.

Chapter 1

Rio Linda *Janine*

A yellow bulldozer creeped over the hill that separated Gram's house from the river. Gram, Martha Williams Stinger, still retained hints of auburn interwoven in her silver hair. Janine adored her grandmother and ached seeing her in despair as her prized backyard was destroyed.

After a year in court battling over mineral rights, the far mound was ordered to be torn up for the removal of a rocky deposit below the top soil. Giant boulders embedded with copious amounts of rare earth minerals lay hidden on her property, and their value proved far too great to win the fight against their removal. Plus, Gram would receive a nice six figure settlement for her portion of the boulders, a quarter of their worth.

Janine watched from the back glass patio as her grandmother *tsked* each time the earth mover jolted. She didn't want to admit to Gram that the disruption of the backyard was a relief. The changing scenery made it easier to face the house again. That dirt mover erased every place Janine had seen the River Ghost.

"Are they going to cut into the green?" Janine watched the machine roll over the edge of Gram's manicured lawn. It erased the sharp edge the landscapers often labored over. The machine smudged out that border alarmingly easy.

"They are cleared to dig all the way to the chicken coop." Gram stood with her arms akimbo and shook her head. "But that TJ Grounder from the county assured me they'd stay in the rough, up on that mound. He also promised to shut down at a reasonable hour each day, but look at the time. He also said they'd cart in a truckload of dirt to reform my mound, but who knows if that'll happen?"

Gram turned her back on the destruction and pulled Janine into the kitchen.

"Come on, girl, tell me what you have planned over a nice cup of tea. Does that look like Camilla hiding in the bush over there? It is!" Camilla was a large Americana hen that dropped blue-green eggs on occasion. She was one of the older hens in Gram's free range flock.

Fresh biscuits cooled on the stovetop, all set to accent their planned picnic dinner of fried chicken. Gram's roommate and house keeper, Misty, made a batch of homemade biscuits every weekday. In the early mornings, she delivered a dozen biscuits and fresh eggs to the small care home down the street. In all the years she lived with Gram, Misty never missed a day with that delivery.

Not until the bulldozer. With the mineral removal activity, Gram said the free range hens have been spooked and flew the coop. Usually, the hens dropped so many eggs they donated dozens to the farmers market in the summer, but for the past couple of days, only a few eggs waited in the rack, and that morning, there hadn't been any.

"Those poor girls are probably terrified of the ruckus. They've all run for their lives. We'll be lucky if we ever see them again. A stressed out hen can have a heart attack you know."

"Oh, Gram, they're probably just hiding in the brush waiting for that machine to go away. They'll be back."

"I hope so." Gram pointed toward the window. "But did you see any of the girls out there, beside Camilla? Think about that. When have you ever seen that hill without a large gaggle walking about? I don't know why men like TJ Grounder think a few dollars is worth spoiling the view, destroying the environment, and obliterating the wildlife."

A few dollars? More like six hundred thousand dollars, and disrupting a gaggle of free range hens was hardly obliterating the wildlife, nor was turning over half an acre of land destroying the environment, but they certainly spoiled Gram's beautiful view with their digging. Janine knew that Gram loved her home and looked forward to spending her twilight years in the peaceful routines of her small town community.

Ever since the rare earth mineral discovery, the entire town had turned topsy-turvy with activity. *Not just rare elements, but maybe even ghostly energy too. Some believed the boulders bore an element mixture perfect for absorbing the energy from a soul.* Janine wonder if any spiritual energy hid in the rocky samples under Gram's mound.

"I'm sorry, Gram," Janine said softly.

Gram patted her hand, "Not your fault, girl, now drink your tea." Gram pushed a small cup across the table. "Me and the gals have taken up tealeaf reading. We became very interested after Kiki Mellow gave us each a personal reading that time."

Kiki Mellow happened to be a self-proclaimed witch and the popular star of a ghost hunting television show called *Spectral Analysis*. Up until several months ago, Janine had been a tech specialist and cast member on the same show. About a year before Janine decided to leave *Spectral Analysis*, they brought the ghost hunting crew to Gram's small town and filmed a very successful documentary on a spirit that haunted the river. Gram and Kiki developed a fast friendship during the documentary's research phase and they still kept in touch. Those two were birds of a feather.

"Kiki gave us a special contact to learn tea reading. Have you met Annelise Batten? Kiki insists that Annelise is the one to study the leaves with. Annie also specializes in the short tarot deck, but that's too much work, She requires students to make their own cards if they're serious about lessons. Can you imagine?" Gram exclaimed. "As you know, Leone is very in touch with technology and has attended hundreds of zoom sessions with Annelise. They drink tea, with others, in an online tea party, then screen share and read the leaves as a group. Leone says people from all over the world join the tea parties. It's very international. Apparently, an interesting older gentleman from France joins once a month. Leone believes he flirts with her, can you imagine that? I want to sit in too, if I can figure out how to use that computer. Of course, Leone shares her lessons with the rest of us. She's our local expert now." Gram tapped the teacup with a spoon. "Drink up, girl, I want to have a try without Leone looking over my shoulder."

Janine bit back the acid that welled up in her mouth. Did Gram forget Kiki's tealeaf reading the first morning *Spectral Analysis* came into her home?

Great fortune is coming your way, but the return may not be worth the investment.

Did Gram even consider that Kiki's reading may have been for both of them? Janine had sipped some of the tea that morning. Did Kiki's tea reading predict everything that happened? It certainly seemed so. Becoming friends with Kiki Mellow had proven life altering for Janine. In a couple of short years, Kiki managed to upset her whole view of the universe.

"Let's put the backyard out of our minds." Gram patted her hand. "Let's focus on what we want to know. Annelise urges a calm atmosphere while sipping our tea, with minds actively on the concerns you want addressed. So, sip your tea slowly and thoughtfully, girl." Gram demonstrated by sipping her own tea.

They clinked cups and enjoyed a biscuit with cream, yum, but the tea, yuck! Gram insisted on her bitter homemade raspberry tea. Janine would have no problem sipping that liquid slowly. She added a generous helping of honey to sweeten it up.

Gram rolled her eyes, then donned her kitchen spectacles. They had been resting on top of the Sacramento Bee. Janine noticed the crossword was barely started. Gram usually completed it before breakfast. A telling sign that Gram's mind wandered, most likely to that machine in the backyard.

"How about I get another look at your ring? I want to see the design up close again." Gram reached out to take her hand.

Janine had gotten engaged barely eight weeks ago. Her fiancé happened to be the other star of the *Spectral Analysis* show, Doctor Ian McNally. He was a professor of paranormal electromagnetic energy and very handsome. He currently ran a research lab out of Berkeley while also teaching a class at Davis, where Janine happened to be finishing her degree. Three episodes into the new season, just after she left the show, it morphed from the filming of ghost encounters to filming research and development. The next few episodes focused on the creation of sensors and devices designed to measure energy associated with ghostly encounters.

Ian and his crew were currently enroute to the haunted orchard in Rio Linda. They planned a field test of prototype instruments and to film clips for an upcoming episode.

"Oh my," Gram exclaimed. "That design is the exact little triangle symbol! I thought so."

"Triquetra," Janine told her. On either side of the beautiful one carat diamond, the white gold metal twisted into delicate Celtic knots.

They were a symbol of Ian's genetic roots. The ring had passed down from his maternal grandmother. When Janine described the ring to Kiki over the phone, she knew it well. Kiki and Ian were cousins, so, the grandmother belonged to Kiki too. Janine wondered if Kiki desired the ring for herself. If she did, she gave no hint of it.

"It's a family heirloom from his grandmother."

Gram nodded thoughtfully. "Have you gotten Ian a ring yet? Perhaps, he would like a family heirloom from you. I need to show you something." Gram sprang from her chair and dashed out of the room, her voice carried back, "You'll never believe what I've found!"

Janine could hear footsteps fly through the living room, followed by a distressed shout, then the steps moved into the study. Janine heard a distinct "Aha!" before the footsteps returned to the kitchen. Gram's bright eyes blazed with excitement.

"You may just flip your lid over this." She waved her finger in the air.

Gram settled behind her tea and took a careful sip. On the table, she placed a simple wooden box, old and weathered, the size of a very small shoebox with an ornate metal clasp system and keyhole. Gram took care not to allow the clasp to seal the box when she set it down. Her beaming expression made Janine laugh.

"So, what do we have here, Gram? What's in the box? Where did it come from?"

"You'll never believe it," Gram let out a long breath. "Since all that poking around the attic last year, I've been clearing things out, sorting through the mess. After Caroline Govant left her own mess, I especially wanted to straighten things out in case something happened to me."

Caroline Govant had lived on the other side of Marysville Boulevard and owned the haunted forty acre almond orchard made famous in the *Spectral Analysis* ghost documentary. Janine felt terrible about the last time she spoke with Caroline. She practically accused Caroline of heading up a cult group that lured kids into the river. Janine will never forget Caroline's dark beady eyes and how she chuckled after that accusation.

Caroline died less than a week later. The sole beneficiary of her property went to a man named Henry Webber, the other person Janine accused of being in the cult group. The more time that passed between her initial accusations and the present, the more idiotic they seemed. Now, she regretted her rash words.

"Nothing is going to happen to you, Gram," Janine said softy.

"I know that, girl." Gram laughed at her. "I just don't want to leave a mess and wanted to find more historic clues. Henry Webber claims there are boxes of things at Caroline Govant's place. Things she wanted destroyed. She was holding out on you guys. He says there are loads of ghost diaries."

Gram pulled the wooden box closer and put it between them.

"This one was hiding in my attic, locked and tucked away in a corner, and for over a week Misty and I tried to open it with a screw driver, and failed. Misty suggested taking a hammer to it, but I couldn't destroy such a lovely old box. Look at that delicate catch."

"It's unlocked now." Janine touched the open clasp.

"It is," Gram told her. "Day before yesterday, when you and Ian asked to stay here after his thing in the orchard, I came downstairs and the box was open. Just popped open like that. Misty says she didn't do it."

Gram's wide eyes suggested a mysterious, unnatural event must have opened the box.

"Gram," Janine chuckled under her breath. "You said you've been jiggling that lock for days? And even took a tool to it?"

Gram nodded. "And nothing. Still locked tight."

"Yes, but all that activity surely loosened it up a bit." Janine noticed the clasp naturally swung down with gravity. "Most likely, you loosened it enough for it to finally to pop on its own. I doubt a ghost came wandering in and opened it for you."

Gram wrinkled her nose in disappointment with that logical explanation.

"Don't be so sure," Gram told her. "Not till you see what's inside. Just so you know, this box came off the wagon train, I'm certain of it by the few things in here. They're labeled with the names Finn and Irene, and there's a perfect ring for Ian, a real family heirloom."

The wagon train! Rio Linda was initially populated with people who survived a horrific wagon expedition over the Sierra Nevada range. Those brave ancestors built part of Gram's house and founded the town and orchard. Gram discovered an old Bible from the original group on their initial attic search. Now, Gram stumbled upon a box with some of their long lost treasure.

"Why would anything of value still be in the box?" Janine asked. "Why wouldn't someone remove it long ago? It doesn't make any sense."

"It's bits and pieces from our lost Lumens," Gram told her. "Leftovers from the family that didn't make it over the pass. Not much, just a couple of trinkets. Perhaps someone planned to deliver them to Christopher Williams someday, when they revisited his history, and then hid it all away when they couldn't tell him that he was adopted. Or, maybe they forgot these things. Or, maybe he didn't care for them. Go on, open it up."

Janine opened the box.

Several pieces of folded yellow paper tumbled out, along with an old pocket watch. Gram impatiently fished one clump to unfold. The paper was stiff and thick and possibly homemade. A slender silver ring spun out on the table and Janine could see the name *Irene* faintly scratched on the paper. Gram chose another clump and opened it. A larger ring, with engraved Celtic knots, rolled onto the table. It was a thick man's ring with a repeating pattern of triquetra encircling the band. Gram retrieved the ring and displayed it on the tip of her pointer finger.

"Here it is." Her eyes glowed. "The designs match your ring perfectly."

She placed the band next to Janine's engagement ring to compare the Celtic knots. They could be forged from the same artistic jeweler.

"It's not silver, doesn't tarnish, and not soft. Maybe some sort of white gold alloy. Can you believe this luck?"

Janine took the ring and turned it in her hand. It really was a perfect match. Just the other day, she visited a jeweler inquiring about finding a ring with that exact knot pattern. She approved of the weight of it in her hand. She also picked up the smaller woman's ring. Not triquetra, but the twists in the pattern complimented the Celtic bends in the male ring, a matched set.

"You might use that one as well, it could be your wedding band." Gram exclaimed. "You take the rings and use them if you like, no problem if you don't. There are other nice things in here that I can give to Juju, she won't mind."

"I like them." Janine smiled. Of course, she wanted to let Ian look at them as well.

Janine reached to the other folded papers and Gram helped her open them. They each contained something special, a hair comb, a brooch, and a silver charm on a slender chain. That charm caused Janine's heart to skip a beat. When it plopped onto the table, it landed face down, but she felt certain she had seen it before. A chill ran down her spine as Gram reached over to right it.

"This one's interesting." Gram caressed the necklace. "Again, it's not silver, but something else, strong stuff, maybe the same metal as those rings. But it's a funny name for a saint, don't you think? Could it be a joke?" Gram glanced up and stopped chatting. "Jaja, what's wrong? Are you okay?"

Good question. Janine could not believe her eyes at what popped out of that banged up wooden box from Gram's attic. *A Saint Comba pendant!* She gasped for oxygen just looking at it.

S, A, I, N, T, C, O, M, B, and A were stamped along the bottom, and in the center was the impression of a woman with long flowing hair. One of her wrists was shackled to a wall with an animal at her feet. It was an exact copy of the ornament a haunted college guy delivered during her last *Spectral Analysis* shoot. A very disturbed young man who popped up out of nowhere and insisted a *ghost* demanded he deliver the charm to her. A scary ghost that seemed connected to Janine through a psychopath that once tried to kill her.

But Kiki had taken the pendant and delivered it to the rightful owners, didn't she? It was a thousand of miles away. How did it end up in Gram's kitchen in California?

"Jaja?" Gram grabbed her arm. "What is it?" She sounded worried.

"Where did you get this charm? Did someone send it to you?"

"It came out of the box," Gram told her. "From the attic. It belonged to Irene Lumen, see the paper?" Gram pushed a slip of paper to her. *Irene* was scribbled in flowing script near the torn edge. "It's been in the attic for over a century."

Janine needed to think. *If Irene Lumen owned a Saint Comba charm, did that make her a witch?* Saint Comba was considered the witch's saint.

"Gram, I saw a charm exactly like this earlier this year."

Janine pulled out her phone and dialed Kiki's number, then remembered Kiki was in Scotland and the time difference was huge. She hung up immediately.

"Crap! She's probably sleeping."

She peered at Gram, then snapped a picture of the charm and sent it in a text to Kiki, typing out where they found it.

"It was an exact copy with the same exact saint. It belonged to a very scary ghost, one that helped me in the woods a long time ago. Remember, I told—"

Her phone chimed loudly, Kiki Mellow, and she answered quickly.

"Kiki! The charm, it's here. I can't explain it, but my gram has it in her kitchen, or one like it. The Saint Comba charm."

"How did she get it? Your message says she found it in a box? Did the box come in the mail? Was it addressed to you? To her?" Kiki asked. "That doesn't make any sense at all. How would the Daily's know where to send it?"

"No, no, it was in her attic. It came out of a box from the attic," Janine told her. "An old box from the wagon train."

That inspired a long silence, then Kiki's calm voice came back.

"Well then, I've got your photo side by side with the one I sent to… *that* detective. It's definitely from the same source, an exact twin, but not *the* exact charm. Look at the top left. The other charm didn't have that wee mark. This is quite a find, Janine. I'm very interested in this charm. It's very rare and I have to say, I'm dumbfounded. Two Comba charms dropped right into your hands. This is no coincidence. What does it mean? I can hardly wait to see you in November and want to fly out right now! But I have the Samhain with the sisters, and my thing that I really must do, very soon. Maybe I'll come early, right after my obligations. Can I call you tomorrow about this? I'm actually on a date right now and I'm hiding in the loo to take this call." She laughed. "You never ever call anybody and you scared me ringing so late. I almost thought something happened because of Ian's talk with his father. I about had a heart attack. Can I ring you tomorrow at a better time, or a little later? I admit it, I'm pished right now. Can you tell?"

"Sure, sure," Janine said.

There was a lot of mystery packed into Kiki's short outburst. Too many key words opening up trap doors in her mind. Ian had a *talk* with his father? When? Implying the Comba charms were *deliberately* dropped into *Janine's* hands? Kiki *hiding* in a loo on a date? Referring to Bob Anderson as *that detective*? Detective Anderson was supposed to be in Scotland, with Kiki, at the moment.

"Kiki, are you on a date with Detective Anderson?"

There was a very pregnant pause before Kiki spoke.

"Well, that particular detective got a bit skittish on me." There was a hint of sharpness in her tone. "I can't stand a skittish man, Janine, it's not attractive. Let's chat tomorrow at a more reasonable hour."

Janine pressed her lips together. She had been hoping that Kiki and Bob Anderson would work out.

She noticed Gram waiting patiently, fingering the Saint Comba charm. Her eyebrows rose at Janine. Her doe shaped brown eyes were unwavering, but sweet. Janine's own eyes were very similar.

"Kiki Mellow? She knows of a charm like this?" Gram inquired. "And what's this about the woods? Do you mean *the woods*, your woods, Thatcher Woods? And a ghost? You're not telling me something, Jaja."

Janine took a deep breath and another sip of her bitter raspberry tea. Several years ago, when she attended the University of Chicago, Janine had gotten involved with a very charming man that turned out to be a psychopath, Richard Wilkens. Quite unexpectedly, their relationship turned violent and Janine found herself running for her life in a wooded area of Chicago. She endured several knife wounds before her *boyfriend* suddenly stopped stabbing her. Janine swore that a woman appeared in the woods and scared Rick away, but no witness ever came forward. There was no trace of anyone being there except Janine and her attacker.

Then came the Comba charm, just half a year ago, and the ghost she summoned with Kiki Mellow and Gwen Murphy. That ghost led them to a set of bones hidden in the woods. Almost everyone, even Detective Anderson, believed the skeleton belonged to a prior victim of Richard Wilkens. And now, a charm matching the first one had suddenly appeared. She recapped the entire story for Gram.

"Gram, you realize that before we opened this box, everything in my world was settling down and flowing calmly for the first time in… in forever. And now, I don't know what is going on."

Gram let out a nervous laugh and patted Janine's hand reassuringly.

"That's the way of life, girl, there are no guarantees. Now give me your cup to read. I want to see what's in there. Then, we need to start frying the chicken."

"Oh, no." Janine quickly took her cup to the sink, ignoring Gram's pout. There was no way she'd have her tealeaves read, not even by a novice just fooling around, not after what had tumbled out of Gram's box a moment ago.

Chapter 2

The Orchard *Janine*

They packed up a basket of homemade fried chicken, corn on the cob, potato salad, and Misty's famous biscuits with a plan to drive into the orchard and meet Doctor McNally's crew. The picnic dinner would give the crew a break between equipment set up and a long night of field tests. Afterward, Ian's crew would stay at Gram's large house and get a good night's sleep before heading back to the bay area.

As Janine steered the old truck down Marysville Boulevard, she noticed changes to the road. Four pole lamps now lined the orchard and a gravel parking area had been constructed.

Gram said a local group of spiritualists pitched in for the parking lot. They began holding séances in the old orchard by appointment. During the summer, time slots were filled every hour of the night. Henry Webber hated that arrangement, Gram laughed, but he was stuck with it. Caroline Govant signed a five year contract with the spiritual guides before she died. The lot appeared empty when they drove past, but Gram predicted that there'd be a few groups arriving later in the night.

"I hope that doesn't spoil Ian's testing," Janine said.

The *Spectral Analysis* van sat along the edge of the trees in the dirt. The back van doors were wide open, and they could see the computers and monitors. Janine stopped the truck a few feet from the back bumper. She stomped on the parking brake just as Doctor McNally stepped into view.

The sight of him put an automatic smile on her face. She was definitely addicted to Ian McNally. His bright blue eyes fixed on her and he said one last thing before slipping his phone into his pocket. He hurried to help her from the truck and pulled her into a close embrace.

"You brought my favorite truck," he whispered with an enthusiastic kiss.

Then, he smiled at Gram and paused to hug her too. Gram appeared pleased as punch with Ian McNally. The next moment, three chatting men and a young woman strolled out of the orchard.

"We've got the cream of the crop from the Berkeley lab here," Ian told Janine and Gram. "Oliver, Chet, Emma, and of course, you know Ben."

Janine gave Ben a brief hug. Ben joined *Spectral Analysis* before she left the show and they had worked on two episodes together. He was a computer expert with a bachelor's of science degree, but was not yet of legal drinking age. He wore his standard *Star Wars* T-shirt, wire rimmed glasses, and jeans. He gave her a big toothy grin. Oliver appeared to be an Asian version of Ben, and Emma was the female version with a pixie haircut. Both were extremely thin, compact, and wore comic-hero shirts. Chet, on the other hand, was boldly bald and stocky. He wore an ensemble of Cal workout clothes and looked a couple of days away from his last shave.

Janine and Gram gave each crew member an enthusiastic greeting before ferrying out the late dinner. They arranged a picnic blanket under the flood lights near the van and everyone gathered around.

"So, the big controversy right now is, who will wear the *mellow-skin*," Ben told them. "Emma doesn't think it should be a girl and Chet believes his arm hair will get in the way, so that leaves Ollie."

Bald Chet made up for his lack of head hair with curly masses on his forelimbs. Ollie did not hide his perturbed expression. He flipped his long black bangs and flashed a frown at Emma.

"I don't know why it shouldn't be a girl. Why not, are we protecting you? What happened to equal rights?" He glanced around. "Girls are more sensitive anyway, right? Maybe the skin will work better on Emma. We might get a better test. Who gets cold first in the lab? Emma does. She's already halfway more sensitive than the rest of us."

"Boom! That's exactly why I shouldn't test the skin," Emma countered. "I might not even need it. I bet I'm already sensitive enough to pick up paranormal energy, and we'd get a false positive. And you're not protecting me, I don't need protecting. I'm not the one scared of ghosts." She passed the chicken basket to Oliver. "Do you want a fork for that potato salad?"

"Oh yeah, thanks," Oliver nodded.

The doctor seemed to ignore the discussion as it vacillated between Emma and Oliver, but Janine knew he listened intently. He refrained from adding his opinion because he wanted them to work out the best solution for testing their own gadgets. Finally, they decided that Oliver would be the *mellow-skin* guinea pig.

The Wheel of Fortune

"I'm just a little old lady," Gram smiled when the discussion came to a resolution. "I have no idea what *mellow-skin* is. I confess that I'm very confused."

The research and development crew erupted into giggles.

"No one knows what *mellow-skin* is." Emma grinned at her. "It's a brand new thing. It might not even be a thing, really. We're just experimenting with an idea."

"Yes, it's something new that we threw together this last month," Oliver told them. "A skin-like sensing device for ghosts. It's one of the main senses people use to detect ghosts, and we brainstormed how to boost sensitivity of spiritual energy."

"The doctor challenged us to review video and audio tapes of people encountering spirits." Emma sat up and pulled her knees up to hug to her chest. Her tone became more commanding than in the previous discussion. "Most mediums first sense a presence through their skin, a tingling. Kiki Mellow was our prime study subject, hence the nickname *mellow-skin*. She does a spectacular job of describing what she feels each step of the way. Well, you already know that." Emma looked a little bashful at schooling Janine on Kiki.

"But what is it?" Gram asked again.

"A thin layer of film, like plastic wrap." Chet laughed.

Oliver ignored him. "It's more like nylon. It goes over your own skin and amplifies signals to your receptors, skin receptors. Kind of like an arm sleeve. Not the temperature or actual touch receptors, but the type that detect vibrations at different frequencies. The *mellow-skin* will zone in on both types."

"Are you talking about Meissner or Pacinian corpuscles?" Janine asked.

"Yes!" Emma exclaimed. "Boom! Exactly. The *mellow-skin* amplifies in the 20-60 hertz range for the Meisser, and 90-420 hertz for the Pacinian, we went a little outside of the box just in case. The skin will take signals from the environment, normal signals that any person would feel, and amplifies them in the film before it reaches real skin. It's basically an amplifier, like wearing earbuds for skin."

The *Spectral Analysis* crew got into many discussions about the ability to see, hear, and detect ghosts. They discussed theories on why Kiki Mellow easily detected spirits when other people didn't. They hypothesized that it had to do with early development of sensory receptors. Plain and simple, people needed to develop ghost sensing talents at an early age, sometimes while still in the womb. The senses of smell and hearing began in the fetal stage, why not ghost detection too? And if the development of those senses failed to occur early enough, then those receptors might not develop at all. Many experiments provided evidence supporting that theory, at least in regards to the other senses. Consider the Harvard Pirate Cat experiment and the visual cortex, Emma challenged.

Janine recalled the cat experiment as Emma relayed it to Gram. In the 1960s, researchers Hubel and Wiesel attested that if a kitten was deprived of normal visual stimuli early in life, their ability to see would be irreversibly altered. They took a number of newborn kittens and sutured one of their eyes shut. They kept the kitten's eye sewn shut for 6 months, until they reached adulthood. At that time, the sutured eyelid was opened to finally allow visual stimuli. They found that the newly opened, perfectly normal eyes failed to send messages to their feline visual cortexes. Unfortunately for those cats, they were blind for life in the eye that had been sewn shut. Further, the experimenters conducted a similar process on an adult cat. One eye was sutured shut for a complete year. Because the adult cat had already developed normal vision, the experiment did not have a similar result. Vision in the eye that had been shut for the adult cat was just as good after the experiment as before. Hubel and Wiesel concluded that early visual stimuli proved critical for the development of vision in cats.

"How terrible for those kittens!" Gram exclaimed, distressed.

"Boom. Right, I know," Emma agreed.

Ian's crew felt certain that early paranormal encounters provided critical stimuli for the development of extrasensory abilities. Kiki experienced ghosts in her youth and likely developed the critical receptors to see, hear, and speak to them. Those Meissner and Pacinian corpuscles, sensitive skin receptors, also developed very early in life, in the very first months. Kiki certainly had many experiences, almost from birth, with paranormal situations. That could be a big factor in why Kiki Mellow was so tuned in to the spiritual world compared to most people.

"We also set up incongruent and antipode motion detectors. They detect odd motions that defy physical logic. In other words, they detect forces that don't seem to be there or don't have a detectable origin," Ben told them. "We also perfected the magnetic antennae for the big EMF box. There are now six spools that will swivel until they lock onto a signal, and then they move with the signal. Not as heavy as the spool of copper that shocked you in that tunnel."

"Oh my gosh, that was such a tight episode!" Oliver gushed at Janine and then at the doctor. "Did you guys ever find out how you took on so much charge? I watched the clip over and over and couldn't see anything supplying that electric charge."

In an episode from the second season of *Spectral Analysis*, Janine suffered a static electric shock on the magnitude of a weak bolt of lightning. It was a much talked about scene. A myriad of theories floated around the blogs speculating on how it happened and where the energy might have originated. Janine shook her head at Oliver.

"Okay, I don't want to pry, but will you settle something here for me? My friends and I have a bet going, and the doctor won't settle it."

Emma's girlish tone and bashful smile gave her age away. She was either Ben's age or less, maybe nineteen Janine guessed.

"When you fainted into the doctor's arms in that tunnel and opened your eyes, my friend Sandy swears that's when you two fell in love. I think she's wrong, I think it was earlier than that."

"At the graveyard in Savannah!" Gram exclaimed, just as excited as Emma. "In season one! All the gals think that's when it happened. Remember the look they exchanged?"

"Yes!" Emma and Gram high fived. "Savannah. Boom! *The look*. I never believed the Kiki spin."

"Oh yes, *boom* on that too." Gram high fived Emma again. "Me and my gals never believed the Kiki-doctor nonsense, either."

Janine couldn't help chuckling at them. She glanced at Ian and caught his eyes on her, smiling, ever the even-tempered professor. When *had* it all started? To Janine, it felt like she had always been in love with Ian, but it took time to trust herself with it. She couldn't really be upset with Emma and her questions, because it was certainly something the tabloids focused on.

When Ian showed up at UC Davis with Janine there as a student, it took no time at all for entertainment reporters to spot her engagement ring and figure out they shared a small apartment. That fact, added with Kiki Mellow being indisposed in Scotland, got the gossip machine rolling on why *Spectral Analysis* suddenly changed focus. When the stories spun out of control about a love triangle breaking up the *Spectral Analysis* team, the doctor agreed to an interview to clear everything up. To the great shock of their viewing audience, the doctor finally revealed that Kiki Mellow was his cousin. Though viewers fondly imagined a romance between those two, people realized the possibility never existed and it became clear why the doctor was never distressed when Kiki went out with famous athletes "behind his back." Instead of being a clueless nerd, he was a care less cousin. Many fans of the show were very relieved for him.

"Gram and I are right, right? It all started in the Savannah graveyard," Emma pressed her. She also peered at the doctor. "Come on, old man, tell us. Tunnel or Savannah?"

"Wrong and wrong." Ian grinned at Emma. He stood up and helped Janine with a hand. "It was love at first sight, the first moment I laid eyes on her. So, be careful who you look at, young lady." He pulled Janine toward the truck. "And you lot need to start tuning up and getting ready." He led her to the truck's tail gate for a little privacy. "Thanks for bringing the picnic. It was a very nice break. Sure you don't want to stay and watch the action?"

"Maybe I'll drop Gram off, help her clean up and then head back. I'll bring Gram's big coffee dispenser. I'm curious about the new gadgets." Janine chuckled. "*Mellow-skin?* Really?"

Ian nodded. "You have to admit, it's innovative. Emma and Oliver came up with that one. These kids are really imaginative. We've got ultralow and ultrahigh band audio and video, and Ben didn't mention it, but he rigged an audio receiver to automatically shift subsonic patterns into the sonic range. There's a three second delay, but it's very close to real time, so it'll be interesting. Maybe we can have an actual conversation with a spirit."

Then he told her about how they designed the thin film for the *mellow-skin*, but she got distracted watching his neck move as he spoke. He recently shaved off his thick beard, and although she had adored it, she was happy to see the lines of his jaw again. She loved how he kept his sideburns just a tad too long. But his mouth stopped moving and she realized that he stopped talking.

"Sorry, I got a little distracted."

Ian leaned in and gave her a nice kiss. "I like it when you get distracted that way."

"Speaking of distractions, did you know there might be séance seekers in the orchard tonight? Gram says they're a regular thing now."

Ian nodded. "We're kind of counting on it. I'm told they've had lots of success with the Mary ghost out here."

"They've actually had success, how? I thought the river stones held the spiritual energy from those ghosts, and the stones have been obliterated," Janine said. "And the dictum. Wasn't the dictum met? Why would the Mary ghost hang around if her purpose had been met?"

Ian shook his head. "Maybe it's an echo. Or, those boulders did not hold the energy of Mary. Perhaps her essence is in the trees, or in that little tombstone. One thing is certain, people are still reporting consistent encounters in this orchard. You remember Angie Minnihan, the redhead from Kiki's séance? Well, she's one of the local mediums. She insists there is still a very strong presence haunting the area. We're expecting her to bring two groups later tonight."

"Angie Minnihan?" Janine recalled Angie.

Angie had been very eager to participate in the *Spectral Analysis* research and production. She consented to an interview, the séance, and she even played a part in the wagon train reenactment skit at the river. She played her own direct ancestor, Ingrid Stauch, the mother of the girl who became the river ghost.

The metal charm from Gram's wooden box popped into her head. The Saint Comba charm belonged to Irene Lumen, that's what the paper scratched with Irene's name implied. In the original diary of the wagon train, it mentioned that Irene Lumen and Ingrid Stauch were related. Janine was certain she remembered that connection correctly. If Irene had been a witch, it's likely that her cousin Ingrid had also been a witch. Either way, the charm suggests there must have been a pagan in their lineage.

"What is it?" Ian noticed her unease.

"Nothing, I'm just pondering something Gram found in her attic," she said. "Old jewelry, possibly from the wagon train. There were some interesting pieces in the box. I may have found the perfect ring for you, but you should have a look at it and tell me what you think."

"You found a wedding band for me?" His eyes brightened and he kissed her deeply. She felt flooded with warmth at his spontaneous burst of emotion. "I can't wait to see it." He kissed her again.

Ian had wanted to marry right away. When he showed up on her doorstep a few weeks before the start of the fall term, he urged her to elope that very day. But Janine couldn't just marry without telling her family, and then her sister and niece vehemently insisted on being present for the vows. So, instead of an elopement, they agreed to a small ceremony at the

Thanksgiving break, hopefully in Gram's back yard if it wasn't still torn up. Her sister Juliana already planned to visit Gram on that holiday and it fell well after Kiki's important pagan events Scotland.

Ian was still being quite attentive with his kisses, and they didn't notice someone had walked up until a deliberate sound interrupted them.

"Ahem."

Chet stood a few feet away holding the blanket and large picnic basket. He gave them an amused pressed-lip smile before shyly looking away. Janine could hear Gram chatting as she got closer. Janine and Ian both jumped off the tail gate so Chet could load up the picnic supplies. Gram came up behind him and added the small cooler.

"I'm going to have a small sticky note on each door with your names on them," Gram said. "And I'll put a big sign on the bathroom door as well. That door looks just like all the others and there's no way to know until you find it for the first time."

"Thank you, ma'am. It was very nice meeting you, Gram. And you too, Mrs. McNally… Miss Stinger… Miss… Janine," Chet stammered.

"You should just call me Janine," she told him.

Chet nodded shyly, then skittered off. He seemed a tad timid for a large muscle-bound man. His bulk probably made him appear older than his years, she concluded. Ian did mention that Ben was the only graduate student in the bunch. Then, Ian helped her close the tail gate and remained by the side of the road, watching them drive off.

Janine returned with a large dispenser filled with coffee and a platter of fresh baked cookies. Gram insisted on whipping out the cookies before heading to bed. She predicted the doctor's researchers would need a little sugar on their late night coffee break.

As she passed the new gravel parking area, Janine spotted a car with people sitting inside. Were they coming or going? Janine continued up the road and parked behind the van again. She spotted Ian standing with his arms crossed facing the orchard. She stepped on the parking break and dimmed the headlights. Chet appeared and waved. He trotted over to help her out of the truck and held the door open for her.

"Thank you." She passed him the large tray of cookies. Chet smiled big.

"I was hoping," he scanned the cookies. "Gram looks like the kind of grandma that always comes through."

Janine laughed, he certainly hit the nail on the head with that remark. Ian strolled over and Janine passed him the large coffee dispenser. She followed them around to the lit area and the table someone set up near the van. She could see the shadows of Emma and Oliver in the trees growing larger and more defined as they came into the light.

"Just in time," Ian kissed her. "We're taking a little break in the action right now. Angie's got a second set of ghost seekers arriving. I need to warn you," he pulled her to the side, "Someone mentioned that you might be back and Angie became very excited. I think she's going to ask if you want to join their small group. She goes by Mistress Mini, by the way."

Janine's encounter with the ghost in the orchard had been a huge highlight in the documentary film of the Rio Linda area. Angie would certainly ask Janine to at least take photos with her guests, it could only help her séance business. But it was just the sort of attention that turned Janine off about the television show, the celebrity. Janine did not enjoy being on camera, or the notoriety that came with it. Sure enough, the small group from the gravel parking area headed right toward them. Janine noticed Emma and Oliver eyeing her.

"How's the testing so far?" Janine asked them.

"We've got nothing, nothing, and nothing." Emma grumbled. She moved to the table to grab a couple of cookies.

Janine moved closer to Oliver to inspect the sleeve on his arm. It looked soft and resembled sheer tights. She could see very thin wires snaking through the seams and noticed very small dots scattered everywhere.

"It feels constantly creepy," Oliver confessed. "It's like a million worms are sliding around my arm. I'm just now getting used to it enough to ignore it."

Emma delivered a cookie to Oliver. Apparently, they had bad luck finding paranormal activity and were disappointed. Angie Minnihan's first group had consisted of two boisterous couples that laughed through their entire hour in the orchard. Even though the séance members claimed to "feel a presence" and "hear faint voices," the *Spectral Analysis* gadgets didn't agree. Angie Minnihan admitted that even though her participants were happy, it was a failed outing. The tipsy California tourists basically spooked themselves with their active imaginations. Angie declared that the night might not be ripe for the orchard ghost to appear.

"Mistress Minni says the ghost only appears if descendants of the wagon train are near. She was pretty excited to hear that you might be back tonight. She felt certain the ghost would appear with the two of you here, even though there's no moon." Emma peeked hopefully at Janine. "But the doctor said you might not be into that."

The new moon affects the tides as vigorously as a full moon. It's no different for the aether of spiritual energy, Gwen once told her.

Angie Minnihan entered the halo of flood lights with a trio of middle aged women. The women each toted a large glass of wine and sipped while chatting and giggling. Angie, clad in a hooded velvet cape, carried a soft mushy bag of items. Janine shook hands with each of the ladies while Doctor McNally greeted them enthusiastically. He asked if they had any objections to having their excursion filmed, and they didn't. When he told them some of the footage might be used on an upcoming show, the women became very excited. He needed them to sign off on an agreement and they were very happy to comply.

Emma and Oliver wore skeptical expressions, probably wondering what a ghostly spirit might possibly have to say to those wine drinking women. As Ian obtained their signatures, Janine allowed Angie to lure her from the small crowd. Before Angie could say a thing, Janine pointed to her velvet bag.

"What do you have in there? Anything useful? Do you have jet or black tourmaline?"

"Yes," Angie said, suddenly alert. "I also have a rose candle."

"Do you have a stone for everyone? One for each of those ladies to hold? And something for the doctor's students?" Janine asked.

"I have five tourmaline stones, and I also have a big bag of bay leaves," Angie said.

Kiki Mellow claimed to be a witch, and all her friends claimed to be witches. Not the worship the devil, cast evil spells, and ride on broomsticks variety. Her coven of friends studied from an ancient book of pagan practices passed down from mother to daughter for generations.

The study and knowledge began before monotheism and then incorporated itself into the folds of society as the world changed into the current male dominated system. Saint Comba had been a witch as well. A witch that met and accepted Jesus as the savior of men, because men needed saving. The world would cease to exist without both the masculine and feminine aspects mixing together, and together they formed the aether of the cosmos and the Trio of Wells.

Janine ruminated on those ideas, because one of Kiki's coven friends, Gwen Murphy, began feeding the information to her little by little over the past months. Both Kiki and Gwen claimed Janine was a gifted speaker to the spirits and might even be able to command them, and Janine felt herself beginning to agree with them. So many unexplainable events contributed to her paradigm shift regarding the paranormal, especially the encounter with the ghost in the Chicago woods. She called on that ghost more than once, and that ghost had saved her life, she was sure of it. That ghost sent her a Comba charm, exactly like the one in Grams wooden box, and in some opaque way, Janine felt that she was being drawn into action for some important event.

A vital lesson Janine gathered after summoning the woods ghost was; that a spirit could be dangerous and unpredictable, like a wild animal. Both Kiki and Gwen had been vulnerable when the woods ghost appeared, so, most of Gwen's lessons revolved around minimizing the danger.

Black tourmaline proved to be an essential mineral for protection. No one knew why it worked, but like gravity, it just did. Gwen's lessons increased Janine's curiosity, and she constantly wondered if she could really do it: summon a ghost at will, whenever she wanted. She'd been itching to try again, since the encounter in Thatcher Woods, but Janine would need someone to see the ghost, a receiver to verify it. Perhaps Mistress Mini was a talented receiver.

"Caroline Govant always insisted that Mary is a kind spirit," Angie said softly.

Janine nodded. "I know, but there's nothing wrong with being a little careful."

"Does this mean you'll participate in my group?" Angie asked.

Janine nodded.

Angie was elated.

The séance participates were excited.

The doctor's research crew became hopeful.

Only Doctor McNally appeared a little apprehensive.

Mistress Mini instructed each of the research crew to place a bay leaf into their shirts, above their hearts, and gave each of her participants a sample of black tourmaline to clutch in their left hands. The research crew laughed about the bay leaves, but placed them as directed before disappearing into the orchard.

The gaggle of séance women stood at the edge of the tree line emptying a fresh bottle of wine into their glasses. Ian watched them, then strolled up next to her.

"Are you sure about this?" he asked. "We're going to be filming and may use some of the clips on the show. You don't have to do this for me, you know, you can run home and warm up the bed. I'm perfectly happy with that, even prefer imagining you there, rather than in those trees. You weren't too fond of the Mary spirit, as I recall."

"I've seen scarier," Janine said.

She told him bits and pieces of the Thatcher Woods séance, but not everything. He overheard Kiki and Gwen refer to Janine as a *dragoma*, a speaker to the spirits, but didn't know how much stock Ian put in their witching beliefs. He seemed to accept most of them, but not all of them.

"Don't you want your students to get something to record? Apparently, I'm the person to call if you want a ghost to appear, just ask Kiki and Gwen."

He kissed her, then strapped a small earpiece over her right ear. He adjusted the microphone so it wouldn't bother her. "Thank you. But at least wear one of these, and I'll come running at your slightest word. I'm going to have you on hot mic. Is there anyone you want to hear?"

"Oliver with the skin," she said.

He nodded. "Good luck, and don't faint."

Janine followed Mistress Mini and her three séance participants into the orchard. Ian lent her a flashlight, but she kept it turned off. The electric lantern Angie carried illuminated the ground plenty for their small group and Janine didn't want to spoil the ambience of Angie's activity. Although her earbud was turned down quite low, she could hear the research crew's excited babble. Most likely, the EMF box picked up some vibes. Janine grinned at their excitement. They would learn soon enough that heavy footsteps could set off a bleep or two on that box, and those drinking women were stepping very heavily. She decided to dream up an original rhyme for the ghost of Mary Miller. What type of charm would woo that spirit out on a dark night?

Angie escorted them to a spot cleared of almond husks and fallen debris. A flat-topped stone messy with frozen wax dribbles lay in the center. The large shadows moving in the trees must belong to Ian's gang, Janine noted.

She could easily pick out Chet, but Emma and Oliver were harder to distinguish until they moved. Emma walked with a bounce in her step while Oliver glided from place to place like a shadowy ninja.

Janine found her spot near the stone, sat down, and nodded at Angie to go ahead and do her thing. Angie positioned a large three-tapered candle on the flat top rock. There were rose petals of red and white mixed into the wax.

"I am going to light this slender candle and pass it to each of you," Angie informed her giggly ladies. "Remember to inhale deep breaths to clear your heads, calm yourselves, then light one of the wicks."

She took her own cleansing breaths before passing the slender taper to her left. The first woman took obvious deep breaths before setting her wick aflame. She passed the taper on and the other two mimicked her. Angie's ladies were very tipsy, Janine noticed. When Janine accepted the taper, she blew it out and set it down. Then, Angie began to sing in a soft sweet voice. Janine could not understand any of the words, but the soft tune succeeded in quieting the giggling women. They listened silently as Angie sang her eerie song, mesmerized.

"I think I'm starting to feel something brewing," one whispered huskily after Angie quieted. The others agreed, and they all proceeded to giggle again.

"Let us concentrate." Angie used an ominous voice, low and halting. "Mary, Mary of the orchard, we desire your presence. Come to us and show us your essence. We call on you to visit and reveal yourself. We come as friends and desire an audience. Come now, spirit of the orchard, come out, come out, and quench our curiosity. As I command it, so shall it be." Angie peered at Janine. "Would you also address the spirit?"

Should she? Could she? Janine drew in a deep breath and let it go slowly. Why not try? Try it all by herself without Kiki or Gwen around. Did she need them to do it? Maybe yes, maybe no. Was Angie a receiver?

"May I suggest holding the gemstones between your palms like this." Janine clasped her hands together.

Gwen advised that a good way to keep a spirit from invading your core was to place your hands together in a prayer or clasping position in front of your chest. *Best done with a bit of jet, very dark amethyst, or black tourmaline between the palms. Some sisters use a Christian rosary made with those very stones.*

"Keep hold of them like that." Janine turned to Angie. "I have a little charm we can recite. It's one that Kiki Mellow would approve of."

That wasn't entirely a lie, Kiki would likely approve of any charm Janine might dream up. She actually encouraged Janine to practice developing them. Bringing up Kiki's name had the desired effect, Angie and her participants were very eager to try anything Kiki Mellow would approve of. Janine waited for them to calm down and then recited her charm made up for Mary.

"To one that spread a dictums dread, to us appear, and come you near. Meet us under this almond tree. So I command, so mote it be."

The temperature instantly dropped and the three women went stone silent. Chet's voice filtered faintly into her receiver, calling out the falling numbers on his thermal-panger. Emma and Oliver were also talking, noting swings and changes in the gadgets they carried, but Janine tuned out Ian's college students to focus around the circle. She repeated the charm.

"To one that spread a dictums dread, to us appear, and come you near. Meet us under this almond tree. So I command, so mote it be."

The facial expressions in the circle went from giddy, to confused, to slightly alarmed. The temperature drop was certainly noticeable without need of any thermal gage. A familiar charged sensation began to develop and the hairs on her arms stood on end. Angie's eyes darted around expectantly, then flew to the rising smoke from the rose candle. It swirled and collected into an unusual wispy cloud above the rock alter. It became thicker and thicker as the temperature dropped faster and faster.

Oliver, in her earbud, complained about the *mellow-skin* and Emma's dim voice noticed something on one of her cameras.

"Ian, Emma," Janine whispered into the microphone. "Is Emma getting something in the middle of the circle? Above the candle?"

"Aye. A bit of light, like last time." Ian's voice filtered over the airwaves right into her ear, soothing her. "Do you see something?"

"It's a form," Janine whispered. Then, she spoke to the spirit, *"Yes, yes, Mary. Come you near and meet us here. Meet us under this almond tree, so I command, so mote it be."*

The smoky cloud morphed and grew thicker and denser by the second. It began to resemble the body of a young girl. Janine watched arms and legs stretch out of the central mass as the ghost took shape. More smoky darkness swirled around, and a head formed. Everything but the eyes filled in on that familiar face. Then, her clothes took on a dingy, murky color.

Is that what happened the last time, when her eyes had been closed?

Angie's middle lady dropped her stone and the sound of the impact echoed to the tree tops. The ghostly girl twirled around and the woman let out a whimper. The woman's eyes grew into wide circles as she cringed from the specter.

"Pick it up," Janine gently urged. "Pick up your stone."

But the lady was frozen with fear and didn't seem able to move. All three of the séance guests seemed frozen in place. Even Angie appeared frightened as she stared toward the nearly solid smoky girl in their circle. Janine watched the spirit move a fraction closer to the woman who dropped her stone.

"*No!*" Janine said firmly. "*Stay away from her.*"

The ghost spun round to glare at Janine. Her sockets had filled in with eyes. It was the familiar sight of Mary Miller. Her dark hair hung over her right shoulder in a single braid. Her eyes were black, and her lips and skin were red.

For a moment, she was a pleasant young child standing in the orchard, grinning, then quite suddenly, her face became a clear grimace of anger. Janine could make out a bit of Caroline Govant in that face. Her heart raced, pounding out of control, and the knavish girl let out a laugh that sounded like Caroline's when Janine had accused her of leading a cult. Janine studied plenty of photos of Caroline as a young girl, and this ghost smiled in the same manner.

Then, the ghostly girl moved out of the circle, toward the trees, her motion was both agitated and quick. Her voice carried back toward the circle, a lullaby, in direct discordance with her choppy dysfunctional movements.

Heed this, her voice wavered similar to guitar strings out of tune. *One each for redemption.*

Then, the ghostly voice was replaced by a human yelp. It was Oliver. He screeched into the cold dark night. Janine could hear Emma's rapid voice wondering what was going on, what was happening to him. Oliver's soft wail echoed painfully.

"My arm, the skin!" he moaned. "Something's grabbing my arm, I think."

Janine quickly stood and peered into the trees, focusing on the area she last noted Oliver and Emma. She couldn't see a thing. Then, she remembered the flashlight and scooped it up. It had three beams, low red, regular dim, and high beam white. She flipped on the high beam white as Angie and the drunk women moved behind her. Janine scanned until she got to the right spot. One of Angie's women screamed, making her jump.

Emma stood like a deer in headlights staring back at them, while Oliver appeared startled and held his arm straight out, the one with the *mellow-skin*. They both seemed oblivious to the dark cloud of mist surrounding them.

Oh my, Janine's blood raced. *Calm, calm, calm*, she told herself. Gwen had warned her once: never let a spirit feel your fear, or they may begin to control you.

Janine forced herself to breathe easy as she watched the ghost phase in and out. The spirit had Oliver's arm in her jaw, like a dog. Then, the spirit let go and grinned at Janine with an unsavory glint in her eye. *That little shit!* She knew he would feel that bite.

"*Go! Leave us!*" Janine yelled.

And just like, that the ghost disappeared, poof! No more mist.

The temperature began to readjust, and the séance ladies started moving. Both Emma and Oliver appeared stunned, backing away in confusion and she realized they thought she had been yelling at them. Ian's voice dribbled through her earpiece, but the blood thumping in her ears drowned him out. She felt woozy.

Janine reached to pull the earpiece away, she needed to control her fear. That entire experience had been so unexpected. *Mary is a kindred spirit*, Caroline Govant had insisted. *I don't think so, Caroline*, Janine thought. She didn't think so then, and certainly did not think so now. Her muscles felt completely exhausted and she just wanted to lie down.

"Not you two." Janine waved Emma and Oliver to her. "Not you two. You two come here."

Angie Minnihan couldn't stay and talk, she needed to escort her shaken up séance guests back to her parlor. One of the guests couldn't stop crying, the woman who dropped her stone and witnessed a very "evil" black mass with glowing eyes. *It wanted to grab my heart, I swear it*, she blubbered between hiccups. She had also been the screamer and watched the dark mass circling Oliver. The other two women only saw smoky fog gather above the candle and got chilled, but they each agreed *a feeling of dread* had closed into circle. Angie visualized Mary. She described a distinct girl outlined in the mist, and she heard the voice warning them to heed the dictum. She'd seen the same apparition many times before, just not as clearly.

Ian's students didn't see anything other than "needle swings" on their devices. Chet recorded temperature changes, noted odd motion on the incongruent detection device, and watched the EMF antenna lock and track activity from the circle to Emma and Oliver.

Emma filmed faint flickers of light on her ultralow IR camera, and "something" on the ultrahigh UV recorder. Emma and Oliver didn't notice anything with the naked eye and were skeptical of the woman who said a mist surrounded them. Oliver felt a terrible pressure from the *mellow-skin*. He believed it had have been caused by either the temperature drop or faulty wiring. Yet, under the thin sheath, distinct red marks stuck out on his arm in a crescent pattern, like a bite mark. Ben took several photos of the marks.

Janine didn't say much about anything, she only confirmed that the ghost of Mary Miller did indeed visit them. She didn't want to scare Angie's ladies any more than necessary. All in all, the research crew would go home with a ton of recorded data to review.

Janine, feeling weak, sat puddled in the truck while they gathered their equipment. She asked Ian to drive her in the F-150 back to Gram's house. Ben and the crew followed in the van.

That woman was not drunk enough to hallucinate, Janine told herself. *Angie witnessed almost everything with no ill effects, so she's a receiver. And I should just accept it, I can summon ghosts.*

Kiki once asked Janine how many experiences she needed before she would no longer question her paranormal abilities. Perhaps, she was finally there.

Typically, after a *Spectral Analysis* shoot, the crew would drink whisky and debrief the encounter in the comfort of Gram's den, or other comfortable gathering place. But with the crew all under drinking age, and exhausted from the excitement, they each went straight to bed.

Chapter 3

Scotland *Kiki*

Kiki woke very late in the day. The previous night had spiraled into a awful disaster. Going on a date with Rory O'Hara, an old boyfriend from her school days, was a huge mistake. Why did she imagine things would be easier with Rory simply because she was familiar with him and he was a coven lad?

He had been thrilled when she called. He always knew she'd seek him out for her awakening, he just didn't think it would take so long. At one point, he laughed at her Kiki Mellow persona and said he found it very *cute*. Nice to see she had melted from the frozen girl he once knew. He always felt there was unfinished business between him and his wee Kiera Lovett.

It was her own fault for listening to Gwen and calling on Rory, but she agreed, there weren't many men that she could trust with the little experiment she needed to conduct. Perhaps it was karma that she needed to suffer through it, because she should have done it years ago when she dated Rory back in school. If she had opened up just a little bit back then, when it was normal behavior to learn the ropes, she wouldn't be so apprehensive now. But she had been completely focused on developing her Core Well, and that entailed shunning any type of physical pleasure. Having an older fellow, a coven lad like Rory to deflect away the other blokes, had been very helpful. He had been quite the gentleman with her, gambling that he'd be called on to attend her sacred ritual someday.

And now, here was Gwen at her kitchen table, fishing for the results of Kiki's experiment. There she was, sitting across the table with her wicked lemon scones and prying blue eyes.

"Come on then, let's have it. How far did you let yourself go before shutting off your base door?"

"You don't need to give me your truth scones, Gwen, I have no ego left in this situation." Kiki drank a bit of the coffee Gwen brought and took a bite of a lemon scone. "Well, Rory brought me home after a fun filled night of tomfoolery and I invited him in for more fooling around, in which I consciously allowed every ounce of energy into my base zones."

Gwen suggested Kiki prepare before her ritual by experiencing passion energy through her base aspects, to get used to it. It might help her resist diverting the energy for comfort's sake during her ritual. She didn't want to cheat herself from the truth of the experience. An awakening couldn't happen with a closed Base Well or without a true climax. Then, it would just be a physical act and not a true awakening. Gwen's colors, aura, hair, everything, ran very red, as her own passions ran deep. No woman had as healthy a Base Well as Gwen Murphy.

"I actually allowed the energy through my bosom, because he seemed pretty focused there."

"Ho ho, so Rory O'Hara finally got to second base." Gwen laughed. "Nice of you to finally give him what he always talked about. Were you able to let that passion flow freely?"

Kiki could feel the heat creep into her face and nodded. "As I said earlier, yes. It was very unexpected, titillating and uncomfortably warm. I really wanted to alter the energy to my core right away. I felt so, so…"

"Vulnerable?"

Kiki nodded. "I had no idea minor massaging up top could quickly flood a body down below."

Gwen laughed again, this time her whole body got into it.

"I could barely sit still, my private areas felt hot, I admit, nice and not nice at the same time. Soon after his ministrations, I completely shut down my base zone. Now I know why men are heavily drawn to cleavage, it gets them quick results."

"You have very nice breasts, Kiki, very eye catching. Are you telling me this is the first time you let someone go there?"

"Yes. I've never let anyone touch me that way before," Kiki admitted. "Is it the same for everybody?"

"Everybody is different, of course," Gwen said sadly. "But I certainly enjoy it."

"Oh, Gwen, I'm so sorry." Kiki came around and gave her tall friend a hug. "I'm such an idiot."

"You really are, Kiera, and a complete minx." Gwen hugged her back. "You need to stop shutting off your passion zone. Believe me, eventually, that vulnerability, the giving in, becomes power. You need to experience these sensations and not run away from them. Just go on and give it another practice or two. I admit to feeling very angry at you right now. Nobody gets to twenty-eight in this day and age, you know. Resisting and avoiding the natural flow of any type of energy is an aberration. Are you going to give Rory another go? Could he be the stag for your ritual? He's always adored you and no one would be surprised if you chose him. Or, will you try to woo that detective back?"

"That one's not interested."

Kiki wished she could woo the detective back. Her experiment would have gone differently with Bob Anderson. She would not have had the desire to alter the flow of energy with the detective. He mixed his energy in a way that she could easily accept, without fear of losing control.

"I can't ask Rory, either. I believe he actually loves me a little bit, and I won't have him chasing after me or break his heart."

"He's always loved you," Gwen nodded. "More than a little. So, a blind stag then?"

"God, no. No blind stag. And I'm afraid to see *the list* that surely awaits me at the cottage. I could never allow a stranger to touch me like that, I'd totally shut down." Kiki stared at Gwen. "I'm floating the idea of inviting Max Colliers. We have a very flirty rapport and I believe I could accept his passion adequately, and it's not like he has a heart to break, not like Rory. I'm familiar with Max and know his intent would be straightforward."

Gwen's shocked, amused face was well worth it. She wasn't expecting that name to come out of the hat. Gwen bit thoughtfully into a scone. "I can actually see that working out fairly well." She nodded, then started laughing again.

Max Colliers was the executive producer of the *Spectral Analysis* television show Kiki starred in. He happened to be a salacious rogue who sported in the seduction of women. His beguiling nature and handsome appearance actually made him very pleasant company. He might not believe in the ideas involved in a witch's ritual, but Max would certainly honor them and play the game to the best of his ability, and he would jump at the chance if she offered it, not just to couple with Kiki, but to participate in a sultry pagan event. One of his life goals seemed to revolve around having various sexual experiences. He had recently fixated on Janine Stinger when he believed her knife scars implied she enjoyed sexual cutting games. He became quite upset when she refused to share anything about those experiences with him. It would be hard for Max to pass up a scandalous sex ritual.

The thought of Janine Stinger brought that late night phone call back to mind. Kiki had been very tipsy when the call came and begged off a little quickly. She picked up her phone to find the message with the photo. There it was, the Comba charm. She checked the clock.

"What time is it in California?" Kiki asked Gwen.

"Oh goodness, that's some quick math you're asking." Gwen pulled out her own phone and tapped away. "I've got a world time app. It looks to be about six in the morning there. What's cooking in California? Ian didn't tell Janine what his arse of a father said, did he? Why does he even talk to that man anymore?"

Kiki went ahead and dialed the number. Knowing Janine, the girl wouldn't be able to sleep with thinking about the charm. Kiki shook her head at Gwen as the connection rang.

"It's not that."

After a couple of rings, she heard a commotion and then a very groggy voice. Ian grumbled through the line, probably still mostly asleep. In a hushed voice, he told her Janine was sleeping and they had gotten in very late. Did Kiki realize the time difference? He refused to wake Janine, she had a big night. She helped summon the orchard ghost in Rio Linda and needed to sleep.

Kiki passed her phone to Gwen. The Comba charm lit up the screen.

"Sounds like your protégé has summoned a spirit," Kiki told her. "Not only that, look what she found at Gram's house. It came out of a box from the attic, she said."

All of Gwen's humor altered into a very serious expression on her freckled face. Her natural reddish aura took on a more anxious orange, and she pushed red wispy strands of wavy hair from her eyes as she pulled Kiki's phone closer. She studied the photo.

"You're joking, she *found* this? Another Comba charm?" Gwen asked. "We haven't seen this one, there's a wee blemish in the corner. Every girl in the coven wanted one of these charms when we were young, how does Janine manage to have two delivered to her?"

They contemplated the photo in silence. Not counting the one in the picture, Kiki had only seen two other Comba charms in her life. The most recent one popped up less than a year ago, in Chicago of all places. It came by way of a haunted man in the service of a ghostly witch, one who had been strangled in the woods. The other charm belonged to her late Auntie Celeste, Ian's mother, and her auntie wore it sparingly, only on a special occasion. Kiki recently asked Ian's father if he knew of its location and Roger McNally claimed it was gone, lost.

"Kiki, remember my vision in the woods?" Gwen asked. "A gathering of women hand in hand?"

Kiki nodded at her.

"Well, I've been dreaming of it, often, since that night."

Gwen picked up her coffee and walked around, pacing to dissipate her anxiety. Kiki watched the orange in her aura wane ever so slightly.

"At first, I imagined it was a celebration, like part of a festival even, but now I feel that it may be a massive summoning to end something, or to start something, something big. Beyond the boundaries of just our coven of sisters. Something dark. Not a happy event."

"With ties to the charms?" Kiki asked.

"We should go see Trinity," Gwen told her. "She's keeper of the books. If something is brewing, she would know, and I should tell her of this vision, write it down in the book, just in case it has meaning. I've been waiting for you to be ready to go to the Isle. Trinity has been asking after you and expects me to bring you."

Oh, Trinity, Kiki grimaced. She needed more time before a visit to her mother. She always felt like such a little girl near her and she had a few issues to work out regarding her awakening before letting Trinity add her two cents.

Kiki made a command decision and sent Max Colliers a detailed message inviting him to participate in her awakening ritual. She didn't mince words, but sent him a link to a website that explained a ceremony similar to what the coven planned. It covered the usual: candles, drinking, singing, drumming, and dancing skyclad in a natural setting with the sexual awakening of a virgin witch. The coven always chose a nice spot near the cliffs of the Quiraing in the Trotternish area of Skye. It included a beautiful and dramatic landscape which the sisters often used at the Samhain and for awakening rituals. But an awakening event was very rare. Not every witch celebrated an end to their celibacy, only those that had taken a vow of chastity at fourteen and kept that vow for seven years, and if that witch persistently kept her vow for seven more years, then the ritual became significant on an exponential level. The tantric power that passed to the coven was a blessing to them all. But it needed to be remedied in ritual before the witch reached her twenty ninth year. If she waited too long, the ritual would lose meaning and her triad might never become balanced.

It was a three hour drive from Inverness to her mother's cottage on Skye. Kiki slept some of the way, but woke to answer her phone. Less than an hour after leaving the message, Max called with questions.

Was she joking? No. *Wasn't she still angry about the incident with Janine?* Of course. *Would everyone really be nude, outside, under a full moon?* Skyclad, and yes, though some wore hooded capes. *Did she imply that she actually planned to have sex with him?* No implications there, that's exactly why she was inviting him. *In front of people?* Only a few others, seven women. *Did she also imply that she was a virgin?* She'd let him determine that during the ritual. Max laughed, then continued, *Would he be expected to have sex with other people?* Only if he wanted. *So, it's a witch's orgy?* No, not usually, but if he inspired another girl in the ritual, and they were both willing, they could certainly do as they pleased. No one would frown upon them. Three sisters would be there to get him warmed up, so he was sure to be plenty satisfied if he was worried. *You are being perfectly serious?* Very serious. The ritual was all about animal instincts and eroticism, right up his alley. *This isn't some sort of joke they're playing? Pay back for Janine? Because he'd understand that and would fly over just for them to get it out of their systems.* Well, he'd have to take that chance then. But she assured him, she was inviting him to a serious pagan event. *And you're definitely going to participate in it?*

"Of course, it's an important pagan rite. This is a very sacred ritual for me, I'm a priestess in my coven and I want to do things right by my sisters. There are other men the Priestess of the Base Well can call on, but I have the right to bring my own male. I could invite anyone, Max, but I really think you'd appreciate it more than everyone I know. You've said it before, many times, we should do this because we understand each other and are physically suited for one another. I want you here. I'm asking you to open the door to my Base Well, my passions, and initiate me into the world of sex and pleasure. Just let me know if it's too much to ask and I'll choose someone else."

"Wow, Kiki, I don't know what to say. I really want to believe this is a real thing and not a joke on me, pay back," Max said over the line. "Let me check my calendar and get back to you."

"Of course," Kiki said. "Think it over."

Gwen glanced at her with a raised red eyebrow. The sun was setting, and they still had twenty more minutes on their drive.

"I see you're brooding about the balance of things," Gwen said. "But don't feel rushed. If you're not feeling right about the ritual, you shouldn't do it. I know the coven is super excited and this is a momentous event for the sisters, but it's also a very intimate experience. Many witches break their vow on purpose, to avoid a ritual. You could easily do the same. You can take things slow and private, call up your detective. Kiki, you have almost no experience here, the other sisters don't quite realize it because of your flirty behavior and that television show. Usually in a ritual like this, it's a young lassie in a heated state, yearning to be released from her vow as quickly as possible. That's not you."

"A high coven virginal priestess run and hide? My sexual awakening belongs to all the sisters. I'm a Core Master. I'm going to follow what's written and celebrate the aethereal energy the old fashioned way. I'm not going to cheat and I'm not going to hide, and it's going to be a true awakening, a true joining of Core, Head, and Base, in ritual." Kiki was angry again. "And the more I think about it, Max Colliers is completely right for this role, he was born for it. Perhaps that's the reason he was placed in my path in the first place. There's a reason for everything."

Her phone suddenly pinged with a message from Max. She read it quickly. Not the man she originally wanted, but she felt relieved that she could now dismiss the vetted list Trinity was compiling. She smiled at Gwen.

"Can you believe it? The bastard has cleared his schedule to frolic wantonly in the glen with me. I told you he was completely right for this role."

Chapter 4

The Coven Cottage *Kiki*

Trinity Lovett resided in an old cottage near the coast of Uig Bay in a small crofting village on the island of Skye. The cottage once to belonged to Trinity's Great Auntie Meg and Kiki visited every summer of her youth. There, she explored the glens and lochs with the children of other pagan sisters. When her great auntie passed, Trinity moved into the cottage and became the new keeper of the coven books. By that time, Kiki had completed academy and followed her peers to the university. Kiki flittered about with classes but never came close to completing a course of study. She bailed out early and ran off with a friend on a traveling adventure. They meandered from festivals to cultural events, dabbling in fortunes, reading auras, and gaining quite a cult following. It lasted until she decided to visit her cousin Ian in the United States, where she found her way to becoming a television star.

Kiki's mother, Trinity, ran a small bed and breakfast with her business partner, Annelise Batten, Kiki's old traveling friend. Annie had remained on Skye when Kiki left for New York. While waiting on Kiki to return, Annie expanded the business to include an online shop and school of sorts. She conducted a series of online lessons on tarot, tealeaf reading, crystal grids, and herbal magic. As herbalists, they expanded the coven garden, cultivating the weeds and old plants and expanded their drying room. They bottled and sold packets of special herbs over the internet. They also managed a website on ethnobotany and were considered a resource in pagan herbal circles.

Trinity gathered Kiki in for a hug before ushering them into her private sitting room. They arrived too late for dinner, but tea and cookies were served in front of a blazing hearth. If they had used their phones, Trinity would have saved a bit of the baked bass for them. Trinity also offered rooms if they wished to stay the night, but Gwen had a shift the next evening and they planned to drive back.

In the far corner of the room, Kiki noticed a familiar older man sipping a dram of golden fluid, likely a batch from a local homemade highlands mash.

He was quite tall, with a head full of speckled salt and pepper hair and wild bushy eyebrows. It was her stand-in father figure, George MacLeod, and Kiki smiled wide at him as he winked at her.

George was one of the many men that circled around her mother all the years of her life. Even after he wed, then divorced, he kept returning as if a tether held him to Trinity Lovett. Perhaps it was because he fancied he was Kiki's real father and often acted as such. George MacLeod boomed with pleasure at the sight of Kiki and Gwen and bestowed generous hugs on them. They both knew George well. He was a local Uig Bay fisherman and, as a young man, he helped around the cottage when Auntie Meg had been alive. He took the girls on outings when they were young and all the locals believed Kiki was his illegitimate love child.

"Well, the wee lassie has returned." He gave Kiki a thorough up and down before kissing her cheek. "Ye're quite an eyeful, my bonnie dove, your mother all over again. And Gwen! Ye're a pleasant sight for my weary eyes."

His accent always thickened with whisky. George made his way to the door. He knew the routine. When the witches dropped in, the men must depart.

"I'll just be gone. I dropped off a fresh batch of the MacLeod cask 345 and a bit-o-bass. I'm off, ladies. If ye'll be stayin' the night, mayhap I'll bring my young nephew, Andrew, aroond. Ye kin get a good keek at him. Young, but he's able." He chuckled at Kiki.

Trinity escorted him to the door, flirting all the while. Kiki watched her mother's emerald eyes flash at the old man teasingly. Kiki grimaced at how Trinity leaned in just barely touching him but kept a scant sliver of air between them as if she didn't notice she invaded his space. One might believe she couldn't resist him. Kiki would be happy if Trinity would act her age for one second. Did she always need to behave so openly ardent with George MacLeod and every other man who happened to drop into her presence?

Then, like a splash of cold water in the face, Kiki realized that George was correct: Kiki was the spitting image of her mother Trinity, in looks and behavior. They both had dark wavy hair, green eyes, and dramatically curvy bodies. Kiki also knew that their mannerisms, mode of movement, facial expressions, and even their auras, were alike. *Her mother all over again*, George was spot on. The only difference between them was their skin tone. Trinity's skin shone ivory white with a sprinkle of freckles, while Kiki's skin was a deep smooth olive color.

Trinity once divulged that Kiki's coloring came from her true father, a Spaniard of Moorish descent, powerfully built, with hazel eyes, a strong square jaw, and handsome beyond belief. Trinity swore his aura often took on a pinkish hue. He was her green man at the Beltane one year and they spent three days of the festival conceiving a baby, but she let him go when he invited her to transplant to an eastern country with him. No way, not after the disaster her sister made by marrying a demon, abandoning the coven ways, and following Roger McNally's orders. Don't worry, Trinity purred, she had loved him a bit, and she dearly missed him after he left. But it was for the best, a man just got in the way with the raising of a daughter, and Kiki was a Beltane baby, a blessing, a true *Next*. And please don't be upset, Trinity urged, she was very sorry that she couldn't remember her green man's actual name. She had called him "mo leannan" and always thought of him with that term of endearment. He will forever be "Leannan" to Trinity, and so he was "Leannan" to Kiki.

Trinity returned with a grin and finally hugged Gwen. She gave Kiki a more careful looking over, during which Kiki rolled her eyes and reached for the bottle of MacLeod 345 to fill their tea cups. Gwen's blue eyes flew open in pleasant anticipation. Nothing ran down as smooth as home cooked highland whisky, especially after a long drive on a cold night, and George MacLeod's batch was always a fine example.

"My darling daughter, how long have you been back? Nearly a month? And you're only now payin' your poor old mum a visit?"

Trinity's green eyes flashed briefly before she spun round to poked up the fire. Then, she accepted a cup of the whisky.

"Really, Kiera! You have Annelise and Gwen, and every girl buzzing about your awakening ritual, are you *truly* still chaste? Is that why you've been hiding from me? I have seen the gossip, and I finally watched a couple of those shows and that documentary movie. If you have broken your vow of chastity, just admit it. Nobody would be upset or think less of you. Well, a few might think a little less, but truth be told, some believe that vow has already been goosed."

"Ugh! Mother, you are impossible."

"Dinna take that tone with me, lass. You've been known to cover your missteps with me, Kiera Lovett. This is nae the time to hide from a broken vow of chastity."

Trinity pulled a magazine from her side chair holder.

"What am I to think, when all these reports are, Kiki Mellow tames this bloke, then succumbs to that one, and look over here, she's hooked the playboy. Dinna get me wrong, lassie, I admit to being a wee proud of this reputation of yours. If you have goosed your vow, at least you've done it in grand style, some of these fellows are nothing to sneeze at."

Trinity flipped to a page with a photo of Kiki and a certain NBA athlete.

"But keep this in mind, lass, an awakening is a sacred ceremony, and I'll not have you make light of it to cover your arse with the sisters. Tisn't unheard of, to hide a broken vow."

"How could you even suggest such a thing," Kiki fumed. "I would never make light of a sacred ceremony!"

"You seem to be making light of quite a lot of our practices in that show. You have no qualms about brandishing untenable tea or tarot readings, and that comical, sultry, witch persona you're pushing? What am I supposed to think? I have seen your behavior on camera, flirting shamelessly with every male in the vicinity, even your own cousin!"

Kiki's arms crossed over her chest and she narrowed her eyes.

Gwen calmly stepped between the mother and daughter to gaze at the magazine. She nodded to Trinity.

"That's a very nice sample of a male in that picture, I don't see how anyone could resist that."

After a pause, they both chuckled.

"Trinity," Gwen added gently, "Kiki has kept her vow beyond a shadow of a doubt. *You know that.* Besides, it's quite clear that this fellow doesn't fancy girls, why do you think she ran around with him so often?"

Trinity pressed her lips together and conceded. She moved to Kiki and administered another hug, a proper embrace, and patted her hair down in her annoying motherly way.

"I'm sorry, my wee yin," she said softly. "You leaving so suddenly upset me. Then, staying away so long got me afraid you lost our ways. You haven't attended one coven event in three years and with the magazines spinning gossip with these odd stories, it got me questioning things. It is not uncommon for girls to fly off and do their own thing, rebel it up a bit, grow up and out of the practice. That's what your grandmother did. I'd understand it."

Trinity took the chair between them and placed her magical green eyes on Kiki. When they looked on her like that, Kiki always felt a surge of love and wanted to please her mother all over again. Why did she need this crazy woman's approval all the time?

"And spending all your time with Ian, I love him, but his father *is* a demon. Never forget that. How do I know what influence the man has on the boy?"

Kiki shook her head. "Ian is a gem, Mother."

"I can't help my bias. Lots of times the apple doesn't fall far from the tree." Trinity turned toward Gwen. "I'm sorry, lass, but I'm not happy with how he left you after all that business, either."

"Trinity," Gwen rolled her eyes. "I'm the one who broke it off. How many times do I need to tell everyone that?"

They gossiped about Ian's upcoming wedding at the end of November. Both Gwen and Kiki planned a trip to California to witness Ian exchange vows with Janine, who was the other girl on the ghost hunting television show. Kiki pointed to a magazine picture of Janine. Trinity believed she resembled a princess, big doe eyes, long auburn hair, long legs and just the right curves to be quite attractive. Intelligent looking. Trinity wondered out loud if Janine might be a little reserved perhaps, even judgmental? Gwen and Kiki both assured Trinity that Janine was very level headed, nice, and loyal. After Gwen, Ian certainly deserved a loyal girl.

"We've actually come in regards to Janine Stinger," Kiki told Trinity.

"A coincidence then," Trinity said. "Because I've been patiently waiting to ask you about her."

Trinity went to her den console and opened the top drawer. She pulled out a large book, one of Great Auntie Meg's chronicles by the look of it. Auntie Meg always kept a hand written loose leafed collection of important events she often called the *Book of Happenings*. Kiki remembered Meg carefully adding a page to the book after an outing near the Pass of Odall. They had spotted an unidentifiable beast eyeing them. Meg called that animal a demon, one that lost its human shape. She swore it was a man she once knew.

Beware, Auntie Meg warned a very young Kiera Lovett, *a man may become a demon if his core slips away.*

"I dinna watch many of your shows, only a few in the first season," Trinity said. "Then Annelise put on the movie, the documentary you won a prize for, that's when I noticed her, your Janine."

Trinity placed the book on the table in front of Kiki. The old leather cover was cut with a spiral Celtic triskelion.

"Now tell me, daughter, have you seen this book before? Peeked deep into it perhaps? Do you know things that are in it? Used something written in here, maybe, to add spice to that movie of yours?"

"Well," Kiki snapped defensively. "This is one of Great Auntie Meg's book of happenings and I recall one incident she added to those pages, but other than that, I don't know anything in there. I would never use a witches diary without invitation."

"I'm not accusing you of anything, Kiki, I only need to hear you confirm that," Trinity added gently. "That you dinna use words found in here for that movie."

Kiki threw her arms up in vexation. "What's in the book?"

"One each for redemption." Trinity's glowing eyes stared at her. "Those words are written in this book, *One each for redemption*. The same curse in your movie, the one that clings to your friend Janine is recorded in these pages, several times, and I remembered it from my youth. Auntie Meg wrote them here," Trinity paused to drain her cup of whisky. "The ghost of the wall, a hag of a witch, appeared to myself and Celeste on one of our nightly romps to the Faerie Glen. The hag said those exact words to us." Trinity's eyes shone with emotion. "It made my skin crawl hearing it in your movie and I'm afraid of what it might mean. So, if you say you read it here first, I'll be quite happy."

Kiki moved closer to the book and placed her hand on the smooth leather cover. She asked Trinity if they could see the entry. Trinity had marked the spot with a purple silk ribbon and quickly opened to the correct page.

"I dinna remember everything at first," Trinity admitted, "because I was terrified and then fainted. I was a very young girl at the time."

In giant loose script, Meg had written a short paragraph. An inked oblong circle hovered at the top right hand corner indicating a waning gibbous moon, a witch's knot on the left was drawn to protect against evil. Near the bottom of the page, Meg had sketched a beautiful figure of a woman in the left margin and an old hag in the right. The paragraph read,

The ghost of the wall did appear to young Celeste and Trinity Lovett. Celeste did give a summoning call. She claims to have said, "Come wise soul, to us appear. Show yourself as we come near. Draw us in to make us three, so I command, so mote it be." To which, the spirit answered. She appeared old and hunched, then young and beautiful. Green eyes and smooth skin. But she grew tall and moved in unusual ways and eventually became a hag with black eyes. She gave a warning. To the best of her recollection, Celeste heard, "One each for redemption, forever, unless the curse be washed away." The wall ghost also claimed that, "A dragoma *called, one to take the curse from the demon's grasp." And she did warn Celeste that the "demon comes for one such as you," meaning Celeste. I did catch sight of a shadow of the spirit when I heard the girls talking at the wall.*

"There hasn't been another entry for the wall ghost since this one," Trinity told them. "But there are many entries further back in the pages. Look here, an entry from over eighty years ago."

She flipped the pages to a spot marked with a different silk ribbon. This time the moon symbol indicated a waxing crescent and the only other picture was a beautiful unclothed woman sitting on the wall. The short paragraph read,

The spirit of the wall appeared before a séance of six. Present were Abigail, Sara, Meghan, Sissy, Gillian, and Katelyn. Not all saw the young woman on the wall, and only young Sara could give a full description, smooth alabaster skin, deep green eyes, nary a stitch of cloth. Her beautiful body curved into the shape of the moon under which she sat. Everyone heard something akin to whispers, then clear words. All agreed on their content and relayed the speaking to the best of their ability. "Tae wear the saint beware. One each for redemption, must feed the dark soul,'til such a one wrests this curse from his hands."

"So you see," Trinity sighed, moving nervously around the room. "It's the same curse, one each for redemption, to feed a demon. Every wall entry repeats it, *one each for redemption*, these are not ordinary spirits relaying this curse. The wall ghost, and that one from your movie, not ghosts, but spirits compelled by a demon." Trinity pointed to the names in the older entry. "You see here, that's Great Auntie Meg. Meg always reminisced on her old friends. Gillian MacDonald was killed, strangled. Meg says that Gillian's lover did it because she was leaving him. Abigail Kirkpatrick also met a violent end, and my dear sister Celeste was strangled too, *I know it*. Don't worry, I won't be pointing fingers, but everyone knew she was finally leaving Roger McNally. I bring it up because all these women heard that warning, the curse, from the demon's mouth, before they met a violent end from someone they loved."

"But Meg heard it too," Gwen said gently. "And you and the others. I knew Sissy and Katelyn, they were very old ladies who passed on naturally. Sara was Diana's great grandmother, Cara's mother. I'm missing your point."

"Aye, my dear, tis true. We heard it as well and live on," Trinity said. "But these three that died had something else in common that the rest of us lacked, and I wonder how the same demon haunts your friend's folks half a world away. If there's more to it than what you think, perhaps—"

The den door flew open, and a burst of vivacious energy entered to break up their serious conversation. A woman taller than Kiki, but shorter than Gwen, flashed a mouth full of white teeth at them. Her golden hair had grown longer and curled wilder, and her laughing hazel eyes seemed brighter. Kiki noticed that Annelise Batten put on a few pounds and changed from a twig of a girl to one with a womanly figure. She seemed very happy and healthy, blossoming. Kiki and Gwen both jumped up to greet their old friend.

"So then, Kiera, shall I call you Kiki Mellow?" Annie asked, "Are you going by Kiki or Kiera here in Scotland?"

"Kiki."

Annelise just finished an online tarot lesson and set her prized cards on the side table. The three chatted a bit and laughed as Trinity brewed more tea. Annelise told them of her online lessons and the herb shop. She thanked Kiki very much for recommending folks seek her council, they've gained quite a following from *Spectral Analysis* fans in their online school. Everyone wanted to glean a bit of the ancient ways these days. Then, Annie came round to see what they were looking at.

"Trinity is asking about the curse," Annie noticed. "I thought she was having a heart attack when we heard it in the movie. She hoped you read it in the book and made it all up." Annelise glanced at Trinity, "But we knew deep down something strange was brewing."

Trinity poured everyone a nice cup of tea and passed the honey around. Kiki had gone back to flip through the pages of Auntie Meg's book. Annie vocally admired Meg's skilled and artistic entries, pointing out the perfect symmetry and bold lines in dark ink. Every page pleased the eye. The paper felt thick and the edges were slightly jagged. Small shapes and colors were sprinkled prettily across the pages. Auntie Meg must have made all of the paper using stem cuttings from unwanted herbs and weeds.

As a very young girl, Kiki often watched Meg cook plant matter in lye and then beat the fibers by hand. Auntie Meg often tasked the summer kids to have at the pulpy mess in that big mortar of hers. It was loads of fun for kids, whacking the mess. Some of those thick sheets might contain the energy of their youth beaten into the pulp. Kiki flipped the pages back to the older ghost entry and viewed the warning again. One line caught Kiki's eye and seemed to jump off the page in an ominous way.

Tae wear the saint beware, Kiki placed her finger on it. Gwen and Annie both nodded their heads at the line she pointed out.

"This must be a reference to Saint Comba." Gwen exchanged a look with Kiki.

"Aye," Annie said. "We figured it out because of the charm necklaces."

"Celeste, Gillian, and Abigail," Trinity named them. "They all wore an heirloom necklace with the Saint Comba charm, passed down from mother to daughter. Each wore one when they died, and the charms emit a faint feeling of their death. It makes procuring all of the charms worth a bother, if we hope to solve more of the puzzle. There are many old diaries in Meg's library, most are written poorly, or writ in the old way, but many tell of the curse. I mean to have them translated better. Cara says she'll have a look and help with the old Gaelic and Latin, but some of it is just gibberish."

Gwen sank heavily into a chair and set her teacup on a saucer. Her red brow furrowed and she shook her red head. Trinity stopped talking and waited.

"I have something for the *Book of Happenings*, a distinct vision recently crowded into my subconscious," Gwen told them. "A gathering is coming, an important one, a gathering involving the charms." Gwen recounted her vision for them.

Kiki came round to sit next to Gwen and pulled out her phone. She called up the photo Janine sent of the most recent charm and held it for Annie's round eyes to see, then passed it to Trinity.

"We found a Comba charm for you, Mother," Kiki said very softly.

The magnitude of that coincidence weighed on the very air itself. Kiki continued in a subdued tone.

"Ian's fiancé found it in an old box in her grandmother's attic. There's your demon's connection to California and perhaps our pagan connection to Janine. Perhaps her distant lineage traces back to this very cottage."

Trinity and Annelise were stunned to see the silver charm in the photo.

"That's incredible!" Annie said to Kiki and Gwen. "Do you know how difficult a time we've had tracking down any of the charms?"

"I can imagine." Kiki glanced at her. "I actually called Roger McNally about Auntie's charm, but he said it was long lost."

"I have it," Trinity told her.

She returned to the console and bent to a lower drawer. Very carefully, she fetched out a carved wooden box and set it atop the leather bound book.

"I have your auntie's Saint Comba necklace in here. Actually, Meg had it. All this time she's kept a collection of them in this box. She may have suspected the unsavory death curse before she died. But she didn't share what she knew, didn't write it down anywhere that I can find. And Meg became a recluse in her old age, shunning people more and more in her paranoia. Maybe she was afraid of what she surmised, afraid to share it, and perhaps she was afraid of the curse herself."

Trinity used a large ornate key on the wooden box. When it popped open, all four women tilted forward to peer inside. Small, sheer, drawstring bags in different colors lay on the bottom of the box. Six bags, Kiki counted, and silver charms could be seen in each of them. Trinity reached inside and fished out a pearl colored bag. She handed it to Kiki.

"Here's your auntie's charm," she said.

Kiki opened the small bag and the Comba necklace spilled into her palm. At the touch of the metal, Kiki got a shock to her heart. A lingering echo of Celeste vibrated in that metal triggering a sudden emotion to well up behind her eyes. Kiki fingered the chain that slithered around the charm. She remembered how she studied the intricate pattern as her auntie tucked her in on a summer night. Kiki drew in a breath and then passed the charm to Gwen.

Gwen had always been very close with Celeste, because her mother had been dear friends with Celeste and passed away too young. Then, young Ian always insisted he'd marry Gwen someday, and when Gwen broke her vow of chastity with Ian at sixteen, Celeste treated Gwen like her own true daughter. Kiki could see Gwen's brilliant blue eyes sparkling with emotion.

"I can sense her." Gwen's ginger lashes fluttered.

Kiki nodded and hugged her friend.

Gwen gave the charm back to Trinity and she held it quietly for a moment before pouring it back into the shear little bag. Then, she returned the bag to the box and stared at the treasure.

"Auntie Meg collected six of these Comba charms. She kept them a secret from everyone. I stumbled on them accidently behind the drying racks in the kitchen herb room. Annie and I were rearranging things. Meg must have suspected their connection to the curse after Celeste was murdered," Trinity said softly. "I'm pretty certain twelve of these charms were made, one for each moon priestess in a traditional pagan coven. With the one in your picture, there are only five to be found. We need to find them before your gathering occurs."

Trinity peered at Gwen. She continued,

"The high sisters believe it'll take all of the charms to obliterate this curse, that was why Meg gathered them. And we'll need a *dragoma*. A real *dragoma* to command the demon. Those writings did advise that it'll take a *dragoma* to *wrest the curse from the demon's grasp*," Trinity added.

She'd found the cask of whisky and poured herself another sample. Trinity's glowing green eyes bore into Kiki's again.

"Have you become a *dragoma*, my dear daughter? It certainly appeared so to me. With the cultivation of your core aspect these fourteen years, did your skills evolve to such an interesting level? Both of us, Annie and I, we recognized your increasing successes on that television show. Is it true?"

Kiki exchanged a long look with Gwen.

A mysterious vortex of aethereal energy revolved around that little cottage near Uig Bay, on the island of Skye. Certainly, it was the nexus of the curse. It had been in that very room when Kiki discovered Ian went to New York, and she became obsessed with visiting him. Kiki ignored the council of every person in her inner circle when she flew off on that trip, a trip that led her to a real *dragoma*, a witch who spoke to spirits and demons. Unusual and rare, and just what they needed.

That *dragoma* led to more charms and might be linked to the coven in ways no one could have imagined. A cosmic energy guided Kiki to find what she hadn't even known she sought. Kiki stared back at Trinity.

"Well, Mother, I'm going to have to disappoint you there," Kiki said.

"It's Ian's girl, then, isn't it," Trinity interrupted. "She's the *dragoma*. Does she even know it?"

Kiki nodded. "She does now."

Gwen added. "She's a powerful caller, even as a novice, but there's something else. There's also another charm. We've seen it."

"One was delivered to Janine in Chicago this past spring," Kiki said. "At the request of a ghost, a witch's spirit. In the woods where the witch was murdered, strangled, Janine summoned her. Gwen and I are witnesses."

"She used one of Celeste's summoning charms," Gwen confessed. "It came from her grimoire, the one she placed in my care. Celeste wrote a special summons for calling out a sister, and though this *dragoma* had no concept of her power, it was a wonderful success. I actually visualized the spirit and she gave me the initial vision of the gathering. All three of us were able to visualize the spirit, just like the testimonies given in Celeste's circles of the past."

"That spirit's murderer also tried to kill Janine Stinger, but failed. We hoped to find the victim's body or bones to prove the murderer's guilt."

Kiki reached to the bottle of highland whisky and charged her cup, sipped, then continued.

"The spirit showed me a vision of her death. She was leaving him, after discovering he was a demon, and running from an intimate situation with someone she had loved. She was strangled. Sound familiar?"

"Like Gillian and Celeste. You're grandmother, Gwen. Perhaps even Abigail would tell something similar, and who knows who else. Does she have both charms? Please tell me the *dragoma* did not wear one, you must call her immediately and warn her not to wear them, to put them aside and then bring them here. She should come too. I wish she could come for the Samhain, we could take all the charms to the castle rock and see what happens. I would very much like to meet her."

Trinity lounged back in her seat, contemplating this new information. The light from the fire flickered over her features. Trinity was still a very beautiful woman, with intense green eyes and dark hair only lightly speckled with grey. Kiki watched her mother's eyes come round to return her gaze, they were hypnotic.

Gwen sighed. "The wood's spirit also spoke out loud, not just in visions. She said that an empty place needed to be filled. What do you think that means?"

Kiki stood up. She needed fresh air, and to warn Janine Stinger not to wear the charm. She also resisted confessing to Trinity that the other charm was gone, slipped through her grasp when she returned it to the Daily family. It was likely somewhere lost in transit, trying to find its way back to Miranda, who most likely died years ago in Thatcher Woods. Kiki shot Gwen an urgent eye, and thankfully, Gwen got the message. She'd take on the task of explaining the blunder to Trinity.

Kiki left voice messages because no one was answering a phone, then slunk back into the cottage and found the three women laughing as they flipped through the entertainment rags. Kiki could see her own image posing at a party. They glanced up with amused eyes.

"Gwen says none of these men are the detective fellow you've mentioned. That he's a bit messy and has quite a slender build and he's not so glamorous at all," Trinity said.

Gwen shrugged her shoulders, what could she do? As High Priestess of the Base Well, Trinity would be very interested in the selection of the male for the awakening ritual.

"Gwen says this is the fellow you've selected."

Trinity pointed to a photo of the *Spectral Analysis* team. Max Colliers's hand was under Kiki's arm in a possessive manner. He had pulled her very close for that group shot, and they definitely appeared to be a couple.

"He's quite handsome. Annelise perked up at the sight of your choice."

Annie nodded, "He is very handsome, and looks refined. I truly like the look of him. But are you positive he knows what an awakening ritual entails? He won't be too prim and proper, or too shy, will he? He looks very proper. It'll be an embarrassing disaster if he's too shy to perform. Is he your love interest?"

Both Gwen and Kiki laughed at all that, answering her questions with their amused chuckles.

"You know," Trinity's voice took on a more sensual tone, and she fluttered the lids above her glowing green eyes, "George MacLeod has suggested his cousin's son, Andrew, for your awakening ritual. He's a couple of years younger than you, but he's a very well made man and knows the way of things. He's popular with the lassies here. A sure success for an awakening. We can bring him around and you can get a good look at him. He's at the top of my short list and he's bound to be as capable as George was at my awakening. He may seem like a simple headed fisherman to you, but the MacLeod men are gifted with an orgiastic pleasing of women and blessed with a fine tool for it. From my own experience, I can tell you…"

Kiki threw her hands over her ears.

"I can't listen to this, you're my mother. I don't want to hear the details of your experiences, especially not with George MacLeod. And I don't know how, or why, George is privy to the details of my awakening. I can only guess who's been bending his ear there."

Kiki watched Trinity's lips continue moving and glared until they stopped, then she slowly removed her hands. Both Annie and Gwen could barely contain their giggles.

"Are you sure?" Trinity asked softly. "A blind stag ensures he'll no follow you for life."

She made a good a point. Trinity picked a friend, George MacLeod, and he has hovered near her hearth since the night Trinity lost her virginity nearly thirty years ago. Sisters often advised girls to choose a blind stag, or they might be choosing their future husband. Then, Annie grabbed up her tarot cards and began shuffling the deck.

"Shall we ask the cards their opinion?" Annie winked at Kiki. "We'll keep it simple. Pull a card for your Max Colliers, and another for our Andrew MacLeod."

Annie Batten's tarot deck was a *one of a kind* treasure. At the university, Annie had been an art major and each of her cards was a miniature original water color with an ink outline.

She created other decks for reproduction, the Kiki Mellow cards for example, but the cards in her hand were for her own personal use. They were sacred to her. Kiki knew the deck well. It had gone with them on their travels and Annie claimed that the images revealed themselves in dreams. There would never be another deck like the one she presented to Kiki. Annie would never give them out to be copied and always replaced a worn card by creating a new original artwork. Annie once tore up a beautiful rendering of her High Priestess card and created a different image, just because the original vision had altered slightly in her dreams. *She has a hint of a smile now*, Annie had said.

"Max first," Annie ordered.

To placate the laughing women, Kiki drew a card and placed it face down.

"Now one for Andrew," she urged. Again, Kiki drew a card and placed it next to the other.

A funny feeling descended on Kiki. That familiar feeling she often garnered from Annie's beautiful cards, that they contained a subliminal message meant to be obeyed. Gwen, Kiki, and Trinity all watched as Annie simultaneously flipped both cards over.

Ace of wands for Max. Three of swords for Andrew.

Max Colliers is the Emperor

"Ho ho, that closes that discussion." Gwen giggled at Annie. "Fine tool or no, your Andrew is off the list."

Then, they recapped a general plan for the upcoming awakening ritual, which would be followed a few days later by a special Samhain in the Faerie Glen. Kiki promised to make a final decision on the seven witches she desired for her awakening, and Trinity delivered a small list of the sisters that vied for a spot.

It was very late, past midnight, when they finally strolled out to Gwen's car. Gwen was scheduled to work the next evening and wanted to get back to the city to sleep in her own bed. She worked the night shift on the children's oncology floor and never liked to call in sick and have someone work a double shift for her.

Chapter 5

Rugby *Janine*

Janine aroused lazily in the midmorning to find Ian spying at her through a small scope of some type. She shifted and pulled the sheet to cover her body better, wondering at his strange behavior.

"What are you doing?"

Ian removed the device from his eye and grinned at her. "Just admiring you through this little toy Ben designed." He passed it to her. "He calls it an ocular prism spectrometer. It's fun. Needs a bit of white light to work, but not full direct sunlight or it washes out. This filtered morning light works nice."

Janine examined the tubular device. It appeared similar to a small monocular telescope, except both sides had similar sized lenses. A little lip on one end identified it as the eyepiece. Janine pointed the scope toward Ian and was startled to see iridescent rainbows surrounding him. She twisted the end ring to bring the light into better focus and watched the rainbows become more distinct. Ian appeared to radiate energy in colorful radiating waves that shot outward in every direction. Certain areas of his body, the top of the head, thorax area, and the groin area, projected brighter patterns that extended the furthest. The rippling rainbow effect waxed and waned in intensity when he moved and she heard herself giggling.

"Aye, right." Ian laughed with her. "It's an infrared signature."

"It's a rainbow," she said, transfixed. The pulsing colorful array outlining him was a bit erotic, and she quite enjoyed the effect.

"A little converter takes each infrared frequency and multiplies it, then expands the scale for the full visible range. Similar to what Ben did with the subsonic audio," Ian told her.

"It's fun, and colorful, but why do all this work for a fancy heat display?" She realized that she was ogling him quite blatantly and handed the scope back.

"He thinks it might be what Kiki sees when she talks about auras. He's fascinated with Kiki, obsessed with her."

Ian aimed the scope back on Janine and tugged the blanket away.

"This blanket is interfering with my assessment," he said. "This is very enlightening, lass, you're radiating lots of heat energy from a very interesting location. Bonnie rainbows, very sweet. After last night, I'm pleasantly surprised to see that you're very warmed and ready."

"I don't think so," she protested, pulling the thick covers over herself.

All this talk of Kiki reminded her of that phone conversation the night before. Kiki might call at any minute, and she wanted to hear her thoughts about the charm, then there was that disturbing comment about Ian's father. Ian remained focused on his little scope and she nudged his arm, but he kept the scope pointed at her and tugged the covers off again.

"I'm still looking, it's very stimulating. I don't think this is what Kiki sees, but there may be a good use for this little scope." Ian grinned slyly at her. "A wee look through this piece and there'll be no confusing if a lass is warmed up, and I'd say you're very warmed up, Janine, eagerly warmed up in fact. That is a very bright rainbow leading to your pot of gold."

"Put that thing down. You don't know what you're talking about."

He set it aside and then rolled over to pull her into a full embrace, tugging the covers out from between them as he kissed her. She put up a feeble fight, but got overwhelmed with the feel of him and ended up wrapping her legs around him instead. His earthy smell, and the sweet taste of his kisses, were intoxicating. The way his hands drifted down her body stirred her blood into a nice state of excitement. Living together for the past several weeks had been the most sensual time of her life. She couldn't get enough of her fiancé, and his closeness had a euphoric effect on her.

"See there, I knew you were hot for me, that scope doesn't lie," he whispered, as he nuzzled her ear.

A loud bang startled them. A door shut somewhere near. Then, another thump sounded, followed by the footfalls of someone walking down the hall. That much mass had to be Chet. Low murmuring voices sounded right outside their door. Janine scooted away from Ian, embarrassed that his students may have heard the bed squeaking with their wrestling. Maybe they actually woke his crew with their activity. Ian glanced toward the door, then back at her.

"Sorry lass," he whispered. "Maybe you'll get lucky after the rugby match."

"Not another rugby match."

Janine detested the rugby matches. Ian enjoyed a very rough game, and she always feared he'd come out of it with a broken bone or something. He got the wind knocked out of him often, and once he lay on the ground unmoving for several minutes before jumping up and running back into play. Rugby was more violent than regular football and often resembled a crazy group of men wrestling in the mud.

"Ian, what if you get seriously hurt or something? I want you intact for our honeymoon."

He just grinned at her.

"Isn't your team a man short? Don't tell me you're playing with a man short again." That'd be just like his mates.

Ian laughed. "No, no, settle down. I've recruited some of the Berkeley kids to fill in."

"You mean Ben and Oliver?" Janine sat up, alarmed. "Tell me you didn't bully those guys into playing rugby. They'll get creamed." Did they realize rugby was a full contact sport?

Ian was laughing, motioning her to quiet down a bit.

"No, no. But Chet. And another young bloke named Andy. He played the line in lots of American football. And Emma. Emma's coming out too."

"Emma! You mean boom Emma in the hall? What is wrong with you? That little girl is going to get hurt."

"She insisted." Ian nodded at her. "Really, she'll be fine. I think she's going to zip around the big blokes quite nicely. We don't discriminate in rugby, if a girl wants to play, that's fine with us, and I'm confident Emma will make a right brilliant scrum half. She's played before too, on a team back home, she says."

Janine stared at him. He never asked her to play on the team. They were short in the last game, and he didn't even consider asking her to fill in, and Janine was a very serious athlete. She played varsity soccer at the University of Chicago for two years and played on a club team at Davis. She could run circles around some of his rugby mates, and she certainly knew how to handle a ball. All this time, she thought his team was a men's only group and now she felt a little rejected.

"Why don't you ask me to play?" she asked. "Maybe I can help too."

"Oh no, you don't like rugby," he shook his head. "Besides, you've already got an important job in the match."

"Really, and what is that?"

"You know, being my sexy cheering section. Watching me show off." He smiled at her. "I always play better when I think you might be impressed with my moves. I enjoy you on the sideline, rooting for me, ready with a cool cup of water and a nice fresh kiss between phases."

She didn't expect that. Rugby always drew out his baser side, but this was outright patronizing.

"You want me to be some sort of sideline, nitwit treat?"

"Crikes, Janine, I didn't mean it like that. I'm your cheering section at your soccer matches, right? Don't you love it when I run cool water to you when you come out of play? Don't you enjoy showing off a bit for me? I certainly enjoy watching you show off."

He took her hand.

"Total truth, I wouldn't be able to play right if you were on the field. What if you got ruffed up? I'd bloody get ejected dealing with the idiot, even if it was an accident. I know you're tough, I just don't like the idea of some bloke knocking you down. And the other players would sense it on me, me watching over you. You'd be a liability. I'm sorry, I know it's a little old fashioned, but girls don't play rugby," he said firmly.

She frowned at him.

"Well, I mean, *my girl* doesn't play rugby."

He just called her a liability. Somehow, she found the conversation both sweet and irritating at the same time. Should she punch him or hug him? Ian sidled up next to her, still a little amused, but cautious.

In a clear attempt to change the subject, he asked, "So, are you going to show me the ring you found?"

That reminded Janine of her conversation with Kiki, and she pulled the covers tightly around herself thinking about it. Kiki let it slip that something was said between Ian and his father, *something bad* by the sound of it. Kiki sounded worried that the conversation may have caused *something to happen* in California.

Janine didn't know how to bring it up. Ian was very tight lipped about his father. It was not an amiable relationship, that was clear. *But Ian must have discussed it with Kiki already.* Why didn't he discuss it with Janine? Would it cause *something to happen* if she knew what was said? Janine finally decided to wait and give Ian time to bring it up on his own. Maybe he was waiting for the right moment, or when they got home. Or maybe it was nothing at all.

Ian loved the Celtic ring Gram found in the box. Finn's ring fit him perfectly and he wanted to begin wearing it right away. He wanted to wear it to his rugby match, which was silly, because he wasn't supposed to wear jewelry during the game. They rushed out of Rio Linda and barely made the start of the match. The *Spectral Analysis* students had outraced them to the field and Chet and Emma were already warming up.

Janine watched from the sidelines as Ian got knocked around that afternoon. She sat in the rooting section with the other girlfriends, drinking white wine and discussing both the gluteus and cerebral assets of their respective partners. At the half, she gave him a nice steamy kiss like the other sideline treats. After a quick dinner with the team, they went home to finally be alone. Ian had just excused himself to a shower, and Janine lounged on the sofa waiting for the after match luck he promised her. That's when her cell phone pinged with a call from Scotland.

"So, this charm you found is just an unbelievable thing," Kiki said. "Beware, though, clues point to it being attached to an ancient curse. Don't wear it and try not to touch it. If possible, I'd like to buy it from you, or Gram, or whoever it belongs to."

"Nonsense," Janine told her. "I have it here. It's yours, just like the last one. And don't worry about me wearing it, I have no desire to even touch it. I can send it to you."

"Thank you, Janine," Kiki said. "But don't send it in the mail. Hold on to it, and I'll fetch it. I'm going to come early for your nuptials, by at least a week or more. Maybe we can go out and celebrate before the big day, like a little hen."

"You mean a bridal shower or something? My soccer team is throwing something next week, I'm covered."

"I want to do something too, and I bet Gwen wants to participate as well. You're one of us now, a sister. Maybe a spa day for the three of us," Kiki said. "And there are things we can discuss, the charms, the curse, the Mary spirit you summoned. Can you tell me what happened? I spoke with Ian and he said you conjured her again."

"It was very unpleasant," Janine confessed. "I told everyone the last time that the spirit was angry. This time it was obviously so. One lady thought the spirit wanted to grab her heart and I'm sure the spirit bit one of Ian's students, because he felt it. Caroline Govant claimed that Mary was a kind spirit, but I think she knew better. Gram says Caroline was holding out on us, that Henry Webber found a pile of old history stuffed in her attic."

"Really?" Kiki sounded surprised. "How do you know she bit this person? It could have been something else."

"Angie Minnihan and I both saw it," Janine said. "When she ran into the trees, she clamped her jaws on Oliver, one of the techies, because she knew that he would feel it. He was wearing a device called…" Janine couldn't say *mellow-skin* to Kiki. "A device that makes the skin receptors heightened, more sensitive. I got the distinct feeling that she chose to attack him because he would feel her and she could hurt him, to make a point."

"Interesting," Kiki said. "Maybe I can sweet talk Henry Webber into letting us ransack Caroline's pile of papers. Maybe others have reported her sinister ways too."

"Whatever you think is best," Janine said.

"I hope you and Ian are still coming to Scotland, no matter what happened," Kiki said. "Make it a point to come to the Isle too, my mum would love to meet you. You can visit the coven cottage and the Faerie Glen. I know you have the end of your term, and then your honeymoon, but promise to come at the start of the year, please. Are you still waiting for next fall to think about grad school, is that still your plan? I don't want to keep you too long, I'm supposed to call that detective about the other charm and I'm not sure that I want to talk to him."

Janine blinked. What did Kiki mean? *No matter what happened?* What was she talking about? What had happened? The *talk* that Ian had with his father?

Is that what she meant? Were they not planning to see Ian's father at the start of the year any longer?

"Yes," Janine said. "Yes. That's the plan. You guys will be on location somewhere and I might come along to watch. But, Kiki, what did you just say? What did you mean by that? What happened? Can you tell me what happened?"

There was a long pause.

"It's my awakening ritual, Janine. I've kept my vow of chastity for two cycles of seven years. That's a lot of mystical power to the coven, but weakened if I break my vow on a whim. There needs to be a ritual, a purification of sorts, because sex can be very spiritual to the coven. And that detective promised he would participate in any pagan ceremony I asked, remember? You're a witness."

Kiki's voice was rising and cracking.

"He broke his promise. It was too much to ask of him. Sure, he'd have no problem bedding me in private, on his terms, but ask him to participate in this very important sacred ritual and it's too much for him to bear! He broke a promise, Janine, a promise!" Kiki sounded very upset. Did Janine hear an actual sob? "He left. He's out of the picture now."

"Kiki," Janine said. "I'm so sorry."

"No, no." Kiki's voice pulled back together. "That was a stupid outburst. Don't listen to a word of it. I'm just pouting because I had it planned so nicely, everything is good. Things are going grand, who needs that detective anyway."

"Kiki."

"No, no. I'm just a little stretched over these charms. Do not wear the charm. Put it somewhere safe. I've got to find a way to get the other one back, and, Janine…" Kiki's voice was calm again. "We're going to need a *dragoma* over here, to break a curse, a curse that seems to bring a violent death to certain women, like what happened to Miranda. I really, really, really don't want to ask you to do it, so just think on it. When we see each other, you can tell me how you feel about it, and don't be afraid to say no," she said. "Anyone in their right mind would say no, Janine. No, to getting involved in a curse. But we don't know another living *dragoma*, so we'll need you to say yes, but don't let that sway you."

Kiki rung off.

Of course she would say yes, Kiki knew that. There were too many omens for Janine to turn around now, and in reality, saying yes would not be Janine helping Kiki, it would be Kiki helping Janine. Those charms found Janine. Janine was the one who barely escaped a violent death like Miranda's, and Janine was meant to participate in whatever was going to happen, she knew it. She could feel it. Whether she truly believed any of it or not, she was mixed up in it.

Ian poked his head into the room with an amorous expression on his face. He was fresh and clean and only wore a towel from the shower, but that phone call dashed any hope of an ardent tryst.

"Are you ready for anything special?" he teased. She nodded.

"I'm ready to hear about the conversation you had with your father."

She had not seen those blinking eyes in a very long time. Ian McNally's eyelids always went out of whack when he felt nervous or stressed about something, and now they were revving up to a nice speed.

Chapter 6

Balance *Kiki*

Kiki shuffled through her notes on the haunting of Rio Linda. According to the wagon diary, Irene Lumen and Ingrid Stauch had been cousins. More, the river spirit had been Ingrid's daughter and the charm had belonged to Irene. They probably shared a grandmother who had been a witch of the coven. Wedding bands with triquetra knots were found with the charm, confirming the Celtic origins of Janine's ancestors. It would not be presumptuous to assume those two women practiced pagan teachings. Janine didn't remember it, but under hypnosis, she said the river spirit mentioned a necklace. *Had she meant the Comba Charm?*

Kiki sipped an Irish Coffee in the Blue Pilot, watching for Gwen. The nurses of the cancer ward often frequented the pub in the morning after a night shift and Gwen promised to meet her there. She'd solicit Gwen to make the phone call, because she didn't want to do it herself, not after breaking down when she mentioned the detective to Janine. How embarrassing was that? At least she warned Janine about the charm and asked about the recent summoning. It sounded very unsettling. The orchard spirit actually sounded sinister.

Gwen poked her shoulder making her jump. Kiki stood and greeted the nurses behind Gwen before they disappeared to their usual spot in the back of the bar. Gwen wriggled into the booth looking very professional in her nurse scrubs. With her long red hair tied neatly in an elegant low bun and her speckled face free of make-up, she looked quite youthful and pretty. None of her colleagues suspected Gwen's practices in the coven community, except Bridget Murphy, the pediatric oncologist Gwen was currently attached to.

"Did you give a mind to your seven awakening angels? Katie Walsh rang me today and is dying to know if she's on the list. That lassie is truly enamored with your media persona and she'll be discussing it for years if she's in the mix. But everyone knows she can't keep a steady beat and the drumming will be all out of whack. You'll want a steady beat to help you along."

"Yikes." Kiki sipped her drink. "She's on my list. What do you think of Katie, Annelise, Diana, Roxy, Liz, Ginger and then you?"

"Poor Trinity, she'll be heartbroken, and not a single one of the older sisters, very unbalanced," Gwen observed. "And only Ginger and Diana in that mix suffered an awakening of their own, kept their sacred vow, those two are great choices, but the others, myself included… Maybe drop a couple of us vow breakers for a mother or a crone. Please, seriously consider Trinity, she'll be pleased as punch, and Diana's mum Kate and her grandmother Cara are lovely women who would be grand at such a ritual, all vow keepers. That old lady is still a stunner and could actually be an initiator if you wanted. Each generation should be represented, Kiki, for the best balance."

"God, Gwen, I can't choose another mother if I don't ask the High Priestess of the Base Well. This way I can claim a maiden centered circle of sisters, only those who haven't conceived. Truthfully, I'd rather have five hundred other witches witness my ritual than one Trinity Lovett. I've so failed her by being so happily asexual," Kiki said. "Did you see her eyes? She was very excited when she imagined I broke my vow. Now, she worries I won't be able to fully open up. I know it. She expects to be disappointed and I can't say I'm not worried about it too."

Gwen chuckled and waved her hand. "She expects no such thing, Kiki. That's your wee lassie taking. Dinna forget, Trinity is often asked to such rituals as High Priestess. You don't like to think on these things, but your mother is a very wise woman when it comes to the passions. She's a proper choice for any awakening ritual. You're a sister who's held her vow for seven and seven, to feed your core, that's a first in her lifetime. You're likely the only Core Master she'll ever know, and your awakening is significant on many spiritual levels. Kiki, she'll want to be there to send you some supporting energy."

Kiki rolled her eyes at that. Gwen spoke a truth she didn't want to hear.

"At least invite a couple of the older sisters so she can gossip with them on it. It'll keep your ritual a mite more respectable with a couple of mothers there. I'd wager Roxy and Liz will cozy up to Max the moment you're done and not let the stag get away without a taste of him. A proper initiator should only look to light the flame, but those two will hope to quench part of the fire as well."

Kiki smiled slyly, "Maybe that's why they're on the list. Why should I be the only one in the hot spot in this awakening? Our roguish hero fancies himself quite the adventurer, right? Let's see how he keeps up with Roxy or Liz. I'd love to see Max squirm his way around those two."

Gwen gave her a stern eye. "Always enticing trouble. Do you really want your ritual to end up in debauchery? Please, include a mother in there, maybe two. You can leave in Liz, if you must, but definitely take out Roxy, she never even made a vow. And take me out too. You'll not want any imagery that might spoil his appetite, not during your ritual. He'll be looking around, that one. Include Diana's mum for sure, she's absolutely beautiful, and Trinity if you dare…"

Well then, Gwen never liked it to show, but she was still coming to terms with it all. Most people never suspected, because she was tall and slender, athletic looking, and had a confident air about her. She kept quite fit and most believed she was naturally flat chested. But that wasn't always so.

Gwen went through a very tough time at the end of her teens, breast cancer that led to a double mastectomy, treatment that required harvesting and freezing her eggs, just in case. Her coarse straight hair had come back very curly, and years later, it was still quite wavy with a deeper shade of red, softer. There was no reconstructive surgery for Gwen, and she'd never be able to naturally feed a baby, even if she opted for the reconstruction. Although Gwen quickly accepted her altered body, she claimed it startled new lovers, especially men, and it was the main reason she left Ian. Kiki could still remember Gwen fuming with anger after a weekend with him.

Ian is a liar, she said. *He lied when he said it dinna matter to him. He closed his eyes, Kiki*, she spat. *Every time we faced each other, in the heat of passion, when his eyes fell to my chest, he faltered and I could feel him soften. He needed to look away to get hard again. I'm never going to fuck him again.*

"Don't give me that look, Kiki."

"I'm not giving you a look, my dear," Kiki said. "I'm preparing to ask for favors."

Kiki pulled out her phone, scrolled to Detective Anderson's number, and wrote it down on a sheet of paper.

"I can't talk to him. You have to call and see if he'll give us his man's contact. A member of the Daily family carried the charm to Turkey, to find Miranda and return it. The detective sent a private investigator to follow along and confirm when, and if, they found her. No news means she hasn't been found yet. We need to get that charm back. Maybe the PI can do that for us."

Kiki slid the number to Gwen.

"Better use your phone, he hasn't been accepting my calls."

Everyone except the Daily family assumed the skeleton that turned up in Thatcher Pond was Miranda, strangled and abandoned in the woods, killed by the same man, Richard Wilkens, who brutally knifed Janine Stinger. When Janine summoned the woods ghost, all indications pointed to the spirit being Miranda, who else could it have been? Even Richard's own sister believed her brother murdered Miranda. They sought proof of Richard's dark deeds when they called out the spirit, proof that might help keep him behind bars.

Gwen dialed the detective and he picked up on the third ring. They exchanged pleasantries and she put him on speaker phone so Kiki could hear the conversation. The detective last heard from his private investigator that morning. The PI tailed the family member into the hills around Mount Palandoken. It was rough country and the cell service was sketchy at best, so it might be a few days until the next message came. The detective agreed to give the PI their request to buy the charm. He'd also send the PI Gwen's number.

"So, I guess that necklace is pretty important to your... your group," Detective Anderson said. "I remember Miss Mellow already tried to purchase it from the family. What makes you think anyone will change their mind?"

"No harm in asking again," Gwen said. "But I get your point. We'll probably need to speak to someone else as well."

"Do you have the number for the family?" he asked, "I can send it to you in a text."

"Thank you, detective, as always, you've been very helpful." Gwen's eyes went to Kiki, flustered about what to say next, then shook her red head. "I'm sure you heard the news about Janine and Ian," Gwen spoke toward the phone. "They're making it official the weekend after Thanksgiving."

"It's wonderful news. I could tell the first time I saw them together, those two are meant for each other."

In her mind's eye, Kiki envisioned the detective smiling with his pink aura flaring. Bob Anderson had a soft spot for Janine. As the detective on site when she turned up a bloody mess, he took a personal interest in her case and always kept in touch with her.

"I agree," Gwen said. "I'll be flying to California for the small ceremony."

"I may attend as well, if I can break free. We'll see." He hesitated a moment. "Please give my regards to—Look, I'm aware that Kiki is probably sitting right there, likely listening in," his voice turned soft. "She is, isn't she? Listening."

Gwen's blue eyes glanced toward Kiki, "You're a very good detective," Gwen said.

That got a small chuckle out of him. "I like to think so. So, hello, Kiki. I want to apologize to you, for avoiding your phone calls." He paused. "I admit to behaving a little childish lately. I guess that's why you needed Gwen to make this call. It's unprofessional of me and I hope I haven't burned a bridge. You should know, I have nothing but fond thoughts of our times together and… well, I do miss you."

Kiki snatched up the phone and turned off the speaker. "I miss you too," she said quietly. "Does this mean you might reconsider and come out here next week, and participate in my awakening? It's not the wild affair you imagine it is. We can —"

"I can't," he cut her off. "You know how I feel about it. What you're asking is something that should be a private affair between two people in love, following a wedding. At least for me, it has to be…"

Kiki thrust the phone back at Gwen, shaking her head.

"I can't talk to him."

She could feel the tears threatening to flow and wiped her eyes just in case. For one bleeping moment, she thought he was going to throw his conservative, romantic ideas aside and come back to Scotland. She didn't need to hear his excuses. *Why did he get to decide what was right*, Kiki steamed silently?

With deaf ears, she watched Gwen complete the phone conversation and she got her emotions under control. Kiki never met a man that didn't follow the script she wrote out for him, and she never felt the sting of rejection before Detective Anderson. She took a small swallow of the Irish Coffee in front of her, wishing it was something stiffer. With the detective, she was guaranteed a true awakening, but with anyone else, she might divert the energy out of unease. She didn't want to disappoint the High Priestess of the Base Well, or herself.

Gwen took a sip of her own drink and shot her a tender smile.

"What else I can do for you?" Gwen asked gently.

"Come with me early to California and help look through Caroline Govant's things, possibly meet the orchard ghost. We should give Janine a little bit of a hen, don't you think?"

Gwen nodded. "Without question, a girls' night. Anything else?"

"Yes. Be the one to fetch Max from the airport and be in charge of him. Annie wants to do it, but I'd rather it was you. Give him a good talk about everything, spell it all out for him. Take him to Trinity, if you must, and to the pastor, he'll need to confess."

Kiki wouldn't interact with anyone for a full day and night before her awakening, and someone needed to manage Max for the time before and after her part in the ritual. Max was an outsider and knew nothing.

"Of course," Gwen said. "Any other favors?"

"Yes," Kiki said. "Please participate in this awakening ritual. I'll invite Annelise, Diana, Diana's mum Kate and grandmother Cara, then Ginger, then you, and… and Trinity. You're right about the balance. So, I'll have them all; a dear friend, a maiden, mother and a crone of one family, a coven witch who's recently had an awakening of her own, the High Priestess of the Base Well, and also, the sister I love the most." Kiki took Gwen's hand. "The most beautiful woman I know. I want you there."

Gwen nodded.

"A perfect list then." Her eyes suddenly opened wide. She sat up straight, alert and amused. She smirked. "Ho, ho, here comes your second baseman. Were you planning to meet him?"

Kiki turned just in time to see Rory O'Hara reach their table.

"Kiera Lovett! I've been trying to get a hold of you. You're back from you mum's! Hey there, Gwen." He grinned at them.

Gwen was giving no more favors that day. To Kiki's horror, Gwen swiftly stood and offered Rory her empty seat. She winked at Kiki and suggested waiting for her blood alcohol level to drop considerably before setting out to practice anything. Then, she begged off to join her lovely nurses group in the back, chuckling wickedly the whole way.

The full moon shines for only a moment in time. It occurs at the instant the satellite passes in orbit 180 degrees from the new moon stage and the entire lunar surface facing earth is illuminated. Yet, to the naked eye, the moon appears in the full stage throughout the night before and the night after that singular moment. Those two nights are called the first and last cusps of the full moon, respectively. During the awakening of the Base Well, a coven virgin will enter into a secluded meditation on the first cusp and will not reenter society until the last cusp completely passes, with the ritual event occurring as close to conjunction of sun, earth, and moon as possible.

Annie drove Kiki into the hills on the Quiraing, in the Trotternish area of northern Skye, and dropped her in a carpark at the end of a single track of road. Kiki disappeared into the hills toward a special secret valley, to a little known cave carved into the jagged stones where a girl could spend her meditation before an awakening. She needed to return to the elements, stripped bare of the fabric of society and the unnatural comforts of a human designed world, to prepare her inner Wells. Her singular goal in seclusion was to redirect her flow of energy into opening her animal instincts and preparing her passion center.

Their pagan ethos specified that energy was focused in three infinite wells called the Head, the Core, and the Base, or the Triquetra of Wells. Each well contained characteristics that pointed in either a masculine or feminine direction and formed a trio that snapped together to make a whole. For her entire life, Kiki focused on her Core Well, the spiritual center, so intensely that her Base, the passions that included her sexual appetites, became tenuous. She was practically asexual. But now her time was up and she needed to acknowledge her primal aspects. It was unnatural and unhealthy to shun part of one's Triquetra of Wells, and Kiki's Base needed to be explored. Her soul might become crippled if her wells remained unbalanced, and Coven teaching only allowed for celibacy until the night before her twenty-ninth year. At that age, a maiden needed to transition into becoming a mother if she hadn't already taken that step. As a coven virginal priestess, the transition occurred with an awakening ritual to initiate her into the physical drives and pleasures that led to motherhood.

The man she initially sought for her ritual didn't understand it. Her Base Well had naturally opened to him and she believed the cosmos sent him to share in her initial sexual encounter and to father her child. But when she described the events of an awakening ritual to him, he refused to participate. It never occurred to her, that her ideal man might not be the one to awaken her. That he'd be wrong for it and another might be better suited for the job.

Annie's tarot never lied. The Ace of Wands pointed to a powerful creative rebirth of her Wells, and Max Colliers's name pulled that card. He was very confident, and naughty enough to jump at the chance of participating in what most might consider a risqué exhibitionist escapade. She knew exactly what she'd be getting with Max, and she had been sexually drawn to Max on several occasions. His Base Well overflowed with passion energy and perhaps he was her perfect opposite.

Kiki slipped into the rocky cave with a special tea and candles. She would cleanse her system with fasting and pray for the next twenty-four hours, at which time, her entire balance of energy would be altered completely. She was nervous, excited, and scared. She knelt down and placed a single candle on the floor of the cave. Then, she began an ancient pagan meditation prayer to pry open her base door.

H idden further in the cliffs lay a small protected flat area which the coven often used for awakening rituals. Porous basaltic rocks lined the outer edge of the clearing providing perfect fire bowls. As the moon climbed higher into the night, Kiki detected the fragrance of smoke from those bowls. *They were waiting.* She emerged from her cave hungry and sore, feeling every cell in her body. Her eyes beheld a cloudless night and she took in the cool air. It was a short walk to the protected clearing and the rhythmic drumming drew her to their call. The drums set a steady pace for her beating heart, keeping her calm but alert, knowing he was waiting for her.

For centuries, the women of the cottage respected the lunar effects on a woman's cycle and an awakening ceremony would only occurred during a full moon, because a full moon increased a woman's sexual desire. She rounded the top of the mound and spied into the small valley. She watched her seven angels drumming in a circle, corralling her stag.

Max felt her and looked her way. She watched his red passionate aura flair and practically flood the entire clearing. Yes, she chose the perfect awakening stag. The moon hung directly overhead and the drummers increased their tempo. The time had come. The small valley radiated warmth and her stag stood ablaze and ready, watching her. She could see that Max still didn't quite believe she was coming for him, but he was ready for anything. Well, then, Max was in for a nice surprise. Kiki drew one last breath as a coven virgin, then obliterated any lingering barrier to her base aspects. She was finally ready to jump into the fire.

Chapter 7

Jane Doe *Janine*

One last set of final exams and her Bachelors of Science in Biology from UC Davis would be complete. Not the fancy University of Chicago degree in Biochemistry she once dreamed of, but who cared? What did the exact title on her undergraduate degree matter? What mattered was that she finally completed something. A miracle, especially after the major detours she took along the way: recovering from a near fatal knife attack, being cross-examined in a courtroom, having her sanity questioned, losing herself in a psychiatric ward, battling a crippling depression, months of weaning on and off mentally foggy medication, *losing Sammy*, and two years of *Spectral Analysis* where she was reborn. But reborn into what? A witch? A medium? A *dragoma*? Janine returned the metal charm necklace to the folded paper. She didn't understand her to urge to study it, but lately, she often felt compelled to look at it.

Janine didn't quite accept any of Kiki's labels, she wanted the regular B.S. in Biology instead. It sounded normal and half a semester away. Afterwards, she'd be free to run off on a honeymoon to the South Pacific with her incredibly attractive fiancé, a man she completely adored. He was sweet, sexy, smart, and loved her. They fit so perfectly together and after finals, she'd be carefree and able to focus solely on him. Carefree, except for wondering what would happen in Scotland.

It took major pulling to get the details out of Ian and his fluttering eyelids, but the gist of it entailed his father's total rejection of their planned marriage. Roger McNally decided that Janine was not the right stock after what he witnessed through the lens of the *Spectral Analysis* film. He noticed Janine *bending* to the influence of Ian's cousin, Kiera Lovett, aka Kiki Mellow. Janine stepped into forbidden territory, according to Ian's father. Roger McNally refused to allow the pagan community to darken his door ever again and wouldn't accept a witch into the family, or any woman who remotely accepted their pagan ways.

Hang him, Ian had said. There was a time his father enjoyed his mother's folks on the isle and begged to be included in their world. But once he got his woman and tied her down with a child, Roger set about cutting her off from her coven background. Ian watched his father control his mother in oppressive ways, cutting off her friends, her funds, her automobile, and hiring help that *discouraged* her from leaving the estate, all in the guise of her own protection.

The final straw came when teenaged Ian and Gwen became romantically involved one summer. Neither Ian nor his mother were allowed back to Skye, and Roger had Celeste *watched* and followed. He questioned her motherly instincts and the faulty parenting of their teenaged son. That's when Celeste finally decided to leave Roger. Ian's father first institutionalized her, and when that didn't work, Ian actually believed…

"You aren't serious," Janine said. "You think he had a hand in her accident?"

"I did at fir-first. Sometimes, I still do, somewhere inside." Ian began stuttering as well as blinking. "I accused him outright of ki-killing her with no proof at all. I know, I know, it was a terrible thing to do. Cost him friends, and clients, and a scandal to live down."

VII

The Chariot

Ian McNally is the Chariot.

Ian got his nerves under control with deep breathing, and his stuttering disappeared.

"All because of my gut feelings and bad dreams, which came from grief. It can make a person believe crazy things, grief. You know about that. He couldn't have done anything near what I had accused him of, because he was out of the country when everything happened. And he was heartbroken too, but I didn't care and kept blaming him. It's idiotic. I was just s-so angry at him for the rest of it too. I'm older now, and realize that a sixteen-year-old boy probably shouldn't carry on with girls the way my mother encouraged me on Skye."

Janine hugged him. She pulled him close and kissed him gently. That was the most he ever conveyed about the bad blood between him and his father, and she now understood why he had been so harsh about her wild accusations when Sammy was lost.

She wanted to help him mend his relationship with his father, if he'd let her. Janine missed her own father terribly and didn't want that for Ian. She had been locked away in a hospital refusing to see anyone when her father suddenly passed and she deeply regretted it. Ian wanted to be forgiven, she could tell by the way his blinking and stuttering came and went. He was upset at himself for believing such terrible things about his own father.

"I think I should meet him." Janine climbed into his lap and cuddled him. "Even if you think he is an ass, he's your father and I should meet him and at least try to win him over. You don't have to protect me from him, you know. I'd like to meet your aunt too, Kiki's mother, I'd love to see what she's like."

Ian agreed to take her to Scotland on the return from their honeymoon, but not before, as originally planned. He didn't want his father spoiling the romance. If she wanted, they could drive onto Skye and meet his Auntie Trinity too, Kiki's mother. But when that happened, she should remember that she had asked for it. If she thought Kiki was a bit colorful, just wait until she met Trinity.

After Ian departed to teach his night class, Janine flipped on the television for background noise as she organized her notes. The Comba charm and the conversation with Kiki crowded her thoughts. Kiki's special ritual must have already occurred, because the full moon had just passed. Janine wondered who Kiki invited and felt disappointed that Detective Anderson let her down. He seemed positively in love with Kiki when they met in Chicago. Whatever happened in Scotland, whatever was said, really hurt Kiki's feelings, she had been very upset during that phone call. Then, Janine's phone pinged, and the caller ID told her it was the detective.

"Detective Bob Anderson," Janine said. "I was just thinking about you."

"I'll bet," he said. "I'm so sorry, Janine. I didn't expect it."

My goodness, Janine thought. Did he have ESP?

"Well, you know, sometimes Kiki comes up with some surprising ideas. It's not your fault for hesitating. It took me a while to take some of her pagan rituals seriously. Not your fault for being put off by it. She's just used to getting her way with people…" Janine heard him take in a breath and paused.

"No, no. It's not about any of that. It's about the commuting of his sentence. The dental results on that skeleton came back and it was not Miranda Daily in the pond. We don't know who the skeleton belongs to, not yet, and the governor decided to immediately commute Richard Wilkens's sentence. He's signing the papers next week. The governor believes the department was out to get him, set him up unfairly due to an ongoing squabble between law enforcement and his family. They've been pushing that narrative for quite some time."

"What?" She was stunned.

"I'm sorry, Janine. Wilkens has been working the governor since before his parole hearing. And I have to warn you, that's just the tip of the iceberg here. Maybe you'd better turn on the news, national news, they caught me outside a moment ago. I believe it's just starting to break."

She switched channels to the national news and the picture on the screen startled her. A reporter stood outside the house on Thatcher Road and a mug shot of Richard Wilkens popped up in the top righthand corner of the screen. He wore a sweet smile with his angelic face, and they actually used a photo of him in a choir robe.

Then came a picture of Janine. It was a promo shot from *Spectral Analysis* in that racy outfit Max Colliers insisted on. *Good grief!* The reporter babbled on, but Janine didn't hear a word. She always knew her secret would get out, being the girl left for dead in the woods who actually survived. In the distant background, she recognized Detective Anderson's voice calling her name and retrieved her cell phone.

"What does this mean? Is this worse than parole?" she asked softly.

"I'm afraid it is," the detective said. "He's still a convicted felon, of course, but his punishment has been erased. We won't be able to tie him down when he gets out. The governor doesn't believe he's guilty and nearly pardoned him."

Janine forgot to say goodbye when she hung up, then muted her phone because call after call after call kept coming in. Her sister, Lauren, Gram, girls on the soccer team, unidentified numbers, Gwen, Misha from her study group, her sister again, Carlos, Doctor Crisper, Max, an old friend from her University of Chicago days, and several unidentified numbers. She muted the chime for texts too, because when people couldn't get through, most sent a message instead. Janine set the phone down. She pushed it away and focused on the news. They stretched the story out, it was their highlight, so the reporter decided to recap the entire Coed Captive case of sex, blood, and deceit.

It was a black Labrador that led Hank Jones to a gruesome scene in a secluded area of Thatcher Woods where a brutal attack had occurred. Mr. Jones feared they had stumbled upon a dead body, until his dog Sparky insistently began licking the face and neck of Jane Doe from Chicago and he realized that she was still breathing, but just barely. The victim was a young student from the University of Chicago, and for years, the court ordered her identity be kept confidential, but today we learn her true identity. Jane Doe from Chicago is none other than Janine Stinger from the hit ghost hunting television program Spectral Analysis. *Janine Stinger went mysteriously missing for ten days before Mr. Jones and his dog Sparky found her. Evidence indicates that she had been shackled by the wrist, beaten, and sexually assaulted before taking multiple knife blows to her torso. She very nearly died. The big shocker for folks following the story occurred when she finally named her attacker. After nearly two weeks of recovery, she finally opted to tell the police that Richard Wilkens, the man keeping vigil by her hospital bedside, was the man who stabbed her. Miss Stinger claimed that Wilkens held her captive in a house across the street from Thatcher Woods, chased her down, and tried to kill her after she escaped. Many people wondered why she didn't name him sooner? Some believe it was to protect the baby she carried. Perhaps she did not want to send the father of her child to prison. Others believed she suffered from hysterical delusions, or perhaps she wanted revenge following a lover's quarrel. Others suggested she stabbed herself in an attempt to abort the baby. What followed next was a long and sensational trial in which the defense claimed Miss Stinger suffered from traumatic delusions and was mistaken in her claims. Many believed Richard Wilkens had been unfairly accused and convicted, and today those people are celebrating. Richard Wilkens will be set free by noon on…*

The reporter continued with speculations about the baby, where was it, who had it, what gender was it and why did Janine Stinger give it up for adoption? Did Richard Wilkens now have the right to demand meeting his child? They showed a few clips from the *Spectral Analysis* television show and reminded the country that Janine Stinger recently announced her engagement to Ian McNally.

Detective Anderson popped up on the split screen speaking to a different reporter, followed by Doctor Crisper from the psychiatric hospital. He nervously patted down his crazy hair while smiling self-consciously. As usual, his buttons were misaligned. Janine turned the volume down and picked up her phone.

She called Gram to let her know she was fine. Then, she called her sister, Juliana. She tried Kiki, but there was no answer, so she called Gwen. Gwen sounded very concerned.

"Will he try to contact you, do you think?"

"I don't know," Janine said. "Maybe."

The real answer was *yes*. Even though he would be told to stay away from her, she knew he wouldn't. When would he show up? Next week, when he emerged from incarceration, or next month? Or would he wait until she became relaxed and unwary? That's probably what he'd do, wait and surprise her when she least expected it. Janine didn't want to think about that yet.

"It's the skeleton I'm calling about, Gwen. They didn't mention it on the news, but Detective Anderson told me a little while ago that it isn't Miranda Daily, the skeleton from the pond. It's somebody else. Is Kiki around? She's not answering her phone. Is she okay? Did her ritual go well?"

"Kiki's in a solitary meditation," Gwen said. "Her awakening was a glorious success, but she's still in seclusion. Sometimes a witch will stay secluded far into a waning gibbous. I'm not expecting to see Kiki until the Samhain in a couple of days. None of this news has touched her ears yet."

"Well, it's not really an emergency, is it?" Janine said. "The notoriety will just be an annoyance for a few days, and Rick doesn't scare me anymore, well, not too much. It's the skeleton I'm confused about."

"I agree, it's very confusing. We'll figure it out. I'm worried about you, lass. You're bound to get a lot of unwanted attention. Shocked folks might try calling you. Do you have a preference there?"

Janine sighed. "I'm going to handle it by ignoring the calls. I mean, it is what it is. I can't stop people from talking, but I don't have to participate in it, right? About that skeleton, do you think it belongs to the spirit? Was it her own death vision, or Miranda's, that she gave to Kiki? Where do think Miranda is? Do you think there's another body in those woods?"

"I truly believe the spirit would only give her own death vision," Gwen said. "And the charm necklace must have been hers as well. At first, Kiki claimed the vision appeared to be two visions woven into one. Perhaps the skeleton is a girl who died after Miranda, or before, another victim he passed the charm to. As for Miranda, there's a private investigator in Turkey right now. If she's still alive, we'll hear of it soon enough. Don't worry about these things, Janine, just focus on your wedding and all the happy events going on around you. Let us worry about the charms and such. I'll make sure to keep you informed of important news. For now, put this stuff behind you, if you can. Move forward."

"Thanks, Gwen."

Then, Ian burst through the door, he cut his class short when someone mentioned the Coed Captive case. She spotted a news van outside, on the curb, before he closed the door. Now it was his turn to comfort her. Janine couldn't help blaming the charm in the bottom drawer of her jewelry box for bringing the negative luck. She never should have taken it out of its wrapper.

Chapter 8

The Samhain *Kiki*

Trinity invited Max Colliers to stay through the harvest holiday, but he declined as business called. He lingered around the cottage for two days, hoping to see Kiki, but she stayed in seclusion and his time ran out. Gwen ferried him to the small Isle airstrip where he caught his private jet. Annelise went along for the ride, practically drooling over the fact that Max owned a private jet, and she answered all his questions about Kiki and their college days, telling him anything he wanted to know. When they returned to the cottage, Kiki had emerged from her post awakening seclusion, ready to rest in luxury before the Wiccan festivities began.

"Well then," Gwen meandered around her room. "Were you waiting for Max Colliers to depart, or did you really need a prolonged seclusion to recover from that very nice awakening ritual?"

Kiki smirked at her, relaxing with a sample of George MacLeod's homemade whisky. She sat atop the bedsheets scribbling in her notebook. Her phone lay charging off to the side with all the alerts still flashing. She hadn't checked a message yet. She noticed Gwen acting a tad uneasy, the sparking green in her aura gave her away.

"Aye, I was waiting for Max to leave," Kiki confessed. "But mostly for Trinity to get busy with Samhain doings. Do you think the ritual went well? I certainly felt a surge of cosmic energy flooding the small valley. How did the sisters take it?"

"Trinity raved that it was the most passionate and powerful awakening she's ever seen. Then again, she's your mother and has always bragged about you. She was very lit up about the way you came in and took charge of the stag, then just let go like that." Gwen chuckled. "It was a highly energized event, and you very nearly shocked me, my wee yin. I've never witnessed an awakening before, but I can't imagine anything to top that business. I hid my eyes most of the time, concentrating on my job as drum leader. Dinna worry, I spied your mother hiding her eyes too, you made the High Priestess of the Base Well quite bashful and proud!" Gwen laughed hard enough to turn her whole face red.

"I very much enjoyed making her proud," Kiki said, and they both fell over in a giggling fit. "I hope Trinity doesn't sit me down to discuss it," Kiki got herself under control. "What did Max do after my departure? Did he dally? I could see Ginger get googly eyed on him out there, hard to imagine he'd resist that toothsome lass."

"Not just Ginger. Annie and Diana got pretty stirred up after that display of yours, but they each had a man nearby to settle them up. Max may be a player, but he's first string from what I saw, and funnily, Max wasn't having any of it when you left." Gwen nodded at her surprise. "When we got back here, Ginger hung about, plying him with drink, but he was waiting on you, acting like a perfect gentleman at the queen's dinner, charming and refined. Your mother approves of him, I must warn you. He charmed the socks off her."

Kiki hooted at that, "Is that so? Maybe I should have come back sooner. I felt an interesting desire to revisit some of his finer points during my seclusion."

It was true. The next morning, she found herself fanaticizing about Max Colliers with very erotic images, which completely surprised her.

Gwen picked up Kiki's phone.

"A natural reaction. You dinna check your messages yet? Shall I tell you what's transpired while you were out hiking the hills?" Gwen poured more whisky into Kiki's copper cup and took a sip for herself. "The results are back on the skeleton in the pond. Not Miranda Daily."

Kiki blinked.

"They dinna know who it is yet. And then I got a message from the private investigator. There's a woman in Turkey, and everyone says the woman is Miranda, even the family member positively identifies her as Miranda. Miranda is alive and well, not dead at all, and definitely not the spirit from the woods."

"How did we get it wrong?" Kiki's eyes were wide. "Who was that spirit, if not Miranda Daily? Do you think she will give up her Comba necklace? Did the investigator ask about that?"

Gwen giggled almost uncontrollably. The very freckles on her face darkened, and her eyes were watering.

"Oh, Kiki," Gwen caught her breath. She took another deep sip out of Kiki's whisky cup. "That girl in Turkey says the charm isn't hers. She never lost her charm." Gwen's blue eyes reflected her unease. "She says she'd like to keep it but knows it isn't hers to keep." Gwen nodded and paced, skin growing redder by the second. "She's planning to come here and bring the charm, to discuss where it really belongs. She actually asked about our Comba charms. Apparently, someone else is attempting to procure them."

"Good god, when is she coming? I don't want to miss it."

"Not till after the winter solstice. The cabal she lives in is very bound to the Samhain and Yule seasons and cannot leave their homeland until after the new year. We'll need to be patient," Gwen told her. "Of course, Trinity is beside herself with the whole affair. She's adamantly looking for a translator for those books. Cara has been a bit of help but doesn't know the language used in some of it. She says it's an old code, long forgotten and they're looking for the cypher. Those ladies have been very busy flushing out the elements of the charm curse."

Kiki suddenly realized something of personal significance. She regained her copper cup, drained it, and smiled at Gwen.

"Do you know what this means?" she asked. "It means that he didn't break his promise to me after all, Bob Anderson. He only promised to participate in a pagan ritual if they found Miranda Daily in that pond. So then, maybe I'll forgive him for standing me up and allow him to sire my baby at the Beltane. Perhaps I'll meet him halfway with that, private and proper."

Kiki stretched out on the bed.

"That spirit, even if the bones weren't Miranda, she's still a victim of that demon in the jail. The spirit affirmed her murderer as Richard Wilkens, remember? And I saw him in my vision. Maybe there's some way to link him to her murder."

"Oh, and that." Gwen closed her eyes. "Apparently, he's not dangerous enough to keep locked up. Some governor decided to let him go."

"So, he got his parole." Kiki grabbed her phone. Should she call Janine?

"Something like that. But they dinna call it parole. And now everyone knows the lass in that story is Janine. It was all over the news. Don't call right away. Give her a breather. Leave a text message, maybe. She's dealing with it in her own way." Gwen gave Kiki a hug. "You'll need to get a bit of sleep yerself, for the Samhain. We're planning something with the charms in Trinity's cabinet."

Back in the wild hills, a large bonfire blazed in an open glen close to the small valley of her awakening. Fast moving clouds swirled in the upper atmosphere and the air felt cool and crisp. Sharp igneous stones poked defiantly from the emerald grasses. She had never seen anything more beautiful, or erotic, as that expanse of highland hills. Kiki inhaled sea salt intwined with oak smoke, an aroma that stirred the life between her legs, bringing back memories of Max and his engorged male appendage. *Shut it off, close the door*, she ordered herself, shocked that her energy drained so easily into lust.

Several small fires littered the landscape, which, along with a waning gibbous moon, cast dramatic shadows over the festivities. Tourist and locals dressed for the occasion with painted faces in red or white, or with adornments that hinted at sacred animals. Children bobbed for apples, and scurried about dressed as ghouls. The coven purposely mixed with the outsiders at the harvest bonfire, the bigger the party, the better. Festive events provided the perfect lure to keep prying eyes from the more sacred aspects of the Samhain. Later, select sisters of the coven would quietly gather in the Faerie Glen to make an offering to the fae, then, at the witching hour, coven members would climb atop Castle Ewen to pray and attempt a summoning. This year, they hoped to summon victims of the charms. Often, they would meditate until dawn on that rocky spire.

Annelise, Gwen, and Kiki carried cups of warm mead and wore long flowing capes. Besides having a bit of fun, the main goal of attending the bonfire festival was to absorb positive energy into their cores. They would need it later, at Castle Ewen, when they prayed for the new year and summoned the spirits. After her awakening, Kiki's energy wells felt very out of whack and her entire focus now dropped to her Base Well, distracting her. She dearly needed to refill her core.

Kiki spotted Trinity in the center of the music, surrounded by her usual collection of male admirers, dancing quite vigorously in a jig some might define as Irish line dancing. Her mother's green eyes flash wickedly at everyone they encountered.

A bit further from the main crowd, a small group prepared for a fire dancing show. Attractive men and women in dark leather clothing placed cans of water in a semicircle, clearing an area for their act. Annie pulled Gwen and Kiki closer to get a good spot.

The fire dancing ritual had become more and more elaborate in recent years. Unlike a Polynesian show with staff torches, the dancers in this pagan arena used fire poi, which consisted of a wick at the end of a long chain. It resembled a medieval weapon. The dancers swung the glowing wicks in elaborate patterns while dancing to drum heavy music.

Kiki's eyes kept falling on a particular fellow with thick black hair and taunt bulging muscles under his leather vest. His black eyes fixed on her, holding her captive. At one point, he poured a flammable liquid across his leather covered chest and lit it aflame before tossing his fire poi about. He glared intensely as he performed, sending a cascade of hot sexual energy at her. Kiki was surprised at how easily her passion well flooded while watching his gyrating movements.

Normally, she'd divert that energy right into her core, but somehow, she had problems closing that door again. The sea aromas, the bonfires, the tight pants on that man, and the night air were doing a number on her senses. She glanced to Annie and Gwen as they dissolved into giggles.

"Your mouth is hanging open, Kiera, and you too, Annie. I take it those fire gods have bewitched the both of you." Gwen laughed at them, but she was quite flushed herself.

"It's my Base Well door. I find now that I've opened it, I cannot seem to close it again," Kiki observed.

Annie giggled and pushed her blond rings aside.

"He's hot, right? Shall we talk to him? That fine fellow happens to be Andrew MacLeod. He might be a bit put off with you, Kiki. He dearly wanted to participate in your ritual awakening and you crossed him off the list pretty quickly. The other man is Sam Welks, he's my fellow. He's pretty exciting, right?"

"Very exciting," Kiki agreed.

Kiki gave Andrew MacLeod another long look. Red blaring passion emanated from his halo as he stared across the short distance. Her mouth watered and she realized that she desperately wanted him in a venereal way. She was flooded with an erotic vision of his thick thighs between her legs. Kiki grimaced at herself and consciously bent his energy toward her core. She shook her head at Annie and they broke off in different directions. She needed to escape from that fire god before she jumped right on top of him.

While Annie skipped over to chat with the fire dancers, Kiki and Gwen slunk off to find a quiet spot away from the main throng of the crowd. Her eyes flitted from one man to another, imagining how each might have behaved in her ritual. Perhaps she should have stayed in seclusion a bit longer, she felt as if the entire cosmos had turned upside down. Here she sat, lusting after everything in trousers when just a few days ago she couldn't have cared less. Kiki stewed a bit, drinking her mead while actually daydreaming about Max Colliers. *How ridiculous.* Gwen's eyes were amused as they passed in her direction.

"Maybe you need to run loose a little," Gwen chuckled. "It happens after an awakening, they say, girls will enter a very lustful stage. I mean, hello, you've been awakened. No worries, I'll keep an eye on Trinity and let you know when we're moving to the glen. Go on and get it out of your system. I hear Andrew MacLeod has a very nice tool for such things."

Kiki set her mead down hard and glared at Gwen.

"I don't have anything in my system, Gwen, at least nothing I can't control," Kiki snapped, but suddenly stopped. She glanced around the hundreds of faces walking in the crowd, something was wrong. "Where's Bridget, the oncologist?" Kiki asked. "I thought she was coming to Skye? I didn't even notice she wasn't here." Kiki studied Gwen.

Gwen might be chuckling, but she wasn't happy.

"I am such an *eejit*, Gwen. A totally self-absorbed *eejit*."

"A flooding of the Base Well can make one a bit self-absorbed, my wee lass." Gwen patted her back. "Bridget is a tad upset at me and decided not to come."

Kiki sidled next to Gwen and put a comforting arm around her, worried. She hoped Bridget hadn't gotten a false idea about Kiki. It's happened before. Kiki and Gwen's friendship was deep and everlasting, coven sisters that bonded since before their memories could recall, but Kiki was not one of the many lovers from Gwen's past. Even so, whenever Gwen chose a girlfriend, they often became suspicious of Kiki because Gwen was not the most faithful partner in a relationship and often succumbed to her spontaneous desires, fouling things up.

Gwen sighed. "My fault again, I had a bit of a snogging session with Max before your awakening and tried to explain it to her. She found my reasoning extremely weak."

"Gwen!"

"It needed doing," Gwen defended herself. "It's the only way I could ease into the situation of showing him my chest, or lack thereof. I dinna want his first glance to be during your ritual. It's the sort of thing that needs to be seen and absorbed over time. You dinna understand, Kiki, the initial sight can turn a person quite solidly cold. I've plenty of experience with this."

Kiki didn't know Bridget as well as she'd like because they only just met when Kiki returned to Scotland. Bridget had a very sweet and serious aura, all blue and golden highlights. Kiki realized that, in her egocentric pursuits, she had been monopolizing Gwen's life, getting Gwen into all kinds of situations and asking for favors as if they were still young girls. Grown up Gwen moved in circles that didn't include the coven, or Kiki.

"Dinna worry yerself over Bridget, she'll come around or she won't." Gwen wrinkled her speckled nose as her ginger eyelashes fluttered. "She knows I couldn't possibly be interested in one such as Max Colliers."

"I bet she's getting tired of me too," Kiki said. "If you need to run off right now, you should do it, and if you really shouldn't fly out to California, especially early, it's okay. I'm starting to realize I might be mucking things up for you, dropping back onto your life like this."

Gwen smiled at her with the familiar expression she always used when she thought Kiki was being stubborn or silly. Gwen took her hand and squeezed it.

"I need to go to the castle at three and see what's to be known when Trinity takes out those charms. You don't have to be sorry, or thinking it's always you dragging me into these things. Celeste was dear to me too, you know, and I want to know the history of those charms. I'm well invested in what's to do about it."

Gwen eyes were quite serious.

"And nothing could keep me from being at Ian's wedding, I've been waiting for it, praying for it. I need to be there. Bridget will be patient with me, or no, and she could come to California if she wants. I invited her. I just need to wait on her forgiveness, and she does make a good a point. I've messed up in the past, and so it wasn't a singular event, fooling around with Max. I can't help it if sometimes I itch for a lad. She's usually very understanding about a lad."

Kiki nodded, "I hope Max wasn't an arse about it. He can be a world class arse."

"He was a wee shocked at first, but recovered in a grand way. He asked a lot of questions, like he was trying to understand things, and he wasn't an arse, he really wasn't. I was delighted and surprised with Max. He wondered why I opted away from a reconstruction and said my reasoning was spot on." Gwen laughed. "I like Max, Kiki."

"That's because you two are very alike in your rooted aspects."

Gwen laughed at that. Then, she stood up and looked to the far side of the clearing toward the bonfire. Kiki could see what got her attention. Trinity was on the move. Kiki watched her mother's head turn, and their eyes met. Time to head to the Faerie Glen, Trinity eyes conveyed, and then to the castle with the charms.

Chapter 9

Castle Ewen *Kiki*

Trinity sent Annelise into the Faerie Glen with several of the younger sisters to make offerings to *them* that reside between the cottage and Castle Ewen. They prepared gemstone bowls with a portion of thick milk, butter, and the dried petals of wild flowers and herbs. Trinity also baked sweet cakes. The offering needed to be made, if they planned to stir the aether on the top of Castle Ewen, and gifts were always placed in the glen on the night of their pagan new year. The tradition went back centuries. After the younger girls left, Trinity gathered the small collection of Saint Comba charms and ten of their twelve coven priestesses converged in her den. Two missing priestesses would put a blemish on their ritual, but a couple of other sisters were thrilled to fill in.

Each moon priestess represented one of the twelve lunar cycles, as well as a Sacred Well. Coven Priestesses of the Base Well included Gwen, Ginger, a mother named Rebecca, and Trinity as the High Priestess. The maiden, mother, and crone from Kiki's awakening, Diana, Kate, and Cara, were all Priestesses of the Head Well, along with another woman named Lisa. Kiki belonged to the Core Well, along with two very old women, and a young mother, Rebecca. Other witches in the coven included virginal priestesses keeping a vow of chastity and those waiting to become a moon priestess someday. They were mostly young girls learning the pagan arts or late joiners to the coven, like Annie. They rarely attended a meeting in the private den, but were always invited to rituals in the glen. The two missing witches, Rebecca and Lisa, were in the midst of motherhood and could not attend the celebration on Skye that year.

Each priestess silently filed out carrying a portion of the alter to be built, while Trinity ferried the box of charms. At the witching hour on the Samhain, the veil between worlds stretched so thin that it was possible to communicate to loved ones long passed. Whispers in prayer resulted in answers. Mostly in the form of a silent touch of a rekindled memory, but sometimes in a full vision. Never, in all her years of ritual on Castle Ewen, had Kiki actually seen, or heard, a ghost. Although the hill vibrated with cosmic energy, it was not the same as a soul stamped with enough essence to form a true entity. But this year was different. This Samhain, they planned a summoning ritual along with the prayer. They hoped the residual energy in each Saint Comba charm would coax out their lost sisters.

Castle Ewen emerged at the end of a narrow dirt trail, which required a single file line for the hike. The castle stood above the brilliant green of the Faerie Glen and rose strikingly into the night sky. Castle Ewen wasn't a castle at all, but a natural tubular rock formation that appeared to be the hardened stone tower of ancient ruins. On top of the rocky hill, there was only enough room for the alter and the twelve lunar priestesses. Any other witch would have to stay in the glen and take their chances among the fae. When the last coven priestess reached the summit of the rocky hill, they began to build an alter on the small plateau.

They built a small fire and placed a cauldron over the flames. Old Cara added water, herbs, and spice to the pot to make a special tea. Next to the cauldron, a small oak plank was balanced on the ground until it lay flat, then a three wick candle was placed in the center. Circling the candle, Kiki and Gwen built a crystal grid of gemstones in the shape of a hexagram, leaving the six points of the star open for each of the Comba charms in Trinity's box. Larger stones, with the Celtic carvings, were placed at opposite the edges of the plank and incense sticks were placed on top of them. A two handled metallic cup sat on the plank while a basket of odd shaped black candles lay at the other end. Trinity slowly pulled the charms from her pockets and named the owner of each charm as she placed them at the tips of the crystal grid.

"Sister Lillias Blair, sister Holly MacLeod, sister Freya Tod, sister Gillian MacDonald, sister Abigail Kirkpatrick, and sister Celeste McNally." She kissed the last charm before placing it, then lit one wick of the thick candle before stepping back with the others.

Cara ignited the second wick before returning to her cauldron to stir the contents. Her granddaughter Diana sat very close to her, at the ready to assist as needed.

From the back of the group, another old woman stepped forward. This woman radiated a brilliant aura, even in the darkened night. Kiki watched swirls of blue intertwined with purple radiate from Eva's core. Her energy was surprisingly thick, even though she was a stooped, wizened woman with silver white hair and a face carved with age. Eva was the oldest living sister in their coven. She neared the century mark but refused to slow down or step aside for a younger witch to step up. Aside from being the High Priestess of the Core Well, she was also Priestess of the Blood Moon, sometimes called the Hunter's Moon, and she ruled the Samhain. She stepped forward and lit the last wick with a shaky hand, then set the sticks of incense aflame releasing a sweet spicy odor which permeated the air.

"Ring in here, ring in clear, all ring in our new year. Night will fall, night will laugh, we welcome in our darker half. Burn the veil, till shriveled and curled, met us from the other world. Come sisters hear, come sisters see, so I command, so mote it be."

Eva's voice came so loud and strong that in Kiki's mind, Eva appeared a giant.

"Sisters Lillias, Holly, Freya, Gillian, Abigail Celeste."

Each witch knelt on the top of Castle Ewen to pray for the six sisters named. They prayed for them to find peace and to bring them word of what must be done. Breathing in the fragrance of incense, each searched and cleansed their own hearts of foul feelings. They each prayed to be worthy of a vision. Eva repeated the names.

"Lillias, Holly, Freya, Gillian, Abigail, Celeste."

Eva kept reciting the names and composed it into a song and the others collectively joined in. From down in the glen, Kiki could hear the music of younger voices echoing the chant. From behind her on the path a few younger girls had climbed the hill to watch, beautiful maidens with bright eyes on high alert, hoping for a vision. The air rang with the melody of those names.

The name chant continued softly as Diana fetched the metallic two handled Quaich and held it while Cara spooned in liquid from the cauldron. Then, she raised the cup high and recited a common oath.

"We share this drink and every breath, to seal our bonds in life and death."

Cara carefully swallowed a sample of the tea, then she passed the cup to Diana. Diana also recited the oath before drinking, then passed the silver cup to Eva, who passed it to Trinity. After her sip and oath, Trinity reached into the basket of black candle stubs and lit one with the flame of the alter candle, then found a spot to settle.

Soon, each moon priestesses moved to the alter and recited the oath, *we share this drink and every breath, to seal our bonds in life and death.* Each took a mouthful of the bitter sweet potion and ignited a small candle. Each carefully cradled the flame back to their place of prayer, forming a tight circle around the center alter.

Kiki sipped the tea after Gwen and felt the warm spice run fast in her veins. Kiki sheltered her candle, thinking of her Auntie Celeste. When the final priestess joined the circle of light, the High Priestess Eva raised her hands and the chanting ceased. Eva bent to the alter and whispered something softly before blowing out the alter candle. Then, she closed her eyes to see what she would see.

"My heart summons you, my auntie," Kiki whispered, then blew out her own candle and closed her eyes. Kiki could already feel the tea coloring the visions in her head.

The air over Castle Ewen grew cold, and the stillness grew tense with concentrated energy. Kiki watched an image of her Auntie Celeste grow very distinct behind her eyes. Celeste's own eyes were the same blue as Ian's, and they shared a similar smile. Kiki felt the warmth of Celeste's embrace. She calmed as the essence flooded her core. She could hear the melody of Celeste's lullaby whispering in her ear. The sound lulled her breathing into an slow rhythm as a vision took form.

Her auntie tending the herbs in Meg's garden in the summer, while sunlight magnified the red highlights in her dark hair. Then, the images cascaded rapidly; her auntie crushing herbs in a mortar, swimming in lochs, spying faeries, designing gemstone grids, brewing tea, braiding hair, walking the hills, holding hands, and on and on they went. But mostly, she saw that beaming smile for Kiera Lovett, her favorite wee lassie. *Kiki*, Celeste called her, whenever Kiera ran from Trinity in a huff. *Oh, dear Kiki, mellow out, my wee yin*, that's how Celeste always began her consolations, even as Kiki grew older. *Kiki, be mellow, your green eyed monster is just yourself, looking back to smooth your path.* Then, her auntie would speak to her green eyed mother and Kiki knew everything would be better, because her auntie was the big sister and Trinity had to listen.

But listen to me carefully, my wee yin. The voice turned very quiet and hard. *You wore the charm and now you are marked. Complete the curse, expel the demon, to erase your mark.*

Then, there were more images of her auntie in the glen, and the cottage, and on the McNally Manor. The Comba charm hung around her auntie's neck glinting in the moonlight, calling for attention. A distorted image reflected in the metal as someone closed in. But who? Surely someone Celeste knew. Kiki watched a large hand reach out to grab Celeste's long slender neck, then another hand reached up to help the first, and Kiki could see the fat ring that might be the one on her Uncle Roger McNally. She could feel her auntie strain with the task of trying to breath and not succeeding. As the life left her eyes, Kiki could see Celeste's recognition of her murderer reflected clearly in those bulging blue pools, and even with the life being squeezed out of her, Kiki knew that her auntie still loved him.

Dawn broke and woke her. The cauldron fire had gone out. Kiki felt the caps of her knees aching and the beginnings of a headache behind her eyes. She came to a sitting position, drained. Around her, every priestess wore a tired and worn face. Gwen stirred, wiping the tears from her lovely freckled cheeks. Gwen and Kiki grasped hands.

"Kiera," Gwen whispered. "Celeste spoke to me. She was indeed strangled by someone she knew. I got the sense that it was Roger."

Kiki nodded. "I saw it too." But it was something they always suspected.

"Celeste urged me to search the grimoire." Gwen's eyes were rimmed with red. "*Her grimoire*. There is a charm that can be used to expel a demon and it *must be recited to the demon to release the death marks*, she said. I'm not certain what that means. She wrote hundreds of charms in her book, how will I know which it is?"

As the sisters began to chat, they discovered that nearly all of them had a vision or heard something in an episode of clairaudience. They began to share stories of what transpired in their encounters.

Eva reported seeing Freya Tod, a lovely young woman from generations past. Freya insisted that *who'll be the last one, must be. And she who can speak the words, must speak. Otherwise the demon will live forever, feasting on the sins of the chosen.*

Diana heard from Holly MacLeod, who warned that those who follow Comba are cursed. There must be an offering, *one each for redemption*, before the curse can be broken. *There is still a missing piece.*

Trinity witnessed the murder of all six of the sisters. Each knew their murderer intimately with love, and lust, and passion.

Kate, Diana's mother, was given a vision from one who may have been Gillian. That spirit warned that the demon will try to weasel away from accepting an agreed payment and will seek to mark more and more. The demon must witness the testimony while in the presence of a strong ring of energy. It will take a collective effort to move the fae.

The lovely crone, Cara, heard from Lillias Blair. Lillias once lived in the cottage and built the stone wall. Her ashes lay scattered under the oak tree near the wall. She had been strangled and burned at the stake. She chose the lustful seed of the wrong man, and her predicament put her sisters in danger. Lillias did say, *do you th' evil deed 'n it wull come back on ye twelvefold. One each fer redemption shall hurl th' curse.* At least, that's what old Cara believed was said.

The others reported similar visions, with similar warnings. Trinity invited the sisters to the cottage, to write their accounts into the book of happenings and to enjoy a hearty breakfast. It had been a long time since such visons touched each of them so equally.

Gwen drove back to the city hoping to patch things up with Bridget before the trip to California, while Kiki decided to stay extra days at the cottage at her mother's request. Most of the coven sisters spent the day in and out of Trinity's house, excited and nervous at the same time. Everyone could feel something brewing in the air. Even the small non-pagan community reeled from the aftereffects of the Samhain Fire Festival.

Trinity organize a small feast and bonfire in the rear yard to settle their agitation, but Kiki opted to stay hidden inside. She hadn't divulged everything about her vision to Trinity, because she didn't want an interrogation from her mother. No one knew that she was warned that she had been marked. Kiki only reported the part where Celeste said, *complete the curse, expel the demon, erase the marks.* Kiki didn't want to admit to her mother that she had worn one of the charms in the spring. *Trinity was right again, Kiki was hiding her missteps from her mother.* She knew her lingering childish pride was a stupid thing, but she couldn't help it.

Kiki lounged in the front parlor drinking more of George MacLeod's smooth whisky. She felt a strong desire to deliver some to California for the wedding, along with an engraved Quaich cup. Ian would love drinking a communal pinch with Janine to seal their union.

Kiki was enjoying her moment of solitude when the door burst open and two fellows carrying flowers stumbled in. Right behind them, Annelise was laughing. Already two sheets to the wind, Annie enjoyed her festival days.

"Ho there, Kiera," Annie giggled under her halo of yellow curls. "Looks like your stag sent bunches of pretty blooms. I think he meant them to come on different days, but with the goings on, nothing's been delivered. They were sitting in the post, as pretty as a garden."

One of the men chuckled with Annie, but the other man stood stiffly, staring at Kiki with dark intense eyes, Andrew MacLeod. He no longer wore his tight leather pants, but his denim was just as form fitting. Kiki spotted the curve of that tool everyone kept talking about. He noticed her interest and gave her a thorough looking over. She felt volumes of passion sent her way, exactly what she needed to recharge her weakened core.

Kiki sat up and smiled sweetly at Andrew, soaking in the testosterone powered surge of energy. It was an old trick some of the witches used, taking in one type of energy and changing it to another. Kiki was very good at funneling any type of energy into her psychic core. Spiritual communication required core energy and the previous night had drained her into a limp mess. She imagined the other sisters were out recharging their own batteries with festive merrymaking.

"We meant to deliver these to your room and surprise you. Surprise!" Annie's big blue eyes blazed with humor. "Come, join us outside? There's a nice fire and a cookout commencing in the back. There's a fiddler and a handsome singer with a guitar. Maybe we can dance slow with these fellows."

"Oh, no, just go on without me. Maybe I'll come later, maybe not."

Kiki stood up and took the flowers from Annie and her chuckling friend, who Kiki realized was Annie's fellow Sam. Andrew held fast to his bunches of blooms and she met his unwavering eye. He didn't blink.

"Are you going to give those flowers to me, or would you like to keep them for yourself?"

"I'm going to carry them upstairs for you." He gave her a devilish little grin. "I wouldn't want you to drop them with being so overburdened."

"Come along then."

Kiki started up the stairs, feeling him follow very close behind. The energy felt good filling into her core, and she believed she may have gotten control over that base door again.

"We haven't met yet," he said. "I'm Andrew MacLeod. George is my uncle, or great uncle. Something like that. I used to live on Islay, but I live here now."

"I'm Kiki," she said simply.

She kicked her room door open and set both vases of flowers on the dresser. Andrew strolled right in like he owned the place and set his vase on the bedside table. He looked around, taking in her messy habits, before turning his dark eyes back to her. He sent a gust of that passion again and she took as much of it into her core as possible.

She felt ten times better than she did before he arrived. It unsettled her that some of his energy seeped into her base, and she felt a wee stirring of actual desire. She could not completely seal off that particular door since the awakening and it caused a measure of uneasiness she wasn't used to in the presence of an admiring man.

"Thank you for the delivery. You're very nice."

"No problem, I usually make the deliveries here, I work on the farm." He moved around slowly. "Trinity often talks about you. You should visit your mother more often."

Kiki stood on one side of the room, studying him. He moved like a giant cat, stalking about in a circle. Andrew was aware that he was a fine looking man, and he had a charming way about him. He cleverly allowed her to get a good look at all his best angles and knew he had her attention.

"The sender is very enamored with you."

Andrew glanced at the flowers. Then, he reached into the bunch by the bed and pulled out the card. The nerve of him! Kiki couldn't help chuckling at his boldness. She loved a rebel.

"Well, he thanks you for the best night of his life." Andrew's playful grin grew wide and even. "Just what did he do to get those exquisite green eyes to notice him? What do you suggest I do? I already set myself on fire. So then, love, are you going to come downstairs and dance slow with me?"

That got her laughing.

"Men and their honey talk. Look here, Andrew. I can see what you're thinking, but if George MacLeod is your uncle, then that means we're very likely cousins. You are aware that George MacLeod may well be my father. So, I must regretfully say *no thank you*, and you shouldn't take it as a big brush off. My tune might be different if there wasn't a chance we were cousins."

She didn't expect Andrew MacLeod to let out such a guffaw. He pushed aside the dark bangs falling in his black eyes and preened up like a rooster. He exuded power and sent a surge of it right at her. Kiki felt her mouth water at the sight of the taunt bulge in his breeches. He stepped a little closer and Kiki watched his aura flare up an even deeper crimson. His other energy, head and core, ebbed significantly to feed his base.

This man is all about sex, she mused, breathing harder, startled at her own physical responses. Every part of her body felt his presence in that small room. Her eyes kept drifting to his large hands.

"Come now, lass," he grinned confidently. "You and George both know he's not your father. Don't get me wrong, he loves you dearly, but knows you're not truly his daughter. He only says such things to keep hanging around Trinity Lovett without causing a stir. He actually reaps lots of respect for tending to the mother of his love child." His volume dropped. "I was completely crushed when they told me you chose someone else." He certainly didn't look crushed.

Three of swords. That was Andrew's card.

Kiki could see it now. If a man like Andrew MacLeod, all heat and fire and passion, wasn't a demon already, he might easily become one. Could she accidently push him into it, if she fed his ardor haphazardly? Could she destroy his fragile core?

Especially now that she was marked, and the demon hunted her? Was some dark energy pushing him toward her? Was that how it happened?

Kiki needed to be watchful and seal her passion door tight. She needed someone else to feed her Base Well. Someone like the detective, a man whose passion mixed with his emotions. One who would only act from love. Or she should accept no one at all, especially not one so mired in his physical plane. She reached up and pushed Andrew MacLeod away. She pushed him right to her door and his face turned startled.

"Whoa there," he stepped back so as not to stumble. "I'm sorry. I thought you were interested. You seemed to be very interested. I can tell that you're interested."

She was relieved to see his aura change. A bit of brown tamped down his red mess, and energy returned to radiate from his core and head. Andrew was no demon, and she felt bad for thinking he could become one.

That was ludicrous, *wasn't it?*

She continued to shoo him out the door and sent him away to the party. Then, she shut herself up in her room.

Kiki needed to be careful with her newly awakened Base Well of passion. She couldn't let herself spin out of control with the wrong person, *she was marked*. The wrong intimate partner could become her murderer. She wouldn't be safe until they *completed the curse, expelled the demon, and erased her mark*. Her Auntie Celeste would not steer her wrong in such things. It was just so hard to push him out that door, because now that she's had sex, she desperately wanted it again.

Chapter 10

The Hen *Janine*

Kiki and Gwen landed in Sacramento one week prior to Janine's scheduled wedding in Gram's backyard. They spent their first two days at Henry Webber's house, the old Miller estate, rummaging through Caroline's old boxes. On Wednesday morning, Kiki sent a limousine into Davis to fetch her and insisted on a full day pampering session at the Isba Spa and Baths.

It'll be our little hen for you, Kiki had said.

Steam room, hot springs, massages, body wraps, facials and nails, then a fancy dinner before conducting a séance to summon a local ghost. Janine hoped the outing in Sacramento would help her decompress from the hoopla surrounding the media. Although the attention died down considerably, people still wanted to hear Jane Doe from Chicago's reaction to the recent release of Richard Wilkens.

"You keep calling him a demon." Janine gifted them Irene's Saint Comba Charm necklace and watched Kiki stow it in her bag. "You use that term a lot. You've called Ian's father a demon too. Do you mean someone possessed, or a person from hell? What exactly do you mean by demon?"

"It's an ancient pagan term," Gwen told her. "In modern times, people don't say demon. They say sociopath or psychopath instead. But a true demon is something worse than a person with just antisocial personality disorder, they have zero conscience and they completely lack empathy. What they're really lacking is a functioning Core Well, and we've always called them demons. The spiritual center is in the core, it's the center of the soul. Having an odd Core Well is crippling in many ways, but it's not always obvious to most people." Gwen crinkled her freckled nose and winked at her. "Of course, a demon might also be an evil spirit from hell."

"True demons don't emanate an aura from their Core, they've got nothing. No soul," Kiki said. "You'd be surprised at the number of near demons running around the world. It's a fair amount. It's mostly those that avoid developing their cores, but an actual demon is rare and scary, and doesn't have a core to develop in the first place."

"Remember the Trio of Wells," Gwen said. "Head, Core, Base. The lack of an aspect, or a very weak aspect, makes for an incomplete person. Sometimes their other wells are stronger, to make up for that lack of energy, and a demon can be very charming and alluring. Most are highly sexed and very smart. Demons are often hard to spot unless you can see an aura, like Kiki, but most people can't see an aura, and demons blend in very well. They often live perfectly normal, productive lives and can be very nice, especially if they're lucky enough to pair with a person with a strong core aspect and that person sticks it out with them. But demons eventually devour the cores of the people around them. They constantly seek that part of the soul they are missing, and their partners suffer the consequences."

"Do you have special vocabulary for people who lack one of the other wells?" Janine asked.

"Idiots and anhedonics," Gwen told her. "Idiot is misused a lot, and a true anhedonic will rarely last into adulthood."

As they entered the Isba dressing room to don robes, Janine gushed about the wedding plans. Ian asked Carlos to be his best man, she asked her niece Ashly to be maid of honor, and her brother-in-law would walk her down the aisle. Her dress might be demure, but Kiki would approve of it. Gram recently dropped an expanded the guest list on them, and there would be an outdoor meal and a live band now.

Ian and Janine planned to escape to Tahoe for only three days because they'd needed to return to Davis to finish the school term. Over the winter break, they reserved a secluded bungalow in Tahiti for a real honeymoon, and then they would detour to Scotland on the way home. Ian didn't need to be anywhere until the *Spectral Analysis* shoot was scheduled, and Janine was completely free until she made further plans.

"Oh good," Kiki said. "My mother is dying to meet you."

After the attendant left them to get undressed, Janine hesitated. Gwen had never seen her knife wounds before. Her back and stomach scars were both very deep and scary. Why hadn't she thought about that when she agreed to a spa day? Did she imagine she would get a full body massage wearing a T-shirt? Gwen and Kiki didn't notice her unease as they continued to chat and get undressed, then Janine saw Gwen's chest and the two long marks where her breasts should be. Janine realized that she was staring and looked away, embarrassed at herself for gapping.

"I'm sorry," she said. "I had no idea."

"Don't worry about it," Gwen told her. "Come on, let's see yours then."

Janine showed them the jagged scars from the knife attack, all seven of the gash marks. Janine lifted her shirt to show them the stomach marks first. Then, she exposed the two large scars on her back to include the deep shoulder gash and the uneven wound down her lower back, near her kidney, the near fatal one. All the rest were basically lighter cuts. Dramatic but survivable lines drawn onto her skin, like the X carved into her cleavage close to her left breast, over her heart.

"Well," Gwen pressed her lips together. "Those are very angry marks. You know, I made up my mind a long time ago to accept that my chest was gone and to stop worrying about it. Most people barely notice after the first look. There's no way I'm going to hide from a nice massage and body wrap over something like a couple of missing breasts."

Throughout their spa treatment, Kiki and Gwen relayed stories of their Celtic Halloween and the six victims who wore a charm from Trinity's box. Then, they discussed Caroline's old house and her stuffed attic. After hours of hunting through useless documents, they barely found any extra information about the local ghosts, just diaries with simple accounts of the orchard ghost over the years. Most entries were limited to a date with the name of a witness. Very few included a short descriptive line or a ghostly quote. Only Caroline described the spirit as *kindred*, all the others found Mary quite sinister.

The oldest ledger was filled with math sums regarding the almonds and contained dated entries from the 1840s. It was created when Mary Miller was still alive. Someone kept an account of the trees, how many survived and how many were transplanted each year. In the back of those pages, they found a very dramatic entry scrawled with a heavy hand. Kiki snapped a photo of it.

Not a blessing, but a devil that fed from unholy flesh while in the womb. She's drawn to watch bodies stuck in the river rocks. Some think it brave, but I spy a curious pleasure in her eye. I fear, for as she grows older, her face becomes his.

"We believe the writer is referring to Mary Miller. The girl would have been six or seven at the time of that writing, right before she died," Kiki said. "I wager it's the mother who wrote it. Apparently, Mary was a morbid girl."

"Kiki, you wore a charm," Janine said bluntly because they kept changing the subject.

It'd bothered her since that phone call, when Kiki warned her not to touch the Comba charm. It bothered her to imagine it folded inside the crinkled paper in Kiki's purse, waiting to be worn again, and Janine knew Kiki gravitated toward those charms. She kept flashing on Kiki in the Chicago graveyard with one between her breasts, caressing it. She had insisted on wearing it with her gothic outfit and now Gwen and Kiki just claimed that six women wore a charm and were murdered. They believed wearing the charm cursed those women.

"You wore it on the last day of the Chicago shoot."

"Is that right? I dinna know that." Gwen glanced at Kiki. They were in the hot bath soaking in the mineral water, faces pink. "But maybe it's okay. Not every lassie who's worn a charm has been murdered, only women who bound themselves to a demon and then tried to leave him."

"Exactly. They were killed by a spurned lover." Kiki chuckled. "It's not like I have a long list of lovers to avoid, right?"

"What about the man from your awakening?" Janine asked. "If he wasn't Detective Anderson, who was it? Can you be certain he isn't dangerous, a demon feeling spurned? Do you know him very well? Can he be trusted?"

Kiki and Gwen exchanged guilty looks as they divulged who it was. She couldn't believe it. Kiki invited that deceitful asshole deviant who tried to coerce her into a sexual relationship by making it hard to get out of her *Spectral Analysis* contract. That's the man Kiki selected for her *important* ritual. Why Max Colliers of all people? He was the last person Janine would have guessed.

"If I couldn't have my triquetra connection, I needed someone with a very strong base aspect who would be open to a pagan sex ritual," Kiki defended herself.

But Max Colliers? "If anyone could be a demon, Max Colliers could be one," Janine spat.

"Well, he's not a demon. He has a strong yellowish core aura," Kiki said firmly, rising from the bath to wrap into a towel. "He's just a very naughty boy. If he had known the real source of your scars, he never would have chased you so ardently. He became fixated on the risky things he hoped you'd show him, Janine. I know that doesn't excuse his behavior, and he'll always be an unsavory arse, but he's exactly the type of arse I needed for that particular ritual."

"When your story broke, Max was devastated," Gwen added softly, also toweling off. "He wanted to ring you and apologize. Remember when we spoke on the phone? He was still on Skye and stewing about what to do. I believe he was truly upset with himself, if that's a consolation."

Janine already knew Max was sorry, he sent her flowers and a letter. She threw the flowers away and only opened the letter because he sent it via a currier to be delivered into her hand. She initially believed Max found some way to reinstate her contract. She opened the letter, expecting to see some type of legal document, instead she found a simple apology drawn in Max's bold artistic handwriting.

My behavior was monstrous, and I apologize. My lawyers are investigating the legality of that governor's actions at this writing. Max.

But she still harbored angry feelings toward Max and was now a little miffed at Kiki.

They decided to drop the subject during the massage and body wraps and focus on relaxing. Gwen relayed stories about growing up with Ian and their adventures on Skye. She described swimming in small lochs, the dangerous faerie niches in the green glens, and fishing off the dock in Uig Bay. Ian always had good luck with the fishes in Uig. He'd still be able to feed her if he ever lost his job, Gwen joked. Then, she recalled the lopsided distilling apparatus Ian and another boy built in Auntie Meg's shed when they were twelve. He wanted to make his own highland whisky and Gwen helped with the mash. They were lucky they didn't burn down the whole farm after making their undrinkable poison. Of course, that one was all Ian's idea.

Kiki said she brought a small cask of highland spirits and a special engraved Quaich for the wedding. The whisky was homemade from the isle, and Ian knew the maker, George MacLeod. George taught the boys secrets of whisky production during the summers when the girls were inside studying the ancient arts.

"What's a Quaich?" Janine asked.

"It's a two handled cup for sharing the whisky," Gwen told her. "It's a Scottish tradition to drink together from the same cup, to seal your bond, and then pass it to your clan."

After their seaweed and mineral body wraps, they headed to the massage room and rounded out their spa day with manicures and pedicures. Their driver suggested a fancy French eatery for dinner, where they made plans for the summoning later that night.

Instead of the orchard, they decided to visit the Old Rio Linda Graveyard and would attempt to summon Susan Miller, the mother of Mary, the orchard ghost. Kiki and Gwen worked out questions to ask Susan regarding the pre-ghost child.

From the wagon train documents, they knew that Susan had been pregnant with Mary during her months in the Sierra Nevada. He group had gotten stuck on the mountaintop during a blizzard and people froze and starved to death. While isolated during the winter, some members of the Hansen Wagon Train resorted to cannibalism to survive. For roughly one month of her pregnancy, Susan nourished her fetus with human flesh from dead companions, flesh that provided the elements that formed the early cells of Mary Miller. After the end of that nightmare, Susan Miller and the survivors descended into the valley where she gave birth to Mary, and the town was born.

"If the spirit in the orchard actually attacked a person, tried to hurt them, then it's not a normal spirit," Kiki said. "It's an evil spirit and it will do us no good to call on a such a spirit. That spirit only repeats the dictum anyway, and little else, according to the recorded sightings."

Gwen nodded. "Aye. Twill only give the spirit a better view of our hearts and it can learn ways to trick our thinking. Best to leave that one alone. We dinna want a demon's false intentions to muddy our minds."

The Miller family gravesite loomed on a small hill in the graveyard. An ominous monument for John and Susan Miller towered over the other markers; a wall of granite six feet high, dark and menacing. One side of the placard was carved with a tree of life symbol, possibly meant to be an almond tree, and both John and Susan shared the gravestone. By the look of things, they lay side by side.

The placard was etched with a short blurb honoring John Miller for founding the orchard and town. Janine noticed they died within a month of each other in 1865. She didn't bother searching for Mary Miller's grave. It was hidden far away in the orchard, a small river stone flush with the ground. Mary had committed suicide in the at the tender age of seven and her body had probably been banned from the consecrated grounds of the church graveyard.

Janine set out a rough cobble and placed Gwen's dark candle in the center of it. Along the edge of the rock, she placed crystal gemstones of jet, amethyst, black tourmaline, and selenite. Then, she pulled out her smart phone and activated the electromagnetic field analyzer app she downloaded earlier. She propped it against a rock. Why not try to get some rough data? If they were summoning a ghost, Ian might be interested in seeing the readouts. Gwen pulled out sachets of protective herbs to place over their hearts and they arranged themselves into a small circle. Kiki lit the candle.

"I'm not sure what type of summoning to use," Janine confessed.

"We don't know much about Susan Miller," Kiki said. "Maybe just a generic summoning charm then?"

"How about the one you always use? We seek yon souls of near to there, we call on you to us appear, reveal yourself for us to see, so I command, so mote it be?" Janine offered. They each nodded. Janine settled herself to recite it.

"Dinna forget tap into your heart." Gwen put a hand on her knee. "Just pause, and take a cleansing breath, and find yerself. Slow down and consciously seek your core. Reach into your well of love, lassie. When you're ready, go on. We'll be ready with you."

Janine drew a few deep breaths and tried to clear her head, but the summoning several months ago in Thatcher Woods kept returning to her mind. The deep dark eyes and long hair of that ghost had been frightening. Who had she been, if not Miranda Daily? *Doesn't matter here, get her out of your head,* Janine told herself. She needed to relax and find her core.

Janine focused her thoughts on Ian and the Celtic rings waiting for them. She recalled Ian's eagerness to wear the thick metallic band right away. She set her mind on how he often cuddled her through the night, breathing softly into her ear after making love. Then, she reached for Kiki and Gwen's hands. They formed a connected ring around the candle, because joining hands allowed witches to share gifts with one another. Holding Kiki's hand meant she'd have a better chance of seeing and hearing something.

"We seek yon souls of near to there, we call on you to us appear, reveal yourself for us to see, so I command, so mote it be," Janine said softly. Then, she repeated it more firmly, *"We seek yon souls of near to there, we call on you to us appear, reveal yourself for us to see, so I command, so mote it be."*

They remained quiet for several long minutes as the sounds of the night emerged; the lonely song of a cricket, the rustle of a branch in the breeze, the hoot of an owl, a train lolling on the tracks several blocks away. Janine opened her eyes and glanced at Kiki and Gwen, both sat perfectly still with closed eyes. Then, Janine felt Kiki's grip loosen and watched those green eyes pop open.

"Nothing here," Kiki sighed.

Gwen also opened her eyes and relaxed.

It was a little disappointing. Susan Miller did not leave any ghostly energy in the graveyard. Kiki suddenly twisted around, stood up and searched across the dark night. Janine was very familiar with that pursed lip look on Kiki's face, and her heart began to beat faster.

"I feel something out there," Kiki stared into the darkness. "I believe someone has heard your summons and is interested in us." Kiki knelt down to retrieve the candle and stones. She glanced at Gwen. "You have the electric torch? Let's go see who's buried over there."

Janine and Gwen followed her. They each carried a flashlight and used them to illuminate the ground. The moon was well past the first quarter, but a thin sheath of low level stratus clouds shielded most of the lunar light and the night was dark. The Rio Linda graveyard emitted a wet musty odor that intensified with their footsteps. Elaborate trees loomed creepily and cast dark shadows across the old burial grounds. Kiki led them toward a series of graves with similar markers, thick crosses with a circle around the center, Celtic crosses. The whiteness of the stones glowed luminous in the meager light.

"Have you noticed these names?" Gwen whispered. "We've left the Miller section and crossed over a variety zone and now these here are mostly Stauch."

She was right, Janine could see Stauch carved on several of the markers. Her heart tightened when she spotted three small stones that indicated children were buried side by side.

Were they victims of the river ghost?

Kiki paused in front of an old weathered Celtic cross. The white stone reflected brightly in the dark night, like an ominous beacon. Kiki knelt down to place the candle in front of the grave and lay the gemstones beside it.

"Look at this. Ingrid Stauch has beckoned us." Kiki smiled and her eyes flashed in the darkness. "This was Linda's mother, mother of the River Ghost. Ingrid may have been a witch, you know."

"That's right," Janine added. "The charm in your purse belonged to Irene Lumen, and Irene and Ingrid were related."

Gwen gave the rock to Janine to rebuild the alter. Janine transferred the candle and gemstones to the top of the stone.

The dragoma *is supposed to build the alter*, they always told her. Gwen reached over to briefly clutch Janine's hand.

"If she's a sister, maybe summon her with a joining charm like the one you used in Thatcher Woods," Gwen said softly. "We'll open our circle for her. Do you remember the words?"

Janine nodded. How could she forget them?

"Remember what happened last time, Janine." Kiki reached into her shirt to adjust her sachet. "Don't release our hands, no matter what. We need to stay connected and share our gifts. It's likely Gwen and I may both go cold again and only be able to see, hear, or have a vision. Those are our talents, audience and prophesy. So, you should ask the questions. Don't expect us to say anything."

"And remember to speak from your core, dinna waver or show weakness," Gwen added rapidly. "Be commanding, but loving. She won't come or participate if she thinks your heart is closed off to her. If you're speaking to a sister, she may be able to feel your intent."

"Okay, okay." Janine nodded. "But what am I going to ask her? We only worked out questions for Susan Miller."

Gwen and Kiki exchanged looks.

"Well," Gwen said. "Ask if she's a pagan sister. What she knows of the Comba charms. If she is aware of a curse and what it entails. What she knows about young Mary."

"Ask her who the demon is," Kiki said. "And who might be marked. What Mary means when she says, *one each for redemption*." Kiki must have seen Janine's agitated face. "Don't worry if you miss something, let's just see what she does. I can already feel her here, or someone, just hovering here. She wants to speak but needs help."

Then, Gwen passed the lighter to Janine. "Cleansing breaths," she coached gently. "Find your core."

Okay then, Janine tried relaxing. *This is Linda's mother here. Mother of the river ghost. Did the spirit of her daughter lure Sammy, my birth daughter, into the river? Good grief, Janine, let's not get into a mom fight with this spirit! Focus!*

Janine drew in deep breaths and let the air escape slowly. She mused about Ian again and their upcoming vows. She concentrated on her sister Juliana and how her sister always stood by her, even when she was upset with Janine. She recalled how Juliana swooped in, adopted Sammy, and cared for her. Then, Juliana shared Sammy with Janine, without a qualm, when Janine was finally ready to wake up. Ingrid Stauch also lost a little girl, at that very same spot in that river. She could surely open her heart in commiseration with Ingrid on that point. Janine reached out and took Kiki and Gwen's hands all over again. Then, she focused on the candle flame and recited the charm.

"Sister come complete our ring, it's assist and ease we bring. Meet us now, and reap your meed. A sister's oath we do concede. Accept our vow to set you free. So I command. So mote it be."

Janine felt the air change, but couldn't describe it. Not colder, not warmer, just stale air. Like the molecules stopped moving and hung suspended in space. Was that why it often felt cold? She noticed a tingling, just very light touches on her face, similar to soap bubbles alighting and popping on her skin. It was an unsettling, unnatural sensation. She glanced at Kiki and Gwen, and they seemed fine. Then, she looked to the empty spot in their circle and saw nothing unusual.

But someone or something filled that void, Janine sensed it, and her heart rate began to pick up. She felt eyes bearing down on her, eyes from the empty spot in their circle. She repeated the summons in a soft commanding voice.

"Sister come complete our ring, it's assist and ease we bring. Meet us now, and reap your meed. A sister's oath we do concede. Accept our vow to set you free. So I command. So mote it be."

Kiki turned slightly to face the empty spot in their circle. *Did Kiki see something?* Janine glanced at Gwen. Gwen's eyes fluttered between open and closed, and her head tilted downward. Janine examined the empty spot. What did Kiki see? Janine strained to distinguish something, anything, and noticed the air become a little out of focus over there, a little evanescent. Or was it only the dim light and the moist night playing tricks on her vision?

"Are you Ingrid Stauch?" Kiki asked quietly. "Can you hear me?"

After a moment, Kiki squeezed Janine's hand.

"I don't think she can hear me," Kiki whispered to Janine. "You try asking."

"Are you Ingrid Stauch?" Janine asked the empty spot.

Kiki's reaction indicated that her invisible friend had answered. On the *Spectral Analysis* television show, Janine and Kiki attempted something similar. Janine spoke to a ghost while Kiki listened and watched for it. If Janine or Kiki exerted an extreme amount of psychic effort, they could do it all, speak, see, and hear a ghost, especially if they held hands and shared their gifts.

But then, how had she managed to see the Mary ghost so easily when Kiki wasn't there?

"Do you know of the Saint Comba charms?" Kiki inquired.

"Do you know of the Saint Comba charms?" Janine repeated.

Kiki posed, "What do you know of the curse? Who is the demon?"

Everything Kiki asked, Janine repeated, and while she parroted Kiki's questions, she kept one eye on the empty space and one eye on Gwen. Gwen appeared to be sleeping and dreaming. Her eyes fluttered beneath her lids in a REM like pattern. The empty space became more and more unfocused. The air took on a wave-like quality, as if atmospheric gasses were turning to liquid or being heated over a very hot surface. Janine could see an outline begin to emerge in the wavering molecules.

"Are you a student of the pagan ways?"

It was a womanly shape, quivering through the surface of a mysterious fluid. Janine could just detect the edges of her body. She could make out the curve of a long slender neck, rolling with the rhythm of her trembling visage. It began to reflect the candlelight and called to mind those female silhouettes on the mud flaps of big trucks, bouncing along the highway at night.

"What does *one each for redemption* mean?"

An oval face filled in with large eyes and a wide mouth. As she became more vivid, Janine could see that her skin was smooth and creamy. Very pleasing. Her hair was shiny, lush, with a bright buttery color. Her entire image oscillated continuously, as if she stood behind a flowing wall of water. Very disturbing. She gave the impression of a young and vibrant woman, but her face was aged and her expression uncomfortable. The image generated sadness which Janine felt it in her own heart, effusive sorrow.

"Who is marked?"

Her agitated movements were odd and inspired fear. Her eyes fluctuated from Kiki to Janine in stop action motion, like a strobe light. It made Janine nervous, and the beat of her heart drummed faster. The ghost moved in such disharmony with her beautiful flowing image. While her likeness rippled steadily in that unknown liquid, her gestures were jerky and harsh. Her hand was here, then there. Her head faced right, then left. There was no way to predict her movements and Janine felt a surge of acid build in the pit of her stomach. Her own limbs became heavy. Core energy began draining from Janine's chest as the sadness overtook her, she could feel her core empty out. Feelings of abandonment, grief, and hopelessness dominated her heart and soul.

"What did Linda die of?" Kiki asked.

"Did Linda lure Sammy into the river?" Janine asked quickly, instead.

The woman's mouth opened, then closed without a sound. The wavering head faced right, then left, then right again. The womanly image began fading from sight because Janine's eyes were blurring and clouding over. Janine felt herself moving further and further away from the situation as her eyes tunneled. Her pulse raced. She knew she should not have tried so hard to see this spirit. Janine lost focus and she couldn't decipher the next question Kiki asked.

"Why can I see the ghost of Mary Miller?" Janine gasped in a whisper.

Then, she heard the old woman's voice, soft, choppy and distinct, one word at a time.

"*You. Can. Be. The. Last. One.*"

Then, the world contracted dramatically and pulsed once before expiring, and Janine passed out.

Chapter 11

Vows *Janine*

When they returned from the graveyard, they found the bar in their Old Town Sacramento hotel pulsing with activity. Gwen and Kiki insisted on finding a back table to discuss the séance. They might be able absorb some ambient energy into their drained cores, Kiki whispered. She didn't fool Janine, Kiki planned to absorb more than ambient energy, she was outright trying to attract attention as they worked their way to a back table. At one point, Kiki glided into a random fellow and gave him a very slow appraisal. Then, she smiled sweetly at him, flashed her bright green eyes and drew in an exaggerated breath.

"Well, aren't you a stimulating sight," Kiki purred in her silky, seductive voice. Then, she hugged Janine with one arm as the man and his friends quickly gathered around. "My friend is getting married this weekend. So, please excuse us for appraising you fellows a little blatantly, we mean no harm. She'll be mourning all the fine blokes she'll be giving up… but that's not till this weekend. I hope we've come to the right place to celebrate."

Kiki winked at them, then she pulled Janine along. Gwen hung back to order the drinks.

"Good grief, Kiki, really?" She still felt weak and irritated from her encounter in the graveyard, and Kiki's remedy of attracting male attention to recharge her psychic batteries was not high on Janine's to do list.

"You're the one that fainted out there," Kiki whispered. "Now you've got a ton of testosterone fueled energy focused right on your ass. Stop deflecting it. Just divert it into your core and thank me later."

Gwen caught up to them as they sat down. She brought three tumblers of neat whisky and scooted into the booth across from Kiki and Janine. She brushed her long red hair aside and grinned at them.

"Well, that wee group is now convinced our lassie is looking for a final fling. I'd wager they're a little drunk." Gwen's pink cheeks glowed as she glanced around. "I asked them to hang back and allow you to decide from afar. I hinted that we may bring over a key with terms of engagement in a wee bit. So then, Janine, they'll be vying for your attention. Soak it up, lass."

"Not you too!" She tried to hide and slid further into the booth. She could see the group of men glancing over, checking her out, starting to strut a bit. "Didn't you advise me not to try this sort of thing without a lot of practice? I'm not soaking up anything from anyone that isn't Ian McNally."

"Oh, calm yerself. No harm in letting those nice lads flood you with admiring energy," Gwen said. "Just try to redirect it to your core. You can practice right now." Gwen glanced over her shoulder. "As long as they stay over there, you'll be grand, no pressure. Ho ho, look at this."

The waiter delivered three new drinks from that small group of five men. He said the group sent them a message.

Congratulations, and they'd be happy to help celebrate as needed.

"I'm going to leave." But Janine was boxed in and Kiki gave her a stern look.

"No, you're not. It's your hen, and you're staying," Kiki insisted. "Those fellows are just flirting. They just want to see who you'd pick. They probably got a bet going by the way they're standing like that. It's just harmless fun. Just try to absorb some of their energy and then we'll forget about them. They'll lose interest after a while."

"I don't understand why I'm the one who fainted," Janine said miserably. "I didn't faint in the orchard. I got weak, but I didn't faint. And I didn't need to hold your hand to see the ghost in the orchard."

"Did you hear the ghost at all? Ingrid's spirit?" Kiki asked them.

"Not me, I was in a trance. I had another vision," Gwen said.

"Only what she said right before I fainted, when she said *you can be the last one,*" Janine grumbled. "She said that to me, didn't she? She meant that *I* can be the last one. Last one for what? To drown in the river? I thought that was part of the river curse and Sammy had been the last one! So, what did she mean then? Is there another curse? Did we get it all wrong?"

Gwen stared at Janine, then glanced at Kiki. Kiki shook her head.

"No, no, you didn't hear everything. It wasn't quite like that," Kiki said.

"I asked her why I could see the ghost of Mary, and she responded with, *you can be the last one.*" Janine felt like Kiki and Gwen had both come to a similar conclusion but weren't sharing it with her. Kiki continued shaking her head.

"That's not what she meant."

Gwen Murphy is Judgement

"What's wrong?" Janine asked. "What do you think it means?" Janine asked Gwen.

Gwen settled comfortably in her seat and played with a stray loop of her red hair.

"It could mean many things, we're still piecing the puzzle together and it'll do us no good to be jumping to conclusions at this early stage. One thing is clear, that dictum was never about your river." Then, her blue eyes settled on Janine a little more tenderly. "Besides, lass, you never wore a Comba charm. The ghost can't mean *you* when she said you. Maybe she meant a generic *you*."

"That's exactly what it was. The Mary ghost has been making that same statement for decades. It's a generic warning. She could have meant me, just as much as Janine, or anyone." Kiki stared at Gwen with her intense green eyes.

Who was she trying to convince, Janine thought.

"Look here. Let's just share what we saw and heard," Gwen proposed. "We'll gather all the information and sit on it for a wee bit of time before drawing any conclusions."

She reached into her purse and pulled out a little notebook.

"We'll jot it down separately, so as not influence each other, and then share it out. We'll draw no conclusions, not tonight. Not until we've sorted through those old tomes back home and discussed it with the other sisters. Not until we gather as much information as we can."

Janine wrote her description of the spirit of Ingrid Stauch, the very beautiful ghost that appeared to be underwater. She also angrily wrote out the one patchy sentence about her being the last one. She also noted that her EMF app didn't pick up anything in that graveyard, probably because the phone app didn't make a very good receiver.

Gwen wrote a narrative of her vision, which was quite disturbing to Janine. A large gathering was on the horizon, with twelve Saint Comba charms brought before a demon spirit to bear witness to everything. Gwen could not identify anyone present, because everyone came shrouded in capes, but it appeared to be their coven sisters in a dark gathering. She saw a witch's dagger and indications of a blood ritual, not something they'd done before.

"Not every charm had a story of redemption," Gwen said of her vision. "At least one pendant was still in need of a redeemer, and it allows the demon to continue marking people who come near any of the charms. Several sisters at the gathering were marked already, we'll see it on them. So, in front of the demon's spirit, a pledge is made to complete the curse before anyone else is tagged for death. I could not see anything past that gathering and I could not see the faces of anyone there."

"Holy crap," Janine cursed.

"A vision isn't always a premonition," Kiki added forcefully. "Sometimes nothing comes of it."

Gwen nodded. "She's right. Remember, we make no conclusions here. Who knows, we may discover something else that'll bend the meaning in that vision. It's likely we've got things wrong. Come now, Kiki, your turn. What did Ingrid have to say about things?"

Kiki wrote a description similar to Janine's, except the spirit appeared crystal clear and not wavy in the least for her. Ingrid's hair was a gorgeous blonde cascade, and her eyes were big round balls of sky blue. She had a dainty nose and pink rosy lips, beautiful. She seemed a little on the shy side, eyes pointed down and away, and Kiki felt that made her slightly shifty, perhaps untrustworthy. But her movements flowed, no stop action for Kiki, and she wasn't scary in the least. The ghost confirmed that she was once Ingrid Stauch, and that Saint Comba was the patron saint of her birth family. The spirit believed a curse followed the women in her family, a curse that bestowed physical beauty on them but drew evil intentions.

"She was marked," Kiki said. "When we asked her who was marked by the demon, she said that every woman in her family was marked, even Linda, the girl. They fled the big city because of the marks. She said that Linda died of being baptized in the river."

"Did she answer my question?" Janine asked. "Did the ghost of Linda lure Sammy into the river, or was it something else?"

"She didn't say anything about that," Kiki told her.

"Did she identify the demon?" Gwen asked.

"She named Hansen as a demon, and his father, but never suspected either of them until the wagon train. Hansen marked others too," Kiki told them. "She said he continues to leave marks, as his child leaves a mark."

"His child? What child?" Janine asked.

"I don't want to speculate, but I got a gut feeling during that whole episode," Kiki said. "I feel like this ghost implied that Mary Miller was the demon's daughter. That Mary became the demon, *in flesh*, when she was born. It makes sense. Remember the scribbling that said, *as she grows older, her face becomes his*. That's got to be a reference to Hansen. You read the wagon train diary. Stanley Hansen was a predator, chasing every woman in that group. The ghost said he marked others. We can be the last to deal with Mary, if the curse is broken. Perhaps that's what she meant with the words, *you can be the last one*."

That was a much nicer interpretation than the one formed in Janine's head. Both Gwen and Kiki didn't want to say it, but clearly, the ghost believed Janine could be the last one to die wearing a Comba charm. She was slated to be the last redeemer of the curse, *wasn't it obvious?* It didn't take rocket science to figure it out. Those charms fell into Janine's lap, both of them, and she successfully attracted a psychopath in her past. She was probably marked already. Holy crap, and her psychopath was out freely roaming the country.

"Hey, ladies."

Two of the flirty men were standing next to the table carrying more drinks. They each wore a mischievous smile. The taller man grinned quite handsomely with an attractive tilt to his lips, but his brow suddenly furrowed in a concerned way.

"Hope we're not interrupting. It looked like a serious discussion going on, so we thought we'd come over and lighten your mood. You're supposed to be celebrating we're told."

"We're happy to help you ladies celebrate." The other one grinned. "Any final decisions over here?"

"Good grief!" Janine slapped her hand on the table. "Do you really think I'm looking for a final fling three days before I get married?"

By the look on their faces, she might have just slapped them on the face instead. They visibly shrank a tiny bit, preparing to bolt, but Kiki quickly jumped up and fluttered her eyes at them, smiling. She leaned in a little close, so they were doubly confused. Gwen also started to rise but stopped about halfway and chuckled. She retrieved one of the whiskies from their hands and flicked her red hair.

"Oh, don't listen to her," Gwen said. "She's a wee vexed because she really wanted to misbehave but is chickening out. She's way too attached and loyal to her man, you understand. And I see you must have guessed, that's why you came over, it was you that caught her eye before losing her nerve." Gwen smiled sweetly at the taller man, the one with the handsome smile.

He didn't appear to quite believe that, but chuckled anyway. The shorter man stared at Kiki with owl eyes.

"Aren't you Kiki Mellow?"

"I am." Kiki maneuvered between the two men and slipped a hand on each of their arms. She began walking them back to their little crowd and appeared very interested in both of them. "Why don't you introduce me to your friends?"

When they had gotten out of earshot, Gwen slipped back down to a sitting position and gave Janine a small smile.

"The task is not yours to be a sacrifice. I can see you're thinking it. Just because we might guess a curse's meaning does not mean we need to follow it. Besides, you never wore a Comba charm, and as long as you don't wear one, you can never be the last redeemer." Gwen split up the rest of the drinks between them. "You shunned those charms instinctively and must have felt the curse. You realize that we are nae letting you anywhere near the charms. There'll be no wearing a Saint Comba charm for you, ever. The spirits and ghosts dinna know all that, you know, and visions do not make a fixed future. So, please relax, it's probably wedding jitters that got you spinning your doomsday scenario." Gwen glanced toward Kiki and the group of five men. "I'm getting a wee bit drowsy and Kiki's stilling running off at the mouth. Is she over there getting her energy reset, or do you wager she fancies one of them?"

"Sorry about snapping. You think I was a little harsh on that guy?"

Gwen shook her heard. "Not too bad, but a good rule of thumb, Janine. Treat nicely the ones replenishing your core energy. It's the least we can do to repay that kind deed."

Gram's backyard was back to normal. After the excavation of large boulders from the hill, truckloads of dirt and soil were carted in to rebuild the mound. At first, the workmen didn't follow Mother Nature's lead and the mound took the shape of a small angular levy wall, but Gram personally redirected the spread of earth to flatten the landscape in a more pleasing way. Afterwards, a landscaper arrived and seeded the soil for grasses and wildflowers. Gram was delighted, because the seeds attracted the hens back to the hill. Their clucking and strutting calmed Gram tremendously. So, she managed to save the wildlife, the environment, and the view from the evil bulldozers.

Gram's five acre manicured lawn had further been transformed for the outdoor wedding and reception with a large tented area. A false floor lay under a canopy of high spires, and the sides of the giant tent were tied open to allow a cool breeze to flow over the diners. Chandeliers decorated the high areas while round tables with tall floral centerpieces were scattered over two thirds of the false floor. The last third was cleared for dancing. Gram solicited a bluegrass rock band, *Joe Craven and The Sometimers*, with a double bass player, drummer, guitarist, and mandolin/fiddler to provide the entertainment. The small wedding Janine and Ian initially planned morphed into something larger than anticipated. Besides Janine's immediate family, and Ian's cousin, Ian's research students, rugby team, as well as Janine's soccer team were all invited. Then, Gram added her own personal friends and local relatives. Close to seventy plus people socialized in Gram's backyard. Not the handful of people they first imagined when they agreed not to elope.

Near the glass back patio, an area with rows of foldout wooden chairs had been arranged to face the elevated wooden deck. A beautiful floral arch of white roses, peonies, and hydrangeas in eucalyptus greens framed the steps off the deck. That was the spot Janine and Ian exchanged vows with the pretty Lutheran minister from Gram's church officiating the ceremony. Gram bragged proudly that her own wedding had taken place in that same backyard in a very similar setup.

Most of the day had gone by in a blur for Janine. Her soccer teammates helped her get ready, along with her young niece, who appeared very grown up in her pinkish bridesmaid dress. Her sister Juliana teared up at the sight of them, while her brother-in-law Adam laughed, looking very smart in his tuxedo. He whispered that it wasn't too late to run away if she wasn't completely sure. Then, Adam escorted her down the aisle, beaming proudly.

Janine felt wobbly as she followed the confident steps of teenaged Ashley. She walked between the rows of chairs with every eye on her and wished that they had eloped instead. The undivided attention was nerve racking. She calmed down when she spotted Gram and Juliana weeping together and the fidgeting Carlos next to Ian. Carlos, with his deep cheek dimples, seemed to be biting back a witty remark. Ian appeared absolutely in love. When his soft blue eyes met hers, she melted all over again, and everyone else become a blur. It no longer mattered whether the others were there or not, all that mattered was the starry-eyed guy staring back at her.

It was getting late and Janine hadn't really chatted with anyone. She'd been tasked to dance with old relatives and rugby players and Ian in between. When she saw Ian dancing with Gwen, Carlos came round to claim her.

"Oh my god, this dress! At first, I was wondering, who is that gorgeous woman the doctor's marrying, whatever happened to Janine? I'm not kidding, every jaw dropped. We all wondered where and when you finally escaped." He finally got his wisecrack out. "I totally expected you to be in clumpy boots and a T-shirt. I'm very disappointed."

"You look nice too, Carlos," Janine said, and they both laughed. "How's being a weatherman?"

Carlos scowled, then smiled. "Early mornings. But I'm home every day. Maria is actually getting annoyed with me. Me, annoying? Tell me you find that unbelievable?" *Not at all.*

They searched the crowd and spotted Maria chatting with Kiki Mellow and a few older women. It appeared to be a nice tea party around that table. Janine spied Leone sitting next to Kiki, peering into a coffee cup. No doubt they were exchanging readings. Janine and Carlos strolled in that direction when Ben rushed up to greet them. Emma and Oliver were close behind. Janine hugged each of the research crew before introducing Carlos them.

"You guys are the tech experts developing new gadgets?" Carlos asked.

"Boom. Yes." Emma nodded and started speaking rapidly. "We actually field tested a few of our tools recently, on a real ghost. Very successful. It was eerie. If you're staying around for a while, we can show you some of the equipment. In fact, we've brought the *mellow-skin* and UV cams and other stuff out here for another try in the orchard tonight. Why not, since we're in Sacramento again, right? Boom! If you like, you can come along. It wouldn't be a problem, and it might be fun. I think you'd like what we've come up with."

Then, Emma gave a quick nod and bee-lined away. She pulled Oliver with her and they disappeared to the dance floor.

"What was that?" Carlos was all dimples, chuckling.

"Oh, just Emma," Ben told him. "She's your biggest fan and has a major crush on you. Are you guys heading to Kiki Mellow? I've been waiting to say hello, but she seems a little busy."

"Come on," Janine grabbed Bens arm and they continued to Kiki's table. Everyone stood up to hug Janine. The small group chatted about the online tea-reading lessons from Annelise Batten. Janine finally gave Kiki a proper hug. They hadn't seen each other since the hotel in Old Town and Janine wished she hadn't gotten so upset that night. Now that the wedding was winding down, and the media had disappeared, her stress lifted and she felt a little silly about everything.

"Hello there, cousin." Kiki engulfed her and then also hugged Carlos. "Hello, you." Then, she smiled at Ben, who had turned a slight shade of red. "And hello to you, you handsome fellow. I was wondering when you'd find the time to come and say hi to me. I was getting very jealous of those girls in your group."

Someone brought over bubbling wine, and they toasted Janine again. Then, Carlos started bragging about his twins' soccer successes. The twins, Milo and Mimi, were off playing in the grassy area with the other children, kicking a ball around. Janine watched the kids for a bit. Her nephew Jack, the oldest of the lot, dominated the action. Two of her soccer teammates played with them, keeping things even. They had kicked off their heels and played in pretty dresses with bare feet. For a brief moment, Janine felt sad.

Sammy should be out there kicking the soccer ball.

She shook that out of her head and pretended to listen to the chatter surrounding her. She searched around and spotted her sister Juliana watching the band, then she watched her niece Ashley dancing with Oliver and Emma in a circle with other young people. Ian still danced with Gwen.

"So, I was thinking," Ben stammered at Kiki, "would you consider coming out with us?"

"Well, it sounds like fun," Kiki said, "but Gwen and I are actually flying to Chicago on the red eye. As soon as the newlyweds drive off to Tahoe, we've got to pack up and run to the airport."

Chicago? Janine finally noticed that Detective Anderson was not at her wedding. Janine glanced around the crowd for him and settled on Gwen and Ian instead. Those two were speaking intimately as they slowly made their way toward Janine. Gwen's face appeared redder than usual and… *Were Ian's eyes blinking? Did he look upset?*

Gram ran up to their little group.

"The limo's out front," she practically squealed. "I have it all planned out! Jaja, I want you and *your groom* to walk out the front door toward the limo. There are bubbles in a basket on the porch, and everyone is going to line up along the walk and blow them at you. The photographer is standing ready and says that the light is perfect right now, perfect! It's going to look magical."

"You want us to head around and gather in the front yard, right now?" Carlos asked.

"Boom!" Gram winked at him before running off to prompt another group to move to the front.

Carlos watched Gram run off with a confused expression on his face. "Did she just say boom?"

"She's convinced it's the new slang for *yes*." Janine giggled. "Gram refuses to give it up because she thinks she sounds very hip saying it. She's got all of her girls saying it now. Right, Leone?"

The tall, thin old lady smiled up from her tea cup. "Oh yes, boom," she agreed.

Ian and Gwen finally reached them. If he had been blinking earlier, he wasn't anymore. To everyone's pleasure, he gave Janine a nice deep kiss. Then, he whispered that the car was waiting out front to take them to Donner Lake and that hotel they once stayed in.

Chapter 12

Chicago *Kiki*

Kiki and Gwen lounged in the rooftop bar of the Lincoln House Hotel enjoying the sunset. They were waiting for Detective Anderson and a woman named Mary Kline. They scheduled a dinner meeting in the restaurant and went up for an early cocktail to cool their nerves. Or, at least, Kiki needed to cool her nerves. She hadn't seen Bob Anderson since he bailed on their budding romance and she was nervous about the dinner.

She noticed Gwen admiring three very pretty professional looking women at the end of the bar. Gwen gravitated toward confident, feminine women, as she was quite graceful herself. Feminine, but with an *Annie Hall* type of flair. Gwen preferred flowing slacks and blouses to dainty dresses. She detested an overtly sexy look and loved a classic, professional, ladylike style. She never tired of chiding Kiki for dressing in silly racy outfits with high hems, sheer material, and revealing necklines.

"Dream on, those girls are as straight as arrows." Kiki laughed. "And shouldn't you mind your eyes anyway?"

"Don't be so sure, my wee yin. You may be the master of the Core Well, but I am the tutor of the Base Well. I'd wager that pretty lass on the left leans my way," Gwen confided. "Besides, I'm a free agent now. I can do whatever I want, without the guilt."

"Tell the truth, Gwen, this new Comba pendant Janine found. Did you feel anything in it? A death? Or do you think it's one that needs a redeemer?" She asked. "Do you think the redeemer can be anyone, or do you think the charm will select a specific soul? Perhaps someone is already marked by that charm. Are we going to say it out loud?"

"No conclusions. Not until we go over everything. Not until we relay everything. There must be another meaning in it all. Janine *shunned* those charms, how could it be her if she was repelled by them? It would have to be someone who is attracted to them." Gwen sighed, "She looked beautiful in that gown, didn't she? A very refined and modest choice. It cut a nice silhouette, don't you think? And Ian. The way he gazed at her. I'm very proud of him. I just want to declare it… that I deserve a little credit for molding him so well."

Kiki started laughing at that.

"Ho ho, I absolutely molded him, you little witch."

"What is it you were talking about at the end there? I saw his colors turn the wrong shade of brown."

Gwen's eyelids fluttered and she wrinkled her freckled nose at Kiki. Definitely something personal. Since Gwen started dating women, she kept her personal business closer to the chest. She freely discussed coven friends, boyfriends, other friends, other couples, but never deeply discussed her *girl*friends with Kiki. This last girlfriend had been serious, and Kiki knew that waves started rocking that boat when Gwen visited back in the spring for Ian's birthday. It's likely that Bridget was jealous of Ian. He had been Gwen's longest relationship to date, and first love, but Gwen rarely discussed those details with Kiki anymore.

"If you must know, my embryos," Gwen said. "Back at his birthday, I told Ian that I finally planned to use the embryos, and he was happy about it. Bridget begged to carry the baby, to make it ours, my egg and her womb. But that's all moot now. Doesn't matter anyway, because he hasn't even discussed it with Janine. After they got engaged so suddenly, I wanted her to know those embryos existed before proceeding, but he's a blockhead and didn't know why she would care about my embryos and I had to explain it to him. Oh no, Kiki, here you are making your face. This is why I don't like discussing things with you." Gwen finished her drink. "You're making things worse with that face of yours."

"Is it really over with Bridget, Gwen? You don't think she'll come around?"

"It's the coven," Gwen told her. "It kills a lot of relationships, not just mine. Look at how your Detective Anderson ran away. Most people fancy dating a witch as cute, but then they delve deeper into things, and they dinna understand it. Best to find someone from a coven family. Annie is the smart one, fixing herself on Sam Welks. He's one of old Cara's grandsons, you know. It's a rare outsider that can truly accept the pagan ways."

Perhaps Gwen was right, but Kiki was still going to give it another try with the detective. His deep, rich aura pointed to a highly spiritual person who she wanted to learn more about. The detective had just gotten a shock at the magnitude of her pagan practices. His conventional religious background made it difficult for him to accept the things she asked of him, and Kiki had dropped too many bombs too fast. They completely connected in their core wells. They just needed to find some sort of compromise between his conventional belief system and her pagan one. Then, maybe, they could conceive a child. Kiki definitely felt that Bob Anderson was the correct man for that task. A powerful core, that's what she wanted for her daughter.

Gwen knocked her arm to get her attention.

"Ho, ho, look who just walked in. Your rare outsider."

His eyes locked right onto her, Max Colliers. She should have known. That'll teach her to use Cheryl from the *Spectral Analysis* office to book all her travel and hotel plans. He pushed his designer glasses back into position and walked toward her with a big smile under his bright happy eyes. He hugged both of them warmly.

"Kiki and Gwen, so nice to see you." He signaled the bartender with a flick of his hand. "Before you say anything, this is my week in Chicago, board meetings every day downstairs. I'm not stalking you, I promise. I was delighted to hear you would be here during our Chicago summit, a little bird told me. I'm going to call it fate, unless you admit that you were actually trying to bump into me."

Max loosened his dot patterned silk luxury tie and unbuttoned his collar. He insisted on treating them to drinks and dinner. They told him they were waiting for the detective and would have to decline the dinner, but they would never say no to free drinks. He didn't mention the texts and phone calls Kiki never returned. They told him a little about the Samhain bonfire festival that he missed, and also about the wedding in Sacramento.

"I'm sorry I missed it, but you couldn't get me to step foot in that cow town again," he meant Sacramento. Kiki knew that he would have gone, if he had been invited. "Did you meet the new tech crew? Ian has some interesting kids in that lab."

The Colliers company was funding the entire grant for *Spectral Analysis* research and development, and Max happened to be the top active executive. Half the kids in Ian's lab received scholarships from his parent company, and Max Colliers was basically paying for Ben's doctorate degree. No one could accuse Max of being tight with his money, but Kiki knew there were lots of thick strings attached to all those investments.

Gwen excused herself to go chat with the three women she had been eyeing earlier, she wanted to give Kiki and Max a private moment. She knew it was their first face to face meeting after the ritual on Skye. Max kept his eyes on Kiki as Gwen walked away.

"I stayed as long as I could, to see you at the cottage, but Gwen said you might be gone another day or another week, no one knew. I already rearranged my schedule and then there were—"

"I wasn't expecting you to hang around," Kiki cut him off.

She found it hard to meet Max's eye, his expression was so happy and earnest. All of his usual Max Colliers flirty sparring was replaced with a bit of maudlin adoration, and it was hard to take. She felt herself being drawn in by his good humor. If her aura had taken on a new red tinge in places, his had developed a bit of soft blue around his yellow core, and she found it quite attractive. Maybe the whole experience had just brought the blue out from hiding. That awakening may have been a good growth experiment for both of them.

His proximity stimulated a sudden flash of the ritual to mind, and the memory tingled all over her. She actually felt a little embarrassed and slightly stirred up. If she felt that way, it was likely he did too.

"Look, Max, I want to thank you for flying to Scotland at the drop of a hat," Kiki said. "There aren't very many men I could have asked…"

"Are you kidding?" He shook his head in disagreement.

"There aren't many men I could have asked that I would have opened with like that. And I needed to open up for a successful awakening," she insisted to his shaking head. "Listen up, I need to say this clearly. Although I opened my passion center to you, and it was an amazing experience, that's all it was. You must know that it had nothing to do with love, or relationships, or anything near that vicinity. That's why I chose you. I knew you could meet me with the passion and not get it mixed up with the other stuff. It was just a fun…experience. Okay? You did me a big favor, and I appreciate it."

"It can be whatever you want it to be." He grinned at her. "I promise to never mix anything up. You can decide what everything means. I love that you believe I did you a big favor. Any time you need a favor…"

He took her hand and kissed it before she knew what he was doing. Then, he paused and kissed her knuckles slowly, more sensually, to remind her of that passion he opened up. She felt her blood bubbling and her breath come quicker. Sitting across from her first erotic partner and inhaling the scent of him caused an automatic response to develop inside of her. She pulled her hand away and slammed her Base Well door shut on him. It was something Kiki had always been able to do, better than anyone else. He didn't seem to notice and stuck his hand in a pocket to pull something out.

"I admit you have an effect on me, Max," she uttered, avoiding his eyes. "But I'm actually interested in someone else quite seriously. I'm talking about love with him. He's going to be showing up pretty soon and I'd like to gather my wits before he gets here, and not have any added complications."

Max nodded, still smiling. "I understand. So, it's a love thing with him? Of course." He set a velvet box on the bar. "But you'll allow me to give you a little gift first? No, don't worry, I promise to get promptly out of your way after you accept my gift nicely."

His boyish eyes danced with amusement.

"That event was a big one for me, the coolest experience ever. And it was especially big for you, I didn't realize that when you said you were breaking a virginal vow of chastity that you weren't kidding. I was floored. First, that it was a true witch's ritual and not some joke, then that you were just… just… You're the sexiest woman ever, Kiki, I've always thought so. And you were really a virgin, I couldn't believe it. But I need to fix something.

I didn't bring you a gift, like an offering. Your mother, Trinity, told me that traditionally the man might bring the virgin a little gift. You didn't mention that part to me. I should have thought of it, but it all happened so quickly."

"Usually, it's just a little food and whisky," Kiki told him. "You brought that, remember?"

"That wasn't my gift," Max said. "Your friends, Gwen, Annie, and your mother put that together, it was their gift. I didn't gather those things. Besides, if I'm going to give you a gift, I want my gift to be more permanent and everlasting, a true Max Colliers gift." He slid the velvet box across the bar to her. "I had it specially made, right when I got home."

Max opened the box and she saw a bracelet of diamonds and emeralds glittering in the dim light. The elongated cut emeralds were set in pairs and the seven princess cut diamonds split up the pairs as they lay in a simple line. The gems sparkled beautifully and she held her breath for a second. Max discovered her weakness: gemstones.

"One diamond for each of those lovely ladies you invited, and the emeralds remind me of you, Kiki. That's your exact eye color when you're angry… or aroused." He glanced shyly into her eyes. "Now, accept it nicely and I promise to get out of your way."

Kiki admitted to herself that the bracelet was a stunner, and she wanted it. It was bad luck to refuse an awakening gift, she reasoned, so she held out her hand and allowed him to clasp it onto her wrist. He gazed into her eyes again and Kiki felt an odd warmth. She expected Max to be gung-ho and a little sentimental, but she didn't expect that she'd develop tender feelings for him in return. But there they were, and underneath those feelings, there was still a bit of simmering lust running through her system. She closed it all down as she watched those jewels slide down her arm.

"If things go south with the love guy, you know where to find me. I'm always available if you need any little favors." He smiled at her.

Gwen came around to look at her new bracelet and two of the women professionals followed her over. Apparently, they had been in the same board meetings with Max earlier, and they all knew each other well. Kiki showed off her wrist as they oohed and aahed. Max told them it was a present, and they assumed it was for her recent birthday. They chatted about the *Spectral Analysis* show until Kiki spotted the detective at the lounge entrance, then Kiki and Gwen begged off for their dinner meeting.

Detective Robert Anderson stood about five foot six, not tall by male standards, but still taller than Kiki. She knew most women preferred fellows like Max Colliers, but she loved that the detective appeared large without taking up so much space. He had wiry curly hair and a bit of a receding chin. His huge white teeth were very bright against his dark skin, and his clothes always seemed perpetually wrinkled. Most people would not classify the detective as a handsome man, but Kiki saw something different when she looked at him. She saw the energy that pulsed around him. His aura was very bright and pulsed pinkish in a thick cloud around his core. It extended about three feet from his center and people visibly calmed when they passed close enough to touch it.

When the detective fixed his eyes on a person, he had a keen way of focusing on them. The few times he sent Kiki passion energy, he had mixed it with his pink core tones, and it made her swoon with feelings of love. It had been a knee buckling experience and very unexpected. Kiki watched him for a full minute before he turned his big brown eyes in her direction. He couldn't help himself and smiled widely. He was happy to see her too.

"Wow, she's cute," Gwen said. "Looks like her brother."

The woman standing next to the detective was an inch taller than the detective and better groomed. Her shoulder length dirty blond hair framed an oval face with eyes that might be light blue but appeared grey in the distance. Her body still looked in good shape, but her hips had clearly let loose a baby or two in the past. Her attention landed right on Kiki and she started walking toward them before the detective moved. The detective hurried after her.

"Miss Mellow, Miss Murphy." The detective gave them each a warm smile.

He introduced Mary Kline and they all exchanged greetings. They were escorted to a table on the outside patio near one of the heat lamps. It afforded a spectacular view of the buildings and river along Chicago's River Walk. The detective pointed out the clock tower at the Wrigley Building, a historic landmark visible from their table. Like Big Ben, it had a clock face on every side and was startlingly white against the blue sky.

The detective retrieved an eight by ten picture of one of the Saint Comba charms. The charm had an imprint of a woman with her left hand chained to a wall and a large animal at her feet. Kiki sent him that photo because she thought the charm might belong to Miranda Daily. A college guy found the necklace in Thatcher Woods and insisted on delivering it to Janine Stinger at the urgings of a scary ghost.

Kiki wore it on one of their ghost hunting nights and it gave her a death vision. The original vision had been confusing, like two versions of the same death, or perhaps two different deaths. Later, Janine, Kiki, and Gwen took the charm back to Thatcher Woods and used it to call up a ghost who led them to some bones. Up until a few weeks ago, they had been convinced that the ghost and bones belonged to Miranda Daily, a girl that dated the man who once tried to kill Janine Stinger. A man Kiki believed was a true demon, a person without a core. Now, they sat across from that man's sister.

"I'll come right out with it," Mary Kline said. "That necklace belonged to my mother. She wore it every day of her life and now it belongs to me. I'd like to have it back."

Her mother?

The Comba charm necklace belonged to Richard Wilkens's mother? Kiki searched Gwen's big blue eyes and she appeared just as stunned as Kiki. Mary Kline waited patiently. She was an attractive woman who came across as tired and worried. Her hands fidgeted around her cup. Her grey eyes darted from person to person.

"Detective Anderson tells me a private investigator contacted the people you gave the necklace to and they know it doesn't belong to them, but they refuse to send it to me because they got it from you. They plan to deliver it to you somewhere in Scotland." Mary Kline leaned forward. "I want it back. You must understand my feelings. It's my mother's necklace and she always wore it." A fat tear rolled down her cheek.

Kiki and Gwen both nodded their heads, of course they understood. If it had belonged to their mother, they'd want it returned as well. Such objects bore an imprint of a person's soul, which made the object invaluable. Kiki detected high levels of energy in that particular charm, powerful and positive energy along with the death vision.

Gwen reached across the table to gently pat Mary's hand. "There, there, lassie."

"I thought Rick gave it away, to that girl, Miranda Daily. I accused him of giving her my mother's jewelry." Mary wiped her tears away. "Miranda was wearing it when I met her and I became livid when she refused to give it back. But the detective says that she has one of her own. I never knew there was more than one of those necklaces. Believe me, I tried to find one for years."

Several months before her father's heart attack, Mary and Rick's mother left with no forwarding address. Mary wasn't worried about her mother, because she always planned to leave someday and said if she ever did, she would need to stay hidden until the senior Richard Wilkens accepted that she was gone. Mary had believed her mother was alive somewhere with no knowledge that the senior Wilkens suffered a heart attack.

So, when her father had that heart attack, Mary returned to the Thatcher house to act as guardian of the junior Richard Wilkens. Mary recently graduated from the University of Chicago and gladly took on the task of managing her teen brother. She always expected her mother to pop up again and wanted to make sure everything was taken care of.

Then, Miranda Daily showed up wearing a Comba charm. That necklace was the only thing her mother never would have left at the house. If that necklace was still in Chicago three years later, it meant something terrible happened to her. Her brother must have known how she disappeared, Mary deduced, if he hid the charm and then gave it to a girl.

"You believe your mother was killed?" Kiki asked. "And that your brother gave the Saint Comba charm to his girlfriend."

Mary nodded, "I looked everywhere in the house for that charm. Not finding it meant she was still alive. Then, unexpectedly, to see it around that girl's neck, I imagined Rick stashed it somewhere the entire time. He hid other things too, and I already suspected him of killing my father. It wasn't a stretch to imagine he killed my mother as well. Why else would he hide that necklace? My mother always worried that Rick might be worse than my father." Mary closed her eyes. "But the private investigator reported that Miranda has her own Comba necklace, so I might have been wrong about my brother."

"Your brother may have given it to someone else then. Whoever those bones belong to…"

Gwen stopped and glanced at Kiki as it finally caught up to her. She turned back to Mary.

"Those bones belonged to your mother?"

The detective confirmed the identity of the victim found at the bottom of Thatcher Pond, Alice Wilkens, wife of Richard Wilkens and mother of Mary and Richard Junior. The DNA report made it certain. How Alice ended up at the bottom of the pond is another mystery. The broken hyoid bone and kettle bell weights pointed to a definite murder. Based on the fact that Alice

Wilkens was never reported missing, her husband would've been the prime suspect.

"I know what I said to you on the phone." Mary drummed her knuckles on the table. "And what I said to that girl, Janine Stinger, but I may have been wrong about my brother. I never understood him because he was disturbing as a kid, but that doesn't make him a mass murderer. He obviously did not kill Miranda Daily, and he did not give away my mother's charm. He told the truth about Miranda running off to Turkey, and my father probably really did die from a heart attack and not because my brother poisoned him as I always suspected."

Mary shot a glance at the detective, "And that girl, Janine Stinger, maybe she really was suffering from post-traumatic delusions and remembered her attack wrong. Rick has always maintained his innocence, even though an admission would have gotten him a lighter sentence. The governor always believed him. And he admitted the other stuff, just not the woods attack."

Mary Kline rung her hands.

"What if Janine Stinger's delusions were my fault because of the notes I sent her? Maybe I planted the idea in her head, that Rick was violent, and I broke them up." Mary teared up again and used a knuckle to wipe the moisture away. "All I wanted was my mother's necklace back."

"We'll try to return it to you, if possible," Kiki said. "But can we ask you some questions?"

They discussed several people during their lengthy dinner, Mary's mother, her father, her brother, Miranda, and Janine. One thing was clear, Mary still feared her own brother. Kiki could see it in her colors when she spoke about him, deep in her gut, she didn't trust him. Her descriptions of their father indicated a sociopathic personality. The home she described was practically a prison for her mother, and she revealed that both her brothers had been the spitting image of her late father, all identical. *Obviously, Kiki mistook the father for the son in that death vision. It hadn't been Janine's Richard, but the senior Richard she'd seen.*

"Yes, Rick locked Janine Stinger in the house before the attack, but that was how my father dealt with my mother, locking her in when they disagreed."

Mary tried to explain her brother's motivation.

"Our father always said that a woman might flee, from weak resolve, unless she was anchored against her whims. Locking the door was one way, but he also said a baby made an anchor that rarely failed. Better than a marriage license. My mother disliked when he said such things, but we could see that it worked on her. Rick may have wanted Janine pregnant, so that she wouldn't leave him. She called it rape, but they were already in an intimate relationship and maybe he thought of things differently. We grew up in a different sort of home and I'm certain he didn't mean to hurt her."

That was a twisted justification for some of what happened, Kiki observed.

Mary also supposed that Janine may have been unbalanced and erratic to begin with, didn't she end up in a mental ward? And Janine admitted to snatching up the knife herself, why? Why would she pick up a knife?

For years Mary believed the worse of her own brother, just because he had similar traits as her father. But some of his actions, the ones he admitted, like keeping Janine in the house, was because he didn't know better. She felt guilty for her presumptions and for adding to the confusion.

But she still fears him, Kiki observed.

The detective leaned in and gently added,

"It's understandable, feeling the way you do. Even the guilt. But listen to your gut feelings, Mary." He gathered up the papers and photographs. "Being wrong on one point does not negate the rest of it. Often, the apple doesn't fall far from the tree."

The apple doesn't fall far from the tree! Kiki stared at the detective.

"There's no family reunion planned," Mary said. "I don't even know where he is."

The detective nodded, "Another red flag, Mary. He disappeared after leaving the penitentiary and hasn't checked in once. That doesn't bode well for his character or intent."

Richard Wilkens had gone directly into hiding. The media speculated that he was afraid of being incarcerated again, due to the efforts of a legal team paid for by the *Spectral Analysis* executives. Janine's former bosses were suing the state and governor for dereliction of duty and a miscarriage of justice.

Chapter 13

Séance *Kiki*

Kiki enticed the detective to have a private drink after Mary Kline left. Gwen disappeared to join a small group hidden in the back of the lounge that included the professional women interested in the séance. Kiki ordered a coffee, like the detective, and they sat at the end of the bar sipping quietly.

Bob Anderson drinks coffee like a Scot drinks whisky, Kiki noticed.

He gave her a nice smile and settled into gazing into her eyes. Detective Anderson was blessed with light brown, almost golden eyes that always appeared wide and clear. It appeared clear to Kiki that he was bothered by something.

"I hoped to attend Janine's wedding," He shook his head. "But things were breaking around here pretty quickly and I needed to hear it all first hand. I'm sorry, because I wanted to see her happy event, and, I hoped to see you as well. In a better situation than talking about skeletons with Mary Kline." He smiled again. "I have to say, you light up a room."

"It was a beautiful afternoon wedding," Kiki told him. "And I'm sure Janine understands. Does she know about Rick Wilkens being unaccounted for?"

He nodded. "That was a hard call to make."

He took her hand in his and she could feel the positive feelings he sent her way. Nothing like when Max held that hand earlier and generated a flash of uncomfortable passion energy. The detective's vibe was softer and sweeter, easier to absorb, *balanced*. She wondered if her body would react similarly with him, as it did with Max, when he finally decided to focus his undivided base energy at her. He noticed the emerald bracelet, then glanced to where Gwen had gone off to flirt with those professional women.

"Your boyfriend is doing a good thing with those lawyers of his." He gently released her hand to hold his coffee cup instead. "There's actually a petition of recall slated to hit the judge's desk in two days. I think he might actually be successful, so I can't be too upset with him."

"Are you talking about Max Colliers? He isn't my boyfriend," Kiki retorted sharply.

"You forget, I'm a detective," Bob Anderson told her gently. He didn't look upset, he looked reconciled. "I find out a lot of things very easily. It didn't take much to find out Mr. Colliers took his jet to Scotland for four days. Right around the time of the full moon."

"That doesn't make him my boyfriend." Kiki sat back feeling a little burned. "You made it quite clear you would not participate in that particular ritual, and I was running out of full moons before my birthday. I explained everything to you and I invited you first. It would have been a very different experience with you, Bob, more balanced and tempered, and that's what I wanted. But I couldn't wait any longer, and it needed doing. Max is a fine friend who came through for me. It was just a raw passion ritual and nothing else. So don't judge."

Bob Anderson chuckled humorlessly and turned his head away.

"Wow."

"I grew up with some very firm spiritual beliefs and practices, Bob. Different from yours, but very important to me. That ritual was a celebration of my personal growth and self-enlightenment. I kept a vow for fourteen years in order to develop my spiritual center, my core aspects. Priests and nuns try it for life, but we consider that unnatural. That ritual was the celebratory release of my vow, and a pledge to finally develop my Base Well, my passions. That event marked a formal transition to my next stage of life, from maiden to mother. Tell me you'd refuse a rite of passage, like a confirmation or some other important spiritual ceremony," Kiki said. "Would you refused it, if someone casually asked you to? If I asked you? Would you stop taking communion if I thought it was a terrible or ridiculous ritual?"

"That's not exactly the same thing," Bob said gently. "You're comparing apples to oranges again. A confirmation is a widely common and socially acceptable event. So is communion. It's not shrouded in intimate activities that should be kept private."

"You mean like the wedding I just attended? That was shrouded in quite a bit of ceremony and intimacy, and though we didn't witness anything beyond that kiss, we definitely expect Ian and Janine to consummate their union. In some parts of the world, even that part of the event is witnessed. Let's just compromise here. You didn't want to participate in one of my spiritual rituals, and I don't want to participate in one of yours. That's fine. Why don't we leave all the rituals off the table, and go on from here?"

"You realize that your religion leaves little room for men. It's hard for me to get behind it."

"I might say something similar of yours," Kiki said. "But to clarify, the coven is a practice, not a religion. And I do get behind yours, your religion. We all belong to the Kirk, to support our men. I'm just not a fan of the male dominated sexism in some of it."

"I don't mean to argue with you." He shook his head.

"I don't want to argue, either. Let's just forget all of that," she said softly. "I'm ready to meet you in private now. My vow has been released, and there's nothing to stop us from picking up where we left off. I've entered a very lustful stage in my development, and I'd like to explore that with you."

Detective Anderson stood up and drained the last of his coffee.

"Balanced and tempered?" He nodded to her, and she knew she had lost him. "That's not part of a lustful stage." He sounded angry. "As always, it's been a pleasure, Miss Mellow."

Kiki fumed as she watched him leave. Her pulse raced a mile a minute. How did that little cup of coffee go so wrong? Why did Bob Anderson feel so justified with his own opinion? She was well aware that the detective was no saint in the area of relationships. He admitted to having lovers in his past, and he didn't need to marry those women before taking them to bed. In fact, when he first met her, he assumed she had an elaborate past as well. Back then, it hadn't bothered him in the least that she might have plenty of experience and had been eager to jump right in. So, why did he act so upset now? It exasperated her, because on top of it all, Kiki had residual simmering energy in her Base Well, passion energy that she had been saving for that particular detective.

She made her way toward Gwen and saw him, Max Colliers cozy between two beautiful women. He lounged at the same table as Gwen, and Gwen appeared to have made a connection with the female executive. Max jumped up when Kiki joined their group. He strained his neck around, searching for the detective. He maneuvered to get closer to her and his eyes were hopeful. He had been patiently waiting for her to seek him out.

"Where'd Detective Anderson go?" Gwen finally noticed that Kiki joined them.

"He went south," Kiki snapped, then glanced at Max. "But I'm not looking for any favors," she added and steered clear of the arc of Max's red hot aura.

The next day, Gwen and Kiki arranged for a small séance in the Congress Plaza Hotel. During the last *Spectral Analysis* investigation, Kiki hosted a very successful séance in the Plaza, thanks to Janine Stinger. Having a *dragoma* entice spirits to the room proved overwhelming. One spirit didn't need a *dragoma* and had desperately wanted to communicate with her.

Having more participants would extract the cosmic energy better, so Gwen solicited folks in the bar the previous night and they lucked out with Max Colliers's colleagues. The women lawyers were intrigued by the idea of a séance and Max was interested in spending time with Kiki. They scheduled an event for right after noon, because the conjunction of the earth, new moon, and sun always affected the aether in significant ways.

Max Colliers invented an excuse to cancel his afternoon sessions for the day and all three women lawyers agreed to attend, Olivia, Michelle, and Theresa-May. They were all employed by the Colliers Empire. Michelle and Theresa-May worked out of the Chicago office and were on a team suing the governor among other things, while Olivia had traveled from Austin with Max.

Up close, Kiki recognized Olivia. She was a common sight in the Austin office building and had even attended Ian's birthday party with Max. She was the stereotypical blueblood; polished, elegant, blonde, and very thin. Rumors revealed that her family had close ties to the Colliers clan and that Max and Olivia had an on-again, off-again, relationship that had gone on for years. At the moment, they were off-again, but all the gossip speculated that one day they'd be on-again for life, after the wild oats were all sowed.

Kiki and Gwen reserved a suite on the third floor of the plaza. They maneuvered the small round table to the center of the room and began placing minerals in a pattern on the surface. Michelle, a dark-eyed woman with wavy short hair, arrived early with Max.

Kiki quickly tasked Max with placing candles around the room. At the table, Gwen explained mineral order in the crystal grid to Michelle, constantly giggling about something, and Max followed Kiki around, administering a constant dribble of blandishments.

"I was sorry to miss the other séance," Max said. He had gotten very intoxicated and couldn't participate the night of the *Spectral Analysis* shoot. "The playback looked very spooky. You're irresistible dressed like a gypsy. I love it when you wear this type of sheer flowy material." He moved very close and admired her gossamer blouse.

"You know that's not working on me right now," Kiki told him. "All your efforts are being sent to my spiritual center. You're having no physical effects on me at this moment."

"Really, you can just turn it off like that?" Max asked.

"That's right," Kiki smiled at him, realizing she was lying a little. "It's the natural state of my Base Well. My passion center, it's closed. I would have to open that door on purpose to feel any of this heat you're sending me. But keep that attention coming, I can use the energy elsewhere."

Olivia and Theresa-May finally arrived, and just in time, the exact moment of syzygy was at hand. Max closed the blackout curtains and everyone helped light the rest of the candles. Kiki admired the cubic grid of jaspers, quartz crystals, and dark amethyst pyramids that Gwen and Michelle created. Kiki noticed Janine's Saint Comba charm in the center of those minerals.

Olivia, on the other hand, chuckled at the sight of the grid. She had been the least interested in a séance and clearly considered Kiki a silly woman. She obviously considered Kiki another itch Max needed to satisfy before finally settling down. Kiki could feel the animosity hit her in the face and felt a bit of hostility in return. *Never blame another woman for the behavior of a man.*

Everyone gathered at the table and Gwen directed each to a different spot. She led them in breathing exercises to relax their bodies, then proceeded to explain the paper and pens in front of them.

"Many mediums call it automatic writing," Gwen told them. "Nae like what you may have seen in a scary film, your minds won't be possessed when you write, only your hand. The crystal grid is arranged to keep disengaged spirits on the table. Notice the placement of the paper, just under the wee pyramid. Keep it there. If your hand moves too far from the grid, it may drift out of the sphere of influence and not feel the spirit."

"Just how big is the *sphere of influence?*" Olivia smirked and glanced at Max.

"Come on, Ollie, keep an open mind." Max grinned at her.

"Almost the size of this table." Gwen smiled at Olivia. "So, only allow your writing hand on the table. I might warn everyone not to lean over the table, you dinna want your heart to drift into that sphere of influence."

Everyone chuckled, thinking Gwen was teasing, but Kiki knew she wasn't. Cracking open the aethereal veil into the darkness could be risky business. Participating in a summoning opened wide one's core door, where a disembodied spirit might easily sneak into a warm body. The core, or heart, was where an essence could stick. Hands were safe, hearts were not. Gwen chuckled and gave Kiki a brief glance.

"Allow your hand to hover over the paper while holding the pen. When I give you the signal, allow your hand to write whatever it desires. Dinna think about what you're writing, just allow your hand to flow freely," Gwen told them. "You won't get more than a word, or two, before your brains take over. The moment you begin thinking about what you're doing, just stop. It'll nae be the spirit writing, if you're thinking about it."

"What spirit are we trying to reach?" Theresa-May asked.

"It's a spirit I met in this hotel before," Kiki told them. "It'll be on the Chicago episode, I believe it airs next week."

"Yes." Max openly admired her. "Next week."

Kiki returned his boyish grin. She could feel him sending his testosterone fueled passion at her and she just fed it into her core. His determination must be hard to resist for most girls. Janine actually hid from Max when he turned his attentions to her the last time they were in Chicago.

"It's a spirit that felt eager to speak to us," Kiki told them. "Keep this in mind, we are calling on one who feels ignored, misunderstood and disregarded, and possibly seeks vengeance for something. We hope the spirit will tell us about a curse mentioned in our last séance and elaborate on the name Irene that was mentioned." Kiki pointed to the center of the table. "See that silver pendant? If you need to focus on something, focus on that."

Gwen coached them through deep cleansing breaths using soothing, lilting words. Her voice resembled a lullaby. Gwen never wrote a summoning charm of her own, she claimed to be a dunce with words and always chose the written charms in Celeste's grimoire. Kiki could hear her auntie's voice whenever Gwen quoted her.

"As the aether flows and opens wide, enter from that great divide, earth, moon, and sun point the way, to ears to hear what you might say, feed us now your potpourri, so I command, so mote it be."

Gwen paused and the room became very quiet. Kiki felt an electric tingling in the air. Max began to speak, but Gwen hushed him with a wave of her hand.

Gwen continued, "We are seeking one who spoke here before. We desire to learn of Irene and the curse, and the vengeance mentioned. *As the aether flows and opens wide, enter from that great divide, earth, moon, and sun point the way, to ears to hear what you might say, feed us now your potpourri, so I command, so mote it be.*"

Kiki felt the spirit. A wisp of air flowed into her fingertips from the crystal grid, intense and strong, and moved very slowly over her knuckles. This spirit felt connected to someone close, or perhaps, it was *attached to that charm!* Kiki noticed Theresa-May's face change into an expression of someone straining to hear something. She felt it too.

"Write!" Gwen ordered.

Everyone scribbled.

"Flip your papers over," Gwen ordered. "Now, inhale for a wee count of three and exhale slowly. Dinna think about anything that just occurred and don't speak, not yet. Keep that writing hand over the table."

Then, Gwen repeated the charm.

"*As the aether flows and opens wide, enter from that great divide, earth, moon, and sun point the way, to ears to hear what you might say, feed us now your potpourri, so I command, so mote it be.* Spirit, tell us what we need to know."

Kiki could feel the energy circling the grid. Did Gwen also detect a minor glow off the Comba charm, or the static charge building in her hand?

"Write!" Gwen ordered again.

Everyone scribbled again.

"I don't want to do this anymore," Theresa-May whispered. She tossed her pen to the table and pulled her hand into her lap.

"Of course," Gwen nodded. "You can drop your pens and move from the table. Just sit quietly for a moment and collect yourselves. I'm going to lean forward a wee bit. Dinna anyone else lean in. Just try to relax." Then, her voice came stronger as she spoke to the spirit. "Come now, whisper into my ear."

Gwen leaned ever so slightly toward the table and Kiki could hear a soft growl trickling from the center of the grid. It sounded like a low growl of a dog, and the density of the air grew heavy. Gwen closed her eyes to focus better.

Be careful, Kiki sent Gwen the silent message.

Theresa-May wore a concerned expression and Michelle fidgeted as she quietly watched. Max glanced around, totally unaware of the changes in the air and stared at their quiet, serious eyes. He exchanged an amused look with Olivia.

Olivia chuckled softly and leaned her thin frame toward the table with her ear pointed to the grid, mirroring Gwen. She tucked her hand behind an ear and Kiki watched her amused smirk suddenly freeze and change.

"I hear something," Olivia whispered and leaned in further.

"Stay back," Kiki said sharply.

But it was too late. Olivia's body contracted and she shot to a rigid stance over the table. *That spirit is at least six inches beyond the grid,* Kiki noticed. Olivia's hands gripped the table and every muscle in her body appeared to contract. Her arms began to shake. Her eyes rolled into her head so that the whites showed large. She appeared to be having a standing seizure. Max jumped up, but Kiki grabbed his arm and pulled him away before he could touch her.

"Don't!" Kiki warned. "It's like electricity and can transfer to you if you make a connection."

Kiki glanced around for something to use and tried to pick up the chair but it was very cumbersome. Max took it from her, but before he could use it to push Olivia from the table she let out a loud long tone that startled them all.

"Ahhhhhhhhhhhhhhhhh." Olivia's mouth hung wide open as the sound emerged. A single note, B flat. Then, she said quite clearly, in a high pitched voice, "One of each for redemption shall atone for your deed."

Max pushed her away from the table with the chair. She stumbled two steps but didn't fall. Her eyes instantly snapped back to normal. She stared at them with the amusement back on her face. She began chuckling at them, especially at Max standing there holding a chair. He set the chair down and stepped closer to rub her arm but Olivia pulled away and gave him a cutting look.

"Spirit depart, spirit go home. I command you, go away!" Gwen said harshly and repeated it.

That made Olivia chuckle again. Everyone stood up and moved away from the table. Theresa-May went quickly to one of the lamps and flipped it on while Max moved to open the blackout curtains. Michelle blew out a few candles. Everyone glanced periodically at Olivia.

"Are you okay?" Michelle ventured with a meek voice.

"What do you mean?" Olivia chuckled. "Of course I'm okay. Are you okay? Why is everybody staring at me?"

Typical, Kiki thought. Many times the one possessed won't have a clue about it.

"What did you mean with that squeaky voice?" Michelle asked her.

"What are you talking about?" Olivia stopped chuckling.

"It's no matter," Gwen smiled reassuringly, yet her skin was very red. Her big blue eyes turned to Olivia. "The spirit gave a wee bit of a message through you. It can happen."

It took several minutes to calm their nerves. All the while, Olivia refused to believe she had said anything in a high pitched voice. She rolled her eyes and refused to fall for any of their jokes. She admitted to hearing a whispering sound, like a harsh voice or the bark of a dog. Gwen heard the same sound, but the others hadn't heard a thing. Kiki heard a voice rapidly repeat *beware the mark*, but would wait to share that with Gwen later, in private. Then, they shared their automatic writings.

In the first round Gwen had written *lured*, Michelle wrote *diverted*, Theresa-May wrote *outwitted*, Kiki wrote *avoided*, Max wrote *served*, and Olivia wrote *the demon*. In the second round, they had written *life, eye, nose, ear, tooth, and wound*, respectively. Max had stashed a few bottles of wine in the cooler and he dispensed the liquid as they discussed the automatic writings.

"Isn't it obvious," Theresa-May's eyes darkened. "The second round of words refer to the idiom, an eye for an eye, a tooth for a tooth, from the holy texts. We're being told that justice must be served. We're all lawyers here, we're familiar with that sentiment. Maybe that was a special message, just for us, because we're lawyers."

"What about ear, nose, and wound?" Olivia chuckled, enjoying her wine. "I don't remember those being in the Bible quote."

"It's in the Quran." Theresa-May appeared unsettled as she realized something strange had happened in that room. "How did we come up with those exact words, in the correct order?"

"What about the first round," Michelle's dark eyes searched out Gwen. "Sounds like someone was tricked, or lured by a... demon?"

"Irene." Gwen nodded at her, then stared directly at Kiki. Even her neck had gone pink, it wasn't the wine. Gwen pulled her long red tresses into a pony tail, and Kiki noticed Michelle's dark eyes drawn to Gwen's long white neck. "Irene lured the demon away. She outwitted and avoided a him by diverting his attention and serving him. That's the image I saw. What do you think, Kiki? That is Irene's charm in the middle of the table, she wore it last, as far as we know."

"Thinking back on the wagon train entries, it would fit," Kiki said. "This spirit felt different than what I felt before, maybe it wasn't the one we were hoping for. It could have been a voice from the charm."

"What is on the back of your neck? You have a tiny tattoo!" Michelle reached over to brush Gwen's curls aside. "It's so cute. I didn't notice it before. Just below your hairline"

"It's a trinity knot," Gwen showed her. "Kiki has one too."

Michelle becoming chummy with Gwen got Theresa-May and Olivia a bit fidgety and they began moving to leave. Then, everyone started moving at once.

"Why don't you ladies all go and I'll help Kiki clean up." Max nodded at the three lawyers. He smiled at Gwen. "You too, you look like you could use a nap. They tell me Kiki gets very taxed after she hosts a séance."

He glanced at Kiki and everyone in the room knew that he was trying to get her alone. Theresa-May and Olivia moved to the door, ready to leave. Olivia openly glared at Kiki and only paused to wait for Michelle. When she realized Michelle was going to wait on Gwen, she left abruptly with Theresa-May.

Max kept their wine glasses full and the conversation rolling as they tidied up. Gwen gathered the minerals and the charm while Kiki gathered up the candles. Kiki accidently smudged soot on her silky shirt and ducked into the bathroom to wash up. When Kiki emerged, she found that Max had successfully shooed Gwen and Michelle out the door. There he stood, with two recharged glasses of wine and the top two buttons of his shirt undone. She felt a sudden surge of his passion energy hit her.

"How about we do a little exploring of your Base Well?" Max smiled confidently.

"Max, we are not going to become a thing," Kiki purred at him. "Just so you know, you are not having an effect on me. That door is closed."

He nodded. "I blame Gwen for reminding me of that little tattoo on the back of your neck. I'm dying to see it again."

He offered her the wine glass and she took it. As always, Max had expensive taste in wine. It went down smoothly. He had provided her so much energy during the séance that she felt terrific. She took another look around the room and spotted a few places where the wax had solidified to the table. Before she could get to it, Max came around with the hotel room keycard and scraped it up. He stood very close to her and she realized that her sexual center easily sensed him. It made her curious. She noticed a force deep inside compelling her to move toward him. She pointed out a couple more spots and he scraped those up too.

"Am I still having zero effect on you?" Max grinned at her. "Because you're having a major effect on me." He reached out and took her hand. He bent down to kiss her knuckles again. "Why don't you do me the favor this time? Brave enough to do a little dare?"

"What kind of dare?" He just said the magic words, she rarely passed up a good dare.

"Open your door, you know the one I mean, just for one minute, and let me in." He stared into her eyes, he was tenacious. "If you can still brush me off, I lose, and I'll back off for good. I'll never bother you again, I promise. And you can ask me to do whatever favor you want. I'll be happy to comply."

"Anything? Such as, lend me your private jet to fly home?"

"Oh."

He laughed, taken back. He looked up and away, he clearly did not want to lend out his private jet. Max Colliers loved his private jet. He shook his head and groaned.

"I don't know, that trip will take awhile and the crew couldn't fly back right away. They'd have to crew-rest a night in Scotland. They'd be tied up for three days, minimum. I'd have to fly back to Austin commercial."

"Well, I guess that's that." Kiki sipped her wine with a grin. "Perhaps, you're not as sure about us as you think."

He took in her grinning lips and let out a long breath.

"No, no, sure, okay, my jet will be at your disposal, if I lose. But you have to promise you'll open your door as wide as you did back in October, out in that wilderness, no cheating. And we should up the time. Two minutes."

Confidence was an attractive quality, and Max had plenty of that.

"Let's get this straight. I open my passion well for two full minutes and if I can resist you in the end, I win. I get to use your jet for a trip back to Scotland and you will never proposition me again. I like that. You truly believe I can't resist you? You're going to lose, Max."

"Who knows?" He grinned. "It's really a win-win for me. I get a couple of minutes to jump into your passion well and have another look at that tattoo, I'm dying to kiss you behind the ears. I get to do that in the dare, right, kiss you? God Kiki, I just want to touch you. I'll be happy if I just get a little reaction from you and see your eyes turn that dark green," his eyes bore into hers, "You know, like they did when you were screaming my name."

His glance shifted to her lips and he licked his own.

"That would be a minor win for me, right? Knowing that somewhere in there, you want me, even if you make yourself walk away."

His eyes drifted down to her sheer shirt and her open cleavage.

"I believe I have a good chance of winning it all, I know where your buttons are. At that ritual, it wasn't normal stuff. Tell me you haven't been thinking about it every minute since it happened. You're going to find out soon enough, we generate something that's very hard to resist."

She would have to take his word for that, and Kiki wanted to see how hard it would be to resist him. Opening her Base Well was new territory for her. How difficult would it be to push Max aside when her desire was fully inflamed? She should find out, for future situations, so she agreed to the bet. Two minutes shouldn't be too much trouble. Kiki pulled out her cell phone and set the timer for one hundred and twenty seconds. She set it on the table and smiled sweetly at him.

"When you're ready, just hit that button and say go. I promise not to block you out. Good luck."

Max suddenly appeared nervous. He drained the rest of his wine and then removed his shirt. He had a beautifully fit physique, smooth, well-shaped muscles, ripples over his stomach. He worked hard at being attractive, at least on the outside. He rubbed his arms and jumped like he was warming up for a boxing match. He grinned at her and shook his head of hair. She couldn't help giggling at his antics and felt a little of his energy already seeping into interesting places, warming her up. She actually itched to touch him. Then, he pressed the button and said "go." Kiki consciously unblocked her Base Well and the feeling was instantaneous.

Kiki Mellow is the Empress

Every nerve in her body was back on the cliffs of the Quiraing. All of his red hot energy flooded into her system and rippled through her veins like a fire. The scent of him caused a heady sensation that made her feel unsteady. His eyes drifted to her neck and she realized he hadn't even touched her, but she felt him everywhere. She was doomed.

Then, his hand came up to gently moved her hair aside as he stepped behind her. Just the one hand, and then his lips made contact as he slowly kissed the back of her neck. A spark shot down her spine right to a spot between her legs, and she melted. She sank into his body, craving the contact. She sensed his hands hover over her hips, then slowly move to her waist before finally grabbing her, claiming her, and she let out a raspy breath. His large hand massaged her and she was disappointed that he did not move them further down, into that fire. But she stayed quiet, statue still, trying to withstand the passion he fanned.

She heard him groan as his hand explored her fully clothed breasts and she felt her nipples pulse in response, aching for attention as they recalled his ministrations at her awakening. The sounds he made were animal erotic to her, wooing the cells of her body into submission. His hand moved back to her neck and he moved around as if he prepared to kiss her. She definitely wanted it, tilted her head for him, slightly opened her mouth in anticipation. Her own hands slid eagerly up to caress his smooth sculpted chest, taking in the shape and hardness of his muscles. Her mouth watered and she resisted allowing her hands to wander further. She was beginning to get impatient and wondered why he did not kiss her. If he would just kiss her, she could calm down. She moved her lips closer, to invite him, but he moved excruciatingly slow, breathing into her ear instead, whispering.

"I want to— "

The alarm suddenly went off startling them both so much that they jumped apart. He watched her, breathing hard, eyes flickering everywhere, and he let out a long breath.

"That went too fast," he chuckled softly. "I guess you win then, but at least I can see it in your eyes. That's a small victory for me, right? That's a beautiful color, Kiki."

She didn't want to feed his cocky attitude and tell him that he had won in the first ten seconds. There was no way she could shut the door on that unbridled heat now. He made a move to retrieve his shirt and she grabbed his wrist.

"Just where the hell do you think you're going?" she snapped and pushed him onto the bed.

Chapter 14

Making a Demon *Kiki*

Waking in the Congress Plaza suite disoriented her. Her cell phone kept beeping and she noticed several missed messages and calls. Kiki grabbed her device from the side table and saw that they were all from Gwen. She turned and Max stirred beside her. She was astonished to see his aura so bright and blue. Sure, his red base was still intact, but the blue pulse he developed around his core had grown. *Oh no, was Max feeling love?* Was it temporary or permanent? Did she fill him with her core energy the way he filled her with his lust? That was not her intent. If she could fill his core, could she empty it too? What was going on here? *Was she falling into a demon's trap?* The phone pinged again and she answered it quickly.

"Kiki, where are you?" Gwen asked. "It's after eight o'clock in the morning. The detective is coming around at nine and then we have to catch our flight. The plane takes off before noon!"

"It's morning?" Kiki spun around to the clock. *She had been holed up with Max Colliers the entire night.* That was impossible! No wonder she was starving. "What, why is the detective coming? I don't want to see him."

"Rick Wilkens popped up in California," Gwen said. "Apparently, your cousin beat him pretty badly. Detective Anderson has the full clip of a video and offered to fill us in on the details. I certainly want to hear what happened, without the media spin."

"Can he come a little later? I don't know if I can get there by nine."

"He actually has to leave by ten, unless we can meet at one, over lunch. He sounds pretty booked. Court in the morning and afternoon. Should I try to change our tickets? Where are you?"

Max sat up with his glasses back on, took the phone, and greeted Gwen. His free hand stroked Kiki in a comforting way, but she slapped it away because she still felt a tincture of the heat between them and that annoyed her. One would think multiple sessions in a row would have sated their desires. Carnal memories flashed through her brain and she had to tamp down an urge to roll up and straddle him. She couldn't believe the crazy night they'd shared, or that her blood was pumping up for more. Her base instincts had a mind of their own and her foolish body yearned for Max Colliers.

"Tell him to meet you at one. I promised Kiki I'd let her use my private jet to get home. If I call right now, they can be set to take off as soon as five. You can be late and they won't take off without you." Max chatted a little longer, then hung up and returned the phone to Kiki.

He reached for his own cell phone and made a few calls. He scheduled the jet and then called to push his board meetings back till the afternoon, apologizing profusely into the phone. Clearly, a room full of people were waiting for him back at the Lincoln House. Kiki tried to get out of bed but he held fast to her wrist and pulled her closer, making her blood race off the charts. He made another short business call, then used the hotel phone to order room service. When he finally set his phone down, he grinned and pulled her into a tight embrace. She couldn't understand why her body desired to mold into his, it made no sense at all, but her skin craved his and she pressed herself into him, savoring the feel of his muscular torso. She ached to have him between her legs but kept them pressed tightly together instead.

"You're a bad influence on me, Kiki," he whispered into her ear. "I've never missed a board meeting at a summit. I'm going to catch a lot of flak back home because of you."

"Max, you know this isn't going to last. I might never agree to a rendezvous like this again, it's an aberration. It's just lust, pure lust. I'm in a lustful state right now, after that awakening. I'm going to get over it. That's all this is. This is going to end very soon."

"Of course. It's whatever you want it to be." He chuckled softly. "It's a lust thing for me too. I find you X rated, Kiki, that's what I've always loved about you. I realize it won't last forever, but it can last another few hours, right?" But his core pulsed light blue while he babbled on and he became incredibly attractive to her on different level. She felt herself opening up to him, head, heart, legs, and she realized that now her own core was getting mixed up in it.

Was this how the demon spirit worked? Was she being used to morph a regular man into something else? Was she creating her own demon? Who could she talk to about it? Trinity, maybe? *Terrific, she would have to discuss all her personal business with her mother.*

Gwen shot her a raised eyebrow when she finally returned to pack, but Kiki just ignored her. She picked out a pretty dress to wear for lunch with the detective, then she carefully applied just enough eye shadow to accentuate her green eyes, and just enough gloss to draw attention to her lips. She finished by rubbing lotion, with a sexy floral scent, all over her arms and legs. Gwen patiently watched her with an eyebrow still raised.

"What is going on here?" Gwen mused. "This looks like Kiki Mellow preparing to yank someone's chain."

"Don't judge me, I'm a bit of a woman scorned," Kiki told her. "I just want that detective to realize he's made a terrible mistake, and his mistake is causing me to make mistakes. I want him to rue the day he led me to this ruin. I am so furious with myself."

"You're a self-absorbed teenager," Gwen said and stood up.

Kiki followed Gwen into the elevator. Of course Gwen was right, what was she hoping to accomplish by trying to tease a reaction from the detective? He made his decision. Their preplanned ideas of what a relationship should look like were very different. She would never consent to moving to Chicago and playing a detective's wife, and he would never father a child out of wedlock. In a way, Kiki respected the detective more for refusing it, but she blamed his rejection for leading her right back into Max Colliers's bed. When the doors of the elevator opened on the top floor, Detective Anderson was waiting for them.

He smiled as usual, then shook their hands. *He shook her hand.* Then, they were escorted to a table. He didn't seem to notice her dress, but when his eyes touched hers, she sensed it. The little flare up of his core aura. Protest all he wanted, Detective Anderson felt love for her. This was the man she wanted, a respectable man in touch with his soul, not a shallow rogue with a flash of fire. She detested her weakness with Max, he was not what she wanted.

"Rick Wilkens attended a night class at UC Davis." he told them. "If you followed the cyber story, then you know he snuck into Doctor McNally's lecture. The news isn't reporting his identity yet, just the fact that the doctor beat someone pretty badly."

Kiki hadn't seen the story at all. She had been too occupied at the Congress Plaza with Max. Gwen could see that she hadn't heard anything and quickly took out a phone. She found the news story.

Kiki read the headline. *UC Davis Professor's harsh reprimand for speaking out of turn.* She scanned the story quickly. An unidentified man crashed Ian's class. When the professor asked the man to identify himself, the man teased the professor with personal questions. That's when the professor punched him and began beating him down. Three students stepped in to pull their teacher back. When authorities arrived, the professor was taken into custody and the unidentified man was taken to UC Davis Medical Center in a state of unconsciousness. Kiki peered at Gwen.

"I already spoke to him, he's fine, he doesn't want to talk about it," Gwen told her.

"He's not facing any charges," Detective Anderson told them. "From the local authorities, that is, but the university might take a different tactic in regards to his standing."

"I don't understand," Kiki said.

"Rick Wilkens left a note," the detective told them. "He doesn't want to press charges."

"Where is he? Is he being sent back here?" Kiki asked.

"He's gone," the detective told them. "No one knew who he was at first. He miraculously woke up and dragged himself out of the hospital before being identified. All he left was a note that said he didn't want to press charges. To answer your next question, if Rick spied on Janine, she didn't notice him. As far as we know, he only dropped in on the doctor. Due to the nature of his incarceration, Janine and Ian are now under police protection until Wilkens can be picked up, or until they depart on their trip. I understand they are leaving the country soon."

Detective Anderson placed his phone on the table between Gwen and Kiki. He hit the play button and they watched a clip of Ian standing in front of a white board with waves and formula's written all over it. He held a gadget with multicolored lights and chuckled at something that just happened. Then, someone on the side of the room got his attention. Ian glanced over, smiled, and ask that person to repeat the question. A murmuring voice, calm but unclear, wiped the grin off Ian's face. Ian stepped toward the speaker with his eyelids blinking rapidly.

"You're not registered for this class. Who are you?"

Just the top of a head poked into the corner of the screen. Even though his voice was muffled, they could hear the man distinctly.

"You know who I am," the man said. "You think you're married to her, but you're not. Not really. I'm the one to…"

Ian jumped at the man with fists flying, and they both fell from the screen. They could hear a crash, and shouting, and different people moving about. Loud words interrupted the sickening smacks and Kiki knew it was Ian cursing as he hit Richard Wilkens over and over again. Then, three fellows pulled Ian toward the front of the class. Kiki barely recognized Ian's furious, murderous face at the end of the clip.

"Only the last bit, starting with the first punch, is being shown on the net," Detective Anderson told them. "The media is in the dark regarding the man's identity and we hope to keep it that way. It might help the story go away if the media doesn't find out it was Wilkens. But, they're already speculating."

"Do you know what he said at the beginning?" Gwen asked. "It was muffled."

The detective nodded. "Several people said that he mentioned a baby, that he claimed a connection through their baby, and that Janine was his soulmate."

They rewatched the clip. Fortunate that the three fellows stepped in before Ian regretted going too far. Kiki had seen Ian in a few fights and he always stopped when the other fellow hit the ground. This time he didn't stop, and Ian's expression had been frightening. He would have a tough time living down that video in the faculty lounge.

Kiki abruptly stood and hurried to the far end of the outdoor restaurant where she could see the Wrigley Clock Tower and the river below. It was a windy day and the air whistled around her. She dialed Ian's number. He picked up on the first ring.

"I'm fine." He sounded dejected.

"You're not fine, Ian," she said quickly, loudly, and instantly wished she hadn't because it sounded very harsh. She shook her head and continued in a softer tone, "You lifted your hip on that first punch, it just screws with your balance and doesn't add a bit of power. I bet you rolled to your toes as well.

How many times do you need to be reminded to keep a firm footing? What would George say?”

She heard him let out a breath.

“Did I tell you, I met up with Rory in Inverness? You were punching like a Rory, Ian.”

Now he let out a little chuckle. “Oh now, lass, be nice. Actually, Rory called me a few weeks ago, when you first went home. But thanks for calling, I really am fine. Don’t worry yourself.”

“Is Janine fine too? Should I call her?”

“Maybe in a day or so. Give her a little break from answering all the questions,” he said. “Truly, Kiki, I’m fine. The only part I’m upset about is that he’s still out there… and for scaring those kids. I think a few are fair terrified of me now. They didn’t need to see that.”

“They’ll come round, if they’re smart. Smart kids in that class, right?” Kiki said. “They know you by now, Ian. The media is going to find out, sooner or later, who that guy is, and then you’ll be a hero. A hero with a lame ass punch, but a hero. Someone will see him and they’ll pick him up.”

“You’re probably right,” Ian said.

They chatted a while longer before Kiki hung up. He sounded upset, but okay. She made her way back to the table and found Gwen sitting alone with an open file of papers. Gwen glanced up from her tuna melt sandwich.

“The detective left a copy of the skeleton report.”

“He left?” Kiki couldn’t believe it. “Without saying goodbye? He knows we’re leaving today. He couldn’t step over there and let me know he was going and say goodbye?”

“He only just left. He’s probably at the elevator now. He has somewhere else to be, court. I tried to stall him.”

Kiki ran to the elevator, but he wasn’t there. She pushed the buttons in vexation, then he was standing right next to her as the doors opened. He had come out of the men’s room. They entered the elevator car together. Another couple followed them in.

“Were you going to leave without saying goodbye?” she asked quietly.

“I was going back and forth on it,” he answered softly. “I didn’t want to, but I’m due in court. I can’t be late.”

The elevator stopped and the other couple disembarked. It was a relief to have a moment alone with him. Kiki stood on one side of the elevator car, staring at him. The only other person she had ever known with a large pink core aura had been her Auntie Celeste, and his was the same exact color. She loved that aura and the feeling it generated in her, and Kiki knew that he felt something for her too. She could see it in the way he gazed at her. Kiki felt angry and sad at the same time.

"I didn't say it earlier, because I know you're very aware of it." He smiled softly. "You look lovely today. Radiant." *He had noticed.*

"You look lovely too," she said.

"I'm not quite sure what you and Miss Murphy are chasing, but I hope you two are careful. Richard Wilkens is a dangerous man, as his father was before him. The senior Wilkens had been on our radar for a very long time."

Kiki nodded and glanced at the numbers. The elevator moved very close to the lobby floor.

"I guess this is goodbye then," she said, and he nodded.

Detective Anderson's hand went out, and he pushed the *Emergency Stop* button on the elevator. The car came to sudden halt. Then, he took the two steps over to her side of the car and she felt his soothing core as his aura engulfed hers. She felt that leg buckling reaction set in. But he didn't let her fall. The detective gathered her into his arms and slowly kissed her. All his soothing, creamy core energy streamed everywhere, covering her like a warm blanket. Completely different from the red hot passion Max pushed through her Base Well. This feeling was balanced, and tempered, and bound to last a lifetime. Then, he stepped back and put his hands into his pockets.

"I couldn't help myself." He shrugged at her. "I guess that was your intent."

"Detective Anderson, you realize that this is a love connection," Kiki told him. "That I feel love for you."

He reached out and pushed the *Emergency Stop* button again, and the car jolted into motion. His eyes had turned serious.

"I believe it, Miss Mellow," he said. "And I feel love for you too. If I didn't feel this way, I certainly would have met you alone the other day. But I'm in a self-preservation state, you realize. There is a lot of variable, unusual activity in your life and I'm not sure I fit in with the scheme of things. I don't envision a role for me in your life, and I don't believe you would be satisfied following a normal life path in mine. So, I'd rather remember you fondly as the one that got away rather than risk what I'm sure will be a bitter broken heart for one of us."

The elevator doors slid open and they were on the lobby floor. He pressed the button for the roof top dining room before stepping out. He motioned for her stay in the elevator. He reminded her that she still needed to finish her lunch upstairs and he needed to hurry away. He enjoyed seeing her and hoped she would remember to be careful doing whatever it was they were doing. As the doors closed again, he kept his steady eyes on her.

Max Colliers's private jet was a Gulfstream G550. It bragged two Rolls Royce BR710 engines and had a range of 6700 nautical miles, which translated into flying from Chicago to Inverness in one hop. Kiki and Gwen were not the only passengers. Max Colliers often allowed people in his business empire to jump on flights if space was available. Eight others were waiting in the airplane when they arrived, all lounging in the forward two sections, chatting and laughing. The two aft sections were Max Colliers's personal area of the airplane and were separated from the rest of the plane by a private screen. One of the two pilots greeted and escorted them to their seats.

"That phone is a direct line to the cockpit." The pilot pointed to a beige telephone attached to the table. "In case you have a concern or want to change anything about the flight plan, or need one of us back here, I'm happy to be of service." He glanced at each of them. "I set our flight plan for Inverness, Scotland. To call on Kathy, the flight helper, just hit that red button." He smiled at Gwen. "If you'd like to visit the cockpit at any time, the door is always open. Just give us a ring and I'll come to escort you up."

He patted the seat with his hand to indicate they should sit down.

"Let me show you how to use these buckles."

He gave Gwen another handsome smile and moved around to adjust the seat belt for the right length. He knelt down and gazed up at her.

"Just like regular airplanes," he demonstrated. He stopped for a moment to consider Gwen. "Can I just say something? You have very beautiful hair, just an incredible color. I bet people tell you that all the time."

Then, he stood. He was very tall. He nodded to Kiki.

"Whenever you're ready, Miss Mellow, we'll get going. We can start up now or standby until you give us the go. Mr. Colliers said that it's your airplane for the next twenty-four hours."

"Well then, let's get going," Kiki said.

"Good plan," he agreed. "I'll send Kathy to get you set up with refreshments. It might take few minutes to get us into the lineup." He gave Gwen another pleasing smile.

Gwen watched him leave with big, blue, amused eyes. Gwen attracted her fair share of men, but not usually when she was standing next to vivacious Kiki. Kiki was so curvy, and exuded so much energy, that most male eyes couldn't resist her. It was unusual for a man to flirt openly with Gwen and barely glance at Kiki.

"You might try a lad this time," Kiki said. "He certainly preferred you."

"Ho ho, isn't it obvious," Gwen chuckled. "He's scared to look at you. God forbid he sends the wrong message to Max Colliers's woman. He probably thinks he'd lose his job if you thought he was hitting on you. Safest thing for him would be to hit hard on your friend instead."

"You think that pilot believes I'm Max Colliers's woman? Well, I would be one of many."

"I don't think many have borrowed his private jet." Gwen smirked.

Kathy, the helper, popped her head in and delivered cold bottled water. She rattled off a list of refreshments and asked what they'd like. Then, she left an inflight menu and said she'd be back to turn down the beds when they reached flight level. Kathy also pointed out a wet bar in the back, in case they preferred mixing their own drinks. Gwen went off to do just that.

Gwen's assessment worried Kiki. If other people saw her as Max Colliers's woman, then Max very likely thought of her that way too, even though he adamantly denied it. He was a terrible skirt chaser, and his aura never deviated from basic yellows and reds around most of those skirts. She had detected softness in his core aura that morning, which unsettled her and made her wonder just how far a person could change. Kiki wondered if the demon's mark attracted questionable people to close in on her, people that could be used to meet the needs of the curse. Max never presented a particularly strong core signature, then he insisted they use his private jet even though she had lost that bet. What did it mean?

Kiki finally confessed her worries to Gwen. She told Gwen about Celeste's warning, that she was marked for death, and about hearing a voice bark *beware the mark*, over and over again at the séance table.

Kiki declared her concerns about the alternate death vision she had in Chicago, how the landscape changed from green heather on a rocky hill to cattails in a meadow. The evergreen heather in her vision was the same as the winter plants along the outer edges of the Faerie Glen on Skye.

She also professed her new theory to Gwen, that she might be making her own demon with her actions regarding Max. Perhaps the dark part of the aether was working toward a resolution to the curse by molding victims and murderers, and the ghost meant either Janine or Kiki could be the last one.

"The apple doesn't fall far from the tree," Kiki said. "Didn't you find that eerie? Trinity saying it about Ian and then the detective saying it about Wilkens. Both of Janine's men were described with the same words. I'm afraid to think what it could mean."

"Just stop right there." Gwen's face flamed red hot angry. "I'm about ready to slap you, Kiki. You cannot turn someone into a demon with your actions. A person either does or doesn't have a core, a soul. Don't start blaming the *victim* for creating their own attackers. You really think Janine caused that guy to stab her seven times? Just because she loved him and then didn't? Even if some mystic energy is pushing people around, it could never force a hand to act in such an evil way. Do you actually believe Ian could be pushed to do such a thing?"

"No!" Kiki said. "I just wondered if dark energy is maneuvering people into position. I was marked, and suddenly, I'm attracted to the wrong type of man. Don't you think Max, and also Andrew MacLeod, are risky men? They're full of physical energy and have very weak spiritual centers. Both are the perfect type of person for a crime of passion, skirt chasers like Stanley Hansen, and Hansen was a demon. Could one of them become my demon if I push them too far? Both those guys crossed directly into my path after I wore that charm and I find myself extremely attracted to both of them."

"They crossed into your path because they are the exact type of man needed in an awakening ritual, guys that are all yang. The type you really need, lots of yang because you're practically all yin. Opposites attract, Kiki. You are the exact opposite of each of them. Don't forget you pulled the Ace of Wands for Max Colliers, that card wasn't only meant for you, it was also meant for him. You both needed to balance your Base-Core aspects. Whatever growth he makes to his core is not going to disappear because you leave him. His base is learning to chase his core better, and he's developing what he already has. It's not possible for you to change Max, or anyone else, into a demon. And there is no way in hell Ian could be changed into a murderer!"

"That video didn't scare you?" Kiki said. "I've never seen Ian so angry. I don't think he'd murder anyone, but something dark has been working on him, wouldn't you say?"

"That something dark is named Richard Wilkens," Gwen steamed at her. "He tried to kill Ian's wife! *He made all those marks on her body.* And did you hear what he said to Ian? He bragged about fathering a child with Janine, and you know how that happened."

Gwen took a deep breath and settled her anger down.

"This is really not your business, but it may help give you more context. The main reason Bridget was so upset at me was because I balked on using the embryos. When Ian suddenly got engaged, I needed him to tell Janine first, but he was having a problem telling her about it. Apparently, he pushed hard to try for a baby right away, but said she wasn't sure about ever trying for a baby." Gwen said. "Then, that guy went and said those things to Ian. Of course it would make him angry. I wasn't surprised at his response at all."

Kathy popped her head in. A call waited on the tan phone for Kiki Mellow, it was Max on the line. Kathy inquired if they were quite comfortable. Did they want a snack or dinner? Anything else to drink?

"Hi, Kiki, I hope everything is going smoothly," Max said. "Dave said that you guys got settled in okay. He found Gwen very captivating. Also, what do you think about *Spectral Analysis* doing a feature on Skye instead of the main island? I hear there's a phantom fiddler in one of the castles out there. We need a location and you haven't put in your thoughts. Ian's crew thinks it's a splendid idea, and so do I."

"It's a phantom piper," Kiki corrected. "Your airplane is a wonderful treat by the way. Thank you for lending it out."

He laughed. "My pleasure. Hey, since McNally is planning to be in Scotland next month, maybe I'll have the *Spectral Analysis* crew fly out to meet you two. I might come along too."

Gwen reclined her chair while watching with annoying raised eyebrows and a smirk on her freckled face. When Kiki finally hung up, Gwen shook her head.

"He's coming up with reasons to see you, and he gave you *emeralds*, Kiki," Gwen said. "Even if he doesn't realized the significance, there it is. It is definitely serious. Just what were you thinking, carrying on with him like that in Chicago? I thought you were all about that detective."

"The detective is looking for a proper wife," Kiki frowned at her. "And I'm in deep trouble here. This Base Well of mine is either on or off. I feel bipolar. I used to have total control and now I have absolutely no control, especially with Max. Once that door opens a crack, the lust quickly becomes overpowering and I cave in to my base urges. I don't want to admit what hearing his voice did to me just now. So, what am I going to do? "

Gwen was laughing. "You're going to have to talk to your mother, my wee lassie. This might be a genetic problem."

Chapter 15

The Manor *Janine*

J anine and Ian both glowed a golden brown. They spent ten days in a beach bungalow on a small semi-secluded Pacific island below the equator. Only one other couple had slept on the island, on the opposite side about half a mile away, but they never crossed paths with them. They spent each day swimming and snorkeling in the ocean, lazing in a large hammock, and making love before falling asleep and upon waking. On three occasions a speed boat came around and took them scuba diving. One afternoon, Ian built a fish trap and caught their dinner. On another night, they pretended to be stranded on a deserted island and camped on the beach next to a small fire sleeping naked under the stars. Ian sparked the fire with a frictional hand drill. He insisted on showing off his survival skills. They wouldn't have matches on a deserted island, he said, and she should know that he could take care of her anywhere. Ian stopped shaving, and she loved how rough he looked after all the sun, and sand, and swimming. Janine barely thought about her scars, and for the first time in several years, her tan covered ninety percent of her body.

Janine lapsed into a sense of perpetual pleasure and joyful feelings in the presence of her new husband. She found him absolutely magnetic. Ian completely mesmerized her with his survival instincts, and she found his efforts to impress her extremely attractive. She giggled at how he wanted to pretend they were the last people on earth and needed to repopulate the world. Really, a deserted island would not have a fully stocked wine cellar to accent the fish on skewers. She couldn't imagine being more blissful. She loved the South Pacific.

Their transition to Scotland was a shocker. They suddenly went from barely dressed to fully covered in winter wear. Good thing they packed an overlarge suitcase of coats and sweaters. Ian insisted on wool and now she knew why, the itchy weave trapped the heat nicely. Even the landscape was dramatically different, rolling hills and startling rock formations broke up the view. Instead of the warm serenity of a flat blue horizon stretching into infinity, her eyes were flooded with contrasting shapes in an agitated skyline.

They landed in Inverness and drove toward Dornoch to meet Ian's father and to visit for a couple of days. Then, they'd stay with Kiki one night in the city before driving onto Skye to visit Ian's aunt. Apparently, the *Spectral Analysis* team would meet them on Skye to film at one of the castles. Ian thought she might enjoy hanging out at his auntie's cottage while that was going on. The coven women were very fun and the local landscape provided nice hiking trails.

McNally Manor included both horse pastures and woodland hills, and it lay near the east coast on the main landmass. The drive from the main road to the front door consisted of a half mile of winding driveway, which Ian seemed determined to attack at top speed. The entire drive to Dornoch had Janine scared out of her wits. If the warm Pacific island had calmed Ian, the cold Atlantic one irritated him. Ian's blinking eyes told her that he was nervous about seeing his father again and his driving had become very reckless. She tried not to snap at him, but the jet lag, cold, and fast driving unnerved her. It made her a little nauseous, and his blinking eyes were causing her to panic. He was not calm, good natured Ian McNally in Scotland.

"We're late," Ian said. "He doesn't like late."

Her hands were on the dash holding on for dear life. He glanced at her tight grip and then into her eyes. He was upset at her for being upset. He flew through another turn and their tires just skimmed the edge of the road.

"Ian!"

"Relax," he said. "I've driven this a thousand of times."

He brought the car speeding into the large driveway and screeched to halt. It took all of her strength not to fling forward too dramatically. She felt her seat belt lock, protecting her from smashing into the dashboard, and she gave him a good glare.

"Can you calm down? It's not going to be that bad," she snapped.

"I'm sorry." Ian let out a long breath. He glanced past her. "Crikes, here he comes."

Janine glanced around to see three people emerge from the front door. Two men headed down the steps, and a woman hung behind in the doorway. Anyone could tell which man was Ian's father, the resemblance was spot on and it made her smile. Janine popped open the door and jumped out before anyone arrived at the car to help. The elder McNally walked right up and appraised her with Ian-shaped grey eyes and had a strong Ian-shaped jawline. He only glanced fleetingly at his son before returning those strange eyes to study her.

"Hello there, lassie, you must be Janine. I'm Roger McNally. That laddie failed to tell us how captivating you are in person." He smiled at her. "Can I get a hug from my new daughter?"

He was just shy of Ian's height and seemed very friendly. She couldn't understand why Ian had been so nervous. His father seemed positively happy to see them. After a brief hug, he pointed out the other man and introduced him as Stan, the manager of the stable. Roger gave Ian a brief hug and survey, then he tucked Janine's hand into his arm and walked her up the front steps asking about their trip. The woman who had been in the doorway had disappeared and Roger McNally turned his head back toward Ian.

"You might have time to clean up before dinner," he said. "You look rough."

Ian shaved off his rough face and she sadly watched it all go down the drain. She got a lot of enjoyment from his whiskers. She asked him not to shave, but he said his father practically ordered him to shave with that *clean up* comment. Ian glared at himself in the mirror. Was he still feeling nervous? His father had been pleasant so far. She didn't know why Ian was still so grouchy. She tried to hug him, but he felt so rigid.

"Ian, I think it's going to be okay. He seems to have gotten over the shock of you marrying someone he's never met."

"I can't help it," he turned around and kissed her. "I'm sorry. I'll try to loosen up."

"Who was the woman in the door?" Janine asked.

"That's a good question," Ian said. "I didn't recognize her at all. I guess we'll find out soon enough. Are you ready to go downstairs?"

The McNally house was actually a small mansion. Ian said that they were staying in his old room and the rugby trophies along the wall were his, but besides those relics, there was nothing else of Ian's on display. It had been redecorated since the last time he visited back when he had been in college. He did find a few of his old things in the drawers and closet. Would she like one of his old rugby jerseys? *Yes!*

Ian led her down the generous staircase, through a large sitting room, and into a formal dining room. His father and a middle aged woman were waiting for them. Roger McNally introduced his good friend, Chloe Kirby, who happened to live on McNally Manor. She helped keep the grounds and the house up, and exercised the horses. Janine wondered at their relationship. He called her a friend but acted very familiar with her. Were they platonic or romantic? It was hard to tell. She admired Janine's ring and asked to see Ian's while Roger delivered cocktails. They waited for the groundskeeper, Stan, then they sat down for dinner.

Janine relayed details about their wedding in California, and also their living arrangements in Davis. Ian answered questions about the research he was conducting, and his father told him about the horses and the drainage problems in some sector of the manor. After polite small talk, Ian's father began asking Janine about her family. He asked detailed questions about her sister and grandmother. Ian got a little perturbed with the interrogation, but she didn't mind. This was Ian's father and he'd want to know about his daughter-in-law's family. All in all, it was a very pleasant evening. By the time they retired to bed, she fell right into a deep sleep, exhausted from traveling.

Sleeping in a new place always brought odd dreams. Unlike the tropical island where her night visions had been sweet and erotic, the cold Scottish winter revealed unsettling images lurking in her subconscious. A familiar nightmare crept its way back into her dreams, spoiling her peace of mind.

She ran in the dark of night, stumbling through the foliage. She was cold and shivering, and knew *he* followed directly behind. If she turned left instead of right, things might end differently, but she always chose wrong and ended up in the same little copse of trees. Perhaps she could hide better. As she sunk into the ground, trying to blend into the foliage, she knew it was no use and the trees receded rapidly, exposing her, the ground spitting her out. Then, he stood in front of her, staring down, ready to strike with the knife she dropped. She needed to remember not to bring the knife next time. She looked up and saw him clearly. It wasn't Rick, it was Ian. He had that look in his eyes and she was relieved. Or was it his father? His eyes had turned grey and she was terrified again.

Janine awoke disturbed. Letting her past nightmare sneak into her present relationship almost doomed them before and she vowed never to let it happen again. She needed to clear those images from her head and decided to sneak out for a run. Running always helped clear out the dreams. It had been two weeks since she last ran, and her legs needed a good workout. She didn't wake Ian because he snored soundly, finally peaceful. She crept out the door, down the stairs, and quietly slipped into the cold dark air. She'd be warm once she stared moving, she knew, and took off in a trot down the drive. She decided on an out and back, down the winding drive and a bit of the road.

It was cold and a little foggy. She couldn't see much of the landscape or the manor. She had no idea how far she had gone, but by the amount of time, she could make a good guess. She decided to limit herself to two miles because the cold air made it hard to breath. She had been spoiled by the warm, dry, California climate. When she turned back down the drive, the porch lights had broken through the fog and she could see the outline of the house. *Was that Chloe in the distance, near the end of the drive?* No, it had been a trick of the fog, no one was there.

Janine jogged up the steps and welcomed the warmth as she entered into the foyer. She pulled off layers in the heat to get down to her full body spandex. When she turned, she noticed Roger McNally standing in the doorway to the sitting room. For one brief moment, she thought he was staring at her body, then he wasn't. She found herself slipping back into her hot hoody, but not the sweat pants, that would be too obvious. What was wrong with her? She must have been mistaken.

"Nice to see you're an athletic girl," he said. "But it's very cold this time of morning. Come and get something warm inside o' ye."

"I think I'll just run upstairs to…"

"I insist." He waved her over. "Have a cuppa coffee or tea, or I can call Cookie to warm up some milk. You don't want to catch a cold. Maybe warm porridge or oatmeal. You can go up in a minute, but first, you need something warm to coat your throat. Come along, Janine."

What could she do? She followed him toward the dining room where he poured her a warm cup of tea and added loads of honey to it. He stirred it, then handed it over. He waited to watch her drink it down and smiled at her. He was right, the warm fluid felt good on her cold throat. He added more tea to her cup.

"The honey will coat your throat well." He nodded, pleased with her compliance.

Janine sipped the tea feeling a little uncomfortable with his scrutiny. Usually, she never gave a thought to her spandex running attire but the dream, and that look at the door, unsettled her. Her idea of personal space was probably wider American rather than closer European. She thanked him for the tea and tried to excuse herself to get cleaned up.

"Let me show you something first."

He reached down and took her hand with an exact replica of Ian's hand. He lightly pulled her through the house, moving from room to room, chatting as they walked. He regaled her with Ian's antics as a small boy and the speech therapist Ian terrorized when he was working on his stutter. He seemed to be sharing simple, humorous anecdotes, but Janine didn't appreciate how he spoke about Ian. He seemed to be mocking his son. They finally ended up in the library where Roger presented a large painting of Ian's late mother. She wore a Comba charm necklace in the portrait and was very pretty with a hint of Kiki in her face and form.

"She was a beauty, don't you think?" He gazed at the portrait. "A little flighty, like Ian, and given to imaginative fanciful yarn." He turned his grey eyes on Janine. "Not unlike his cousin Kiera and the women that hang about that cottage on the isle. I hear it's great fun spinning the tales they do, but more than one woman has confused herself out there." He pointed to the painting of Ian's mother. "Celeste for one. She actually suffered from delusions and needed to be hospitalized. She took her own life. Ian blames me for that. He wasn't quite a fully grown man, in the storm of adolescence, rebellious and wild. Ian's likely told you a bit of it. He was a little hard headed to remember everything, but the doctors believe she drank hallucinogenic teas. Those women at that cottage encouraged Celeste that way. I'm only telling you this because I know that you're planning a trip to the isle soon. *Don't drink the homemade tea.*"

He noticed that she finished her own tea and took the cup to carefully set it down on a desk. Janine found it hard to continually meet his eye. Her skin crawled because his eyes were exactly like Ian's but they weren't the same color. He squinted and moved his head similar to Ian, which further unsettled her. Janine took a step back. She was wary of Roger McNally. Although he appeared to be an older version of Ian, there was something missing in him, something she couldn't see. *Kiki and Gwen both called him a demon.* Maybe it was his Core Well she couldn't sense. Then, his expression became cautious. His eyes bore right into hers, locking her into place. His voice dropped very low as he leaned in.

"Ian would be upset at me for asking, so please don't share this, but I would like to see something before you go upstairs. I'm afraid I must insist."

"What?" She was shocked. What did he need to see? Janine tensed, ready to spring from the room.

"The back of your neck," he said quietly. "It's where they place their witch's mark. Ian assured me that you weren't involved in their nonsense. His cousin, and her friends, and her mother, are a terrible influence. Easy to get caught up with them. I know you're friendly with Kiera. I just need to confirm that you're not part of that cult."

Janine took a shaky breath. He only wanted to see if she had that tattoo. What was wrong with her thinking? It must be some of Ian's nervousness rubbing off on her. She pulled her hair up and turned around to give him a good look at her neck, then became suddenly upset at her own easy obedience. She dropped her hair and turned back around.

"Thank you. Thank you." He was visibly relieved and extremely happy. "Forgive me, lass, but for many years, I feared he would marry into that cult and meet the same misfortunes I have. You may not know this, but Ian was bewitched by one of them, as a young lad. Very wild behavior with those girls, especially with that one. Fortunately, God saved him. She was disfigured. You've made me very happy. Very happy. When you go see his auntie, just remember, they often spike the tea."

Disfigured? Was he referring to Gwen? His tone almost sounded like he blamed Gwen for her own misfortune. *Would he consider Janine disfigured if he saw her scars?*

"I'll remember that." She gave him her best try at a smile. "Now, I think I'd better run upstairs and get cleaned up."

Roger and Chloe took them on a driving tour of the local landscape and sights, then they went into town for lunch. Ian seemed considerably more relaxed in the glow of his father's good humor. As time separated her from that disturbing dream, Janine chastised herself for getting so uncomfortable with Ian's father that morning. Her father-in-law came across very likeable in the light of day. She could clearly see that Chloe was more than a friend and they were being modest to spare Ian's sensitivities. Although, Janine didn't think Ian would mind at all if his father had a companion.

That afternoon, Roger urged Ian to go on a walking pheasant and partridge hunt over the north end of the grounds. There were flocks of birdies and they could get in a good chat. Chloe offered to take Janine on a horse ride if she liked, or perhaps she'd like to nap after all the traveling. Janine opted for the riding. It would get dark soon enough and then they'd be cooped up in the house.

The barn was large and Roger owned four horses. Chloe exercised each of them at least two days a week. That meant two rides a day for four days. She missed a morning ride, so Janine was helping her make up for that session by coming along. Chloe even lent her a pair of breeches, but she didn't have the right sized boots. Janine threw on her tennis shoes and said that she wasn't planning anything fancy. No jumps or gallops, just walk, trot, and canter if that was okay. Chloe nodded and smiled, then asked if she was familiar with an English saddle.

Unlike a western saddle, the English saddle was very small and lacked a horn to grab. Although Janine had ridden in an English seat as a kid, she was nowhere near as proficient as her sister Juliana. She was confident that she could still sit well enough not to fall off.

The barn manager saddled up two Cleveland mares when they arrived. He helped Janine mount and adjusted the stirrup straps for her. He raised an eyebrow at her sneakers.

"Mind you don't go past the red marked fence posts," he said. "These here have a chip in the ear. It'll sound the alarm if you take her out of bounds."

Janine chuckled. "Horse thieves a problem out here?"

"I think it's more to keep us girls corralled in." Chloe chuckled in a matter of fact way before trotting away.

Chloe and Janine spent the next two hours trotting around the grounds, mostly over very green pasture lands, but there was a nice section of trees within the horse boundaries that they zig zagged through. Riding in nature was much more fun than strutting about in mock shows in a ring. Chloe didn't talk much and that was okay with Janine, they were both just enjoying the quiet exercise. Janine fantasized about living on McNally Manor with Ian someday. Her sister Juliana would love visiting. Better yet, maybe they could reproduce a McNally Manor somewhere back home.

Ian and his father each bagged a couple of pheasants and they put them on the menu for the following day. *Ugh, the menu in Scotland was not agreeing with her.* Everyone went off to clean up and change for dinner. She was happy to see Ian calm and peaceful. Maybe he'd get his South Pacific mojo back. He grabbed her when she came out of the shower and snuggled with her on the bed for several minutes.

"Thank you for making us come here," Ian said. "I think he's forgiven my wild accusations and he's actually behaving himself, right? He's been very nice and polite to you, right? No funny stuff. He seems so normal with Chloe, it's not how I imagined it'd be at all. Finally getting on with him is just… just brilliant."

"He's very nice." Janine didn't want to mention the neck incident, or the dig about Gwen. "The bottom line is he loves you, and is worried about you. He wants to make sure I'm right for his son. Do you think he approves?"

"Absolutely." He kissed her. "He'd be an idiot not to. He can clearly see you're very intelligent and well grounded. Not to mention a stunner. I think you've given me a little clout with my old man. I think maybe he was expecting a frivolous airhead or something. He's got to be amazed at the brilliant bird I managed to capture." Ian looked so happy she decided to try to get over her uneasiness around his father.

Janine couldn't sleep again. She either felt someone stirring in the house, or the heavy air kept her from sleeping. Plus, she had another disturbing dream. She dreamt that she was riding horses with Ian's mother, Celeste. But they couldn't talk on the manor grounds, they needed to find a place right outside the perimeter, out of earshot of the grounds. Apparently, Roger McNally's ears could pick up anything said within the red markers of McNally Manor. They needed to find someplace outside the red posts that wouldn't set off those alarms. There was a spot near the perimeter fence and they rode the horses there. It looked just like the entrance to the main arena at Gold Country back in Rio Linda. Then, Celeste whispered and Janine needed to lean very close to hear, almost slipping off the English saddle.

He'll bend you to his will, she said.

Janine didn't know who she was talking about. She couldn't ask for clarification because the mare's ear went just outside of the red posts and they were caught. She woke up.

It was four o'clock in the morning and pitch black outside. After laying wide awake for more than thirty minutes, Janine decided to go for another jog. Why not, no one would miss her. After that horse ride, she knew the grounds pretty well and she had a small flashlight she could take. It wouldn't be totally crazy to jog so early in the morning. All the traveling had likely gotten her internal clock out of whack, so she decided to go. She had been feeling blah lately and knew it must be from of lack of exercise. Janine slipped into her warm jogging gear and tiptoed down the stairs.

A layer of low level clouds trapped the earth's heat so it did not feel as cold as the previous morning. She decided to jog past the stables and toward the little gathering of trees, then she'd turn around and run along the fence back toward the house. That would be between two and three miles.

She set out at a nice even pace. She always found it a good time to think things over on a private run. She didn't know what to make of Roger McNally. She wanted to feel comfortable around him, was happy Ian was getting on with him, but deep down, she had reservations about him.

His comment about Gwen upset her. Was that because of the word he used, *disfigured*, or was it something else? Janine didn't want to process the thought, but there she was, on her private morning jog and she had to. Roger implied that Ian left Gwen because of the double mastectomy. Was it just too much for Ian to accept? Did Gwen push him away because of it? Ian and Gwen were certainly very bonded and something was being said between them at the wedding.

Janine wondered if Ian would still desire her if she was as altered as Gwen? *Damn! Why would she even think that*, she chastised herself. Ian had not even blinked the first time he saw her knife wounds. *But Ian did enjoy all of her womanly parts*, she admitted. Would he feel differently if one of her womanly parts was missing?

Janine reached the small woods and paused to drink the water in her flat flask. It had been tucked into her belt and her body heat kept it warm. She took a few slow sips and looked around. It was very quiet in the highland hills at night. She tucked the flask back into her belt and started jogging again.

The portrait in the library popped into her mind. Roger still displayed that overlarge portrait. In fact, Janine noticed Celeste's image in several rooms of the house. Janine wondered how Chloe felt about that. Celeste appeared intelligent in that portrait, not fragile in the least, as Roger claimed. Every story Gwen or Kiki told of Ian's mother painted her as a strong caring woman, and she actually wrote a book full of summoning spells. Gwen promised to give Janine that book soon, because Celeste hoped to pass the book to her granddaughter.

But was that even possible, with only one ovary and a damaged womb? Janine found herself wishing she could have met Ian's mother.

When she reached the perimeter fence, she turned toward the house. The jog was going to be a good three miles. Either that, or she was out of shape. She spotted a dim light in the barn house. Someone must have left it on. Then, she saw a woman standing along the fence again. Was it Chloe? No chance of calling out, the crisp air was too cold and her vocal cords felt stiff. Janine would catch up soon enough. Maybe Chloe enjoyed an early morning walk.

In the pitch black?

Janine glanced up again, but no one was there. The woman suddenly disappeared as Janine drew closer to the house. Janine glanced around. Had she been mistaken two nights in a row? *Could it be a ghost? Celeste?* More likely, the bent pole with the flag fooled her at a distance. Janine just shook it off and went inside to warm up.

Roger stood waiting in the foyer. He already poured the tea and urged her to sit with him in the den. He hoped to catch her alone again. He actually had a tray of steaming hot oatmeal waiting for her. He noticed her odd appetite the night before and predicted that she would be hungry.

"I thought I saw Chloe out there," Janine told him. "But it must have been a trick of the light and shadows. The past two mornings, I could have sworn she was standing right at the end of the fence when I was at a distance. But then no one was there when I got closer. Maybe it was that pole with the flag on it."

Roger chuckled. "You don't think it was a ghost? After your adventures on that show, I'd guess your first reaction to be that you saw a ghost. Nice to know you steer clear of the fanciful. Must be hard to take Ian seriously sometimes, eh? Just so you know, lots of folks have mistaken that post for a woman when it's dark. The wood bends similar to a lass."

He handed her a small bowl of steaming hot cereal sprinkled with fresh berries. Once again he put a large helping of honey in her tea.

"Do you often have problems sleeping?"

"I think it's the time change." She felt uneasy again. "The traveling."

"Worried on something?"

"Well, no. Not anything to keep me from sleeping," she said. "What about you? You rise pretty early. Are you worried about something?"

"Aye." He locked his grey, Ian-shaped eyes on her.

Janine considered him.

"What are you worried about?"

"Neither of you have mentioned it," he said. "The man my son beat in California. I'm aware of who he was to you. Your story broke everywhere. Anyone can google anything these days. I reviewed all the news articles and brushed up on your secret scandal. I'm trying to understand it."

Janine let out a long breath and said softly, "I'm still trying to understand it too." *How awkward.*

"Did you know that you were pregnant when you ran away from him?"

"What? No." *Oh good lord, was he going to interrogate her about it?*

"Was finding out about the pregnancy what made you finally blame him?"

"I blamed him because he tried to kill me." *Did he mean to be insensitive?*

"Then, why did it take you ten days to point him out? You let him sit next to you and feed you in the hospital for ten days before saying anything. That's unusual. Isn't that when you found out about the baby?"

"I was scared. Not fully lucid at first, and then, I didn't want to believe it happened." *He doesn't believe me,* she could see it in his eyes.

"Is it possible that he's innocent? That governor thinks so."

"No, he's guilty." *He thinks I made it up.* She felt her anger bubbling up.

"What did you do to him, to inspire that kind of violence?"

"Nothing." *He thinks it was my fault.* She was fuming, *couldn't he see her reaction?*

"Would you like more tea?" He picked up the pot with a benign expression. "You look a little low there."

"No, thank you," she said sharply. *Was this just a social talk over tea for him? Was he oblivious to her reaction?*

"Where did the baby go?" he asked softly.

Janine couldn't speak. She just stared at Roger McNally, completely stunned that he had asked that question.

"That man was very angry, lassie. I saw the clip of Ian punching him down, you've got my laddie wound nice." He chuckled. "But that little brawl is not going to stop that man. He has not let you go." Roger poured himself more tea. "He's going to hound you for years to come. It's okay if you tell me what you did to him. You're my daughter now and I'm on your side no matter what it was. I'm just curious."

"Are you trying to scare me?" she asked softly.

Roger chuckled again, and he sounded strangely like Ian when he chuckled.

"I'm trying to reassure you. As long as you stay here on the manor, he won't get within an inch of you, I can guarantee you that. My men are good at keeping out the strays. They chased a fellow off the hill the day you two got here. Not to worry, probably just a laddie hiking around. Ian tells me that you finished your degree and you're between plans. Perhaps you should consider making this home part of your plan. Stay here and relax as long as you like. Why go to Skye and mix with those crazy women? Nothing good can come of it."

Janine stood up quickly and backed away. She set the bowl down and could see those grey eyes studying her. He stood with her.

"Need to get cleaned up?" He nodded at her. "Let's keep this conversation between us. Ian gets oversensitive about things, he's always been an emotional lad. Another good reason he shouldn't go hanging around that cottage on the isle."

They were bickering on the drive to Inverness. Ian suggested she might stay at McNally Manor for several more days, but Janine insisted on sticking to the plan; stay with Kiki one night and then go to Skye to stay at the cottage. But Ian didn't want to disappoint his father. He requested that Ian's wife stay at the Manor and skip Skye. Everyone was getting along so brilliantly, Ian said, they should ride that wave as long as possible. Plus, she could completely avoid the *Spectral Analysis* business that way. Max Colliers would be on Skye, and she detested Max. It might be better for everyone if she stayed near Dornoch instead of at Uig Bay. Ian believed she had the right touch with his father, he had warmed up to her nicely.

"As long as your wife does exactly what he wants her to do."

"What does he want you to do?" Ian asked. "Relax, ride horses in the meadow, get to know him better, it doesn't sound like too much to ask. I've never seen him so polite and nice. I think he really wants to make amends and be a part of my family. It would only be for a few days and I'll come back in the middle. Are you sure you won't change your mind about it?"

"I just want to stay with you and visit when you see everyone," Janine said softly. "I feel like you mean to hide me away up there in Dornoch. Are you hoping for a private meeting with someone? Like, with Gwen, perhaps?"

Oh goodness, why did she say that? She didn't mean it, not really. She just didn't know how to tell him that she wasn't wild about his father. She actually disliked Roger McNally.

Ian glanced at her, a bit angry. "What are you saying?"

"What were you two talking about at our wedding? I saw your eyes blinking, Ian, so it must not have been good. What was going on? What did Gwen say to you?"

He started blinking all over again. He was going to get them into a car accident with his fast driving.

"Slow down!" she snapped.

"She just wanted to wish us well," he said. "Why would you ask that? Did my father say something to you about Gwen?"

He had such a crushed looked on his face that she felt she must have hit a nerve. Maybe it was true, that he still loved Gwen and Gwen loved him. Maybe their chances were damaged by her cancer. Ian must feel like Gwen would never take him back, and she must feel like Ian still desired a woman with an undamaged chest.

Good grief, she thought, *married barely a month, and it's already over!*

"What is this, are you crying?" He sounded exasperated. "Oh, Janine, this is ridiculous. What in the world are you thinking? My father doesn't know anything about anything. I barely even talked to him back then. What did he say?" He glanced at her. "Gwen and I were just kids, experimenting too soon, that's all it was. We've been friends for as long as I can remember and we were just trying to figure it all out. And my mother, she encouraged us."

"I don't want to talk about it," she was sobbing. Why was she sobbing so uncontrollably?

"You're scaring me here," Ian said. "It was just youthful nonsense, that's all. We crossed some lines when we were young, but that wasn't really us. I…

Please don't be upset with what happened with me and Gwen. What exactly did my father say?"

"I don't want to talk about it!" she snapped.

"Janine…"

"And slow down!"

He yelled back, a terrible curse word, but he did slow down for a several minutes. But his knuckles turned white as he gripped the steering wheel, and the speed inched up again. His jaw stayed clenched, and his eyes were blinking, and she really just wanted to apologize, ask him to pull over, and have a kissing session. She didn't really believe he still loved Gwen, not in a romantic way, did she? A minute ago, she had, and now that her tears were winding down, she didn't anymore. It suddenly seemed like a ridiculous idea. What was wrong with her?

Chapter 16

Unexpected News *Janine*

Kiki, Gwen, and a tall, handsome fellow with a receding hair line and hazel eyes greeted them at Kiki's apartment door. They were all smiles, until they noticed Janine and Ian were miserable. Ian fought his way into Kiki's apartment with some of their luggage and tossed them haphazardly to the side. Then, he smiled big at the tall handsome fellow and high fived him.

"Rory O'Hare!" Ian yelled.

"Ian McNally!" Rory roared back.

The two fellows gave each other a boisterous hug. Ian introduced Rory to Janine, and then gave Kiki and Gwen quick brutal clutches before grabbing Rory's shirt collar. Ian practically dragged Rory to the door. He glanced back at Kiki and Gwen, avoiding Janine's eyes.

"We're going to the pub!" he announced. "We've got some catching up to do. It'll give you three some time to get your sass out and get ready for dinner. Get out there, Rory." Ian pushed his old friend out the door and then followed him, letting the door slam shut at their departure.

Kiki and Gwen stood shocked with their eyes on the door and their mouths hanging open. They turned to gaze at Janine. *Oh ,sure, leave her with the fallout,* Janine fumed. Neither Kiki nor Gwen moved a muscle.

"Trouble in paradise?" Kiki asked softly.

Janine had to resist throwing her purse at the smirk under Kiki's beautiful eyes.

"We got into a huge fight in the car. He wanted me to stay at the manor, but I can't help it, his father creeps me out, and I can't tell him that, because they were getting along so famously. Then, Ian has to drive like a lunatic and it just drives me crazy. What is wrong with going the speed limit and staying in your own frigging lane?" Janine stomped.

"He's always been a terrible driver," Gwen agreed.

"Just tell me one thing, Gwen, because I need to know, and don't sugar coat anything." Janine let out a long breath. "Just very plainly, tell me. Did Ian leave you because of the cancer, the surgery, because of what happened to you? Is that what happened? Because, deep down, I think he might regret it. So, if you're still in love with him, I want to know about it right now. What did—"

"Janine—" Kiki interrupted.

"No, no, let her go on and get it out." Gwen stopped Kiki and nodded to Janine. "Go on."

"I saw you two talking at my wedding, and I've seen you and Ian many times before, and you cannot tell me that there isn't something there. I just want you to be up front about it, okay, be honest. Because this has been bugging me, and right now, all I can do is snap at him, and I don't want to snap at him about stupid things. If I'm going to snap at him, and cry uncontrollably, I want it to be something worth getting upset about. Half the time, I am absolutely certain he completely loves me, then I start thinking about his blinking eyes while you two were dancing at my wedding."

She felt herself crying again, tears streaming down her face.

"And what is this! I can't stop crying. This is ridiculous, I don't even feel like crying right now, so why am I crying like this! Let's be absolutely clear here, these are angry tears, not crying tears, okay? So, don't try to be all sensitive with me, just tell me the truth."

Gwen and Kiki exchanged looks. Gwen reached down and handed her purse to Kiki.

"I've got a box in there," Gwen said, then turned to Janine. "The first answer is *no*. Ian did not leave me because of the cancer and my mastectomy. And *yes*, I do love Ian, dearly, but I'm not *in love* with him and he certainly isn't in love with me. He is totally in love with you."

Gwen moved closer and put an arm around Janine. She started leading her to the bathroom and handed her the pregnancy test stick Kiki had retrieved.

"Okay, lass, I want you to go in there and pee on this little thing, then bring it out to us," Gwen told her. "While we wait, I'll tell you everything Ian and I discussed at your wedding. He obviously didn't know how to broach it with you."

Gwen pushed her into the bathroom, and Janine heard them tittering on the other side of the door. She sat down. They thought she was pregnant. That was ludicrous, it took people months, years, to get pregnant, and Ian and Janine had only started trying since their wedding night. But, it would explain her mood swings. It would even explain her recent nausea, *not a travel tummy, but a baby tummy?* She felt like a complete idiot. But in only two months, was it even possible? She peed on the stick, then washed her hands and emerged from the bathroom calm and rational again. Kiki took the test stick and placed it on the bathroom counter.

"A watched pot never boils," Kiki said stupidly.

They went to the sofa to wait.

"We've only been trying since the wedding," Janine confessed. "So, it's a long shot."

"I think it's quite obvious," Kiki told her. "Even though you're crying, you're absolutely beautiful. I've never seen your colors so bright."

Gwen leaned over and took Janine's hands.

"At the wedding, Ian and I were discussing my zygotes. They told me that zygotes had a better chance of surviving the freezing process than eggs. So, Ian donated his sperm and I had zygotes frozen just in case. Last spring, I finally decided to use those zygotes and Ian was fine with it, but then you two suddenly got engaged and I thought you should know about it first. Maybe you might not like the idea. It's okay if you don't. I might not use them after all, and I might have them destroyed, to take away the tease. I never should have asked him to speak with you again, especially after you got married, but I panicked. I'm sorry about that. I suppose he was afraid to tell you."

She did not expect that, but it made total sense.

"No, don't, don't destroy them," Janine said slowly. "If you're infertile, and they're your only chance…"

"They might not be my only chance," Gwen said. "The doctors say I might have a few good eggs lingering in there, so there's a slight possibility that I dinna absolutely need those zygotes to have my own child. I could find another donor to fertilize an egg."

"Like your pediatric oncologist, right?" Janine said. "Isn't that better? Or is he infertile, is that why you wanted to use the zygotes?"

"She," Gwen said. "She's plenty fertile. I thought you may have caught on by now. Ian and I were doomed from the start. We were always just best friends, really. I've always preferred a bonnie lass to a lad. If I try hard, I can certainly fall for a fellow, but it's so much easier for me to love a woman."

Gwen leaned back, a little perturbed at having to explain herself, and Janine felt like an idiot for being so dense.

"I'm going to go get that stick."

Kiki grabbed Janine's hand after Gwen went off.

"Gwen's girl Bridget was supposed to carry the baby. Gwen's egg and Bridget's womb. Almost as easy as a simple fertilization because the zygotes were already waiting. The big bonus was that the baby could be both of theirs, in a way."

Kiki told Janine that the whole episode broke them up for a spell. Bridget felt like Gwen betrayed their relationship by halting the use of her zygotes.

Gwen emerged from the bathroom and brought the test stick with her. She placed it on the coffee table.

"What do you think about that?" She smiled.

Double positive. What did that mean? Was that a yes or a no? The box said yes, but was it a definite yes? Her blood started racing and she wasn't sure what she should do. Panic set in. Holy crap, she had been drinking wine off and on for days, and when was the last time she took a vitamin? Kiki and Gwen were both chattering, but she couldn't hear a word they were saying. She put her hands on her belly and realized that Ian's little child was in there, and she had just been yelling at its' father. She began to hyperventilate.

Kiki sat beside her and rubbed her back. Janine didn't realize how desperately she wanted to be pregnant until that very moment. When she told Ian they should wait, she had been frightened that it would take a very long time to conceive. Her sister Juliana and Alan tried for five years, both times. Or worse, Janine feared that she might never conceive because one of her ovaries had been stabbed to death in Thatcher Woods several years ago and part of her womb had been wounded.

"Breathe easy, Janine," Kiki said. "Here, are you okay?"

Kiki dabbed Janine's eyes dry with a tissue, then Gwen gave her a wine glass of ice water while Kiki and Gwen had the real stuff, because they could. They toasted her good news and then laughed together. After a while, Gwen grabbed her purse and pulled out a small book. Gwen handed it to Janine and urged her to open it. It was a diary.

"It's perfect timing," Gwen said. "She always wanted her granddaughter to have her grimoire and now she has it right away. But there is something written in there we need to find. I'm hoping you can help me find it. A charm Celeste wrote. Maybe, as a *dragoma*, you can figure out the one we need, kind of sense it out."

Janine's phone buzzed. She could see it was Ian and snatched it up. What would she say? She should wait to tell him in person. Goodness, what if he was calling to say he wasn't coming back right away because he was fed up with her? She had been horrible to him on the recent drive.

"Ian?"

"Janine."

"Ian, we need to talk. Where are you?"

"I'm downstairs," he said. "Before you say anything, I want to apologize and…"

"No need for that, just come right up so we can talk," Janine said. "I need to tell you something."

Then, she hung up. She picked up the book and gave it back to Gwen.

"Don't destroy your zygotes. It's okay with me if you use them, then maybe you'll have the girl for the grimoire. I imagine that's what Ian's mother wanted."

"We'll see," Gwen said.

There was a knock on the door. Kiki picked up her bag and pulled Gwen along.

"We'll come back to cook supper in say, an hour?" Kiki opened the door.

Kiki pushed Rory back into the hall and stepped aside for Ian. Both Gwen and Kiki gave him a pat on the rear as they giggled and ran off. Ian stood there looking sorry and sad and very worried. Janine picked up the test stick and walked over to him.

"I'm so sorry about snapping at you. I know why I've been so irritable."

"Is it because I've been acting like an idiot?" He noticed the test stick in her hand. He kept glancing down at it, confused and blinking. "Gwen told you about the fertilized eggs? Is that? What is that?"

"It's mine," she told him. "It's mine and yours. We're going to have a baby."

Ian, Janine, and Kiki drove together onto Skye for a visit with Trinity. They received word that the *Spectral Analysis* team was on schedule to show up the next day and booked rooms at the hotel in Uig Bay. That establishment was located roughly between the two castles they meant to investigate, Duntulm Castle ruins on the northern tip of the isle and Dunvegan Castle, a tourist attraction about midway down the island. They would easily find folks to interview regarding the specters in those two places. Skye was riddled with MacDonalds and MacLeods, all privy to the spooky old tales regarding each location.

If the main island of Scotland was beautiful, it had a rival in the island of Skye. The rolling green hills were speckled with sharp boulders cutting into the skyline. The granite peaks were dramatic and pleasing to the eye, and salt water saturated the air. Scattered along the hillsides, fancy fluffy-haired cows grazed the emerald grasses comically shaking overly long bangs, very different than the cows they had in Texas.

Ian gushed that the roads were not as crowded and lacked the erratic touristy drivers in the winter, so the trip should go smoothly. Janine bit back any comments about his driving. She knew her hormones were making her crazy, because she was just as annoyed with his slowed down overly cautious driving as she had been with his speeding.

Kiki's mother lived in a cottage on the outskirts of a fishing village. They veered off the main road prior to the town and went into the hills. Ian steered down a small single lane road that seemed squeezed between two green mounds. A small farm magically emerged from between those hills. A cottage that might be a giant replica of a gingerbread house with a round topped front door, generous eaves, and lavender painted shutters over the windows sat at the end of a long drive.

Trinity ran a bed and breakfast at times, Kiki said, but she was very selective regarding who might stay in the main cottage. There were two other dwellings close to the main house and a very large garden area between them. The surrounding land consisted of gentle rolling mounds. A wood fence cut through the hill on the right, while a mossy stone wall meandered over the hill on the left.

"Wow, you're mother lives here? It's so pretty." Janine felt like they just drove into a fairy tale.

"Keeper of the coven cottage and books." Kiki pointed to the two fences. "Follow the wood fence to Uig Bay, the closest pub, shop, and post is nary quarter of a mile at the end of that fence. Follow the stone wall to the Faerie Glen, it's about half a mile away, but be sure to take a little milk and honey the first time you venture in that direction, you don't want to offend *them that live in the glen.*"

Janine glanced at Kiki. "Are you serious?"

Kiki smiled at her, "I'm always serious, Janine."

People emerged from the rounded door, two men and two women.

Kiki was a near carbon copy her mother. The only difference, besides age, was the older woman had pale skin and cheeks speckled with freckles instead of Kiki's smooth bronze color. They both shared deep green eyes, oval shaped faces, generous bosoms, and curvy hips. Trinity and Kiki even stood the same way and wore a similar expression of suppressed humor.

Next to Trinity, a woman with long blonde curls and a big smile waved enthusiastically. The two men were both tall and well built. One had very dark piercing eyes that seemed to invade her space, even at a distance. He flashed a handsome grin before turning his undivided attention to Kiki.

Ian knew everyone except the dark eyed one. He introduced Janine to his Auntie Trinity, then Kiki's old friend from the university, Annie, and then Sam Welks. Ian used to go fishing with Sam in the summers when their mothers brought them to Uig Bay. Annie told them that Sam was the Postmaster and lived just over the hill. Apparently, Annie and Kiki were college roommates and had gone hitchhiking through Europe at one point in their lives. Now, Annie helped Trinity run the Inn, an online herb store, and taught online classes in tarot and tea reading. She knew Leone from Rio Linda and had met Gram in one of her zoom sessions. Annie insisted that the ladies from Rio Linda were very serious students and quite funny.

"This is Andrew MacLeod, George's nephew from Islay. He's the cottage groundskeeper now that George has retired," Sam introduced the dark eyed man. Andrew shook their hands.

The small group remained on the drive, chatting. Between the thickening accents and the inside stories, Janine couldn't follow much of the conversation, but she did enjoy watching their animated faces. Then, she noticed Kiki's mother holding up a small stone, peering at her right through a hole in the center. *Strange.*

"Mother!" Kiki also noticed.

"You've got a bonnie air, my dear," Trinity called over, then slipped the stone into a pocket on her dress. "Why don't we all go in for a spot of tea?" Trinity opened the round topped door and disappeared inside.

"That was only a hagstone, Janine," Kiki whispered to her, sounding very annoyed. "It's how my mother can get a glimpse of your aura."

It reminded Janine of Ian's rainbow infrared scope. She wondered if the *Spectral Analysis* team had packed that little gadget? It might be a fun device to share. Everyone meandered into the house as Sam and Andrew helped carry bags. Janine noticed Andrew insisting on taking Kiki's bag out of her hand as he whispered to her.

Trinity offered tea and small cakes in her large kitchen. The room was an interesting mix of modern appliances and cast iron pots stacked along the wall. A large window gave them a view of the backyard and patio area.

Off to the side, a smaller room, which might have been a breakfast nook for a different resident, was open for inspection. Many different plants hung on twine and closed topped jars lined the wall shelves. It resembled an herb and potions room from medieval times.

Trinity came round to personally deliver a special cup of tea to Janine. She chatted about the herb business Annelise expanded online. At the moment, Annie was in the process of taking photos of each herb from the picking stage to the dried stage and then the powdered stage for the eighty-two herbs and plants they grew. She was building an online photo catalogue. She dubbed it *Herbs, from Ground to Ground,* Trinity laughed at the pun. Janine noticed a couple of beautiful drawings of flowering herbs on the wall.

"Is the tea too hot? Need more honey? Maybe milk?" Trinity asked.

Trinity noticed her reluctance to drink the tea and Janine felt awful. Roger planted the idea in her head and that herb room didn't help. *Did they really spike the tea at the cottage?* People spiked tea and coffee all the time with a bit of alcohol, so it was possible that Kiki's mother might believe it normal to add an *extra spice* to the tea. Janine wouldn't put something like that past Kiki, and Ian did say that Kiki was a toned down version of Trinity. If there was any possibility of an odd chemical in the tea, Janine didn't want to chance it going to the baby. She glanced at everyone else enjoying the tea and cakes.

"I'm just hesitant because…"

Janine noticed Ian watching her. This wasn't going to make a very good first impression, being suspicious of the tea. She moved closer, speaking very softly to Trinity, so that the others wouldn't hear.

"Roger McNally said that you might spike the tea sometimes. I just wanted to make sure it's not spiked with the wrong stuff for… Because I'm… We're expecting a baby, and I need to watch what I drink."

Trinity laughed with eyes that flashed similar to Kiki's.

"Roger McNally, you say." She shot Ian a raised eyebrow. "I wouldn't listen to that old goat, but at least this time he's a wee accurate. Aye, the tea is certainly spiked, lassie, with a little ginger and mint. Someone revealed that you were feeling a wee whoosie in your pregnancy and this will settle you down nicely and mayhap brighten your dark colors. Dinna worry, we only drink the interesting stuff in ritual, and we never waste it on the men." She patted Janine on the back reassuringly.

Ian and Kiki departed on a *Spectral Analysis* errand. They drove to the Castle Duntulm ruins to scope it out and speak with possible subjects for the upcoming shoot. They planned to spend the day rounding up witnesses before the *Spectral Analysis* crew arrived. While they were gone, Annie offered to take Janine on a hike around the hills and show her the Faerie Glen. She wanted to point out Castle Ewen, because it was a beautiful and sacred monument in that glen.

Annie regaled her with stories of hitchhiking through Europe with Kiki. They earned money fortune telling and reading auras at fairs and festivals, and lived a wild life. Annie said Kiki adopted the stage name Kiki Mellow for the first time back then, it came from a nickname her auntie gave her. Annie never met the famous Auntie Celeste, Ian's mother, and didn't have a pagan education like the others in the coven. Her sketchy interest in the tarot was fueled into a full obsession with the encouragement of her college roommate, Kiera Lovett. Their first year, the housing lottery paired them up and they have been tight friends ever since. Annie's father had been the son of a highland witch, so the ways came natural to Annie, and many of the older coven women had known her grandmother.

It was an easy hike to the glen. They followed along the low stone wall up and over a gentle mound. The dramatic rise and fall of the land, sprinkled with stones and lochs, gave the area a magical appearance.

Annie carried a bowl carved from polished wood. It was an offering bowl for the faeries in the glen. They used a smooth shelf in a large boulder to leave a milk and cake treat for the faeries. Annie passed the items to Janine and she arranged the present. By dawn the next morning, the cakes should be eaten and the milk bowl drained, Annie said, and if the faeries were pleased with her, they might leave a shiny trinket near the bowl as a thank you, but that didn't often happen. Annie's tone came off completely serious, without any hint of humor. Janine planned to jog out early the next morning and check it out for herself.

"In a week, or so, these hills may be covered in snow," Annie told her. "A light little flutter, and it becomes magical in a different way. Then, in a couple of more months, the full green returns. Then, the winter heather will be replaced with summer colors. It can get quite purple along this mound. In the summer, the aroma becomes heady and earthy, the air muggy."

"It's beautiful out here," Janine said.

"Did you feel her at all?" Annie asked. "The spirit of the wall? As we walked by?"

Janine glanced back down the hill to the low stone wall stretching toward the cottage. She hadn't felt a thing.

"The tale goes that the remains of a witch is buried down there," Annie told her. "Aboot halfway down by that old tree. She was burned at the stake and her ashes and bones were scattered there, near the wall. She was keeper of the cottage in her day."

"Really. How long ago was that? The cottage doesn't seem extremely old."

Annie laughed.

"I suppose it's been redone a few times and added to, but something has been in that spot for hundreds of years, persevered through weather and war. During the early witch hunts, the Isle avoided most of the ruckus, except for this one area here. A wee scandal occurred with the ladies of Saint Comba when someone accused them of witchcraft. The original group had to be broken up. We discovered that a woman named Lillias Blair was burned in the heart of this Faerie Glen, probably where the tourists always lay the rocks in spiraling circles."

"Ladies of Saint Comba?"

They continued walking slowly into the glen. Annie pointed out the rock formation they called Castle Ewen. There were a few hikers on the top taking photos.

"The pendant necklace you gave Kiki belonged to one of those ladies, they all wore one. We've been researching and translating cryptic writings. The ladies of Saint Comba were a close knit group of women who followed pagan healing and the sciences of the stars, among other things. They're our coven ancestors. They left writings deeply rooted in the Celtic traditions. Having a female saint who accepted both Christ and the ancient teachings was important to them, as, the times were changing. Unfortunately, the coven women didn't change fast enough. They became targets in the witch hunts and had to disperse to save their own lives."

Janine asked to hike to the top of Castle Ewen, so Annie took her around back to the narrow trail. As they tramped up the path, they could see people along the edge of distant trees and around a little loch. Janine didn't feel the wall spirit, but she did feel something in the Faerie Glen. It could be the beauty of the place, or the cold crisp air, but something was there.

The winter heather crunched under her feet and a few birds fluttered into the sky. The Gulf Stream current must keep the island warmer than normal for such a northern latitude, she wasn't nearly as chilled as she had been on McNally Manor. She suddenly wondered if Annie had been given the task of bringing her up to speed on the curse of the charms. The thought of Gwen's vision clouded her mind.

"Have they figured it all out?" Janine asked when they reached the summit of the small rocky castle. "About the charm curse, how to break it, what needs to be done? I've had two ghosts tell me that I can be the last one. Another ghost told me to fill an empty spot. Do the women in the coven talk about that?"

Annie shook her head.

"I didn't know that. I'm not privy to everything said in Trinity's den, just what I manage to eavesdrop on. All I've heard about you is, that you're a real *dragoma*. That's a rare thing."

Annie's eyes were wide.

"And I know there's a debate on whether to ask you to speak in a summoning. I admit, I have been running around it out here myself, but would it be too farfetched to ask you to whisper to the spirit of Lillias as we pass by her tree on the way home? Not a real summoning, just a little whisper?" She shrugged nervously. "I've never seen an actual ghost, you know."

Janine smiled back.

"I'm not sure if should. Isn't there some sort of protocol or something? Trinity advised me not to summon spirits while I'm pregnant. Of course, she said it was only taboo in my second trimester. Would you tell me everything you know about those charms?"

Annie didn't take part in the discussions, but she listened in on the translations of the old books and the gossip from the older ladies. From the records written by Lillias Blair in old Gaelic and Latin, there existed a tight net coven of women from all over the isles, the *Ladies of Saint Comba*, who studied together and met every full moon.

The group consisted of twelve unmarried women who took a vow of chastity, yet they were responsible for producing and training their own replacement, a *Next*. The wording was very confusing, but most believed those women were only chaste until they decided to produce a single daughter to replace them, then they would pass the ancient knowledge and the Saint Comba charm, from mother to daughter.

"No one ever gave birth to a son to pass on the knowledge?" Janine asked.

"There wasn't one mentioned in the translations, as far as I know," Annie said. "Lillias Blair became very concerned with witch hunters because the world seemed to be in a fever to root out and eliminate evil devil worshipers. The worldly devil was a new invention, spawned by male oriented religions. Foul men bred fear of the devil to amass wealth through the hunting of witches. Lots of people, women especially, were strangled and burned at the stake. Unmarried women were highly suspicious, because a male dominated world doesn't like an independent woman. The high social status of the Saint Comba Ladies made them prime targets. With their ancient knowledge and pagan ways, their lives were at stake if a witch hunter targeted them. Lillias felt it was inevitable that one of them would be accused, and she realized, if one fell accused of devil worship, then sooner or later, they all would be accused of it."

"Guilt by association," Janine said.

"Exactly," Annie said. "That's exactly what Lillias wrote in the book, so they hatched a plan to save themselves in case a witch hunter came for a sister of their circle. It's in the book. They made a pact to eliminate any threat and to safeguard the ancient teachings."

Annie paused and glanced over the glen.

"Then, they did it, right down there. They murdered four witch hunters who came to the isle. They got blood on their hands. Lillias believed their actions spawned a curse on the group. They disturbed *them of the glen*, and the *fae* granted a demon's last wish for revenge."

An emerald green stretched over the valley floor and grey stones were placed at the spot Annie had pointed out. A stone spiral radiated from the center. Hikers appeared. They nodded a greeting before starting a climb down the rocky spire. They strolled silently back to the low rock wall. Janine could see the tree in the far distance, stretching into the sky. She did not want to whisper to Lillias Blair, a murderer. They sat on the rocks to rest and enjoy the view.

"In her last entry, Lillias wrote that the coven broke up and the women ran for their lives. They dispersed because new witch hunters were on the way. The locals were also privy to sins of the glen and wanted it covered up. The magic of the glen had been spoiled and highlanders are very careful of the faeries, more so back then, than now. People were truly afraid."

"I'm surprised they didn't burn the house down, with that book and all," Janine said.

"Who can say exactly why, but the locals helped her," Annie said. "Her books were carefully tucked away in the house with other writings and her Saint Comba necklace was preserved. Someone added a few stray sentences to her book, a short tale of her death. A less educated writer by the look of it. They wrote that Lillias was strangled by her lover in the heart of the glen and burned, then laid to rest on the stone trail. An Oak sapling was planted to mark her grave, which is now that large tree. So, are you going to call on her, Lillias Blair?"

Annie searched her face with big bright eyes. Janine thought about the orchard ghost, and the woods ghost, and the ghost of Ingrid Stauch. She wasn't quite ready to see another unnerving spirit.

"Maybe we should do it another day," she told Annie.

Annie laughed in a good-humored way. "That's what I thought you'd say."

Chapter 17

1649 *Lillias Blair*

Eric Lyndae, the avid apprentice of Mathew Hopkins, lay trussed up in the Faerie Glen along with three holy men. That small commission hoped to kill Lillias Blair, for nothing more that birthing a baby boy and passing the lad to his father. Lillias sat cross-legged in a circle with her moon sisters, Iona, Gavina, Anice, Lyndsey, Elspeth, Aileen, Fiona, Inghinn, Caroline, Robina, and Muira. Their names were each scribbled on a decree in the witch hunter's sack, along with those of their daughters. Each one of them was slated for death.

Other decrees lay folded in the sack as well. A few bore the names of cranky old mothers and one unruly wife, each accused of evil, but Lillias knew them well. They were only lonely women whose sole crime was being bitter at the many losses life bestowed on them. The sack also contained two books, a Bible and the book *Daemonologie*, along with a box filled with pins, three needles, a jar of sulfur sticks, and two small daggers.

The sisters circled the sleeping men, waiting patiently so they might plead their case, but they knew their hope was folly. Still, if even a dim chance of a peaceful resolution remained, they needed to try for it. Perhaps the magic in the glen would open the eyes of those dark men.

Not far away, inside her cottage, Feandan MacDonald's wife waited with his bastard son, tending the baby. Feandan MacDonald himself had scampered off quite suddenly, upset that folks in the surrounding area now held him in such low esteem.

"I brewed too heavy a tea." Anice squirmed in her seat, she often struggled with patience. "We must settled this before the veil thins and the Fae awake."

In the beginning, her voice stood alone against their present action, but when she witnessed all their names on the warrant, including her own Next, her mind turned. The writ list was not title *suspected*, it was titled *confirmed,* with a death sentence plotted out for each of them. It made little sense, as Anice's daughter was only a babe barely weened. On the back of the warrant a long list of evidence gave witness against each sister. It began with Feandan MacDonald and the accusation which lured the witch finders to the isle in the first place.

Feandan MacDonald accuses Lillias Blair of bearing the devil's child and trying to pass it as his own, smearing his good name and enticing him in salacious ways.

Seeing those words drawn on paper tore at her heart. Lillias had trusted Feandan and believed that his actions had contained love. He easily consented to father her daughter and agreed to the ways of the coven ladies. Lillias would not take him to marry, only to father her Next. If something went amiss, and the baby was male, then as the father he was obligated to take the child into his own home and care for him there. Many men had wives who understood and accepted that fate, because the Saint Comba Ladies were an integral part of the land. Coven women often became chaste after a daughter was made, refusing to settle with anyone. Their unions were temporary, only agreed to last until the conception of a girl child. The Comba ladies were healers, and seers, and helpers to all. They kept the peace between the world of men, the faeries, and from the energy that seeped into the world through the cosmic veil.

Unfortunately, Feandan MacDonald persistently laid claim to Lillias Blair and desired to keep her bound to him for life. He feared that Lillias might seek her Next with another man after birthing the boy. He wished to abide in her cottage, abandon his barren wife, and bind Lillias to him. He was heartless in the matter. He commanded that Lillias raise their son and act according to his wishes.

All of those things went against their compact, and she told him *no.*

That's when Feandan accused her of bewitching him, of casting a spell and being in league with the devil. He carried on and on about it until an official of the commission overheard his rantings and wrote down his statement. The commission collected several stories about the Saint Comba women and a warrant was signed ordering each of them to death.

When Lillias informed Feandon that those men sat in the glen awaiting a correction to his accusations, he fled and hid. It didn't worry him that twelve women and their daughters were slated for death galvanized on his word. He only wished to conserve his reputation. A false accusation would cost him his title and land, and he would never admit a lie in front of *them that live in the glen*, that was bad luck. He became livid because the coven's rash actions brought danger to him. As a man with prospects, he ranted, he had more at stake than twelve pagan hags.

That's the moment Lillias Blair realized that Feandon MacDonald was bereft of a soul.

Dusk settled into night and the stars lit one by one as the four men began to stir. Disoriented, the three clergy men wormed their way to a sitting position, staring out of wide fearful eyes. The witch finder attempted to stand, but the tea Anice feed him still affected his limbs. His face burned with a hateful glare as he growled at them in a terrible voice. The ladies waited patiently for him to exhaust himself.

"No one can hear you except the faeries, and they pass their own judgement," Iona said softly. She had lived long enough for her hair to become infused with silver, and her Next had recently produced a Next, but Iona still wore her Comba charm. "You are not in mortal danger, as long as we are not in mortal danger."

"You've bound us and fed us a potion," one of the men squeaked.

"Only because you've passed judgement before introducing yourselves," Sister Aileen told them. "We seek to discuss this matter and expose the weakness in your warrant."

"You must pay for your evil deeds," the witch finder, Lyndae, spat out. "Dallying with the devil, you made your choice. Abjure your ways! Give way to what you've reaped. These actions against our holy decree prove your evil intentions."

"You've never exchanged a word with a one of us," Iona continued softly. "Yet, our names fill that decree written *confirmed of witchcraft* and acting as the devil's concubines, reeking of evil, with a recommendation for each of us to be strangled and burned to dust."

Iona gripped the paper in her hand, crushing it.

"We do not *reek of evil*. You realize that there is no devil here, not unless he comes with you. How many people met their fate in a similar way as this? From the weak testimony of strangers?"

"Did you murder every person on your list?" Sister Caroline asked. Caroline was a mother, and both herself and her teen daughter were accused together. "Did you not find any of them innocent? Did you speak with any of them before passing sentence?"

"Repent," one of the men said weakly.

"Your group is an abomination," another added. "Repent your unnatural lifestyle. A proper path is to follow the spiritual leaders placed before you by the church. By refusing a husbandly guide, you've wed yourselves to an evil influence. You poor women know not how your weak constitution draws you down a wicked path into ways that are unnatural. The evidence lies in how you bring unblessed fruit into the world, dark fruit that must be eliminated. Repent for your own souls and give yourselves to God and be saved."

"Look at this." Lillias held up her Saint Comba pendant. "This woman met Christ on the road and accepted His word as we accept His word. Our two sides can merge as one. We are not followers of a devil, we are healers and students of nature and our paths are interconnected."

Stubbornly, the witch hunter and the clergymen were deaf to the women of the coven. They refused to back down the accusations and were willing to die in the name of their god rather than admit they might be wrong. The holy men declared the witch finder a divine guide and they felt justified in their actions. They followed their leader blindly, fooled easily by Lyndae's unwavering confidence and steadfast declarations. His brazen confidence reassured them.

Lyndae showed no fear, and sensed their desperation. He believed he possessed the upper hand. He counted on their woman's weak resolve and forgiving nature to release him. With a little patience, he assumed he would gather them up, torture, strangle, and burn them to ashes for the bounty it would bring... And now, also for the vengeance. His eyes could not hide his intent from Lillias.

"How dare you claim a witch met Christ," he yelled at her, "Release us now, you evil woman. You hold a royal commission unlawfully and dare to question the word of the king!"

He hopped manically up, working his way to looser bonds. Soon, he'd be free. As time drifted deeper into the night, the women realized it was a pointless discussion. Feandan ran away instead of testifying in front of the holy commission, and these men were deaf to a woman's voice.

The sisters nodded to each other, accepting the time had come. They gave the commission a chance to walk back their warrant and now had little choice but to kill them instead. Each elder sister would contribute, because members of a coven shared their sins and guilt together. Each carried a dagger for the sacrifice of herbs and they already prepared the blades with traces of *hemlock and nightshade and snakeroot and caster bean.* All twelve of the moon sisters drew their blades with their left hands, to avoid committing a foul deed with the offering hand.

Lyndae finally realize his mistake and he went still. He definitely deserved his fate. He murdered the innocent knowingly and darkness engulfed him. He journeyed to the isle hoping to torture them in evil ways, to feed his pleasures, and then kill them when he was done, to erase all possibility of reprove.

"I curse you!" he growled, spinning round to glare at each of them. "I curse you all! I call on all the forces of divine rage to curse your outrageous ambition! How dare you hold a dagger to me? How dare you! I act for the good of the community. I act in the name of a higher order than your dark lord. I have a royal order and I speak for God!"

The women closed in, humming softy to cover the sound of their pounding hearts and the pleading liar. They swayed to give each other courage. Each sister pledged to mark each man with a groove deep enough to draw blood. If they failed to bleed to death, then the poisons would close their air pipes and halt their hearts quickly. If they still clung to life, then they would reach their conclusion when their bodies were consumed by flames in a similar sentence as the one drawn out in the warrant.

"Heed this warning. I, Eric Lyndae will haunt you into eternity lest you release me! I warn you. If you proceed any further, each of you will meet me on this very road you walk and I will prevail again and again until you and yours are all dead!" His eyes were wild, desperate, angry.

The coven moved slowly, dancing in a delicate circle, singing softly to each other. Each Saint Comba sister, all twelve, did their deed and the glen floor slowly drank in the poisoned blood. The holy men whimpered as they flailed and gasped, but the witch finder continued to curse. He called on his god. Then, he called on his devil. Then, he called on *those that live in the glen.* In a stricken voice, he cursed the coven women again and again as the spittle flew from his lips. His vile energy flooded their circle with a blackness that tasted bitter in their mouths and with an air that parched their skin. As the poison constricted his air pipes, the witch finder used his last raspy breath to beg a favor from the fae, *a curse…* and they answered.

An eerie sound cried from the hills.

Stunned eyes watched as blue-green lights fluttered angrily around their victims. In that moment, each woman realized they saved their own lives, but lost their souls in the process. They were no better than the men they snuffed out. They lingered in the glen with the poisoned bodies, unsure of what they wrought.

Unsettled images manifested in their minds and they shared a similar vision. Their path to redemption would require an eye for an eye, a tooth for a tooth, a life for a life. With the first atonement, a script would be written and must be repeated twelvefold, one for each blood soaked Saint Comba charm. The demon would be granted his revenge because the fae were angry.

The following morning, the coven women burned the dead men and then made hasty plans to disperse. As long as one member of the coven lived, the ancient knowledge could be passed on. The link between worlds was already tenuous, and reaching across the void a delicate endeavor. They would not let the pagan teachings and the ancient learning disappear. Someday, they would meet to right their transgression in the glen and attempt to balance their foul deed.

Lillias remained at the cottage, vowing to divert any new witch seekers from the rest of the coven. She informed Feandan MacDonald's wife that when the new commission came for her, the cottage would belong to the boy. So, if Feandan MacDonald's wife promised to care for the boy, then the cottage would be hers. She could move in right away and no longer be dependent upon a man, or go her own way.

The king sent a new commission the following year. They arrived specifically for Lillias and she lied to them. Lillias testified that she was the lone woman left of the Comba Coven. She swore on a Bible and told them Lyndae successfully murdered her sisters as writ in their decree, then Lillias killed him and the others in retribution, because they acted on false testimony. She swore that she alone burned those men in the glen.

The new commission summoned Feandan MacDonald to face her. He writhed in anger that she made him a fool once again and that his word was being questioned. To prove his truth against hers, the commission insisted he be the one to strangle her. If she spoke truth and they had been lovers, he would not be able to do that deed, in which case, they would not burn her as a witch, but only hang her as a murderer.

Rick Wilkins is Death.

No need to fear the noose, Feandon easily stared into her eyes as his hands encircled her neck. When he tightened his hold and closed off her air pipes, he insisted their fates were wrought by her own actions, not his. Lillias drove him to this low state when she betrayed his love for her. Why couldn't she do as he asked and be an obedient woman?

When she finally lay dead, they burned her body in the center of the glen and scattered her ashes on the trail to the cottage. Her death redeemed the first of the twelve Saint Comba sinners and ignited the redemption sequence of the demon's curse.

Chapter 18

Dark Energy *Kiki*

Ian and Kiki returned late from their excursion to the north. Most everyone had gone to bed and Ian eagerly ran upstairs to check on his pregnant wife. Kiki decided to take a stroll to the pub for a quiet drink away from the cottage. So much had happened in just a short time and she fancied a nice drink without thinking about curses or babies or Roger McNally.

On the outing, Ian tried to convince Kiki that his father had changed. He insisted that Roger had been very nice, accommodating, and normal. He couldn't recall his father mentioning Skye, so wasn't sure when Roger warned Janine about spiked tea. Ian insisted that Roger never cornered Janine for a private chat.

Kiki countered by saying that Roger has always been clever at cornering people alone and then warning them to keep mum about it.

A couple of familiar old men were in the pub. Kiki waved at them before heading to the opposite side of the bar. The pub was just an old wooden room filled with fishing plaques, dart boards, and little else besides the long bar and stools. Kiki could finally check her messages in peace. The bartender nodded at her.

"Were you supposed to meet that American fellow here? You're too late. He asked if you might be coming around but I didn't think you'd be in tonight. He ran off a little while ago. Quite a handsome bloke you got there, lassie." The barkeep winked as he brought her a pint of dark ale and a dram of whisky, the usual in Uig Bay.

Kiki shook her head. Who was he referring to? Was Max Colliers already on Skye looking for her? He should know they would be busy checking locations and speaking with people.

"Or maybe you're looking for Annie, she's next door with Sam. I don't think they'll be back tonight."

Kiki leaned up to the bar and purred at the bartender, "I'm just here to see you, James, you know how I love your special blend. I hope this dram is from that old batch."

"Aye, lassie. She's a sweet one." He grinned at her.

She deleted a ton of messages, mostly from different men, some from media people, and a few from friends wanting to meet in either Austin or Inverness. None from the detective. She deleted every message from Max, unread. He absolutely irked her with his annoying confidence. His texts might be show related, but if they were, he'd message Ian as well. The last thing she wanted was to encourage Max Colliers. An interesting sensation flared between her legs when she imaged Max might be nearby searching for her and she grimaced at her own weakness.

She also deleted the messages from Rory. Rory had taken to hanging out in the pub near her apartment and had the temerity to invite himself over when he discovered Ian was on the way. Hopefully, he finally got the message that Kiki was not interested in another romantic encounter.

There was one message from an unknown number. She hesitated over the delete button. It was a couple of days old and she decided to open it.

Janine is a nice girl, and I don't like your influence on her. Stop confusing her.

She got shivers. She tapped in a response.

Who is this? She waited, but whoever it was didn't respond.

What should she do? She could call the number. She tried, but there was no answer, just a generic message response, so she hung up. She could trace the text, but how would she do that? It was a Scottish number, so that narrowed it down. Could it be her uncle? Who else could it be? He always called the coven a *bad influence*, but why would he use a random number and not sign the message?

"What are you doing there, love?"

Kiki nearly fell off the stool she was so surprised. She hadn't notice him approach and sit down. She had been too focused on that little screen. Andrew MacLeod sat next to her, having a pint of his own. He raised his glass to the two old men and they grinned at him. They probably thought she had been waiting on Andrew by the salute they gave him.

"Checking my *private* messages." She smiled sweetly at him and put her phone down. Andrew MacLeod might be good for a little energy boost.

"Whoever he is, he seems to have gotten your ire." He gave her that devilish grin of his and let his eyes drift to her lips.

"You think you're pretty charming, don't you?" Kiki made sure to lick her lips to draw in his interest.

"You're the charming one, love."

Andrew shifted to fully face her and stretched himself out to remind her of just how tall and broad a physique he had. Why did she find arrogance so attractive? He was nearly as annoying as Max. His dark eyes stared at her lips intensely.

"I'd be willing to kiss you," he offered softly. "It could help erase some of that ire."

"We've been over this, Andrew," she purred. "I've said no thank you, remember?"

His eyes never left her lips as she spoke, and so she took a sip of her ale to give him something to watch. His intensity became a little unnerving. Kiki set her glass down, suddenly worried that her Base Well door might crack open. She didn't want to dissolve into unbridled lust like she did in Chicago.

"I should probably go," she said.

He reached out and took a hold of her wrist, keeping her seated.

"I know what you're doing," he said. "You're going to run away because I'm getting in, ain't I? Having an effect on you."

"You're very handsome, but I must say *no thank you.*"

"You think what you're doing is okay because nobody gets hurt. Just a little flirty fun, right? But you've used me, I know it. You used me to power up your ego, your core. I know all your tricks, I've been around you pagan lasses long enough. I see how Trinity keeps George and the others on a leash. Well, I'm no George." He let go of her wrist and then stood up. "You say no thank you, but your face belies your true meaning. You're scared of losing control to me." He took a step away. "Go on and finish your pint. I'll get out of your hair now."

He gave a short wave to the bartender, then left. The two old men gave her confused looks. It was probably the first time they'd seen Andrew MacLeod strike out. What a complete arse. How many times does a girl need to say no thank you? Perhaps if she shouted it with an explicative he'd get the hint. There were probably twenty girls in Uig Bay that'd take him in a second, why waste time with her?

Because it's the demon's curse placing people into position, the thought popped into her head.

Both Gwen and Trinity insisted she couldn't forge her own demon. However, Trinity and Gwen were not always correct and *they were not marked.* They didn't felt a constant urge to wear one of those Comba charms.

Kiki finished her pint and decided to head back over the hill before it got too cold. She popped out the door and admired a waxing moon in the star filled sky. Home again, the isle air calmed her. She only got about four steps before a large man grabbed her and pushed her against the building. He had a hand over her mouth and she could feel his warm breath in her ear. She was more incensed than frightened and she struggled. His grip became so tight she could barely move.

"Listen here, love," Andrew MacLeod whispered into her ear. "I'm inviting you over to that door there. That's my place. It's warm in there and I've got some nice whisky. I can assure you a very pleasant time. Now, whatever you do, don't say *no thank you* again, it's upsetting to me."

He maneuvered around so that his entire body pressed against hers. She could feel his red intensity and his famous MacLeod tool. She tried to worm away from him.

"Settle down, we're just playing here. You played your game, now I get to play mine. You will nae say no thank you again."

Then, Andrew MacLeod kissed her and her entire body flamed up. He had a hand on her head, so she couldn't get away and held her firmly in place with his body. She squirmed, but it was no use. It was outright assault. His lips hovered near hers and she tried to bite him, but he moved away chuckling. He lay tickling kisses along her neck and behind her ear, then gently trailed his nose just under her jaw. Kiki considered screaming but she was suddenly out of breath. She felt her mutinous limbs melting.

Her neck! That was her weak place.

Then, his mouth found hers again and his kiss became more stimulating, and sensual, and she flashed on Max Colliers of all people, and she actually started kissing him back. But he wasn't quite as potent as Max and she stopped. He loosened his grip a bit and turned his dark intense eyes on hers. He wore a smirk. He was devilishly handsome.

"You're eyes are lovely deep pools, Kiera Lovett. And your lips are like the soft petals of a rose," he said softly. "I suppose fate would have us…"

Kiki sent a swift knee into his groin, hard, and he yelped.

"Idiot arse! Let me go. You think you're going to get away with raping me?"

"Rape? This isn't rape! This is a seduction!" He let go of her abruptly and backed away. His dark eyes were alert and upset, and he stood slightly crouched over. "I'm sorry if that's what you think. Don't worry about it, I've changed my mind." Then, he turned and walked away very quickly.

"That son of a bitch!" She cursed under her breath, debating if she should chase him down and kick him again.

The next morning, Kiki found Gwen and Annie sitting on the stone wall close to the old oak tree. She could hear Annie dribbling on about the arrangement of her new herb garden and how certain plants should not be grown in the same soil as others. Kiki could see the new greenhouse in the lower field. It was the work of Andrew MacLeod, Trinity had bragged, Andrew was a very handy young man. The sky was clear and it was a beautiful crisp day. Annie and Gwen seemed surprised to see her.

"I thought you were going with Janine and Ian to Castle Dunvegan," Gwen said. "What happened?"

"I want to be here when Miranda and her group arrive." Kiki sat on the wall beside them. "Ian can work out a good guide for Dunvegan. I was just too tired, and frankly, I don't really care about making contact with the phantom piper. I don't want anything to do with the family MacLeod for a spell."

When they were small girls, George MacLeod took them to Dunvegan Castle where they browsed many artifacts from the clan MacLeod.

George told them stories on that trip, and one tale revolved around the Faerie Flag, a yellow silken scrap. According to George, the sidhe in their Faerie Glen wove that flag to grant the MacLeods three wishes. *Kiki recalled seeing the flag glow*, it had an aura of its' own, and no one but Kiki saw it. *Maybe they could use the Faerie Flag to help with the curse.* Kiki's pulse began to quicken.

"Ooch," Annie giggled. "Sounds like Andrew made his move then. He's been planning a seduction for quite some time. Says George knows how to slip into Trinity's Base Well and so he's going to figure how to slip into yours. I guess he bombed royally then, I warned him."

Gwen was laughing. "Ho ho, I hope you spoke with your mother about this."

"This is no laughing matter," Kiki told them. "Andrew MacLeod basically assaulted me last night, right outside the pub. I can't believe that bastard's nerve."

Gwen and Annie jumped off the wall, both surprised and concerned. Annie started talking,

"Are you okay? Oh my goodness, Kiki, did he hurt you? I'm so sorry, I never thought Andrew would do any such thing. Should I go find Sam to question him? Do you want to report him? I can't believe Andrew would attack a woman. I'm so incredibly upset at this."

"No, no, no," Kiki said. "I'm fine. He just held me up for a minute and kissed me without permission. There's no need to report him, it wasn't a terrible assault, and he backed off easily enough. I just wanted to point out that he assaulted me outside the pub, and it's not a laughing matter."

Both Gwen and Annie seemed very confused and concerned.

Kiki pulled out her phone to find the messages from the mystery phone number. She didn't want to discuss Andrew anymore, especially with Gwen. She wasn't sure why she brought it up in the first place. Instead, she showed them the text thread from the mystery number.

"Take a look at this message sent to my phone. I don't know the number, but my first guess is that it's from Roger McNally. But it seems odd, because I have his number, and he always signs it Uncle M. The only other 'R' I can think of is Rory… or Richard Wilkens."

Janine is a nice girl, and I don't like your influence on her. Stop confusing her. The mystery number.

Who is this? Kiki's message.

I'll give you one hint. R. The mystery number.

"Can you take a screen shot of that message thread and send it to me?" Gwen pulled out her own phone and began clicking away. She glanced at Kiki. "You should have sent it to Detective Anderson right away, I bet he can have it traced. See what other numbers are linked to it and figure out who it's from. The police can uncover digital tracks all over the world these days.

Are we going to show this to Janine, or Ian? I think we have to, don't you think?"

They were interrupted by the sound of Trinity's alert bell. That could only mean one thing. The guests they've been expecting have finally arrived.

The coven High Priestesses met in the cottage sitting room along with Diana, Gwen, Kiki, and Annie. They welcomed a small group from the near east, two women and a man. The man appeared Middle Eastern with dark skin, thick dark eyebrows, and short dark hair. His eyes were a pretty hazel, and although he seemed fairly older, he kept strong and fit. He introduced himself as Dominique Diaz and Kiki felt something familiar in his manner.

The two women, although dressed modestly in the style of Turkish women, were easily Caucasian. By their accents, one might be from Germany and the other American, Bertha and Miranda. Miranda Daily was tall, thin, and angular. Her dainty wrists stretched out of her sleeves as she reached out to touch hands with each of them. Miranda gave Kiki a slight nod when they were introduced and Kiki could see that she was nothing like the specter in Thatcher Woods. Her eyes were calm and serene.

Dominique Diaz placed a Saint Comba charm on the small table. A tincture of energy seeped from the charm and Kiki knew it was the one that gave her a vision of death back in Chicago. The three visitors delivered it to Scotland, personally, for a reason. They were seeking information regarding the charm coven.

Their cabal in the Turkish mountains had been founded by women of the Comba coven, Dominique conveyed. Their doyenne always wore one of the charms and taught the sciences of nature and other spiritual theories. Her charm passed from leader to leader, mother to daughter, and the education went almost exclusively to girls, but there were a few males as well. Their retreat provided a safe haven for women who had been marked by darkness in some way.

"My grandmother described the retreat when I was a young girl," Miranda spoke. "She warned me that demons followed our lineage and that I might meet one someday. Then, I would have a choice, either become his slave or run as far away as possible and hide."

"So, you ran and hid?" Cara the crone asked.

"Yes," Miranda said. "When his sister recognized my Saint Comba charm, I knew for certain what he was, because I already had my suspicions. My demon is the same one your Janine Stinger has encountered. I was told she might be here." Miranda glanced around but settled her gentle eyes on Kiki instead.

Trinity answered, "She'll be along later, please continue."

"I fled to the retreat. I always planned to go because that's where my great grandmother was born and I've heard tales of it. Tucked away in a faraway land, a magical kingdom dedicated to female wisdom. Much more than a nunnery or monastery, it is a place of true mystic science and a true safe haven for women like us. As long as we remain mindful that a demon spirit stalks us, we can be safe. All of us at the retreat remain reclusive and cautious."

Kiki exchanged glances with Gwen.

"There is a question of ownership," Dominique said, pointing to the charm on the table. "This one belongs to a woman, the question is… who, which woman? We would like to keep it, to safeguard it, but it must be given in good faith." He turned to Kiki. "Miranda's brother says that you delivered it to him and that you desired it's return."

"Someone gave Janine Stinger that particular charm." Kiki glanced at Miranda. She resembled Janine a little bit, tall, long hair, big eyes. "It once belonged to Richard Wilkens's mother."

Miranda nodded, "His sister accused me of stealing it from his house."

"Mary Kline claims the charm is hers. It did belong to her mother," Kiki nodded.

"But the last owner gave it to Janine Stinger?" Dominique asked.

"In a way. So, perhaps it belongs to Janine now. Only, Janine never wanted it. She refused to accept it and she gave it to me," Kiki said.

"Never wanted it? She has very good instincts. Then, that makes it yours." Dominique smiled at her and Kiki couldn't resist smiling back.

She wasn't sure if she'd like him, but she did, and that pleased her. His expression grew slightly concerned.

"I can see that it has already touched you, which means that it is definitely yours. Yours to keep, or yours to give. We are seeking these Saint Comba pendants, if you would agree to part with it."

The other woman, Bertha, gave him a signal, and he became quiet. Kiki realized that Bertha must be the leader of their small group. When she uncovered her head, they could see that she was a very old woman, maybe as old as Cara, Diana's grandmother, and yet her aura appeared vitally young and strong. Bertha slowly nodded to each woman in the room. Her thin lips bent into a smile.

She can see energy, our auras, just like me, Kiki realized.

"It's a puzzle that has been pieced together over many decades." Her voice was soft and unassuming. "You have obviously fit the pieces together well and sensed that each pendant carries a small portion of a strong curse. A curse that begins with intense carnal love, followed by a violent death. Long ago, our group discovered that only young women in the bloom of fertility are marked and the mark will follow the women for life in the guise of a dark shadow urging the curse to be fulfilled. A mark can only be erased by death and the longer it takes to fulfill the curse, the more marks each charm bestows. We also discovered the phrase, *one each for redemption*, and know it to mean this: a blood sacrifice must occur in proximity to each Saint Comba charm."

Bertha locked eyes with each sister, one after the other.

"Our groups are tributaries feeding energy into the same stream, and our groups share the burden of damming the flow of this curse. We need each other to end this."

Everyone agreed. Bertha explained the two sure ways to protect against the curse. Avoid intimate relationships or stay in a single committed relationship with a trusted partner. Bertha also conveyed that the Saint Comba charms were interconnected in energy. They seemed to reach out to each other and were able to form a lattice pattern covering a vast area.

Many in their group believed the dark net of energy could be significantly shrunk by keeping the charms condensed in a singular location. Until a way to expunge the curse is found, they hoped to keep them in the mountains at their retreat.

"Buried?" Gwen asked.

"Oh no," Bertha said. "That was once done, and the effect was like a pressure explosion, seeming to work at first, until the day an entire community woke with the demon's mark. It is written in our history. It is better to handle the Comba charms every so often. This allows the dark energy to move through the aether of life and believe it is getting somewhere. Worn by an elder woman who is well past the phases of her moon cycles, or one already marked, is best. It minimizes the proliferation of marks. We personally came to you because we know you have other charms," Bertha said. "We are interested in them and hope to eliminate the net of darkness by keeping them closer together."

Dominique added, "Or perhaps the curse can be purged. We would need to gather all the charms for that. History indicates there were a dozen women in the original coven, so there must be a dozen charms. Your collection might bring us closer to that number."

"If we can break this curse, then the mark these girls bear might be erased." Bertha glanced momentarily at Kiki and then Miranda. "Fulfilling the curse would mean a death for any charm that still needs a blood sacrifice. I have a fear that the curse may never be fulfilled. The dark energy has grown greedy and may desire to hunt for victims into eternity."

"Do you believe you can do such a thing? Cleanse the curse from the charms if we acquire all twelve?" Trinity leaned forward.

"We can certainly make an attempt." Bertha nodded. "It would require a strong speaker. Without a *dragoma*, I could try, but I would need a powerful circle to aid me. And even then a demon spirit may not listen. There is tale that at one time your coven had a speaker to the spirits, we heard stories about her. Dominique was sent to recruit her many years ago, but said that she had already been marked and was in the hands of her demon. She refused to leave. Perhaps she left an apprentice."

"That's what you were looking for, my sister." Trinity's eyes were on Dominique. Kiki felt the energy between them, major conflict. "And Comba charms."

He nodded. "I was desperate to help end the curse. My dear mother fell victim and so did my sister. Our elders have always known the coven originated on this isle, and so there must be more charms close by. We have collected five, including the one here on this table. Would you be willing to give your Comba charms to lessen their lattice of energy? We would keep them safe and far from the general population. Or, you could safeguard them here, near their original home. We will trust you."

With the five he mentioned, all twelve charms were accounted for, Kiki realized. If Bertha knew of a way to cleanse the curse, then they had a chance of ending it instead of letting it play out. *Maybe no one need be the last one.*

Both groups shared everything they discovered about the curse. Trinity brought out her small box from Auntie Meg's collection, and Bertha and Dominique added all the charms in their possession to Trinity's box for safe keeping. They planned an immediate summoning in the glen. Every moon priestess would be called and every member who wanted a hand in breaking the curse would be invited. They would need all the positive magic they could muster.

Later that night, Kiki, Ian, and Janine drove the short distance to the Uig Hotel. The *Spectral Analysis* tech team arrived that afternoon and a welcome dinner was planned in the hotel restaurant. Ian assured Kiki that the plan was firm for the next day. The tech crew would head out in the morning to set up sensing devices at Castle Dunvegan, rest in the afternoon, then at nightfall, *Spectral Analysis* would head north to the ruins of Castle Duntulm to attempt contact with the MacDonald ghostly family. Donald, his nephew Hugh, and his first wife Margaret were all said to haunt the ruined remains.

The previous day, they filmed locals retelling the story of how the castle became haunted. The nephew, Hugh, betrayed the Chief of Clan MacDonald in an assassination plot gone stupidly wrong and was chained and tortured in the dungeon, so, his spirit haunted the dungeon area. His uncle, Donald, also haunted the grounds, likely from being such an arse all his life. One person told a terrible tale of how Donald abandoned his first wife, Margaret, after she did not bear a son their handfasted year. In her own defense, she revealed that his impotence was to blame and he knocked out her eye in angry retaliation. He then sent her home to the MacLeod lands with only one eye, riding a one eyed horse, with a one eyed servant, and a one eyed dog. So, she returned to Castle Duntulm after passing away and haunted him the rest of his days. On the ruins of Castle Duntulm, they could expect one big family ghostly spat.

As for the Castle Dunvegan, Ian and his team would set up devices to attempt a recording of the phantom piper and the eerie music said to emanate from the Faerie Flag. They would monitor for music over a three day span and then follow up with a visit to conduct interviews with the castle staff.

Ian and Janine enjoyed their outing to Dunvegan and stayed so long they missed the cottage visitors. When Ian caught wind of the coven's planned summoning, he asked the elder women if he could bring some of his gadgets into the glen during their ritual. So, there was that to think about as well.

Chapter 19

Calling a MacLeod *Kiki*

Before joining the dinner, Kiki shared the phone messages from the unknown number with Ian and Janine. Ian called his father right away and Roger adamantly claimed innocence. Janine said she wasn't going to worry about it because Kiki often got messages from mysterious senders. It was probably a rogue fan upset that Janine dropped out of the show. Kiki noticed that Janine had transitioned from the *easily sad and mad* stage to the *nothing can bother me* stage in her pregnancy. At least the hormones were good for that.

Ian's new crew included Ben, Emma, Oliver, and Chet. Emma and Oliver were replacing Janine and Carlos as the tech assistants on camera, and Chet became the new cameraman. Kiki noticed that Lauren, the hair stylist, Sally, the costume designer, and Guy, the makeup artist, had also come, plus two extra helpers and Max Colliers. When Kiki spotted him, she glanced around to see how Janine would respond, and Janine did a very good job of acting like she didn't notice Max at all.

But if looks could kill, Max would be dead by the glance Janine shot him when he rushed over and tried to take her hand in greeting. He instantly diverted his hands to his pockets and paused a safe distance away. He then nodded and offered his congratulations on their recent wedding before moving to the other end of the table to sit between Lauren and Sally. Always between two pretty girls, that was where to find Max Colliers.

After dinner, they retreated to the bar where Kiki found herself between Ben and Emma. Ben asked Kiki her opinion on setting up remote cameras in the Faerie Glen. Lots of folks in the immediate area relayed stories of faerie encounters and Ben thought it might be worth a bother. Janine divulged her own experience with making offerings to the faeries in the glen. She offered cakes and milk one day and found them gone when she checked the next morning.

"Every crumb and all the milk consumed. Plus, there was a shiny coin left in the hollowed rock." Janine nodded to Emma's wide eyes. "I suspect it may have been the work of a woman named Annie."

"Oh no," Kiki interjected. "It's bad luck to take a faerie offering. Annie would not have done anything of the sort."

"Then maybe it was the birds," Janine said. "Do you think they'd leave a coin?"

"Only if they like you." Kiki turned to Ben and caught him admiring her again. "The answer is no, Ben. Nobody should plant a camera or any other sensing device in the glen. The Faerie Glen is populated by real faeries and they'll be angry if they're spied upon," Kiki told him. "You'll just raise their ire, and we would not want that. Did you know the flag at Castle Dunvegan was given a special magic by the faeries in that glen?"

"Boom!" Emma said with energy. "I read up on it. Three wishes, right? The first wish was used to increase the MacLeod numbers, to aid them in a battle against the MacDonald clan after some church fire or something. The second wish restored their livestock after a plague. Rumor has it, the MacLeods have one more wish. I wonder why no one has ever used that last wish. What are they waiting for?"

Boom, Kiki thought. *The Faerie Flag has one last wish. What are they waiting for?* Was the flag real or just another tall tale? She had certainly seen an aura coming off that flag more than once. All they needed was a MacLeod to make the wish for them. She knew two MacLeods that might be able do it. As if the faeries themselves agreed, he came strutting into the hotel bar searching for her, Andrew MacLeod. *You've got to be kidding me*, Kiki fumed.

"Who *is* that?" Emma perked up and her eyes grew wide at the sight of Andrew.

Everyone watched him make his way to Kiki. He gave every woman in their group an appraising look. He paused on Emma, taking in her very short pixie haircut, and he winked at her. Then, he set his eyes on Kiki.

"Hello there, love. I've been looking all over for you," Andrew said.

Before she could respond, Max came around and gave Andrew a discriminating eye. Andrew smiled nicely at Max and nodded. Kiki took a moment to introduce Andrew to Emma, Ben, and Max. Kiki could see the two men sizing each other up. Max had not been concerned in the least about the detective, but he seemed very concerned about Andrew. *Was it because they were basically the same man, full of passionate base energy and little else?* What did Andrew think showing up uninvited? He had a lot of nerve smiling at her like that, especially after his assault the previous night.

"Your mother asked if I could persuade you to come home soon," Andrew told her.

"Really, is it such an emergency that I need to leave right now? Is everything okay? I thought she was visiting with George."

Andrew smiled at her. "I'm not sure what's going on, but it didn't look like anyone was falling down dyin'. A few minutes more won't hurt. Go on and finish your drink. I'll drive you home when you're ready."

Max did not like Andrew, Kiki could see it in his face and in his energy. All evening he had been sending her waves of passion from across the room. Max definitely came to Skye looking for another illicit rendezvous, and in a way, Andrew showing up was her perfect escape. Her only hesitation was wondering if Andrew really came at the bidding of her mother. He seemed like the type to invent a reason to get her to leave quietly. Max pulled her aside while Andrew chatted up Emma, Lauren, and Sally.

"Kiki, you're not really going to run off, are you?" Max glared toward Andrew. "Did you get that kid to come in here to prove something to me? Trying to make me jealous?" He grinned at her.

"Is it working?" Kiki laughed. "Because it better not be. I told you not to expect anything from me. There's nothing here, Max. We're not a thing, remember? What did you need to talk about? If it's another little dare, I can't. We already know I can't resist you, and I won't get caught up like that ever again."

Kiki turned and waved Andrew over, better to avoid Max as much as possible, he could be her demon. Maybe she could go back to flirty avoidance, and hopefully he'll get bored with that.

"What if I told you that there might be something here? Would that change your mind?" Max whispered in her ear.

"Did you say something like that in the pub when you went looking for me? I don't appreciate it, Max, you could start a rumor. This is my home, people know me here," she whispered back.

"What pub? I don't know what you're talking about," he said innocently. She rolled her eyes at him. Then, Max stared down Andrew, "Her mother needs to see her, you say? I can take Kiki home in a few minutes. I need to drop in and say hello anyway, no need for you to hang around."

Andrew stood about an arm length away, watching them. His dark eyes flittered back and forth and he wore a simple smile. Then, Andrew nodded at Kiki and turned to go as if it didn't matter to him one way or the other.

Kiki did not want to let her "out" get away. She knew Max would stay glued to her side if she let him drive her home. Resisting him would be very difficult and she didn't want to chance it. She could not be alone with Max Colliers.

"Wait a minute, Andrew." Kiki reached out and pulled Andrew back. "I'm going with you."

Kiki pulled Andrew along to fetch her coat and held his hand as if he was her boyfriend. Max needed to get the hint that she was a free agent, like always. Kiki made sure to give Max a stern gaze to keep him away, and she could clearly see that he was bristling, even though he kept a very pleasant face. Andrew followed along, knowing exactly what she was up to. Outside, she saw that he had driven over in George MacLeod's old truck. He helped her up, then went around to climb in himself.

"Are you sure you want to offend Mister Moneybags in there?" Andrew glanced at her. "He seems very determined. It could be a good match."

Kiki laughed, "He's only interested in one thing. He's an arse in real life and is a very bad match for anyone. Did my mother really send you to fetch me, or will I be kneeing you again?"

Andrew laughed in a way that hurt her feelings a little.

"Yes, she did. There's a little storm brewing at the cottage, and she wants to see you before it gets out of hand. Don't worry, did you think I meant to bother you again?" he asked. "I'm sorry for grabbing you last night, I've never done anything like that before. Something made me imagine that you wanted me to be forceful. You may not believe me, but something strange has gotten hold of me in regards to you, controlling me like. So, maybe I better stay away from you."

Now, that got Kiki's attention. Andrew felt like something was controlling him? *Like a demon spirit?* Annie mentioned that Andrew's obsession with Kiki began before they even met. His initial interest began around March. *Right after she wore that Saint Comba charm.* He pushed to be considered for her awakening and when that fell through, he began plotting a seduction instead. Regardless of Gwen and Trinity's beliefs, the demon spirit seemed to constantly twist people into doing its bidding. Could that negative energy actually make someone murder her? Andrew came from a coven connected family and seemed very in tune with the pagan beliefs.

"Do you believe an evil spirit induced you to seduce me? You probably had little control over your actions then. Do you feel like it's pushing your hand right now?" Kiki asked him. "I've been marked, you know. I'll likely be murdered by a lover before long, unless the curse is broken," she said it half joking, but he wasn't amused.

"Well, it won't be by me," Andrew said quickly. He looked worried. "Do you think you'll be able to break this curse? Annie told us everything. It's what all the to-do is about, isn't it, breaking this curse? Annie told me the sequence the other day. Love, betrayal, death."

Kiki nodded.

"Do you know why I'm here, living with my Uncle George instead of back home?" he asked. "My own cousin was almost strangled to death on Islay by a man I'd never expect it from. Then, I almost killed the man in revenge. Nobody knows it was me that beat him so bad. I'm actually in hiding." He nodded to her. "Everyone believes that I came to learn the family mash from George, but I really came to hide. They say she was marked by a curse. It's supposed to be a secret, my violent past."

"Then, why are you telling me?"

"So that you know what I am and what I'm capable of," he said. "I don't want an evil spirit working through me. So, we can both make sure of it. No love for us, love. Keep your green eyes off of me, okay?"

"I'm not the one sending out erotic energy." Kiki glared at him.

"Don't be so sure about that." Andrew laughed. "That's about all you send out. Do you think I could help in some way with this curse before it gets the better of me? I saw that other fellow, the Turk. He's at the cottage right now and Trinity will let him help, but not George, or me, or Sam. Why? Do the old women think the demon might work through us because our mothers belong to the coven? I don't like that. I want to break that curse too. What do you think I can do?"

The Turk? Why would Trinity let any man help? Was it because the Turk could see the marks, or because Trinity had a special past with that man?

"Do you believe in the Faerie Flag? Ian is going down there tomorrow morning and will be placing sensors behind the big glass barrier," Kiki said. "I'm sure Ian would let you tag along. As a MacLeod, you can make a wish on the Faerie Flag, if you think it's important enough to use the flag wish, that is. If you can believe in this curse, maybe you can believe in the flag as well."

Andrew stared at her. She was happy to see that he was not amused.

"I've always believed in that flag," he said softly.

George, Trinity, and Dominique conversed in the sitting room, drinking. The tension in the room foretold a storm lurking on Kiki's horizon. Dominique did not drink whisky with Trinity and George, he sipped tea from a small mug, and they were patiently waiting for her. Andrew did not go into the room with her.

"Kiera, come in here." Trinity sounded tipsy. Something must be amiss, her mother usually only accepted a dram or two, unless it was a festival. Kiki noticed that George appeared tense and upset, while Dominique seemed calm and happy. Dominique rose and beamed at her when she came in.

Were they really going to do this, Kiki thought.

"Good evening, Miss Kiera Lovett," Dominique gushed.

Kiki nodded at him, then gave her mother and George a hug, she always did. For all intents and purposes, they were her parents as far as anyone in in the village was concerned. Kiki sat between the two men and faced her mother.

"You probably wonder why we called you here," Trinity said.

My goodness, did she need to drink so much whisky? Kiki could see her mother acting spacey. Did they really think she didn't already know and needed to sit down and air it out? Their auras gave everything away at that first meeting and Kiki hoped they'd just let it go. Why rock the boat now and upend perfectly peaceful relationships. Kiki glanced at George, worried.

"Out of respect for George, please do not talk about what we're going to tell you," Trinity said.

George rose suddenly. "You know, I've always loved you, lassie."

"Of course. I love you too, George." Kiki rose quickly and gave him another hug.

George smiled down at her, then turned to Trinity. "This changes nothing between us. Isn't that right?"

Trinity nodded.

Kiki stared at Dominique Diaz and felt incredibly upset. Who was this man to come and spoil George's peaceful life? Kiki always knew George wasn't her real father, but he always acted like he could be and seemed proud at the possibility. George kept very close company with Trinity, for as long as Kiki could remember. He loved her mother deeply and naturally loved Kiki as well. He was loyal to Trinity, even when he married briefly once before. Kiki was sad to see her fake father walk out the door, finally and totally exposed. A connection was severed, and she realized they could never pretend he might be her real father again.

"Kiera. My green man, Mo Leannan. I want you to…"

"Mother, please be quiet for one second." Kiki sadly stared at the door George just exited. Then, she glanced at her mother gazing fondly at Dominique. If she had loved him so much, then why didn't she go with him? Or, why didn't he stay with her? "Just give me a wee moment to get over the one father."

Dominique became concerned.

"It is natural for you to feel this way. He has been here your whole life. You can still think of him as your father," Dominique said gently. His aura changed to soothe the air. "I just wanted to know you. And for you to know me, for who I am. No one else need know of these things, unless you want it. George has asked that we keep the status quo in the village."

Kiki smiled at him and took his hand.

"I've always known that George wasn't my real father and that you were out there somewhere. This is not so much of a shock," she told Dominique. "But, I didn't realize, until just now, that I've always taken George for granted. Maybe like a real daughter might, I suppose. And I'm sad about that, disregarding George. He always behaved like I was his little girl. But I'm happy to meet you too," Kiki said. "Tell me why I've never met you before?"

Dominique glanced at Trinity, then turned back to her. "I never knew about you. Trinity never told me. I suppose I did not leave a forwarding address," Dominique confessed. "Truthfully, I'm not sure what I would have done had I known. Your mother did not want to be burdened by a man or follow me on my quest. I invited her, I assure you, but she refused. Now my quest has led me back here to the both of you. Maybe it worked out the way it should."

They talked into the night. Her father was the son of a very wise woman, a woman who decided to teach both her son and daughter the pagan arts. His mother had once been the leader of their group in Turkey, so he had ancestors from Scotland. Kiki should know, she had three half siblings, all sisters. If she ever wanted to meet them, she was welcome. Just like Kiki, two of those sisters were marked by the demon spirit. Dominique was very determined to see those marks erased.

The next morning, Ian agreed to take Andrew to Castle Dunvegan with the crew. He didn't understand why Andrew needed to go, but Kiki said it was important coven business. As a MacLeod of the clan from Skye, Andrew had ties to that castle and could trace his linage to the laird of the land. George MacLeod always said that the MacLeods on Islay were closer to the seat of Dunvegan than the MacLeods left behind. Kiki suggested the crew interview Andrew in front of artifacts in the castle. Andrew was a very pretty man, very photogenic, and he could recite all the MacLeod stories. Plus, Emma seemed to have taken a shine to Andrew.

That meant Kiki and Janine could run through the summoning spells Gwen marked in Celeste's grimoire. Dominique, joined with them as they perused the book. He was very interested in charms written by a *dragoma*. Trinity avoided her that day. Sitting with her biological father, listening to his gentle nature, she wondered if her mother might have been shaped differently paired with him. Instead of the radical town matriarch, she might have become a quiet, gentle, retiring, satisfied soul. Or bitter. One or the other. It made Kiki think about the detective.

"Have you spoken to many spirits?" Dominique asked Janine.

They lounged on the wall that connected the cottage to the Faerie Glen. It was near noon and a few tourists hurried past. The Faerie Glen had become very popular in recent years and it was worrisome. Janine read through verses Gwen marked, but no one knew what they meant and Janine proved to be very little help. She was preoccupied with euphoric feelings of love and pregnancy and could barely concentrate on serious matters. Janine flipped to a random page, not one Gwen marked.

"I really like this one. So short and simple. *Come wise soul, to us appear. Show yourself as we come near. Draw us in to make us three, so I command, so mote it be.*" She smiled at Kiki. "My type of charm, simple and sweet. I think she wrote it as a little girl."

Kiki felt a cold breeze and glanced at Dominique. Did he feel it too? His brow creased. Did he recognize the summons? Surely, the coven women would not let a man read Auntie Meg's book of happenings. Janine had hit directly on the charm Celeste used to call out the spirit of the wall. Janine recited it again, sitting right on that very wall.

Looking up and down the mossy rocks, Kiki expected to see an old woman, but all she saw were a few tourists. A woman by the old oak tree stood up and walked toward them purposely. She moved differently than the others and Kiki got a funny feeling about that woman. She stopped about three feet away and sat on top of the stones, glancing at them. She was young and beautiful. She pulled her long hair out of a ponytail and shook out the wavy tresses. Her aura had a shimmery, silvery outline to it. The woman nodded before tilting her head back to soak some sun onto her face. After acknowledging her, Janine and Dominique returned to their conversation about Janine's experiences.

"Good afternoon to you," the woman greeted Kiki. "I understand a couple of women live in that cottage over there and sell herbs and teas. Do you know anything about that?"

Kiki nodded. "Trinity Lovett and Annelise Batten. If you go around to the back blue door and knock, Annie should be in the drying room grinding herbs and taking photos. She's working on the web page. Have you seen it? The website for the cottage."

The woman nodded her head slowly, smiling sweetly. Kiki suddenly noticed her beautiful green eyes, her long dark lashes and porcelain skin. Mixed together, they gave her a striking appearance. Kiki felt an odd sensation. *Did the woman resemble Trinity a tiny bit?* No, her hair was auburn with a reddish tint, and she was tall and twig-like, *but her face.* When she spoke again, her voice had changed.

"A mix o' hemlock, nightshade, snakeroot 'n caster bean. Just a wee smear on each blade to touch the blood." The woman grinned at Kiki and her eyes sparkled beautifully. "That's how it's done." The woman nodded her head toward Janine. "She is meant tae be the last one, and th' Faerie Flag wilnae help her. But it may help ye. Ye tae take her stead can save that one."

That set Kiki's heart beating wildly, who was this woman? Kiki wondered why Janine and Dominique paid the woman no more attention than they would any other tourist sitting on the wall. Could they see her? Of course they could, they had greeted her. Kiki was very confused, but her throat felt too stiff and dry to speak. Her own eyes were locked and unable to move from the hypnotic green jewels gazing at her.

"Hey, babe!" A man trotted toward them. He waved to the woman. "Why'd you take off?"

The woman stood to greet the man. She turned briefly to nod goodbye, and Kiki noticed her eyes were no longer green and her face was no longer familiar. Kiki watched her walk away, holding the hand of her man. She was just a regular woman on an outing. Kiki searched the wall to where the woman had been before walking toward them, sitting under the old oak tree. *Had the spirit possessed her there?* She watched the couple walk toward the cottage and silently calmed her beating heart.

That was a message, wasn't it?

Janine patted her arm.

"Kiki, are you okay? Janine asked. "You look a little spaced out."

"Did either of you hear what that woman just said?" Kiki asked them.

"She was nice." Janine nodded. "Loved the web site, and I agree, Annie has an artistic eye."

Chapter 20

A Betrayal *Janine*

It was another early morning and Janine decided to jog around the Faerie Glen. She wanted to go all the way to the top of Castle Ewen and back. She brought another offering of bread for the faeries and tucked it in the niche rock as she passed. She loved running over the gentle mounds and enjoyed the added fun of rocky obstacles. It was much more interesting than the flat surfaces of Davis back in California. She also figured out the faerie offerings. She spotted a couple of hooded crows hopping around the rock the previous morning, each eating crumbs. If she timed things right, she would get back just as Kiki and Ian rolled into the cottage from their *Spectral Analysis* investigation of the ruins of Castle Duntulm.

It was only a mile to the top of Castle Ewen, so Janine ran just outside the edge of the glen to add distance. Annie told her that the faeries would appreciate that. She took the winding narrow trail up the back side of the hill and was soon on top looking down at the glen. There were three spiral rock designs on the glen floor, looking very like a Celtic triskelion. Janine paused at the top to sip some water. It was then that she spotted him, a lone man standing far off in the hills, not moving. What was he doing out so early? Janine could barely see him, but it appeared like he was watching her. Something about his posture troubled her, he seemed familiar. *No, no, just a random traveler.* Janine ignored her paranoia and turned around to begin her jog back to the cottage, then she spotted them, the two hooded crows. They were sharing her bread crumbs. As she passed, one of the birds paused and carefully watched her movements.

She could hear the ruckus before she came over the hill. Ian and Kiki were in the parking area speaking with Roger McNally. They were not having a pleasant conversation. Everyone stared at Janine when she came over the last mound and jogged happily into the drive. Roger watched her for a second, then turned to Ian.

"You see, Ian? This is what I'm talking about." He pointed at Janine. "You let your young wife go running in the wee hours of the day, who knows what could happen in that wilderness? *That man* is still out there. You're busy here, lad, I should take the lass back to the manor. It's large, and it's protected."

"I'm fine. I just…" Janine was amused, but Roger McNally cut her off harshly with an upheld hand.

"Just be quiet there, lass," he said firmly. "Ian already had to settle a scuffle with one past fellow, I don't want any more of that happening. Hanging about with these women is bound to wrap you into even more trouble. I know their ways and I cannot sleep thinking about it, especially since your good news. Best if you come to the manor where I can help keep my eye on you."

"Not everyone is safer on that manor." Kiki glared at her uncle.

"You watch your tongue, Kiera," Roger glanced from Kiki to Ian. "I'll not have you spinning evil gossip. This discussion is not your business, it's a discussion between myself and my son. You mind your manners."

Roger held his hand up and he commanded silence. His Ian-shaped grey eyes froze on Janine.

"You can make this easy, lassie, and come along with me. You can run all you want on the manor, ride horses with Chloe, and have an easy time. There are several men that watch the grounds, so there'll be no trespassers to bother you."

Kiki shook her head and turned to the cottage entrance.

"And no leaving without permission. I can see you'll probably let those fellows tell you exactly what to do."

Janine watched Ian squirm. His soft blue eyes searched hers. He clearly hoped she would go back with his father, not because he wanted her to leave, but because his father insisted on it. Ian didn't want to lose the recent reconciliation they acquired. But Janine didn't want to go to the manor and be trapped there with Roger and silent Chloe. She enjoyed the chattering women in the cottage and hoped the coven would invite her to participate in the summoning they planned.

He will bend you to his will. Who will?

"I don't trust her influence on you," Roger said to Janine. "That one is just like her mother. Trinity relentlessly urged Celeste to disrespect me, and it caused a lot of confusion and pain in our lives. I'm just looking out for you, and Ian. It's been weighing heavily on my mind and I drove all night. You carry the McNally heir in your belly and we must protect you. We are obligated to take care of you. Why not make that easy for us? Make it easy for Ian. He's busy here."

Janine took Roger's hand and squeezed it, then glanced at Ian's blinking eyes.

"You mean well," she said softly to Roger. "But I'm going to stay here with my husband."

Then, she ducked into the house.

Trinity, Kiki, and Annie stood waiting with their hands on their hips. Kiki sighed, relieved to see her. Trinity seemed worried, like she wanted to go outside and tell Roger off, but felt it might be better to leave it alone. Annie nodded, then disappeared so as not to intrude. The door flew open and Ian stepped in. He swayed back at the sight of the three of them standing akimbo. He scowled briefly at his aunt, then turned to Janine.

"Are you sure?" Ian pleaded. "It'll just be for a couple of nights. I'll drive up day after tomorrow. We don't have to film anything at Dunvegan. We can wrap up early. He's just so set on it, on you going to the manor. It's nice that he's taken an active interest in my life again."

"Bollocks, Ian," Kiki said sternly. "The detective told us that the original text message came from a cell tower in Dornoch, and so he lied to you about that. What else is he lying about?"

"He's concerned," Ian snapped. "He drove up because he was worried about that text message too. He couldn't sleep and drove all night because of it. He thinks whoever send it was spying on us."

"She doesn't want to go, perhaps she can feel something is not right," Trinity said. "You know what happened out there before."

"I don't know," Ian snapped at her. "I had a dream, okay? You never should have told me my dream was real, I was a kid in mourning, Auntie. Angry at my father, and heartbroken about my mother. He was hard on us, everyone knows that. That made it easy to believe that dream."

Ian bit back whatever else he wanted to say. He looked at Janine.

"He's just trying to make amends. I like getting on with him more than hating him."

"Please, Ian," Janine said gently. "I just want to stay here with you. Is that okay? I want to be wherever you are."

Janine could see that he was disappointed, but he nodded. He told her he was going to take his father out for breakfast and try to explain it to him. Then, he banged out the door.

Janine let a breath go. She was very relieved that Ian didn't press her. She had been very close to giving in and she did not want to go back to McNally Manor without Ian. Janine glanced at Trinity and Kiki.

"I can't explain why I don't want to go back there."

"No need to explain it to us," Trinity said. "I'm just happy you followed your gut on it."

Kiki stayed awake to tell Janine about the ghost hunt in the old ruins. They sat in the overlarge kitchen, drinking coffee and eating fried eggs. Kiki told Janine that the remains of the castle were on a small cliff overlooking the North Minch. The ocean was very violent at night, and the crashing of the waves was scarier than any ghost. Kiki said it had been freezing cold and her teeth pretty much tried to chatter themselves out of her head. Her scanty lace up leather top was probably not the best outfit choice, but poor Emma and Oliver, she chuckled. Sally designed some sort of furry animal suits for them. At least they were warm.

The wind made it impossible for Ian and his rotating new antennae and forget about any audio sounds in the howling wind. As for herself, she didn't feel any spirits. Kiki got the sense that any lingering ghostly energy faded with the elements long ago. She used her standard summoning charm, but it didn't urge a single MacDonald to come out to bicker. Only Emma and Oliver came out to bicker, over who would use which tools in the ruins. Did Janine know that the tech geeks had some sort of arm sleeve that they called *mellow-skin?* Janine couldn't stop giggling at the look on Kiki's face.

"I'm supposed to take it as a compliment," Kiki said. "But it's a little disturbing. Ian's crew was quite disappointed. Max is going to press for a request to film one night at Castle Dunvegan now. He's upset at the dud of a night we had on the cliff. Of course, if the sisters agree to filming the summoning, then we might be okay. Max plans to woo the old girls regarding that. My mother pretty much adores him, so it's very likely a done deal."

Janine's laughter subsided.

"Are you still involved with him, Max? He seemed pretty focused on you the other night. It's none of my business, and I'm not really upset anymore. I realize how gullible I can be. I've been quite a stupid girl when it comes to men."

"You're a trusting soul. My Auntie Celeste was the same way," Kiki told her. "I'm glad you put your foot down about going back with Roger. I half expected you to cave in. To answer your question, I'm trying to avoid Max."

"I am weak with men, I know it," Janine admitted. "But I felt something odd going on at that manor. Chloe is just too quiet, and I had weird dreams and strange conversations. Ian's father actually believes I did something to inspire the stabbing. He actually questioned me about it."

"I'm sure he believes Celeste caused everything he did to her," Kiki said. "Isolated her, institutionalized her. Maybe even…" Kiki let that last thought hang.

"Kiki, tell me the truth. The women have all discussed it here, I know they have. The redeemers for this curse of the charms, am I supposed to be the last one? Both the Mary spirit and the Ingrid spirit said it. The woods ghost gave me the charm and said there's a place to be filled and told me to fill it. Am I destined to fill a place in the redemption curse? Is that what everyone thinks? Because that's what I think."

Kiki moved away, and Janine could see it in her eyes. The coven concluded the same thing.

"It would make sense that a demon would mark a *dragoma* for death. Only someone like you can command it to listen and the curse won't end until the demon sits in witness to the stories of redemption locked in the charms. If there's a story in all twelve charms, then that's it. The demon must concede. That's what we're hoping."

"What about this talk of a last one?" Janine asked. "Even I know it must mean that one charm doesn't have a story to tell, and there's one place to be filled. What's the plan then?"

"There are a few ideas stewing in the cauldron. Not one of them include you wearing that charm. Everyone believes it's an obvious trick. Hoping we'll sacrifice the *dragoma* so there's no one to command it. Eva says there will not be a sacrifice. She was adamant that she would take on the last charm if there's no other way. She's old, very old, but still has a lover. She has tasked him to kill her if need be." *And then Andrew will make a wish on his faerie flag to bring her back.* Kiki raised an eyebrow. "Not really, though. It's a last resort, and not something anyone is seriously considering. Bertha, from Turkey, proposed a ritual that has worked before. No death, but one that calls on the blood of twelve or more sisters, a compurgation of sorts. A blood sacrifice. The shedding of blood works wonders against dark energy. There doesn't need to be a death, the blood of an entire coven united can do it. Very few of the sisters have actually participated in a blood sacrifice, so we're a little nervous."

"Is the coven going to ask me to help?" Janine asked.

"Trinity doesn't want you near a demon spirit and has pressed for not including you. She feels her sister's essence in your belly," Kiki told her. "She's very protective of you. But it's clear we need a *dragoma*, and so you may be asked."

"Well, I want to do it," Janine told her. "I'm not sure how effective I'd be, but I want to do whatever is needed to erase this nonsense. So, if anyone asks you, tell them I want to help any way I can."

Kiki nodded, then went off to bed.

After Ian returned and fell asleep, Janine escaped to the herb room to help Annie. Ian had been a bit grumpy and she didn't want to spoil her mood by arguing with him. He'd be better after a good nap. Janine enjoyed Annie's company, she was always funny and bright. Her artistic photos of the herbs in different states, fresh, dried, chopped, and pulverized were very pleasing. Plus, Annie filled her in on gossip from Trinity's den.

"I'm going to use a blue background for this one, that blue sheet over there." Annie pointed out the paper. "We want to bring out the reds in this powder. Blue will give it a softer, more romantic appearance."

Annie sprinkled the brownish powder on the slightly blue background. They watched the reds pop out, warming up the tones in her red clover. Annie used a digital camera suspended from a tripod to snap pictures. Her workroom felt cozy and warm. The hanging herbs created an interesting potpourri and Janine loved the ambience in that little room. She knew a larger drying room sat off the patio house, but it was not as cozy as Annie's nook off the kitchen.

"Kiki said you were an art major," Janine said. "Do you ever think about completing your degree? I finally completed mine this past December, so it's never too late."

Annie's wide eyes glanced up. "Don't tell Kiki. I finished my classes before we left on our Europe adventure. She was never going finish anything and we would have been stuck there forever." Annie shrugged sheepishly. She went to the window to adjust the light entering the room. "How's that?"

"Very romantic," Janine smiled. "Any more news on the summoning? Anything Kiki's worried about? She tends to treat me like a child about these things."

"You and everybody else." Annie passed the powder, and Janine transferred it back into a bottle. "She's a gifted girl, beyond compare. But she's does have her ego. Has she mentioned her fears about creating her own demon? No? Well, she's convinced that the demon spirit is placing people in such a way as to complete the curse, or to garner more victims anyway. She thinks your husband's father is being used to cause dissension in Ian."

"I don't follow. What does she mean by create your own demon? I thought a demon was a sociopathic or psychopathic person or something like that."

Annie nodded. "Kiki believes that people are being compelled to act outside of their normal nature. That we are puppets of the curse and will act out the roles written for us. Marked girls will gravitate toward the wrong men and then find an excuse to leave their lovers. Jilted lads will find themselves compelled to attack the lass that left them. Kiki's not the only one with such theories. The younger moon sisters agree, and so do the Turks. Even Sam and Andrew believe it to be so. Of course, I believe a person has free will. Just because a demon spirit compels a person doesn't mean they will act on it. Gwen is of the same mind as me, as are some of the older sisters. Andrew told me that he feels drawn to Kiera, but he is not going to touch her and become the demon's puppet. That's proof enough, don't you think?"

Trinity peeked into the kitchen. She advised Annie to take a nap, every woman in the coven would be needed at the summoning. She gathered up a tea service and lured Janine to her private den for a chat, she had a very important favor to ask. Janine was pretty sure she would be asked to participate in the night's ritual.

Chapter 21

The Summoning *Janine*

Faerie Glen's upper parking lot was crowded with Doctor McNally's tech crew and their rental cars. The coven leaders gave permission for *Spectral Analysis* to film and monitor their ritual from the outer edge of the glen floor. The paranormal investigators received strict orders to avoid the main clearing and to stay off the rocky hill dubbed Castle Ewen. Annie meandered into the parking lot to bid the crew hello and to advise them on how to leave an offerings for the fae. Annie brought breads and dried petals in a large woven basket and wore a crown of flowers in her hair. She set the basket on the ground near one of their rental cars.

"Place your offering in an inconspicuous spot, near where you plan to sit," Annie instructed. "Make the offering yourselves, personally, just a wee crust of bread or a sprinkle petals will do. Always include a soft thank you. Doesn't hurt to compose a verse, the fae always enjoy a bit of a rhyme." Annie gave Janine a hug before walking off again.

"Is she for real?" Oliver scowled at her receding figure, brows lined. Ian's crew appeared unusually irritated.

"We're guests here," the doctor told his crew. "We'll follow Annie's directions and take them seriously. The locals truly believe in the faeries, so maybe there's something to it. It's smart to be discerning, but we must always keep an open mind. We are trying to record the paranormal, so let's assume something extraordinary exists in that glen. Don't forget what happened in the orchard back home."

"Boom!" Emma lambasted Oliver with a finger in the chest. "When in Rome, Oliver, when in Rome. We don't want to piss off the faeries. We are not talking about Tinkerbell or tooth fairy types. Highland Faeries are mean and harsh. Better to be safe than sorry, Ollie."

Oliver grimaced at Emma, Ian's students were not getting along. Janine noticed that neither of them took out the *mellow-skin* wrap, the opaque sleeve remained on the trunk floor of their rental car. Janine watched as they pull out other familiar gadgets. She itched to help, but remained off to the side, out of the way. Ian opened a map of the glen on the hood of the car. He already marked out the placement for equipment and observers. He grinned at Janine.

"For tonight, would you prefer to hang out with me near the stone wall," he pointed to a spot on the map, "or up here in the lot with Ben and the master controls? Max is going to be here with Ben, if that helps you decide."

Janine hadn't told him yet. She planned to be right smack dab in the center of the green meadow. She worried about his reaction to that information. She wrapped her arms around him and kissed him lightly.

"Don't be angry," she whispered into his ear and felt him stiffen. "It's just this once, that's all. I need to help with this summoning because of those Saint Comba charms. They were given to me, you know, so I have a stake in what's going on here."

"Janine." He stared right at her. "You realize that we are filming this. We need to use the footage in the show. If my father catches sight of you in that witches' ritual, he's going to feel betrayed. I assured him that you were not the pagan coven type. He'll think I'm either a total idiot or a total arse." His soft eyes pleaded with her. "Come on, lass, watch from the side with me, I promise you won't get bored."

Janine turned away because he could persuade her very easily with his beautiful eyes. But, she was the *dragoma* and she needed to help. Trinity revealed that since she entered the cottage, they've had all kinds of interesting occurrences. Did Janine realize the faeries were leaving trinkets in the offering rock? Coins, threads, shells. That rarely happened. They were appeasing Janine. Not just pagan sisters, but *them in the glen* valued a *dragoma* too. Did she realize she called on the spirit of the wall the other day? Kiki wrote out the encounter for the big book of happenings.

They needed her. Trinity didn't want to ask, but there was no other way. It made perfect sense that the demon marked Janine, only a *dragoma* would be able to command a bad spirit to sit, listen, and accept the testimony required to break the curse. The demon spirit wallowed in a state of resistance, and it grew greedy for victims. Surrounded by the fae, that glen was the safest place to meet a dark entity and command it. They needed her.

Janine resisted the urge to give in to her husband because Ian's arguments really came from Roger McNally, and whether he knew it or not, her father-in-law might be in league with the demon spirit. Janine would have to disappoint Ian and she stepped away.

"At least stay on the periphery of the crowd," Ian could see her mind was made up. "We might be able to splice you out of the picture."

Janine didn't know how to tell him that she would not be on the edge of the crowd.

"What if you get faint?" Ian said suddenly. He pulled her away from the tech crew and started walking her away from the cars. "Have you thought about that? This is bound to be a very intense paranormal event and you've fainted in intense events before. Aren't you worried about our baby?"

"It's only the first trimester," Janine said. "Trinity says—"

"What if I just say no, then? *No!*" Ian had a hold of her arm. It was unusual for him to be so forceful. "As your husband, what if I demand that you not participate? How am I supposed to protect you if you're down in the middle of it? I'm not allowed down there? Men are never allowed in the glen during a ritual."

His blinking eyes were breaking her heart. What drove this intense insistence of his?

"Are you joining the coven now?"

"Ian, you're overreacting. I'm not joining anything," Janine told him. "I'm just participating in this one summoning event. We've both done this sort of thing before, many, many times."

"This is different and… These women have been doing these things for years, they don't need you to participate." His angry voice rose. "Crikes, Janine, I should get back over there and help set things up, you can see those two kids are at each other's throats, and I need to keep you and our baby safe. Don't forget you've fainted in paranormal situations! Why take that chance with our baby? You'll make me very happy if you change your mind and stand right next to me tonight, or stay in the cottage. You'll be safe and cozy in there."

Janine's eyes followed him as he walked away, the man she loved. She felt an uneasy lump in her gut as she remembered Annie's words. *Love, betrayal, death.* When Ian sees the significant level of her participation in the ritual, will he consider it a betrayal? According to Annie, a few sisters speculated that the demon nudged people to act out of character. Even so,

Ian would never, ever harm her. She would not make that mistake again, letting her past fears paint him that way, and she tamped down her racing heart. As she turned back toward the cottage, Janine rubbed her arm where Ian had held it so tightly.

All twelve moon priestesses arrived in Uig Bay for the ritual plus many casual members of the coven. Bertha and Miranda were also present, and Dominique would be allowed to observe from a distance. Doctor McNally invited him to sit with Ben and Max near the control monitors. He thanked them gratefully.

Janine already met the three leaders of the coven, Eva, Trinity, and Cara, and one of the moon priestesses, Diana, but besides Gwen and Kiki, every other coven member was new to her. She tried to remember their names, Ginger, Roxanne, Kate, Lisa, Rebecca, and Elizabeth, as they congregated in Trinity's private den. The women studied Janine with obvious curiosity. Annie popped in briefly, with her bright eyes easing the mood. She wasn't a moon priestess, but she would lead the younger girls into the glen to set out offerings for the faeries. Trinity and Cara whisper instructions to her. Annie paused to nod encouragement at Janine before she left.

The coven women dressed in flowing skirts, silken scarves, and gemstones. They wore protective minerals as jewelry and sachets of protective herbs as belts or wrist bands. Gwen passed a familiar sachet to place over her heart and Trinity gave her a necklace strung with round beads and one hagstone. Trinity claimed that things were more easily seen through a small stone window. Then, each of the moon priestesses took turns handing Janine a piece of jewelry to wear. She soon found herself decorated with two anklets, four bracelets, three rings, and three strands of beads around her neck. Over the top of everything, Trinity delivered a red velvet hooded cloak.

"You don't think this is overkill?" Janine showed Gwen the rings.

Gwen smiled, "Everyone wants to be connected to the *dragoma*."

"I feel like everyone is staring at me," Janine whispered. "Does everyone know that I could be the last one? Is that common knowledge in this room? Or is it the *dragoma* thing?"

"A little of that, but more because everyone knows that you're Ian's new wife," Gwen whispered. "Half these girls had their eye on Ian McNally once upon a time. He was always a favorite lad around here." Gwen chuckled. "That's why a few of them are staring."

Eva called for a moment of silence. Janine was very familiar with Kiki stepping aside to "center" herself before a séance. *Deep breaths, and clear your mind with the exhale,* Janine told herself. Gwen hovered near Janine to comfort her. She felt glad, because she was getting nervous.

Miranda studied her from across the room. They met briefly, but Miranda still seemed a mystery. *Had she been fooled by Richard Wilkens as easily as Janine?*

Soon, the women began picking up the pieces of the alter. As they now had a *dragoma* present, Janine would be tasked to build it after leading them into the glen. Each priestess would hand her one small part and indicate where to place it. Earlier that day, Trinity led her to the exact spot on the glen floor to build that alter. It was in the same location many of the tourists chose to start a spiral rock design. Trinity laughed and said that the faeries guided hands on a daily basis in that glen. That spot happened to be a central location for faerie energy and the spiral was an ancient sacred symbol.

Janine donned her hood and led the women toward the glen with Gwen right next to her. The old crones following first, then the guests, then the rest of the moon priestesses. Kiki brought up the rear. Janine followed the low stone wall and wondered what Kiki wrote regarding her encounter with the wall spirit. The moon hovered overhead, well past the quarter stage, and the sky appeared banded with a greenish glow just on the horizon, the northern lights, beautiful.

Janine spotted Ian up ahead. He was not fooled by her low hood and stared directly at her with a disappointed face. His lips were pressed tightly. For a second, she feared he was going to stop her from walking past, but he didn't. *Keep going,* she urged herself. She hated the look on his face, but too many ghosts had warned her that she would be the *last one* and she didn't want to live with a curse hanging over her head for the rest of her life.

Janine meandered to the prescribed spot and stopped. She instantly spotted Annie among the women scattered in the glen and their eyes met briefly. Gwen gave Janine a wooden board to place on the center stone. A large spiral of rocks still lay on the ground and Janine used it for guidance. Gwen stood just to the left of Janine, close enough to whisper an encouragement.

Trinity stepped up and delivered a three wick candle, which Janine placed in the center of the oak plank, then Trinity chose a spot to the left of Gwen.

The lovely grandmother, Cara, delivered a small ornate dagger with a carved wooden handle. Janine placed it on the far right edge of the plank, then Cara went to stand to the left of Trinity.

Weathered old Eva gave her twelve purple amethyst stones to circle the edge of the candle, then the old woman moved to the left of Cara. Janine could see that the women arranged themselves into the beginnings of an arc.

Bertha delivered twelve brownish smoky quartz stones. Janine would slowly build a design with those stones, a crystal grid, a twelve armed spiral to match the one on the ground. Bertha instructed her to place the stones in such a way that they curved and radiated outward, clockwise.

Gwen's friend, Ginger, brought twelve green jasper stones. She paused to kiss Gwen lightly on the lips and whispered something softly, then found her place in the circle.

Roxanne, with the dyed blue hair, delivered yellowish stones.

Tall, slender Kate gave Janine small black tourmaline chunks. *To ward against harm*, she whispered.

Lisa, a tired young mother, produced twelve selenite mini-pyramids, smiling shyly.

Rebecca, behind owlish glasses, surrendered polished corundum in reds and blues, blinking at Janine before she joined the circle.

Elizabeth, thick and sturdy, delivered a nervous smile and a stone carved with three triskelion spirals, which Janine placed at the left side of the wood plank.

Diana brought a stone carved with a trinity knot, which Janine placed on the right side of the wood plank. Diana gave her a brief hug.

Miranda delivered sticks of incense, which Janine placed on each of the carved stones. She also paused to hug Janine.

Kiki opened a silken scarf full of the Saint Comba charms and instructed Janine to place one at the end of each arm in her crystal spiral grid. She stood very close as she watched the charms being placed.

"It's not too late to bow out, my dear," Kiki whispered. "I can see your husband is fuming at us all, and I can't say he's totally wrong to be worried."

Janine didn't bother with an answer. She just stared into those feline green eyes of Kiki's and sent her to a place in the circle. Building that alter gave Janine an odd sense of power. She felt a surge of energy tingling below her skin and the hairs on her arms were standing on end. Then, she stepped aside for Gwen. It was the month of the Wolf Moon, and Gwen happened to be the Priestess of the Wolf Moon. In coven tradition, Gwen would lead any coven ritual during the cycle of her moon.

"On this night in winter's clutch, beyond the veil we seek to touch, I light the candle set for thee, so as it burns, so shall you be." Gwen lit the incense sticks and one wick of the candle, then delivered the taper to Janine.

"On this night in winter's clutch, beyond the veil we seek to touch, I light the candle set for thee, so as it burns, so shall you be." Janine lit the other wick.

"Come now, spirits, light it three," Gwen said softly.

"Come now, spirits, light it three, so I command, so mote it be," Janine echoed.

The third wick spontaneously ignited, and *something entered into the glen with them.*

Excitement permeated the air. By the way Kiki's eyes focused on the center of their circle, Janine knew it must be there. Many of the women noticed something and Janine spotted Trinity spying through a hagstone. It wasn't the demon, whatever it was, that much Janine knew. Gwen cleared her throat.

"We demand the spirit who tainted these charms to be obedient. Hold open your hands." Every woman in the inner circle opened their palms to the circle. Gwen looked to Janine and nodded. They chose three written charms from Celeste's grimoire and decided that Janine would choose one of them, whichever felt right at the correct moment.

"Come thee that spawned an evil deed, the blackened soul to which it feeds, witness now which was agreed, we call on you to now concede. So I command, so mote it be."

An audible gasp floated from several women in the glen, and the night became extremely still. Janine couldn't see anything, but clearly, others could. Kiki's eyes locked onto the center of the circle, and by the way her eyes tracked, Janine knew something moved around in there.

Janine resisted envisioning it. In the past, she lost precious energy trying to visualize a spirit, and it was too early in the ritual for her to lose energy. Earlier, Trinity advised her to remain aloof and ignore the taunts from the demon, her only goal was to command it. The coven women glanced at one another, and some frowned at each other. Janine couldn't see what caused the distress. Even girls outside the circle, the ones with Annie, were upset.

"What is it? What's going on?" Janine whispered to Gwen.

"The demon's mark." Gwen peered at her with gloomy eyes. "You have it, Kiki has it, Ginger has it. Nearly half the sisters bear the demon's mark. You can't see it?"

Janine shook her head. *Try not to see it*, she told herself. *Preserve your energy.*

"We shall summon the sisters of the charms to reveal each story of redemption," Gwen announced. "A blood sacrifice will be made on each charm, and the demon will be compelled to listen and accept them." Gwen nodded at Janine.

Janine addressed the inside of their circle.

"Thee that spawned an evil deed, the blackened soul to which it feeds, witness now which was agreed, I demand that you shall now concede. So I command, so mote it be. All that is present will witness the stories that absolve each woman who wore a charm. Every soul present will bear witness! After which, the curse will dissolve and each mark will be erased."

Gwen took up the short dagger and pierced the skin of her palm. She held the wound high over the alter and allowed several drops of her blood to spill onto a few of the charms.

"With this blood, I call on your testimony," Gwen said.

The entire circle moved counterclockwise, keeping the circle tight. Cara came toward the alter, and Gwen passed the knife to her. Cara spilled her blood and recited the charm, *with this blood I call on your testimony*, then passed the knife to Trinity as the circle moved steadily. After each high priestess made their blood sacrifice, the rest took their turn. Finally, at the end of the line, Kiki handed the blade to Janine. Gwen nodded to her. The dagger burned along Janine's palm and it brought a sting to her eye, but Janine was happy to leave a drop of herself on the charms.

"With this blood, I call on your testimony." Janine watched her blood steadily drop onto the charms. She made sure to soil each one of them.

She returned the knife to the alter and took up the hagstone attached to her necklace. She slowly raised the hole to her eye and spied something dark and hunched in the center of the circle. It was the shadow of a person, bent over, curling into himself, but it shivered and had no discernable features. Janine noticed a red mark on Kiki's forehead, a glowing red light, not unlike the dot from a laser pointer. Janine turned to Gwen and saw that she did not have a mark. Janine dropped the hagstone and waited, breathing hard. She needed to calm herself and remain aloof.

Suddenly, one of the women in the circle began speaking in a loud voice. It was Cara, the beautiful crone.

"*I, Lillias Blar, met mah death at the haun o' mah lover, who did strangle me oan this very spot. His was the last eyes I glimpsed in life. And in his eyes, there wis na remorse fur whit he did, only anger at myself. And in death, I redeemed my own soul.*"

Then, another of the women called out, "*Anise Glindale, I was murdered because I refused to move far from home and my lover felt trifled with and betrayed. He slit my throat after dinner on the night I refused to leave, and he buried me in our backyard. And with my death, I redeemed a soul.*"

And then another, "*My name is Celeste. I was strangled on the front steps of my home by the one I loved. He bent me to his will, then held my throat until the world disappeared from me. He covered his foul deed by sending me over a cliff. With my death, I atoned for a soul.*"

Other women in the circle called out more names and stories. All of the women had been strangled, or stabbed by a lover, a husband, or fiancé. Freda Tod, Gillian MacDonald, Lisa Michelle, Abigail Kirkpatrick, Iona Fraser, Blaire Beasley, Jennifer Smith, and Holly MacLeod. Each told a tale of love, betrayal, and murder, and their deaths each redeemed a long lost soul.

Then came a long silence. Too long. No one recited a final story and that meant one of the charms did not have a redeemer. Janine searched Gwen's face.

"Order him to accept each testimony of redemption and to erase the marks," Gwen whispered.

"Hear me," Janine spoke to the center of the circle. "You will accept each story of redemption. You will erase every mark. You will accept the end of the curse. The blood we shed demands it."

The night suddenly grew darker. Patched clouds flowed in to cover the moon. Janine reached for the hagstone and again put it to her eye. She could see the dark figure squirming, moving quickly toward the alter and Janine dropped the stone, heart suddenly racing.

"Calm, Janine, breathe easy," Gwen whispered. "Dinna let it know you're afraid. Now tell the demon again what you want. Search your core, and latch onto a strength."

Janine took a deep breath. She glanced toward Ian and thought about their baby. She knew that even though he was upset with her for being in that glen, Ian would always come running to catch her if she should fall. He was an expert at catching falling women, and she had nothing to worry about, not with him close by.

"You will accept each story of redemption. You will erase each mark. You will honor the end of this curse!" she said firmly.

Another of the grimoire charms suddenly blazed into her head, the words glowed behind her eyes. Her voice took on a calm commanding tone.

"Blood for blood, life for life, we now seal up this seam. Eye for eye, nose for nose, fading to a dream. Ear for ear, tooth for tooth, wound for wound is cleaned. Each weak soul is now atoned, each dark soul is now reformed, and each lost soul is now redeemed. All in witness here to see, So I command, so mote it be."

Something happened, because the women in the circle let out a collective sigh of relief. Janine raised her hagstone, but she could no longer see the dark figure. She turned to Kiki and could no longer see the red mark. Janine maneuvered the small stone around and could not see any of the marks. Her heart felt tremendously lighter.

As she maneuvered the stone toward the alter, she jumped. Through the hagstone hole, two beady red eyes glared at her. Then, the dark shadow moved close to her, turned, and blew out the candle. It instantly vanished with the flames.

Gwen began chanting in a thick accent, a simple song, and soon, all the women in the glen joined the chanting. Janine stood quietly, steadying her heart, not understanding the old language. Gwen kept hold of her hand, clutching it firmly, sending her calming energy. When the chant dimmed away, Gwen turned and hugged her tightly.

The pagan circle broke up and Eva, Cara, and Trinity moved quickly to the alter and searched the charms. Kiki also hurried over, her green eyes glowed with concern. Janine's heart rate pounded at top speed and though Gwen stopped hugging her, she did not let go of her hand.

"Do we know which one?" Cara whispered.

"It's this one." Eva pointed to one of the charms. "I feel that it is this one."

Kiki gather the charms from under the old women's noses and they started moving back toward the cottage. As they passed Ian, he avoided her eyes, still fuming. Not only would his wife be a prominent figure in the summoning shoot, but a nice story about how his mother was strangled by a lover on the front drive of McNally Manor would make it into the clip. Janine didn't blame him one bit for being upset. Gwen and Kiki walked closely on either side of her as they passed him.

"Maybe you'd like to hide in my room," Kiki whispered.

"I didn't see or hear hardly anything. Just those women reciting stories," Janine told her. "Were we successful? What happened? It looked like we were successful."

Kiki and Gwen exchanged glances.

"Pretty much successful," Kiki said. "The demon accepted all the stories of redemption and erased every single death mark as you ordered. The blood ritual worked."

"Pretty much?" Janine said. "What does that mean? Is the curse over or not?"

Kiki and Gwen led her around to the back of the cottage, away from everyone else. They stood under the lattice patio, just outside the kitchen nook doorway, in the shadows.

"There's still one more thing I need to do," Kiki rummaged around the silk scarf.

"All the marks were erased, as you commanded." Gwen stared straight into her eyes. "But then he came close and left his mark on you again. Don't take it personally, it's probably because you're a *dragoma* and forced it to listen. It's a trick."

Kiki told Janine everything she saw. Every mark was erased and as long as a final redeemer fills the empty spot, there will never be another mark. But the demon won't wait forever, only until the last cusp of the full moon, when the blood they shed dispersed, dried, and flaked away. If the final witch wasn't redeemed by then, then marks would begin to appear again. Hide the charms if they must, but the dark magic will seek out victims sooner or later.

"Give me the charm," Janine snapped. *So, the demon still wanted Janine to be the last one.*

"No." Kiki clutched the scarf to her chest. "You're not wearing that charm. No one with a brain expects you to wear that charm. It's a ridiculous attempt to get us to sacrifice our *dragoma*. The demon doesn't understand that we would never sacrifice anyone. That's not going to happen."

"I don't want anyone wearing it," Janine demanded.

She was a lot taller than Kiki, and stronger too. She was not letting Kiki walk away with that charm.

"You already told me what Eva planned as a last resort. She wants to wear it and end the curse, and I won't have it. So, give me the charm, Kiki, I mean it. It's mine, you know it. Don't worry, I won't wear it, but I'll not have someone else wearing it, either. Give it to me so I know it won't be used for something stupid. Clearly, I'm supposed to be the last one. No one else is marked now, so no one else needs to touch it. Until we figure something out, something that makes sense, I'm keeping the charm with me. The full moon is when? Day after tomorrow? That gives us at least three days to work something out."

Kiki opened her scarf full of charms. They were still stained with blood. She wiped one of them off and gave it to Janine.

"Even if you don't wear it, you're still in danger," Kiki said gently. "The demon is trying to find a way to work around us, Janine. Ian is very angry. Everyone could see it. It's out of character for him to be so angry. Maybe you should hide from him for a day or so, until he cools off."

"I'll never hide from Ian. He may be angry, but he would never hurt me. I'm safe with him. You're being absolutely ludicrous."

Gwen seemed very upset, her face was red.

"Kiki, what is going on in your head? You're making me nervous, please don't disappear without telling me." Gwen could see the lights go on in the cottage. "We'll need to go in. Bertha and Miranda will want to discuss storing these, and the old crones will want to discuss everything, and I need to get back to Inverness tonight. Why don't you come back to the city with me? Get a little distance from this."

Kiki hugged Gwen quickly and then passed the scarf of charms to her. They went in through the back kitchen door and Kiki paused inside the herb room. She desired to make a special tea to calm her nerves and urged them go ahead. Gwen did not want to leave Kiki in the kitchen, but as the Wolf Moon Priestess, Gwen was needed in the den to discuss the ritual right away, and she was required to add an entry into the old book. Kiki pushed Janine to follow Gwen and pulled a cup from the kitchen shelf.

Chapter 22

The Faerie Flag *Kiki*

Kiki found Andrew MacLeod in the pub. She rushed over to grab him and all the old men chuckled as they watched her drag him out the door. It wasn't uncommon for a witch to seek out a lad following a special ritual. She could hear the laughter chase them out of the bar, but she could really care less. They needed to resort to plan "BFF," Bring on the Faerie Flag. Eva's plan would not work, as the demon demanded the *dragoma*, or a maiden in bloom. In the eyes of some of those women, Kiki could see they felt the needs of the many outweighed the needs of Janine. There was no way she would allow Janine be a Comba Charm victim, or to continue mixing in this dark business, not with her Auntie Celeste's grandchild growing inside of her. Kiki could already see the baby's aura. She was already a beauty. They should never have allowed Janine to participate in their ritual!

The wall spirit said that the Faerie Flag could not help Janine, but it could help Kiki.

The wall spirit had been instructing her. Perhaps there was a reason Janine always shunned those charms while Kiki constantly itched to wear one.

Andrew followed Kiki to his room around the corner. When he went to the Castle Dunvegan with Ian's crew, Andrew swiped the Faerie Flag. He replaced it with a replica flag he had treasured since he was a boy. As long as no one looked closely, it would be okay until he could return the original. The crew planned to go back to the castle the next day, and that was when Andrew hoped to switch the flags back.

Kiki could clearly see an aura radiating off that flag. It pulsed with faerie energy and was definitely the real thing. Kiki watched it glow brighter in Andrew's hands. It knew Andrew as a true MacLeod. Kiki had no doubt her plan would work, as long as she could get her lover to kill her.

"I don't know about this Kiera, something happened." Andrew shrugged. "Suddenly, I'm not as obsessed with you like I was. I think the summoning was a success. It's like that vise that had me locked down is gone. Maybe we dinna need to use the wish. Maybe everything will turn out okay."

"It's temporary," Kiki told him. "The marks are erased for now, but after the full moon comes and goes, the marks will be back. If the demon tried to use you before, he'll likely try to use you again. It's not like anyone is ever going to use that last faerie wish, Andrew. You're a MacLeod, right? Tied to the women in the coven through hundreds of years of history. There needs to be one last victim. Maybe that wish was waiting for you. We don't want a real victim, do we? Don't you want to help destroy a curse that has plagued our kin for hundreds of years?"

"I'm not laying my hands on you, lassie. That part I'll not do."

"Dinna worry about that," Kiki said. "I only have one lover in the world and I think I can easily trick him into cutting me with a poisoned knife. How's that for a betrayal? If that doesn't work, then he's already upset at me, regarding you. I can lure him into the glen and get him very riled up if needed. If the demon wants a victim, I can make that happen. I just need you to be ready with the flag. To wish it away."

Kiki coated a dagger with poisons she stashed in a lower drawer in the herb room. The spirit of the wall instructed her to poison a knife for a reason. That spirit knew what must be done, and it made total sense.

Max Colliers had been obsessed with Janine's knife marks. He imagined the scars had come from some sort of risky sex play and his curiosity had been inflamed. He practically begged Janine to allow him to participate in that type of play, even tried to coerce her. Kiki could easily lure Max into the glen with an invitation he couldn't resist.

It was the perfect place to end the curse, because the faeries had attended the summoning and desired an end to it as well. Andrew could be waiting in the wings with their Faerie Flag, and, as a MacLeod, he could make a wish. He could wish the poison out of her system and bring her back from death. Kiki also brought a portable, personal defibrillator to help. Trinity kept one in the herb room in the case of an accidental poisoning. Kiki told Andrew that he probably wouldn't need the electric shock machine, as the flag would probably be enough, but it was there, so she brought it. Didn't hurt to hedge their bets. If she was completely wrong about all of it, then so be it. At least an ancient curse would be put to rest.

Perhaps that's why things didn't work out with the detective. Perhaps Kiki was never meant to transition from maiden to mother or to crone. Her carefully nurtured core might be the final sacrifice needed to satisfy the thirst of this ancient curse.

"I'm going to take him to the top of Castle Ewen. It might get dicey if he sees you, so hide out in the glen, or in that little cave just below. You need to be close enough to hear what's happening so you can come up as soon as I'm a goner and use the flag."

Kiki took another look at the Faerie Flag. It definitely glowed with energy. *If she survived, she was going to go to Chicago and do whatever was needed to win that stubborn detective back and make her baby.*

"I'm counting on you, Andrew. Meet me in one hour. If the plan falls through, I'll call you."

Kiki had no problem contacting Max. He picked up on the first ring. She knew that he was waiting for her call. He had been hanging around the cottage, and he dropped in to visit her mother more than once. He had sent Kiki flowers with a cute note that said, *okay, there's nothing here, I promise. You should call me.* Kiki hated to use Max in this awful event, but she needed him, and he was just the sort of rogue that would come through for her, reckless, spontaneous, and full of passionate base energy.

Max once yearned to cut a design on a lovely bosom. The wall spirit knew that and then practically instructed her to poison a knife.

"Well, Kiki, I'm not sure if I can meet you right now. I'm actually having drinks with someone, and it's very late. Maybe we can get together tomorrow."

So, Kiki thought, he was going to play hard to get, make her wait and squirm. How charming. But she didn't have time to wait. At the cottage, they likely figured out that she took a charm from the pile and would be wondering what she was up to. They'd wonder if she passed the right one to Janine or kept it for herself. Only Gwen knew how that transaction went and she wouldn't keep quiet forever. She would expect Kiki to wait until the full moon before trying anything, so she couldn't wait another night.

"No problem, lover," Kiki purred into the phone. "I'll just ring Andrew. He's quite young and vigorous, a prime stud. That summoning really stirred me up. It reminded me of our night in the sacred valley, was it the same for you? Before the sunrise, I hoped to reenact a little of my awakening, and, perhaps, add a little extra spice into the mix. What do you think about a little erotic knife play? A wee blood ritual on the top of Castle Ewen with our reenactment. I recall that you once yearned to try something like that, carve your mark on a bosom. Well, my bosom is screaming for you, Max. But if you're too tied up with someone else, I can call Andrew. He's always ready to please a lass in need."

She could hear him swallowing. He must have dropped something.

"Are you pulling my leg?"

"You know I'm not pulling your leg, Max." Kiki used her special sultry voice. "But I can certainly pull something if you meet me. My base door has been thrown wide open and I'm fantasizing about you. You know I can't control my desires when that happens. Will you come? You can make a nice design between my breasts with my silver dagger, I'm very set on it. Tell me now if you can't, so I can ring Andrew. I'm in a heated state and need to be satisfied soon. I'm dying for you, but Andrew can easily step in if I need him."

"Don't call Andrew." She could hear Max shuffling around. "I'll meet you. You say on that little rock tower in the glen? No one's going to be out there?"

"No one should be out there, but I don't care if they are. I'm not planning to be shy."

Kiki texted Andrew that they were on schedule. He texted back that he would be there with the flag. She avoided the main cottage on the way to the glen. She found a few soft wool blankets in the outer herb house and snuck away quickly and quietly. Although the house appeared dark, someone might still be up and about. Likely, a fair amount of whisky had flowed in Trinity's den, then many of the women probably found warm arms to settle into. Kiki wondered if her mother gravitated to the attentions of Dominique after that ritual. For some reason, Kiki was rooting against that. She was rooting for George.

The waxing gibbous moon dipped well past its apex but still illuminated the area well, even with the clouds. She was happy it wasn't too cold.

Kiki observed someone skirt across the glen and jump into the trees. How did Andrew beat her there? The crisp night air carried sounds well and Kiki heard a far off car engine. She hurried toward the narrow trail that led to the top of the rocky hill. She wanted to be up top, waiting for him. Andrew, in the trees, ducked down when she glanced over. Hopefully, he'd be prompt with that Faerie Flag when she needed it. Why was he so far inside the tree line anyway? She asked him to be just below the top of the hill or in the little cave. She texted him to get closer. In the distance, she heard the car door slam and knew Max was on the way.

At the top of Castle Ewen, Kiki laid out wool blankets to make a warm nest between two large boulders. She carefully placed the poisoned dagger on one of them. She retrieved the Saint Comba charm and clasped it around her neck. The metal felt cool against her skin. It felt right. It calmed her. It was the charm Janine had asked for, the one from Gram's attic box without a redeemer, Irene Lumen's charm.

The night was mostly clear. She had a beautiful view of the valley and cottage roof. She watched Max hurry across the glen floor and felt a little jolt of something in her chest. Here he was, running to meet her again. She could not take her eyes off him. He carried a blanket, or a bag, or something.

After a few minutes, Max appeared at the top of Castle Ewen. He slowed down when he spotted her and began to swagger toward her. He glanced around, then fixed his eyes on hers.

"Another great spot." A handsome, mischievous grin spread across his lips. He pulled a bottle from his pack. "I remembered to bring gifts. Whisky and cheese. Does the lady desire a little nip?"

Kiki couldn't help smiling at the rascal and accepted the whisky. Now that she was no longer rushing, her brain had slowed down to think.

What was she doing? Would Andrew make it in time with the Faerie Flag? He should be just below the top, listening.

Kiki suddenly felt tired and all she really wanted was to lay down with Max, cuddle him, and fall asleep in that soft wool. But neither of them climbed the towering rock for that. Max bent down to initiate a slow, sensual kiss that stimulated a tingling in her core. She felt her knees give out. *Holy crap*, she thought, *he's mixing love with that kiss*. Some part of her began to yearn deeply for him. Kiki pushed him away.

"Come on now, don't get romantic on me," Kiki chided him. "I'm looking for my bad boy. Come lay down with me on these blankets and we'll put on a nice show for the faeries."

He grinned. "I feel inspired to romance you, Kiki."

He followed her onto the wool blankets and kissed her passionately. He moved very differently than before and sent her more than just passion energy. Thing were not going the way she expected.

She pushed him aside again. *Keep that door shut.*

He pulled her back and kissed her again, taking his time, caressing her skin. She felt a creamy bit of warmth coat her core and she imagined tumbling into those blankets, kissing him deeply, and straddling his engorged… Kiki did not like how things were playing out. Max was chipping away at her resolve. If he kept up his loving caresses, she might not be able to follow through with the plan.

But she had to, because back at the cottage half those witches were hoping Janine would slip the charm around her neck and *be the last one.*

Kiki squirmed out of Max's arms and glared at him.

"Come on now. Let's get this going"

Kiki unbuttoned her top and exposed a generous portion of her voluptuous assets. There's the reaction she wanted, much more lustful. She grabbed the dagger and handed it to Max.

"Go ahead. Carve in your mark. Do a good job now." She helped him unbutton his shirt.

Max put the knife down and focused on kissing and caressing her instead. Kiki took up the dagger and pushed it into his hand.

"Max, don't make me wait. Let's get this blood sacrifice going. I want you to hurt me like I've hurt you. I want to see my crimson red smear across your chest while we kiss. Aren't you eager to make your mark on mine? I know it's a fantasy of yours. If you make the cuts deep enough, they'll always be there, and I'll always think of you whenever someone touches them."

Max chuckled and put the knife aside, shaking his head.

"I like the sound of that, but I don't want to cut you, Kiki, I wouldn't dare. I just want to make love. I've been dreaming of this moment for a long time." He started kissing her all over again. Kiki pushed him aside.

"Max. Would you please cut me? I know you've always talked about doing something like this, do it to me." She pushed the knife back into his hand. "Please."

Max sat up. He tossed the knife away. *The idiot!* He stared at her and his expression turn serious. *Where was the roguish Max Colliers she was counting on?* He actually gazed sweetly at her, longingly, core aura pulsing blue.

"I don't want to cut you and I don't want anyone else to touch you. I know you keep saying that we're not a thing, but maybe we could be. Can't you feel it a little bit? This thing between us? I can't even look at another woman without thinking about you. I think…I think we should do something drastic." He chuckled softly. "I mean, drastic."

Kiki sat up and pulled her clothes back together. So, he wasn't going to cut her. Then, she'd have to humiliate him into strangling her or something. That was probably best anyway, it followed the curse better. Why did he have to bring love energy into it? How had he even mustered that up? It made the effort to push him into anger much harder. She actually enjoyed his romantic overtures, they felt so nice. She couldn't look at him or she'd waver. Kiki took a deep breath.

"Don't be an idiot, Max." Kiki grabbed her phone. "I guess I'll just give Andrew a ring. You may have heard around town, the MacLeod tool is legend. He'd be more than happy to carve something on me and satisfy this craving of mine. I probably should have called him to begin with, instead of a squeamish prat like you."

Max stared at her and she could see the light dimming from his eyes. She hated herself.

"Kiki, I think I love you. Does that mean anything to you?"

No, no, no! She couldn't lose her resolve now. She kept her eyes glued to her phone.

"Don't be such a sap." She made herself laugh, and it sounded hollow. "I'm sorry, but you're just not love material, everyone knows that. And what I need from you, maybe Andrew is a better bet after all."

"I can't believe you said that." Max pulled his shirt together. "Are you trying to make me lash out at you?"

Then, she saw him flinch with understanding. Max drew himself up to sit on one of the rocks, considering her.

"What's going on? What are you playing at?"

Well then, Kiki thought, he's not going to fall for her game. Kiki grabbed his bottle of whisky and had another taste. Then, she set it down. She was fingering the Saint Comba charm dangling from her neck.

"There needs to be a final victim, before the end of the full moon. I know you don't believe any of it, but many women will be marked for death if the curse isn't broken. You can help me here, as my lover. I've betrayed you terribly, don't you agree? If you would just strangle me, or cut me with the poisonous knife you tossed away, the curse will be over. Don't worry, I won't be dead long. *We have a plan.* Andrew is waiting down the trail with the Faerie Flag. He's a MacLeod and can make a wish on that flag. So you see, no problem. I'll only be dead for a few minutes, but it should be long enough to break the curse."

He stared at her as if she were crazy. He picked up the whisky and took a long sip. Then, he stood up and buttoned part of his expensive tailored shirt.

"Andrew is down that trail, waiting for me to kill you? And then he's going to run up here with a Faerie Flag and wish you back to life?" Max summed it up out loud.

He started laughing in a mean way. Stumbling and laughing. He finally got a hold of himself and glared at her.

"You're being serious. That numbskull is waiting just down the path with his magical Faerie Flag? And this is what you think of me? You actually believe that I could harm you. I'm the villain." He looked completely brokenhearted. He threw the whisky bottle and after a long moment, the crash echoed in the glen.

"Under the influence of the demon," Kiki said softly, realizing her folly.

She could see his sadness transform into anger. Then, he moved toward the trail and started hurrying down, growling for Andrew. Kiki could hear a scuffle just over the rise. It was a disaster. They were fighting down there.

In her head, Gwen was calling her an *eejit*. *You cannot turn someone into a demon.* Why did she think she could get Max to kill her? Gwen would say they needed to be patient and find another way. Well, she tried. The plan would have worked with the right man. *The right man, or the wrong man?*

Kiki stood up and gathered the wool blankets together. She could see the moon had grown huge as it dived toward the western horizon. It was close to dawn and people would come around soon. She hoped Andrew and Max were not hurting each other down on the path.

Kiki faced the trail and saw someone's head popped up. It wasn't Max, and it wasn't Andrew. She had seen that aura before, and it lacked a core with a frightening emptiness. Richard Wilkens, bright eyed and handsomely flushed, stared at her. Kiki clutched the blankets and searched around, but she knew the top of that rocky hill well. There was only one way up and one way down, and that soulless man was blocking her exit. She suddenly felt terrified. Clearly, he could see it.

"I was watching you," he said softly. "I asked about you in the pub. You have everyone fooled."

"What do you want?" Kiki asked.

"I want what's mine," he said softly. "And to clear up what was done."

"Well then, I'll leave you to that." Kiki moved forward to pass, but he stepped in her way.

"I don't think so." He tilted his head slightly, looking at her cleavage. "You're wearing my mother's necklace. My sister will want that back."

He stepped over and grabbed her neck with a fast firm hand. He held her high so she had to roll to her tip toes. He grabbed the charm and yanked it off her neck. The chain burned as it cut through her skin. He tucked the necklace into the deep layers of his clothes, next to his heart, while keeping a firm, strong hand on her throat. He squeezed her neck as his lips bent into a tense smile and his eyes narrowed.

"You corrupt people, do you know that?"

She could not answer. She could not even gasp. His grey eyes were like glass and she could see the reflection of the moon perfectly.

"I followed you around Inverness a bit. You enjoy toying with people, don't you, like those two losers down on the trail? And what you did at that river. It was your influence that caused it, don't try to deny it. That child was my daughter. My beautiful little girl." He put both hands on her neck now. "I saw you at my parole hearing, sitting behind her and urging her to keep blaming me… and you continue to confuse her, just like her sister. Did you tell her that she could talk to ghosts? You did, didn't you? You enjoy playing these games, don't you? You led me here."

Kiki suddenly had an *aha* moment as she recognized the scene. Winter heather edging the hill top. A swollen moon descending toward the horizon. The soft breeze flowing over the grass as the stars dimmed. Kiki recognized her alternate vision from that night in the Graceland Cemetery in Chicago. The interwoven death vision she experienced as she stared into the metal face of the statue of death.

The moment of her death was at hand!

Well, how about that Gwen Murphy! Kiki experienced a bona fide vision of her very own future and not just a spirit's jumbled message. She clearly foresaw this very event. Kiki felt so pleased with herself. She really was the most gifted sister in the coven, *ha!*

Rick continued to squeeze her neck and she began to choke. He continued talking, but her ears were no longer listening. He forced her slowly to the cold ground. The interwoven images made sense now. The glen for Kiki, the woods for his mother. The moon in the sky for Kiki, the moon reflected in the pond for his mother. Heather for Kiki, cattails for his mother.

The son for Kiki, the father for his mother. Kiki tried to struggle, but she already knew how it ended and it was no use. She found herself following the script, look at the moon, then to his eyes, then at the stars. Soon, the light would narrow into pinpoints before going out. Kiki realized that she hadn't drawn a breath of air for a very long time and her field of vision had grown incredibly small. Her hands gripped his wrist, trying to pry his fingers from her neck, but Richard Wilkens was a very strong and determined man. If there was something she forgot to do, it was too late now.

She remembered everything clearly, faeries lighting up the night by a loch in the glen, her auntie in the garden showing her how to arrange the weeds, her mother holding her hand as she went to school that very first day, realizing the man in that boat on Uig Bay was really a ghost, her cousin blinking as he coached her on how to throw a dagger, Gwen's freckled face laughing hysterically, the Nimble Men dancing across the winter sky on her fourteenth birthday, herself dancing at a fire festival, and on and on the clips flashed through her mind, right up to Max's brokenhearted eyes staring at her, sparking an unexpected feeling deep inside her core.

Her lover possessed a heart after all.

Fascinated, Kiki watched her world view grow smaller and smaller and smaller, until there was nothing left but silence.

VIII

Justice

Janine Stinger is Justice.

Chapter 23

The End *Janine*

Ian slept on the living room couch. He accused her of completely disregarding his feelings, not only had she participated in the ritual, she had been a key player in the ritual. There was no way to block her image on the screen and his father was sure to watch the show. And Roxie, calling out his mother's name, did Janine know she was going to do that? Why did Janine insist on helping him make amends with his father if she was just going to dash it all to pieces immediately afterward? He didn't understand her vacillating attitude regarding his father. Ian had been so annoyingly righteous that Janine finally attacked back.

Sit on his high horse all he wanted, but when did he plan on telling her that he knew half the girls in that ritual once upon a time? They were all very curious about her and she got very distinct vibes that a few of them had known him pretty darn well. Was that the real reason he didn't want her mixing with the coven women, afraid they might gossip about him? He should leave her alone or just fess up.

But she didn't really believe any of that, and when he stomped away, she instantly missed him.

Janine couldn't sleep with worrying about it. Then, like clockwork, she was wide awake an hour before the sunrise. Every day in Scotland the early morning called her out to run. Why stew in bed? She'd sneak downstairs to check on Ian. If he was still awake, she'd try to make amends; if not, she'd go for a run and wake him when she got back. She needed to pump some endorphins into the baby before she got too far along in the pregnancy.

Janine heard Ian's gentle snores before she got to the bottom step. Run first, talk later. She quietly left the cottage and began a trot. Her thoughts went to the summoning. Many of the women were both happy and upset at what occurred in the glen. Like Janine, not everyone had been able to witness things. Many needed Gwen and the older ladies to repeat what had happened.

But everyone did wonder about Kiki disappearing. Where had she gone so suddenly? Someone claimed she ran off to meet a man, and the fellows at the pub confirmed it. Gwen believed Kiki had a very bad idea brewing and hated leaving with the carpool back to Inverness. But Gwen had obligations that needed attention, and she couldn't control Kiki anyway, even if she did find her. Not to worry, she'd return before the full moon and intervene in whatever nonsense Kiki was hatching.

As Janine passed over the last mound into the Faerie Glen, she spotted activity in the distance at the top of Castle Ewen. Two people already climbed the hill, even though the sun had not yet popped over the horizon. Maybe they wanted to watch the sunrise.

Janine gazed at them and realized that one of them was Kiki. Who was the other? She didn't know, but his posture seemed familiar. Was it the guy in the hills she had seen the day before? Something set off an alert in Janine's head. Kiki's stance suddenly appeared defensive. Instead of taking the long way around the glen, Janine decided to cut across instead. She lost sight of the two on top as she went around to the trailhead.

She found Max sitting near a rock, holding his brow. Blood trailed down his neck and he was trying to stand up. Another fellow lay a few feet away, it was the dark eyed guy, Andrew MacLeod. Janine ran over to check on Andrew. Someone broke his nose and the front of his head was bloody. She noticed the bloody rocks and glanced at Max.

"Did you guys bash each other with rocks?"

"No," Max wobbled, but sat up straighter. "Andrew was already like that. There was another guy. He looked like that guy," Max spoke sluggishly. "That guy, you know, *the* guy!"

He was obviously very disoriented and upset. Janine picked up a rock and ran up the trail. Whoever bashed rocks into Max and Andrew was up top with Kiki. She sprinted to the top and saw someone bent over Kiki with his hands on her throat. She only saw the back of his head, but she knew it was Richard. An ice cold fear froze her for an instant, then she stepped on something, a witch's dagger. Janine traded the rock for the knife and felt dizzy, but she looked up anyway and yelled,

"Get off her!"

Richard turned quickly and rose to a full standing position. His grey eyes brightened at the sight of her. He broke out in a grin, happy to see her. Janine noticed that Kiki remained limp and made no sounds. What did he do to her? Richard took a small step in Janine's direction and she waved the dagger in a threatening way. He paused.

"There you are," he said. "Right on schedule. You always loved to run just before the sunrise. I didn't want you to see me like this, to meet this way.

I'm sorry about this, but you can see that I didn't plan this, right? This is not my fault. They were here already, doing these things. I didn't expect any of these people. I only came to meet you during your run and they were already here." He glanced guiltily at Kiki, then back again. "I was defending myself. Those guys, they both tried to jump me, and she…she's responsible for —"

"Stop. Back up."

He stared at the knife in her hand and Janine felt a terrible déjà vu, they had done this before. For a moment, she felt the resolve drain from her limbs knowing what came next, but she stopped herself. She stood her ground instead of shrinking. She wasn't weak and feeble, she was strong and capable. There was nowhere to hide anyway and she needed to get to Kiki.

"Please put that down," he pleaded with her. "You're completely confused and you remember everything wrong, you do. We could rewrite our story, Janine, we… We had an unfortunate episode, but we can put that behind us and forgive each other, we can get past it. We're soulmates. There hasn't been a single day that I haven't thought about you, and it's no use fighting fate. These people, they have been poisoning your mind for a very long time."

He took another step toward her and she waved the knife wildly at him. It sliced him on the hand making a cut similar to her wound from the blood ritual. Did it sting him? He flinched back. His slate grey eyes began to darken as he took another step toward her. Then another. And another. His eyes fixed on the dagger in her hand, and she felt herself wavering. Just like before, she knew she couldn't stab him. She swiped at him again and made another cut. It only angered him as he howled at her. His eyes were in agony. She would not be able to drive that knife into flesh, she knew it. So, she threw the dagger far away instead and his eyes tracked it flying through the air. It went over the edge of the drop off, out of reach.

She decided to ram him instead. She was strong and fast, and had been studying Ian's violent rugby matches. In her head, she practiced a rugby front tackle for weeks in anticipation of being asked to play.

This time, when Richard sprang toward her, she bent down to take the hit with her shoulder, crashing down, and caving backwards while twisting so that they hit the ground with Janine on top. A surprise move that he didn't expect. Janine instantly sprang up and sent her foot into his crotch as hard as she could, as if she were making a long pass in soccer. She made a good connection with his balls and watched his face cave in agony. He was sweating profusely, and his face went terribly red. Her tackle couldn't have been that effective. Why was he gasping oddly and writhing in pain like that? He was precariously close to the edge of the plateau and squirming crazily. He was going to fall off. She didn't care and ran to Kiki.

Kiki felt completely limp. Janine checked for a pulse and couldn't find one, nor could she detect any breathing. Her own pulse pounded in her head and her vision tunneled into total panic. Janine heard herself yelling at Kiki to wake up, to open her eyes. Then, Max stumbled up the trail and the sight of his wobbly steps calmed her a little bit. She watched him use a foot to help send a motionless Rick over the edge of the hill top. They heard a sad thump as Rick hit the floor of the glen. Janine yelled at Max.

"She's not breathing and I don't feel a pulse!"

Janine opened Kiki's airway and gave her thirty chest compressions. Then, she gave Kiki two large breaths and more chest compressions. More breaths, more compressions. Crap, she thought, how many compressions was that?

Max's voice boomed next to her ear. It took a moment to comprehend what he was saying. He yelled into his phone, then he yelled down the trail as Janine gave Kiki more breaths and more chest compression. She kept losing count and needed Max to *shut up*, but she didn't have the breath to tell him that.

"Andrew!" Max screamed. "Get up here with your fucking Faerie Flag and make your wish right now! We need that flag!"

Janine stared at Max and could feel the sweat on her brow. *Did she hear that right?* Then, Max reached over, gently moved her hands aside and spoke softly in his gentleman's voice.

"You need a break, I got it." Max gave the next two breaths and started compressions.

Janine counted out loud for him, and he nodded a thank you to her. When she got to thirty, he paused to give more breaths, then went back to the compressions. He seemed calm and focused, even though she knew he had a concussion. She could see the dried blood on his neck, and his pupils were each a different size.

"Come on, Kiki," he said softly with the rhythm of his movements. "Just breathe. Come on, I dare you. It's a win-win for you. Whatever you want, just breathe."

Then, Andrew MacLeod was there with laggard movements. He stumbled in close and emptied out his bag. Janine watched a small square portable medical device tumble out.

Was that a defibrillator? She had just been wishing for a defibrillator.

Andrew ignored it and placed a ratty cloth on Kiki's stomach instead. What in the world was he doing? He threw his head back and yelled into the air.

"I, Andrew, of the Clan MacLeod, call on the faeries of Skye! I hereby use the third wish of this flag, given to my clan, the Clan MacLeod! Bring her back! I wish it! I wish it!" Then, he fell over from the exertion, breathless.

Janine grabbed the portable defibrillator and tore it open. She stopped Max in his compressions and attached the pads to Kiki's chest. Then, she plugged the leads into the device and waited for the full charge light. When the green light blinked on, both Max and Janine moved back a tad. Then, she shocked Kiki. Her whole body convulsed.

Andrew struggled to a sitting position and asked if it worked. But Janine wasn't watching him. She was watching Kiki's chest and trying to find a pulse in her arm. Just in case, she set the defibrillator to charge again. How long should they wait? How many more charges did they have? She glanced at Max and could see him crying. It made her want to cry, but she didn't, not yet. Janine restarted CPR and stared at Max.

"After two minutes of CPR, we'll try it again," she said, and Max nodded.

"Thirty," Max sobbed, and she was grateful because she hadn't even been counting.

She gave the two breaths and then went back to the compressions. Max counted softly. Then, they shocked Kiki again as Andrew shouted out his wish again. Janine whispered to the faeries to please listen to Andrew and his wish. As Max and Janine searched for a pulse, the sun cast the first beams of morning light over the Faerie Glen and started a brand new day.

Richard Wilkens and Kiki Mellow both died in the Faerie Glen just prior to dawn. Kiki from suffocation, and Richard from cardiac arrest caused by the toxins coating Kiki's dagger. They were both evacuated by helicopter to the nearest hospital. Max Colliers and Andrew MacLeod were also taken to the hospital, but they were ferried away by ambulance and treated for concussions. Janine spent a couple of intense hours answering questions from authorities before she could finally escape into her husband's embrace.

"I'm sorry, Ian," she sobbed uncontrollably as he held her. "I should have listened to you. Your father's instinct was right. He was here."

"Oh no, lass, I never should have snapped at you." He was crying too. "You took care of yourself pretty good. Maybe even… maybe we can hope Kiki's okay. Let's not ever fight about anything ever again."

Ian, Janine, and Trinity drove to the hospital the moment the authorities released Janine from questioning. She would have to stay in Scotland for a while, but for all intents and purposes, it appeared to be a case of self-defense in the alleged death of Richard Wilkens.

Max and Andrew sat draped over seats in the hospital waiting room. Gwen sat with them, speaking softly to Max. She jumped up and ran over to embrace Janine and Trinity the moment they entered the room. Then, Gwen escorted Trinity and Ian to the nurse's station to alert the doctor that family had arrived. After a moment, all three of them disappeared behind the big doors separating the waiting room from the patients and medical staff.

"No one is telling us anything," Max grumbled. Both Max and Andrew wore matching head bandages. Neither of them opted to be admitted for observation. "They were waiting for family, for her mother. I'm afraid to get my hopes up, but why wouldn't they say anything?"

Janine sank onto the seat next to Max and gently took his hand in hers. He peered at her with a terrible sadness in his eyes.

"Thank you for trying so hard." Janine squeezed his hand.

Max nodded, trying to be brave, but he looked like a lost boy without his glasses. Andrew had his head tilted back. A torn yellow cloth covered his eyes. *Did he swipe the fabled Faerie Flag from that castle the other day?* He wasn't moving, and it was hard to tell if he was awake or asleep. Janine put her arm around Max because he was shaking. What were they waiting for, a final confirmation? Kiki did not have a pulse on that rocky mound and Janine had resigned herself that the worst had surely occurred. She felt completely numb.

Then, Gwen burst from big double doors. Her eyes were big and bright, and Janine's heart started racing. What did that face mean? All three of them jumped up expectantly to greet her, afraid to hope.

"It's a miracle!" Gwen's big eyes bore right into hers.

"She's alive?" Max asked tentatively, and Gwen nodded vigorously.

Max and Andrew began jumping up and down.

"It worked!" Andrew yelled. "I can't believe it, it worked! Thank the faeries and their flag, it worked!"

The guys hugged each other and then hugged Gwen and Janine. The adrenaline rush felt overpowering, Janine couldn't possibly sit down. She wanted to run through those big doors and see what was going on.

"Is she awake? Can we go see her? Is she okay? Did she say anything? What's the prognosis?" Max asked his questions in rapid succession. "Will they let us go back there?"

"She can barely say a word or open her eyes." Gwen chuckled. "But her ego is bigger than ever."

She stared gleefully at Janine.

"She turned right to me, pleased as punch with herself. Guess what she was babbling about. She was bragging that she had a vision, not a message from a spirit, but a vision, perfect and acted out according to script. More accurate than any of the sights I've ever had, she bragged. She claims to be the new mistress of prophecy now. Can you believe the ego on that wee lassie?"

Tears were rolling down Gwen's freckled cheeks as she spoke.

"Then she begged Ian to fetch her a wee dram to coat her throat, but I don't think she's going to get it."

Kiki Mellow returned from the dead with only the bruise marks on her neck to show for it. The doctor placed her on blood thinners to alleviate possible blood clots and her voice was weak for about a week. The doctor lauded the chest compressions for keeping her brain cells alive, and the paramedics couldn't say how her heart restarted. When the helicopter got into the air, they suddenly detected a pulse. By the time they made it to the hospital, Kiki had become quite stable. Kiki couldn't tell them anything about being dead. No bright lights, no lost relatives, all she remembered was blue-green sparks similar to the light glow worms emit around the lochs in the glen. She winked when she said it.

Epilogue *Kiki*

Four months later, Kiki and Gwen were excited that Janine and Ian were staying for the Beltane Festival. They met at the cottage on Skye and crowded the grounds with friends. Gram and Leone both came from California, as well as Emma from the show, and Gwen's partner Bridget was there, plus a few locals, George, Andrew, and Sam, and several other coven families.

Kiki invited two men to the Beltane that year, Detective Bob Anderson and her boss Max Colliers. After recovering from her hospital stay, Kiki found herself quite confused on matters of love and could not resolve which man should sire the baby she desired. She decided that if they both showed up, she'd sample each of them, then let her egg decide on the father.

The coven women and the visitors from Turkey agreed that the demise of Richard Wilkens satisfied the 300-year-old curse placed on their ancestors. Gwen reasoned it out to Janine. Richard Wilkens passionately loved her, then he completely betrayed her, and while in possession of the last charm, Janine dealt him a fatal blow. Janine became the last one to vindicate the Comba Ladies and fill the empty spot of redemption. Not by being a sacrifice, but by delivering the fatal blow. The dictum never required that the victim be a woman, and the killer be a man.

Every spirit had always been right about Janine. She was, indeed, the last one.

The End

About the Author

Joanne Alain Cook is a mother, wife, sister, teacher, artist, officer, and writer. She retired from the USAF after serving both in the active duty and reserves as a C-130 navigator, executive officer, and maintenance officer. Joanne is of Korean/American heritage and has lived in Texas, Japan, Georgia, and California. Her adventures have taken her to every hemisphere on Earth, and she has spent many hours flying in the air and scuba-diving under the sea and lounging on her sofa while reading. She lives in Sacramento with her very handsome husband of twenty-plus years, beautiful brainy daughters, goofy Labrador, angry bearded dragon, frightened chickens, and clueless fish.

Author Drawing by Alaina Grace Batten

www.ingramcontent.com/pod-product-compliance
Lightning Source LLC
Chambersburg PA
CBHW032057310726
48972CB00001B/6